Philip Friedman is a practising attorney and the author of four previous novels, including *Rage*, which was made into a film starring George C Scott and Martin Sheen, *Termination Order*, which the *New York Times Book Review* called 'one of the best spy stories of the year', and *Reasonable Doubt*. He lives in New York City.

Also by Philip Friedman

Reasonable Doubt
Termination Order
Act of Love, Act of War
Rage

Inadmissible Evidence

Philip Friedman

First published in Great Britain in 1993
by HEADLINE BOOK PUBLISHING PLC

First published in paperback in 1993
by HEADLINE BOOK PUBLISHING PLC

A HEADLINE FEATURE paperback

10 9 8 7 6 5 4

All characters in this publication are fictitious and any resemblance to real persons, living or dead, is purely coincidental.

ISBN 0 7472 4171 6

Phototypeset by Intype, London

Printed and bound in Great Britain by
HarperCollins Manufacturing, Glasgow

HEADLINE BOOK PUBLISHING PLC
Headline House
79 Great Titchfield Street
London W1P 7FN

For Jeanne.
No one could have been a better teacher
or a truer friend.

As I keep rediscovering, the world is full of generous people.

No one could have given more, in time and expertise, than Dan Castleman and Mary Corrarino and William Hoyt. Without them, this book wouldn't exist.

Others in the law who have more than earned my thanks are Linda Imes, Jim McGuire, and Baruch Weiss. Also, the New York State Association of Criminal Defense Lawyers and its executive director Anthony Cueto.

Invaluable education and assistance came from Francisco Drohojowski, Molly Ivins, Katharine Muir, Mike and Ellen Parish, Gidion Phillips, and Arthur Kern and Andrew Klein, and from Malvin Vitriol of New York City's Office of the Chief Medical Examiner and Drs Jon Pearl and Robert Shaler.

The people of Williamsburg, to many of whom I was introduced by their able and gracious assemblyman Joseph Lentol and his remarkable staffer Ann Townshend, have shown me hospitality without stint. Particularly helpful in Brooklyn were Luis Garden Acosta and everyone at El Puente. My gratitude goes as well to Adam Vanesky and the People's Firehouse, Msgr Thomas Foley, Martin Needleman, Thomas Kline, Richard Aniero and Thomas Montvel-Cohen, David Pagan, Mike Rochford, Inez Pascher, Marsilia Boyle and Isaac Abraham.

It is to the people who have helped and advised me that the credit for what is accurate in these fictional pages belongs. The mistakes are mine.

My thanks go as well to William Smart and the staff of the Virginia Center for the Creative Arts, where this book was conceived and where a large part of it was written, to Owen Laster for keeping me sane and shielding me from harm, and to Judith Mintz for her insight and hard work when it really mattered. Many years' worth of thanks, for many reasons, to E. W. Count.

The usual suspects, a hardy and understanding crew, have continued to nurture me as a person and a writer. I give my love and thanks to all of them, both old stalwarts and new, and especially to Margit Anderegg, who was an indelible part of the process.

And, as always, my gratitude for inspiration and comfort in times of confusion goes to Lynne Bundesen, to Robert Geller and to Lawrence Block.

A double-minded man is unstable in all his ways.

James 1:8

INVESTIGATION

1

He made himself start with the pictures. Sooner or later you always had to look at the pictures.

Joe Estrada got no kick from photographs of murder scenes. He was not one of the assistant D.A.s who passed them around for fun. After four years prosecuting homicides, death was still a problem for him. Bad enough when it was an anonymous male body askew on a grimy sidewalk, its life drained out through neat bullet holes. This time it was a woman – abused and cruelly slashed.

Experience had taught him to be wary of surprises. His first pass through the stack of photographs was no more than a rapid glance at each one, just enough to let him know what was in them.

Blood was everywhere. He had an impression, too, of thick, red-gold hair and long, pale legs. In one closeup he could not avoid the sparkle of a reflection in a blindly staring green eye.

He put the pictures down and walked the long corridor to the vending machines for a cup of bitter coffee, letting his first impressions sink in before he went back for more.

Mariah Dodge had been raped and murdered on an office couch high in a Manhattan skyscraper. Alive, she had been a woman of distracting beauty. The police photographs showed that beauty horribly violated, obscenely parodied. Her coppery hair was fanned out around her face, gleaming richly in the light of the photographer's flash. Her body was brutally displayed – skirt yanked up around her waist, underpants gone, blouse and bra slashed open, all of it haphazardly painted a grisly red.

Estrada absorbed all this gradually, going through the pictures over and over, more thoroughly each time, until finally he was numb enough to the human reality to see only the details of a crime, evidence to be used or protected against at trial.

After the pictures came the words. Five newly arrived file boxes crowded the back wall of his office – the official record of the investigation following Mariah Dodge's murder, and of the trial a year later. *People of the State of New York versus Roberto Morales*.

The jury had convicted Morales of first-degree manslaughter; they had acquitted him of intentionally murdering the woman who had been both his employee and his lover. Only weeks later a fresh team of defense lawyers had gotten him released on bail pending appeal. Now, more than three years after Mariah Dodge's life had been gruesomely torn from her, two years after the first verdict, there was going to be a new trial. And it was up to Joe Estrada to make sure Roberto Morales went back to jail and stayed there.

By the end of a day immersed in the appeal briefs Estrada was ready for some relief. He got his messages and returned as many calls as he could. He did not reach either of the defense lawyers on the two pending armed robbery prosecutions he wanted to plead out as soon as possible. There was a message with a lawyer's name he did not recognize and a reference to a defendant he did not recognize, either – not the first time the name of some mope he was supposed to put away had blended with the names of all the other mopes he was supposed to put away, or had already put away.

He stayed in the office trying to catch up on paperwork, but he could not keep his mind off his new assignment. Retrials ordinarily had all the appeal of bad movie sequels. *People v.*

Morales was different. It more than made up for its lack of novelty in the passion of the people who cared about the outcome.

At the time Roberto Morales was charged with the rape and murder of Mariah Dodge, he had been a hero of sorts in the Hispanic community, a self-made millionaire with a plan to bring new economic vitality to the Brooklyn neighborhood where he had grown up. His flamboyant defense lawyer had worked hard to turn the first trial into a focus for the city's economic and racial hostility.

After the trial Morale's grand development scheme had fallen to ruin. Now, with his conviction thrown out because of the judge's errors favoring the prosecution, Morales was even more the martyr. Three years of well-publicized volunteer work in the community while the system ground out his trial and appeals had only increased his following. His retrial would be a hot ticket, and not only among the pro-Morales faithful. The front office, having anointed Joe Estrada, would be monitoring his progress without mercy.

He checked the clock. Almost eight, seven in Texas. A good time to catch the victim's parents at home. It was not a call he was eager to make. At best, he could offer them a measure of revenge, a sense of order and closure – nothing like real solace, particularly for people who had seen an earlier guilty verdict evaporate.

He took a deep breath and reached for the phone. It rang long enough for him to think he had been spared this time.

'Hello.'

'Mrs Dodge?'

'Yes. Who's this, please?' A light, pleasant voice. Homey. Hospitable.

'Mrs Dodge, this is Joseph Estrada, I'm with the Manhattan District Attorney's office and I'm going to be prosecuting Roberto Morales. I just wanted to let you know that I'm here and I'm happy to answer any questions you might have, now or in the future.'

He stopped to give her time to respond. There was silence on the phone.

'Mrs Dodge?'

After a moment, a new voice: 'This is Samuel Dodge speaking. Dr Samuel Dodge.' A strong, hard voice. Not hospitable. 'Is there something you want?'

'Hello, Dr Dodge. I'm Joseph Estrada, I'm—'

'I know who you are. Is there something you want?'

'No, not really.' Estrada hesitated. 'I'm calling mostly as a courtesy. To let you know we're going forward and we hope to put Roberto Morales in prison for a very long time. We try to be in contact with the family of the victim and keep them involved if they want to be.' He felt tongue-tied despite the rush of words, knew he was going about this wrong – too impersonal, too abstract – thrown off by Dodge's coldness.

'Mrs Dodge and I have been through this before,' Dodge said. 'Involved, as you call it, the first time they brought the man to trial. I don't see where we'd want to endure that again.'

'I can understand that.' Understand it, maybe, but he could not imagine what it felt like: the pain and the frustration, the sense of futility. Crowds of people up in arms on behalf of the man who had brutally killed your daughter.

'They told us the lawyer they assigned then was the best they had.'

'It's true. He's as good as they come.'

'Not good enough to win for Mariah, though, was he?'

'It was a difficult case—'

Dodge cut him off. 'Are you the best, too, Mr Estrada?' Acid in his voice.

'Well, I don't know if I'd say that myself . . .'

'I don't suppose it matters. They're going to get another radical lawyer and stir up another racist fuss and make a worse fool out of you than they made out of that smart Jew.'

'Look, Dr Dodge, I didn't call to argue with you. I want to make myself available . . .'

'It's Estrada? Did I get that right?'

'Right. Joseph Estrada.'

'Mexican?'

There was an official answer, a small gem of disingenuousness: The details of my heritage have nothing to do with the case. It would not do, now.

'If you must know, Dr Dodge, it's a Spanish name. From Spain. My father's ancestors were dukes of Castile and Aragon.' Or so Big Jim Estrada had claimed. 'My mother's name was Smithfield. She's a Daughter of the American Revolution, since those things seem to matter to you. Oh, and my maternal grandmother was Jewish.' An exaggeration for effect; she had been Unitarian, a quarter Jewish via her mother's mother.

'All right, son, no need to get testy. I said a smart Jew, I meant it to be a compliment.'

There was an uncomfortable pause while Dodge waited for a response he was not going to get. He cleared his throat, a reaction to the silence, preparing to start again.

'Now, listen, young man, Mrs Dodge and I want to see this . . . this . . . we want to see him squashed, the way he deserves. I don't speak his name, and I don't care to hear it spoken. I don't care to speak about what he did. Most of all, I don't see the point of putting Mrs Dodge through the heartache of watching a trial every day and hearing all those stories, and then have that scum get off a second time without spending so much as a whole month in jail. Do I make myself clear?'

'Yes, sir, you do. I can only assure you I'm going to do my best to get the highest penalty there is.'

'Still no death penalty in New York, is there?'

'No, there isn't.'

'Pansies, every damn one of them.'

Estrada did not ask who he meant. Legislators, maybe.

'Listen to me, young man. I don't want you calling here, disturbing Mrs Dodge. I'll give you my office number and you can reach me there if you need anything. Understood?'

'Understood.'

'Something else I can do for you?' A way for Dodge to get off the phone, as sincere as 'y'all all come back.'

'You know, actually, there is. I'd appreciate having a recent photograph of your daughter.'

'Why would you want that?'

It was a good question. The request had just popped out of his mouth.

'I'm going to be looking for new witnesses,' he improvised. 'People who might have seen them together, but who might not know her by name. I think there was a picture of her in the file, but it must have been returned.'

'I don't know. We don't have many pictures of her. Pictures are all we have now.'

'I could have it copied and send it back. Or if you have the negative I could have prints made.'

No response.

'Or you could have prints made, and I'd reimburse you.' He did not know why he was insisting. Maybe because he wanted an antidote to those crime-scene photos, a better image to have in mind when he thought about her.

After another pause, Dodge said, 'I'll see. Is there anything else?'

'No, not right now. Thank you very much.'

'Goodbye, Mr Estrada. Remember, don't call at home.'

Not much chance of my calling at all, he thought as he hung up. And yet, as unpleasant as the conversation had been, he knew there had to be real pain behind Samuel Dodge's behavior. And he came away feeling even more sympathy for Mariah Dodge. He knew all about stern, bigoted fathers: he'd had one himself.

He was still in the office almost two hours later, going through the file, beginning to worry about the holes in his case. When the words began to blur he decided he'd had enough.

As usual, even after ten, Broadway near his apartment was bustling with life and light. Another wave of late-night food stores had invaded in the last year, lining the sidewalks with displays of fresh fruits and vegetables, enticing shoppers inside to try overpriced specialty foods of all nations. Estrada, far from immune, bought himself a melon and some grapes, fresh bread and a bottle of wine-dark wild blueberry juice from Sweden.

He had been living in the same apartment since law school, long enough so he did not see it accurately anymore. It felt comfortably spacious to him, though people told him he should get himself some furniture. His former roommate had all but denuded it moving out when he took a job with a Wall Street law firm. A couple of years later they had chipped in to buy the place for Estrada to live in; when he sold it they would share the profit. Choosing the D.A.'s office had not made him poor, but his starting salary had been less than half his former roommate's. That was not so bad: in the eight years since then the starting-salary ratio had become more like one to three.

Estrada did not intend to let the earnings gap last forever. He looked at it as the price he was paying for the courtroom experience that came with working in the D.A.'s office. No beginning associate in a big law firm could hope for a fraction of the courtroom time Estrada had put in by the end of his third year. And in the following five years, getting into major felonies and then homicides, Estrada had been multiplying his experience in both quantity and quality, waiting for the case that would really establish him.

He opened a beer, put his feet up on the leather couch and turned on the television. The screen warmed up on what looked like a cop show of some kind. Good for a laugh, if not much insight into law enforcement. The scene switched to the bad guys. They were arguing, apparently over what to do with a kidnap victim. One of them stalked off menacingly and slammed through a door into a room whose only furniture was a bed. Tied to it was a beautiful woman in as little clothing as the phantom censors of TV would allow. As he approached her the man took out a large knife.

Estrada changed the channel. Closeups of a sweating woman's body, working out: a commercial for spring water. Changed it again, caught a glimpse of long, swirling red hair and turned it off.

He thought about Mariah Dodge. Her red hair was not swirling any more. She would never work out again. No man would ever be tempted by her body, or prompted to destroy it in unreasoning anger and frustration that led him to violence like the kind he saw emulated everywhere, every day.

There was too much of it. It was too easy to get away with. He felt like the Dutch boy trying to save his country from drowning. No leak was so small you could ignore it. Roberto Morales had to be put away for a long, long time.

The phone dragged him out of bed just after midnight. It was his girlfriend, calling from a printing-industry trade show in Chicago.

'Hi. What's new in the world of cops and robbers?' Michelle sounded wide awake and right in the room.

'I was saving it to tell you in person.'

He heard her take a deep breath. 'Joey . . . I'm not coming back right away. I'm going to L.A.'

He did not ask for how long. More or less, he knew the answer: It all depends on if they offer me the L.A. job, if I'm coming back to New York to pack or to stay. He did not want to think about it. 'And here I am, too tired even to be sexy.'

'You sure? I was just taking off my skirt.'

He could hear the zipper, then the faint sibilance of silk sliding over pantyhose.

'Tomorrow,' he said.

'I bet I could persuade you.' Her voice was lower now, intimate.

'Any other night.'

'Because of your news? Now you *have* to tell me.'

'I had a personal audience with the Bishop the other day.'

It took her a moment. 'Your boss? The Big D.A.? He didn't *fire* you?'

'No.'

'Then what . . . ? Wait, don't tell me, he's quitting to form a law firm. Bishop and Estrada.'

'That's next year. First he's going to make me the most famous prosecutor in New York.'

'What? How?' Excited.

'You remember the Mariah Dodge murder? Woman raped and killed in an office building? The Skyscraper Slasher.'

'It was a black guy? Her boss? That one?'

'Hispanic. Name of Morales.'

'He cut her up because she wouldn't go to bed with him?'

'That was the first theory. The way it turned out they were lovers and she was dumping him.'

'I remember it was real gory.'

'That it was.'

'Didn't they put him away?'

'The conviction was thrown out on appeal.'

'Why?'

'The judge let in some testimony about how the victim told a friend that Morales told her to meet him at the office that night. Hearsay twice removed. The prosecutor offered it as proof Morales intended to go there, and the appeal courts decided it was inadmissible.' That was the official reason.

'You're telling me they're going to let him out on a technicality? A guy who did that?'

'He's already out. He's been out almost the whole time. I'm supposed to put him back in.'

'Really? You're prosecuting him?'

He was almost awake now, enjoying her reaction. Worry about the case nibbled at the edges of his pleasure; he made himself ignore it.

'I bet you'll have great stories to tell.'

'Life of the party, as always.' For a while he'd been flattered that she liked his courtroom war stories and liked having him tell them to her friends – her customers, really. Recently he had begun to feel like the court jester.

'It's going to look terrific on your résumé. And just in time.'

Just in time because she would be moving to L.A., he was sure she meant. For some reason, it killed his good mood. 'So that's my news. I spent most of my day studying the crime-scene pictures. Very detailed and very vivid, and they're still right there in front of me.'

'Oh, Joey, how awful. You go back to sleep and try not to have nightmares, and next time we talk I'll give you something else to think about.'

He had the feeling it was going to be harder than she thought to get his mind off this case. He did not say so.

2

In the morning he dove into the trial transcript, starting with the opening and closing arguments to the jury. It was easy to get carried away by the rhetoric. Lawrence Kahn, who had prosecuted Morales the first time, was a master of argument even with a weak case.

Estrada was startled out of Kahn's closing argument by a sharp knock on his office door. Dan Mahoney poked his head in past the dirty blue partition wall.

'Hey, guy. Ready for lunch?'

Estrada was astonished to see him. 'You can't be here. You're in the Caribbean.'

'Yeah, well . . . Kath and I split up Monday night, so I figured, why take a chance on too much sun?'

'I don't believe it. You guys were forever.'

Mahoney shrugged his heavy shoulders. 'Every day is its own surprise. And speaking of surprises . . .' He handed Estrada a brown paper shopping bag.

The box in the bag said EXECUTIVE DART BOARD. 'Just what I need.'

'Open it.' Basketball-tall and still muscular, Mahoney's imposing frame often seemed to camouflage a prankish twelve year old.

Estrada pulled out the dart board. It was metal and the darts had magnetic tips, nothing an outraged defense lawyer could use to take revenge. Pasted over the target's bull's-eye was a photograph: a prosperous-looking man in his forties, the kind of man an executive dart board was intended for. A man whose face Estrada was learning to recognize. He laughed. 'News travels fast.'

'Even on the tiny island of Vieques they know who's prosecuting Roberto Morales.' Mahoney was on his way to the door. 'Let's get some lunch.'

The two prosecutors had become friendly sharing a cramped office as D.A.'s-office rookies eight years before. Now, with Mahoney in Appeals and Estrada in a trial bureau, they stayed in touch by having lunch together at least once a week.

They went across the playground behind the courthouse to a small, dark Italian restaurant Mahoney liked. Mahoney, not usually a lunchtime drinker, ordered a double scotch on the rocks.

'How's it going on *Morales*?' he said quickly enough to keep Estrada from asking about him and Kath.

'It's weird,' Estrada confessed. 'You wish for one of these, dream about it from the moment you get here, the kind of case people would kill for. And then you have it and you're the focus of attention and everybody's waiting to see what your next move is going to be. That's the part that's not in the dream. What the hell do you do then?'

'Throw up?'

'Regularly.'

'What does Michelle think about your good fortune?'

'She thinks it's going to look great on my résumé.'

'Assuming you don't screw up.'

'My thought exactly.' About to tell Mahoney that Michelle was probably moving to Los Angeles, Estrada stopped himself. Given his friend's romantic problems, his own uneasiness seemed trivial.

'You know what bothers me?' he said. 'This case is big, but it's all because of Morales. Usually, you get a big case, it's because of the *victim*. That's how this one should be. I look at the crime-scene pictures and I think, what can that have been like for her?' Empathy for the victim had always been one of his strengths as a prosecutor, one of the forces that drove him. It was also one of his weaknesses. 'And all these people yelling about poor Roberto Morales. It makes me sick.'

'Wally Kubelik's idea of a defense' – Mahoney caught the waiter's eye and pointed at his already empty glass – 'inflame everybody and hope they forget the facts.'

Aware from the beginning of the case's community-relations dangers, the front office had assigned it to one of the city's sharpest and least volatile prosecutors. Lawrence Kahn was known for his ethical correctness, the thoroughness of his preparation for trial and his persuasive, low-key style in the courtroom. But despite the care and tact with which he had tried to handle the prosecution case, the evidence had forced him to paint the widely adulated Morales as a thin-skinned macho with a violent temper, ready to use the first sharp blade that came to hand.

There had been immediate cries of 'racist stereotype,' and defense lawyer Walter Kubelik had made sure that the whole trial was conducted on the verge of explosion. Mercifully, it had not been long as major murder trials went, less than a month from jury selection to closing arguments.

The jurors had quarreled for a week before finding Morales not guilty of intentional murder. They had found him guilty of first-degree manslaughter, as a lesser included charge of intentional murder. On the charge of rape they had deadlocked, as they had on the indictment's second, distinct, murder count, which combined rape and killing to yield the crime sometimes called felony murder.

Not quite a year and a half later, the court's Appellate Division had decided that trial judge Luz Martinez had allowed the prosecution to use evidence she should have excluded as inadmissible, and that she had compounded her error by encouraging the jury to give weight to that same evidence. And now the Court of Appeals had affirmed that judgment.

Morales's supporters, including an impressive number of

national and state legislators and city council members, had been quick to claim that the results on appeal proved not only that the first trial had been unfair and the verdict wrong, but that Morales had been falsely accused.

'I already had a visit from the office thought-police,' Estrada told Mahoney. 'Our colleagues in El Grupo Latino think I should refuse the case because I'm in it as a token. And the truth is they're right.'

'What! You're going to turn it down?'

'Not right about that, right that I got this because of my name.'

Estrada noted his friend's skeptical expression. 'There's – what? – six hundred of us, give or take a few, every last one sure he's the greatest? He or she. And a big chunk of them dying to have a shot at Morales.' The cowboys and the risk-takers, especially. Nothing got their blood running like one where there was a real chance it could go the other way. 'So it had to be more than my pretty face and my fancy footwork.'

'A pretty face and fancy footwork go a long way,' Mahoney said. 'Look how far they got you already.'

'Hey, listen, I'm a sucker for a compliment, but I saw the truth, talking to Bishop.'

'You speak Spanish,' the District Attorney had said, looking for verification.

'Yes, sir. Three years in high school and four in college, and I get plenty of practice right here in the office.'

'Well . . . good. Keep it up. It's important.'

'But I could tell by the way he said it, he wished I'd learned it at my mother's knee.'

'I guess he never met your mother.' Mahoney had. 'That's a funny picture, her feeding you Spanish with your bottle.'

'She didn't think so.'

Nor had she been impressed by the case's importance. 'That's very nice, I'm sure,' had been all the congratulation she could muster. Abigail Smithfield Estrada was no longer patient with her son's assurances that he was going to move on from the D.A.'s office.

'And my father's got to be rotating in his grave,' he told Mahoney. 'I remember, when I wanted to take Spanish at Classical High, you know what he said? He said, "They'll think you're a P.R. or some damn thing, talking that language, with your name." He really said that. A man who kept framed relics of his aristocratic Spanish ancestors all over the house.'

Almost sixteen years after his father's death, Estrada still had not figured out how to feel about him. A strapping man who always smelled of the chemicals he worked with as an electroplater, Big Jim Estrada had been an offhand tyrant with his older kids; he had spared little time for his afterthought youngest son, born a decade late. As soon as Joey Estrada had learned where babies came from and how they were prevented he had labeled himself an unwelcome accident. Nothing in his father's manner had ever told him otherwise.

Then, at the height of his high-school success in the classroom and on the football field, his father had in two short years dwindled to nothing, poisoned by his work and consumed by his drive for revenge and restitution. He had fought death and his employers' insurance company with equal desperation. At the end he had displayed an instinct for manipulation no one had ever guessed at: rewarding the young son he had so often ignored with a legacy freighted with guilt and obligation, charging him to travel the long, bumpy road through college and law school.

He could still see his father in the hospital bed, I.V. tubes in his arm, breathing tube in his nose, tubes under the blankets leading to the plastic sack clipped to the side of the bed.

'Look at me good, Joey.' He had gripped his teenage son's arm with a strength that brought back memories of his robust days. 'This is what they do to you if you don't have power. Don't let this happen to an Estrada, ever again. Always remember, we were born to great things.'

'The closer he got to the end, the more he talked about "our noble Castilian name." And now the District Attorney of New York County wants the whole world to think Big Jim

Estrada's little boy Joey is Puerto Rican.'

'It's not healthy to be bitter, Joseph,' Mahoney said.

'It's not healthy to be the one they throw to the wolves when a big press case goes sour. And you want to know the real joke? Bishop was in such a hurry to find someone who could pass for Latino but wasn't so Latino he'd feel used and make a stink, that he went too far. You think they're not going to check up on me? How hard is it to find out that my mother's family goes back almost to the *Mayflower*, or that the Estradas got to this country five generations ago? How's Bishop going to look? How am I going to look?'

'Did you point this out to anyone?'

'I damn well should have. Right then all I could think was, When's the next time I'm going to get a case this big?'

'Never, if you're lucky.' Even through the scotch, Mahoney sounded like a man who knew what he was talking about.

'Did you work on the appeal? I didn't see your name on the brief.'

'We all kicked it around. The way I remember it, the case was so weak there was a real chance the verdict would be thrown out as not supported by the evidence.'

'It wasn't *that* bad.' But Estrada was talking to make himself feel better, and he knew it.

'I remember we decided the trial was so political no one would dare say the verdict was against the evidence. We figured they'd reverse the conviction on the hearsay instead, in which case there wasn't going to be anything left for the next guy to use.'

'It could be worse,' Estrada said. 'All they knocked out was the part where Morales said he was going to be at the office and she should meet him there. That hurts a lot – the jury relied on it to place him at the scene – but it doesn't mean I can't win. As long as there are no big surprises.'

'Hey, you can do it. If anybody can do it, you can.'

'I've got to do it. This is why I'm still here after all these years, to get one like this, so nobody would say Joe Who? when they saw my résumé.'

Mahoney grinned evilly. 'You don't have to win for that. They'll know who you are for sure if you blow it.'

On his way to Lawrence Kahn's new office to confer about the case, Estrada went to the men's room to wash up and take inventory. Times like this, he needed to remind himself that his internal uncertainties were masked by the view from outside: high brow framed by light brown hair, large brown eyes set slightly wide, straight nose, ready smile, strong jaw. The kind of face that inclined people to be receptive, or so he was told. He could never quite see it himself. The pieces were there but when he looked at them they added up only to today's version of the same face that had always stared back at him.

Waiting for the elevator, interminably as usual, he was spotted by Gerry Lomax, the defense lawyer on one of his pending armed robberies. Lomax's stock in trade seemed to be dragging out plea deals past the point of endurance.

'Hey, there you are. They told me you weren't in.'

'I wasn't. I'm not.'

'Look, Joe, I need to talk to you.'

'We've already talked.' He poked the elevator button again. 'I told you, five to ten. Right now I've got an appointment.' He turned back to the elevator.

Lomax grabbed his arm. 'Wait a minute.'

He pulled free. 'I said I've got an appointment. You want to talk, come back later.'

'I can get him to plead if he can have rob three and two and a half to five.'

'Are you crazy?' Where the hell was the elevator? 'I told you – rob two, and five to ten.'

'You told me four to eight.'

'That offer expired a week ago, and you know it.'

'You want the plea, don't you?' Lomax challenged. 'You don't want this case dragging through the system and getting in the way of the Morales trial.'

Estrada had been watching the elevator doors. Now he turned to the defense lawyer.

'Is that a threat?' It was ridiculous: if Lomax's case went to court, a different A.D.A. would take it there. Nobody was about to put the whole Morales prosecution at the mercy of some other judge's schedule for the sake of a routine armed robbery. 'Because if it is a threat—' Behind him, the elevator bell chimed. In mid sentence, he lunged for the already closing doors, glad to leave Lomax behind.

He checked his watch as the elevator released him into the downstairs lobby. He could still make it to Kahn's on time. He pushed through the revolving door into a day that had turned gray and cold. A dozen years had not taught him what to expect from April in New York.

He was whisked up to the offices of the Kahn Commission in an ornate old elevator with dark wood paneling and polished-brass fixtures. The illusion of luxury stopped at the commission's spartan reception area: pale blue walls, a government-issue metal desk and a security guard doubling as receptionist. Some kind of cop, most likely a state trooper. He took Estrada's name and told him to sign in and have a seat. Estrada sat there waiting to be fetched, uncomfortable on the plastic chair's unyielding curve, trying not to feel like a jerk for having worried so much about being on time.

The Kahn Commission had been created as a result of the death in police custody of Abdullah Timmins, a reluctant murder witness who had reportedly died while an assistant district attorney waiting across the hall to question him had done nothing to intervene. Under pressure to name a special prosecutor, the governor had gone a giant step further and formed a panel that would investigate and prosecute not just the Timmins case but every significant allegation that the city's police department was mistreating members of minority groups. Besides prosecuting the most serious cases, the commission was to generate a report on the current state of police-minority relations, with recommendations for improvement.

Snatching Lawrence Kahn from his job as the mayor's criminal-justice coordinator, where he'd gone from the D.A.'s office, had been a conscious gamble by the governor. The other seven commissioners he had appointed were civic leaders from minority communities, chosen to represent their constituencies and to see that the commission lived up to its mandate. For that reason, the logic went, the person at the top had to be a well-regarded prosecutor, and he had to be white, to keep the white middle class from writing the commission off as simply a way to pander to minority voters.

It was a delicate balance, and it had been left to Kahn to meet the initial onslaught of criticism – noisy claims that the commission was a fraud, that anything it did would be a whitewash. He had taken it head on, inviting the skeptics to watch him as closely as they wanted, making integrity and openness points of honor for himself and his staff.

Waiting for Kahn, Estrada did his best to put the coming meeting in perspective. He had been trained in part by Lawrence Kahn, had worked on his first murder trial under him. That had been almost five years ago, soon after Kahn had stepped down as deputy chief of the Trial Division to return to the daily challenge of trial work as a senior trial counsel. The trial had ended well, with a murder verdict and the maximum sentence – twenty-five to life – but not before Estrada had come too close to scuttling it and making serious trouble for Kahn, as well. Since then Estrada had done his best to avoid his former mentor.

He consoled himself now with the thought that Kahn had put in a lot of courtroom time since then, had bullied a lot of young A.D.A.'s into something approximating experience. Probably they had made stupid mistakes, too.

Eventually, Kahn appeared. He was a big man, wide and thick, with a slumping posture that made him seem shorter than he was. His wavy hair had been silver-gray since law school, and he radiated a fatherly aura he had somehow acquired not long after his thirtieth birthday.

He led Estrada back to his office, a wide room with a desk and conference table arranged in a T, mimicking the executive style at the D.A.'s office. He indicated a worn vinyl couch for Estrada to sit on and lowered himself into an equally broken-down easy chair. 'I see you're coming up in the world.'

'It's a big responsibility. I hope I'm up to it.'

'If you remember any of what I taught you, you should be all right.'

Estrada was not sure Kahn meant that as praise, but he pushed ahead. 'I'll be using your transcript as a guide, as far as how to use the evidence. I only wish I were half as good as you are with a jury.'

Kahn let the compliment pass unacknowledged. 'Is there anything in particular . . .' He said it with collegial interest, but the unstated message was clear: my time is valuable.

'I don't have any specific questions, not yet. Just one general one. Is there anything that isn't apparent in the transcript, any traps you can think of, ways I might trip up that I'd be likely to miss?'

'Like what?' As if to deny the very point of the question.

'I don't know . . .' A dumb thing to say. He had not been sure whether he should ask for this meeting, and the way it was going the answer was a clear no. 'Personalities of the cops or the witnesses, for one thing. People I should be careful of, evidence that isn't as strong as it looks in the transcript. And especially anything you didn't get a chance to follow up on that might be useful.'

'You're looking for a shortcut.'

'I don't think of it that way.'

'The modern plague. The problem is, shortcuts have a tendency to lead in the wrong direction.'

Estrada had no response.

'You know, Kubelik really caught me, putting that neighbor on the stand,' Kahn volunteered out of the blue. 'The cops on the case never could find that apartment, the one Morales and Mariah used as a love nest. We heard about it from Mariah's friends, but Morales covered his trail so well that all I knew was there was an apartment the two of them used. There was no way I could be prepared for Kubelik putting the downstairs neighbor on to say the two of them had been there that afternoon making the bedsprings creak. I did him some damage on cross – enough, anyway, to keep them from throwing out the rape charge. But he'll be harder to catch when you go after him this time, unless he's a complete idiot, and Morales's lawyer, too . . . Who *is* Morales's lawyer this time?'

'Nobody's filed an appearance yet.'

'It'll be interesting to see who turns up. The point is, you'll want to concentrate on that neighbor. The way they popped him on me I didn't have time to come up with a rebuttal that was worth anything. And he's crucial because if they were together at the apartment that afternoon then the defense has an explanation for all the evidence of sexual contact – semen, pubic hair, all of it. You're liable to lose the rape, and without the rape there's nothing to goose the manslaughter up to felony murder.'

And without felony murder there could be no life sentence, because the first jury had acquitted on intentional murder. The defense got to retry a conviction now and then, but acquittals were forever.

'There's bound to be something you can use against the neighbor,' Kahn continued. 'Morales bought him or put pressure on him or applied some other influence – something you can use to impeach him besides that he's got an old man's memory and it's a busy neighborhood.'

Estrada made notes as if it were an approach he had not already thought of. 'Thanks. I'll follow it up.'

'Well, I don't want to rush you out, but I'm in the middle of a crisis. One of my many.'

Estrada stood. 'I appreciate your taking the time to see me.'

'Any questions as you go along, feel free to call. I'll do my best to get you an answer in a reasonable amount of time.' He held out a hand. 'Good luck with it. The bastard's a murderer. He belongs in prison.'

'I'll do my best, sir.' The honorific came out unbidden. Could it be that in some recess of his mind he still saw the older man as a mentor, still hoped for his approval? The idea did not make Estrada happy: he already had enough trouble propitiating his father's shade. 'Thanks again.'

Estrada walked to the door alone. His hand was on the knob when Kahn called to him.

'Joe.'

He turned back. Kahn was at his desk dialing the phone.

'One more thing. Watch out for the sister.'

Estrada wanted to know what that meant, but Kahn was already on the phone.

3

Estrada found as he took care of the case's routine details that he was thinking constantly about Roberto Morales. He wanted to know how Morales had become rich and prominent, what made him tick, how he could have first jeopardized and then thrown away what must have been the culmination of a lifetime's work. And for what – an occasional nooner and a moment's anger at being rejected?

He dug through Kahn's files and found a thick folder of newspaper and magazine articles. He paged through it, getting a sense of Morales's progress from the Brooklyn barrio through a scholarship-funded Ivy League education and a postgraduate career that had taken off from early successes rehabilitating residential housing and soared to the presidency of Phoenix Enterprises, a development company that had planned to revitalize a chunk of the Brooklyn riverfront. It was a saga that would have thrilled a junior chamber of commerce audience anywhere in the country, and it had prompted a fair number of awards from various Hispanic organizations, the kind of awards you did not get unless you were a major benefactor.

Since the murder, Morales had armored himself in volunteer work. When he was not managing the out-of-state real-estate holdings that kept him prosperous, he was working hard at local projects he had founded and helped finance: a drug-rehabilitation center, a resource center for small businesses and a housing renewal program.

Estrada picked up the hefty police file to review what the cops had learned about Morales during the investigation. The detectives' follow-up reports – recorded on the form called a DD–5 – were, as usual, in reverse chronological order, listed only by the interviewees' names, no clue who they were. If you were not already familiar with the case, it was impossible to tell why any given person had been interviewed. He looked for a compilation of the hundreds of interviews, a cross-index of some kind listing areas of information and the DD-5's that were relevant. He did not find one. He walked down the corridor with the file.

Lisa Stein was at her desk in the paralegals' office, her long blonde hair pushed back out of the way of the earmuff headphones she was using. She was transcribing an evidence tape from some other case into the word processor, the last of the old jobs she was wrapping up.

She was the brightest of the Ivy League paralegals spending two years in the office to decide whether they wanted to become lawyers. Despite her relative lack of experience, Estrada had chosen her as his full-time paralegal on *Morales* for her lively intelligence and inquisitiveness. His job was going to be hard enough without having to fight the inertia of a blasé career paralegal.

She saw him standing in the doorway and found a place to stop.

'Okay, Stein, I've got some real work for you.' He dropped the police file on her desk. It made the computer keyboard jump.

'I know, you want me to index it.' She made a face at her computer. 'I have to finish this first. Is tomorrow okay to start? Or else I can stay late if you want.'

'Tomorrow is fine.' But he was pleased to see how eager she was.

He got back to his office just in time to get a phone call from Tommy Clemente, the Task Force detective who had been responsible for the case during the original investigation and the first trial. They set up a meeting for four-fifteen that afternoon. Estrada went back down the hall to retrieve the police file so he could skim through some of Clemente's reports.

Just after three the phone rang. 'A Mrs Dodge calling person-to-person,' Ginny, the bureau receptionist, told him.

'Put her on.' He wondered if her husband knew about this call.

'Mr Joseph Estrada?' an operator said.

'That's me.'

'Just a moment, please.' Silence, then some clicks on the line. 'Mr Estrada? This is Sylvia Dodge. Mariah's mother.' The same pleasant voice, more youthful than he remembered.

'Yes, Mrs Dodge, what can I do for you?' As warm as he could get without laying it on too thick.

'Well, I'm not supposed to do this – call you, I mean – but I do have a question or two?' There was a hesitation. Estrada could almost see her gathering herself to begin.

'About this new trial . . . I simply don't understand why. The Doctor says it's a bunch of no-backbone liberals giving in to racist pressure, but even if that's true there has to be a *reason*, doesn't there? Tess – Mariah's sister? – tried to explain why they threw out the first trial but I guess I'm just slow because I heard everything she told me and I purely didn't understand it at all.'

'Let me see if I can help.' He gave her a quick rundown on the need to place the accused at the scene of the crime. Then he described defense lawyer Walter Kubelik's specific attacks on the physical and I.D. evidence that Kahn had offered.

'Yes, I remember most of that from the trial.'

'Good. Now, Mr Kahn's problem' – and mine, now – 'was to convince the jury that Morales went to the building to see Mariah.' Too late, he remembered the rule about not using Morales's name. 'Sorry about the name.'

'That's all right. That's the Doctor's problem. You just go

ahead and don't worry about anything but what you're telling me. I want to get it all before I run out of change.'

'Are you at a pay phone?' That would explain the silence and the clicks: time out for her to deposit a pile of quarters.

'Well, I couldn't do this from . . . Yes, I am.'

'Give me the number and I'll call you right back.'

'Okay,' he said when they had reestablished contact. 'Now the story gets more complicated. To keep out unreliable evidence there are rules about what the jury isn't allowed to see or hear. We call anything like that "inadmissible evidence." It's for the judge to decide how to apply those rules.'

'I understand that.'

'Most of the time we only let the jury listen to the words of people they can see for themselves, people both sides can examine in the jury's presence. That way the jury decides if the testimony is reliable based on what it sees and hears. Witnesses don't usually get to testify about statements other people made outside the courtroom, much less statements about *other* statements made by third parties.'

'I suppose that makes sense.'

'Okay. Good. Now, you probably remember there was a witness, a friend of Mariah's, who testified that Mariah said she intended to go to the office because Morales had asked her to come and had said he intended to be there himself.'

'Yes . . .'

'Now, if Mariah told a friend she expected to see Morales at the office, that's probably a good indication that *Mariah thought* he was going to be there. The problem comes with the second step. She said *he said* he was going to be there. The question is, should that be admitted? Does it tell us something reliable about *his* intentions?'

'Doesn't it? If he said that?'

'Well, as it happens that's an area of the law where there's plenty of disagreement. In our case the judge not only admitted the statement into evidence, but when the jury asked specifically about it later, the judge said yes, Mariah's alleged statement about what she said Morales said to her could be taken as evidence that Morales did intend to go to the office to meet her. The Court of Appeals said the judge was wrong, she'd gone too far.'

'And that's it? That's the reason we have to have another trial?'

'You have to bear in mind that the jury asked the judge that question because the answer was important to them. In a way, the whole trial hinged on that one statement. It kept Morales's lawyer from casting doubt on the witnesses who said they saw Morales in the building that night.'

'Mariah wouldn't lie,' her mother said. 'Why would she lie about a thing like that?'

'It isn't just whether she lied, it's whether she misunderstood him, or whether *he* was lying to *her*.'

'Why? Why would he?'

'That's where the trial judge and the other judges disagreed.' It was an oversimplification, but he hoped it would do.

'I don't understand. The truth is the truth.'

She said it so earnestly it made his heart ache. How many times had he wished it were that simple? How many people had been brought to grief because it wasn't?

'There are a lot of things that are true – sometimes things straight out of the written public record – that are still inadmissible as evidence.'

'I don't see how anyone can talk about justice if that's true.' She sighed. 'I do appreciate your being so kind as to help me understand all this, though I must say it seems to me a person is guilty or he isn't, and if he's guilty they ought to put him behind bars and be done with it, none of this second-guessing and doing it over. Making people live through their pain over and over again. That's not how it should be.'

Not how it should be. He contemplated the truth of that while he waited for Clemente to arrive. He wished he could be sure that even a murder conviction was enough to justify suffering that repeated pain.

* * *

At first glance the man who walked through Estrada's office door promptly at four-fifteen was less than impressive. Average height and build, he was wearing a baggy suit that he must have thought was hip but that succeeded only in looking too big for him. A closer look at the weathered face made Estrada think of a Revolutionary War flag: picture of a viper – DON'T TREAD ON ME, the motto said.

He came around his desk to greet the detective. 'I'm Joe Estrada. I'm going to be retrying Roberto Morales.'

Tommy Clemente made no move to shake Estrada's hand. 'What can I do for you?'

Estrada waved him to the visitor's chair. Clemente slumped into it and reached inside his jacket. To pull a gun, Estrada thought for a single absurd moment.

'Mind if I smoke?'

It was against the rules, against a city ordinance in fact, and Estrada's office was close and stuffy at best, but saying that was not the way to begin with Clemente.

'I don't know how much you know about why the conviction was reversed . . .' Settling in behind his desk again.

'Not much. Hearsay problems, if I remember. And the judge fucked up some way. Bullshit technicalities.'

'Bullshit or not, we're stuck with it. And one of the results is that we're hurting for evidence the man was at the scene. I'm not too happy with what we can say about his motive, either.'

'You kidding me? You see her? The deceased? The guy had a mighty powerful Jones for that woman, and you won't catch anybody wondering why. She cuts him off at the knees and calls him nasty names. He's a hot-blooded Latin type – no offense – so he puts it to her good, one last time, and then he cuts her throat so she can't give him any more grief. Seems pretty simple to me.'

'Maybe if we had somebody who actually heard what she said, instead of a couple of friends who heard her say she meant to say it. Secondhand reports won't buy us much if the judge spends a lot of time telling the jury about hearsay and what a lousy form of proof it is. Which is exactly what she's going to do, considering the way the appeals courts went after her.'

Clemente spread his hands. 'Look – I bring in the witnesses. I can't do a damn thing if some judge tells the jury not to listen to them.'

'Nobody's blaming you. The question is, is there any better way we can prove motive?'

'You don't need motive. That's gravy. Means and opportunity is all the law requires.'

Estrada leaned forward, elbows on his desk. 'Don't play dumb with me, detective. I need to know what I can find on Roberto Morales. I have two women who can tell me about how Mariah Dodge felt about him, and how badly she *said* she wanted to get out of their affair. But I have no witnesses to any arguments or any mistreatment in the past. I don't have any evidence that he ever threatened her. I don't have anyone in the building overhearing an argument that night. You name it, I don't have it.'

'Look, counselor' – the title was slick with sarcasm – 'Larry Kahn did fine with what he had. We got him what evidence there was to get, and he brought in a verdict. And if you think we're going to find anything now, three years later, that we didn't find then, well, maybe you're in the wrong line of work.' Clemente stood up. 'Now, if you have something you want me to do on the case, you want me to go talk to witnesses from the first trial, you want me to go over the file with you, explain what you don't understand, that's fine, I'm your guy. Otherwise, I got to get back to work.'

The meeting with Tommy Clemente reinforced Estrada's worries about depending on a detective who had a record to protect. He talked to Lou Collins, his bureau chief, about getting someone from the D.A.'s-office detective squad.

'It took some arm twisting,' Collins told him after a talk

with the squad commander, 'but I got you the best. Stash McMorris or Richie Eilewitz, take your pick.'

Estrada had not worked with either man, knew them only slightly. 'The best' was an exaggeration. By reputation Eilewitz was the smarter of the two, McMorris the more reliable.

Estrada picked McMorris for the worst of reasons. There was tension in Brooklyn between the Hispanic community and the Hasidic Jews who were their immediate neighbors. Estrada did not want to send a Jewish detective to Southside, where Morales had his most loyal and passionate following. McMorris was Catholic, which would help on Southside, and with his Polish mother and Irish father he would be welcome on Northside, where Morales had planned to build the Phoenix Project, his riverbank Oz.

It was the curse of the Morales case once again: ethnic politics as prime directive. Estrada hated it, even though he knew it had gotten him the job.

At week's end Estrada had a meeting with Collins and Collins's boss, Natalie Muir, one of the Trial Division's two deputy chiefs.

'I've been going through the transcript,' Estrada told them. 'Without the testimony that Morales intended to meet Mariah Dodge at the office, we're relying on a couple of security guards who can't do better than placing him in the building lobby – and maybe in the elevator. It makes a borderline case significantly weaker.'

'That's not unexpected.' Muir was a solid, squarish woman whose hairstyle, makeup and clothes made no attempt at adornment. She was perpetually impatient, all business.

'It's going to be a problem scrounging up anybody new at this late date,' Estrada continued. 'If I'm going to do that I can't take time to learn about matching body fluids with DNA testing and PCR enhancement and the rest of it. I've never had a blood case, and it looks to me like it's worth a lifetime's study.'

'If you want something, ask for it,' Muir told him.

'I need a second seat. Not for the legal issues, I don't expect a problem there. I need somebody who knows the whole drill on rape, somebody with DNA experience.'

Muir looked at Collins, too smart not to guess that Estrada had brought this up before.

'All right,' she said. 'We'll see what we can do.'

She was barely out the door of Collins's office when he rounded on Estrada, eyes narrowed. 'What the hell was that for?'

'What?'

'Don't give me that shit. You know *what*.' Medium-short, muscular and bald, the bureau chief intensified his resemblance to a bulldog by carrying his head well forward on a thick neck, his lower jaw thrust out pugnaciously. 'You need a second seat, you talk to me about it.'

'I have been.'

'Nobody loves a wiseass, Estrada.' Collins turned abruptly and walked back to his desk. 'Sit down,' he commanded.

Estrada sat.

'All right.' Collins poked a finger in Estrada's direction. 'Facts of life. Natalie Muir is leaving the office this summer, late July or early August. She's not coming back.'

'No kidding?' Estrada had heard some rumors; he did not think it was politic to say so.

'*No kidding*.' Full of sarcasm. 'Do you want to think about what that means, or should I paint you a picture?'

'You're in line for her job?' That had not been in the rumors.

'The way I hear it, there are two names on the list, and I'm one of them.'

'Nice.'

'Maybe. As somebody said one time, there is no second place.' Collins's eyes narrowed again. 'I'm going to spell this out for you so I'm sure you have it right. If I move up, then my job goes to Talley or Bloch' – his deputy bureau chiefs –

'and if you don't screw up, you're in line for the slot that opens up. ¿Comprende?'

It was the trickle-down effect at work on the organization chart, and even though Estrada's future lay elsewhere, the promotion could make a major difference in where he went and at what level. It could be a giant step toward fulfilling his family obligation: position and money to satisfy his dead father's dreams and repay his brothers and sister their lost legacy, and as a plaintiff's lawyer the ability to give people like his father a fighting chance against the companies that oppressed them and betrayed them the way Big Jim Estrada had been oppressed and betrayed.

'I don't want you to think you can do something smart and get me this job, because you can't,' Collins pointed out. 'But if you screw up you can sure as hell lose it for me. And if I don't move up, neither does anybody else in the bureau, and that means we're all stuck here together exactly the way we are now. You got that?'

Estrada nodded.

'Good. The front office wants this case over and done with yesterday, so that we can forget about it and move on. I've already been running interference for you, keeping them off your ass. The drill is, you keep me posted and I'll keep them posted. And you don't go over my head or behind my back. To anyone, for anything. You get that, too?'

'I get it.'

'You'd better. Now. This business of a second seat. I know what you need and I've been trying to figure out how to make this work for you and for me. Now that you opened your mouth to Muir, there's no question how it's going to go. And I have the feeling you're not going to be happy with how it comes out.'

'What do you mean?'

The bureau chief ignored Estrada's question. 'That's all for now. Everybody gets a mistake or two at the beginning. You've had yours.'

4

Estrada took home some of the file material on Roberto Morales for the weekend. Reading about him only increased Estrada's fascination with the man. On Sunday Estrada gave in to the universal prosecutors' temptation: playing detective.

He sat slouched in the front seat of the office sedan he had signed out, using its rearview mirror to watch the door of the Park Avenue building where the Moraleses lived. He was thankful for the unseasonably warm weather, hopeful that it would bring them out to play. It was certainly bringing out the rest of the neighborhood.

The longer he sat, the harder it was to keep his attention from wandering, but for all the distractions of the upper-class street scene he noticed the family Morales the minute the doorman ushered them out of the building. It was Morales's wife who drew Estrada's eye – tall, slender and long-limbed, with creamy pale skin and rich brown hair tied back in a pony tail. There was no missing the fact that Marti Morales was a fashion model, and it was easy to believe that before the demands of motherhood had distracted her she had been near the top of her profession.

The kids, a boy of seven and a five-year-old girl, were dressed, like their mother, in bleached-out jeans and white shirts, and also like her they moved with a smoothness too natural to be learned. Morales, in khakis, a blue button-down shirt and a navy blazer, was last out the door. He looked trim and athletic, younger than his forty-six years.

Estrada waited until they had crossed the avenue before he got out of the car to follow them. He gave them a good lead, assuming they were headed for Central Park. Morales and his wife were walking together, the kids skipping on ahead.

Estrada stayed behind them as they strolled through the park. The main roadway, closed to traffic, was thronged with joggers and bicyclists. The dogwoods were beginning to bloom, and there was a dusting of pale green buds on some of the trees. The Moraleses continued their flawless imitation of ordinary privileged people.

When they queued up for the zoo, Estrada decided it was time to call it a day. He got in line a dozen people behind them, anyway, feeling reckless. He continued to keep his distance after they had all passed through the turnstiles. The kids, who had been restrained as they walked through the park, seemed full of new energy, running ahead of their parents, then back to grab their hands, then off again. They wanted to see the seals first, and then the polar bears.

Then they wanted to see the monkeys. Again, Estrada knew he should not follow, and again he did. Being inside the tropical rainforest exhibit was far more confining and unpredictable than strolling the outdoor spaces of the zoo. Here, Estrada felt conspicuous for the first time. He was dressed not much differently from Morales, but he was by himself – a man past thirty, no kids and no girlfriend, alone in an imitation paradise. He tried to look like he was enjoying the birds flying free among the trees and the furry black-and-white monkeys behind the almost-invisible glass wall, while at the same time keeping track of his quarry.

The seven year old darted past, chased by his little sister, giggling. She ran full into Estrada and sat down abruptly from the impact. His instincts took over and he bent to make sure she was all right. Her face was screwed up in distress and fast getting red.

'Are you okay?' he asked in what he thought was a soothing voice. She began to cry.

Marti Morales came up from behind him and kneeled to take the little girl in her arms. He was close enough to count the hairs on the nape of her neck. Her perfume was the scent of woods and wildflowers.

'I'm sorry,' she said, turning to Estrada. 'They get so excited.' The little girl was smiling now, holding her mother's hand.

He could not speak. Doing his best to smile, he got up and turned to move off, almost colliding with Roberto Morales, who was squatted down to talk with soft intensity to his son. Estrada made his way against the flow of people and out into the air, where after a while he began to breathe again. He filed under to-be-solved the question of why a man with a family like that and a wife like that would want to get involved with another woman.

Michelle did not think it was such a mystery when he posed it to her on the phone. 'You don't know what their marriage is really like. Besides, guys are like that. You should see it out here. In New York I have it down, so guys know to leave me alone. Out here they're so into it I'm having to develop a whole new technique to keep them off me. The awful truth is, most married guys can't keep it in their pants. And there's always somebody dumb enough to be a willing partner.'

'She's right,' Mahoney agreed. 'It takes two.'

They were in the locker room of the Y where Mahoney had just decreed they should become members, drying off and dressing after sharing a lane in the pool, groaning about how out of shape they were. Estrada, concerned that his friend might be sitting alone brooding on his suddenly womanless state, had called to suggest a movie; Mahoney had goaded him into this attempt to regain the past. Neither of them had ever been a competitive swimmer but both had been pushed into swimming-team workouts by their college coaches as a result of injuries playing ball. They had both still been at it, irregularly, when they became officemates. Long hours processing complaints and handling arraignments and unwinding in nearby bars had quickly changed their habits. It had been years since Estrada had worked out regularly in a pool or anywhere else.

Mahoney zipped up his gym bag. 'Only I wouldn't be so quick to blame it on the guy every time.'

'I'm talking about *this* time. Anyway, blaming the victim is for defense lawyers.'

'I didn't mean poor Ms Dodge. I was talking generally about who seduces whom in the wide world of sex and betrayal. Now that you mention it, though, maybe you ought to follow up on how they got started with each other. It might have something to do with how they ended up.'

Estrada's week started with the first meeting of his complete prosecution team. He was reminded of the old adage: Be careful what you wish for – you might get it.

Gathered in his office were Lisa Stein, Stash McMorris and Tommy Clemente. And Nancy Rosen, the requested second-seat A.D.A., the last person he would have asked for and the reason why Collins had predicted he might not be happy with Muir's intervention.

Nancy Rosen and Joe Estrada had come to the office at the same time, and she had an excellent courtroom record in the Sex Crimes Unit. Two years earlier she had second-seated Larry Kahn in the first Morales trial. That experience made her a logical choice to work on the retrial, but not as second seat to a lawyer in no way her senior.

She had been famously enraged when she'd heard that Estrada had been given the assignment instead of her. Somebody had to have leaned on her awfully hard to get her to come aboard in the second seat, Estrada was sure. The result was likely to be a gift horse full of angry Greeks.

With the trial staff crowded in, Estrada's office was full beyond capacity. The second day of the unexpected April heat wave had left the building's heating and air conditioning system even more muddled than usual, pouring out full winter heat. Estrada hoped he could get through the high points before the temperature frayed their patience too badly.

He started with the crime-scene details: no murder weapon, no usable fingerprints except of people with regular access to the office. Bloody streaks on the back of the couch, as if it had been wiped with a cloth after the murder, and the same on an end table next to the couch. Presumably the killer had tried to obscure any signs of his presence – though the tweed-covered couch was unlikely to show prints, even in blood, and no one had a good theory about why he had wiped off the table, which was at the end of the couch past the victim's feet. Fiber evidence indicated that the cleanup had been done at least in part with a garment made of black nylon and black cotton. The missing underpants, probably black lace.

There were shapeless bloody footprints leading to the shower in Morales's private bathroom. Mariah Dodge's blood was in the shower drain along with her hair and Morales's and a few unidentified hairs and fibers. The significant points about the body were the neck wounds, some smaller cuts on her chin and two long scratches on her left cheek which Kahn had used as signs of pre-rape threat with the murder weapon. There was an area on her right wrist relatively free of blood, indicating that it had been covered at the time her throat was slashed. Semen and pubic hair. The pubic hair was almost useless as evidence. It did not exclude Morales, but neither did it exclude millions of other men.

'There's one thing we all need to keep in mind,' Estrada said after he had reviewed everybody's initial assignments preparing the case. 'The weakest part of the prosecution case the first time was motive. We need as much corroboration as we can get on that. Strong language and sexual rejection have been the motive for plenty of murders, but murderous jealous rages aren't the kind of behavior juries associate with people like Morales.'

'Why not?' Clemente wanted to know. 'Like I said before, he's a hot-blooded Latin.'

Rosen, her moon face flushed with the heat, had been sitting in resolute, sullen silence. Clemente's words brought a smile to her lips.

'That's exactly what he is, Tommy.' Estrada was damned if he was going to rise to Clemente's bait. 'And it's what we want the jury to think he is, too. But God help us if we ever come out and say it. Even imply it. The best thing that could happen to us would be to find a different motive altogether.'

That produced a chorus of groans. Estrada plunged ahead.

'The point is, we all know what a bitch retrials are. Witnesses forget, they die, they disappear. Evidence deteriorates. Without something new it's damn hard not to do worse the second time around. And much as I respect Larry Kahn, reading the record I can't help thinking he was one lucky prosecutor on this one, getting any kind of conviction.'

He looked at Rosen as he said it. She stared back.

'The moral of the story is we've got to do better on everything. Especially on motive.'

A large, flat envelope arrived with Estrada's mail the next morning. It had a typewritten address label and a return address in Texas that was not the Dodges'. He ripped it open: it contained a note and a photograph.

The picture showed a woman in her mid-thirties with precise, regular features, an abundance of red hair and compelling emerald-green eyes. She was wearing a soft white blouse unbuttoned only enough to show a graceful neck and a hint of delicately curved collarbones that complemented the precision of her features. She was beautiful in a wholesome, open way: her whole face shone with an eagerness for life. Mariah Dodge as she had been . . . before.

The note said, 'Thank you for your kind explanation. I made this copy of our favorite picture for you, because the Dr told me what you said about wanting one. He doesn't know I did this. Please don't mention it if you talk to him.' There was no signature.

Stash McMorris arrived as Estrada was putting the picture on his bulletin board. Beefy and florid, McMorris made Estrada think of the strongman in a teeterboard act, the one who caught the others on his shoulders and at the end of the act supported a pyramid of ten.

'Jesus,' he said, 'isn't she something.'

'Was.'

'Yeah. What a waste.'

'That's why I'm putting this up. So we remember what she was like, alive. So we never think of her as a piece of meat on a morgue slab.'

McMorris pulled out his pocket notebook.

'I called Santos again,' he said, flipping pages. 'He's still giving me a hard time.'

Ramon Santos was the security guard who said he had seen Morales coming into the building around the time of the murder. The I.D. witness who knew him best and who had seen him most clearly.

'He claims he has to care for his sick mother, that's why he can't come in. I talked to the neighbors, and sure enough he's got a sick mother. Nobody thinks he spends a lot of time with her, though. His girlfriend, more likely.'

'He's jerking us around.'

'That's what it looks like.'

'Tell me about the girlfriend.'

'Name of Rosita, works for an accountant in the building, lives in Brooklyn.' He named an address in the heart of Morales's constituency.

'Tell me you're kidding.' But Stash McMorris was anything but a kidder. 'That's all we need, is to lose Santos because his girlfriend is from Southside.' Not sure if he should be taking it seriously. 'You'd better bring him in so we can see what this is about. I don't care what his excuses are. What about old man Censabella? Anything?'

McMorris found a new page in his notebook. 'He lives alone, in that building where Morales kept his apartment. Morales had a floor-through, parlor floor. The best apartment in the place.'

'That's no surprise.'

'Awful big place just to get laid in. Censabella lives right under it, on the ground floor. He still sits there in the window like an old lady. It's nuts, you ask me. All the times I ever sat on places, you could die from boredom, watching the same street for hours.' The detective's lament.

'Censabella have any friends, any regular visitors?'

'Not so far. Goes out to the grocery, goes to the cleaners. Neat, clean, dresses good for an old guy.'

'He's got to have some people in his life.'

'Maybe the people he watches in the street.'

'Maybe Morales,' Estrada proposed.

'Once upon a time, maybe. Not any more. Not if Morales has any sense.'

The phone rang as McMorris was leaving. 'It's Johnson at the security desk. I've got somebody here name of Castillo, walking around like he owns the place. He's got a press card, says he's got an appointment to see you.'

'Not me. I don't make appointments with reporters.' The amazing thing was that security had stopped him. Half the time they nodded hello to anybody walking by who didn't look as if he'd just escaped from the Tombs. 'Tell him I'll be out in a minute.' Estrada was curious, and he did not want to alienate a reporter named Castillo any more than necessary.

'Pancho Castillo, *Noticias Diarias*,' said a smiling man in a gray sharkskin suit. Under a pile of frizzy brown curls his face – the color dreamed of by hordes of pale sunbathers – was deeply creased, but not with age. Estrada thought he might be thirty-five, at most.

'You get points for initiative, Mr Castillo,' Estrada told him. 'But you'll have to get your stories through Public Information.' He walked the reporter toward the public elevator lobby. 'Everyone does, so don't take it personally.'

'Life is too full of random cruelty to take anything personally,' Castillo said. It made Estrada stop.

'I'm not interested in press conferences and canned stories.' The reporter's voice was soft, with only the slightest trace of an accent. The smile looked to be perpetual. 'I'm interested in you. Joseph Estrada is the new spice in this stew.'

'Nothing to justify your interest, I'm afraid.'

'I write for the Latino community. No, that's a misnomer. There's no single Latino community in New York, as I'm sure you know. But *Noticias* is widely read in all the communities. And my readers will be interested in an assistant district attorney of Latino heritage who is going to prosecute Roberto Morales, so admired for what he's done for our people.'

Estrada wondered if Bishop's misguided political stratagem was going to backfire immediately or only after they were all too deeply into it to survive the embarrassment.

'I'd like to help,' he said, 'but I really can't have any contact with you as a reporter, on the record or off.'

Castillo handed him a business card. 'Perhaps you'll think of some way I can be of help to you.'

The phone was ringing again when Estrada got back to his office. 'It's a Ms Miller,' the receptionist told him. 'From Pane, Parish, Eisen & Legler.'

He did not know a Ms Miller and he had never heard of Pane, Parish, Eisen & Legler. Another reporter being clever? He leaned back and put his feet up. 'Put her on.'

'This is Kassia Miller,' she said. 'I represent Roberto Morales.'

His feet hit the floor. 'Yes, hello.'

'I thought you and I should have a conversation about schedule. Judge Martinez is going to want to see us soon.'

'Well . . . I'm not quite up to speed yet, but I suppose we could have a chat with the judge in a couple of weeks, maybe three.'

'That's fine, as long as you and I can meet before that.'

'If there's something to be accomplished.' He was resisting as a matter of course. It was too easy to be steamrollered when you didn't know what was happening.

'I don't intend to waste your time.' There was an edge to her voice now. 'Or my own for that matter.'

'Suppose we talk on Monday and set something up then.'

'Why not agree on Monday right now?'

'Why not?' No harm being reasonable. Besides, he was eager for a chance to size up his new opponent.

He thought of calling Lisa Stein but instead went downstairs to the library himself to look up Miller in the national lawyers' directory. There were a lot of Millers, and he was not sure how to spell Kassia, but he found her. It was not the most recent edition of the directory; she was listed as working with a small firm headed by Andy Andreg, a well-known and flamboyant criminal defense lawyer. That information was obsolete, but the basics of her CV would not have changed. She had been graduated from a fancy women's college, and an unusual seven years later from a plain-wrap law school. She had been a practicing member of the bar for nine years. He calculated that she was in her late thirties, five or six years older than he was.

He looked up Pane, Parish, Eisen & Legler. They did not list a criminal department in this edition of the directory. He was about to close the book when his eye caught a familiar name on the firm's list of partners: Michael Ryan. Could this Michael Ryan be the same one who had precipitated the fall of Franky Griglia, H. T. Bishop's predecessor as D.A.? And hadn't that Michael Ryan had a woman associate working with him on that trial?

He went back upstairs and told Lisa Stein he needed a complete file on a lawyer named Kassia Miller – he spelled it for her – everything she could get from the major database services.

Michelle called to report that she was back from L.A. 'I've

had enough eating out for a lifetime. I'm ready for a night at home.'

So was he. When he had first met her, at an April Fool's party given by a friend of a friend, she had looked cool and self-contained, polished and in control. But there was an impetuousness about her, and a sensuality, that had been camouflaged by her severely tailored gray silk suit, the elegant French twist in which she had done her chestnut-brown hair, and her simple pearl earrings.

In the year since then he had found that her needs were complex, her pleasures sometimes unexpected. She touched something in him he had not known was there. And as far as he could tell she found him as exciting as he found her. He was always ready for a night at home with Michelle.

On impulse he bought a bottle of champagne on his way to her apartment. She opened the door wearing an oversize T-shirt and nothing else, her favorite at-home costume.

They began kissing before they had the apartment door closed. He broke off and backed away enough to be able to admire her. She was noticeably tan, and her hair had streaks of sun-bleached lightness. The tan made her long, firm legs look even longer and firmer.

'What's in the bag?' she wanted to know.

He pulled the champagne out and slipped it under her shirt, touching the cold bottle to the tip of one full breast. She squealed and jumped back, then moved forward, pressing the bottle between them and kissing him thoroughly.

'I'll get glasses,' she said. 'Meet you in the bedroom.'

They used the glasses, but not before he had taken his first sip from the hollow of her navel. It was an hour before they stopped for a second glass of champagne.

Back in her T-shirt, she led Estrada, in his shorts, into the kitchen, where they threw together a quick meal of spaghetti and salad and hot, crisp bread. They carried it and the rest of the wine into the living room and sat down at her glass dining table to satisfy their remaining hunger.

'Why the champagne tonight?' she asked between bites.

'To celebrate your glorious return.'

She stuck her tongue out at him. 'Flatterer.' Then: 'We do have something else to celebrate.'

'Oh?' This was it. Their phone conversations had been about the fun she was having in Los Angeles; they had both kept away from her reasons for being there.

'I got the job offer. Much better than I ever dreamed. To start with they're giving me the three biggest accounts we have out there – just turning them over to me. All I have to do is service them. Plus they're putting me in charge of the whole L.A. sales force. Not just records – movies, too.' As a printer's representative, her main job was to handhold the customers through seemingly constant disasters as they assembled artwork and copy and prepared it for the printing presses, and at the same time to do her best to get her company to meet the customers' invariably unreasonable production schedules. Between crises she entertained current customers and courted new ones. The result of all this effort was a stream of colorful CD boxes, record jackets, videotape packages and movie posters and press-kits – the marketing essentials of the entertainment business.

'We've been losing market share out there, and they want me to turn it around. It's a fantastic amount of work and responsibility, but it's also a fantastic amount of money.'

'That's great. Congratulations.' He got up to kiss her, not sure he was being convincing. Her fantastic new job was not good news for him. 'When do you leave?'

'They want me out there right away, but I can't just walk away from my customers here. I'll go back and forth for a couple of months and be out there for good by the end of summer.'

He sat back down in silence, feeling poleaxed. He had anticipated this, had thought about it and what it would mean. The reality was different.

'Joey.' She came over and sat in his lap, arms around him.

His face was momentarily buried in the soft skin below her collarbone. She smelled enticingly of fresh garlic and sharp cheese and sex. 'Don't look so sad. We can still be together.'

He leaned his head back to look at her. 'I can't afford the commute.'

She kissed him. 'You can be a lawyer in L.A., too, you know. You'd do great there.'

He did not mention the need to pass a new bar exam: you couldn't learn to be an L.A. lawyer watching them on TV. And leaving New York had bigger implications than just learning new law and procedure. It meant abandoning the complex web of connections built up over the years, the network of colleagues and friends moved on to private practice and the bench. Leaving all that behind was no small thing. And even that wasn't the whole point. The point was, he was surprised to realize, that he didn't know if he wanted to go at all. And right now he was in no position to think about it with anything like a clear head.

She noticed his silence. 'It's this new trial, right? I wish you could let somebody else do it, but we can still use the time to start checking around out there for a place you can work. And by the time you come out I'll know all about where to live and everything like that.'

He kissed the corner of her mouth. 'You're very impressive when you get rolling. No wonder you do so well.'

She poked him in the ribs. 'It *is* sort of the same thing, you know – I only sell what I really believe in. I know this is right for us. For both of us.'

'At this red-hot moment,' he said, 'the important thing is how wonderful it is for you.' He kissed her. 'Ready to celebrate some more?'

'I am if you are.'

Physically, he was. He took her hand and led her into the bedroom, his stomach knotted around the knowledge that before long he would have to make a major decision, about Michelle, and about his life.

5

The next day Lisa Stein delivered a heavy sheaf of database printouts. Almost all of them were about the Ryan trial – he had guessed right about Kassia Miller's having worked on it with Michael Ryan. Estrada picked what looked like the most comprehensive article. Written by Allen Crown, who had been covering the courthouse since Estrada was in grade school, it was a long glossy-magazine postmortem of the whole scandal.

The trial of Jennifer Ryan had been, in its own way, as spectacular as the first Morales trial: a well-known former federal prosecutor had been defending his own daughter-in-law, accused of killing his son. Franky Griglia, then Acting D.A. and looking for a springboard to a full elected term of his own, had chosen to reenter the courtroom and run the prosecution himself.

Kassia Miller had been Michael Ryan's second seat for the trial. According to Crown, who clearly did not like Ryan, she had also been his tutor in the rules and procedures of criminal trials in New York courts, all Ryan's prior experience having been under the different rules of federal court.

Miller was an interesting choice for Morales: the opposite of the flamboyant, political Walter Kubelik, who had defended him the first time. Allen Crown painted Miller as a no-nonsense legal technician, though paradoxically his physical descriptions of her tended to the pixieish. Most of her courtroom work in the Ryan trial had been cross-examining the police witnesses and the prosecution's forensics witnesses, including the DNA experts.

There had been no defense witnesses at all, apparently. Ryan and Miller had relied on making the jury disbelieve the testimony of the prosecution witnesses and on otherwise poking holes in the prosecution's case, arguing in summation that the prosecution had not proved the defendant's guilt beyond a reasonable doubt. It was a gutsy way to go, but in the right case it could be very effective.

Estrada thought that from a jury point of view Miller was much better for Morales than Kubelik. It was the defense equivalent of Bishop's picking an apparent Latino as prosecutor. In Miller, Morales had a woman to defend him who was a contemporary of Mariah Dodge's – an attractive, thirty-something woman with a background not unlike the victim's. Some jurors, at least, were bound to feel that she would not be defending Morales if he had done something so horrible to someone so much like herself. Not a proper thought for a juror to have, but a hard one for a prosecutor to counter.

Estrada walked downstairs on his way to lunch rather than wait for the elevator. He was waiting for a gap in the slow-moving traffic on Centre Street when someone called his name. He did not recognize the voice; a harshness in the tone stiffened him against the impulse to turn to see who it was.

'Mr Estrada!'

He stepped out into the street, hoping one of the drivers would leave enough room to let him cross. No one did.

'Mr Estrada.' The man did not have to shout now. He was standing beside Estrada.

He was short – a good six inches under Estrada's five eleven – and stocky. His face was round and brown, his features blunt.

'A decent man does not hurt his own people.'

'What?' For a moment, intent on thoughts of Kassia Miller and their coming courtroom rivalry, he genuinely did not understand.

'Roberto Morales, Mr Estrada. How can you do this to someone who has done so much good? How can you make yourself the slave of the norteamericanos?'

It had to start sometime. He had known the visit from El Grupo Latino was only the beginning. The public had been bound to get into the act, too. 'Look, Mr . . .'

'Condado. Luis Condado.'

'Mr Condado. Roberto Morales was convicted of manslaughter. It has nothing to do with his heritage.'

'It was thrown out. He is innocent.'

'If he is, I'm sure the jury will acquit him.'

'I am not a stupid child, Mr Estrada. Do not talk to me like one.' Condado was angry now. 'I am a man the same as you. Better than you. I do not betray my people.'

Estrada sensed more than saw Condado's hands ball into fists. There were court officers and cops by the dozen in the courthouse behind them but almost before the idea formed Estrada rejected it. He was going to handle this himself.

'Do you want to fight, Mr Condado? Is that it? Is that how you help your friend – by showing me how violent you can be? To convince me Roberto Morales is not violent?'

Condado's fists uncurled. 'I did not come to fight with you. I came to tell you Roberto Morales is innocent.'

He turned and stalked off, muttering in a Spanish too heavily accented and too rapid for Estrada to understand, except for the words he turned and shouted: '¡Volveré! ¡Y no estará solo!' I'll be back, and I won't be alone.

The incident stuck with Estrada. Despite the ethnic circus Walter Kubelik had made of the first trial, Estrada's sense of the case so far had been that all the attention to Latinismo was a red herring. Roberto Morales might have been developing his Phoenix Project in Brooklyn, but his life and Mariah Dodge's had been in Manhattan, and nobody central to the case was Hispanic except Ramon Santos, the security guard. After seeing Morales and his family on Park Avenue – where the main ethnic group was the wealthy and privileged, and national heritage was barely a footnote – Estrada had begun to hope that he might be able to navigate safely through the ethnic shoals. Now it seemed he had been prematurely optimistic.

He decided it was time to know more about the Brooklyn community for which the Phoenix Project had been planned, to give himself a better idea of what had made Roberto Morales a hero despite his manslaughter conviction and the failure of his dream.

Estrada could either go over and poke around by himself, or he could get hooked up with someone from the Brooklyn D.A.'s office or the P.D. The first way he would be an outsider; the second, an enemy.

He took a chance on calling Pancho Castillo. 'I'm looking for a tour guide,' he told the reporter.

'And when do you want this tour?'

'Soon. Sunday?'

'No habrá problema.'

While working on the reluctant Ramon Santos, McMorris had also talked to the two other building employees who had testified at the first trial. Unlike Santos, both were being cooperative.

Willard Boynton was an easygoing man with wrinkled brown skin and sparkling eyes. Sixty-four years old, born in Alabama, raised there and in Harlem, eighth-grade education – a night-shift janitor of visible intelligence. He had seen Morales leaving the building some time around nine that night. His testimony in the first trial had been brief but clear, and he seemed ready to do as well again. He left behind a considerably encouraged Joseph Estrada: at least there was one witness he could count on to do a decent job of testifying.

Estrada's optimistic mood did not outlast the visit three days later from Bernd Petersen, the other security man. In the first trial Petersen had said that he had seen a man in a dark coat getting into the elevator at some time around eight o'clock, the time Ramon Santos had named. Petersen had identified Morales later in a photo array and, still later, in court. His testimony had been vague and uncertain, far from what a prosecutor dreams of.

The man made the transcript look like something to pray for. His memory was worthless, his attention span minute, his attitude surly and uncooperative.

Estrada's attempt to get a coherent story out of him was interrupted by Ginny, the bureau receptionist, calling to say there was a woman asking to see Estrada – Mariah Dodge's sister. 'She's very insistent.'

The word brought back Kahn's warning.

'Sorry, Ginny, but I really can't interrupt this.'

'I'll do my best.'

As he began to wrap things up with Petersen, the phone rang again.

'Ms Dodge says she's going back there and find you herself. You want her restrained?'

'Are you sure who it is?'

'I didn't ask for a driver's license.'

'Try to delay her a little, if you can.' Estrada hung up again. 'Mr Petersen, your testimony is going to be very important in this new trial. Detective McMorris will be in touch with you, but right now my next appointment is on the way in.'

Petersen was slow to respond.

'I don't want to rush you.' Estrada steered him to the door. 'I'm sure you've got plenty to do yourself.'

At the door Petersen had to turn sideways to keep from colliding with an animated jungle of strawberry-blonde curls.

'Mr Estrada.' An accusation from the neighborhood of the curls.

He gave Petersen a parting clap on the shoulder to speed him along, then retreated quickly behind the barrier of his desk where he began rearranging papers.

'Mr Estrada.' A command this time.

He looked up as if just discovering her, as in some ways he was. Under the hair was a medium-tall woman with green eyes. Other than the eyes there was not much resemblance to Mariah Dodge. This woman's face was square, her mouth generous, her nose definite. Nothing like the slim, oval face and precise features in the photograph on the wall. For the first time he could appreciate the concept of eyes throwing off sparks.

'Yes?' he said as if she were an ordinary visitor.

'What are you doing about Roberto Morales?'

'Why don't you have a seat, Ms . . .'

'Dodge. Tess Dodge.'

'Ms Dodge. I'm glad you could come in. Please sit down. I'm sure we've got a lot to talk about.'

'I don't sweet-talk, so you can cut that out.' She sat down in the chair recently occupied by Petersen. 'You planning to do better than that jerk they gave us the first time?'

He was trying not to react; it wasn't easy.

'Understand something, Mr Estrada – my sister is dead and the bastard who killed her is walking around free. I'm here to make sure you don't let him get away with it.' Her wide mouth twisted with distaste. 'The prize prosecutor before you cut it awful damn close. Some of those jurors I talked to said it was a pure miracle they weren't deadlocked beginning to end on the whole thing, not just on rape.'

'You talked to the jurors?'

'Ten. The other two wouldn't see me – the two biggest holdouts. Four of those cretins held out on rape, and the two that wouldn't talk to me damn near tied them up totally. They were ready to let Morales walk out of there convicted of *nothing*, that's the kind of job your Mr Kahn did. I was there, I saw every single day of it. Is he like that all the time? Pretending to be a country doctor, or somebody's uncle? He's got a murderer sitting right there, and there's a woman in the prime of her life who's been tortured and mutilated . . .'

She gulped a breath, her face suddenly full of pain. She

looked away. 'It's three years and I sometimes . . . I still . . . it gets to me.' She closed her eyes a moment, opened them and was going again. 'That's why I get so mad seeing people treat it like some no-big-deal everyday thing, worrying about the politics and maybe they'll offend some group with a lot of votes. That bastard *killed* her and they ought to fry him for it, not take his bail money and let him out there in the world so other men can see that you can rape and slash and do anything else you think of to a woman and nobody gives a damn.'

She paused, out of breath. 'You have something to say?'

He was not sure he did.

In repose, she looked younger and more vulnerable. He remembered from the file that she was twenty-nine, not quite ten years younger than her sister, who would have been thirty-eight now if Morales had let her live.

'She's beautiful, isn't she?' Tess Dodge said, her eyes on the photograph. 'That's Mom's favorite picture of her. I didn't know there was another print. Where'd you get it?'

He did not have an answer ready.

'She sent it to you, didn't she? Mom, I mean. God, if Dad found out he'd have a fit.' He saw the ghost of a smile, gone almost before it appeared. 'It's okay, I'm not going to tell.'

Fierce again, she said, 'Now we're in trouble with the judge, too.'

'What are you talking about?'

'Because of the appeal. Because she got reversed. Because there's this dumb rule you have around here that the same judge gets the trial who screwed it up before.'

'Look' – finally feeling on home ground – 'I understand your frustration with how things have gone, but please don't make it harder on yourself by jumping to conclusions. If anybody on this case is in trouble with the judge it's the defense. They're the ones who wrote a brief about how badly the judge misunderstood the law.'

'Maybe so, but it was *your* evidence that got the judge in trouble. The prosecution told her the evidence was admissible.

That showboat Kahn argued for it. The way I hear it, you're not supposed to get stuff like that wrong – a prosecutor's supposed to protect the judge, not put her in a place where the defense can jam her up like that.'

'You're exaggerating this all out of proportion. It was a close question. Judge Martinez went for our side, the appeals judges went the other way.'

Still, he knew she was right: Luz Martinez might well hold it against the prosecution team that she had gotten a dressing down first from the Appellate Division and then from the Court of Appeals, publicly and in print, in a decision that would probably find its way into future briefs and arguments on the question. Most judges looked for a different sort of immortality.

Tess Dodge was not finished. 'If you're not going to do something serious to put that sack of dirt away, don't expect me to sit by and keep my mouth shut. People'd be real interested to know how you're not doing your job because everybody over here – Mr Elected-official Bishop included – is afraid of being called names by some minority group.'

For all his usual sympathy for victims and their families, he'd had enough of this. He was about to say so when he remembered what her mother had said about being forced to live through the pain over and over. The least he could do was hear her out.

'Don't get the wrong idea,' Tess Dodge was saying now. 'I'm here because I want to be helpful. Mariah was my sister. I know things about her. I don't think your Mr Kahn told the whole story at the trial.'

'What do you mean?'

'My sister could have a sharp tongue sometimes, but she wasn't like me. She was really kind of quiet. So maybe it's true she got him so mad calling him names that he cut her throat, but maybe there was more to it than that.'

Estrada was suddenly paying close attention. 'More? Do you know what?'

'All I can tell you is that Mr Know-it-all Kahn didn't ask

that question, and when I tried to get him to he showed me where the door was and I was so stupid and so upset I let him.' She glared at Estrada. 'Not this time. I backed down once, but not again.'

She pulled a spiral notebook out of the saddlebag she used for a purse. 'We have to talk about the trial. I don't want to see this one have all the same mistakes as the first one.' She dragged her chair around to the side of the desk where they could both see her notebook. She did that, as she did everything, as if she were on home ground, in charge.

She was well into her litany about the first trial before Estrada looked at the clock and saw it was past time for him to meet Michelle. They were having a quick dinner before her plane back to Los Angeles, so there was a limit on how late he could be.

'Ms Dodge, I'm sorry to cut you short, but I'm late for an appointment.'

'I won't take a whole lot longer.'

'We can pick it up again another time. I really have to go.'

'Where are you going?'

'I'm meeting someone.'

'Who?'

Could she be serious? 'I have an appointment.'

'If it's about the trial I should come along. I want to know everything about it. I have a right to know.'

He had to cut this one off at the pass. 'I promise to keep you up to date on what's happening. But under no circumstances can you be with me while I'm getting testimony or participating in the investigation, or working with my colleagues. It's not work that can be done in the presence of outsiders . . .' He heard his mistake and held up a hand before she could protest. 'I know you're not an outsider. I know you have as much interest in this case, in how it comes out, as anyone in the world. I mean an outsider to the process.'

'I'm no outsider at all. I've worked secretary and paralegal for a criminal lawyer almost two years now getting ready for this. And I've been studying this case ever since the beginning.'

Unbelievable. *Watch out for the sister* didn't begin to cover it.

He stood up. 'I'm doing my best to be accommodating. To make you a part of the team. But you can't expect to have everything you want in exactly the form you want it. And now I really have to leave.'

She stood. 'Don't think I'm letting you off the hook, because I'm not.'

Michelle was waiting for him at a restaurant in her East Side neighborhood; it was decked out to look like an Adirondack Mountains hunting lodge and jammed with noisy people unwinding after a hard day at their desks. She was not happy that he had surrendered any part of the little time they had together before she left. He did his best to banish his own dark mood and amuse her with his day's adventures. She was barely listening. After his third time fighting the din with the intro to the story about Petersen he gave up and tried Tess Dodge. That got her attention.

'Is she pretty? As sexy as her sister?'

'That's not exactly the point.'

'It isn't? Are you sure?'

He changed the subject to her trip and the job in L.A., but she was not very talkative even about that.

'All you can think about is your big murder trial,' she said abruptly as he signed the bill.

'It's turning out to be a lot more complicated than I expected.' He reached across the table for her hand. 'It's the most important trial I've ever had, but I don't want it to come between us.'

'Oh, Joey.' She lifted his hand to her lips. 'I'm sorry, I don't mean to be a bitch. It's just . . . I'm scared. This is such a big step for me and I keep thinking, if I'm alone, if I don't have you there with me . . .'

He caressed her cheek. 'I'll be there. I'm always there, even if I'm here.'

She tried a smile. 'These days you're barely here when you're *here*.' The smile took hold. 'It's okay, I understand, I don't blame you. Well . . . a little. You know what I think about a lot? It's good that we both like our work and we have real lives that we care about. But sometimes I worry that it comes between us. Now, most of all. I'm going away right at the time when you're more tied down here than ever.'

'Only until this trial is over.'

'I know. But it still scares me. I'm afraid this dumb trial is going to take up your whole existence.'

'Hey – this dumb trial is going to make my fame and fortune.' He said it lightly, trying to break the mood.

She managed another smile, stronger and warmer than the last. 'It better.' She stood up, suddenly in a hurry. 'We ought to go. After all this fuss it'd be silly if I missed my plane.'

In the taxi on the way back from seeing her off he thought, She's right, this trial is going to take up my whole existence. He did not see how it could be otherwise.

The trap he had to avoid was being distracted by the career pressures that went with a case like this, by thoughts of publicity and of a promotion and how much that might mean when he was ready to leave. For now, he had to concentrate on only one thing. A woman was dead. The man who had been convicted had to be retried, and Joe Estrada had the responsibility of seeing that he was convicted again. The calculus seemed clear: however much work was necessary, he had to do it. For Mariah Dodge and her impassioned sister and gently earnest mother. And for himself – his career, and his peace of mind.

6

The subway to Brooklyn hauled itself up out of its tunnel for the trip across the East River. Estrada stood by the window looking back toward Manhattan. The skyline still moved him, after a dozen years. He wondered if part of the reason was that, living inside it, he only rarely saw its splendor.

He turned to see Brooklyn, somewhat less splendid, as the train rattled along the elevated tracks leading away from the bridge. Low brick buildings; factories at the edge of the river; a defunct garage, its driveway cluttered with refrigerators. Then buildings pressed close to the tracks: the colonnaded second story of a limestone bank building followed by open windows displaying bright bedspreads and votive statues and cramped kitchens to the train clattering by.

Pancho Castillo was waiting for him at the station. They went down a long flight of stairs to a street darkened by the shadow of the elevated tracks, lined with narrow stores and pizza counters. The sidewalk was neither crowded nor empty, the pedestrians mostly Latino.

The street curved to the left and brought them out from under the el. The stores were hid behind corrugated metal shutters, whether for Sunday or because they were out of business Estrada could not tell. In the gray evening of a gray day they looked deserted and forlorn.

Castillo turned left, along another street of shuttered stores, some of them in buildings with their windows covered with metal or bricked and mortared shut. Empty. Deserted.

A few blocks farther along, a housing project rose on their left: red brick buildings set in bleak plazas. Here the pedestrian mix changed. Latinos still predominated but now there were many people with starkly pale skin dressed in severe black. Little boys in skullcaps with curly sidelocks, white fringes swinging from under their black vests. Little girls in long gray dresses and coats.

'Here we are,' Castillo announced, and unlocked the door of a blue sedan.

They drove west toward the river, then headed north. After a few blocks Castillo pulled up and pointed across the street. 'One of Mr Morales's charities. Over there between the bakery and the joyeria.'

Estrada saw a plain storefront, the plate-glass window shrouded on the inside by a grayish curtain, the thick housing of a steel security shutter like a metal eyebrow over door and window.

'Drug rehab. He calls it La Esperanza. Hope. Grand names are the thing these days.' He drove on. 'Speaking of names, Mr Smithfield, tell me about yours.'

Estrada had anticipated this, predicted it to Mahoney; still, it jarred him. 'My name is Estrada,' he managed. 'Smithfield is my middle name.'

'Also the maiden name of your mother.'

'You've been busy.'

'It's my job.'

Joseph Estrada was all the name he used in the office, but his official bar admission used the full three names. Once Castillo had the Smithfield, the rest would not have been hard. 'What difference does my name make? I prosecute accused criminals. I don't care about their background, they don't care about mine.'

'This time we all care. Roberto Morales is a symbol. You're prosecuting him, therefore you're a symbol, too.'

'You know, I have to say – I don't get it about Roberto Morales. He's rich. He lives on Park Avenue. His wife is

Puerto Rican, but she lives and works in a world a long way from Southside. His children go to a fancy private school. What kind of ethnic symbol is that?'

The reporter glanced over at him but said nothing.

They took an indirect route so Castillo could point out more of the sights – a vacant lot where a Latino community organization was putting up prefabricated housing units; a factory by the river, still active after more than a century; the firehouse that had been occupied by local residents for eighteen months to prevent the city from closing it during the city's money crunch in the Seventies.

'This is not one of your neighborhoods where everyone is lost and directionless. It has never been a place where people sit around in despair. Even some of the places here that look vacant are occupied. People don't like to advertise it, but there's a lot of renovating, sweat-equity rehabilitation going on.'

He pulled around a corner. Estrada could see the river ahead of them. Castillo parked in the lee of a concrete-block structure that looked like an old warehouse. They walked around the side of the building.

A vista opened in front of them. They were a good hundred yards from the river, nothing between them and the water but a flat, grassy expanse of land, lightly strewn with loose bricks, tin cans and similar rubble. Looming beyond the choppy gray water was Manhattan, from the downtown skyscrapers to the ones in midtown.

Estrada turned to Castillo. 'Is this it?'

'This is it.'

Estrada followed the reporter closer to the water. The flat, empty land stretched north, many times as long as it was wide. A couple of old one-story buildings, like cinder-block sheds, were the only obstructions until the lot was cut off at the north end by a broad building like the one they had parked behind. On the river side there was nothing – no fence, no abutments. The grass seemed to extend to the river itself, where it ended in a clean line: grass and water seemingly all on one level. It was only when he reached the very edge that suddenly, dizzyingly, he saw that there was a substantial drop to the water.

He had never seen the skyline from the edge of the land like this, with no barrier to define where this side ended and the view began. It made everything seem uncannily close and immediate. 'I can see why people would be interested in building here.'

'It's been vacant a long time,' Castillo said. 'People have had plans, before Roberto Morales.'

'What stopped them?'

'Lack of money, lack of will . . .' Castillo spread his hands: who knows?

'Murder,' Estrada offered.

'Yes – that doesn't help. And there is something else. Some things are not what they seem.'

'What do you mean?'

Castillo waved an arm to encompass the tract. 'Nobody knows what's under here. There are stories about toxic chemicals under the ground from decades in the past. Even five years ago, nobody thought about that too much here, but all the same, there were stories. And not too many blocks away is a hazardous waste storage facility. Chemical waste and nuclear waste.'

'Nuclear waste – here?'

'Why not here? Nuclear and chemical waste, both. In the same building, though the owners can call it two. A convenient regulatory fiction.'

Estrada turned to look again at Manhattan. The river looked narrow enough to take at a single stride.

'Scary to think of it that close to the city.'

'This is the city, too.' Castillo was smiling.

'So it is. I wouldn't want to invest in a housing complex right near a nuclear waste dump, in the city or out.'

'Perhaps that has something to do with this.' Motioning again at the vacant lot they were standing on. 'Though I don't think you should be sure of it. There's a public school almost across the street from the waste facility. The firehouse that the city wanted to shut is only a few blocks away from it. People have unexpected priorities.'

They stood in silence for a few minutes. Castillo said, 'Ready to go?'

'Give me another minute.' Estrada walked again to the edge of the grass. Almost beneath his feet the river slapped against the concrete breakwater. He looked again at the lines of buildings on the other side.

There was something dynamic about it, an urge toward motion embodied in stone and steel and glass. The tall new buildings at the island's tip were like huge sails, like the prow of a remarkable ship. The whole island seemed as if it were poised to cast off and sail forward into the harbor, out to sea, bound for some better future.

Walking back to the car, Castillo said, 'A piece of advice: I know you're not supposed to have direct contact with reporters, but this time you'd be smart to have an ally who can see your side of things. Your superiors made a mistake about this case. It's not like last time, all noise and no real heart, people stirred up because Walter Kubelik came along banging a drum. Then, many people didn't know how to feel about Morales because he was rich, just as you were saying. Some thought he might be guilty. Some wanted to punish him for being with a roja from Texas when he was already married to a Latina who made everyone envious. When he was convicted many said, Te lo dije – I told you so.'

They got into the car and Castillo drove back toward Southside. 'So. Morales had enemies. They were not unhappy to see him in jail. Now, it is not the same. The court said the conviction was wrong because the judge helped the prosecution. ¡Atencion! The judge!'

'Born in San Juan, I understand.'

'In the Southwest they would call her Tia Taco, maybe. Like Uncle Tom.'

'That's not her reputation in my office. Usually she's good for defendants.'

'Tell that to Roberto Morales.'

'That's a point.' A point that had been made often at the time of the first trial. Reverse prejudice was the press's most common explanation for Luz Martinez's uncharacteristic receptivity to the prosecution's arguments, that she had bent over backward to avoid appearing to favor Morales because of their common heritage. Whatever her reasons had been, the question now was how far her treatment at the hands of the appeals courts would swing her back.

Castillo found a place to park near where they had started from. 'Join me for dinner?' Smiling: 'Dutch treat, to keep us both pure.'

He led Estrada into a storefront restaurant with a takeout counter and display cases along one wall. Before Estrada had registered where they were, a portly man wearing an apron over his street clothes came to greet them. Except for the apron and his size he was a match for the pale little boys Estrada had seen earlier on the street outside.

'Señores, bienvenidos. Señor Castillo, it's been too long.'

'Too long, indeed. I miss your good food. This is my friend, Joseph Smithfield. Joe, Mr Rosenberg.'

Rosenberg inclined his head. 'A pleasure. Sit down, please, sit down, be comfortable.' He waved them grandly to a table by the wall, its plain black surface adorned with disposable placemats, simple flatware and paper napkins.

'Do you think this is strange?' Castillo asked him. 'Here I am, a Puerto Rican, and when I come to Southside I come to a restaurant run by Hasidim.'

'It's not what I expected, I'll admit that.'

'Think of it as a culinary adventure. As much a part of your education as rice and beans or rice and chicken.'

Estrada looked at the menu. There was little he could identify with any confidence. 'An adventure for sure.'

'And it's good for them to see Puerto Ricans up close now and then.'

'I didn't have the impression that either group saw too little of the other around here.'

Castillo laughed. 'This is different. Here we're not competing. And we're not looking through each other, pretending the other is not there.'

Estrada let Castillo do the ordering. Rosenberg went off and returned almost immediately with a steaming platter of pungent meat. In bowls were a vegetable that looked like shredded cabbage and bowtie noodles mixed with dark, aromatic nubbins of grain.

'Enjoy,' he said.

While Estrada explored his dinner, Castillo picked up their conversation about Morales. 'He still has enemies, but far fewer than they were, and now many more people believe he is innocent. Now, they understand better why the white establishment persecutes a man like Roberto Morales.'

'They understand? What does that mean?'

'They understand that the Anglos think he's dangerous.'

'Why?'

'Because he's rich. Because he's powerful. Because any Latino young person can look at him and say, *I can do the same*. This is not a message the white establishment can accept. The message must be no, if you climb as high as Roberto Morales we will cut you down.'

'You can't really believe that.'

'It doesn't matter if I believe it. Others do. And you are not helped by your Kahn Commission. Why? Because the very soul of that commission is the idea that the police and the district attorney's office are guilty of doing bad things to people of color.'

'But the whole point is that we want to expose it when it happens. Punish the people who do it. Stop it from happening again. That must count.'

'No, because people assume the commission is a lie, a whitewash. And to need a whitewash is to admit that something is dirty.' Castillo interrupted himself to take some food. 'Before you eat it all.' He tasted the meat. 'Ropa vieja was never so good. You like it?'

'Terrific. I don't know why I never tried it before.'

They ate in silence awhile.

'The outcry about Roberto Morales is going to be worse this time,' Castillo predicted. 'Latinos are tired of being the forgotten minority, the *polite* minority. Prejudice and racial conflict are hot subjects. In a slow week for real news, a cover in a newsweekly isn't impossible.'

'You're pushing it,' Estrada said.

'If Roberto Morales is the symbol of the futility of Latino aspirations, then he can be made the symbol for other new immigrants of color, a test of the American dream. If Roberto Morales must be cut down, then everyone else like him must be cut down, too. A comfortable life may be possible for a few, fitting in at some level that threatens no one. A token or two appointed to high public office, but not real power.'

'That's nonsense.'

'Are you sure?' Castillo challenged. 'Can you be sure?'

'Yes.' Estrada said it quickly, definitely, but it was just a word. Castillo was not speaking of truth, but of appearances. In public discourse, there were no rules of evidence. Nothing was inadmissible.

'You see how this trial can be manipulated, starting from the premise that the judge and the prosecutor conspired to gain a verdict that was unjust.'

'That's crazy. Who *reversed* the conviction, for God's sake? Another court.'

'We are not talking about logic. And isn't the Manhattan D.A.'s office a great bastion of the white establishment, where all you children of privilege go to rub elbows with ordinary people? All you sons of dead presidents and movie stars and WASP aristocrats?'

'Is that what you think I am? Because my mother's great-something grandfather marched in Washington's army?'

'Am I wrong?'

'Damn right, you're wrong.'

'Then make me right. Tell me what I don't know.'

'Not on the record. Not for you to print.'

'I'm a journalist. That's what I do.'

'You just gave me a lecture about how the whole world is going to make Roberto Morales a martyr to norteamericano exclusivity. And the subtext is that he is being prosecuted by WASP-supremist stooges. Have I got it about right?' Estrada did not expect an answer. 'So here I am, son of a Daughter of the American Revolution, S.A.R. myself, I suppose, if I wanted to be. And you want to embellish that for your readers, to convince them that having me prosecute Morales is a cynical trick. And you expect me to help you do it?'

'This D.A.R. business is no secret, amigo. I don't have that from you, off the record or on. I can publish that when I please. Wouldn't it be better if you put it in some context?'

Estrada pushed his chair back from the table and stood up. 'I didn't come here to be threatened.'

'Sit down, I'm only trying to provoke you.'

'You're doing a fine job.'

Suddenly Estrada was genuinely angry. Not with Castillo for his manipulation, but with Bishop and Muir and Collins. With whoever had decided, without bothering to give thought to the consequences, that it would be clever to make Joseph Smithfield Estrada the prosecutor of Roberto Morales.

'Okay,' he said. 'I'll tell you some things. First of all, I'm no child of privilege, as you put it. My family is all blue-collar working people in central Massachusetts. I have two older brothers and an older sister. My mother may be descended from the original colonists, but she's nothing like rich. There are rich Smithfields in Massachusetts. Not us.'

'And the Estradas?'

'From Spain. Long ago.'

Castillo laughed. 'We all come from Spain long ago.'

'In my case it's about as long ago as possible. Sixteenth century, and they didn't go native.'

'This is documented?'

'My father was very proud of it. He kept the family crest on the living room wall.' Estrada paused, not happy to be doing this but seeing no alternative. 'The last true born-in-Spain Spaniard in the line was the second son of some kind of duke in Castile. Came over with the conquistadores and never went back.' Though stories about him were hard to come by, because Big Jim Estrada had refused to acknowledge three centuries of family history in Mexico. 'The best I can work it out, some of the conquistador's descendants settled in Texas when it was still part of Mexico. So if not for Sam Houston and his friends I'd probably be a Mexican. In college I got myself down there and looked up my Estrada cousins as a way to catch up on the family history.'

'Did you find it enlightening?'

'Unfortunately. But not about my history. The cousins I met were not too interested in a relative from a branch of the family they'd lost track of so long ago they couldn't believe it existed. Without exception they were smug and prosperous, happily exploiting their servants. Not very different from the way Latinos are exploited up here, except down there it was other Latinos doing the exploiting.'

Castillo regarded him thoughtfully. 'You're saying you reject that part of your heritage?'

'I'm saying some people find any reason they can to be shitty to other people. No matter what they have in common.'

'Yes, I agree.'

'Then you should agree that my weird background has nothing to do with the trial.'

'It's not the same. Besides, if it doesn't, why did you get the case?'

'Maybe because I win more trials than I lose. Or didn't you do that part of the research?'

'There are others as good or better.'

'Thank you.'

'Why *did* you get the case?' Castillo persisted.

'Ask Mr Bishop.'

'I tried.' The reporter made a face. 'His secretary told me he respected your ability.'

'You see?'

Estrada noticed that Rosenberg was waiting near their table and that they were the last diners left in the restaurant. It was not much past nine.

Castillo noticed, too. 'Mr Rosenberg, we're sorry if we kept you past closing.'

'It's all right. So long as you aren't fighting any more, another few minutes won't kill me.'

Back in Manhattan, Estrada went swimming. He took it slow and easy, changing strokes every few laps. He needed to clear his mind.

There was a lot to assimilate. His picture of the Phoenix Project had been transformed. He had not been prepared for the impact of the site and its vistas of the river and the Manhattan skyline; he was astounded that it could exist in virtual obscurity.

He had been even less prepared for Castillo's catalog of the site's hazards. Morales and the others behind the Phoenix Project had to have known about them, and yet they had proceeded even after the economic climate had turned against them.

About the press and the trial's implications for ethnic politics, Castillo was certainly exaggerating. Still, it would not do to neglect that side of things. There was no knowing how many Señor Condadoses there might be, or how active they might become. How much influence they might have on public opinion and the jury pool. Or on the prosecution's witnesses – Ramon Santos, for one. And it was not a favorable sign that the Kahn Commission was already being dismissed as a whitewash.

Nothing about this case was turning out to be uncomplicated.

7

McMorris brought Ramon Santos in first thing on Monday. A bull of a man, thirty-four according to the file, he was wearing work pants and a bright colored shirt with a baseball jacket. A drooping Pancho Villa moustache failed to add an air of menace. He seemed uneasy, but being in the D.A.'s office made a lot of people uneasy.

Estrada had decided to approach him as if nothing was wrong, and deal with the trouble when it came. If it came. He started by saying that even though Roberto Morales's conviction had been overturned, that didn't mean anyone was less sure that Morales was guilty.

'Laws are complicated and people make mistakes. So we have another trial. This time – no mistakes.' He was talking in English, keeping it slow while trying not to sound patronizing. There was no indication in the file that Santos had needed a translator.

'I apologize if this is inconvenient for you. I want you to know that we thank you for your cooperation.'

The security guard shrugged. Except for a slight raising of the eyebrows, his expression did not change noticeably; his mouth was mostly obscured by the moustache.

Estrada plunged ahead. 'I'm sure that Mr Kahn, the man who was in my chair last time, told you that your testimony was very important. Because people made mistakes before, your testimony is more important now.' He reached for the file folder that held a copy of Santos's DD–5 and his testimony at the grand jury and the first trial. 'You did very well. You were strong. People listen when they hear someone who is sure of himself.'

He paused. Santos was facing him blankly, a wariness in his eyes.

'Do you have any questions?' Estrada asked. 'Anything you don't understand.'

Santos shook his head. Still not a word.

'Okay, let's go back over it. You testified that you were on duty that night and that you worked the four-to-twelve shift every day except Friday and Saturday. You knew Roberto Morales because he worked late a lot. That right so far?'

'Yeah.' Flat, almost grudging.

'Okay. And you were eating your dinner that night when Roberto Morales came in, and you said hello and you didn't bother to have him sign in.'

'No, that's not right.'

Estrada looked up. 'Isn't that what you testified?' Not pushing it. He knew it was not what Santos had said.

'I wasn't eatin' no dinner. The delivery guy was there. I was payin' him, you know, shootin' the shit – How you doin', shit like that.'

'My mistake.' Santos's catching him was a good sign, a test passed. 'I'm glad you corrected me. Don't let me say anything that isn't what you remember. Okay?'

Santos nodded. Sat waiting.

'Okay. You were paying for your dinner and Roberto Morales came in.'

'No.'

This time Estrada's surprise was genuine. 'No?'

'I don' know if it was him. I don' know who it was.'

Estrada took a deep breath. 'Let's take this a step at a time. You testified that you saw Roberto Morales at the building that night. You said so in the grand jury, and you said it again at the trial.'

'I don' know what I said. You tell me – you the one readin' it there.'

Estrada controlled his anger. 'That's what it says here. You identified Roberto Morales from a photo array that the detective showed you, and you said it was him in the grand jury and you pointed him out in court. You said he was the man you saw that Sunday night while you were paying for your dinner.'

'Maybe that's what I said, but I'm tellin' you now, man, that's not right. I don' remember that. I remember this guy, I don' know who it was. Guy in a black coat. I never got a good look at him, you know? I was facin' the other way, I was talkin' to this guy, the delivery guy. That's all. Some guy in a black coat.'

'You're telling me you don't remember.' If that was the game he was playing, it was bad, but not fatal. People forgot things they'd seen three years before. Though considering the reinforcement of twice testifying formally and the media coverage of the case, this was the kind of memory a person might be expected to retain.

'Whatever you saw then, you don't remember it now as clearly.' Willing him to settle for that. 'Right?'

'No, man, it's not right.' Santos was leaning forward, his voice tight. 'You got trouble with your ears? I'm tellin' you, I remember what happened. I *remember* I din' see the guy.'

Very bad. 'That's not what you said in court.' Harsher now. 'You swore on the Bible that you saw Roberto Morales.'

'I was wrong.'

'It's a crime to lie under oath, Ramon.' No more Mr Santos.

'You going to put me in jail? Huh? You sayin' you going to put me in jail. ¿Por que? Porque . . . I make this *mistake*?'

'Three years ago, right after the murder, you told a detective you saw Roberto Morales. You swore an oath on the Bible in the grand jury to tell the truth, and you said you saw Roberto Morales. A year later, two years ago, you swore an oath again, and you said you saw Roberto Morales. The defense lawyer asked you many questions about it, hard questions, and you were very sure who you saw that night. You were an excellent witness, and you were very sure of yourself.'

'I'm sayin' I din' see.'

'It could have been him.'

'I don' know.'

'I believe you're a good man, Ramon. You came forward and testified honestly in the past. That was the right thing to do. A woman is dead. That's not right. Somebody killed her. That's not right. Roberto Morales killed her. I know that, and you know that. Just as you know you saw him in the building that night.'

'No,' Santos interrupted. 'I din' see.'

'Look, Ramon . . .' He switched to Spanish, hoping it might crack the barriers a little. 'A man of honor does not break an oath. A good man does not swear falsely on the Bible. You swore an oath to tell the truth. Now somebody, some friend, tells you this is bad. Bad for Puerto Rican Pride, bad for your people. So they tell you to lie. But they are not good people who tell you this. They are not your friends.'

Santos was out of the chair, his face red, fists clenched. McMorris was up, too.

In English Santos said, 'Nobody tells me nothin'. Nobody tells Ramon Santos what to say.'

Estrada stood up slowly behind his desk. 'All right, Ramon. You can sit down now.'

Santos stayed on his feet. Estrada waited. McMorris hovered.

'Sit down,' Estrada said again, more sharply. 'There are a few more things I need to say, then you can go.'

'I go now. I go when I want.'

'If you go, I can make you come back.' A simple statement of fact. 'The police can make you come back. We work all hours here. Who can say what time we'll need you? When you're working, or sleeping? When you're home with your family? With your girlfriend Rosita? It's easier to stay and listen.'

Santos flinched at the mention of Rosita. He sat down.

'I want you to think about this,' Estrada said. 'No matter what you say now, the jury is going to hear what you said before. Everyone knows that people remember things better right after they happened. The jury is going to believe what you told the detective and what you said in the grand jury, when this was fresh in your mind.' He gave that a moment to register.

'If you change your story now, you must be guilty of lying under oath. Because if you tell two stories that are not the same, one of them has to be a lie. And I promise you that the first thing I'll do is go to the grand jury and tell them about it. The penalty for lying under oath is up to seven years in prison.'

He paused. Santos sat staring at the top of the desk, saying nothing.

'I don't know who told you to change your testimony, but they weren't doing you a favor. I'll tell you something else – whoever they are, they're wrong. This trial is about one man. One bad man. A man who kills a woman because she calls him names – porque ella lo está *insultando*' – the Spanish word far stronger than its English look-alike – 'such a man does not bring pride and glory to his people. Such a man deserves to be punished. And anyone who lies in a court of law to protect that man brings shame on himself, and on his people. Not Orgullo Puertorriqueño, *Vergüenza* Puertorriqueña.' Not Puerto Rican Pride, Puerto Rican Shame.

He paused again. Santos looked up at him. 'Can I go now?'

'Yes. The detective will drive you back.'

'No. I go myself.'

'However you want it. Make sure you think about all this. Detective McMorris and I are going to stay in touch with you. I'll have to arrange for him to come and get you again, because we have to talk about this again.'

So he had been right to worry about Santos. Whoever had changed Ramon Santos's mind had done a good job of it, and

Santos was too macho to yield directly to the threat of a perjury charge.

There had to be a way to turn the heat up. The girlfriend was clearly a sensitive spot, but that might not be enough. Nothing in the cross-examination at the first trial had seriously impeached Santos's credibility, but it was possible that Kubelik had missed something, and that was more than two years ago: a lot could have happened since.

Estrada would not be able to impeach his own witness, but knowing about Santos's criminal past could be useful for putting more pressure on him before the trial. Estrada told McMorris to see what he could turn up, and to arrange for somebody to sit on Santos for a while, get a better idea of how he spent his time and with whom. How he worked having a girlfriend and a family. You could never tell where you might find a lever to move even the most stubborn potential witness.

This was more like Estrada's usual line of work, dealing with witnesses who were skells and mopes. The kind of people – men, mostly – who needed frequent applications of both stick and carrot before they would testify that the sun rose in the morning.

He thought of the line his mother used whenever her impatience with his career path and his pace traveling it got the better of her: 'You know, Joseph, when your father insisted we use his insurance money for your education he didn't mean for you to end up in a civil service job, dealing with the lowest of the low. He wanted you to be a *lawyer*.'

He realized that he was sweating. The interview with Santos had not been that bad. He checked the radiators: going full blast again. And the windows were stuck, as they had been since he got the office and for no one knew how long before that. At the beginning he had hoped Maintenance might come by to unstick them in response to his repeated requests; he had given up long ago.

The heat was a problem. His first meeting with Kassia

Miller was scheduled for early afternoon and he did not want to have it under these conditions. And he had another witness coming in after that. He called Mahoney.

'Can you breathe down there?'

'Got the window wide open.'

'Good, I need to borrow your office.'

'Where am *I* supposed to go?'

'You can come up here.'

'What a pal.'

'The library? You can do some research.'

'Okay. But it goes in the ledger. You owe me.'

Kassia Miller was not what Estrada expected. From the press clips he knew she was short, but short did not cover it. She was tiny, five foot one or two in high heels, at most. The heels went with an off-white tailored suit and a peach blouse. No little bow at the neck, but an oversize silk scarf. A lot of style, very individual.

'Nice to meet you,' she said.

'Nice to meet *you*. I've heard a lot.'

'I hope you don't believe it.'

'It's all very favorable.'

Smiling, she said, 'That's why I hope you don't believe it.'

He laughed.

She said, 'I assume you heard about the Ryan trial.'

'That I did.'

'It was all Michael, really. I was just along for the ride.'

'I'll bet.' Lisa Stein had gotten the transcript from storage for him. He'd only had a chance to skim over some of the testimony; it had been enough to impress him.

Miller grinned. 'Okay, now that we've established that I'm an amateur.'

'And we can assume I am, when it comes to a big press case like this.'

'Well . . .'

'No, really . . .' He was glad not to be meeting her for the first time in his office, every surface piled high with papers, the floor cluttered with boxes of files. Better to be sitting in Mahoney's high-back pseudo-leather executive chair, the kind you didn't see outside the front office, than his own rickety typing chair. Leave it to Mahoney to have furniture a bureau chief could envy. Still, it would have been good to sit her down where she could see the portrait of Mariah Dodge and the clippings about her death that covered the bulletin board. Next time. 'This trial is such a lock for us the front office just picked somebody at random.'

'Nothing to do with your name, I suppose.'

Straight for the jugular. 'Not that I know of.' He almost wanted to compliment her. 'Speaking of how we got to be adversaries, did your client come to you, or to the firm?'

'There's not much difference. There's really only me and Michael and a couple of associates in the criminal department.'

'He's lucky to get you. Criminal defense work is still such a man's game I have to guess it's hard to find a good woman criminal defense lawyer. Harder still to find a woman who'll defend a rapist, much less a rape-murderer.' His counter-thrust.

He saw anger flash across her face before she controlled it. 'I'm not defending a rapist, or a rape-murderer. I'm defending an innocent man wrongly accused of rape and manslaughter.'

'The first jury didn't think so.'

'The first jury's judgment was distorted by improper instructions from the bench,' she rapped out. 'The verdict was vacated. Unless another jury says otherwise, Roberto Morales is an innocent man. And I expected better than a cheap shot like that. That trial is a nullity, at least as far as judgments of guilt and innocence are concerned.'

'Okay,' he said, smiling. 'Now that we've taken a couple of shots at each other, can we get down to business?'

'Fine.' Her own smile was back. 'Do you have anything new I should know about?'

'Not yet. I just got handed the case a week or so ago' –

compressing the reality – 'and I don't know yet what I'll have before trial.'

'I'd appreciate it whenever you get it. I hope we're not going to play games that way.'

'I don't plan on it. And you? Anything new?'

'We have some lines we're following.' Not quite taunting him. 'I thought we might talk about what we're going to stipulate from the first trial. No point tiring out the jury.' Agreeing on evidence and testimony that had been presented at the first trial would allow them to skip those witnesses at the second. 'We could stipulate the uniformed cops, the crime-scene diagrams, the document authentication, all that. I'd even be willing to give you the M.E. Read the testimony into the record.'

Estrada was about to say all right but before the words were out, he reconsidered. 'I'd like to wait.'

She tilted her head to one side. 'I assumed you'd be putting on basically the same case . . .'

He nodded, trying to look knowing. Had he ever been naive enough to fall for that one? 'Still, I'd like to wait a bit . . .'

'Sure.' Briskly. She bent to extract a datebook from her briefcase. 'Let's talk about a trial date. We're still in April. I could be ready for the first of June, but we can put it back as far as the tenth if you want.'

'Next June, you mean? A year from now?' He was trying to smile. He had been counting on her to delay, like every other defense lawyer. He needed as much time as he could get to develop a case where now there was none.

Miller's own smile looked effortless. '*This* June, actually. I wanted to give us plenty of time before August. I figured a week or a week and a half to pick a jury, at most. I'm usually a quick picker. Then two or three weeks for testimony, less if we can stipulate a fair amount of it, which I really think we can. With any luck we can get them deliberating by mid-July.'

'Sounds good, the way you describe it.'

'Great.' Her pen was poised. 'If we can get to Judge Martinez soon enough . . .'

'Wait a minute.'

Her head tilted again, barely perceptibly. The gesture made him think of an intelligent bird. A very intelligent bird. Predatory.

'I said it sounded good. I didn't say it was realistic.'

'Why not? It's just a question of assembling your witnesses. They've all testified before. How long can it take?'

She was fishing again, in the wrong pond.

'For one thing,' he said, 'my witnesses are not all in the jurisdiction. I have to coordinate their schedules, and I've got to give them a good month's notice. Six weeks, probably, if I'm going to get them all here. That's for starters. I don't see a trial before September, the absolute earliest. I don't know what else I'm going to run into, and this is too important to rush.' Collins would not be happy if he could hear this, but the way things stood Estrada's only hope was buying time.

'Roberto Morales is entitled to a speedy trial,' Miller insisted. 'He's a public figure and he has a terrible cloud over his head. We have an obligation to remove it as fast as possible.'

'He's not in prison, he's never been in prison – there's no hardship of that kind. As I understand it, he's independently wealthy thanks to his real-estate holdings, so his livelihood isn't impaired' – when she started to object, he held up his hand and barreled ahead – 'and he's been under this cloud, as you call it, for more than three years, so another month or two isn't going to make a difference.'

'Every *day* makes a difference. This whole proceeding is a travesty. There was never enough evidence to convict him. Not enough to indict him if grand juries didn't lie down for any prosecutor who asks them to. An innocent man accused of a heinous crime is in agony every minute until he's cleared. Think of his family. Two little kids. Beautiful, smart kids. And they go to school and the other kids call them names because in nursery school and first grade there's no presumption of innocence. In the schoolyard, their daddy's a murderer.'

'Their daddy *is* a murderer.'

'No he isn't!' She was almost out of her chair with the force of the denial. Her vehemence took him by surprise.

'All the more reason not to rush the trial. Maybe it will improve your case to have a few weeks' extra preparation time.'

She busied herself putting her datebook back in her briefcase. 'I have an obligation to my client to honor his insistence on the earliest possible trial date.'

'If we push for June, even late June, you're squeezed to almost no time for making pre-trial motions.'

'I'm prepared to deal with that. The main issues were covered the first time around.'

He could believe she was all set to begin, motions all drafted and ready to be filed, witnesses all lined up. The fact that she was first making a formal appearance in the case now did not mean she had just been hired. She could have begun working on a new defense as long ago as Morales's victory in the first appeal, or even before.

'In any event,' he said, 'Martinez isn't going to make me put on a case if I'm not ready.'

'We'll see.' She stood up.

He came around the desk. She held out her hand.

'I enjoyed this,' she said, smiling again. 'I think we're going to have a good trial. I'm sorry it has to be on this case. Roberto Morales should only be in court as a spectator.'

8

As short as Kassia Miller was, Lynne Schelling was tall: over six feet, lithe and graceful. She sat in the chair Miller had used, crossing her legs carefully so the skirt of her burgundy wool suit did not ride too far up her thighs. Excellent legs, Estrada could not help noticing.

'How can I help you, Mr Estrada?' A low voice. Musical. If she had a good story to tell she would be a perfect witness, and judging by the transcript her story would be a good one indeed.

'As I told you on the phone, Roberto Morales's conviction has been thrown out, and I'm going to be prosecuting him. I wanted us to get to know each other a little before I put you up on the witness stand. I don't think we ought to be strangers when that happens.'

She was following him alertly, nodding in the right places, but not too much or too enthusiastically. 'All right. Do you want to ask me questions now?'

No wonder Kahn convinced the jury. With a witness like this . . . 'I do have some questions,' he said. 'But first, do you have any for me?'

'What kind of questions?'

'About why we're doing this again. About me, what I'm going to expect of you. About the timing – when we're going to trial on this, when you're likely to be called, how much time it's likely to take.'

'Schedule, of course. I'll need to know about that

eventually.' She paused. 'There is something else.' Her hands were crossed on her knee, holding a small, elegant purse. She looked down at it, long fingers manipulating the clasp. 'I hope you understand that when I testified at the trial two years ago it wasn't pleasant for me.'

'I'm sorry to hear that, but I won't say I'm surprised. Testifying at a trial can be very gratifying in the end, but it's almost never pleasant while it's happening.'

'It's not something a person wants to do more than once.' She looked at him – a silent attempt to make him her ally in some way. She had the darkest blue eyes he had ever seen, mysterious and inviting. She was forty-two years old, a decade older than he was; it did not diminish her appeal at all.

'Believe me,' he said, 'none of us is happy to have to do this again.' He smiled, the soul of reasonableness. 'Unfortunately for us all, the state's highest court decided that the judge made a mistake and the trial has to be repeated.'

'I don't see why I should suffer because the judge made a mistake.'

'I hope that this time it won't be suffering. If we talk about what bothered you, maybe we can keep it from being so unpleasant.'

'To be honest with you, I'm not inclined to do this at all.'

Two reactions flashed through his mind: anger at her presumption – declining as casually as if this were an invitation to a cocktail party – and a quick spike of fear that he was going to lose another crucial witness.

He leaned forward, elbows on his desk, his earnest posture, coupled with an earnest expression. He thought, If she's got good ears she can hear my heart pounding.

'Ms Schelling, when a person has evidence as important as yours, you have to understand that the trial can't proceed properly without it.'

He wanted to hold back the threat of a subpoena as long as possible. Once the word was spoken it became very hard to reestablish the illusion that the witness was a voluntary ally, not a coerced one.

The implicit warning seemed to be enough. She shifted in the chair, recrossed her legs, less concerned about her skirt. 'All right, I suppose I understand that. As long as you understand that I'm not happy to be here.'

'As I said, I'll do my best to make it as easy on you as possible.' He tried not to show his relief.

'I appreciate that.' Smiling. Again, her eyes seemed to reach out. 'I do have a question.'

'All right.'

Another examination of her purse, slender fingers working the clasp. And, suddenly, Estrada was worried. Something was wrong and he had been too busy being dazzled to sense it. She wanted out, but there was a bigger reason than her discomfort.

'I was wondering . . .' she began. 'Suppose I remember something now I didn't then.' A glance up, then back to the purse. 'Suppose I change my testimony.' Another glance up and then, quickly, 'I'm not saying I will, I'm just saying suppose.'

He could not believe this was happening. 'It would depend on what the changes were.'

'Suppose Mariah said she might not want to break up with him that night.'

Estrada took a moment to absorb it.

'What are you saying?' Not entirely keeping the horror out of his voice.

'I said . . . I'm not saying anything. Just suppose.'

'You testified that she said she was going to break up with him. That she couldn't wait. That she wasn't going to pull any punches.' He tried to remember the phrase from the transcript. 'Give it to him with both barrels.'

His tone made her flinch. 'Yes, but' – she struggled with the next few words – 'suppose now I say something else.'

Estrada took a breath. He had to back off or he wasn't going to get anywhere.

'Okay, suppose you say something else, now. Like what?'

'I *said*. Like she told me she was going to break up with

him, but then she sort of took it back. The first time we talked, she was going to, but not the second time.' Her eyes widened and she hurried to add, 'I mean, suppose I said that.'

Joe Estrada was not a happy man. He was staring perjury in the face, and it was the face of his most important witness.

'There's more than one question here,' he said carefully. 'What would actually happen depends on how much you change your testimony, and why you gave testimony at the first trial that was different from what you're now saying happened.'

She clearly wished she had never brought this up. 'Just suppose, that's all. Suppose I say what I told you just now.'

'Okay. Technically, lying in court under oath is perjury, and that's a serious crime.'

'I didn't mean to.'

'Well, we'll get to that.' You lied to Larry Kahn, too, he wanted to say. Lied over and over, despite having plenty of opportunity to change your mind and tell the truth. 'The first thing we need to do is find out what the truth is.'

'I don't want to go to jail because my memory isn't perfect.'

'That's what I meant before. If it's a question of your remembering the conversations better this time, that might get by. Although plenty of people are going to wonder why your memory is so much better three years later than it was right after all this happened.'

'I was confused then, and upset and anxious. Somebody had just killed my best friend. Since then I've had time to think about it.'

Estrada leaned back in what he hoped was a gesture of nonchalance. 'And what do you remember now?'

She shifted in the chair. Uncrossed her legs and recrossed them the other way.

'The first conversation was the same as I testified in court. I didn't lie or make anything up. Mariah was furious with him. She wanted to give it to him with both barrels.' She smiled faintly at the echoed phrase. 'But then' – she fidgeted again with the clasp of her purse – 'I don't know for sure. This is just what I think she said. What I remember now.'

Estrada waited.

'Suppose she said there was a big meeting at work the next day and maybe she wasn't going to break up with him after all, because she wanted to talk to him about the meeting. Something like that. That maybe she was going to wait because she didn't want to rock the boat at work.'

She stopped. She was watching him, waiting for a reaction, but he was too frozen to respond.

It's not the end of the world, he told himself. This wasn't a definitive statement. Mariah had said *maybe* she wasn't going to break up with him. *Maybe* she wasn't. Which left maybe she did, anyway.

But he was kidding himself, and he knew it. Because all that really mattered to him was what the jury heard, and what they believed. And he wasn't sure he was getting the straight story yet. *Maybe* was as likely to be Lynne Schelling covering her butt as it was to be the truth.

'Did she really say "maybe"? Are you sure she didn't say she'd changed her mind – that this meeting, or whatever it was, was more important to her than whatever satisfaction she'd get from breaking up with Morales. Wasn't it more like that?'

'It might have been.'

'*Might have been*? You'll have to do better than "might have been". You can hope for the benefit of the doubt – that people will believe your memory got better, not that you're correcting a lie – once. But change your story a second time and you're not going to find a lot of sympathetic listeners.' He had to press her, had to be sure he was getting the truth, whether it helped him or not, because if he didn't and she changed her story again it would surely be disastrous. 'So you want to think hard about whether it was *maybe* or whether she said something more definite.'

'Suppose it was more like what you said.'

'I don't want to put words in your mouth.'

'No, really, that's how it was.'

Suddenly her face clenched up as if she was holding back tears. 'I don't know why I didn't say this . . .' She caught herself, on the verge of an admission she did not want to make. 'Sorry.'

'You were saying . . . you don't know why you didn't say this . . .'

'It's not important.'

Estrada let it pass. 'Tell me something . . . What would you say her demeanor was when you had that second conversation? The way you remember it now.'

She looked blankly at him, so he led her into it.

'When she said she might not break up with him, did she sound happy or sad? Did she seem to be focused – hot on the track of something – or was she confused? Do you think she'd actually changed her mind about Morales, or was this just something she was doing to better herself at work and if she didn't break up with him right away she was going to do it as soon as she had what she needed from him?'

'I don't want to make her seem like she was cold and manipulative about it.'

'Just tell me what you honestly remember.'

'She said she was just about to tell him to fuck off forever when he said, Hey, I have some news for you, and then he told her about the meeting. So she kept quiet until she was sure she understood what the meeting was about and as soon as she did, she knew that she couldn't let the meeting happen with him hating her for the way she'd just trashed him.'

'She thought he'd hate her?'

Her expression clouded. 'She thought he'd hate her but she didn't think he'd *kill* her.'

Estrada gave her a moment before he spoke again. 'So she was going to wait.' Leading the witness again.

'Yes.'

'And how did she sound when she talked about the meeting? Tense, worried?'

'I don't know. She sounded . . . tense? I guess so, maybe. Excited. Big doings.'

'And did she say anything about Morales?'

'Like what?'

'How she felt about not breaking up with him?'

'Just that it wasn't a good idea right then.'

'And when was the meeting?'

'The next day, I think. Monday.'

'And your impression was that she was not going to break up with him until after that.'

'Yes.'

'And is this the truth, this time?'

She started to look hurt but seemed to decide it wouldn't play. 'Yes. As far as I remember.'

'Do you expect to remember anything else – anything different?'

'No, I don't. I mean, I don't know. It was a long time ago.'

Estrada stood up. 'I'm glad you came to see me. We'll have to get together again and talk some more about your testimony. In the meantime you might want to be careful whom you talk to about this, at least until you talk to me again.' Being careful himself, not wanting to step over the bounds of what he could advise her. 'The press, in particular. If they get in touch with you for any reason, you can always tell them you have nothing to say. And you have no obligation to talk to the defense lawyers, and certainly not to Roberto Morales.'

'Morales! You think I'd talk to him?'

He hoped she meant it.

After she left, Estrada sat at his desk and threw darts at his executive dart board. For a change they hit the target, but none of them stuck. It had to be something to do with the magnets.

He tried to assess what had just happened.

He couldn't counsel her to stay with her original story. But it was no more than his duty – if he wanted to stretch things in that direction – to tell her that if she changed her story now he could not protect her from a perjury charge. Let her work out what that really meant.

If she took the hint and decided she'd been right the first time, could he put her on the stand? Condoning a lie in the service of some ultimate truth was a slippery slope indeed.

On the other hand, if she persisted on this new tack he might well have to steer her straight to Miller. And once Miller had her it was all over, because she would be testifying about a change of mind that had happened after Mariah's last conversation with Carlyn Sims, her friend in Texas, the other witness to her intention to blast Morales. If the jury believed Schelling, then Sims's evidence was worthless. The most Estrada would be able to prove was that early in the day Mariah Dodge had intended to break up with Morales. But, the defense would say, after Dodge and Morales made love that afternoon and he told her about the meeting she had changed her mind. So where was the motive for savage rape and murder?

He tried to work but found himself staring at the murky shadows beyond the windows. He went home. If he was not going to accomplish anything more at the office, at least he could beat the rain.

He'd had a worse day, but he didn't know when. He was facing the loss of both his motive evidence and his evidence placing Morales at the scene of the crime. If he had to go to trial with no more than he had now, he would have to consider recommending that the charges against Morales be dropped. Without Ramon Santos to place Morales at the scene, and with Lynne Schelling ready to testify that Mariah Dodge had changed her mind about breaking up with Morales, he doubted there was enough prosecution evidence for a legally sufficient case.

He had been prepared, he thought, to endure a loss. This was something else. To be counted out before the starting bell was not tolerable.

At home, he popped open a beer and called Michelle in Los Angeles, hoping for a little consolation. She was not at the office. Phone tag was getting to be their regular game, the time difference conspiring with their schedules to deny them any free time in common. When they did connect, at least one of them was invariably in a hurry or exhausted.

He did not finish his beer and he did not try to watch television. He leafed through some newspapers without paying attention to what he was reading.

He lay on his living room couch staring at the ceiling, playing through what he knew about Roberto Morales and Mariah Dodge. Not enough. If he looked at it honestly, he had to admit that he didn't know enough even to be sure that Roberto Morales was guilty.

Somewhere in what he did not know was the answer. All he had to do was find it.

9

Arriving at work, his mind churning with doubts about his case, he walked past Tess Dodge sitting in one of the blue-vinyl chairs that lined the corridor wall opposite Ginny's reception desk.

'Hey! Estrada.'

He turned. She was starting toward him, smiling broadly, her hand out. He shook it, perplexed. The curls were the same, and the bright green eyes and the generous features, but this was a different woman from the one he had seen only a few days before.

'I came to apologize.'

'No need for that.'

Her smile widened. 'Oh, yes there is. And don't you pretend there isn't.'

They were drawing attention from the cops and his bureau-mates passing them in the narrow hall. 'Maybe we should continue this in my office.' And get it over with, whatever it is.

It was, it turned out, an apology, just as she had said. 'It's been weighing on me . . . I don't want you thinking I'm some kind of monster. I honestly want to *help*. I care how this comes out, a lot. I tried to be all nice and ladylike with that awful Kahn person – some of the time, anyway – and he didn't listen at all, so I thought this time I'd try something different.'

'It certainly was different.'

'I know toward the end there all you could think of was

how to get rid of me. I don't blame you.'

'You're being too hard on yourself. Of course you care. Of course you want to be involved. But I have to set some limits.'

'As long as you listen to my ideas, and as long as I can know what's going on, I'll try not to get in the way. I'll be around. I have a place to stay in New York until this is over.'

'Let me know where to reach you, and I'll keep you posted.'

'How about I'll call *you*?'

He had to smile. 'Fine.'

'And I want you to think about what I said, that Kahn missed part of the story. I don't know what, exactly, but there's got to be more.'

'Like what?'

'All that money, for one. And Cuyler Jadwin, the man behind the money . . .' The Texas banker who had put together the financing for Phoenix Enterprises. 'I hear he's kind of slippery.'

'Why do you say that?'

'I got it from one of my former employers. Slick as deer guts hangin' on a doorknob, is what he said.'

It was a slender reed, but he was ready to grasp it. He called Nancy Rosen.

'Did Larry ever talk about any motive besides sex?'

'You mean you weren't kidding about that?' He could not read her tone. 'What kind of motive are you looking for?'

'Money. Did Larry ever talk about a financial motive? Ever explore it at all?'

'Not that I know of.'

'Could you ask him if he ever considered it?'

She hesitated. 'It's *your* case.'

'Thanks,' he said.

'Any time.'

He called Kahn.

'In a meeting,' the secretary said.

Phoenix Enterprises was Tommy Clemente's assignment.

He had already been tracking down the few executives and other employees of the defunct company. Estrada called him. 'I want to look harder at the company. Let's see what we can turn up in the way of business records or anything related.'

The detective was slow to respond. 'I'll ask around.' He did not sound pleased by the assignment.

Kahn called back within an hour. 'What can I do for you?'

'Your Morales investigation.' Estrada did his best to make his reply as crisp as the question. 'Did you ever look for a financial motive?'

'I *had* a motive, remember?'

'Phoenix Enterprises was planning to spend hundreds of millions of dollars. There was already fifteen million or so pledged or actually invested at the time of the killing. And it was a racially touchy project. Lots of room for motive there, too.'

'I'm in the middle of preparing my first case for the grand jury and you want to know if I was chasing phantoms three years ago? Listen to me. Carefully. It was a sex killing, a love killing – call it what you want. Don't confuse yourself. Don't waste your time and mine. Just stick to the straight and simple.' He hung up.

Estrada could see Kahn's point. The rejected-lover motive had worked with the first jury – or had seemed to work. And, most likely, Kahn believed the story he'd told in court. Still, that didn't excuse not pursuing any other motive. Especially since the evidence for the motive he had used was so second-hand. It would be a hard mistake to overcome, with the Phoenix Project long dead and its ashes scattered.

'It's an interesting twist,' Mahoney said when Estrada told him about the possibility of a financial motive. 'As long as it doesn't lead you way out into left field.'

He paused, distracted by a passing woman. They had walked over to the South Street Seaport and Mahoney had insisted they sit outside so he could appreciate the human scenery. 'Nice,' he said with a note of wistfulness.

'If we were upstairs, where we belong on cloudy, windy days, you could admire the waitresses.'

'Or the manager.'

'Spoken for, the way I hear it.'

'So was I, once.'

'You and Kath are really over. I still don't believe it.'

'You don't give up, do you?'

'I guess I don't want to believe it didn't last.' Estrada pressed on despite his friend's annoyance. Mahoney and Kath, living together for four years, perpetually on the verge of marriage, had been his proof that two people could form a warm, stable connection that diminished neither of them. With Mahoney playing it silent about the breakup, Estrada had called Kath to find out what had happened; she would not talk to him. 'I need all the good examples I can find,' he told Mahoney. 'And I liked seeing you happy.'

'You want to know why?' Mahoney burst out. 'She cheated on me. Okay? Not just once. I mean – one guy, but for months. All right? Satisfied?'

Estrada gripped his friend's arm. 'God, Dan. I'm sorry. Really.'

'Yeah, well, so am I. And that's all about this, okay? No more.'

Estrada paid attention to his fish, feeling stupid for having pushed too hard. Sometimes life wasn't so different from court that way: you didn't ask a question unless you were sure you were going to like the answer.

Mahoney waved the waitress over. Ordering a double scotch, he read his friend's expression. 'I'm a grownup, Joseph. I make my own decisions, about drinking to drown my sorrows and everything else.'

'Speaking of decisions, I have a legal question for you.' Changing the subject as quickly as he could.

'I'm open for business.'

He told Mahoney about Lynne Schelling. 'I want to know

at what point it stops being a question of my prime witness going bad on me and becomes something I have to tell the defense about.'

'Am I hearing that you're worried about our old friend *Brady v. Maryland*?'

'Precisely. Bad enough if I don't have Schelling to say Mariah intended to break up with him. But suppose she's ready to testify that Mariah wanted to hang on because of what was going on at the office. At what point does that stop being the absence of motive evidence and become something that could help the defense create a reasonable doubt that Morales did the crime?'

'Good question.'

'Because if her evidence goes to help the defense case in a material way, then under *Brady* I have an obligation to inform them about her. To make her available. Don't I?'

'You're reaching.'

'Humor me for a minute.'

'You know, Joseph, being in the Appeals Bureau I find that sometimes it's my job to learn what the answer is, and sometimes it's my job to make sure the answer comes out right. One way or the other, I like answers. I like black and white, and I worry about people like my friend Joe, who see moral dilemmas everywhere they look.' He finished his scotch and chased it with water.

'Now, having said that, I will deliver an opinion. The story you just told me falls squarely in the gray, as you have apparently divined on your own. It depends on exactly what she says, but from what I've heard I think you shouldn't worry about it too much. If you can't use her in court the effect on your case will be plenty bad enough. If I were in your shoes I'd be running after that financial motive as fast as I could.'

He reached across the table for Estrada's beer and drained it. 'The oracle has spoken.'

In the afternoon Estrada heard from Clemente. He had talked to three of the four former Phoenix Enterprises executives he had been able to locate. None of them was admitting he knew where the company records had gone. Some papers had been destroyed or thrown out, they all said. Others might still be in storage. Somewhere.

'Keep trying.'

'There's only one I didn't talk to. Don't get your hopes up.'

Federal and state law said that tax-related documents had to be kept for longer than the two years since the Phoenix Enterprises' final tax return had been filed, but that did not mean the records existed. Often enough, when a company went bust the way Phoenix had, everyone simply made for the nearest exit.

'They must have had outside lawyers,' Estrada said. 'Accountants. They'll have something.'

Prompted by the call from Clemente, he decided it was time for an investigation of Phoenix Enterprises. Grand juries were not for post-indictment investigations, but it was relatively common practice to issue subpoenas for another crime involving the same people. Then, if you happened to pick up a useful lead for your trial, you were ahead of the game.

Waiting his turn outside the grand-jury room to open the new investigation formally, Estrada thought about his conversation with Mahoney. Even in a system of law where the opposing sides went at each other like medieval knights at a joust, unfairly tricking your opponent was not supposed to be the way to win, particularly not for a prosecutor. Prosecutors were the guardians of the community. If you had evidence that could set the defendant free, hiding it from the defense was not the way to do justice and serve the people.

Simple ideas, hard to argue with, it seemed to Estrada. The rule established three decades before by the U.S. Supreme Court in *Brady v. Maryland*, and even earlier in New York, did not tie a prosecutor's hands, did not mean going easy on criminals. It was the right idea. The question always was, how to decide what qualified.

Because it had another side. There was precious little objective truth to be had in the world, especially in the highly artificial world of a trial. Instead, there was appearance. What *seemed* to be. What could be proved by admissible evidence.

This case was a perfect example. To make Roberto Morales appear guilty to a jury while playing according to the rules was proving to be no easy task. If you did too much to help the defense create doubt in a case like this, you were likely to end up with a wrong result. You had to be very careful.

For years now, Estrada had preferred to err on the side of disclosure, to give the defense the benefit of the doubt. It was a lesson he had learned the hard way, and he had learned it from Lawrence Kahn, working with him on a major murder trial—

A tourist from Boston, a prominent doctor, had been gunned down on a Manhattan sidewalk at lunchtime on Memorial Day weekend. The doctor had been in New York, as he was every year, to revisit the scenes of his New York childhood. He had been walking with his sister, one of the stars of a popular daytime soap opera. The grand jury had indicted the gunman – one Guillermo Pandolce, a low-level Mob hanger-on known to friends and family as 'Billy Cakes' – and an accomplice.

Kahn, having just resigned as deputy chief of the Trial Division, had put in for it at once, knowing the front office would take it out of the normal homicide rotation. Being put on the case under Kahn had been a real honor for Estrada, a sign that he was well regarded in his bureau. A sign, too, that he had impressed Kahn at least a little during the year Kahn had been his bureau chief.

Estrada had expected to have the time of his life; it was his first homicide trial and his first real taste of prosecutorial celebrity. The reality had been that he had been working too hard to notice. Kahn had been constantly demanding, incessantly critical: nothing Estrada did was right.

Driven by Kahn's precept and example, twenty-eight-year-old Joe Estrada had compensated in part by painting himself as a merciless prosecutor when he talked about the case outside the office. In the process, he had convinced himself. It had worked well for him, up to the point where he had become Kahn's intermediary with a jailhouse informant.

Billy Cakes Pandolce had made the mistake of bragging to the snitch and now his lawyer was offering his testimony. The way Estrada heard the story from the A.D.A. the snitch's lawyer had talked to first, there was no quid pro quo. The snitch expected to get a break sometime, but no specific promises had been made.

Estrada had told all this to Kahn, who, relying on it, had put the informant on the stand to testify that he hoped for benefit from coming forward but no promises had been made. Kahn brought it out in direct testimony because he didn't want the jury to think anything was being put over on them, and the defense was sure to cover the ground.

They did, pounding away at the 'no promises' testimony until the judge, prompted by Kahn's objections, made them stop.

That was in the morning. At lunch, Estrada got a call from the snitch's lawyer. They needed help right away with a judge in New Jersey, and they expected to get it from Larry Kahn. So far, Kahn had not been responsive, saying wait until after the Pandolce trial. But now they couldn't wait, and the lawyer believed the D.A.'s office had a legal obligation to provide that help. If it wasn't forthcoming, he was going to make a stink. And what was all this in the snitch's testimony about no promises? He might not have been promised results but he had damn well been promised a good word to the judge in Jersey.

'I'll take care of it,' Estrada said.

Kahn heard him out, then grabbed him by the arm like a wayward schoolkid and marched him in before the judge to tell his tale. The judge listened, grim faced, and agreed with Kahn that Estrada's failure to reveal the snitch's shading of the truth was the kind of thing that led to censure and disbarment.

Estrada was barely able to speak as he tried to explain that he had been sure, from what he had been told, that no 'promises' had in fact been made.

Luckily, the snitch had not yet been sent back to jail. He was brought over from the Tombs, next door to the courthouse, and Kahn called him back to the stand. Once the truth was out, the defense did its best to twist the snitch's earlier testimony into perjury. Kahn worked to keep it a matter of misinformation and misunderstanding.

After court that day, Kahn treated Estrada to a fiery lecture on a prosecutor's responsibility to the truth and the defense's right not to be sandbagged or deceived by a malicious adherence to a constructed reality; this was not a game of playing with dictionary definitions, the way civil disputes sometimes were. People's freedom was at stake. Savage as Kahn was, teaching the lesson, he did not once refer to the danger Estrada had created for him – that Lawrence Kahn himself might have been accused of suborning the snitch's perjury.

As things turned out, Kahn had gotten his conviction. The defense's appeals based on the snitch's flip-flop testimony had been rejected. All's well that ends well, Estrada had tried to convince himself. The bad guy was in prison and Joe Estrada had escaped with his skin intact, saved by the very man whose career he had jeopardized.

But he had never felt comfortable around Lawrence Kahn again, and his confidence in his own judgment had been badly damaged. It had taken him years to build it back up, and even now it was not that secure.

10

In the morning, Estrada showered and shaved and tried to pep-talk himself out from under his cloud of doubt and frustration. Santos could be dealt with: the right combination of inducement and threat would bring him back to the truth. And maybe there was hope with Lynne Schelling, too.

He called her as soon as he got to the office, on the principle that friendly attention from an assistant district attorney was a good way to keep her mind on the consequences of perjury.

'I was just going to call you,' she said. 'I want to talk to you again.'

'When can you come in?'

'Lunchtime. It's hard for me to get away from work.'

'I'll be here.'

He spent the morning following up on the business and financial aspects of the relationship between Roberto Morales and Mariah Dodge. He hunted out Clemente's contact data for Cuyler Jadwin, the money man behind the Phoenix Project. A Texan, and a slippery one, according to Tess Dodge.

'I'm sorry, sir, he'll have to get back to you later,' Jadwin's secretary drawled.

Jadwin called back immediately.

'Mr Estrada. My apologies. My secretary didn't realize who you were. How can I help you?'

'I'm trying to get a clearer picture of Mariah Dodge and Roberto Morales, and what they did at Phoenix Enterprises.

I imagine you can answer my questions better than anyone.'

'You flatter me, Mr Estrada, but I'll be glad to help you if I can. Glad as a man can be on a subject like this.'

'Are you going to be in New York any time soon? I'd much rather do this in person if we can.'

'Well now, I don't think . . . Hold on, let me not be hasty here. I do have a trip, but not right away. Couple of weeks, maybe.'

'Sooner would be better.'

'It could change. If it does, I'll let you know.'

Estrada reread Clemente's reports of his interviews with Jadwin: The meeting that Mariah Dodge had told her friends about, the one that Lynne Schelling now said was important enough to make Mariah consider *not* breaking up with Morales, had been about restructuring the company's financing. The gyrations of the stock market and the looming economic slowdown had cost the Phoenix Project its most important sources of capital. Jadwin had wanted to make the project smaller and more practical. More commercial, less altruistic, he had told Clemente. He had drafted a series of suggestions and he had found a potential investor who might buy a piece of Phoenix's interest in the restructured plan. Jadwin had been surprised to learn that Morales wanted to oppose him at the meeting.

Morales had claimed he was upset because he thought the changes would hurt the area's Latinos, Jadwin had told Clemente on the morning after the murder, but Jadwin thought the real reason was that selling off a big piece of Phoenix would threaten Morales's position.

Jadwin had not volunteered anything about Morales's affair with Mariah Dodge in the first interview, the day after the murder. Interviewed again after Lynne Schelling had called in with the information that Morales and Mariah Dodge had been lovers, Jadwin had said yes, he had known about it for months, but 'as long as it wasn't getting in the way of work, I didn't care what they did.'

Jadwin had not himself been a serious suspect at any point, though he had arrived in New York from Texas in the afternoon. His alibi for Sunday night had been two meetings with potential sources of financing for Phoenix Enterprises plus contact with room service waiters. Not airtight, but good enough.

Estrada lobbed darts at Roberto Morales, then got up and walked the length of his narrow office – six short steps, skirting the file boxes, from desk to target – and retrieved them to start over. He needed to know about Jadwin and Morales and how they had come together. And he needed to have a good overview of the company's structure before he could decide what to focus on.

Lisa Stein had been a business major in college, if he remembered it right. Something like that. It looked as if he might have been smarter than he had realized deciding to use her instead of Olga Gomez, the eight-year veteran paralegal who for years had been his regular partner for practicing his Spanish.

Clemente came by to report, wearing another of his somber gray oversized suits. Estrada remembered a description he had once heard: a clown on his way to a funeral. In Clemente's case a dangerous clown, indeed.

'I talked to the accountant who did the audits on Phoenix's books. Can't help us, he says. Doesn't want to reveal client confidences. Privileged information, he says.'

'What'd you tell him?'

'That accountants cut no shit with law enforcement and he should think it over and I'd be back.' Something like a smile touched the corners of Clemente's eyes. 'He didn't like the way I said it.'

I'll bet, Estrada thought. 'First these people get their clients to treat them like priests and then they decide their offices must be confessionals.' It was ridiculous. This client was a dead corporation. Even if there had been an accountant-client privilege, there was nobody left to claim it. 'It just so happens that I've opened a new grand-jury investigation of Phoenix Enterprises. Why don't you go back and see the accountant with a subpoena in your pocket. Make it easy for everybody.'

'I wasn't worried,' Clemente flipped out a cigarette and lit it. 'You going to push hard on this business angle?'

'It looks like I have to.' Not ready to say why.

'That's not my kind of case. I'm no accountant.'

'I'm going to get one assigned.' But that was not Clemente's primary message. 'You want out?'

The detective took a deep drag. Estrada was sure he was considering the question.

'Ah shit. No, I'm in for the ride.'

'Look, Tommy, don't do this just so you won't be some kind of quitter. If you're going to see this job as criticism of what you did last time, then you're not helping me, or yourself.'

Clemente took another deep drag. 'I don't stick with stuff I don't believe in, not if I have a choice. If I thought this was a waste of time, I'd be out of here in a minute.'

Estrada did not think he had time to eat before Lynne Schelling arrived; he went down the corridor for a bottle of juice from the vending machines. To keep his mind off what she might have to say, he read about Phoenix Enterprises. He was struck again by how much more he needed than was in the file. He called Lisa Stein. She was out to lunch; he left a message for her to do some research on Phoenix Enterprises, starting with newspapers and magazines.

Lynne Schelling arrived at one o'clock, hungry.

'I'm sorry,' she said. 'I didn't plan this very well. Could we get some lunch somewhere? It's the only chance I'll have to eat until at least eight.'

It was not what he had in mind. He wanted to keep the heat on her, and going out to lunch was not the way to do it.

'Maybe we can grab a sandwich and come back. It's not fancy, but it's private.'

The idea did not please her. She named an Italian restaurant, a major D.A.'s-office hangout. 'If it's too crowded to talk we can come back.'

On their way out, he was struck by how imposing she was. As they entered the crowded restaurant, conversation all but stopped. She did not deign to notice it, moving gracefully to meet the maître d'. There was a table unoccupied and he was only too happy to snatch away the RESERVED card for the toweringly regal woman in the red suit.

It was a booth for two, in an alcove slightly apart from the rest of the room. On the wall a brass plaque announced that this had once been the chosen table of one of H. T. Bishop's predecessors as D.A.

'See. We have all the privacy we could want.'

'I'm beginning to think privacy is something you don't get much of.' Hard to make small talk, knowing he was about to threaten his lunch companion with a perjury indictment.

'I'm used to it.' She opened her menu. 'I'm starving.'

'Whose meeting is this?' she asked Estrada when they had ordered. The question sounded show-businessy to him; according to the file she had worked in the movies before her current job in 'executive placement.'

'I called you because we needed to talk more about your testimony. You said you were about to call; you didn't say why.'

She was playing with the silverware in front of her, her slender fingers turning it this way and that, small movements like playing with the clasp of her handbag.

'I've been thinking about what you told me, and I've been trying to remember what really happened. What Mariah said and what she didn't. It's hard, you know, to sort things out after more than three years.'

'I'm sure.'

'I kept hearing you saying I had to get it right this time.' Turning her fork over, then back. 'That I couldn't change my story more than once.'

She looked up, an appeal for some sort of reassurance. This wasn't the time to give it to her.

'What I said to you, in your office' – she looked down again, slid the blade of her knife between the tines of the fork and rested it there – 'when I said Mariah might have decided not to break up with Robbie?'

He remained silent, waiting.

'That's really what she said. That she wasn't going to do it.'

He locked his face against showing a reaction.

The waiter arrived with their food, generous portions of robust southern Italian cooking. Estrada could not look at his.

She inhaled the aromas of garlic and oil, tomatoes and spices, took a forkful. 'Wonderful.'

'I'm glad you like it,' he managed to say.

'Aren't you going to eat?'

He picked up his fork and speared a piece of sausage without lifting it from the plate. 'I'm in suspense.'

'There isn't much more.' She took time for another bite of her calamari, the sauce red as her suit. Or blood. 'The thing that's been bothering me is, *when* exactly did she say that? That she was maybe not going to break up with him. And what I kept coming back to was, I was mixing up different conversations. That's what I had to figure out, and now I think I have it straight. The important part is that when I last talked to her about him, she was still planning to break up with him that night.'

'She was.'

'Yes. Just the way I said when I testified at the first trial. So I didn't commit perjury after all.' Grinning like a kid with a perfect report card.

His whole body relaxed; he was sure she could see his relief. His first bite of sausage and peppers tasted very good.

'Is this the final version?' he had to ask.

'I swear. It's the truth.'

'Good.'

'Honestly, it is.'

Why did they insist on gilding it? The bigger the lie, the more earnest and frequent the protestations of honesty. But maybe this was different: she hadn't been sure, she was reassuring herself as much as him. Right now, he would take whatever was offered, as long as she wasn't going to torpedo his case.

'Last time we talked, your memory was that she'd changed her mind. Why do you suppose you thought that?' Hoping the answer would be a good one.

'Oh. Didn't I say? It was another time. About a month before. She was pretty fed up with him already, and she was going to break up with him. Then something came up at work and she kind of pulled her punches, but it was only temporary, a matter of time. That's what she was saying the Sunday . . . the Sunday she was killed. That she couldn't stand him, and that he just wouldn't let go. But I can see her having one last time with him, even so. She didn't say anything about it when we talked, but I can see her doing it.

'And then, later, when she was telling me about the big meeting, she said that if she broke up with him he was going to hate her. That's what I told you, that she was afraid it was going to spill over into the meeting on Monday. So that's why I put it together with the other time, in my mind. But then she said something like, "Too bad. He needs this meeting more than I do." And I think she said something about remembering the mistake she made the last time. She definitely didn't say anything about changing her mind that day. That was the other time. Really.'

She smiled at him and went back to her calamari.

Her story wasn't perfect, but it might be true. He would have to convince himself it was.

'When you testify, I'm not going to ask you about our other conversation. The mistake you made when you talked to me last time is human enough, nothing to worry abut.'

'I'm glad you feel that way.'

'The important thing is to get straight in your mind the parts of that Sunday conversation that have a bearing on the trial. There's no need for extras, no reason to embellish the story. You'd only confuse the jury.'

'I understand,' she said with an ounce too much stress.

He'd had enough sausage and peppers, and more than enough Lynne Schelling. If he could have he would have left. It was not an option: he needed to stay and consolidate his gains and, for the moment, at least, banish from his mind the thought that he might be colluding at perjury.

To help himself put Schelling in perspective he called Tess Dodge to ask about her sister.

'I'm trying to get a better sense of Mariah and how she dealt with decisions. Did she make up her mind and go ahead, or did she change her mind at the last minute a lot?'

'I'd have to say both. She could be real impulsive, that's for sure. But when she truly set her mind on something she wouldn't let go. That's how she was when we were growing up, anyhow. What's this about?'

'I want to understand how she decided to break up with Morales, and how she felt about it that last Sunday. From the evidence we have, she told two friends that she was really fed up with him. That last Saturday night and Sunday morning, the friends say, she was working herself up not just to breaking up with him, but to being as strong about it as she could, to be sure he'd get the message. Then we have testimony that she met him in the afternoon at the apartment, made love with him and then told one of her friends she was going to meet him at the office that night and carry out her plan to break up. I need a way to explain that to a jury.'

In the first trial Kahn had managed to slide by the afternoon lovemaking by ridiculing old Mr Censabella. Estrada was not going to count on duplicating Kahn's luck, and he needed an explanation he could believe himself before he could convince a jury.

'I don't know,' she said. 'The thing is, Mariah and I spent a lot of years not talking to each other all that much. It was only the last few years we were getting to be friends again.' There was a silence, broken by the faint rubbing sound of a hand covering the mouthpiece.

'Sorry,' she said when she was ready. 'It's like I said, it just comes over me sometimes. I was going to say – that's one reason I took it so hard. We'd been doing real well fixing up what was wrong between us and we didn't have time enough to finish, and to enjoy it. We just didn't have time.' She sniffled, cleared her throat. 'So I'm no authority. Maybe her two friends who testified would know better.'

'I just talked to one of them. She says she can see Mariah having one last time with Morales, even though she said she wanted to turn him off so completely that he would never think of bothering her again. Does that make sense to you?'

'After Mariah went to New York we had a long-distance telephone relationship, a couple of times a week, mostly. We talked some about Morales, not a lot. I think it confused her some, being with him. She thought he was kind of a hero, the way he wanted to do good things for his people. That was what made him attractive, after all those Texas big-rich types who only knew about money, and easy money at that.'

'Did she talk to you about wanting to break up with Morales?'

'I didn't think they were about to ride off into the sunset together, that's for sure, but she didn't say anything specific about it.'

They poked and prodded the subject, with no success. Estrada asked her to think about it some more and promised to be in more frequent contact.

By the end of the day he had sent grand jury subpoenas for documents and other records to Phoenix Enterprises' lawyers and accountants, to the lone executive still in New York and to the architects who had designed the project.

Late Friday afternoon he got a call from a lawyer representing Alexander Blair, formerly director of finance of Phoenix Enterprises: Was Mr Blair a target of this investigation? Not at the moment, Estrada assured him. 'All I need for now is to have an informal talk. We may not need to have him appear before the grand jury.'

Mr Blair wanted to cooperate, the lawyer said, and he also wanted this out of the way. He had no papers relating to Phoenix Enterprises and did not know where any might be. He would be willing to come in to talk to Estrada, but only on the basis that he was not a target.

Based on the information I currently have, he isn't, Estrada said. He hung up thinking, the poor bastard would have been better off without the lawyer: now I want to know what he's worried about.

Before leaving the office Estrada called Pancho Castillo at *Noticias Diarias*. 'I thought I might go back out to Brooklyn, on my own. I'll need to find Morales's drug treatment center, to start, and I'd like to talk to some people, get a sense of the community.'

'I have just the man for you. His name is Carlos Ramírez, he runs a youth education program called Adelante. He started out in a street gang, just a niño, in the late Fifties when the gangs were fighting over turf and honor. Like in *West Side Story*. Bicycle chains, switchblades and zip guns.'

'Quaint, compared to automatic pistols.'

'For those days, very violent.'

'And now he's running a youth program? Does he know Roberto Morales?'

'You might say so.' Castillo gave him the phone number. 'I'll let him know you'll be calling.'

On the way out Estrada stopped by the paralegal office. Lisa Stein was stapling documents together. Next to her on the desk was a pile of reprints from financial magazines and newspapers.

'Stein, how's your Spanish?'

She made a face. 'What Spanish?'

'See if you can get Olga Gomez or somebody else who speaks Spanish to check out a reporter named Pancho Castillo for me. *Noticias Diarias*. I need to know if there's any slant to his reporting, especially on *Morales*, especially if he covered the first trial.'

'To see if you can trust him?'

'To get a better idea of how his mind works. He's a reporter, so trust doesn't really come into it.' He picked up one of the reprints on her desk: WATERFRONT CITY TO RISE FROM ASHES, from a citywide financial newspaper. 'What have you got for me?'

'Everything you asked for,' she said, pleased. 'Phoenix Enterprises, Cuyler Jadwin and Roberto Morales.'

He stuffed it all into his briefcase. 'Thank you.'

'Some way to spend a weekend.'

'No rest for the wicked.'

11

It only took him one turn around the block in the office car to see that he wasn't likely to go unnoticed if he parked it on the same block as Morales's storefront drug center. He had dressed in jeans and high-tops and a white T-shirt under a worn old jeans jacket, but that didn't keep him from being an unyoung guy with a too-pale face slouched in the front seat of a bottom-of-the-line American sedan. Might as well put up a sign that said THE LAW.

He parked a block and a half away and adjusted the rearview mirror so he could just make out the drug center's door over the tops of the cars in front of it. When his neck started to hurt from straining to see – and seeing nothing – and when shifting around in the seat no longer helped, he got out and walked over to the playground that was diagonally across the street from the storefront. He stopped on the way to buy himself a tabloid newspaper, a container of coffee and a pack of cigarettes. He had not smoked since law school, and not much then, but the props made him feel more comfortable.

Saturday was apparently a slow day for drug treatment. In the hour he sat in the car and the half hour he spent in the chilly, damp park, four people went in the drug center and five came out. No sign of Morales.

He checked his watch: almost time for Carlos Ramírez. He dumped his newspaper and the cigarettes in the park's single trash basket, already overflowing. On impulse he walked across the street to get a closer look at La Esperanza.

Three kids came up the block toward him, clearly headed for the drug center. Their faces were pinched and gaunt. The boy in the middle was being supported by the other two; his eyes were half closed and his nose was running. Estrada started to step aside for them.

'Open it, open it!' the strongest-looking of them said in urgent Spanish.

Even before Estrada had the door open for them, the boy was shouting to someone inside, 'Hector! Hector! Call the doctor. Gordo's in bad shape.'

The trio pushed past him, shuffling sideways through the door. A fast glance showed Estrada only a poster on the wall: a teenage couple heating a bent spoon over a candle. The poster kids look haggard and miserable, though not as bad as Gordo and his friends. NO CUECAS TU FUTURO, the legend said. Don't cook your future.

Walking to the car, Estrada wondered how long ago the human skeleton he had just seen had acquired his nickname and whether his friends felt the pathos of continuing to call him Fatso.

Adelante was housed in an old church, Carlos Ramírez had said on the phone, not preparing Estrada for a building marred by years of warring with graffiti painters and vandals, its high, wide doors replaced by featureless metal plates.

Estrada gave his name to the girl behind the desk just inside the door – fourteen or so, he thought, plump-cheeked, bronze-skinned and smiling. In a few minutes, a dark slender woman with long black hair twisted into a single braid and wide, almost Asian eyes came out to greet him.

'I'm Dolores Acampo. I'm director of our art and theater programs here. Carlos asked me to meet you.'

She led Estrada through an inner door into the disorienting space of an empty church, the pews all stripped out long ago. The altar and the area in front of it had been converted into a stage. Banners hung from the choir loft and the balcony railings. ORGULLO LATINO, and EL PUEBLO UNIDO JAMÁS SERÁ VENCIDO, and MEJORATE CADA DIA and, in several places, ADELANTE.

'Carlos will be with you in a minute. I'll be in my office if you need anything.'

He wandered around under the vaulted roof, reading the signs and newspaper clippings posted on the partitions along the sides of the naked space.

'Mr Estrada?'

He turned to see a man, thin and stooped, coming toward him from a stairway that led up to the choir loft, limping slightly. A full beard streaked with gray did not obscure the scarring on his face: shiny burn scars and the blanched ridges left by an edged weapon. In plain olive-drab fatigues he looked like a battered and emaciated Fidel Castro.

'I'm Carlos Ramírez.' His voice was raw, as if his battles had scarred his vocal cords, too. His handshake was firm. In a face much older than its owner's forty-odd years the deep brown eyes were startlingly young.

'I understand you want to know about Roberto Morales.'

'I want to know about a lot of things, Mr Ramírez. Roberto Morales is one of them.'

'Please call me Carlos. Pancho Castillo tells me you are sincere, and he is only sometimes wrong. What do you want to know about besides Roberto?'

'About the community, about your work. About the Phoenix Project.'

'If I know the answers . . .' He made a gesture of accommodation.

'Do you know why I'm asking these questions?'

'Of course.' He walked toward the altar. 'Come, we can start here.'

On a lectern at the back of the stage he showed Estrada a massive scrapbook: Adelante's beginnings as a storefront walk-in consultation center for neighborhood kids with drug and alcohol problems, the first grants it had received to expand its work, the addition of education programs, after-school tutoring. Then it had branched out into art exhibits, plays, concerts, dance recitals – all created and performed by the members of Adelante. Shop classes in the church basement, even a campaign to reopen a neighborhood public swimming pool. Among the newspaper stories, press releases, fliers and photographs of Adelante in action, Ramírez's name appeared rarely, his picture never.

'You've accomplished a great deal.'

'Hard work by people who care. And there is so much more to do.'

'How would the Phoenix Project have affected all this?'

'A good question. They hired me as a consultant. They said they wanted to understand the real needs of the community.'

'Did they follow your advice?'

'No bird ever rose from those ashes. Who can say what it would have looked like? Or whether it would have fed on its young.' Ramírez smiled, as if to take the bite out of his metaphor.

'How did the community feel about the project?'

'Some thought it was a good idea, an exciting idea. Bring housing and commerce and light industry to the area so that the Latinos were the strong group and all the other groups benefited, too. Use the waterfront land on Northside to help both Northside and Southside and make sure that participants from *out*side were kept to the smallest numbers. Prosperity and opportunity for everyone. It sounds good until you take those few words and add details. And then you learn that every detail that pleases one person makes another one angry. And there was no leader strong enough to forge a compromise.'

'Not even Roberto Morales?'

'Especially not Roberto Morales.'

'Why not?'

Ramírez did not answer at once. When he did it was slowly, as if he were finding his way over unmarked terrain.

'You have to understand that this part of Brooklyn is a complicated mix of cultures. Latinos, Hasidics, Italians, Irish, Polish . . . artists from Manhattan gentrifying some of the worst blocks near the river. A lot of constituencies, and the groups themselves are splintered. Especially the Latinos.' He paused, gathering his thoughts, deciding which way to go next.

'The Phoenix Project had an army of supporters and it also had an army of opponents. Roberto planned his New Jerusalem in the last big open tract on the river. The land is on Northside. Most of the residential occupants were coming from Southside. People were upset by the way the project was disrupting neighborhood ethnic patterns, pulling people from the place where they had settled into another place where they were not necessarily either welcome or comfortable. It threatened a system of mutual accommodation built up over years of quiet strife. People who had used the current way of things as a route to influence in the community expected to see their power diminished or destroyed. And all this upheaval was being created by outsiders.'

'Why outsiders? Wasn't it the brainchild of a man who grew up in the neighborhood?'

'In the press, yes. In the publicity. In reality, to many people here, it did not matter that one of the outsiders had been brought up in the community. He had left. He had made his fortune in another place. Now he was coming back with norteamericanos from Texas and money from England and Germany and Japan. "Imperialism for the new century," some people called it.'

'So he wasn't a hero to everyone.'

'I don't mean to mislead you. Roberto had a large following. They thought, he is a native son and an outsider, both. He is not crippled by loyalties to one group or another here in Brooklyn. He is the right person to bring us together. Now, these same people think Roberto was badly wronged. Wronged by the police and the court, and wronged by his Anglo partners for abandoning him and his plans. Also, his enemies then are not all of them his enemies now. Then, he was a threat. Now he is an upholder of the status quo.'

He smiled at Estrada's reaction. 'You're surprised to hear me say these things? You think I am being too cynical or too blunt or not respectful enough of my compañeros?'

'I'm surprised that you're talking to me at all.'

'There are those who will think less of me for it. But I think that we're all better off if you start with something like the truth. And I've seen too much to fool myself about Roberto or the Phoenix Project, or the motives of my neighbors, be they allies or enemies.'

'I was at La Esperanza, his drug center, before I came here. Does that help how he's seen?'

Ramírez shrugged. 'We always want things to be simple: he helps addicts, he is a good man. But the people who are not eager to think so well of him say it's simply another way he is exploiting his people.'

'What do you think?'

'I don't think his reasons matter. What counts is how many lives he can save. La Esperanza's job is a lot harder than ours. We try to keep them away from the drugs, they try to reclaim them after they are already gone. Some of them, it's more than anybody could do.'

'You said before that Morales wasn't the person to forge a compromise here. What did you mean?'

'Many people felt he discovered his concern for his fellow Latinos when it was convenient for him. And so, many did not trust his motives, did not believe his words. As I was saying about La Esperanza, there were those who thought he was exploiting his people.'

It was an answer to a question Estrada had been asking himself since he started to learn about Morales. He had seemed too good to be true, exactly the kind of paragon who would invite jealousy and resentment.

'In the biggest days of the Phoenix Project,' Ramírez continued, 'people called him *perfumado* – it means "perfumed one". It is a term of contempt for a person who travels the cocktail party circuit pretending to help the less fortunate. Some called him names even less flattering. He did not mix his Hispanic and Anglo lives, people said: he surrounded himself with lacayos who had Spanish names, but they were all trying to pass. His wife, also, they said, a fashion model playing Elegant Lady as if her mother had not been Roberto's cleaning woman. And, sadly, it is true about Marti. She has no use for the local people. The only ones she sees are the ones who work for her in her duplex on Park Avenue. She hangs out with the downtown art crowd and with the big-time partygoers from Wall Street.'

Ramírez sighed. 'It's so hard to please people. But you'll find many to tell you that Roberto is a good man at heart. A thing you have to understand about him, thinking about this sad business of the murder, is his weakness for women. He has always had it. Marti understands this, and she understands that it has nothing to do with how he feels about her and the children.'

'You know them well.'

Instead of answering, Ramírez led him to the center of the stage where a row of chairs was set up for a panel discussion. Ramírez settled onto one of the old library chairs with evident relief, offered Estrada the one next to him.

'When Roberto was younger, he was always with a blonde woman. A blonde woman of quality – tall, beautiful, elegant. Sometimes, not often, a redhead like poor Ms Dodge. He did not like women who might be thought of as tramps. It was sad to watch, because it happened so often. He promenaded everywhere with them. It was always pure love, meant to last forever. And always, in the end, the woman left him because he was unsuitable. He began to laugh about it – it was his curse, his calamity. He called it "mi calvario." My Calvary.'

'Why do you think he kept on doing it?'

'Who knows why men do such things? Maybe he liked to

show himself he could. But once he succeeded with one of them he didn't seem to care any more what she thought of him, and perhaps that's part of why they left him, because they understood that. But I cannot believe he would kill a woman because she called him names. Lots of them called him names over the years. He could have given her lessons.'

First thing Monday morning Estrada got a call from Cuyler Jadwin. He was going to be in town the next day on a quick trip, tightly scheduled. If Estrada could meet him at his hotel, he was free from two to two thirty.

Later in the morning, there was a call from one of Kahn's assistants asking him to clear the decks for six to eight that night, so he could meet with Mr Kahn. Why? Can't say now, we'll call you later.

Spare and erect, wearing a blue blazer and gray trousers, Phoenix Enterprises' former finance director Alexander Blair could have modeled for a glossy clothing ad, the kind set at a yacht club or a polo match. Estrada had met Smithfields who looked like that, distant cousins of his mother's on the rich and privileged side of the family. Blair had a reserved manner, but he did not hide his patrician condescension for a civil servant named Estrada. Having apparently decided this visit was not worth his lawyer's hourly fee, he had come alone, informing Estrada that he had been instructed to refuse to answer any question of a doubtful nature.

Mariah Dodge's title at Phoenix Enterprises had been associate director of finance, and nominally she had reported to Blair. Actually, he said, she had worked with Cuyler Jadwin. Jadwin had been the one who brought her to the company; she had worked with him before, in Texas.

It was a piece of information that appeared nowhere in the reports of Blair's interviews with the police at the time of the murder. Estrada pointed that out to him.

'I don't lie,' Blair said coolly. 'At the time it was my perception that the future of Phoenix Enterprises depended on our maintaining an appearance of . . . regularity. Nuances seemed unimportant. To say Mariah was my associate was not incorrect. She worked in my part of the company. Her duties were related to mine, and she had some training in economics and finance. Business college, I presume.

'A company like Phoenix Enterprises operates in two stages, one that covers everything up to the initial leasing, another that covers everything after that. The financial considerations are very different. I was involved in setting up procedures for the long term. The first part – buying the land, selling the deal to equity partners, financing the construction – Mariah had far more to do with that than with my nuts and bolts sort of thing, though one of her duties was to act as a liaison between the two staffs.

'There was a certain tension, I must admit. She was a Texan – one of them, not one of us. She did have some knowledge of accounting, though, and she knew how the overall deal was being put together. That was never my area, they kept me outside of all that. I briefed her regularly, to keep her up to date on what I and my small staff were doing, and she sometimes brought me reports from Cuyler. She also worked closely with the marketing people, that was a second hat she wore. Of course, if they – if *you* – hadn't found the murderer so quickly I would have felt that it was my obligation to come forward about all this. To be more complete.'

'The way you're being now.'

Blair crossed his legs, careful to lift the crease of his trousers free of his knee.

'There's no reason not to be, now. And you seem a good deal more interested in how the company worked than the detectives who interviewed me at the time.'

They talked more about Mariah Dodge. Blair confirmed what Estrada had read in the DD–5's: that she had not had any obvious enemies or rivals at work. Estrada switched back to the amount of time she had spent with Cuyler Jadwin, the meetings he insisted she attend – ostensibly as the representative of the company's financial planners.

'I don't know exactly what she did for him. Perhaps it had more to do with her marketing responsibilities than with finance. People said that in her earlier days with Cuyler she took care of whatever business details he was not willing to entrust to others. I assume she was performing tasks of the same nature at Phoenix. She was with him whenever he was in New York, in his office for private meetings. There was a certain amount of speculation about that.'

'What sort of speculation?'

'Oh, you know.' A man-to-man smile, though he was clearly not at ease sharing whatever it was with a man named Estrada.

Estrada waited.

His discomfort grew more visible, Blair said, 'You know, jokes about what they were doing. Whether she was on the desk or under it.'

After Blair left, Estrada reviewed the meeting. *She took care of whatever business details he was not willing to entrust to others.* That sounded like it had potential.

He flipped some darts at Roberto Morales without much success and thought about that and the other things he might ask Cuyler Jadwin tomorrow. The phone interrupted him. It was Emilio Perez, the architect Morales had hired to give form to the Phoenix Project. He wanted to cooperate but bringing his plans and other records to the D.A.'s office was a hardship. Could Mr Estrada come to see them at Perez's office? Estrada said he could and made an appointment for the morning on the chance it might provide extra ammunition for the meeting with Jadwin, though what Blair had provided was plenty by itself.

Just before five, Mahoney called. 'You hear about the arrests?'

'What arrests?'

'Your friend Kahn. His first victims – four cops and an

A.D.A. Beating up on a bunch of suspects and covering it up.'

'What flavor suspects?'

'Hispo.'

'What'd they get them on?'

'The cops, assault two. The A.D.A. got official misconduct.'

'That's it? D felonies and an A mis?'

'That's it.'

The woman from Kahn's office called minutes later to tell him there would be a party starting at six-thirty, not six, at a Chinese restaurant on the Bowery. She apologized for the morning's mystery: the indictments had been sealed pending the arrests, which did not go down until four in the afternoon.

It was a subdued gathering: these were cops and prosecutors who had just indicted other cops and prosecutors. A woman came in, thin and tailored, blonde formally cut hair set off by a black-and-white dress. Her arrival created a stir. Estrada wondered who she was, realized with a shock that she had to be Sarah Kahn, Larry's wife. Estrada had not seen her for years, not since *Pandolce*. He thought she must have lost at least twenty pounds, and she had not been noticeably overweight then. He remembered hearing that she had been sick, though he didn't know the details. She was, as he remembered her, a pleasant woman, quick to laugh.

He felt a tap on the arm. Jake Berger, former bureau mate, moved to Rackets. They had not seen each other in months. Estrada waved off Berger's congratulations on *Morales* to ask what had brought Berger to the party.

'I'm on the team,' Berger said. 'I was on my way out of the office anyway so Larry asked me if I could get a leave from my new job to do some cases with him. My future partners weren't all that happy, but I didn't want to miss the chance.' He looked around the room. 'It's a great bunch of people. Tough work and nobody loves us for it, but we know we're doing something that matters. This isn't about guys taking money or stealing from the evidence room, it's a lot more important than that.'

Sarah Kahn stopped in front of them. 'Hello, boys. Jake. Joe. How are you?'

'No complaints,' Berger offered immediately. 'You look terrific.'

She smiled with real pleasure. 'Thank you, Jake. I'm feeling terrific, and I can't tell you how nice it is to have a handsome young man pay me a compliment I don't have to think of as charity.'

'Straight from the heart, Mrs K.'

'And you, Joe. You've been a real stranger. We haven't seen you since that sad case where the tourist got shot. The one with the funny name, Cupcake Bobby . . . ?'

'Billy Cakes.'

'That's it. Billy Cakes. Where do they get those names? And now you're an important man, taking over for Larry prosecuting that horrible man Morales.'

'I wouldn't say I'm taking over for Larry. Nobody could do that.'

'Don't be so sure.' It was Kahn, just arrived, finding his wife before he was discovered by his staff. They kissed, and then he stood still for a round of applause.

He held up a newspaper for everyone to see. By some miracle of electronic journalism the indictments were already on the front page. KAHN SLAPS COPS' WRISTS, the headline sneered.

'I guess you've all seen this. We're taking our first hits, nothing we didn't expect. I want you to know that I'm proud of all of you and I think we're making the right start. The idea was to open with one that was airtight and that would not be controversial in any way. We accomplished all that, and I can tell you that in the morning we'll be seeing a headline in a rival paper that says KAHN TO COPS: LAW COUNTS.'

At that they all cheered long and loud. Estrada could feel the relief that fueled it.

'So we're not going unappreciated,' Kahn assured them. 'Anyway, I don't want to make a big speech. Just thank you. We're starting right, and we're going to show this city a thing or two before we're done.'

More cheering and applause. As they were about to go back to their drinking and eating, Kahn said, louder, 'One more thing.'

Groans. With Larry Kahn there was always one more thing.

'We've got one guest here today, somebody I want you all to meet, because next to us he's got the hardest, most important prosecuting job in the city. I give you Joseph Estrada, Joe to his friends and enemies, my able successor in the job of prosecuting Roberto Morales.' During the dutiful applause Kahn went off to join his senior staff, without a further word to Estrada.

'Want to get out of here and have a quiet beer?' Estrada suggested to Jake Berger.

'Can't.' Berger checked his watch. 'Got a date in twenty minutes. Let's grab a cold one here.'

'What's up?' Berger asked when they were off alone.

'No big deal,' Estrada said. 'I was just wondering about Mrs Kahn.'

'Great, isn't she? Seems to have a sweet spot for you, Joey boy.'

'I've been kind of out of touch with them. She was sick, right?'

'Cancer. I don't know exactly what kind, but it nearly killed her. A couple of years ago. She pulled through – a lot of chemo and radiation, I think. You sure wouldn't know it from looking at her. Amazing woman, the way I hear it, really on the edge there for a while, and now she's in remission. I don't know if it's supposed to last, or how long. But I'll tell you, I was on a case with him when it first looked like she was going to make it through, and you wouldn't believe the way she could smile when she looked like she'd just had a quick turn around the dance floor with Mr Death. And Kahn – boy, was he proud of her. Flowers all the time, that kind of thing.' He chugged his beer. 'Gotta go. Don't be a stranger.'

'Share a cab?'

'What – one more thing? Sure, let's go.'

On the way uptown Estrada asked, 'When exactly was this?'

'Mrs Kahn? A couple of years ago. Why?'

'Do you know what he was working on?'

'Before the case I had with him, you mean? Sure I know. *Morales*. He was already working on it when she started to get sick, and she hit the worst of it before the trial started. He took a leave after the trial and only came back when things began to look good for her. That was when I was with him.'

'So she was sick while he was preparing this case.'

'And all during the trial. He kept it real quiet. Hardly anybody knew about it at the time. Only after, when things looked good, people began to find out. And everybody who knew was flat-out amazed that he could have maintained his focus.'

12

Cuyler Jadwin turned out to be the perfect picture of a Texan. Tall, wearing tooled boots under the long legs of an expensive suit, and a string tie with an intricate jade and silver slide. His gray hair was cut short, military style, over a weathered, suntanned face. His Southwestern politeness betrayed a steely edge as he greeted Estrada at the door.

Estrada had said he was going to bring a member of his staff. Jadwin, unprepared for Lisa Stein, took a visible moment to adjust his manner to include a young woman whose golden-girl freshness he clearly found appealing. He ushered them into the living room of a suite decorated in a vaguely modern style. He got them settled in deep easy chairs, then sat down on the couch, boots on the glass top of a coffee table.

'What can I tell you about, Mr Estrada?'

'Mariah Dodge, and where she fit in at Phoenix Enterprises.'

'Associate director of finance. I guess you know that.'

Estrada nodded.

'I gave her that title because if she was right under the CFO then it made sense to include her at all kinds of meetings. She kept up with Alexander Blair, too, knew everything that was going on in his department. Sometimes I had her give a little presentation at the meetings she came to. Financial stuff. Cash flows, interim investments. Mostly she sat and listened.'

He looked at Stein, then leaned back, a faint smile at the corners of his mouth.

'She was very good. Sometimes she even corrected me about

financial details right there in the meeting. The real reason she was there was to keep an eye on all the players. Kind of read the dynamics of the meeting . . . Like Miss Stein.'

Her face colored. Jadwin seemed to enjoy the effect.

'Mariah was as good as they come. She'd been with me a long time – almost ten years. She grew into it, but she was valuable right from the beginning. Somebody I could rely on.'

There was something about the way Jadwin was talking about Mariah Dodge and about the way he looked at Stein that made Estrada think of Alexander Blair's nervous office gossip.

'Were you lovers?' Going straight for it.

Jadwin's expression wavered for an instant; his eyes narrowed and his mouth hardened. Then it was gone and the country-boy-made-good was back. Smiling at the very idea.

'What makes you think . . .' he began, then thought better of it. 'I guess I can't make that fly, can I?' He sat forward, focusing on Estrada, man to man. 'Sure we were lovers. A long time ago, at the beginning, when we first met.' He paused, smiling fully this time. 'It was a genuine pleasure, but it wasn't meant to last and neither of us thought different. She made me give her a job, though, right at the beginning. It was easy enough back in those days, we had more money than we knew what to do with. The surprise came when she made herself indispensable to me, in a business way. She was a smart woman.'

He stopped. 'Sure you don't want a beer or something?'

'No, thanks.'

'Well, this makes me thirsty.' He crossed the room to a wet bar and drew a long-neck bottle from the refrigerator. 'You sure? Miss Stein?'

'No thanks.' She was locked on him, fascinated.

Jadwin returned to the couch, put his feet up again. 'By the time our romance was running through its last act, Mariah had seen to it that she and I were joined at the hip.' He pulled contemplatively at the beer bottle. 'I came to think that right from the beginning she was looking for a way to prove what she could do. Not manipulating me or anything. Knowing what she could do and knowing she'd have a hard time proving it to anybody. She did the romance part right, though, stuck with me till I was ready to move on, then she made it easy for me to get out. Even put me in the way of a replacement. I have no hard feelings, never did. No jealousy, either.'

'How did you feel about her and Morales?'

'I thought it was stupid. He wasn't worth the parings from her fingernails. Understand, by that time we'd been friends, Mariah and me, going on ten years. I'd seen her with other men, some of them better than others. But Rob Morales was a pure phony. She could have done a whole lot better.'

'Did it bother you?'

'Only the way I just told you.'

'But you were in business with him – this phony.'

'I wasn't always so all-fired happy about that, either.'

'What do you mean?'

'Can I be honest with you, son?'

'That's why I'm here.'

'Okay. Maybe this'll give you a better sense of Phoenix Enterprises, too. I came to New York looking for a deal I could put together in some neighborhood that was way underdeveloped. Where real-estate values were depressed in a major way. I knew I was going to need a Rob Morales, somebody like that. I had a list, and he was on it. I talked to a bunch of them, and he was the best by a long stretch. Cool, but not cold, with a track record in real estate and development and a decent-enough idea for the kind of development I had in mind. Only thing was, I never confused him with an honest man.'

'How was he dishonest?'

'I'm not saying he was a crook, just he struck me as a man who was out for himself while he was pretending it was otherwise. And he's not a hundred percent easy with who he is, either. Not a bad man, I'm not saying that. Not a good one, either. Not good enough for Mariah, that's for sure . . . I have to tell you, though, I was surprised he killed her.'

'What makes you say that?'

'Because I knew him, I worked with him. For the purposes that mattered to me, in a business way, I trusted him. And the people I trust aren't murderers.' There was no conviction in Jadwin's words.

'You say you trusted him in a business way. Did you trust him to get you a clean site?'

'I'm not sure I get you.'

'Would it have hurt Phoenix Enterprises if there were, say, poisons in the soil of the site, or hazardous wastes stored nearby?'

Jadwin laughed. 'Where'd you get that? That's some scare talk people were spreading because they didn't want to see us succeed. Sure there's that old storage place down a ways. It ain't bothered anybody so far, near as I can tell, and it's been there a good long time. As for poison in the soil, nobody ever had more than a scare story about that. And we were going to do tests for it before we built.'

'Did you ever ask Emilio Perez to increase his estimate of the construction costs?' A tip he'd gotten in his brief meeting with the architect.

'That's not my style. I like things cheaper, not more expensive. I did ask them to use better materials a couple of times, if that's what you mean. It was something for the investors, an attraction for major tenants. Some kinds of things you don't want to pinch your pennies too hard.' Jadwin consulted his watch. 'I don't mean to be rude, but I think our time's about up.'

Slick as deer guts hanging on a doorknob, Tess Dodge had said.

'You said Mariah Dodge was indispensable to you,' Estrada said as they were getting up to leave.

'Yes.'

'Was there anything she did for you in your business besides sitting in on meetings, the way you described?'

'She did all kinds of things. Financial things. She was a sounding board. You have something particular in mind?'

'Maybe things you could trust her to do that you might not trust to somebody else.'

'Sure. You don't get somebody like that every day.'

Estrada waited for more.

'You want examples?'

'If you can.'

Jadwin stood there, ostentatiously trying to remember. 'Nothing comes right to mind.'

Estrada gave him a card. 'If something does come to mind, let me know.'

'What did you think?' he asked Stein in the car on the way back to the office. He was eager to have her opinion, though that was not why he had brought her along. Interviewing an unknown quantity like Jadwin, it was a good idea to have him on the record at an early stage. Estrada could not testify in his own case to what had been said; his paralegal could.

'Some character,' she said.

'I got the idea you liked him.'

'Me? He's so obvious.'

'Some women like that, I'm told.'

She started to snap at him, saw his grin.

'He doesn't like Morales much,' she said.

'Doesn't seem to care who knows it, either.'

'That part at the end, about whether Morales killed Mariah Dodge? What do you think he really thinks?'

'I'm not sure,' Estrada said. 'He didn't have to say that, and I don't see what it gets him. It's odd. What about Mariah Dodge?'

'What about her?'

'I need a woman's point of view on that story.'

'Not exactly politically correct feminist behavior, if that's what you mean.'

'Is it believable?'

'Sure. Women still have a hard time getting noticed, especially smart women who also happen to be pretty and sexy. The brains part tends to get overlooked. And we're talking about ten, fifteen years ago, in *Texas*. If she liked the guy anyway and she didn't have a great opinion of herself . . . I think it's disgusting that women get put in that place, but I understand how it might have been for her.'

'And the part about how there was no jealousy between them, and how she let him off the hook and found him a new girlfriend?'

'It's an easy way out for her if he was ready. She must have liked him at some point, so why not introduce him to somebody? She had a job she wanted to keep . . . And you have to figure *she* was ready.' She shot him a quick glance. 'Even if he did take me in a little at the beginning.'

The meeting with Jadwin sharpened Estrada's desire to know more about Mariah Dodge. He called Carlyn Sims, her friend in Texas.

'I need to know about Mariah and men. How she knew Cuyler Jadwin, and what she said about working with him. And about the romantic part of their relationship, too, how long it lasted and if they started up again.' A rivalry with Jadwin might have sharpened Morales's anger at being dumped.

'Why do you want to know all that?'

'To understand her better. I think what happened that night may have come from more than just one moment of anger.'

'And you want me to tell you about her love life?'

'Well . . . yes, I do.'

She made a noise that sounded like a suppressed giggle. 'Maybe we don't know each other well enough for that.'

For a moment he was at a loss.

'You know . . .' She drew the words out, considering something. 'If you really want to find out about Mariah like that, you ought to go look in her diary. I bet there's a lot of *interesting* stories in there.'

Diary? This was the first he'd heard of a diary. What diary? he almost blurted. He said, 'I'll bet you're right.' Blandly, as if the idea of a diary were not a complete surprise.

'Well, great,' she said. 'Then you can ask me about what you read, if you want, and I won't have to feel funny bein' the one who's lettin' you in on her secrets.'

'You can be sure I'll call.' And then, as much an afterthought as he could make it, 'By the way, did you say anything about a diary to Mr Kahn when you talked to him before the first trial?'

She had to think about it. 'I can't say as I remember, one way or the other.'

Estrada went back over the old evidence lists and the notes of the detectives who had gone through Mariah Dodge's effects; he did not find a diary. He reread the DD–5's covering interviews with Mariah Dodge's friends and found no mention of a diary there, either.

He called Tommy Clemente. 'You vouchered a box of books and papers from Mariah Dodge's apartment. Do you remember anything about the contents?'

'Remember? Three years ago? If I knew anything about it, it'd be in my notebook, and that's in your file.'

'Okay, thanks.' He had wanted to know more about the diary before he called Larry Kahn, but that was not going to happen.

'Do you remember anything about Mariah Dodge's diary?' he asked when he finally got through.

'Isn't there anything in the file?'

'It says miscellaneous books and papers. No details.'

Kahn did not answer right away. 'It rings a faint bell, but I couldn't say why.'

'If you remember anything, could you call?'

'Of course.'

Estrada was not going to hold his breath.

The next step was to call Mariah Dodge's parents and ask if there had been a diary among her effects. Even though he was doing fine with Mrs Dodge, it was not a call he was eager to make. He was too likely to have to deal with her husband on this.

He called their daughter. He owed her a call anyway. 'You said you wanted to help. Did you mean it?'

'That's an awful dumb question.'

'Here's one not so dumb – did your sister keep a diary?'

'I think she did when she was younger. I remember something before she left home, some book she kept locked up.'

'Nothing more recent?'

'Not that I know about.'

'Did everything from her apartment go to your parents?'

'Everything like that.'

'Could you ask them if there was a diary?'

'Sure.'

'You don't have to bring me into it yet. We just want to know if it's there.'

'Don't teach your grandma to suck eggs, Mr Estrada,' she said sharply and hung up.

The next afternoon he got a call from Lawrence Kahn.

'About that diary. It seems to me I remember some kind of notebook, more than one, I think. Miscellaneous jottings. Nothing of any value, if I remember it right.'

'What happened to them?'

'I can't be certain. There was so much to keep track of that the minor stuff doesn't stick in my mind. Chances are it got boxed up with whatever else we didn't keep.'

'Then what?'

'We sent her effects to the family.'

Notebooks. Miscellaneous jottings. Nothing of any value.

Mariah Dodge's relationship with Roberto Morales had

ended with enough passion to provoke him to murder. Presumably, then, it had caused enough emotion along the way to provoke her to making diary entries about it. Anything along those lines was bound to give some insight into why Morales had killed her. So why hadn't Kahn thought what was in the diary – if it was a diary – was useful?

Tess Dodge did not call until Friday, and when she did it was from Texas.

'There's a diary, you were right. Volumes of it. I asked Mom if you could see it, and she said she'd have to talk to my father. I knew he'd tell her no – just to keep in practice, even if he didn't care, only this time he does care. So I asked him myself. I said you had to see it to make sure the murderer was going to get what he deserved.' She stopped there.

'And . . .' Estrada prodded, thinking he hadn't asked her to do that, hadn't wanted her to do that. He'd wanted to keep this low-key and simple. Unimportant. 'What did he say?'

'He said no.'

'No?'

'At first. I worked on him, and Mom did, too, and he finally said yes. He doesn't like it, he says it's invading Mariah's privacy, but if you need to know what's in the notebooks to put Morales in jail, then all right, you can see them.'

'Great.' He wondered if she worked at being infuriating or if it came naturally. 'I appreciate it.'

'Wait till you hear the conditions.'

Inevitably. 'What are they?'

'You can't tell anybody. And you have to come out here to their house and read it here.'

That was not so great. What would he do if the diary contained evidence he wanted to use? How would he get past her parents' reluctance to see their daughter's words made public? He could subpoena the diary but it was an interstate procedure and you could never tell how long it would take. A lot could happen to some notebooks while the paperwork was making its way between jurisdictions.

He put in a travel request to Lou Collins. He made it vague: interview family of deceased, possibility of testimony.

Tess Dodge met him at the plane and drove him to her parents' house. Hazy sunlight emphasized the warm, rich colors of neighborhood flowerbeds and carefully tended greenery. She turned into a driveway across a broad, landscaped lawn screened from the street by a line of poplars.

Dr Samuel Dodge was as straight as the porch columns of his solid plantation-style house, white haired with broad hands and a powerful grip. Ice-blue eyes looked out of a strong, square face lined by his sixty-six years. It was easy to see which of her parents Tess Dodge favored.

His wife was small and round, with a smooth, clear complexion that would have flattered a woman half her age. Her hair was dyed red, a tepid homage to the flame Estrada had first encountered in the crime-scene photos. Her green eyes were the incarnation of the ones that stared at him from the picture on his wall.

Mastering his desire to see the diary, Estrada sat smilingly through the lunch Sylvia Dodge had prepared – salads and sandwiches and a pitcher of iced tea. Not a word was said about Mariah or the upcoming trial.

Finally, Tess said, 'Mr Estrada came a long way. We shouldn't keep him from the work he has to do.'

Samuel Dodge led him to the study, where a side table next to a narrow straight-backed chair held a stack of composition books, the marble-patterned kind that made Estrada think of grade school.

'Those are the books you wanted to see. If you have questions I'll be right here.' Dr Dodge eased his large-boned frame into an oversize leather chair and picked up a book from its arm. 'You don't have to worry about disturbing me. I'm used to having Mrs Dodge here in the room with me doing her embroidery.'

There was nothing Estrada could do but sit down and start reading. He opened his briefcase and took out a legal pad and a pen.

Across the room, Samuel Dodge cleared his throat. 'Mr Estrada? Sorry to bother you. I see you've got a pad there. When Mrs Dodge and I agreed to have you come here, reluctantly as you must know, we said you could read Mariah's books. I don't recall anything about copying.'

Estrada swallowed his surprise. 'I don't intend to copy them, Dr Dodge. But it would be helpful if I could take a few notes.'

'See if you can do all right without.'

The notebooks covered the last thirteen years of Mariah Dodge's life: it came to sixteen volumes. He decided to start with the most recent and work backward. Useful leads were likely to be close to the time of the murder.

Most of the entries were short, phrases and fragments, with a rare sentence and rarer paragraph and occasionally a few lines of copied poetry. Mariah's own writing was sometimes plain, sometimes flowery. Her subject matter was more varied than her style and even less predictable. It was as if these notebooks were the utility closet of her mind, holding bits and pieces of everything she wanted to save, whatever the reason, all thrown together in no particular order. She seemed to write regularly for a while and then go long periods without writing anything. Dates were sparse: it was hard for him to tell when a given series of entries was made.

He was afraid as he skimmed pages full of cryptic references and indecipherable abbreviations that he would miss something valuable. More than once he caught himself skipping over a comment about Phoenix Enterprises or Roberto Morales because he was beguiled by one of her incidental observations. He sensed that there had been far more to Mariah Dodge than was implied by the limited picture Cuyler Jadwin had offered.

* * *

Sylvia Dodge brought iced tea and cookies just before five o'clock. Estrada was glad to have a break. The tight letters in which Mariah Dodge had printed her entries were neat and legible, but he was feeling the strain of uninterrupted concentration.

'Dinner's at seven-thirty.'

'You're very kind, Mrs Dodge. There's no need for you to feed me.'

'Nonsense. I know you're here to help us, and you've come a long way, just as Tess said. It's no bother to set an extra place at dinner. And you can sleep in the spare room.'

'Oh, no. That's really not necessary.' He had intended to get off to a motel where he could read the diaries in peace. 'I have no idea how late I'll be up with these.'

'That's quite all right. Dr Dodge doesn't use much sleep these days. He hardly ever comes to bed before two in the morning. That's what he tells me. I'm asleep by then myself. Isn't that right, Samuel?'

Dr Dodge nodded stiffly, not encouraging this personal chatter.

Shifting position often on the uncomfortable chair, Estrada accumulated references to Morales – assuming that R, ROB and ROBBIE were all Morales – a man Mariah Dodge seemed to have found intriguing at first, though also vain and self-important. In the most recent notebook she had written that he MKS ME SHUDDER. It lent credibility to the testimony Kahn had used in the first trial, but it wasn't much on its own. Estrada had to fight a growing disappointment at how few entries looked like they might lead to anything useful.

The most likely candidates were a series of notes that paired R and CJ – Morales and Cuyler Jadwin, he assumed. Their thrust was that R was trying to outsmart CJ and would not succeed. In the same rough time period, not more than a month or two before the murder, Estrada estimated, there was an entry about Mariah and CJ. FEELS LIKE TEXAS AGAIN, she had written.

What did that mean? Had they resumed their affair? And if so, had Morales found out?

At seven, Dr Dodge ushered Estrada into the dining room and excused himself to check with his answering service. The long mahogany dining table was covered with a lace cloth and set for four, as it had been at lunch. Now there were flowers on the table as well, and candles – tall white tapers, their wicks still clad in wax. Sylvia Dodge came into the room carrying a fresh roast ham on a silverplate tray; the carving set was already laid out above her husband's place. She smiled tentatively at Estrada and seemed about to speak.

'That smells good,' Samuel Dodge said heartily on his way back into the room, startling his wife.

'Thank you, dear, I hope you enjoy it.'

There was mashed potatoes and gravy with the ham, and peas and carrots. Dinner passed slowly, with only the stiffest conversation. No one mentioned the diary.

Over coffee, Estrada thanked the Dodges for their hospitality. 'I only had a chance to skim most of what I looked at so far, but I saw things that might be very helpful to me, making a case for the prosecution.'

'I'm glad we can help,' said Sylvia Dodge.

Estrada decided to go for it. 'Mrs Dodge, Dr Dodge, what I really need, what I'm going to ask your help with, is this: I need to take the notebooks back to New York with me. I think there may be important information in them. About the company Mariah worked for, not anything personal.'

Sylvia Dodge looked at her husband, clearly uncertain about proceeding without his approval.

'Mr Estrada,' he said, 'I thought we agreed that you would discuss your needs with me and not disturb Mrs Dodge with the details.'

'It's all right Samuel, Mr Estrada's not disturbing me.' She looked at Estrada. 'They're all we have of her.' A sad smile. 'Well, not quite all, I suppose. But they mean a tremendous lot to us, her own words, almost like letters she wrote to herself.'

'You've read them, then?'

She glanced again at her husband. Sharing some guilty knowledge? Estrada wondered, for no reason he could name.

'We didn't read all of them. I read more than Dr Dodge did.'

'None of my business,' Dr Dodge said. 'Nobody's business but hers, if you ask me. *I* wouldn't give them to you.' There was no compromise in his voice.

'Now, Samuel . . .'

'I understand what you're saying, Dr Dodge,' Estrada said. 'I don't want to invade anyone's privacy. I promise you, no one but me will see any part of the notebooks unless it's absolutely necessary.'

'That smart . . . *lawyer* who ran the trial last time out – the one you said yourself was the best – he didn't think there was anything so important.' Samuel Dodge was emphatic.

'Did you talk to Mr Kahn about it?'

Mrs Dodge answered. 'He was very understanding. He said there was no point dragging every last personal thing about Mariah out into the open for the press and everybody to pick over.'

Or for me to pick over, either, Estrada thought. He said, 'All I want to do is see what these books can tell us about why this awful thing happened. So we can make sure justice is done, for everyone's sake.'

He left it there, to let them think it over.

After dinner, when he shifted to some of the earliest notebooks in the stack, an idea in the back of Estrada's mind was drawn to the fore – there was no sex in these notebooks. She mentioned men, time spent with them, even affection and some quarrels, but the incidents described always stopped short of the physical, sometimes seemingly in the middle of an entry. 'A lot of *interesting* stories,' Carlyn Sims had predicted, secrets about Mariah's love life that Sims was reluctant to tell a stranger. She must have expected he would find spicier revelations than these.

The entries in the earlier notebooks were more like stories than were the later, more telegraphic entries, making it easier to see that pieces were missing. The gaps, he now began to suspect, might be related to the absence of details about her sex life. It seemed likely that pages had been removed from the notebooks.

He closed the books at midnight, eyes smarting. He thanked Dr Dodge for his patience and asked again for permission to take the books to New York. He said nothing about his suspicion that the notebooks had been tampered with.

In the morning Samuel Dodge told him he could not take the diaries, but he could stay as long as he wished and make whatever notes he wanted. Estrada suggested a compromise: since they were worried about keeping the books, why not let him make a photocopy? Dr Dodge did not like the idea – how could he know that Estrada would not release it to the press or quote from it in court?

'I don't conduct my trials in the press,' Estrada told him. 'And in court we have a rule that if the real document exists you can't use a copy as evidence.'

He persisted until they agreed. Dr Dodge drove him to a copy shop equipped to make copies that would be hard to reproduce. Hard to read, too, Estrada noted.

With the copies bulging the sides of his briefcase and his overnight bag packed to leave, he decided to ask the question he had been holding back. Had anything been cut out of Mariah's notebooks?

Her father was indignant. 'I've got a fair mind to take those copies back from you, if you haven't got any more sense than to say such a thing.'

'I'm sure Mr Estrada doesn't mean anything by it, Samuel, isn't that right, Mr Estrada?'

'I wasn't accusing anybody,' Estrada said. 'If there are pages missing she might have cut them out herself. I just wondered if you knew.'

'Not really,' Mrs Dodge responded. 'How would we?'

Estrada left it at that.

He reread the most recent sections of the diary on the plane home. Despite the initials and abbreviations he could not decipher, he sensed that this woman who lived now only in the words he was reading had been intelligent, observant and funny. Often confused, angry even more often. She recorded her happiness when she had some notable success; otherwise she recorded her frustration. She wondered about meanings and reasons. And always she was curious, fascinated with the contradictions of the people around her and their vaguely sketched intrigues. Intrigues Estrada still hoped might help him convict her killer.

13

He called Michelle when he got home. 'Did you ever keep a diary?'
'That's an odd question.'
'Just curious.'
'When I was a kid.'
'For a long time?'
'Till I got tired of it. I threw it out, must be almost ten years ago, if you were hoping for a look at my lusty youth. But I can tell you stories if it turns you on. We haven't had any fun together for weeks.' She started to talk teasingly about what she was wearing. He teased back and then she did and then they weren't teasing. When they had calmed down again, he got back to the subject of her diary.
'Did you make entries every day?'
'You really have a thing about this. It's got to be related to your trial.'
'It's why I went to Texas.'
'About a diary?'
'Yes.' Grudgingly.
'Mariah Dodge's diary?'
'It's not something I can say much about.'
'You want my help about it, though, don't you?'
'Just one question.'
'What a fab deal for me.'
'I'm sorry I brought it up.' Her being away was making them both edgy, ready to snap at each other in a way they never had before.

'Ah, hell, it's no big deal. I don't tell you everything, either. What's your question?'

'Okay. When you were keeping your diary, did you make entries every day?'

'Pretty much. You miss some days, but then you try to make it up, filling in what you left out. And then there'd be whole weeks, months sometimes, with no entries at all.'

'When you went back to it did you write a comment about it? Dear Diary: Sorry I've been away so long.'

She laughed. 'No, I just went back to writing.'

So maybe the missing pages were in his imagination.

Tess Dodge called the next day to find out what he thought of the diary now that he'd had a chance to study it more carefully. He asked if she had read any of it.

'I was afraid to. And I kept thinking about what my father said. They're her private thoughts.'

'None of us would be reading them if it wasn't important.'

She was quiet for a moment. 'I suppose not.'

'I could really use your help with it.'

That struck a chord. 'How do you mean?'

'Some of it's personal shorthand, abbreviations, names and nicknames of people. I don't know what it means. You probably will.'

'I wouldn't be so sure. We were out of touch a long time, and she was nine years older than me, almost ten. I know I said I want to help, but . . .'

'You don't have to read it all, just the parts I can't figure out.'

'Let me think about it, okay? I'll let you know.'

When Estrada called Kahn about the diary, Kahn proposed that they have lunch.

'I've been thinking about the question of a diary since you first mentioned it,' he told Estrada over generous bowls of

Chinese noodle soup. 'If I recall correctly, a lot of it was very personal. You know Kubelik – he would have labeled it a sex diary and the press would have had a field day with it. And for no discernible purpose from a prosecution point of view. So I decided to give it to the family and forget I ever saw it. There was nothing to be gained by causing the family more grief. We'd just come off the same kind of thing in that prep-school murder in Central Park, where the judge finally read the diary and decided it was completely irrelevant, and not even a sex diary at all. Meanwhile the family went through hell.'

'What I read wasn't a sex diary either.'

Kahn stared at him for a blank moment. 'Then they can't be the notebooks I remember.'

'Unless the sexy parts were cut out between when you saw them and when I did.'

'I don't see how that could have happened.'

'Once you gave the notebooks to the family, what was to prevent it?'

'I warned them to preserve everything. I told them that if they destroyed something and we needed it later, people were going to want to know what there was to destroy and why they destroyed it.'

'It obviously didn't make a big impression.'

'I understand why you're upset, Joe, but bear in mind that even when those notebooks were intact there was nothing in them of any value for prosecuting Roberto Morales. Not a word about him that was as strong as what her friends testified to. If there had been anything like that, I would have used it.'

Estrada thought about bringing up the diary material about Phoenix Enterprises, the possibility that it might point to a money motive. He decided he didn't really have anything solid to talk about. And Kahn's opinion on the subject was clear, and fixed.

* * *

Estrada needed to talk to the Dodges again, and he needed to be careful about how he did it. When Tess called to talk about reading the diary he asked her how to approach them about missing diary pages they had already denied knowing about.

'Dad's hopeless,' she said. 'If there was anything about Mariah's sex life, he'd have burned the whole business, and he'd never admit it. Mom's the one you have to talk to.'

'Will she talk to me?'

'Not if Dad knows about it.'

'I have to know what happened. If those pages were destroyed and it comes out later somehow, it could be trouble for everybody.' Taking it as a given, not ready to think in specifics.

'I'll call back.'

It was the end of the day before she did.

'Okay. She says she's going to think about it, but if she calls she has to pick her moment. Maybe some time early tomorrow afternoon. No promises. Don't do anything until you hear from her.'

He came to work the next morning in a fog. He had lain awake alternately hoping he'd be able to learn something about what had been in the missing pages and convinced that the information was lost forever. Until Sylvia Dodge called, he was locked into that turmoil. He hoped she would be prompt: he had a meeting with Kassia Miller and the judge at two thirty.

By two twenty Sylvia Dodge still had not called. He left a message for her with Ginny.

He arrived early for the informal pre-trial conference and found Kassia Miller already there. They leaned against the corridor wall waiting for someone to unlock the door. At two forty-five the judge's clerk emerged from chambers to let them in.

Acting Supreme Court Justice Luz Martinez was a large

woman, comfortably padded. Her hair, black streaked with gray, was sculpted into a wavy hat that seemed to sit on her head. Brown eyes shone from under brows plucked thin and shaped with eyebrow pencil. Crimson lipstick set off skin the color of rich cocoa.

She said hello absently, arranging papers on her desk, peering at them over the half-lens reading glasses that were her courtroom trademark. At her desk, out of her robes, she made Estrada think of a high-school principal.

'Okay,' she said, looking up at them. 'I wanted us to get a look at each other before we got into the formal part of this.' She scrutinized the two lawyers. 'I see I'm not going to have a lot of trouble telling the two of you apart.' Smiling as she said it.

'I try to run a happy, efficient courtroom. I'm not going to be arbitrary any more than I have to, but when I make a ruling, the ruling's made. If I didn't mean it, I wouldn't say it. Generally speaking, you're going to catch a lot more flies with honey than with vinegar, as the saying goes.

'I'm acquainted with the defendant in this case, as you know. He was well behaved during his first trial, and I don't see any reason for that to change. We can expect a lot of attention from the press. I'm going to rely on your good judgment in dealing with them. I don't want either of you trying this case in the media, or contributing to any publicity that would make it hard for us to impanel an impartial jury or force me to impose any unusually severe sequestration. I like to avoid gag orders, but I know how to use them if it's necessary.'

She looked hard first at Estrada then at Miller until they both nodded agreement. 'All right, then. Now what can I do for you?'

'I'd like to talk about a trial schedule,' Kassia Miller said.

'Both parties ready for trial right now?' The judge reached out for a desk calendar, pressing the joke.

'I was thinking of June,' Miller said.

'You were?' Martinez reached again, for real this time. 'That's very ambitious. Mr Estrada, what do you say?'

'I'd love to say yes, judge. The People are all for the speediest trial that's reasonable. But as I told Ms Miller when she first suggested June, I think we'll be lucky to start in September. October is more realistic, when you consider how little anyone is likely to get done in August. I have witnesses to assemble. Evidence to retrieve. I'm conducting further inquiries into the forensic evidence. I doubt I can be ready for June, and I don't see any point in making an artificially optimistic schedule and then having to change it.'

'This is a retrial,' Miller countered. 'The prosecution has all the evidence and all the witnesses already laid out for them. They can pull up the evidence they need tomorrow.'

'It's not that simple.'

'Try.'

'And I have at least one major witness coming from a long distance who's already anticipating a September or October trial.'

'You see, your honor, he's setting it up this way. My client has a right to have his name cleared—'

The judge held up her hand. 'I want this trial done and over with as bad as anybody. The uncertainty is a blight on this city, and it's going to cause all of us a lot more trouble before we're done.' She paged through her calendar, not really looking at it. 'This book is already too full. I have a three-week trial I'm starting Monday if the stars are in the right place and the defense doesn't have an unexpected funeral to attend. Then I have two weeks to fit in short trials and other housekeeping, and then I have another longish trial, and that uses up June. I don't see how I can get you in before the summer, so let's say September. That ought to give you both plenty of time.' She made a note in her calendar. 'I didn't hear anybody say anything about motions. I'm assuming all the questions about evidence were settled by the first trial and the rulings on appeal.'

'I've got a further demand for discovery for Mr Estrada,' Miller said, reaching into her briefcase. 'Otherwise I don't have anything for now.'

She handed copies of the papers to the judge and to Estrada.

'Mr Estrada?'

'I don't have anything at the moment.'

'Good. Let's say the first week of June for a progress report. Bring your client, Ms Miller. I'll see you then.' She pushed her glasses up her nose and began to shuffle the papers on her desk.

Waiting for the elevator, Miller said, 'She seems to know what she wants. And I hear she's a major nut about punctuality.'

'Be on time is all I heard.'

'On time every time, and expect her to be late.'

'As if life isn't hard enough.'

'It didn't sound like you expect a very hard August.' She was smiling. 'Going to be at the beach?'

'That's not why . . .'

'It's okay, Joe, I'm not looking for trouble. I can live with September.'

The elevator arrived, jammed with lawyers and defendants and cops and miscellaneous employees of the criminal justice system. There was room for Miller, no way Estrada was going to make it.

'Call me on that discovery demand,' Miller said as the doors closed. 'See you in June.'

Petite and precise, he thought – the Swiss watch of criminal defense lawyers. He liked her. She made him smile. It was a reaction she probably counted on. He would have to watch out or it would make him careless.

He went back to his office and checked his messages. Sylvia Dodge had not called. He found it increasingly hard to concentrate as time passed. He stayed late, on the off chance that she might have forgotten the time difference. She did not call.

He left Kassia Miller's discovery demand unopened on his desk and closed up for the night.

Sylvia Dodge called in the morning, while Estrada was reviewing Kassia Miller's demand for materials in the possession of the prosecution.

'Tess told me you wanted to talk to me.' Her voice was hesitant.

'Yes. About the notebooks.'

'I'm sorry, Mr Estrada . . .' He heard a catch in her voice. 'I simply could not let Samuel know what was in those pages. Mariah . . .' – again she had to pause – 'Mariah was a spirited girl. She was that way from when she was small. She wanted to have her fun. I was a girl once myself. I never had her spirit, but I understood. Her father would never. Mariah's gone now . . .'

There was a sob and a long silence. Estrada thought she might have pressed the phone's MUTE button.

'Forgive me, Mr Estrada, I'm a silly old woman,' she said when she had composed herself. 'I was saying, Mariah can't speak for herself now. She can't explain to her father . . .'

'I understand,' he made himself say. 'But . . . it may be a problem. When Mr Kahn gave you the notebooks, didn't he say anything about preserving them? About what might happen if you didn't?'

In the silence that followed the question he wondered why he'd asked it. To protect Kahn and the record? Did he think that was going to be necessary?

'To tell you the truth, Mr Estrada, I don't remember what he said, exactly. Dr Dodge and I were terribly upset we didn't quite know what was happening those days.'

'Mrs Dodge, exactly what did you destroy?'

'Oh my . . .'

'Not the details. Just give me an idea what it was and how many pages you think it was altogether.'

She told him in the most general way – Mariah had had

several boyfriends. She had done . . . adventurous things. Sylvia Dodge spoke haltingly and in fragments, a blush bright in her voice, mixed with something Estrada thought might be unacknowledged pride. Sex confused everybody, it seemed.

'How many pages would you say you took out?'

'Twenty or so in each book,' she ventured, then quickly added, 'No, not that many. Ten, I'd say. That's more like it.'

Twenty, at least. 'When did this happen?'

'Oh. Not long after she . . . Not long after.'

'Do you remember if there was much about Roberto Morales?'

Silence, then: 'I'm sorry. I couldn't say. Whenever I saw his name or those initials she uses I stopped reading.' Her voice stiff and closed. Not a subject she would pursue. 'I am sorry, Mr Estrada. I had no idea those matters were anything but private. But it would have broken Dr Dodge's heart . . .'

'There's something else,' he said. 'In what I read, there was usually more than one subject on a page. On the pages you took out there must have been entries that didn't have anything to do with the reasons you took the pages out.'

'Well, yes, I suppose . . .'

'Do you remember any of that?'

'It's a long time ago.'

'Let me tell you what I was looking for. There are stories in the part I've seen that aren't complete. I was hoping that if I told you where they were in the diary you could read them in the original that you have and with luck you might remember the parts that are missing now. Remember *something*.'

'Well, perhaps . . .' she began and then stopped herself.

'No,' she said after a pause. 'No, I'm afraid I can't. I'm sorry. I hope it's not too much of a disappointment.'

'It could be very important. Can you do this much, can you think about it some more? Look at Mariah's notebooks, see if there's anything you remember . . .'

He knew he was making no headway. 'Anything at all would be helpful.'

'All right, Mr Estrada, I'll try. But you shouldn't hope for too much.'

So there it was. He had part of a diary written by the deceased. It contained what looked like veiled and oblique intimations of intrigues at or around Phoenix Enterprises. There was no way to know if what was missing might have led him to the reasons for Mariah Dodge's death or if it would have been too obscure to understand, or simply meaningless for his purposes.

Once upon a time, the same diary had held descriptions of Mariah Dodge's sexual activities, presumably including sexual contact between her and Roberto Morales. Sylvia Dodge had said the diary referred to several boyfriends over the years, and to the 'adventurous things' Mariah had done. Could that include boyfriends who were jealous or resentful, the kind of men a clever defense lawyer might try to claim had killed Mariah Dodge?

Kassia Miller's request for discovery asked for all 'papers, correspondence, writings, diaries, journals, etc., of Mariah Dodge, in the possession of the prosecution and bearing on her sexual activity prior to the date of her death, particularly her sexual activity with Roberto Morales, any indication that such sexual contact as she may have had with Roberto Morales on or about the date of her death was consensual, or indicating in any way the defendant's innocence or the possible guilt of others or containing any other information favorable to the defense.'

Lawrence Kahn had known about the diary, and he had not notified the defense in the first trial of its existence, in the face of a virtual duplicate of the discovery language Miller had used. A prosecutor of Kahn's experience and ability would certainly have noticed any explicit reference to a violent boyfriend, or anything else that might have led the defense to an alternative suspect. And as Estrada knew all too well, Kahn did not believe in holding back material the defense was entitled to, or even just *thought* they were entitled to.

So if Kahn hadn't turned over the diary, he must have believed that the defense had no valid claim to seeing it, that it was so valueless he could safely spare the Dodges the pain of having their daughter's private life made the subject of a thousand snickering media reports.

Still, Estrada had to be sure, Kahn had been preoccupied – more than preoccupied – and the diary was no easy read. There was the possibility he had missed something. Estrada needed reassurance about what the diary contained. He called Carlyn Sims. She was not in.

To fill the time, he called Clemente. Was there anything on that subpoena to Phoenix Enterprises' accountants? Would Clemente please lean on them about it?

He called McMorris. Anything on Censabella? What about his neighbors?

Carlyn Sims called back. 'Did you see the diary?'

'All I can tell you about that is I feel I know Mariah much better now.'

'I bet.' Amused. 'What do you think?'

'It's hard to think just one thing.' He was beginning to feel like an expert at evasion.

'She was a complicated girl, wasn't she? Knew how to have a good time, too.'

She was fishing, and Estrada thought he should let her catch something.

'You weren't so bad yourself. How about that time the two of you went to the beach with the twin brothers?' He did not know their names, only that Mariah called them the 'TTwins.' In his version of the diary the story had ended after half a page, when the foursome arrived at the beach.

Sims let out a whoop. 'The Thomas boys? Did that naughty girl put that in there? Well, I hope you don't think any worse of me for it, Mr Estrada, just a good ol' gal kickin' up her heels a little.' Sims paused and her voice turned sad. 'We had so much fun together. I sure do hate to think of her being done to that horrible way. What's wrong with men that they can do things like that?'

'That's what I want to talk to you about. Violent men in Mariah's life. I want to know if anybody she dated was violent, that you know of. Any seriously jealous ones. Anything like that.'

She thought for a moment. 'That's a hard one. Right off, I'd say no. Mariah liked to be treated well. Some women like men who make them feel bad. Mariah liked men who made her feel good. But you never know what people do in private. I do know that once or twice we kidded around about maybe having guys tie us up for sex' – she took a long audible breath – 'God, I don't believe I'm saying these things. But you must've read all this.'

'Some, not everything.' He figured that was close enough to the truth. 'That's why I'm asking.'

'Well, she did talk about that a little, but that's not the same as being *violent*. It's kind of like play acting, something you'd do for fun. Jealousy, that's harder. A lot of boys fell for her real hard. When you fall hard for a gal like Mariah, it's real easy to have reasons to feel jealous if you're inclined that way, and some of those boys surely were so inclined. You want to know if they were the kind got to hitting people when they were in the mood? Going out back of the bar and knocking somebody down?'

'Like that, yes.'

'I don't get it. It was that scum Morales that killed her, wasn't it? You're not looking to say somebody else did it?'

'I'm wondering if somebody else might try to say that.'

'If that's what you want to know, I don't think so. These were all well-bred boys. She used to say she wouldn't go out with anybody who drove a pickup truck. That was one funny, classy lady. God, I miss her . . . I'm sorry . . . I think I better go.'

He hung up feeling slightly better. It wasn't as good as having the pages back, but it might be some help if they became an issue.

Tess Dodge called to say she was back in New York, ready

to come to the office and look at Mariah's diary.

'It's not here,' Estrada said. 'For now I don't want anyone seeing it and wondering what it is.' He couldn't argue with Kahn's basic reasoning. The diaries of beautiful murder victims held an irresistible fascination for the press, and where there was mystery about the contents they would speculate without mercy, causing the Dodges unnecessary anguish and probably getting Kassia Miller in an uproar. Until Estrada knew more about this one, he was going to do what he could to keep it to himself. 'The easiest thing would be for me to drop it off on my way to work tomorrow.'

The address Tess Dodge had given him was a tall, white-brick apartment building on the East Side. Its unadorned, styleless design dated it as late Forties or Fifties. The doorman called her on the house phone to verify that Estrada was expected.

She was standing by the open door of her apartment, looking bright and scrubbed, her curls fluffy and shining. 'I have coffee, if you want to come in for a minute.'

He handed her the package of diary pages. 'I really should get to work.'

'Afraid to be alone with me?'

She was not far wrong. The mere appearance of being too close to the victim's sister could cause him trouble at work and lead to problems at trial as well.

His silence made her smile. 'If it'll set your mind at rest, I don't have any designs on you.'

'I didn't think you did.'

'Then why are you so nervous about this?'

'This morning, I'm in a hurry. In general, it's unethical for me to have anything but the most professional relationship with you.'

'Never fear.'

He let it go at that. 'Let me know when you're ready to talk about the diary. The sooner the better.'

'I'll do my best.'

* * *

Ginny wished him happy birthday on his way by the bureau's reception desk.

He stopped. 'Birthday? It's not my birthday.'

'Well, you got a present.'

He hurried down the corridor to his office. The meager floor space was almost filled with cartons, stacked three high. He looked for a label, saw only a shipper's tag with no name on it that he recognized. He clambered around and over the boxes to his desk and called Ginny.

'What is all this?'

'Did you issue any grand-jury subpoenas recently?'

'Oh. Thanks.' It was the papers from Phoenix Enterprises' accountants. Having been denied their self-anointed confidential status, they had apparently decided to bury Estrada in paper.

Olga Gomez came to his door and stood there, an imposing figure, making no attempt to navigate the barrier of cartons.

'Buenos dias,' he said, remembering belatedly that she had never given him a report on Pancho Castillo. He opened his mouth to ask about it, but she beat him to it.

'You want a report, go get it from somebody else,' she said in English. She flung a newspaper at him. It opened before it had crossed the boxes and fluttered to the top of the stack nearest to him. He could see the headline: FISCALES PERSIGUEN MORALES – EMPLEAN LATINO FALSO. Prosecutors Persecute Morales, Employ False Latino.

'¡Que vergüenza!' she spat and stormed off.

Feeling more persecuted than persecutor, Estrada gathered up the newspaper. It was *Noticias Diarias*. The byline on the story was Castillo's. He considered calling the reporter but there was nothing to be gained by it and anything he said was liable to end up in tomorrow's paper.

Collins called. Bishop was beside himself – what was this 'fake Latino' business? Didn't Estrada have real Hispanic ancestors? Didn't he know how much damage this could do?

'Nobody ever told me being a recent immigrant from south of the border was a prerequisite for the job.'

Collins did not say anything.

'Is it? Is that why I got the job? Because somebody didn't do his homework about my background?' Estrada was working up a good head of steam. It was their stupidity, and now they were going to blame him for being who he was.

'You were very highly recommended,' Collins said.

'Really? Tell me who, so I can say thank you.'

'Look, Joe, this isn't about getting your nose out of joint. We've got a problem and we need to fix it.'

'Bishop never said a word. He had me standing there in front of him and all he asked me was did I speak Spanish and where did I learn? Tell me – what kind of Latino learns his Spanish in high school and college?'

Collins laughed. 'I guess it's not funny,' he said.

'Sure it's funny, I meant it funny. It's hilarious.'

'Is all that in the article true, about your being descended from some Spanish duke?'

'I didn't read it all. Everything I read is more or less the family story.'

'Then that's what I'll tell him.'

It took Estrada the rest of the day to get Lisa Stein set up in a partitioned-off corner of the bureau's paralegal office with the cartons from Phoenix Enterprises' accountant.

Sitting down at her new desk for the first time, she was trying not to look dazed.

'You want this all indexed by tomorrow, right?' Her attempt at humor.

'If you think it'll take that long.' Deadpan.

She looked at him hard, then realized he was kidding, too. 'It's an awful lot of boxes. What are we looking for?'

'Whatever there is to find.'

'No idea at all?'

'I don't want to restrict your imagination.'

'Thanks.'

'Okay.' He looked at his watch. 'You have until noon tomorrow.'

She grinned. 'As long as I get full credit for what I discover in this mountain of paper.'

'I'll talk to Collins about a finder's fee.'

He did talk to Collins, but not about a finder's fee. Ginny had a 'see me' message for him from the bureau chief. Collins was packing up his briefcase to go home when Estrada knocked on the door.

'Joe. Glad you caught me. I talked to Mr Bishop. He wants to make a statement on this "fake Latino" thing. The phones have been ringing off the hook about it.'

'That's nuts. Making a statement only gives the whole thing power.'

Collins snapped his briefcase closed. 'It's not open for debate.'

Tess Dodge called as he was leaving the office.

'Busy tonight?'

'That depends on you. Are you ready to talk about the diary?'

'About the part I read so far, yes.'

'I'm at your disposal.'

'I thought we could talk over dinner, or after dinner, only there's still the problem of where.'

'We can go out somewhere.'

'If we're talking about Mariah and paging through this super-secret diary, maybe we shouldn't be out in public. Besides, I'm liable to get weepy or something and I'd rather do that in private.'

It was one of those problems with no good solution. He needed to maintain appearances but he also needed her help, and that meant keeping her comfortable.

'Okay, I can come there.'

She vetoed the idea of ordering in and gave him a shopping

list. 'I feel like fussing around in the kitchen. Something to calm me down.'

The press ambushed him as he left the office. Not the biggest bunch of reporters he had ever seen, but bigger than he wanted to deal with. They hurried after him, clamoring to know why he was helping Bishop fool the public about his background, and what did his D.A.R. mother have to say about it?

He shouldered his way past, trying to look grim enough so they would let him by and not so grim that he would come off badly in the living rooms of thousands of potential jurors.

14

Tess Dodge answered the door wearing an apron and led him into the kitchen. The apartment had the low ceilings and small boxy rooms typical of the breed. The generic furniture and framed posters he glimpsed on his way through lent an air of impermanence.

'Do you live here alone?'

'I have four roommates. They're all off flying somewhere.'

She took the grocery bag from him and unpacked it. When he offered to help with the preparations, she shooed him away. 'We can talk, if you want,' she said, seasoning the fish filets.

'Did you get to read much of it?'

'Some. I had to stop to cry a lot.'

'I'm sorry it upset you.'

'I knew it was going to take me a whole bunch of hankies. She was my sister, even if we were kind of not talking to each other for all those years. Don't you have a sister, or a brother?'

'One sister, two brothers.'

'Well . . . then you know.'

He didn't know, not really, wasn't sure how he would react if something like that happened to his sister. Disbelief, horror and anger were easy to predict. But three years and more later would he be camping on the prosecutor's doorstep, crying over Betty's diary?

His family's style had been cool and distant even before his father had bequeathed them all an extra measure of resentment, and his brothers and sister were all more than ten years older than he was. He had shared very little with them, growing up. Though there was almost that much age difference between Mariah and Tess, he had the feeling they'd had a different sort of life together.

'Did you understand what you read?' he asked for lack of a response to her question. 'The abbreviations and the people's initials?'

'Not much, no.' She was doing something to the pot of rice she had cooked before he arrived and putting the fish he had brought into a skillet. 'You want to set the table?'

Ten minutes later they sat down to a meal that looked and smelled as good as any he'd had in a long while.

'One more favor,' she said. 'Let's do our eating before we talk any more about Mariah. I'd like to get my food down while my stomach is feeling easy.'

The food tasted as good as it looked and smelled, and he said so.

'Thanks.' She was not attacking it with much gusto herself. 'Tell me about you, where you grew up, how you decided to be a lawyer, all that.'

'That's more than a short dinner.'

'Tell me the abridged version.'

He did, leaving out his life at home and emphasizing high-school sports and college. He made a small comedy of his trip to Mexico to visit his stuffy, overbearing cousins.

'Okay,' he said when she stopped laughing. 'Your turn. Tell me about you.'

'Not much to tell. I grew up half in Ohio and half in Texas. Mariah was in high school by the time we moved. She hated the idea of moving but Mom was having trouble with the cold weather and Dad had a friend in Texas from medical school who offered to make him a partner in his practice if we came down. The next thing you know we were Texans. Mariah got to like it quicker than I did. She went to college there, too, and turned herself into a real Texas gal. Not me. I was moody and sullen and a loner. Skinny and plain too, and there was my big sister being Homecoming Queen and doing all the right social things. She kept telling me I'd be happy if only I'd get my nose out of my books and learn to smile and get ready for when I'd be going out with boys like she did. Whenever she did that to me, I'd go off in a huff.'

She stopped. The memories made her smile. 'I must have been at least as insufferable as I thought she was, in my own gloomy way.'

'Gloomy isn't exactly the impression you give now.'

'But I was. Secretly I wished I could be like her. Big surprise, right? The ugly duckling sister wishing she could be like the swan. She sparkled like no one else I knew. She knew how to have fun without hurting anybody. That was the special part. Except I suppose a boyfriend or two got hurt, but that was mostly because they had such big opinions of themselves they couldn't see how some airhead girl could keep from thinking the sun rose and set on them. Only *she* wasn't the airhead, *they* were.'

She poked at her food. 'And Mariah never stopped trying to include me, no matter how bratty I got. Until I had to go and open my big mouth.' She stopped again, not smiling this time. Her face wrinkled and a tear squeezed out of one eye. She flicked it away. 'Damn,' she said, sniffling.

She stood up. 'I'm going to clear the table.'

'I'll help.'

'You don't have to.'

'My pleasure.'

'You don't have to, damn it!' Crying for real.

He stood there, wanting to be comforting but hesitant to touch her. 'I'm sorry, I didn't mean to . . .'

She looked at him hovering there and began to laugh. 'You do look silly. It's okay. I get emotional about this sometimes. I can stand it. I have to stand it if I'm going to be any help, and I surely do want to be. Let's just finish up with the dishes and all, and I'll tell you what that was all about, and then we can go in and look at the diary.'

Carrying dishes into the kitchen, she said, 'It happened when I was nine and she was eighteen. She came into my room real late one night and gave me a big hug and said something about being a real woman at last and how wonderful it was. And she hugged me some more and said how much she loved me and started to cry. We lay there in my bed, her hugging me, and me tired and confused and thinking she was going to suffocate me but knowing it was important not to complain. And then she got up and swore me to secrecy and went to bed. In the morning she was just like nothing had happened. And that would have been all except a couple of days later I was having a fight with my mother and I must have said something about when I'm a real woman like Mariah is now. And Mom said what do you mean? She kept after me until I told her a little about what happened. It all seemed so innocent to me, but what did I know? I was nine years old.'

She put the last of the dishes in the washer. 'It was years before I figured it out. All I knew then was that later that week my mother and my sister were yelling at each other, and then there was a family conference with just Mom and Dad and Mariah, and Mariah was grounded for the rest of her senior year in high school, no prom or anything, and after that nothing was quite the same. Mariah was very nice and proper around the house but she hardly spoke to me, and once she was in college she arranged not to be around hardly at all. It was more than ten years before we got to be like sisters again. So that's why I get all weepy . . .' She blinked back tears. 'Excuse me.' Hurrying from the room.

'I'm okay now,' she said when she came back. 'All cried out for today.'

In the living room she sat on the couch and made room for him so they could both go over the pages at the same time.

'Here's what I did.' She picked up the top stack of pages. 'If I thought there were pages that went together I made a little pile like this, and then I turned them different ways.'

She handed him a section. The first thing he noticed was

that she had penciled dates at the top of some of the sheets next to the page numbers he had hurriedly jotted. The pages he was looking at were from about five years before the murder.

'See, that bunch there, she was still working directly for Cuyler Jadwin, CJ she calls him. Whenever there was something like that, an abbreviation or something, I put one of those little yellow sticky notes by where I saw it the first time. There's a whole lot about buying and selling land, and everybody's making a lot of money and she seems to think something's funny about how they're doing it. She makes one comment like that, I almost missed it . . . Here, let me find it.' She took the pages and looked through them.

'Here. See where she says "Church of the Heavenly Blessing"? Well, it's one of those little churches that's really kind of a storefront. The preacher is some old reverend with an idea how to make himself some money, and how he does it is he'll bless just about anything or anybody. Any kind of monkey business you want to get up to, you can get that sanctified, too. So when she said these old boys look like they go to the Church of the Heavenly Blessing, that's what she meant, that there's something about them or what they're up to that's not right. And then I didn't see anything about that same business again, so I don't know what happened with it.'

She looked at him. 'I guess that's maybe not much help, but I thought it was the kind of thing you wanted.'

'It's terrific. Exactly what I want. And I would never have got it myself.'

'I don't want to mislead you,' she said. 'That's one of my best, I couldn't understand all of it, who people were, because of the years Mariah and I were apart.'

They kept at it, but none of the other sections she showed him were as intriguing as the Church of the Heavenly Blessing. He asked her about the fragmentary nature of what Mariah had written, bits and pieces with no logical connection an outsider could see.

'She was that way. Everything that attracted her attention was the most important thing in her life right then. When she lost interest she lost interest completely.'

'In men, too?'

'I don't know how she turned out but that's how she was when she was young.' She yawned. 'Excuse me.' She looked at her watch. 'Do you know how late it is?'

He checked his own watch. 'You're right. I should be going.'

They packed up the part of the diary he was taking with him and she showed him to the door.

'You've really been very helpful,' he told her. 'I can't thank you enough.'

'Don't thank me. I'm doing it for Mariah, and I'm doing it for myself.'

In the morning Ginny had a stack of messages for him. Most were just call-me's. A few clever people had left 'fake Latino' jokes. Nancy Rosen's name was not among the message slips. He could imagine her gloating to her friends: the D.A. had passed her over to get Estrada, and look what he'd bought.

There were two messages from his mother, who almost never called him at work. 'Call ASAP,' Ginny had noted on the slips. He did, and got a busy signal.

He returned some of the other calls, then tried his mother again. Still busy. He asked Ginny to keep trying and if necessary to have the line checked.

'No conversation on the line,' she reported. 'Out of order.'

He did not know what to make of it. Whatever it was, it couldn't be good. He thought of calling his sister or one of his brothers to check. His mother saved him the trouble by calling a third time. She sounded tired and snappish.

'Mother, is something wrong?'

'I've never seen anything like it. Reporters calling every five minutes. I had to take the phone off the hook. Then one of them came to the house. I tried to be polite but he was so rude I had to ask him to leave. It's frightening, I don't mind saying, a person like that in your own home and he won't leave until you threaten to call an officer. I'm afraid he'll come back, or someone like him, so I've gone over to the Briggs's to stay for now. They're bothering your brothers and sister, too, with the most personal questions about our background. Who do these people think they are?'

Thank you, Hamilton T. Bishop. 'Nobody you have to be polite to. Tell them you have nothing to say. I'm really sorry about this, but I think it'll go away soon.'

'It can't be soon enough for me.'

He tried to make it all sound like coincidence and misunderstanding. 'Mr Bishop is issuing a statement to straighten it out. After that, I'm sure they'll leave you alone.'

'I don't want to say I told you so, Joseph, but that job of yours is nothing but a vexation. I don't know why you stay there.'

He checked in with Lisa Stein to see how she was doing. She had the front page of *Noticias Diarias* tacked up on the wall over her desk.

'Very funny, Stein.'

She giggled. 'Everyone else thinks so. Have you ever been in a headline before?'

'Not since high school?'

'What did you do in high school?'

'I helped win a football game.'

She was wide eyed. 'You must have done more than help.'

'It was a small town. How's old Phoenix Enterprises doing today?'

'Not so good. All I'm seeing is numbers. Tax stuff, banking transactions, filings for investment offerings, plus general cash flow. I'm separating it as I go, but there's so much of it. And when you consider they weren't even really in business yet . . . I don't know what we're going to find or how we're going to find it.'

'One step at time. Let's get a sense of what's there, first. We'll worry about how to tackle it then.'

He would have to talk to someone in Rackets or Frauds about doing a paper chase like this one. And an office accountant would be a big help if they would ever assign one.

When it was evening in California he called Michelle, his turn in their constant game of phone tag. He caught her, not by much.

'Joe. I was just on my way out. I called last night because I heard you were on the news. Are you okay?'

'I'll survive.'

'They're calling you a phony.'

'Phony Latino, is all. First they blame me for betraying my own kind, then they blame me for not being that kind.'

'You're not having much luck with this case, are you?'

'Not so far.'

'What happened last night?'

'I got home late and exhausted and went straight to sleep, didn't listen to my messages until this morning.'

'Where were you, getting all exhausted?'

'I spent the night with Tess Dodge, going over evidence.'

'You what!'

'Not *that* way. Working.'

A copy of Hamilton Bishop's statement to the world was hand-delivered in the morning by one of the D.A.'s secretaries. To Estrada's astonishment, Bishop was treating the *Latino falso* incident as an insult to Joe Estrada.

Estrada wished that Bishop had let it die an obscure death. Estrada had begun to hope that the second *Morales* trial would sink into retrial oblivion, but if there had ever been a chance of that, it was gone now. If the diary became an issue it would be in the full glare of the media spotlight.

He had thought he had put his problems in perspective, now he was not so sure. He needed an outside opinion. He went to see Mahoney about it.

'Okay,' Mahoney said, making room for a legal pad among the stacks of books and papers on his desk. 'First of all, what do we know about the information that's missing from the diary?'

'It's about sex, right?' Mahoney answered himself. 'And the top count in the indictment is murder?'

'Felony murder and man one.'

'Okay. Start with man one. Sexual behavior in the past doesn't help the defense there. But there's a rape count, too.' Mahoney made notes. 'Okay. Prior consensual sex with the accused is favorable to the defense – if she said yes before, why not now? And if she consented now, there's no rape. And that's your felony, and no felony means no felony murder. Except that here we have a situation where the prosecution is *admitting* prior consensual relations. The whole prosecution theory is that they were having an affair, right? Right. So it's no help to the defense to show they were lovers.' He tapped the pen on the pad.

Estrada was about to offer his theory, but Mahoney stopped him. 'I know you have ideas. There'll be time for that.'

'Ah,' he said. 'Sex. Not only with the defendant. Who else? Some rough cowboy type who might come up north to claim his honey, only to find her in the arms of a repulsive Hispanic type guy. Tex gets all crazy and messes her up and leaves it to be blamed on the Latin lover.'

'That's pretty colorful.'

'Okay,' Mahoney said. 'Suppose we use Tex as a possible alternate killer. Then we have a problem, because then our old friend prosecutor number one may have committed a no-no. *Definitely* committed one, in fact, if (a) he had a diary describing terrible Tex *and* (b) the diary was in his possession at the time the defense asked for it. Even if he'd gotten rid of it by then – which he shouldn't have done if it was potential *Brady* material – he probably had an obligation to get it back, or at least to tell the defense about it so they could take steps to secure it.

'Your real problem, as perhaps you've speculated,'

Mahoney went on, 'is that the destroyed pages may lift this beyond minor misconduct. If the first prosecutor should have given the diary to the defense – because it might have been helpful to them – and if as a result of his wrongfully withholding it the defense is now deprived of the helpful missing pages *forever*, then that could be grounds for a ruling that the defendant could no longer get a fair trial. Throwing out the indictment entirely. Why? Because the defendant was denied due process of law. The defendant walks, period. Permanently.'

'This is getting awfully gloomy.' Mahoney was confirming Estrada's own unvoiced fears.

'Not so fast,' Mahoney hurried to say. 'It's not as if prosecutor number two is going to roll over and play dead. He's going to say that the defense's claim is a crock – it's too remote and too speculative. Who knows what was in those pages? There's no reason to suppose, given what's in the part we have, that there was some deadly defense ammunition in the rest of it. Besides, the prosecutor can't be expected to preserve everything that turns up in an investigation, and returning an intimate diary to the family of the victim is not like feeding it to the shredder.'

'Wrong. The defense is going to argue exactly that – he gave the diary to the family, in a distant jurisdiction, as a way to conceal it. And the pages were destroyed *precisely because* they pointed to the defendant's innocence.'

'But you have somebody who can say that's wrong, right? I mean, that *isn't* why the pages were destroyed, is it?'

'No, it isn't.'

'And the people who did the destroying . . .'

'The victim's parents.'

'Okay. They had some other reason.'

'To protect their daughter's reputation.' Close enough.

'That sounds a little slippery. If her reputation would be spoiled, maybe she was living a fast life. A *dangerous* fast life.'

'I don't think so.'

'No Tex?'

'Not the kind you were describing.' Estrada hoped it was more than wishful thinking.

'And these people read the pages they destroyed, before they destroyed them?'

'The mother did.'

'Get her to testify.'

'Not likely.'

'Subpoena her. You have to get her in here. It's the only way. Give the defense as much of the diary as you have now. Admit that the pages were destroyed, and claim that the missing stuff is meaningless for the trial.'

'I don't like it.'

'Nobody said you had to like it.'

'I can't do it. If I reveal the diary, I'm putting it right out there that Kahn had it and didn't turn it over. Right away the defense is going to start talking about the bad reasons he might have had for concealing it. Every other word out of their mouths is going to be *misconduct* or *bad faith*. And the first thing they're going to do is get the whole Dodge family on the stand and put them through hell about what they read in those pages. And you know who they'll call after that? Larry Kahn. You said just now, who knows what was in those pages? Well, Larry Kahn does, or at least he ought to. And the defense is guaranteed to make the biggest circus they can out of this. They'll get him up there on the stand and do their best to make him the villain of the piece. They'll call everybody who ever read a word of the diary, me not least. And since I can't be a witness and an advocate in the same case . . .'

Mahoney did not have a response.

Estrada said, 'I'm going to check again with the mother and the victim's friends, to make sure she didn't have a boyfriend like your Tex. I'm going to find out as much as I can about what was in those missing pages. But until I learn different, I have to believe that our friend prosecutor number one did the right thing, and if he made a mistake, it was a good-faith mistake that didn't hurt anybody. And it won't hurt anybody unless somebody reveals it now.'

'What about these intrigues at the company? How far is it from intrigue to illegal? The defense is sure to claim that suggestions of criminal activity in the workplace – or even serious corporate backstabbing – might lead them to motives for alternate suspects, at least likely enough to raise a reasonable doubt about the defendant.'

'The only thing I see in that is more motive for Roberto Morales. Valuable to the prosecution, not the defense. I think I have to sit on the diary for now, until I have more information.'

'It could blow up in your face if the defense finds out some other way.'

'Who's going to tell them? Not the family. Not the prosecutor at the first trial. No one else knows about it.' Almost no one.

'Hey, you asked for what I thought, you got it. After that it's your call.'

'I can't let it out, not yet. It's too dangerous and it's too final. I need more information – about the diary and about the consequences of revealing it. What happens if I jump too soon and give Miller a reason to accuse Larry Kahn of misconduct?'

'If it's for nothing, he walks away from it.'

'Not a chance. He couldn't be a juicier target right now. Anything they throw at him will stick long enough to do damage, maybe serious damage, right when integrity is his most important asset. And even if he does walk away from it, what does anybody remember? That Joe Estrada blew the whistle.'

'For the best of reasons.'

'You know that and I know that . . .'

'Just for argument's sake,' Mahoney persisted, 'suppose it *wasn't* for nothing. Suppose he *did* hide something that was inconvenient for his case.'

'All right, suppose. Even suppose the defense could find testimony to show it. You don't destroy a career like Larry Kahn's for one mistake, and that's what this would do.' Thinking, too, about how Kahn had dealt with Joe Estrada's nearly stumbling into misconduct. 'And the people who've grabbed onto *Morales* as a club they can use to beat the Establishment – the same ones pushing the idea that the Kahn Commission is one more trick to lull oppressed people into complacency – those people would pump this up as big as they could to prove their point. Kahn wouldn't survive it . . . and I wouldn't survive the aftermath.'

They both contemplated the prospect in silence.

'It's a puzzlement,' Mahoney admitted.

'Ah, wisdom.' Estrada did his best to smile. 'I feel better already.'

Mahoney gripped him briefly on the arm. 'Be careful, okay?'

15

The conversation with Mahoney reinforced for Estrada how important it was to have the strongest case possible. If the prosecution case was vague, the shadow of possible misconduct would obscure it altogether.

He got McMorris into the office.

'What's the holdup on Censabella? By now you ought to know how many times he shakes it when he's done.'

The investigator's fleshy, pale face colored. 'Yeah? Well maybe I got something.'

'Like?'

'Like a girlfriend.'

'Censabella? Has a girlfriend?'

'This old lady down the street, comes over for nooners.'

'You dreamed it. You've been watching an empty street too long.'

'God's honest truth. I seen them a couple of times. Not like they're doing anything where I can see, just, you know, kind of hanging out. She sits with him in the window.'

'Tell me about her.'

'Nice old lady. Mrs Iannacone. You'd figure she never did anything but knit and drink tea, only there she is, shacking up with this old man, at least the way it looks.'

'You talk to her?'

'We're buddies. I help her carry her groceries, stuff like that. She's sharp for an old broad. Polish.'

'Iannacone?'

'Wojiewicz, actually. Nada Wojiewicz. Iannacone was her sainted husband. She calls him that, only like it was a bad joke.'

'The two of you talk about the old country?'

'We both got relatives from near Krakow. Small world.'

'What about Censabella?'

'They been an item maybe three, four years.'

'She knew him on the day in question?'

'Most likely. I'm not pushing too hard on that. Don't want to scare her off or anything.'

'Good.' Maybe he had been underestimating McMorris. 'What else? Anything about his habits – drinking, falling asleep by the window?' Maybe he was an habitual liar.

'From the bottles, looks like he drinks el cheapo Italian wine. Enough of it for a good buzz, but not enough to stay pickled.'

'Depending on his capacity. What does Mrs Iannacone say?'

'About his drinking? Nothing, so far.'

'See if you can move the conversation in that direction. We need any kind of unreliability we can get.'

'What do you think I'm doing there?'

'Right.'

The press was lying in wait for him again, brought out by Bishop's statement. There was more of them this time, and they were more insistent. Estrada tucked his head behind his shoulder like a prizefighter and bulled through the crowd. As he had the night before, he headed for Canal Street and dove into the first subway station stairway he came to. He changed trains unnecessarily, enjoying the idea of throwing off pursuit. Above ground, he took two cabs and had the second one let him off blocks from his destination.

Tess Dodge had left an envelope for him with her doorman: keys, and a note that said she would be back soon and he should go upstairs and look through the pages.

The diary was on the coffee table. Instead of reading it he

sat back on the couch, feet up on the ottoman, to think about where he stood and what he was going to do next.

Tess Dodge woke him. He splashed some cold water on his face and joined her in the living room. She had the television on.

'I'm watching to see if you're on the news. You're a headline on the radio.'

He had to laugh when he saw himself push past the cameras. 'I look like a fugitive.'

'Very sinister,' Tess agreed. She turned the set off.

'Did you find anything new today?' he asked.

'Nothing as much fun as the Church of the Heavenly Blessing. I sure wish we had those other pages. I kept thinking I was following a story and then it would just stop and there'd be one of these big holes.'

'I wish we had them, too. I wish your mother would talk to me about what she read before the pages were destroyed.' He reached out and pulled the stack of diary pages closer.

They went through it all. He was left tantalized by the deal that had prompted the reference to the Church of the Heavenly Blessing, and by some of the references to CJ and R. The comment that it felt like Texas again with CJ. None of it concrete enough to be useful – to him, or to the defense. Not without more.

'There's one thing I'm curious about,' he said as he was leaving. 'How can you afford all this coming and going between here and Texas? Having an apartment here . . .'

'The apartment part was easy. There's some girls from home – they work for the airline and they're not around a lot. They had this place they'd been sharing for years and they had a bedroom that was empty because one of them just got married, so they rented it to me.'

'But you're not working. Not that I know about.'

'Well, it's like this – I saved up some money when I was working for those lawyers. Saved it up so I could come and go as I needed to when it was trial time again. And then . . . Mariah must have really forgiven me, because she left me with enough so I don't much need to worry about working right away. And I can't think of a single better way to spend money than helping to make sure the bastard who killed her gets what he deserves.'

Friday he was greeted with an avalanche of mail condemning him for pretending to be what he wasn't. Some of the letters, against all logic, wondered how he could be so disloyal.

While he was reading them, Collins came in. 'Fan mail?'

Estrada held one out to him.

'No thanks.' The bureau chief was grinning. 'Read them already.'

Estrada was not amused. 'You do that a lot? Read my mail?'

'Get used to it.' Collins was not to be deprived of his good mood. 'I figured you ought to enjoy the first day, but after this we'll have these read for you, just to be sure there's no real threat.'

'You going to watch for any that might help the case?'

'Why? You expecting some?'

'You never can tell.'

He had persuaded Lisa Stein to come in over the weekend by promising to work with her. They succeeded in separating out everything in the Phoenix Enterprises files that was related to tax filings, and separating that by jurisdiction: city, state and federal.

'They weren't exactly well organized,' Estrada said.

'Maybe they mixed it up just for us.'

'You're learning fast.'

Estrada knew from talking to Alexander Blair, Phoenix Enterprises' former finance director, that the company had taken in almost fifteen million dollars in initial capitalization, for paying the architects, making option payments on the tract of land they needed and other necessary start-up expenses.

The first million of it had come from Jadwin personally and from a consortium of Texas banks he had put together. Keeping track of the money at the level of the largest transactions interested Estrada the most. Fifteen million dollars was more than enough money for a host of murder motives. Estrada wanted to know where it had gone, and if any of it had shaken loose along the way.

The paralegal put her head on her arms atop a stack of mortgage documents.

'Stein? You okay?'

She did not lift her head. 'I keep thinking – this could all be a wild goose chase.'

Abruptly she sat up. 'What was that?'

'What was what?'

'Rustling. I heard rustling.' She was scanning the loose piles of papers on her desk apprehensively. 'There!' She pointed at the back corner of her desk. A page moved.

'Oh no.' She rolled her chair back from the desk, grabbed a stapler and lobbed it toward the offending corner. It hit and bounced, producing an immediate shifting in the nearby papers. Something small and gray scooted across the top of the desk and vanished behind one of the Phoenix Enterprises file boxes. She jumped up.

'Damn!' Her face was red under her blonde hair. 'I mean, bad enough finding mouse turds in the file boxes, but now they're walking across the desk in broad daylight. I've had it, I really have.'

'Come on,' Estrada said. 'You've done enough for one day. Let's quit and I'll buy you a beer.'

Tess Dodge called on Monday morning. 'I'm trying to find out more about those Heavenly Blessing people. It's hard with just initials, so I was going to get Cuyler Jadwin on the phone about it and see what he knows. Seems to me there was something about him there, too.'

'I don't know,' Estrada cautioned. 'We don't know what

role he played in it, and I don't think it's a help to us if people start asking him about it. There must be some other way to find out who those men are.'

'This was eight or nine years ago.'

'Mariah had a friend back home called Carlyn Sims. You know her?'

'The one Mariah used to hang out with? She only started to come around after my great betrayal, so I didn't get to know her all that well.'

'Even so, it might be worth trying her.'

There was a going-away party for an A.D.A. from Narcotics whom Estrada and Mahoney had both known when they'd all been starting out. A long table occupied most of the floor space in the party room of the dim, old-style Little Italy restaurant. Standing A.D.A.'s with bent elbows used up what little was left.

Over huge platters of generic Italian food, Mahoney regaled the nearby Narcotics A.D.A.'s with the details of his latest case, a new appeal by an ex-cop named Williams who had been convicted of murder more than a decade before, after appearing as a prime witness for an earlier version of the Kahn Commission.

'There were cops lining up around the block to testify against him,' Mahoney said. 'He was not a popular guy.'

'It's funny that Larry Kahn isn't having that hard a time of it so far,' one of their tablemates remarked.

'Give it time,' another Narcotics A.D.A. offered. 'Have you talked to any cops lately? They're not exactly pleased.'

Estrada pushed himself back from the table. 'I'm going to get some air.' The atmosphere was dense enough with blue cigar smoke to cut into chunks and serve for dessert.

'Me, too.' Mahoney followed him into the cool air of evening. 'Speaking of Larry Kahn, I did some research on your problem.'

Estrada looked around quickly.

'It's all right,' Mahoney said. 'No need to panic.' He made a mock production of patting himself down for a wire. 'We're clean.'

'Learn anything interesting?'

'That the law on the subject is a mess. The good news is that the Supreme Court, the federal one, is making life easier for us prosecutors on this, the way they are on everything else. They decided a case a few years ago making the destruction of potential defense evidence okay as long as the prosecution didn't act in bad faith, destroying it.'

'But before you get carried away with relief,' Mahoney warned, 'I have to tell you that our own wonderful Court of Appeals in Albany has not been following the Supremes in this area. There's a more recent case here that specifically carves out a standard that's a lot harder on prosecutors. There's a ton of language that says if there's *any question* whether the evidence will help the defense, the prosecutor should turn it over. *Err on the side of disclosure*, they said, plus a lot about the need for heightened prosecutorial care protecting any evidence that might help the defense.'

'Just what I wanted to hear.'

'It still comes down to what was in the diary.'

'Which is what I was saying last time. Once the defense hears there's a diary with missing pages, they're going to do everything they can to make what's missing seem important.'

'You might be able to save yourself by saying your case is so strong and the value of the diary so speculative that it couldn't possibly raise a reasonable doubt about Morales's guilt.'

'Right. Only, the best case I can manage right now is a house of cards on a foundation of sand.'

'Good and solid.'

'Same as before. A DNA match on the semen found on her body, which the defense will claim got there earlier, the hearsay motive evidence from the first trial, and a couple of I.D. witnesses who are getting amnesia or otherwise backing out.

At this point just enough to make out a legally sufficient case. Maybe.'

'What makes you think the guy is even guilty?'

It was exactly the question Estrada had been trying not to ask himself. It had been there, just beneath the level of awareness, at least since his first meeting with Lynne Schelling. The unthinkable – maybe Morales didn't do it after all. Estrada hadn't wanted to face it then, and he didn't want to face it now. It was the kind of negative thinking his football coaches had always warned against. 'Loser thinking,' his high school coach had called it, the sure way to defeat.

In the morning he dropped in on Lisa Stein with a long, skinny package. 'A present.'

She tore away the blue-and-gold paper, uncovering a plastic flyswatter to whose business end he had glued a badly drawn caricature of a horrified mouse with the block-letter legend MASTER MOUSE MASHER. It made her laugh.

'The perfect present,' she said, immediately flailing away at her desk with it.

He noticed the headline from *Noticias Diarias* still posted over her desk. 'About time to take that down.'

'I like it. It reminds me how important all this is.' Her mood was clearly improved.

'How's progress?'

'I'm learning a lot about land transfers and option contracts and title insurance. I'm concentrating on the big real-estate transactions, the ones about the land in Brooklyn, trying to pull the related papers together.'

'Does it have a shape?'

'Not yet. There seem to be a lot of contracts and notations about options and sales and prior mortgages. It looks interesting, but I don't have any idea how it all fits.'

'Keep after it,' he said. 'And keep your eyes open for the gray intruder.'

* * *

The phone was ringing when he got back to his office. 'Visitor,' Ginny said cheerily. 'And she seems agitated.'

'Ms Dodge?'

'The same.'

'I'll be right there.'

'Don't bother, she's on her way.'

Tess Dodge blazed into the room.

'Is it true that Morales's lawyers could use the missing diary pages as a way to get him off?'

'Whoa. Hang on. Where'd you get that?'

'My old boss.'

'Why don't you sit down and catch your breath?'

She glared at him, but she sat down.

'Now, your old boss. Who's that?'

'The lawyer I worked for the past couple of years. I thought he might be able to help me out with those Heavenly Blessing people. He knows about real estate and banks and all.'

'So you told him about the diary and the missing pages.'

'Well, yes.' She studied her lap guiltily, then abruptly looked up. 'What's wrong with that? I trust him. He's more on my side than you are. You didn't tell me about this.'

'And what did your old boss say?'

'He said it's some kind of misconduct for a prosecutor not to tell the defense about evidence they could use, and that if the evidence was destroyed because the prosecutor didn't protect it, knowing what it was, the case could be thrown out for denying the defendant due process of law. He said Morales would go free if the defense found out.'

If the defense found out was an interesting way to put it. Estrada did not point out that the current prosecutor was supposed to *tell* the defense about it, just as the first prosecutor had been.

'His going free isn't as automatic as all that, but basically that's true.'

'That's terrible. What are we going to do?'

'The first thing we're going to do is stop telling people about the diary. Unless you want the defense at our throats and Mariah's life on the cover of every sleazy tabloid in the supermarket.' He fired one of his magnetic darts at the portrait of Roberto Morales. It bounced off the wall.

'Great shot.'

'Not my sport.'

'I swear,' she said, 'if he goes free because of this, I'll get him myself.' She went to pick up the fallen dart, whirled and threw. The dart stuck to Morales's forehead. 'And I've got good aim.'

'It's not going to come to that.'

'Why not?'

'Because if we can come up with enough evidence to prove convincingly – really convincingly – that Morales is guilty, then the negative effects of missing evidence the defense can only guess about won't be that important.' He was winging it; after last night's conversation with Mahoney he was no longer sure what rules applied.

'Can you make your case that strong?'

He studied her, wondering whether he should tell her the truth, after all. He decided that he had no choice. If things didn't look up, she'd have to know anyway.

'So far the evidence looks much weaker than last time. Worse than usual for a second trial. The truth is that if this was a less visible case and all I had was the evidence I have now, I'd have to recommend that we drop the charges.'

'No! You can't!'

'I sure don't want to.'

'We can't let that happen,' she said firmly. Then she sat down and cried.

He stayed at his desk, unable to comfort her, staring at the picture of her dead sister.

McMorris called to say he was on his way with an update on Censabella and his girlfriend.

'I was over talking to my friend Nada before,' he said

when he arrived. 'She was bitching about how cheap old man Censabella was. Something about he wasn't paying her for the groceries she bought. She makes him dinner sometimes.'

'And?'

'She says he used to watch the apartment for Morales.'

'Isn't that what he said at the trial?' Corroboration for Censabella was not what Estrada was looking for. 'That he watched to see when Morales came and went?'

'No, I mean, yeah, that's what he said, but it's not what she means. It's like you know, water the plants, clean up now and then, let him know if a pipe broke, make sure nobody busted in. There was never anybody there at night, so Morales didn't want the place to look deserted.'

'Censabella didn't say a word about that at the trial.' It might help. Potentially it destroyed the illusion that Censabella was just a neighbor who happened to see things. If he had done one kind of favor for Morales, he might have done another, like telling white lies in court.

'If I got it right, Morales gave him a couple of hundred a month for his trouble,' McMorris added.

'Say that again.' Censabella on Morales's payroll! Finally, a real break.

'We were talking about it and she said Morales paid him a couple hundred bucks a month for the service.'

'Did she say how long it lasted?'

'He kept on paying for a while after the murder.'

'Until the trial, do you think?'

'She didn't say.'

'Do you think she'd testify to any of this?'

'Who knows? She's a gossipy old lady, but court, that's something else.'

'If we subpoenaed her, would she lie?'

McMorris shrugged.

'Let's just sit on it for now. Keep in touch with her, okay? Not too often, and no really big favors. We want her to trust you, but we don't want the defense to call it undue influence.

And while you're at it, see if you can pin down how long Morales kept on paying him.'

McMorris looked at him as if he had just offered a lesson on how to open a beer can.

Estrada went down the corridor to tell Collins. 'With luck I'll be able to neutralize Censabella with it.'

'I'm glad somebody is making progress on this,' the bureau chief said. Somebody, not Joe Estrada.

In the afternoon the whole *Morales* prosecution team got together. Rosen, distant as usual, did not say hello. We have to work together, Estrada wanted to say to her, why make it harder than it has to be? But part of him was glad to be spared having to deal more directly with her resentment.

She led off with the DNA evidence. She seemed to have it all under control. After McMorris told the others about Mrs Iannacone, Estrada asked for suggestions about how to deal with her.

'You need her to testify, you got to tell her straight out,' Clemente said.

'You have to be careful though,' Lisa Stein advised with her usual bright certainty. 'You don't want her to worry that her boyfriend is going to think she betrayed him. If he finds out she's been spying on him, he might walk out on her.'

'Nobody wants her to *spy* on him,' McMorris protested. 'This is stuff from years ago.'

'She'd be betraying a confidence.'

'For all we know he brags about it all over town.' McMorris did not have a lot of patience with paralegals.

'The first thing we need,' Estrada said, 'is to find out how she knows about this money Morales was paying him. If she's going to testify she's got to have seen it happen with her own eyes. She can't get up there and say he told her about it, or she heard him tell somebody else.'

'You can do it without calling her,' Rosen said, breaking her silence. 'If you blindside Censabella with it on cross, he ought to admit it. And if he denies it, you ask him if he ever told people that he got money from Morales. Even that much should make the jury wonder how believable he is. If he denies *that* you can call the woman on rebuttal and worry then about what she'll say. Right now she doesn't seem to think talking about it amounts to spying on her boyfriend or betraying a confidence.'

'Maybe,' Estrada conceded, 'but I think Stein's got a point. Serving your lover up for a perjury charge isn't the same as gossiping over the backyard fence.'

Stein's remark about Mrs Iannacone spying on Censabella stuck with him. He was ambling past the Foley Square courthouses after work, enjoying a warm spring breeze and the bright new leaves on the trees, when some of the pieces he had been turning over earlier fitted together.

Mariah Dodge had been Cuyler Jadwin's eyes and ears in the meetings she had attended with him over the years, and she had done other things he had not trusted anyone else to do, things so far unspecified by Jadwin. Suppose that being Jadwin's eyes and ears had been Mariah's assignment all the time, not only when they were in meetings together. Suppose she had been observing Phoenix Enterprises in general and Roberto Morales in particular when Jadwin was in Texas. Suppose she had gone to the office on Sunday night – presumably to help Morales plan his opposition to Jadwin for the Monday meeting – and Morales had found out she was there not to help but to betray him to Jadwin.

Now *there* was a motive for the kind of explosive anger that might end in murder.

Estrada went back to the office to call Jadwin. His secretary took Estrada's name and put him on hold, quickly came back on the line to say Mr Jadwin was in a meeting. Estrada told her he would call back.

At home he took out his bicycle and pedaled over to Central

Park. The more he thought about his new theory of Morales's motive, the more he liked it. It felt right. As he made circuits of the park in the deepening glow of sunset he wondered how difficult it would be to get Jadwin to say what Mariah Dodge had been doing for him.

He tried Jadwin again as soon as he got home, not taking time to put the bike in the back bedroom: it was past quitting time in Texas.

Jadwin was still there, and he took the call. 'What can I do for you today?'

'Did Morales know that Mariah Dodge was reporting to you about what went on at Phoenix Enterprises when you weren't there?'

Jadwin laughed, loud and hearty. 'Well, now, that's some kind of question. Don't you want to know when I stopped beatin' my wife?' He laughed some more. 'Nice try, I'll give you that. Who says poor Mariah was doing any such thing? You must be listening to people run their mouths on matters they don't know the first thing about.'

'That was what she did for you when you took her to meetings, tell you her version of everything she saw. She'd have been a whole lot more valuable to you doing that when you were fifteen hundred miles away.'

'Don't you figure the people at the office'd work that out, too? That'd make her about as useful as a hip pocket on a hog.'

'Only if they already knew you relied on her for that kind of thing, and that's one assignment I don't guess either of you talked about much. It's true some of the people at Phoenix thought you and Mariah were lovers, and that might have made them careful around her, but I'll bet she had a story all worked out.'

'Well . . . it'd hardly be gentlemanly of me to say you were right about any of that, now would it?'

Estrada took it as a concession. 'I'm going to ask you to think about something. When we talked in New York you said you were skeptical about Morales as Mariah's killer. Suppose it was more than a reaction to being rejected as her lover. Suppose on the eve of this important meeting with you he found out that Mariah was betraying him to you not romantically but strategically.'

He gave that a moment to sink in. 'I have the feeling that's exactly what happened. I can probably get it in front of the jury without direct evidence that she was reporting to you, but it won't be nearly as strong that way. You're the one who knows what Mariah was really doing for you. Think about it, and about how Morales might have reacted if he knew.'

There was a long silence. Estrada wondered if he had pushed too hard and lost Jadwin instead of persuading him.

The Texan chuckled. 'Okay, José. Like you said, I'll think on it and then we can talk some more.'

All right!

He called Michelle in California, got her answering machine. 'Hey beautiful, it's Joey. Want to go out and party?' he asked the tape.

By the time he was out of the shower he had calmed down. This would not solve all his problems. Still, he was moving in the right direction.

There were two messages on his machine. Michelle: 'My place or yours?' And then, 'Call me after nine. My time.'

'I remember this Joe Estrada,' she said when they were on the phone. 'What brought him back?'

'I finally got a break in this damn case.'

He started to tell her about Jadwin and Mariah Dodge, realized how long it had been since he had told her anything about the case, or she had seemed interested.

'There's a lot. You want to hear it all?'

'If it's your life I want to know about it. Up to and including the beautiful Ms Dodge.'

'Is that what this sudden interest is about?'

'Just teasing.'

'Okay,' he said, unsettled. He told her about his witnesses – the good, the bad and the unreliable – about Alexander Blair and the avalanche of paper from Phoenix Enterprises' accountants. About Cuyler Jadwin and the role Mariah Dodge had apparently played in his Texas business life. He told her about octogenarian Mr Censabella and Mrs Nada Wojiewicz Iannacone, his Social Security sweetheart. And he told her about his deduction, spurred by the idea of nice Mrs Iannacone telling tales about nice Mr Censabella, that Mariah Dodge had been betraying the confidences of Roberto Morales, her current lover, to Cuyler Jadwin, her former lover.

It feels like Texas again, Mariah had written in her diary. He had forgotten that part. It had to be about reporting to Jadwin.

'Maybe she meant both,' Michelle said. 'Being Jadwin's lover again *and* spying for him.'

'All the more motive for Morales.'

'Is that what spending the night with the sister was about? The diary? The one you wouldn't tell me about?'

He had mentioned the diary in his excitement. Now he was stuck with telling her about it. And why not? If he couldn't trust her . . .

Talking about the diary made the world look considerably less rosy. 'The real problem is, I'm probably supposed to tell the defense about it, missing pages and all.'

'Why?'

'For the same reason they'll say Larry Kahn should have let them know it existed in the first place. If the prosecution has information that might help the defense, we're supposed to say so.'

'You're supposed to help them beat you?'

'The theory is, we're supposed to be on the side of right and justice, and hiding evidence is neither right nor just.'

'This must be awful for you. Why didn't you tell me sooner?'

'You have other things on your mind.'

'That doesn't mean I stop caring about you.'

He could feel the relief. He had not realized how much strain he had been under, thinking she didn't care about the case or about his problems with it.

'What are you going to do?'

'The best I've come up with is to make my case as strong as I can and tell the defense as little and as late as I can. Hope we can convince the judge that no matter what was in the diary it couldn't have gotten Morales off.'

'I don't see why you can't just forget it exists.'

'That's as bad as what Kahn did.'

'And no one ever found out about it until now.'

'Except now someone has. Me.'

'Kahn must have had a reason.'

'He says he thought the diary wasn't important.'

'You talked to him about it?'

'I needed to hear his opinion. *Why* he thought it wasn't important.'

'Maybe it just *wasn't*.'

'I've found things in the pages I have. About Morales trying to outsmart Jadwin. And maybe about what we were just talking about, Mariah spying on Morales. Indirect, but valuable, anyway.'

'Valuable to the defense, or to you?'

'To me.' But Miller might find a way to twist it around.

'Joey, listen, it doesn't make sense to ruin your life over some abstract rule. Not just your life. *Our* lives. This man Morales is an animal, no matter how many charities he's helping. And Larry Kahn is someone who could be important to you. The only thing that makes sense is to put Morales in jail and take the credit you're entitled to. Let Larry Kahn go on being the big public crusader, and when you're ready let him give you a terrific letter of recommendation. Then you can get out of that awful place and we can live a decent life.'

What she was saying made sense. It was time, and more than time. But even if he was finally ready to pack up and move on, the first order of business was still putting Roberto Morales away. For life.

16

He slept badly and got to work late, groggy and full of unease. Tess Dodge was waiting opposite Ginny's reception desk, sitting hands folded and eyes down, visibly avoiding the two detectives just as visibly looking her over. When he said her name she stalked ahead of him down the corridor.

'Those jerks are enough to ruin a person's good, happy day,' she said when they arrived at his office.

'I hope you're here about the good part. And I hope it can wait until I get some coffee.'

'I talked to my mother. She didn't destroy them.'

'What? What do you mean?'

'The missing pages from Mariah's diary. She still has them.'

That woke him up, better than coffee.

'Hallelujah!' He grabbed her in a bear hug, lifting her off her feet.

'Hey! Hey!'

He put her down.

She made a face at him. 'Is that my reward? I bring you great news and you maul me.'

'It's wonderful news. I didn't mean to maul you. I'm just happy, myself.'

'I guess now I don't have to go out and shoot the man.'

'I wish you'd stop saying that. I don't want to be worrying you mean it.'

'Oh, I mean it all right.'

'You can throw darts at him any time you want, right here in the comfort of my office.'

'Weren't you going to get coffee? I could use a cup myself.'

'Not the coffee you can get here.'

They went to a pastry shop in Little Italy, not far from where Mr Censabella was courting Mrs Iannacone. They had cappuccino and biscotti at a marble-topped table against the wall, as isolated as they could be in the bustling shop.

'How did you get her to admit it?' he wanted to know.

'It scared me half out of my growth hearing that Morales might go free because those pages were gone.'

She dipped a biscuit into her cup. 'I thought about it a lot and I thought, if I was right about my mother, she might have kept the pages. I didn't think she had it in her to destroy something that was a part of Mariah, no matter what it said.'

She held up the eroded stump of her coffee-soaked biscuit. 'There must be a better way to do this.'

'Try a spoon.'

She did. 'Not bad . . . So – I called Mom and told her about how Morales could go free. I kind of pushed it, made it sound even worse. She started to cry and I was afraid I pushed too hard. Then she calmed down some and she said, well, was it too late? And I said, I think it's only too late if you burned it all. Only, if you've got it somewhere, you've got to let me know right away. So she cried some more and said she was sorry to cause trouble but it was all to spare my father. And then she said yes, she still had it all, locked away where nobody could get it.'

'I'm sorry you had to go through all that.'

'I'm sorry we had to go through any of this. I'm sorry Roberto Morales ever drew breath.'

After a moment she smiled faintly and took a sip of her cappuccino, licked off the white moustache of milk foam.

'When can I get a look at these missing pages?' he asked her.

'Oh. I don't know.'

'You don't know?' He put his cup carefully in the saucer.

'She said she had it, she didn't say she'd let anybody look at it.'

'What are you talking about? It's not enough to tell people the pages are in a shoebox in somebody's closet in Texas.' His voice was getting louder. 'The whole point is what they *say*.'

'Don't you dare yell at me.'

'I'm not yelling at you. I'm yelling at . . . I don't know . . . life.'

She put a hand on his arm. 'It's okay. I'm kind of feeling that way myself.'

They left and walked over to Canal Street. 'I have to see those pages,' he said as they waited for a gap in the stream of shoppers. Across Canal Street they walked slowly back toward the courthouse. 'Jealous ex-boyfriends make great red herrings for a defense lawyer in a case like this,' he explained, 'especially if there's any sign they're inclined to violence. I have to be able to rule out anything like that.' And any hint that the intrigues at Phoenix Enterprises might have given someone else a motive. 'And if worse comes to worst, if there's anything like that I have to let the defense know about it.'

She stopped. 'You can't do that. I didn't put my mother through all this so you could use it to help the defense.'

'If you're willing to risk having the man go free . . .'

'Right. I keep forgetting.'

He started walking again. 'I need you to call your mother and make it clear to her that I *have* to see those pages. It's not that I want to snoop around in Mariah's sex life. It's everything else.' They were at the courthouse. 'You coming up?'

'No, thanks. I've had enough for one day.' She reached up to give him a peck on the cheek and strode off.

There was a message slip waiting for him from a Nathan Masouros. Nobody he knew, but it was a number in the office. Masouros was out when Estrada called. He called Lisa Stein.

'Thanks for getting the accountant,' she said.

'We got an accountant?'

'He's right here. I'm showing him what I've been doing. He wants to see you.'

Nathan Masouros was at least four inches shorter than Estrada's five eleven. He had curly black hair and a belly that challenged his belt, and he smelled like a half-smoked cigar.

He shook hands perfunctorily. 'I'm on loan. You can have me for a week, the most, unless we find out this guy was robbing from the mayor and the pope, both.'

'Probably just his investors.'

'I see what this pretty young lady has been doing. Good work, it'll make my job quicker. I'm going to need her to work with me overtime. No time out for errands for the boss.' Masouros turned to her. 'You hear that, little lady?'

'Yes.' Her voice did not have its usual happy confidence.

Estrada smiled at her. 'I'm sure you'll work very well together. And the sooner you two find us a smoking gun, the happier we'll all be.'

He went back to his office and made a list of things he needed to follow up. He got as far as DIARY, wrote it over and over, block letters and script, drew boxes around the word, drew it trailing behind a little airplane, the kind he used to draw in junior high.

He tore the page off the pad, balled it up and threw it into the wastebasket. On the new page he wrote LOS ANGELES. He thought about his phone conversation with Michelle, heard himself agreeing with her that he should conceal the diary. For now, he did not have to wonder if he would have followed through. No potential evidence had been destroyed. The problem now was to secure the missing pages – through Tess Dodge, if possible, or with a Texas search warrant, a risky alternative he hoped to avoid. Once he had the pages he could make an informed judgment about whether the diary should go to the defense or not.

* * *

Luz Martinez's regular courtroom was closed down for repairs. The temporary courtroom she had been assigned was across the street in a newer building. Estrada flashed his I.D. on the way in past long lines of people impatiently awaiting their turn to pass through the metal detectors. The lobby space between the elevator banks was as crowded as the elevator cars themselves would be, if one ever arrived.

'Good morning, Mr Estrada,' said a familiar female voice. He turned to see Kassia Miller smiling up at him.

'Quite a crowd,' she commented. 'Want to walk?'

He checked the elevators: all still going up. 'Let's do it.' He pushed his way through, glancing back over his shoulder to make sure she was taking advantage of the momentary space he opened up for them.

'That's better,' she said when they had broken through to the stairway.

'Where's your client?'

'Upstairs, with an army of supporters. I made the mistake of ducking out for a minute. It's too easy to get stuck in that lobby.'

The smallish courtroom, wider than it was deep, was packed to capacity. In the well of the court two lawyers were packing up their papers while a court officer led out a handcuffed defendant. Luz Martinez was on the bench, looking displeased. She consulted a list. '*People versus Morales*? Anybody here?'

'Yes, your honor.' Estrada let the departing lawyers pass and waited for Miller and her client to precede him through the gate. Morales looked calm and confident in a gray business suit. Standing with his lawyer, he seemed taller than Estrada remembered him from the walk in the park.

'I want to warn you,' the judge said. 'I'm not in a flexible mood this morning. I expected to give that case to the jury today, and we haven't so much as finished hearing testimony. I don't need any new annoyances. Am I clear?'

Estrada nodded.

'Yes, judge,' said Kassia Miller. Estrada was aware of Morales standing next to her, but he did not turn to look.

'Good,' the judge said. 'Now, we need a trial date.'

Whatever she was starting to say next was obscured by a sudden chant of '¡Libertad! ¡Justicia! ¡Libertad!' A group of men and women, all now wearing black-and-red armbands, were standing up in the midst of the seated spectators. They held aloft banners hastily unfurled: FREEDOM FOR ROBERTO MORALES, PATRIA Ó MUERTE, JUSTICIA, FREE PUERTO RICO, JÍBARO SÍ YANQUI NO.

One man – nut brown, squat and solid, with blunt features that Estrada found somehow familiar – began declaiming in a surprisingly loud voice.

'This trial is a trick of the Anglo establishment to bring confusion to the Latino community. We demand that the District Attorney drop all charges . . .'

Martinez banged her gavel and shouted for order. The court officers came to life and sprang toward the demonstrators, who were protected by a phalanx of women, arms linked, between the banner-bearers and the aisles. Burly men with black-and-red armbands held the big double doors closed against the pounding of court officers on the other side. The officers in the room shoved to get past the defensive screen of women.

'. . . against Roberto Morales and disband the WASP-Jewish leadership of the fraudulent Kahn Commission. We demand a special prosecutor . . .'

Estrada knew who the man was now. It was Señor Condado, the man who had accosted him in the street a month before. The man who had warned he'd come back and bring his friends.

As the tumult continued, Estrada realized he was not hearing anything from the front of the room. Judge Martinez had left. Moments later, court officers streamed into the room through the back door she had used to make her retreat.

Estrada turned to look at Morales, to gauge his reaction to

the melee, but he and Miller were already gone. A court officer approached Estrada. 'This isn't a good place to stay. I think they want you in chambers.'

As Estrada came into the judge's chambers she was in the middle of a stern lecture to Morales and Miller. '. . . I'll hold you both responsible. I don't care if you've never seen those people before. Spread the word. That doesn't happen in my courtroom.' She noticed Estrada. 'Ah, mister prosecutor. Thank you for joining us. Let's get back to business. I'm putting you on the calendar for September twenty-first. Ms Miller, since you've already said you could be ready by now, September should be no trouble. Mr Estrada, I trust that you can give your witnesses ample notice between now and then, and I also trust that you can find all your evidence in that time, even in the hopeless chaos of the police evidence room. This should be plenty of time for both of you. If it's not, tell me now and give me a damn good reason.'

Miller glanced at her client. 'It's fine with us, your honor.'

'I'll do my best,' Estrada said.

'I'm not interested in your best, Mr Estrada. I'm interested in compliance. And let me make myself clear. September twenty-first. I don't want to hear different down the line. I'm going to put you down for three weeks, including jury selection.' She pushed her half-glasses up her nose and made a notation in her calendar book. 'I'm gone for August, so I want to see the papers for your *in limine* motions before I leave. We anticipating any other motions in the meantime?'

'I want to renew my discovery motion,' Miller said.

'Done. Anything else? Any reason to anticipate problems?'

'Nothing here, your honor,' Estrada said, crossing his fingers that he could resolve the question of the diary without the court having to hear about it.

'I'm fine,' Miller said. 'As long as Mr Estrada doesn't hold anything back.'

'He'd better not. Hear that, Mr Estrada?'

'Yes, judge.'

'Good. See you all in September.'

Tess Dodge called from Texas sooner than Estrada had been ready to hope.

'Victory. Mom said you can read it. But I had to promise her that you weren't interested in the sexy parts.'

'You're great. You've been a tremendous help. I don't say it often enough.'

'Often enough? Hell, mister, you don't say it at all.'

His doorman handed him an air freight package when he came home from work the next day. He started to unwrap it in the elevator. The thick envelope contained photocopies of Mariah's notebook pages, with large sections obscured by a wide black marking pen. He riffled through them, not believing what he was seeing.

He slammed into his apartment and dialed the Dodges, thankful for the time difference, hoping Dr Dodge was still at work. *If a man answers, hang up.*

Sylvia Dodge answered. Estrada forced himself not to snap at her. 'I got the pages you sent. Thank you very much.'

'Thank Tess,' she said stiffly. 'I still think some things ought to be sacred, never mind your rules about missing evidence.'

'Mrs Dodge, the last thing I want is to invade your privacy or Mariah's. My hope is that there's nothing of use to anyone and I can pretend the diary doesn't exist. But I really do have to make sure. About everything.'

'I understand.'

'There's only one thing, ma'am. I see that you've crossed out some of what you sent me.'

'I sent what you asked for. Tess told me you didn't need to read the parts about Mariah's private life.'

'I didn't say that.' The words came out too harsh. He hurried to soften them. 'When I said Mariah's personal life didn't interest me, I only meant I had a serious purpose for this. I didn't mean it was all right to cross things out. How can I know what was there?'

'Only the parts about sex.' Her tone brooked no argument. Sylvia Dodge might play the sweet little Southern lady, but she knew what she was doing, and why.

He would have to get the unexpurgated version from her before he was done. For now, he would read what she had given him. At least these copies were clean black letters on bright white paper.

He spent the night working on the diary. He put the new pages in with the old ones and tried to make sense of the stories that previously had been fragmentary. Now that he had both parts in front of him, one source of confusion became much clearer. There were some places where Jadwin seemed to have opposite opinions on the same subject, or to be in Texas and New York at almost the same time. And if Jadwin was her J, then – unless Estrada was reading something wrong – he seemed to have been in New York a lot just before Mariah's death.

Estrada went back to the earlier material, before Phoenix Enterprises, and verified that CJ and J both referred to Jadwin. Then he worked his way forward and found that in the most recent pages he could no longer be sure if that was true. Nor was there anything to make it clear that Jadwin referred to two different people, except for a passage that said either 'J wants to tell CJ now' or 'S wants to tell CJ now.' Whichever it was, Mariah had not thought the telling was a good idea.

Tess called him in the morning. 'I hear you're not happy.'

'Of course I'm not happy. I have to have it all.'

'She won't show you the rest.'

'Doesn't she understand how important it is?'

'She says she doesn't care.'

He wanted to yell at someone, or to break something. He

was not accustomed to feeling powerless like this. He was a district attorney – ordinary citizens did not defy him except at their peril. But his power was diluted outside New York, and he could not, for now, risk reaching out to an ally in Texas even if he'd had one.

'I don't think she believes Morales could really go free because of this,' Tess said.

'It's still a long shot but that doesn't mean it isn't real. It's crazy to take the chance.' He was beyond being tactful. 'Does she think I'm making it up?'

'I don't know what she thinks.' Tired.

'I have to know what's in those sections she crossed out. I've already come up with questions I can only answer if I can read the parts I'm missing.' He told her about the J's. 'It could make a major difference if it's two people.'

'Suppose I could read the pages and tell you about them,' Tess proposed tentatively.

'It's not enough.'

'It may be the best we can do.'

'Then you'll have to be very thorough. I have to know what's in those entries. *Have to*.'

The moment he was off the phone, Lisa Stein was in to see him.

'Nathan and I are dying to talk to you.'

'You have something?'

'Nathan thinks maybe we do.'

Masouros joined them looking disheveled and sweaty, reeking of cigar. He spread a file folder open on Estrada's desk. 'You want the blow-by-blow or just the bottom line?'

'Let's start with the essentials. I can get the details later.'

'Fine by me.' The accountant paged through the file. 'What you've got here is a title survey, an option to purchase and a series of assignments. What it comes down to is that somebody was passing this piece of land around, charging more money each time it changed hands. Building the price up that way.'

'By how much?'

'About twenty-five million dollars on the buyout and two-point-five on the option. They weren't actually selling the property itself each time. It's a series of options. In each one the deal is different: the length of time varies, some other terms change, so the cash option price is all over the lot, nothing you can point at from one deal to the next. But the final price goes up every time. It's very cleverly done.'

'And the bottom line is that they added twenty-five million dollars to the price.'

'Right. They would have gotten that when the land was actually sold to the company. The two and a half they added to the option they'd already taken out.'

'Who got the money?'

'That's hard to say. You've got the usual bunch of dummy companies and nominee officers. I didn't go too deep into it. What I checked, the companies are all out of business, have been for a couple, three years.'

'You have any guess who was behind it?'

'It had to be somebody right at the top. More than one person, not necessarily all from Phoenix Enterprises. I'd say your man Morales was the most likely suspect. You'd have to dig that out.'

'Will it take long?'

'The real question is, can you do it at all? You'll know that in a couple of weeks, maybe less. You make a list of the people who signed the papers, you follow it down until you hit somebody who knows what was happening. You've got a conspiracy charge to lubricate their tongues with. Of course, somebody has two and a half million reasons to keep it all quiet.'

'Thanks, Nathan,' Estrada shook Masouros's hand. 'It's a big help.'

'What they pay me for,' the accountant said gruffly. 'Happy to do it.'

Twenty-five million dollars, two and a half up front. That

was something for Morales to protect.

Estrada called Clemente. 'Tommy, what's up?'

'That was my question. My boss is on my tail, wants me back on the chart full time. I wanted to know if you still need me.'

'Yeah, I do. We've got something new. Stein is going to make up a list of people for you to hunt down and have a chat with.'

'About?'

'Tying Morales into a major swindle going on at Phoenix Enterprises.'

'No shit. You have something?'

'It looks that way.'

'And we missed it completely the first time?'

'Tommy, I keep telling you this isn't about somebody screwed up before.'

'Thing like this, it's always about that. Somebody's got to look like an asshole.'

'I'm not planning to play it that way, I can promise you that much.'

'Yeah, well . . . Good for our side, I guess.' He did not sound enthusiastic.

'I don't want any rumors running around about this case,' Collins said at the bureau's monthly homicide meeting. 'Anybody talks out of turn I'll personally hang them out to dry.'

It was the first time Estrada was presenting the case at a bureau meeting, and he was giving them only a limited look. He described the way the price of the Phoenix Project land had been inflated. His bureaumates pushed him hard about how far he was from tying this particular bell around Morales's neck. He detected a certain coolness in their reaction to his news, a failure to be impressed. They preferred to think of this as a crime of hot sexual passion and operatic anger. That was exciting and glamorous; killing to cover up a swindle was merely tawdry.

But exciting or tawdry wasn't what counted, Estrada

thought on the way back to his office. What counted was a theory you could sell to a jury.

17

In the morning a message from Tess Dodge was waiting for him at the office: 'On my way to Texas. Don't call me, I'll call you.'

When she had not called by the end of the day he stayed late, distracting himself with his overdue end-of-the-month paperwork for May. Finally, the phone rang.

'I did it! Mom finally gave in.'

'Terrific. Have you had a chance to read it?'

'I just started, but I think maybe I found your second J. Name of Johnny, came to work at Phoenix about a year before Mariah was killed, in the finance department. Seems like they were soulmates from the day he rode into town.'

'Lovers?' That would make Johnny an alternate suspect for the defense. A real problem.

'Oh no. Not a chance.'

'You said soulmates.'

'He wasn't interested in girls.'

'How did he get into the censored parts of the diary?'

'The Doctor thinks all that's against nature. So Mom says she cut out all the times Mariah mentioned Johnny where you could tell it was him. One notebook toward the end had so much about J in it she put the whole notebook aside.'

'You're saying your father wouldn't accept it that his daughter was *friends* with someone who's gay?'

'I know it sounds . . . extreme. I asked Mom about it and she said he'd be more upset about that than almost anything.

It was the part of the diary Mom came closest to burning. More than once, she said. She's still afraid of how he's going to react if this all comes out in public. You'd think a doctor would know better.'

'I need to know more about this Johnny,' Estrada said.

'Okay. Only one thing – it makes me crazy to have to leave messages at your office, having to watch every word I say so I don't give this away . . .'

He did not like it, but he had already bent the rule that said keep home and work separate by giving her his home address. And there was something to be said for not having extended conversations about the diary on the office phones, or having the messages pile up.

'Have a pencil?'

'Shoot.'

As soon as he got off the phone with her he pulled out Lisa Stein's index of the case materials. There were two people listed in the finance department of Phoenix Enterprises besides Mariah Dodge. Alexander Blair, the director of finance, and Juan Alvaro, associate director, the same title as Mariah Dodge's. Estrada paged through the police file and found his DD–5. Clemente had interviewed him.

He had worked moderately closely with Mariah Dodge, Alvaro had told Clemente, and they had become friendly outside the office, occasionally going to the theater or ballet together, having dinner together now and then. They were just friends, not lovers. He had been devastated by Mariah's death, but had no idea who could have killed her.

Clemente had included Alvaro's home address and phone number for follow-up, without recommending any further action. Estrada dialed the number. He did not expect to reach Alvaro at home in the middle of the work day, but he wanted to reassure himself that the man was where he could be reached.

The phone at the other end rang four times. A machine answered. Loud rock music. An androgenous voice, barely discernible under the music. 'You found me, sweetie. Don't waste the chance.' More music and then the usual signal tone. Estrada hung up. Juan Alvaro? He had no way of knowing.

He called information for a check of the residential and business listings. There were plenty of Alvaros, but no Juan or J, which proved nothing. He tried Brooklyn and Queens and came up similarly empty.

When he tried Alvaro's old number again, he got the machine. He did not leave a message.

Michelle was back in town, unexpectedly. Her best New York customer was in the midst of a crisis over a complicated promotional package, and she was the only one in her company the customer trusted to deal with the various suppliers and to get it done right and on time. She had left Los Angeles early so she could have dinner with Estrada before her first meeting with the panicky customer.

Estrada felt unaccountably awkward over dinner and sensed that she did, too. He attributed it to his preoccupation with the diary and hers with the pressure of her crisis at work, and to the effects of her having just stepped off an airplane.

The restaurant was in the West Village not far from Juan Alvaro's last known address. After dinner they walked to his block. The day's soaking rain had passed, and groups of young men clustered on the sidewalks outside overcrowded bars.

Alvaro's address was a townhouse on a narrow street around the corner from the bars. In the entrance hall there was an intercom with six buttons. Number four was Alvaro. Estrada pressed the button.

They waited. He pressed the button again. Waited. Pressed again, then turned to go.

'I heard you the first fucking time,' came a voice from the intercom. A harsh baritone, nothing like the voice on the phone message.

'Mr Alvaro?'

'Who?'

'Alvaro? Juan Alvaro?'
'Fuck, no. He's long gone.'
'You sure?'
'I *live* here, don't I?'
'Can I talk to you?'
'What are you doing now, asshole?'
'In person.'
'What for?' A challenge, not a question.
'To talk about Juan Alvaro.'
'Bye bye, asshole.' The intercom clicked off.
'Too bad,' Michelle said as they left.
'People move. We'll find him.'
They stopped on Sixth Avenue to hail separate cabs.
'Don't wait up,' she said. 'I have my key.'
He kissed her. 'You have permission to wake me.'
He kept himself up with the diary. When she came in they tumbled into bed, both exhausted, and fell asleep in each other's arms.

He woke up full of unfocused energy. Michelle was curled up in sleep, chestnut hair splashed over the pillow. He tried to move gently off the bed. Her eyes opened and she looked at him sleepily.
'Morning,' she murmured. She uncurled, stretching languorously. He reached for her, his energy finding a focus.
The phone rang. He heard it distantly. It kept ringing, more insistently each time.
'Let it ring,' Michelle said softly in his ear.
'Can't. Machine's not on.' He forced himself out of bed.
It was Tess Dodge.
'You're up early,' he said, willing his head to clear.
'You're not. I was about to give up.'
'I'm glad you didn't. What have you got for me?'
'More about Johnny and Mariah. And something else.'
'Can you give me a minute?'
'Oh, my,' she said. 'I didn't catch you in the middle of . . .'

'Don't worry about it.'

'I can call you back.'

'It's okay. Tell me what you've got.'

'Mariah and Johnny. I can't tell exactly what, it's just little hints here and there.'

'What kind of hints?'

'Something to do with Jadwin. They knew something that he needed to know, or that they wanted to keep from him for some reason. Or maybe they knew something about him that they didn't want him to know they knew. You'd probably understand it better.'

J wants to tell CJ. Not a good idea, Estrada remembered. He had been pondering that part of the diary the night before, wondering about it. It came after FEELS LIKE TEXAS AGAIN, so Mariah was presumably reporting to Jadwin. And keeping secrets from him too, it seemed.

'I have to see those pages.'

'I kind of thought you'd say that.'

'And?'

'I'd do better selling outdoor humidifiers in summer.'

'Now's not the time to give up.'

'I didn't say it was. Oh shit. I gotta get off. I'll call back.' She hung up before he could ask when.

Michelle was in the shower. He joined her. 'Am I too late?'

She caressed him with a soapy hand. 'Right on time.'

'My father almost caught me,' Tess said when she called back. 'I should have known better than to call before he left the house.'

'Won't he notice something on the phone bill?'

'I'm using my credit card. Now that I've ruined your sex life and upset you about my sister and her friend Johnny, how else can I help?'

'You said there was something else.'

'Right. It seems as if her friend Johnny got her interested in playing nursemaid to little kids with AIDS.'

'Really? Did you know anything about it?'

'I had no idea she had it in her.'

'Does the diary give any indication how long she was doing it?'

'I'd say less than a year when she got killed. She seems to have liked it. I can't believe the things she did. I mean, babies can be kind of gross even when they're healthy, leaking stuff top and bottom. And these kids had HIV germs. It takes your breath away. I mean, she talked about putting them right next to her skin, so they would be in contact with her body.'

'At least your father should be proud of that.'

'You mean because he's a doctor? I told you how he feels about gays. Drug addicts are even worse.'

'But little kids . . .' He stopped himself. 'Sorry.'

'It's okay. Dad's attitudes have that kind of effect on a lot of people. You still want to hear about dangerous boyfriends?'

'Need to, not want to. Did you find one?'

'This one shitkicker. I didn't think she ever went out except with, like you know, gennulmin in the awl bidnis, but here she is with this rodeo-star type. He hit her, couple of times. She was so surprised by it. That's what she wrote, how surprised she was. The second time she told him never to come near her again or she'd shoot him.'

'Ouch.'

'That's not good?'

'Let's say it's a higher level of verbal violence than I'd like to see. Anything else like that?'

'This one fella slapped her because he said she was teasin' him. She never saw him again. Men can really be creeps, you know?'

He was not going to get caught in that one. 'Did you read anything about her boyfriends being jealous? Maybe violently jealous?'

'She was a smart, beautiful woman who went after life with both hands. Plenty of men wanted to own her. A person could figure that much without any diaries to read.'

'I'm talking strictly from a lawyer's point of view now. Could some clever lawyer use what's in the diary to claim that one of those guys killed her in a jealous rage?'

'Not that I can see. Rich men out here don't get killing crazy over women. Except for that one cowboy, any man Mariah went out with could write a check for a bushel of pretty women. It's sad, but it's the truth.'

Estrada went to Mahoney's office when he got to work, to get a reaction to the latest news.

'You're still walking a tightrope,' Mahoney said. 'Or the edge of a knife, more like. If you slip you're likely to get cut in a very tender place. It's good you located the missing pages, but from what I'm hearing the defense still has reason to cry foul.'

'I was thinking,' Estrada said, 'it might help if there was a way to discover the diary now. At least then it would be brand-new information and it wouldn't reflect badly on what anybody did in the past.'

'It might make life simpler – if you could do it. Only, where would you say you found it? In the bottom of whose box of prom programs and yearbooks? And why wasn't it discovered sooner? And what if somebody talks to the folks in Texas about it?'

'Good questions.'

'Here's another one. Did Kahn ever talk to this guy Johnny?'

'Not that you'd know from the file.'

'And Johnny was conspiring with Mariah Dodge against the boss, what's his name?'

'Jadwin. That's what it looks like.'

'It might not lead anywhere, but I'm telling you, the longer you hide it the worse you look.'

Estrada went back to his office and thought about Mahoney's good questions. He did not come up with any good answers.

For the first time there was something in the diary that looked like it might be useful to the defense. But before he could risk letting the diary out he had to try harder to find out what the suspicious entries actually meant.

He called Clemente and left a message, called Kahn and got through.

'Do you remember anything about a man named Juan Alvaro, a good friend of Mariah Dodge's, also known as Johnny?'

'Is he in the file?'

'There's a DD–5, but that's all.'

'Nothing comes immediately to mind. Why?'

'He's in the diary. He and Mariah seem to have been conspiring at something. I hoped you might have talked to him.'

'If I did, I don't remember. And I have to say again, I think you're wasting your time with that diary.' Kahn sounded more weary than annoyed. 'It's completely irrelevant, and it's going to be nothing but trouble unless you drop it.'

Estrada said thank you and hung up.

He called Alexander Blair. 'Did you have anybody named Juan Alvaro working for you at Phoenix Enterprises?'

'If you know his name you know he worked for me.'

'For long?'

A sharp laugh. 'No one worked at Phoenix Enterprises for long, for me or for anyone else. We were only there three years. I'd say Juan was there half that time. He left before we started laying people off. He must have suspected it was going to happen. I don't know where he ended up. I had other things on my mind at the time.'

'That was after the murder, wasn't it?'

'About four months after, perhaps slightly less. Why do you ask? Is he involved?'

'I'm just tying up a few loose ends. Did anybody call him Johnny, that you know of?'

'I didn't. But Juan does mean John.'

'Do you know who his friends were?'

Blair hesitated. 'He may have been friendly with Mariah Dodge. I didn't keep track of how he spent his free time.'

Beyond that, all Estrada could get out of Blair was a bland endorsement of Alvaro's job performance.

'Do you have any idea where he might be now?'

'None at all. Sorry.'

Clemente came by in a pair of jeans and a T-shirt, a belt pack heavy around his waist, the first time Estrada had seen him in anything but a baggy suit.

'I have somebody for you to find,' Estrada told him. 'I think he can help us tie Morales into the land-price swindle. That makes him priority one. Find him, but don't talk to him. Let me know where he is and I'll decide then how we approach him.'

'Find him? That means somebody lost him.'

'Could be. He's not resident at the address of record as of the DD–5, and he's not listed in Manhattan, Brooklyn or Queens. I'm not a hundred percent sure about the old phone number, but I'm guessing it's not him any more.'

'People move all the time.'

'His name is Juan Alvaro. He's gay, if that's any help, and his nickname is Johnny.' Estrada gave him the old address and phone number.

Clemente was writing in his notebook. 'No problem.'

Estrada hoped he was right.

Toward the end of the afternoon he got a call from Mahoney.

'Kahn's finally coming out with a biggie. He's going to nail a whole squad.'

'A whole squad?' A dozen or more detectives. Hard to believe.

'Up in the South Bronx. Seems there's this lieu – guy name of Ellis – he made it S.O.P. for them to whale the tar out of suspects and potential informants. Not always for something specific. It's not like they're beating confessions out of them, more like to let them know how tough the cops are. Who they ought to be afraid of.'

'That's beyond the beyond. Did Ellis's bosses know he was doing it?'

'Somebody knew, 'cause somebody told Larry Kahn. Now everybody's going to know.'

'Where'd you get this?'

'I have my sources. It's still a big secret, but it's going to come out next week.'

'If you know and I know, how long till Ellis knows?'

'Too late for him. Maybe he can run, but he can't hide. Anyway, the smart thing for all of them is to stay put and tough it out.'

'Who were they beating up?'

'In the South Bronx? Rich Episcopalians, maybe? Try guys named José and Jesús.'

He called Michelle's answering machine.

'I've been hearing things all day that make me think how fragile life is and how hopelessly stupid we all are, hating each other for no reason.' He could not get it out of his mind that Dr Samuel Dodge would not have wanted to hear that his daughter was helping sick babies. Mahoney's news had only compounded it. 'I was feeling bummed and I just wanted to hear your voice.'

He brought home copies of the Phoenix Project land-option documents. After a while the real-estate boilerplate began to blur. He dozed off at his desk, was brought back by the telephone.

'Hi.' Expecting Michelle.

'Hi. You in bed again?' It was Tess Dodge.

'Napping at my desk. Working on the case.'

'I called to say I just got done learning some things. Save dinner for me tomorrow.'

'You're coming back here?'

'Lordy, you *are* asleep. How else are we going to have dinner together?'

Just before noon the next day a florist delivered a bouquet of spring flowers to Estrada's office. The card said, 'Don't feel bummed. Not everybody hates each other. Love, Me.'

Michelle called at five. 'I'm about to perform a miracle. I'm making myself disappear. I'm out of here in an hour, max. Home for a shower and then I'm all yours until these clowns absolutely need me again, which might not be until almost nine.'

'Oh,' he said. 'That's great.'

'You don't sound overwhelmed with joy.'

'It's just that Tess Dodge is flying in. She's got some new information and I promised to have dinner with her.'

'I see.' Michelle's voice was flat. 'Fine.'

'No, Mich, don't be mad.'

'No? I bent myself in half, called in a dozen favors because I was worried about you, I thought you were upset and I didn't want you to be alone, and what do I get? You tell me no thanks, you've got a date.'

'It's not a *date*, it's work . . . I can probably put it off until the morning.'

'No . . . If she's flying in to see you I'll just keep working. There's plenty I can do, and everybody will be overcome with gratitude that I'm not leaving.'

Tess Dodge called him from the airport.

'I'm assuming this is important,' he said, too sharply.

'I have something I kind of think you'll want to hear about.' Matching his impatience. 'Getting hold of it wasn't exactly a church social with hot supper on the lawn.'

He quickly suggested a meeting place. One woman angry with him for being unappreciative was enough for the day.

He had picked a notorious tourist trap, a place where no one would have a clue who they were or what they were talking about. 'Tell me your story,' he said when they were seated.

'After I have some wine in me.'

He waited, not eager for small talk.

'You truly are in one foul mood, aren't you, Mr Estrada?'

'I've been better.'

The waiter arrived with their wine, sparing him the need to elaborate.

'Okay, story time.' Estrada sat back to listen.

She took a moment, swirling the wine in her glass and sniffing it before she sipped it. 'You know, last time I had wine this raw I was maybe a sophomore in high school. And we're talking Southeast Texas, not Bordeaux or someplace.'

'Glad you like it.'

'The wine I got plied with while I was learning what you're about to hear was something else entirely. Vintage grade A–1 French champagne the whole way through from cocktails to dessert.'

'You deserve no less.'

'Yeah, well, what I deserve is not to have every peckerwood who buys me dinner try and crawl into my drawers before we get out of the parking lot. Out of the restaurant, even.' She noticed his bewilderment. 'Not you, Estrada. This Bubba asshole tryin' to pass as a cowboy entrepreneur.' She was stretching her Texas accent to its broadest. 'I'm talkin' about one of the boys from the Church of the Heavenly Blessing.'

'You found them?'

'Betcher buns, boddy. One of them, anyway.'

'Tell me about him.'

'Truth is, I found him half by accident, half because ol' Morty, this lawyer I worked for, the one you got so upset about, knows damn near everybody in Houston. I talked to Ms Carlyn Sims, like you said I should, only she wasn't a lot of help. Morty did better. It took him a while to figure out who maybe it might be, and then damn if the guy doesn't come right into the office and ask for some help on a new deal. Morty has a conflict on it, so he turns him away, only first he checks him out about this old real-estate deal. Sure enough, it's him.'

'Amazing.'

'Bidnis as usual in the li'l ol' awl patch. So Morty introduces us and next thing I know I'm invited to a quiet dinner for two in this godawful gold-plated eatin' place that hasn't noticed it ain't boom times any more. My big slick operator doesn't have a clue I'm there for anything but an overpriced meal, and it seems as if he likes curly hair enough not to care. When I asked him about that deal in Mariah's diary he just about fell all over himself impressing me with his high-ticket sneaky doin's. I didn't have to push, or anything. He just up and bragged at me.'

Estrada refilled both their wine glasses.

'Am I supposed to drink this stuff?'

'Wine of the country.'

She drank some more, made a face. 'So here's what he told me: It's kind of a game. Used to be, anyhow. You get four, maybe six guys in a room, all sitting at one side of a long table. Across from them you put two, three bankers. Then the first guy sitting there takes out the deed to a piece of land or some buildings. He says to the guy next to him, "Hey, cowboy, how 'bout I sell you this here valuable piece of property, for a whole lot more than it cost?" And the second guy says, "Sure thing," and he takes the deed and gives it to the guy next to *him*, and he says, "How about I sell you this here real valuable piece of property for even more money than I just got done payin'?" And the third guy goes, "Sure thing." And they go on like that till they come to the end of the table.'

'What are the bankers there for?'

'Oh. That's for, every time the property gets sold, the guy buying it looks across the table and says, "Banker, good buddy, how about you give me a big mortgage on this here piece of property?" And the banker says, "Sure thing." No problem for him, 'cause the next guy who buys it's gonna get himself a mortgage, too, and he's gonna use that to pay off the mortgage from before. So every time a guy passes the deed to the guy next to him the price goes up. The way I get it, sometimes they go around the table two, three times, raising the price half a dozen times each round.'

Estrada followed it through. 'Then, at the end, everybody's got a big pocketful of money and one bank is holding a huge mortgage on a piece of land that's not worth a fraction of what the bank loaned on it.'

'Hey, you're not so dumb, after all. And you know what happens next? The last guy doesn't bother payin' back the mortgage. And the papers are in the name of some corporation, so when the bank puts the screws on, tryin' to collect, the corporation goes bankrupt. So sorry, no money, and the bank forecloses on this land that isn't worth hardly a penny. And the beauty part, according to my host, whose hand kept crawling up my thigh like some albino spider, is that all the bank's depositors are insured, so even if little games like that make the bank go belly up, nobody's actually out any cash money.'

'And this guy told you all that, about this specific deal?'

'He must've thought I'd be so dazzled by his brilliance and daring that I'd hop right into bed with him. This particular buying and selling and defaulting was over and done with almost ten years ago, he said, so nobody could touch him any more. He could talk about it all he wanted and get away with it. He got off on it, and he didn't even pretend not to.'

'Are you sure this is the transaction Mariah was writing about, the one with Cuyler Jadwin?'

'Well, Jadwin was for sure involved in it and it's at least the same kind of deal.'

And a variation on the fraud Nathan Masouros thought had been worked on the Phoenix Project land option: repeated sales of the same property to inflate the price. Had Morales picked up the trick from Jadwin?

He lifted his glass to her. 'Nice work.'

'Thank you, sir.'

'Now,' he said. 'Not to be greedy, but what about the diary?'

She contemplated her wine glass. 'You see me the way I am – pageless.'

'You brought your notes.'

'Not them either. Left them with Sylvia for now.' And before he could protest: 'Don't you get in my face about this, mister. I'm doing this the way I think'll do us the most good, get us the most of what we want. Did you stop to think it costs poor old Sylvia Dodge half the paint off the inside of her stomach to let you see this stuff? Not to say the risk she's taking that my father will find out. Maybe it's worth something to humor her a little bit now and then.'

Estrada's trial bureau experience ran to assault, robbery and murder – other people prosecuted fancy white-collar schemes. He called an acquaintance in the U.S. Attorney's office to talk about the Heavenly Blessing scam.

'It's a classic,' the federal prosecutor said. 'For a while there, it seemed as if every savings and loan in the Sunbelt had at least one of those going.'

'We're talking major fraud here, right?'

'We're talking the kind of fraud that happened often enough, with variations, that it helped bring the whole system down.'

'How are you doing, prosecuting them?'

'That's a joke, right? A few of the absolutely biggest thieves are making headlines. Past that, we don't have the manpower to make cases, and Washington keeps cutting our budgets. You probably know how it goes from your office.'

'Suppose somebody handed you one with all the players named and good leads on times and places and other details.'

'If it went down any time recently I'd jump right on it. It's always a hard case to make, but if somebody's going to hand it to us, that's different. Why? Do you have one?'

'I do, but it's not recent.'

'No surprise. Most of this happened in the early Eighties. The statute of limitations is five years on bank fraud, so if it was a one-shot and they defaulted fairly quickly, they're home free. Tell your informant he should speak up a little sooner next time.'

'Unfortunately, my informant's been dead almost four years.'

'Then I guess he doesn't care much about the statute of limitations.'

He packed up some papers for the weekend. Before he left he called Michelle at home, ready to leave a message. When the machine did not pick up, he let the phone ring, absently flipping magnetic darts at Roberto Morales.

Michelle answered the phone. 'We finished,' she told him. 'Just as well I stayed last night. It got really nuts and I didn't sleep a wink. I'm going to bed and sleeping till morning. We can talk tomorrow.'

His first round of darts had gone wide of the mark. He collected them and tried again. He scored an immediate bull's-eye, his first ever. An omen, he thought. We missed once. This time we're going to get the bastard.

18

On Saturday, a perfect June day, Estrada and Michelle went bicycling in the park. At the lake south of the outdoor theater, she turned off the road and stopped. They walked their bikes to a small wooden shelter at the edge of the lake where they sat on a slat bench, nothing but a low rail between them and the water.

'We've both been under a lot of strain,' she said, looking out at the lake. 'It's harder than I thought, pulling up stakes like this.' Her voice was controlled, purged of emotion. 'It doesn't help that I'm not getting anything from you about whether you're coming out, or when.'

'I've been distracted. This case is tougher than anything I've seen.'

'I feel bad about how hard it's turned out to be. I wish I could be here for you.' She touched his hand. 'But I can't. I'm going. I really am going. I gave my landlord notice, and I'm arranging for movers. They need me out there full time, right away. And it's where I want to be.'

'I can't say I'm surprised.' He felt blank. He looked at her – skin rosy, hazel eyes clear with purpose, her brow drawn together in appropriate concern, or was it sincerity? She was beautiful and he hurt with wanting her, and he was, he realized, furious with her.

Not for wanting a better job, he could understand that. Not for doing this to him now, the timing wasn't her choice. For the style of it, he thought, for the way she was doing it. He remembered the intro to an old rock 'n roll song. *We can do this for you easy, or we can do it for you hard*. She was not doing it easy.

They sat in silence, watching rowers go by on the lake, then she reached over to kiss him lightly and stood up. 'I understand you've got things on your mind. Just please don't take too long. I have the feeling that my life is racing along, and I don't want to get too far ahead of you.'

Estrada began his week in the office with Clemente. The detective took out his notebook, flipped the pages.

'Checking up on those names I got from Miss Lisa on the land deal. I pulled a bunch of blanks – people gone, people didn't know what I was talking about. I reminded them they put their names on these contracts, responsible officer for some company, and they still didn't remember. People sign anything you put in front of them.'

He settled into the visitor's chair, lit up and puffed the smoke out in a series of perfect rings, watching them drift toward the ceiling. 'I found you one live one, though. Nice lady lives over in Park Slope, remembers every bit of what happened. She said she only had to sign for one deal, something to do with a big piece of land in Brooklyn. Right on the river, she said. She was working for a stockbroker at the time, guy who put his clients into high-interest CDs at banks in the South and Southwest.'

He paused to consult his notes. 'The stockbroker takes her to lunch with this banker from Texas, on the board of directors of these banks where they put their deposits. He invites her to be secretary-treasurer of his corporation. No risk, and a nice designer handbag and a silk scarf to start with as a token of gratitude, promise of more to come. She wants to be sure there's nothing illegal, so the banker explains to her about nominees and like that. She thinks it's a kick, signs all the papers.'

'A Texas banker? Nothing about an Hispanic developer from Brooklyn?'

'Nope. Tall guy, good looking, smooth, rich, gray hair. From Houston or someplace near there.' He put away his notebook. 'We know anybody like that?'

Next on Estrada's agenda was a meeting with Roberto Morales's former publicity agent. She had already canceled three appointments; if this one had not held up she would have gotten a subpoena.

Margo Banner was as understated as her surroundings, a graying medium-height brunette in a purplish pastel suit. The only vivid notes in her office were her long, fire-engine-red fingernails and a huge vase on her desk overflowing with bright yellow lilies.

Before Estrada could begin asking her questions she launched into a long preamble about how gratifying it had been to work with Roberto Morales on behalf of the Phoenix Project. Estrada let her talk.

'Am I getting through to you?' she said finally. 'Does this mean something?'

'I'm waiting to see what you're really selling me.'

She glared at him and then burst out laughing. 'All right, I'll try to come to the point. It goes against all my professional instincts, but maybe it's best.' She lit a cigarette, held it poised, then gave it a sharp look of annoyance and stubbed it out.

'Frankly, I think Roberto was in over his head. He was being used, and I'm not sure he knew it.'

'What makes you say that?'

'I couldn't begin to tell you specific things. I've thought about it a lot, but all I have are my personal instincts.'

Opinion like this was inadmissable as evidence. She probably knew that, had probably been counseled about how to present this to keep herself out of court. That did not mean he would not find a way to use her. 'Please, go ahead.'

She reached for her silver cigarette box again, stopped herself. 'His partners were manipulating something, I don't even know what. Roberto was there to legitimize it for them, but he seemed to think it was all above board and that they were as eager to make the Phoenix Project work as he was. I was on the point of saying something to him about it, but then there was the murder and Roberto was accused and all of a sudden we were representing him and his defense lawyer, Walter Kubelik.'

'How did that happen?'

'It was Cuyler Jadwin who first suggested it, actually. Roberto was reluctant, didn't think it was appropriate. Kubelik's only problem with it was that he didn't have faith we could deliver. He was too used to making his own waves in the media.'

'Were they happy with your work?'

'Roberto never stopped feeling awkward about it, but he came to see it was doing good for him. He was worried about his kids, that all they would get was the negative stuff about him, and it made it easier for him to know that the public was seeing another side, especially after the conviction. After the first appeal exonerated him in a way, he fired us. He didn't want anyone to think his community service work was only a matter of image. And as far as I know he still believes he can make the Phoenix Project happen. It seems crazy, but I suppose that's how things get done in the world.'

'So what you're selling me is Roberto Morales.'

She furrowed her brow. 'No. It's not that simple. Yes, I believe in him, but what I want you to come away with is the sense of wheels within wheels. Roberto can have the kind of abrasiveness that goes with being driven to accomplish something important. He doesn't like things or people that get in his way. But that doesn't make him a murderer. The thing is, I'm convinced his cronies were playing some kind of high-stakes game that he had no connection with. I'd bet anything that's where the murder came in. Not Roberto, not some romantic disappointment. He had more important things on his mind.'

'Tell me about this high-stakes game.'

She shook her head. 'I don't have any specifics, except that from the bit of contact I had with the Texans I got the feeling that they were most interested in how Roberto's image, and the Phoenix Project's, played overseas, in Europe and England and Japan, where the big money was coming from.'

She stood up. 'I don't know if that's any help, but I feel a lot better getting it off my chest.'

The office was a-buzz with news that Kahn had announced major indictments, a whole detective squad in the Bronx, as Mahoney had predicted. The detectives Estrada saw in the elevator and the halls all wore dark looks.

He tried to get Clemente and McMorris on the phone; neither was available. He wondered if there were any cops in New York going about their normal duties.

By the time he got home in the evening and turned on the news, both the Patrolmen's Benevolent Association and the Detectives Endowment Association had issued statements condemning Kahn and his commission for exaggerating the situation out of all proportion and inflaming the city's already tense race relations.

Kahn, confronted with the police response, had defended his actions unflinchingly: This was not a kind of police activity that could be condoned. But he had added a clarification: The crimes he was exposing were individual and unconnected; there was no citywide pattern of police discrimination against African-Americans or Hispanic-Americans. That, in turn, had provoked minority-advocacy groups into charging again that the Kahn Commission was a whitewash and a tool of the white Establishment, obscuring real and pressing problems of discrimination and repression.

Half-listening to the angry charges and countercharges, his mind percolating what he had heard from Tommy Clemente and Margo Banner, Estrada saw what common sense should already have told him. Whatever Cuyler Jadwin and his Texas cronies had been up to, they were not about to include in any but the most superficial way a Latino they barely knew, certainly not one who had prompted Jadwin to say 'I never confused him with an honest man.' Their separate goals might have made them partners in a public and apparently legitimate venture like Phoenix Enterprises, but if there was fraud or other criminality in Jadwin's plans, he would not have made Roberto Morales a part of it. And it now seemed clear that Jadwin had to be the prime mover in the crookedness at Phoenix Enterprises.

While Morales was not likely to have been his partner in crime, the same could not be said of Mariah Dodge. If Jadwin had needed an accomplice who was in New York full time, she was the most likely candidate. And if Jadwin's scam was one that endangered the Phoenix Project's successful completion, Morales's response to learning about it might have been violent indeed.

Interesting. A motive for murder that rested on the murderer's fury at his victim for thwarting the murderer's deeply held dream of helping his people. It had a perverse ring of truth to it, but how did you sell it to a jury without creating sympathy for the man you were trying to condemn?

On the other hand, if he could make this theory work, he could jettison the image of Morales as a macho hothead enraged by wounds to his virility. Pulling it off would be tricky, but done right it would steal the defense's thunder, leave them with no emotional issues to manipulate.

He called Cuyler Jadwin, not ready to confront him but needing to get a better sense of the dynamics at Phoenix Enterprises so he could put what he was learning into context.

'I'm not due in New York anytime soon,' Jadwin told him.

'I can come to Houston.'

'It's a free country.' Nothing like y'all come down. Then, reconsidering, 'Look, if you're that hot to talk, I'm going to be in D.C. on Thursday.'

'Good enough.' He could drive down in an office car and

skip having to justify another excursion to Texas.

Thursday at seven he arrived at the private club where he was meeting Jadwin. Behind a heavy wooden door was a dim room dominated by a long bar, all polished dark wood and brass. High-backed horseshoe banquettes of tufted red leather provided islands of privacy under a ceiling high enough to be lost in the gloom. Estrada was greeted by a tall blonde woman in a skin-tight black creation that seemed barely high enough on top and long enough on bottom to qualify as a dress.

'I'm meeting Mr Jadwin.'

'This way, please.'

Jadwin was in one of the larger horseshoes, sitting behind a long-neck beer bottle and a whiskey glass the size of a small fishbowl.

'Hidy. Pull up a chair and tell Melanie here what you want to drink.'

'Beer's fine.' Estrada slid into the horseshoe opposite Jadwin.

'Bring my friend what I'm having. And I'll do another round myself.' He patted her hip. 'Thanks, honey.' He appreciated the view as she walked back to the bar, his eyes evidently better accommodated to the dimness than Estrada's.

'Good lady. Good place, too, reminds me of home. Calmed down some since the boom days. I kinda like it this way. I miss the money, but there'll be more of that down the line. Maybe not like ten years ago, but enough. Hell, there's enough now, if you know where to look.'

'Nobody in here seems to be hurting. As far as I can see.'

'That's why they keep it so dark.' Melanie arrived with their drinks. 'Ain't that so, honey?'

'Sure is.'

He patted her hip. 'Smart girl. Knows who to agree with.' He slipped a bill into the top of her dress and watched her walk away again.

'I was saying, why they keep it so dark is so you can't see

the frayed places on folks' cuffs. A man ought to be able to make his deals without anybody reflecting on the immediate state of his checkbook.'

'Most people I know prefer the light of day.'

'Maybe so, but we've all been on the balls of our ass one time or another, and I like to see a man have a chance to come back. Now what can I tell you about that'll make it worth your while comin' down here to see me?'

'Let's start with the meeting you were supposed to have with Roberto Morales on the day after Mariah Dodge was killed.'

'The famous Monday Meeting? I told your detectives about it back then. I was going to restructure the financing, and I wanted Morales to sign off on it. I didn't *need* him to, you understand – only it was going to make life a whole lot simpler if me and him came through the swingin' doors together, if you see what I mean.'

'I'm not sure I do.'

'Well, you have to understand – after the stock market bucked a whole bunch of people off that Phoenix Project deal I pulled it back together some, only it turned out the economy didn't have the stamina of a day-old colt. We had bankers pulling out on us all over the world. I'm talking about the capital we needed to build our dream. We were hemorrhaging future money, you might say, and I was trying to put a tourniquet on it. Keep things going so the people who already had put money in with us wouldn't get wiped out.'

'From what I've read, a lot of that was your own money, or your bank's.'

Jadwin drank down the last of his first whiskey, pushed the glass away. 'Sure it was my money – some of it. Plenty of other people's money, too. Banks just hanging on that didn't need any other loans to go bad right then. I felt like I had some kind of responsibility.'

'I can understand that.' Even if I don't believe it.

'Robbie Morales was a symbol to some of the money people I was trying to keep from leaving us. If not, I'd have sooner done it without him. I think I told you that already.'

'Not in so many words.'

'But you got the idea.' The Texan started on his second whiskey. 'The meeting that Monday was for making sure he'd memorized the playbook on this restructuring. Only thing was, when we finally got it together to have that meeting, after the murder and all, it turned out that he wasn't even on the team.'

'What made him oppose you?'

'He figured he had a better way to fix our troubles than I did. He wanted to show me the error of my ways, so to speak.'

'I'd like to hear about that.'

'Not much to it.'

'It's what brought Morales and Mariah Dodge together that night.'

'Who knows what brought them together? Or what they thought they were doing.'

'Aren't you curious?' Estrada asked, thinking, Didn't Mariah tell you about it before she went to meet him?

'Why should I be?'

'If you're interested in why Mariah Dodge was killed.'

'I thought it was sex and rejection. Hot-blooded Latin shot in the machismo. No offense.'

No offense. Clemente had said it, too. A lot of people had said it to him over the years, mistaking him for what he wasn't. 'I think it was more than sex. I think it was business. I have an accountant going over the Phoenix Enterprises books to help nail it down.'

Jadwin sat forward. 'You think he'll find something?'

'What do you think?' Estrada concentrated on drawing a line in the condensation on his beer bottle.

'Hard to say. There weren't a whole lot of us there, but we had plenty of money floating around. Tends to stick to people's fingers, I've found.'

'You have any ideas what he should be looking for?' Seeing how far Jadwin would go.

'Nothing comes right to mind.'

'Nothing Morales might have been up to?'

Jadwin seemed to consider it. 'Not that I know.'

Estrada decided not to push it. 'Tell me something.' Keeping it casual. 'Was Mariah Dodge reporting to you about Morales?'

'You back to that again?'

'It's my job.'

'How do you figure that?'

'I have to prove that Roberto Morales killed her. If she was reporting to you and he found out about it, that's a better motive than sexual rejection. If he was opposing you – about the refinancing or anything else – and if she was repeating their pillow talk to you, supporting you, betraying him . . . That spells murder to me.'

Jadwin drank more beer, covering his reaction.

'Let's go back to the Monday meeting and your take on Sunday night. Was there anything odd or significant in the papers they were studying?'

'Mostly it was what you'd expect. Financing the purchase price of the land, and the construction financing, too. A couple of memos about the approvals we needed to get us past the city fathers. I was never sure what they had to do with it.'

'Was the rest of it part of your restructuring?'

'The land was the heart of it. The option on that land was our biggest asset.'

'Yes, I noticed that the price had been going up.'

Jadwin's eyes fastened on him in the gloom, trying to read past the words. 'It was a quality site.'

'How did it figure into the refinancing?'

'I said before, we had some bankers getting set to sail for home and take their money with them. It was mostly the ones who were lending us the capital to close on the land. I needed guarantees for those loans, and I needed them right away or I was going to lose the land altogether. Morales didn't want to go along with what I worked out.'

'Did he have an alternative?'

'Not that I heard about. If he did, he had plenty of chances to let me know. Just because Mariah got killed didn't mean we stopped doin' business and went home.' Jadwin sat back. 'Trouble was, Morales had a whole bunch of blind spots. Funny, for a guy who made the kind of money he did. Makes you wonder how he got so rich.'

'Sounds like you have some answers.'

They were interrupted by Melanie. 'How's everything, boys?'

'Just fine, sweet buns.' Jadwin reached for her waist. She eluded him with a twist of her hips that barely seemed intentional. 'Bring my friend here another beer. And me, too.'

'And some peanuts, if you have them.' Estrada did not want the beer, but he needed something to do with his hands.

'Coming right up.'

'Answers about Morales?' Jadwin said. 'I have some ideas. I think when he was in B-school he figured out where he could go and suck on the public teat, where the deck was stacked in his favor. Where he could pass as a white man at the same time he took advantage of loan guarantees for minority-owned businesses. He put himself in the right place at the right time. He had a lot of luck. Not to say he didn't have some smarts. He can't be all dumb.'

Estrada registered it without comment. 'What happened to your loan guarantees?'

'They got held up. The murder didn't help, and Morales being opposed to them didn't help, either. I got an extension on the option and eventually I got within reach of the guarantees, too, but I was giving away a lot more of the company than I would have if Morales had been on board from the beginning.'

A new waitress brought the beers and a silver bowl of mixed nuts. Melanie was evidently keeping her distance.

Estrada took some nuts from the dish and lined them up on the tablecloth. 'You were saying: Morales was opposed to the loan guarantees.'

'No big mystery. I went to some people in Canada who used to be big players in New York real estate. Happens they're Jewish. Religious, too. Orthodox, whatever you call it.'

'Is that what bothered him?' Estrada broke a cashew in half, then in half again, and again.

'Loan guarantees for maybe a couple hundred million don't come free. I was giving them a big chunk of the company. I mean, hell, without them we were nothin'. Straight down the tubes once that option expired.'

'And that's what Morales objected to – that you were selling part of Phoenix Enterprises to some Orthodox Jews?' He went to work on a second cashew.

'What he said was, "The community board's not going to like it." They've got a whole fucked-up system: This "board," they call it – fifty-some people from around where you're building – has to give you the okay. Every kind of person you could imagine – black, Spanish, Jewish, Polish, Italian, even some organization of artists or some such happy horseshit. That was Morales's job, to gentle that board down and keep them that way. And he said the only way he got them to go along in the first place was because he was Spanish and he was the president of the company. The way he saw it, once we got a big, rich bunch of Jews from out of town owning a chunk of the company, the Spanish were going to smell something fishy. That's what he said. Nobody's rich out there, where we wanted to build, but the Jews save, and pool their money and buy buildings. They understand politics, bloc voting and like that, so they get more space in public housing. It makes the Spanish twitchy every time a new project comes up, competing for space. The idea was, this was going to be different for them.'

'Did you ever resolve it?'

'The murder made everybody slow down. We got some bridge loans, we got the option extended, I was negotiating some new guarantees, like I said. Then we went down for the count anyway, right after the trial.'

'Do you think Morales was right?'

'I think the business about the community board was pure bullshit. Morales was worried about himself. Worried he was going to lose control, get pushed into the background. He wasn't so far wrong, either. This time we're talkin' about, these Canadians and some of their friends up there owned half the damn city. They knew more about doing business in New York than the mayor. They didn't need Morales for shit.'

'He must have had something in mind for the Monday meeting. A way to counter what you were doing, a different proposal. Do you know what it was?'

'Not a clue.'

'I'm assuming that means Mariah didn't have a chance to tell you.'

Jadwin laughed. 'Hang on like a terrier, don't you, boy? How could she have time to tell me? She was dead.'

'But she *was* reporting to you.'

Jadwin finished his whiskey and made a production of looking at his oversize gold watch. 'I'm having a grand time here, but I'm afraid I have me a date to keep.'

Estrada took out his wallet.

Jadwin waved it away. 'They don't take money here. It gets put on my bill. Maybe I'll remember to pay it sometime.'

19

He called Tess Dodge. Still wanting to avoid the office for anything to do with the diary, he arranged to meet her at an outdoor café at the Seaport.

He spotted her the moment she crossed the road onto the pier. Her curls, fuller even than usual, gleamed in the sun, gold alloyed with copper. She was wearing a sleeveless white dress of some soft material with a full skirt that swirled around her legs as she walked.

He waved her over. She had to detour around a crew setting up for a free rock concert that night.

'Life in the big city,' he said as she sat down.

'There's always something. You had a question for me?'

'Yes. Did you see anything in what you read to indicate that Mariah might have been working with Jadwin on his swindles?'

'How do you mean?'

'There was that comment she made about Jadwin, "It feels like Texas." I took that to mean she was working with him here the way she used to there, maybe even being his lover again. You told me there were places in the diary where she and Johnny seemed to be keeping things back from Jadwin. I was wondering if there was anything where she and Jadwin seemed to be up to something together.'

'What's this all about?'

'Motive. Mariah may have been working with Jadwin even more closely than I thought before. Logic says Mariah was his eyes and ears in New York, and she may have been helping him manage Morales so he wouldn't interfere with Jadwin's scams. Morales may have found that out, and that's why he killed her.'

Tess's response was drowned out by a sudden wail of loud-speaker feedback that made them both jump. Even so he could see that she was angry. It did not take her long to confirm his guess.

'You're telling me my sister was *guilty* of something, is that it? And you want to use me to get information to back you up? You've got some colossal set of huevos, mister.'

'I'm not saying she was guilty of anything. If anybody was guilty, it was Jadwin. I think she may have suffered from too much loyalty, no more than that. What's important isn't what she was actually doing, it's Morales's perception of it. If he thought she was betraying him, him and the Phoenix Project both, that's a pretty damn powerful motive.'

Tess pushed her chair back from the table and stood up.

He stood quickly and took her arm. 'Wait a minute . . .'

She looked at his hand until he took it away. 'Where do they keep the ladies' room around here?' she asked.

He pointed.

'Let me spell it out for you,' she said when she came back. 'I don't want you smearing my sister in public – not even if it's true. And what you're talking about sounds like nasty business to me.'

He had no answer for that.

'You know,' she said, 'there *is* one thing. It stuck in my mind because it was sort of curious, something like "I guess we're not in Texas anymore, Toto." I figured it had to do with living in New York. I don't know why I didn't connect it with "It feels like Texas," but I didn't. Anyhow, maybe not being in Texas any more means she and Jadwin were on the outs. What does that do to your story?'

'It doesn't help, if you've got the meaning right. When did she write it?'

She shrugged. 'I was looking for Johnny and abusive boyfriends, the way I was told to.'

'If she wasn't with Jadwin, I have to know it, or I'm going to shoot myself in the foot with this new theory. If you want to see Roberto Morales in jail, you've got to help me with this.'

'You know, I'm getting damn tired hearing what you need and what I have to do.'

He could feel his face redden. 'Listen, lady, I've got my neck stuck way out on this diary, trying to do my job and protect the Dodge family at the same time. I could just as well go to my boss and tell him about it and let somebody else worry.' That wasn't precisely true, but for the moment he wasn't worrying about what was precisely true. 'I'm trying to nail the man who killed your sister. You say you care. Hell, you say you care enough to kill him yourself. So what the hell are you giving me grief for now?'

She smiled weakly. 'Seems we're both kind of on edge.'

He took a long breath and smiled back. 'Hungry, probably.' He waved for a waiter.

Back at the office, he called the Task Force and asked the detective who answered to beep Clemente for him. Lynne Schelling, next on his list, was not in her office.

Carlyn Sims answered on the first ring.

'A couple of months ago I called to ask you about Mariah and Cuyler Jadwin,' Estrada reminded her. 'We got onto other subjects and never talked about Jadwin. I'd still like to know if she ever got back with him after they broke up.'

'You're talkin' romance, now?'

'I am.'

'I'm no expert, you know. Mariah was funny that way – about talkin' about her men. All the things we did together, and she'd still go all shy on me. All I can tell you is, if she went back with Jadwin that way, and I think maybe she did, it wasn't for long. By that time I think he'd turned into kind of a father figure for her. She might have slept with him for old times, but she was too easy with him for it to last as a romance. She needed more excitement than that.'

'What do you mean?'

'That was how she was. She needed some danger to keep her going. Not *physical* danger, mind you. Emotional danger. She used to joke about how dumb I was, picking guys. "Almost as dumb as me," she used to say. God, I miss her.'

Clemente returned Estrada's call. 'We got an emergency?'

'Juan Alvaro.'

'Nothing so far. I checked DMV, utilities, the post office, the usual. If he's in the state, he's using somebody else's power and phone. If he's out of state he's driving illegal. He's not collecting social security or unemployment. He was never in the service and the FBI doesn't have him. It might help if I had a court order for credit records.'

'I'll take care of it.' Not through Martinez. 'I need him, Tommy.' Need someone who can tell me what Mariah Dodge was up to. 'Sooner, not later.'

'Ain't it always the way?'

In the morning Tess Dodge called to say she had an express package from Houston.

'I told my mother you were going to tell the world her poor deceased daughter was some kind of crook unless I showed you you were wrong.'

When he arrived at her apartment she had already found Mariah's entry about not being in Texas anymore. As he had suspected, it had been written after the one about how it felt like Texas again. So, whatever magic she and Jadwin had found, it had evaporated again. Still, romance or not, Mariah could still have been working for him, or Morales could have thought she was.

Looking through more of the pages, Estrada came to some blacked-out sections. 'I thought this was the unexpurgated version.'

'All it is, is some parts about Johnny's being gay. She didn't do near so much of that as she might have. Do you care? I promise you it has nothing to do with the murder.'

'There's a lot I'm interested in now that I wouldn't have thought mattered not so long ago.'

He skimmed the rest of the new material. Except for the book that had regular entries about Johnny and about Mariah's visits to the hospital, he had read large parts of all these pages before. Now he was seeing them with the most personal entries made visible.

He stopped reading the intimate passages almost at once. He would have to get through them sooner or later; for now, they were not his priority. He was looking for something about Mariah and Jadwin, Mariah and Johnny, and the three of them.

He was on the verge of asking Tess to point out some of the important Johnny passages when his eye was caught by a notation that said, A KND OF POETRY TO BEING LANDOWNER. LANDLORD. NT WT I XPECTED.

He asked Tess what property Mariah had owned.

'She didn't own any property that I know about.'

He showed her the notation.

'Does stock count? If she owned a lot of stock in a company that owned an apartment building, does that count when you're asking if she owned property?'

'How much stock is a lot?'

'Eighty-five percent. And the family owned the rest. Me and my folks.'

'What happened to her share?'

'She left it to me.'

'Is this stock worth something?'

'Judging by the money I get from it, I guess so.'

'What kind of money?'

She looked at him. 'Didn't your mother teach you that isn't polite?'

'This is purely professional.'

'It's enough to live on.'

'Why didn't it show up in the estate? I didn't see where anybody thought money was a factor at all.'

She shrugged. 'I don't know about any of that. They point me and I sign the forms and the checks, and that's it.'

'I need to talk to the lawyer who handled the will.'

When he made the call he was put through immediately. 'Tess Dodge telephoned earlier – at your request, I gather,' the probate lawyer said, all formality. 'She released me from my obligation of confidentiality where she is concerned. I must tell you, though, that I'm concerned about divulging anything to a prosecuting attorney.'

'I can assure you that Tess Dodge is not a target of any investigation by this office.' Estrada fell automatically into a matching pattern of speech. Law schools needed no courses in lawyerspeak, law students absorbed it on their own. 'This is purely to help me develop my case against her sister's murderer.'

'So she told me, though I don't see how this will help.'

'Mariah left a piece of real estate to Tess, as I understand it, with the ownership in the form of stock in a holding company. It may help me if you can explain how the initial financing was arranged, while Mariah was alive.'

'All I can tell you is what appeared to me at the time of her death.'

'That's close enough.'

'Well . . . There was a corporation involved, but as you suggest, it was essentially a device for tax purposes and so on. When the stock came into the estate there was a mortgage on the property, and a balance on a bank loan that had been used to make the down payment on the building. The mortgage payments and other expenses were being covered by the revenues from the building, with very little margin. It was a difficult time economically here, and there were a lot of vacancies in the building. It would have run at a loss except for the fact that Mariah was not having to make any payments at all on the loan. In the long run, if Mariah had lived chances are she would have ended up in the plus column, as long as the bank continued to let her postpone making those loan payments. But from the point of view of the estate the most important fact was that the corporation had key-person insurance on her. It covered both the mortgage and the initial down-payment loan. It's not easy to get that kind of insurance, and the premiums are high. Somebody paid the premiums on both policies in advance, for five years.'

'Is it common to postpone payments on a loan like that?'

'It's why a lot of savings and loans went under. They made sweetheart loans no one ever planned to pay back. In this case, there was a guarantor, a corporation that went out of business not long after Mariah died. Of course, by then it didn't matter to the banks. The insurance paid everything. In effect, Tess owns that building free and clear, except for her parents' small share.'

'Did Tess know about all this before it happened?' He hated having to ask the question. Judging by the thick silence on the other end of the line, its implications had not escaped the probate lawyer.

'No. Not from me. I can't say what Mariah might have told her. I can tell you that when I read the will to the family and explained about the terms, they were all quite amazed. Tess the most. I don't think she could have been acting.'

Estrada was more than a little relieved to hear it.

'Of course,' the lawyer went on, 'at that time we thought the stock had quite limited value because there was no indication of the insurance I mentioned. That didn't turn up until months later and then we had to scramble to redo all our tax documents.'

'What can you tell me about the bank that made the loan, or the corporation that was the guarantor?'

'What sort of information are you looking for?'

'I want to know who was doing her favors like that.'

'Yes, that would be at the bottom of this for you, I can see that. I believe it was a man called Cuyler Jadwin. I've never had any dealings with him myself. He was a middle-level player in the savings and loan business in the southeastern part of the state. I believe you might find him on the agenda over at the U.S. Attorney's office. Mariah worked for him for quite a long time. In fact, I believe she was working for him, indirectly, at the time she died.'

'Yes, she was.'

'Silly of me. Of course you would know him.'

'We've met. I didn't know he was so . . . prominent.'

'I may have been guilty of letting my mouth get ahead of my judgment, a minute ago.'

'Don't worry about it. Nobody's going to know you said any of it, and if it proves out, then you've done me a big favor, and Mariah, too.'

'She was a lovely person. It's a tragedy for such a vibrant life to be cut short so cruelly.'

Curiouser and curiouser. Jadwin was beginning to look like a real desperado, even if he was only middle level by Texas standards. Estrada held the receiver button down only long enough to break the connection and then dialed the internal number for Lisa Stein.

'I need you, Watson,' he said.

'What? Oh. Right away, Mr Bell.'

She appeared almost at once, dressed as always in clothes of appropriate cut and cost for a top-paying law firm. He handed her a pad and a pen and pointed to the extension phone. 'I'm about to call your favorite Texan, and I wanted somebody on the line who's immune to his charm.'

'That's me.' She cleared the stack of transcripts off the visitor's chair and sat down next to the extension phone with the pad propped on her knee. 'Ready.'

In due course, an annoyed Cuyler Jadwin came on the line. 'You know, Estrada, you're gettin' to be more nuisance than a swarm of no-see-ums at a nudist convention.'

'Mr Jadwin, a woman you claim to have cared about was

brutally murdered. I'm doing my best to build a case against her killer, who happens to be a man you introduced her to.'

'You accusing me of something?'

'I'm asking for your cooperation.'

'Okay. Go ahead.'

'A couple of months before Mariah was killed, you arranged for her to own an apartment building. As I understand it, one of your banks provided the mortgage and another made a loan that was used for the down payment. I also understand that the bank that made the down payment made it based on a guarantee from a corporation of which you were a principal, and that the bank allowed an indefinite payment forgiveness. In addition, you advanced money for premiums on life insurance that covered both the loan and the mortgage.' Guessing a little.

'Well, well,' Jadwin said. 'I keep hearin' about New York push and initiative. I guess now I see what they're talking about. All that's mostly right. I didn't pay for the insurance out of my own pocket, that was another bank loan, but it might as well have been me. So where's the question? You seem to know all about all that already.'

Estrada looked over to be sure Stein was taking notes.

'The transactions we're talking about are not what you'd call normal business behavior for well-run banks.'

Jadwin laughed. 'Hell, no. When the hell did we ever have well-run banks down here? Look, I loved Mariah in my own half-ass way like she was my daughter. Except for the times she was more, that is. She did me a lot of good over the years. I paid her good money, and I gave her presents, but here I was gettin' a little bit rich and she was still livin' from paycheck to paycheck. So I saw a way to throw some honey her way, why not? I coulda picked up that building for myself and done fine with it, but a man can be too greedy. So I figured, hell, here's a little something if it works out will be security for a fine lady's old age. Some joke. Her old age.'

'It's a pretty story,' Estrada said. 'You're saying you weren't worried about the ways you were misusing the banks where you had a fiduciary obligation.'

'You got some kind of hair up your ass, boy? I liked you better when we were kickin' back together, drinkin' sour mash and pinchin' pretty ladies.'

On the extension phone, Stein gave Estrada a hard look.

'Look,' Jadwin said, 'People been doin' that kind of thing around here for years. I was in a position to do a favor for a friend and I wasn't going to be in that position forever. Nobody lost a penny. The directors of those banks wish all their loans were that good to them. I'm not talking about the insurance, you understand. I'm talking about how well she did by the banks when she was alive.'

Estrada was happy to get off the phone. 'You get all that?'

'I got most of it. What does it mean?'

'Mr Jadwin seems to have decided it was a good idea to make Mariah Dodge a little bit rich.'

'He gave her an apartment building?'

'Using other people's money.'

'Why?'

'He says, because he liked her. Because she did a good job when she worked for him.'

'I guess I should have been nicer to him.' She giggled.

'He's probably in the market for another daughter. Or more than a daughter, I think he said.'

'On second thought, maybe I'll go out and earn an apartment building some other way.'

20

Estrada left the office early and went back to Tess Dodge's to pick up the diary pages.

At home, he took a long shower and went out to enjoy the river and the community garden in the summer-evening sun. The neighborhood was out in force on the promenade overlooking the river. The playground was thronged with happily shrieking children, and the line of wood-slat benches was full. Dogs and people romped on the grassy median, and joggers weaved in and out among the parents with baby-strollers.

He leaned on the sun-warmed stone wall and watched boats sail by on the river. The vibrant life all around him was an antidote to the death and worry that he lived with every day without being able to do much to control it.

And nothing was more out of control than his case against Roberto Morales. Every revelation raised more questions than it answered. If Mariah and Jadwin had been close enough a few months before her death for him to give her an apartment building, why was she telling her friends she was breaking up with Morales? Wouldn't Jadwin have wanted them to stay close until the refinancing questions were resolved?

Suppose Lynne Schelling had been telling the truth when she said that news of the Monday meeting had changed Mariah's mind about breaking up with Morales. Changed her mind so she could report to Jadwin about him one more time.

And yet, Schelling's impression was that Mariah had expected to be on the same side as Morales at that meeting.

Had Mariah been fooling her friend? And if not, if Mariah *was* on Morales's side, what had turned her against Jadwin, in the face of his apparent generosity? Was that change of heart why she had written 'I have the feeling we're not in Texas anymore'? And if so, how might Jadwin have responded?

Estrada felt like a circus equestrian riding two horses, one foot on the back of each – two horses no longer going in the same direction.

He turned away from the river to go back home. Pulled himself up short to keep from colliding with a stroller. 'Sorry,' he said to the petite, attractive woman pushing it. And realized who it was.

'Hello,' he said to Kassia Miller, mastering his surprise. 'I didn't know you lived around here.'

Smiling, she pointed at one of the tall old apartment houses visible on the hill beyond the treetops. 'You, too?'

'West End.'

'We used to live there. It's nice, but I like being able to see the river.'

He could not resist looking under the stroller canopy. The pink-faced little person strapped into the seat was wearing a tiny T-shirt and red overalls. A squeeze-toy bunny was wedged between the seat and one chubby arm. His eyes were firmly closed.

'He's adorable. What's his name?'

'Alex.'

'How old?'

'A little over a year.'

He looked at the baby again. 'I think he's waking up.'

'He's going to be thirsty.' She rummaged in the bag on the back of the stroller and came up with a bottle.

'Which reminds me,' Estrada said. 'I was just on my way home. Nice to see you. Neighbor.' He turned to go.

'Joe.'

He turned back.

'I probably shouldn't say this. It's not something I do. Never.' A brief smile. 'Well, almost never.'

The baby started to cry. Miller ducked her head under the canopy and unbuckled the straps, straightened up with the baby in her arms. Patting her baby's back, she looked Estrada in the eye. 'Roberto Morales is innocent.' The words were calm and matter-of-fact.

She leaned the baby off her shoulder so she could give it the bottle, looked up again at Estrada. 'Something to think about when you're wondering why your case is so weak and full of holes.'

He was vaguely aware that he was staring.

'I really wouldn't say so if I didn't believe it.'

Still at a loss for words, he tried for a smile. 'I'm sure. See you.' He waved at the baby. 'Bye, Alex.'

Normally he would have ignored a defense lawyer's claim that a client was innocent. Most of them repeated it so constantly it lost all meaning. And it seemed that even the others needed to believe sincerely in the innocence of one client every so often, salve for the corrosive effects of representing an army of the guilty.

This time felt different. Was it because of his own doubts, or his impression of Miller? He tried to push the questions out of his mind, told himself he was only paying attention to this because Miller had caught him at a moment of confusion about what he was learning.

He sat himself down at the desk in his back bedroom to read the new diary pages, carefully and slowly. He needed to find something to resolve his doubts, to make sense of the inconsistencies. Try as he might, he could not focus on the words in front of him. He got up and paced around the room, tracing a path among bike and skis and the rest of the clutter. He got on his long-unused cross-country ski machine to burn off some of his frustration.

* * *

He wondered whether to tell Collins what had happened in the park. Face to face with the bureau chief, reporting progress for the week, he saw that he would be reporting not the remark but his own reaction to it. He held himself to telling Collins about the office building Jadwin had given to Mariah Dodge.

'Where does it fit?' Collins asked.

'I'm taking the position that the sister isn't a possible suspect – she was in Texas when the murder happened – so this isn't information useful to the defense.'

'She could have hired it done.'

'There's nothing to indicate she knew in advance about the terms of the will, or the value of the building, or the insurance. I want to use this as evidence that Jadwin was rewarding Mariah for spying on Morales.'

'You seriously want to go with the money motive, don't you?' Collins was aggressively skeptical.

'You bet I do. It takes us out of relying on hearsay about her wanting to turn Morales off so bad he'd leave her alone forever.'

'You're going to confuse the jury.' The bureau chief was not letting up. 'This is even more speculative than what we have. How do you prove Morales knew anything about it?'

'I want to follow it up. There's still time to flesh it out, and I may have another witness. Tommy Clemente's out looking for him now.' Too late, Estrada saw his mistake.

'Who?' The response he should have predicted.

'Somebody she knew at Phoenix Enterprises. I'd like to leave it at that until I'm sure what he's got to say.'

Collins frowned. Estrada scrambled for something to say about Johnny that did not refer to the diary. It had been a bad idea even to hint at his existence.

'I don't like mysteries,' Collins said, but he let it go for the moment.

McMorris came in with a report on their reluctant I.D. witness, Ramon Santos. The brawny investigator was looking even bulkier lately, straining his buttons. 'Remember how I said Ramon had a good record for being on the job and all?'

'Right.'

'Yeah, well, it's bullshit. They've got a bunch of them up there cover for each other.' He sat down and guzzled from a can of cola. 'I found a guy who's not part of it. Has to work a full shift and it pisses him off. He says Ramon comes and goes when he likes. He's got a little business on the side, peddling happy dust to the office workers. Nothing big, but he's off his post now and then running errands. And the guy I talked to thinks maybe Ramon is his own best customer.'

'Do we know if he was doing this three years ago?'

'Nope. My informant's only been there eight months.'

'This is not the kind of lever I was hoping for.' Thinking about how this would affect a jury's view of Santos's credibility.

'Tell me about it.' McMorris drained the cola can and let out a satisfied belch.

'How talkative a guy is this? Is he singing to the defense, too?'

'He might. I don't get the idea he likes Ramon a whole lot.'

'Thanks, Stash.'

The detective hauled himself to his feet. 'Hell, I'm just glad they don't kill the messenger any more.'

'I'd rather hear it from you, now, than from Kassia Miller in court.'

Estrada spent the weekend going through Mariah Dodge's diary, new pages and old, looking for anything that would help him understand where she and Jadwin had stood with each other in the days before her death, and where Juan Alvaro fit into the picture.

There were entries that looked interesting but that were so out of context he did not see how he could understand them without talking to the principals. One said J→CJ+FDS COMG UP ON MAGIC 5 YRS. The best he could do with that was

'Johnny pointed out that Cuyler Jadwin and his friends are coming up on the magic five years.' But FDS could just as easily mean 'funds,' or even 'feds.'

There were variations on the theme of Morales trying to get the better of Jadwin. Nothing about where Mariah stood, though her opinion that Morales was no match for Jadwin was clear.

There were several entries suggesting that Johnny and Mariah might have been up to something, as Tess had said. J SERIOUS ABT GOING AHEAD and J HAS MORE DETLS and J CHKING SCHED. I'M NOT SURE HE GETS WT'S AT STAKE left Estrada tantalized, as did FEELS LIKE J + I TIED TOGETHER. SCARY TO THINK ABT and especially, NOW J WANTS ME TO TELL CJ WILL XPLODE, and the old familiar J WANTS TO TELL CJ. NOT A GOOD IDEA.

Uneasy as he had felt about reading the intimate passages, he could not skip anything to do with Morales. He learned that Morales had been a good lover, at least at the beginning, though not as good as he thought he was, Mariah had noted. At the beginning, too, she had found his macho posturing funny and endearing. Later it had palled increasingly. More than once she had asked herself why she was not breaking up with him.

Reading about that part of her life, even in the detached, abbreviation-ridden style she used, made Estrada feel uncomfortably as if he were peeking through a keyhole, but he made himself keep reading, looking for something to tell him where Mariah stood with respect to Morales and Jadwin on the night she died. With every new entry he worried that he would find something that was a clear help to the defense.

Among the troubling entries were the ones about how firmly Morales insisted on using condoms. Mariah had been pleased by his caution until the first time he had refused to have intercourse with her because they had none. Morales, it seemed would make no exceptions. He had been tested for AIDS, he had told Mariah, he donated blood regularly to be sure he was all right and he was not going to take any chances.

He had been skeptical when she told him she had been tested and she had apparently been unwilling to tell him that it was because of her regular contact with the kids in the AIDS facility.

During the time when she still found Morales appealing, the diary included complaints about the way condoms interfered with feeling him, skin to skin. She complained too, about being deprived of contact with his vital fluids. Those entries especially disturbed Estrada. A defense lawyer could argue they supported the theory that the semen found on the body came from the time Mariah had allegedly spent with Morales in their secret apartment that afternoon. 'Some people like it, they roll around in it,' Walter Kubelik had argued at the close of the first trial, without the diary entries to support him.

Estrada convinced himself that those entries were more than offset by descriptions of how strongly Morales insisted on using condoms. Because the diary was so unequivocal on that subject, Estrada was ready to argue that it *contradicted* the defense theory that Morales had left semen behind during an afternoon encounter. Morales could still have left semen behind when he raped her, later – either because the violence of the attack had ruptured the condom he was wearing, or because, in his frenzy of violence, he had given no thought to anything so mundane as a condom.

Estrada was less sanguine about the diary's material on Mariah and Johnny and Jadwin. In the hands of a clever defense lawyer the entries about Mariah's collusion with Johnny, apparently against Jadwin, would make Jadwin a possible alternative suspect. And Estrada had no doubt that Miller was more than clever enough to make the most of that theory.

Until Johnny was found, Estrada was in a nasty ethical limbo. His rationale for not giving the diary to Miller was that he needed Johnny's testimony to know if the entries about him were helpful to the defense or not. But the longer Johnny stayed missing, the more he himself became the issue, and the less Estrada could justify not turning the diary over to the defense, or at least to the judge.

He still saw no way to do that without a substantial risk that the diary would become a huge cause célèbre – needlessly hurting the Dodges and exposing Larry Kahn to charges of misconduct at the worst possible time. With the diary to point at what Johnny's testimony might have been, Johnny, the missing and unavailable witness, was potentially an even more fatal flaw than the missing diary pages had been.

Without Johnny, Estrada saw no way to avoid a defense motion to dismiss the indictment because Lawrence Kahn's misconduct had deprived Roberto Morales of due process of law.

Estrada decided to take a chance on calling Kassia Miller to see if he could get her to say more about why she thought her client was innocent. Morales's version of all this was a complete unknown, and sometimes people told you more than they meant to – in the spin they put on their stories, in what they put in or left out.

'I'm intrigued by our conversation in the park,' he told her. 'I wanted to hear more about it, about why you feel that way.'

'A lot of reasons. Mostly, I just really believe in this guy. You know how that is – some people you believe, some you don't, and it doesn't always take much to tell you which is which. And I know your case against him can't be that good.'

'I might surprise you.'

'If you have something that would hurt us, I *would* be surprised. I'd like to know what it is.'

'At the right time, in the right place.' He was on familiar ground with this kind of sparring.

'You're making a mistake.' She was departing from the script. 'The man's not a killer. I mean that very specifically.

He didn't do it. It's written all over him.'

'Too bad I can't read it myself.' It just came out, a wordplay response to what she was saying. He was not thinking about where it might lead until he heard the words himself.

'What are you suggesting?'

'If he's so obviously innocent, bring him in so I can see for myself.' It was never going to happen, so he made it a real challenge. 'Let *him* tell me about it.'

She did not respond. As the silence lengthened, Estrada wondered if she could be considering it seriously.

'I don't think so.' She was speaking slowly and deliberately, a marked change from her usual crisp delivery. 'It's a non-starter unless we have the right kind of protection.'

He played along. 'If you bring him in for a confidential conversation I can agree not to refer to any part of it in my direct case. But I have to be able to use it on cross-examination if there's testimony that contradicts what he says at the meeting, and in my rebuttal case if it's relevant there. That's it. I'll listen to what he has to say, and I'll have questions for him to answer. If he points me at something I think I can use, I'm going to follow it up.'

Another silence before she spoke again.

'It won't fly. I have an obligation to tell him about your offer, but I can tell you that on those terms I'll advise him strongly to say no.'

Estrada was impressed by how effortlessly she had transformed this into his 'offer.'

'They're the only terms I have.'

'I'll call you when I have an answer.'

He had not expected this. Defense lawyers sometimes brought their clients in, hoping to avoid an indictment, but that point was long past. This late in the game, Miller had to have an awful lot of faith to go even as far as sparring with him about it the way she had. On the other hand, in the unlikely event that such a meeting happened, it would give Joe Estrada a far better chance than he'd ever expected to pick up the kind of information that might help put his questions and his doubts to rest.

He caught Mahoney before he went out to lunch and the two of them slogged through the heat to a downstairs dumpling parlor on Bayard Street. Ignored by restaurant guidebooks and courthouse regulars alike, it served decent, cheap food; there were even tablecloths and cloth napkins, though there was never anyone there to use them. He and Mahoney had speculated that it had to be a front for something; they did not care to wonder what it might be.

'What new disaster do you have for me this week?' Mahoney asked him after Charlie the waiter supplied them with a preliminary assortment of dumplings. Estrada started with the story of Mariah Dodge's office building.

'You're telling me he *gave* this woman an apartment building?'

'It cost him zero to do it, just more of the manipulations that seem to be his specialty. And on paper, at least, it was worth zip at the time. Her dying made it valuable.'

'The point is, he gave it to her. He could have kept it for himself, or given it to somebody else. From what you were saying, if things look up a little economically it's going to be worth a ton of money. Would have been even without the insurance.'

'True.'

'What did she have on him?'

'Sorry?'

'Mariah Dodge. What did she have on Jadwin to get the building out of him?'

'I'm assuming it's what Jadwin said it was – a reward for a job well done. A job well done on Señor Morales. One more reason for Morales to kill her.'

'That's not what the defense is going to say. They're going to say she had something on Jadwin. And that makes *him* a suspect.'

Estrada dipped a dumpling in mustard. It slipped from his chopsticks before it reached his mouth, splashing when it hit the plate.

'It's an ugly tie,' Mahoney observed. 'You're better off without it.'

Estrada blotted the tie with cold water. 'You have this knack for pointing out exactly what I don't want to see.'

'An ugly tie is an ugly tie.'

'I mean about Mariah Dodge and Cuyler Jadwin. It's been on my mind since I found out about the apartment building. I've been trying not to think about it.'

'No surprise. It's uglier than the tie.'

'And there's more.' Estrada told him about Mariah's undefined conspiracy with the missing Juan Alvaro.

'My son,' Mahoney intoned, 'you've got yourself a major problem. What are you going to do?'

'I still think I need more information before I open this up to the world. Once I do, it's going to cause a lot of pain and trouble.'

'You're likely to have a pile of pain and trouble yourself if you keep all this secret much longer. Assuming you aren't *already* committing some misconduct.'

'I know it's risky, but there's an awful lot at stake.' The Dodges were first in his mind but he could not ignore the Kahn Commission – Jake Berger and the others trying to do the right thing at considerable personal sacrifice. 'If Larry Kahn gets blown out of the water he takes a lot of good people with him. And he had a lot on his mind when he was trying that case. It could have been an honest mistake.'

'Could be. But if you cover it up, it won't be an honest mistake for you. If that's the choice you make you'd better pray that diary never comes out. And in case it does you'd better be ready with a great reason for why it couldn't possibly have helped the defense.' Mahoney picked up a dumpling and lost it the same way Estrada had lost his, freckling his tie and shirt with soy sauce.

They both laughed hard enough to bring the waiter hurrying over to see what was wrong.

They went back to the courthouse together but Estrada did not go upstairs. Instead he walked over to Foley Square and around the triangular plaza, trying to get his mind to settle down.

He was going to have to find Juan Alvaro, the sooner the better. Only Johnny himself could make it clear what the diary's value was and to whom, because no one else could say what he and Mariah Dodge had been plotting together.

That question had taken on a new importance. Once Mahoney had said, 'What did she have on him?' the other pieces of the puzzle had fallen into place: Cuyler Jadwin and the rest of the crew from the Church of the Heavenly Blessing had been involved in bank fraud just about five years before Jadwin had given Mariah Dodge and her family all the stock in a corporation that owned an apartment building. And at about that same time Mariah had told her diary that Jadwin and his friends, or Jadwin and the feds, were coming up on the magic five years.

Five years was the federal statute of limitations for bank fraud, as his friend in the U.S. Attorney's office had reminded him. Five years after the crime was complete, the criminals could no longer be prosecuted. With the magic date approaching, Jadwin's only fear would have been that at the last minute someone might run to the U.S. Attorney with a list of names and numbers, dates and places – something to bring the feds down on him in a hurry.

It all fit, almost too perfectly. As the prosecutor of Roberto Morales, Estrada did not welcome it. As a person interested in finding Mariah Dodge's murderer, he could not ignore it.

He called Kassia Miller in the morning. 'How are we doing on our meeting?'

'You're getting help from an unexpected quarter. Roberto

says he might be willing to talk to you, but he doesn't want to be worrying that something he tells you in good faith may turn around and bite him.'

Badly as Estrada now wanted to talk with Morales, if he made it easy for Miller he would give himself away. 'If he's not guilty he has nothing to worry about.'

'Since when does being innocent protect anyone from a hotshot prosecutor?'

'If that's how you feel,' he came back sharply, 'why are we talking?'

A pause, then: 'Look, Joe, maybe we should just duke it out in the playground after school. That's what this feels like. I'm right on the verge of saying, "You started it." '

Estrada smiled. She kept slipping under his guard.

'Okay – truce. But I really can't make any promises about not following up on what I hear.'

'This is a man who's been convicted of rape and manslaughter, wrongly and wrongfully. I'd say he's earned the right to be careful, especially where your office is concerned.'

'All I can say to that is nobody over here has pangs of conscience that they railroaded him. If we have enough to convince us, and convince a grand jury, we go ahead. If we don't, we don't. We play by the rules. The jury makes the final decision.' Words he was ordinarily proud to say. This time, it was hard to get them out.

'And with Roberto Morales the court has put you back to the beginning of that process.' She was being low-key now. 'There was a bad call in the first trial. The verdict is worthless. Those rules you were talking about say Roberto Morales is still presumed to be innocent.'

'By the jury. That doesn't mean by me.'

'I need to know you have an open mind about it. If not, then there's no point saying any more.'

He did not answer. It was an admission he could not have afforded to make, even if it had been true. But though he had doubts, what he wanted now was to restore his faith in the idea that Morales was guilty, not to be convinced he wasn't. Still, with the possibility that Mariah and Johnny had been blackmailing Cuyler Jadwin looming in the background, how could he be sure of anything?

'I'm interested in what he has to say.'

'I think you will be. More than you expect.'

'And you want me to see him, or we wouldn't be talking. You knew the risks when we started down this road.'

'Exactly. And if the risks are too great, we stop right here.'

'I've told you what I can do.'

'Too bad,' Miller said. 'If you had talked to Roberto you could have saved the taxpayers a lot of money, and saved yourself and your office time and effort. And embarrassment.'

'I don't have room to be more accommodating. It's not my choice. I'll have to get any deal approved, and the front office is not exactly pro-Morales.' Leaving the door open for her, just a crack.

He walked down the hall to Collins's office to ask how much leeway he could expect on this.

'He'll be right back,' his secretary said. 'You can wait inside if you want.'

He sat at the small conference table. It was littered with the file folders Collins always seemed to be consulting, organizing or consigning to storage. Estrada glanced over them. A few were tabbed with the names of cases he recognized from the monthly homicide meetings. Off by itself there was a file labeled MORALES. Just out of reach.

Estrada looked at it, tempted to see what was inside, then twisted around to look at the open door to the secretary's anteroom and the corridor beyond it. He walked over to stand by the windows. He could see the new federal courthouse going up. Construction had been delayed when the crew excavating the foundation had dug into the site of a famous nineteenth-century slum. For months, archaeologists had been picking through the remains of this notorious sinkhole of poverty, violence and lawlessness. Now that they were done, the site would be home to the largest courthouse in the country.

He went back to the conference table and sat in a chair that faced the door. He used the back of an extended finger to raise the cover of the MORALES file. Just to see what kind of material was there. Upside down, he wouldn't be able to read much, anyway. He glimpsed a letterhead: GOVERNOR'S SPECIAL COMMISSION ON LAW ENFORCEMENT PRACTICES. Only a few words of the letter registered, almost subliminally, before the sound of footsteps pulled his hand away. He was getting up as Collins came into the office.

'Joe. What's happening?'

About to tell Collins that he and Kassia Miller were negotiating a meeting between prosecutor and defendant, Estrada held back. Once the bosses heard about it they would want to supervise every word. It was inevitable, but later was better than sooner. Instead, he asked Collins's opinion about following up further on Morales's former sex partners, an area that Kahn had barely explored.

'What for?' Collins wanted to know.

'See about his sex practices.'

'You think maybe he raped and murdered a lot of them? It's inadmissible, anyway, unless he did them all on their office couches with a razor knife.'

'There's all this in the air about safe sex. Suppose he used condoms all the time. That would help us fight the idea that the semen was from an earlier encounter.'

'It's still propensity evidence. So what if he used condoms with Carmen and Rosa? It proves squat about Mariah Dodge. Anyway, condoms break.'

'Right.'

'Listen, I'm not saying no. Who knows what you'll turn up? If you have the time and your people have nothing better to do, go ahead.'

Estrada got out of there as fast as he could. The words

he had seen under the Kahn Commission letterhead were '. . . none better than Joseph Estrada. I have observed him . . .'

'You were highly recommended,' Collins had said when Estrada challenged him about getting the Morales case because of his ethnic background. At the time, Estrada had thought that was simply a way to deflect him. Apparently not. Apparently there *had* been a recommendation – from Lawrence Kahn.

Estrada waited until he and Kassia Miller had straightened out the terms of his meeting with Roberto Morales before he talked to Collins about it.

The bureau chief's jaw tightened. 'Morales wants to come in and talk? Why?'

'To show me he's innocent, according to Miller. More likely, so she can scare me with what a great witness he's going to be. And I assume they've got a story to tell. Morales has never made a statement more complete than "I'm innocent." '

'I don't like it that it's just you and a paralegal, no investigator.'

Estrada noticed that Collins had not objected to Nancy Rosen's being excluded. There was a good chance her boss was Collins's rival for Muir's job. 'Those were the terms.'

'You think Stein's up to it? I know she's easy to look at . . .'

'She's as smart as they come. I'm not worried.'

Collins was still not happy, but he let it go. 'I want to see a list of questions. We've got to pin him down on everything, so if he does get on the stand he's stuck with what he told you.'

'Right.'

'This ought to open their eyes in the front office.'

As Estrada had expected. 'One of the conditions for this meeting was secrecy. If you take it to the front office, it's sure to be all over the media in a minute.'

'I don't have a choice. Bishop has to approve whatever you agreed to.'

'Nothing beyond the usual.' As if any of this were usual. 'The only thing Morales gets is that I make no public mention of the meeting, including in court, unless he says something different on the stand. I can follow up anything I hear, and use anything I find in evidence. I gave them rebuttal. Otherwise it's the standard agreement.'

'You gave them rebuttal? That means you can't use Morales's statement if that old man contradicts him.'

'I'll take care of that on cross.' Estrada was being optimistic but he thought it was worth it. 'It was the only way to get the meeting. They wanted more but I said I wouldn't get approval. They took those terms because they didn't want me even to *ask* for approval.'

'Bishop still has to know.'

'As long as you can promise me he won't tell anybody.'

'Just when did you start making rules for the District Attorney?'

Estrada spread his hands. 'I promised secrecy. If I'm not sure I can deliver, I'm calling the whole thing off.'

'Hey, take it easy.' The bureau chief was suddenly all smiles. 'I'm not trying to make it hard for you. We're talking facts of life.'

'The facts of *my* life are I keep my word.' He stormed from Collins's office, wondering how much longer he would be able to say that with a clear conscience.

He reached out for Clemente. Finding Johnny before the meeting with Morales could make a big difference in how the meeting went.

'Juan Alvaro?' Clemente said when he called back. 'Same as before. Nothing. Nada. Zero. Not even a credit card. Not at that address, not in Manhattan. Not yet anyway, I only got one report so far. Maybe you ought to put him on one of those TV shows, unsolved crimes. Has the guy got some reason to hide?'

'I won't know that until I can ask him myself.'

'Look, I'm not saying we'll never find him. Only, now that we're past the obvious, it's all a question of time and manpower. You have to decide how important he is.'

And how visible I'm willing to let the search become. 'He could be an important witness on motive.'

'Yeah, well, that's what I'm saying. How important?'

'Very important. I don't want you calling out the militia, but I don't want you to give up, either. Most of all, I don't want the other side to know how much we care.'

'Sure – make it easy for me. I'll keep looking, just don't expect quick results.'

Estrada filled the blank spaces in the next few days reading about Roberto Morales. He took a walk with Mahoney to kick around a strategy for the meeting. There was not that much to say, the walk mostly a way for Estrada to put the meeting in perspective. Talking to defendants and judging the truthfulness of witnesses were meat and potatoes for him, and from that point of view, he told himself, Roberto Morales was no different from anybody else.

21

Unwilling to risk having Morales seen at the D.A.'s office or Estrada at hers, Kassia Miller had arranged to borrow space in a midtown law office. She met Estrada and Stein in the reception area and led them to a room walled in glass, its interior curtains drawn to conceal it from the rest of the law firm. The door was opened for them by a man in his late twenties. Miller introduced him as Barry Burns, her associate.

Roberto Morales was looking out the broad windows at a view that extended northwest past a cluster of office sky-scrapers to Central Park. He turned as Miller finished intro-ducing Barry Burns.

This was the first good look Estrada had gotten of Morales, more face to face than their brief encounters in court or the panic of a closer encounter at the zoo. He looked more his age, forty-six, than Estrada remembered. He was about five nine, slim hipped and broad shouldered, with the physical poise of a dancer. He was wearing a navy blue blazer and dove gray slacks. Rich, not gaudy, Estrada thought.

Miller introduced him quickly. Morales nodded, serious, seemingly relaxed.

As they stood by the conference table, a slab of rosewood with gently convex sides, Estrada looked pointedly at the windows. Miller drew the blinds, banishing the distraction. Prosecution and defense seated themselves on opposite sides of the table. Except for Miller's recitation of names when they came in, no one had spoken. It was as if violating the silence would tear the already strained web of civility that held them all.

Estrada opened the slim leather portfolio he had brought and slid out a folder. He looked directly at Morales. 'I know your attorney has gone over this with you, but for the record I'm going to read it to you now. If you have any problem with it, now is the time to say so.'

He waited for a response. Morales nodded.

Estrada read the substance of the agreement they had worked out. 'Should any prosecution be brought against Roberto Morales by the District Attorney's office, the prosecution will not offer in evidence on its direct case any statements made by Morales at this meeting. However, the prosecution can use information derived from the meeting directly or indirectly for the purpose of obtaining leads to other evidence, which evidence may be used by the D.A.'s office against Morales at any prosecution of Morales by the D.A.'s office, and the prosecution may use Morales's statements for the purpose of cross-examination should Morales testify.'

He looked at Morales. 'Is that the agreement that your attorney described and explained to you?'

Again, Morales gave the smallest of nods. Estrada slid copies of the agreement to him and to Miller. When Morales had signed them, Miller passed them to Barry Burns and Lisa Stein to sign as witnesses. Estrada made no attempt to collect them. He sat forward, elbows on the polished rosewood.

'Suppose we start with your background.' He had already decided that he would question Morales as unthreateningly as he could manage. However this ended up, he did not want to give defendant or defense attorney an accurate preview of how Joe Estrada conducted cross-examinations.

Morales studied the window blinds behind Estrada for a moment, then looked straight at his antagonist out of wide, dark eyes.

'I grew up in Brooklyn, partly on Southside, partly on the edge of the Heights. I was born on the island, Puerto Rico, in a small town by the ocean.' His voice was smooth and well modulated, without a trace of accent, but the words were stiff. 'My mother brought me here when I was small. My father was supposed to join us but he never came. It was hard here for my mother, so she had to put me with someone else. When I was seven I went to live with Tia Inez. She was a distant cousin of my father's. Her husband was Italian, a construction worker.' He shifted in his chair, giving physical form to his discomfort.

'Tia Inez cleaned houses. She believed in education. I spent a lot of time in the library. I loved it there, and it was better than being home alone with Tio when he was out of work. I was good in school, and I had a scholarship to Harvard. That was in the late sixties, when people were first beginning to think about minority students.'

As he listened, Estrada modified his opinion that Morales had no accent. His words carried the faintest spice of foreignness, more in the rhythm of his speech than in his pronunciation.

'When I got out, I was between going to business school and getting some real business experience. I was 4-F from the army thanks to a trick knee and a sympathetic doctor, so I didn't have to worry about that.

'I didn't want to stay in New York because I thought then that if I stayed I would always be just another spic. I had some money I saved from working in college and in the summer – you'd be surprised how much money you can make delivering sandwiches and pizzas in the middle of the night. I used it to get into the residential real-estate market. I got the idea working summers for a man who rehabbed houses in neighborhoods that were coming back from the dead, before anyone called it gentrification.' He shifted again.

'I started in Baltimore, because I'd worked there one of those summers. At the beginning, my old boss helped me. Then I branched out. Philadelphia, Atlanta. It was a business that didn't take a lot of capital, if you did it right. I got some help from the federal government, being a minority businessman. These were cities where the major racial problem was with blacks. I hired local contractors to do the work. I took the trouble to dress well and speak well. I look white. The neighbors didn't have anything to worry about.'

He smiled at the notion and turned briefly to include Lisa Stein. 'This was the mid Seventies, the late Seventies. The oil crunch was on. Inflation was everywhere. That helped me. It sent prices sky high on some of the buildings I bought when prices were low. I made a lot of money and I plowed it all back. I started buying apartment complexes. I rehabilitated, extended, whatever was needed. I got as much help from the government as I could, mostly as loan guarantees, sometimes as tax breaks. I started to sell the buildings to the tenants as condominiums. Flipping, it was called. It wasn't original, people were already doing it in New York, they had been for years. I used the same kind of techniques outside the city. I was getting rich, and I was also getting frustrated. I needed something more, I wasn't sure what. I came back to the city to find it.'

Estrada did not want to seem too captivated by Morales's recitation. Without missing any of the details, he was letting his attention seem to wander – to Kassia Miller and to the stripes of sunlight on the walls. The bright patterns did not register on him; Kassia Miller did. She was sitting quite still, her attention mostly on her client as he spoke. Now and then her eyes would go to Estrada or to Lisa Stein. Her petite body did not move, her hands were quiet. She did not seem tense or nervous, simply focused.

'It was in late 'eighty-four, early 'eighty-five that I came back,' Morales was saying. 'I was ready to rediscover my real roots and do something for my people. I don't want to praise myself or pretend to be some kind of do-gooder. I did these things for myself. I needed to do them. I got involved with Carlos Ramírez and some other community activists. I married Marti. I looked for ways to use my experience to make a difference. I saw what they were beginning to do in the Navy Yard, bringing in small manufacturers, and I saw what some of the housing groups were doing. I visited the new movie studios in Queens and the big center they were starting over there for interior design. I wanted to see what was possible. Then I thought of the empty tract of land on the East River, and I knew what I had to do.'

He had grown visibly more comfortable as he spoke, his voice less tense, his delivery less hurried. Talking about the Phoenix Project brought a glow to his eyes.

'Once I had the idea, I had to put together a plan that made sense. Then I needed a heavy hitter to help with the financing. In the real world, on that scale, I could never have managed alone, and I knew it.'

He sat back in his chair.

'How did you feel about the Phoenix Project?' Estrada asked.

'Excited. Committed. It was . . .' Morales trailed off, searching for the right word. 'It had the potential to be a lasting contribution, to change many, many people's lives for the better. If it worked, it was only going to be the first.' He paused a moment as if to savor the dream, just enough to be convincing. Then, almost apologetically, he said, 'I would have made a lot of money off it, too.'

'How did you find Jadwin?'

'You could say we found each other. I was putting out the word any way I knew how. I got some business and real-estate reporters interested enough to do pieces about what I had in mind. I never thought about looking in Texas. It was beyond my reach. Even if it wasn't, the boom was over down there. The whole savings-and-loan ugliness was starting to come out. But Cuyler Jadwin had his net out. He had an idea about raising money in Europe and Japan, and he was looking for something to hang it on. He read about me and my dream.' Morales looked at Estrada. 'A marriage made in heaven.'

'It didn't work out, though, did it?'

Morales closed his eyes and shook his head. 'No. That was the sad part. I was sure it would. I've been a confident person all my life. Sometimes when I shouldn't have been.' He said it simply, without the obvious elbow-nudge of irony. 'In all my life I was never so sure of anything as I was that the Phoenix Project was the right thing in the right place at the right time.'

'Tell me about you and Mariah Dodge,' Estrada said.

'Mariah.' Morales took a deep breath. 'I've known a lot of women over the years. For the past eight years I have been happily married to a wonderful woman who is the mother of two children I love more than my life. They were tiny when this happened, barely two and four years old. Now one is five and the other will be eight soon. They have had to live with it almost all their lives. I cannot describe how horrible it has been for them. Every minute of my life I feel guilty about that.'

He held up a restraining hand. 'When I say I feel guilty, please don't misunderstand. I don't feel this guilt because I killed Mariah Dodge – I didn't kill Mariah Dodge. I feel the guilt because my relationship with her is the reason this awful mistake has been made.

'Apart from that I have no remorse about my relationship with her. It was part of how Marti and I chose to live, from the first day. We have . . . I believe people call it an arrangement. She has always known I have sex with other women. She doesn't mind. She prefers . . . to be left alone. It has nothing to do with the respect we have for each other and our love for our children. Except for Mariah, Marti never knew who the women were. In this one case we made an exception because Mariah worked with me and sometimes they had to be social with each other, at parties or other gatherings for the company. It would hardly have been fair to put Marti in that position if she didn't know about Mariah.'

Was it more fair that she knew? Estrada wondered: Am I supposed to think that's admirable?

By Morales's account, the affair between him and Mariah Dodge had not begun until they had been working in the same offices for almost five months. 'There was electricity between us from the first time we met. We didn't act on it. Then there was a party, I forget the occasion, and I took her home and I didn't leave. I think at the time Marti was in Paris for the spring collections.'

From there, the affair had grown quickly. Mariah had not wanted him to come to her apartment regularly. The building had a large staff – doorman, elevator man, concierge. A significant proportion of the apartment owners were foreign and corporate, leaving their apartments vacant much of the time, so that the regular, full-time residents were of constant interest.

Morales had found the townhouse apartment in Little Italy and under the name Robert Messina he had rented it month to month. Altogether he had held it for ten months before Mariah's murder. He had quickly come to know Mr Censabella, his downstairs neighbor, and had paid him to look after the place when it was empty. No big deal, Morales said. Not a lot of money.

It was nicely done, Estrada thought: slipping it in casually, serving subtle notice that they would be drawing the fangs on that issue.

'Did you ever sense that Mariah Dodge was prejudiced against people of Latino heritage?' he asked.

'She was from Texas. People there grow up with attitudes like that. Let me explain something. I try not to think in those terms. I know there are stereotypes of Latino men. I've been fighting them all my life. My life is an example that there is nothing to any of it.'

'Did you fight?'

Morales leaned back in his chair, his eyes unfocused, remembering. 'Everybody fights.'

'Did she want you to leave your wife and marry her?' Nothing like that in the diary.

Morales sat forward. 'Where did you get that idea? That never happened.' Emphatic, but fully controlled. 'Mariah was not the marrying kind, and certainly not to me.'

'Why certainly not to you?'

'Mariah was a complex woman. She was happy to be helping Latinos in New York, though in Texas she had been taught to hold them in disdain. Even in Texas, she had done her best to put that aside and treat Chicanos with respect, but the negative ideas were there, under the surface. When we fought she said the thing that hurt most. With me that had to do with being stupid, lazy, greasy, insensitive, self-satisfied, selfish and overbearing. And treating women as if they were subhuman. There were some others, I don't remember them all. Once or twice she even tried some of the Spanish insults about mothers. I'm not completely immune to such things, and she was determined to get a reaction. If I tried to let it all roll off my back, she would keep on. So I learned to let myself get angry enough for her to know she had reached me. It was a kind of dance we did, part of what we had together. We were passionate with each other.'

He stopped again, smiling at some memory.

'Passionate, yes, but not destined for an eternity of passion. We enjoyed what we had. Neither of us expected it to last. But to have it end as it did . . .'

They took a break, moving to two small offices on opposite sides of the conference room.

'This is amazing.' Stein was full of pent-up energy. 'I can't believe I'm sitting across the table from a murderer.'

'What do you think of him?'

'You know what's really gross about it? If I didn't know what he was I'd think he was a nice guy. He's so . . . charming. Easy to like. That's what's so creepy. Because I *know*.'

Estrada, no longer so sure he *knew* anything about this case, was intrigued by how similar her basic reaction was to his own: there was nothing obviously phony about Roberto Morales.

'Suppose you were on a jury. Suppose he was on the witness stand and you were trying to figure out if he was telling the truth. What would you think then?'

She took a long time with it. Estrada would have preferred a quick answer like *I wouldn't believe a word*.

'I don't know what I'd think. I'm afraid I might believe him. Sorry.'

'No need. We can't afford to fool ourselves, even if the truth hurts.'

'Tell me about you and Cuyler Jadwin,' Estrada said to Morales as soon as they were all sitting down again. 'You come from such opposite backgrounds. Was it hard working together so closely?' Giving Morales the rope, to see what kind of knots he'd tie.

Morales glanced at his lawyer, then looked steadily at Estrada. 'He's a crook. I knew that from the beginning.' A more direct response than Estrada had anticipated.

'Why did you get involved with him?'

Morales tried a wry half-smile. 'I thought I could outsmart him. Mariah said I was crazy. She was right but I didn't know it then.'

'She knew about this idea of yours, that you were going to outsmart Jadwin?' No surprise, but not something he had expected Morales to volunteer.

'We talked a lot about work.'

'And she knew you thought Jadwin was a crook, as you put it?'

'Yes.'

'You told her that?'

'Yes.'

Estrada opened his mouth to ask another question, realized that he was beginning to cross-examine Morales and revised his approach.

'I'm not sure I understand.' As perplexed as he could manage. 'She had worked for Cuyler Jadwin for a long time. You must have known about that.' Unstated but clearly implied: How could you trust her? Hoping for: We were lovers, she was on my side.

'I knew she'd worked for him. I knew they'd been lovers, too.' He was watching Estrada for a reaction. 'Do you wonder why I took the chance she would tell Jadwin the things I said?'

Estrada waited, expressionless.

'It didn't matter to me. I knew she might tell him.' Morales took a long, sober look at Estrada before continuing. 'I only said things to her about Jadwin I was willing for him to hear.' He shook his head at the memory. 'It was part of the fun, trying to decide what was getting through to him and what wasn't.'

Estrada could feel a lump in his stomach where the lunch he'd eaten too quickly sat undigested. This was not good. This meant his spying motive was not going to work. Not if Morales was willing to get up on the stand and contradict it this calmly.

'So you were using her as a pawn in your war against Jadwin?'

Morales smiled fleetingly. 'It was nothing that calculated. I couldn't know exactly when she was going to talk to Jadwin, and I couldn't very well ask her.'

'You said you were going to beat Jadwin at his own game. How?'

'The project was going to take an enormous amount of money. To make it happen I needed a public presence, community support. General credibility. For Jadwin to do what he wanted, he needed those same things. He could get them in ways I couldn't. So at the beginning I needed him more than he needed me.'

'But if he took the money he raised . . .'

'That was where I thought I could outsmart him. I thought that the threat of exposure gave me some leverage with him. I didn't think I could stop him entirely from skimming money.' He looked at Miller. She nodded slightly, permission for him to continue.

'It was something I could live with if he skimmed a little

from the English or the Germans or the Japanese. If that was the price I had to pay to make this dream happen, I was willing. I'm not proud of it; still, I was willing. I wanted him to know I knew what he was up to, and that I wouldn't interfere with it as long as it didn't interfere with the success of the project.'

'How could he take money without hurting the project?'

'While we were in a boom economy, with people fighting to put their money into New York real estate, I didn't think it mattered if he was skimming some of the investment. As one example, he pumped up the cost of the tract we were using before he put it in the deal, profit he took for himself. The extra cost meant that the project had a slightly higher indebtedness but not enough to hurt.'

'But the project *was* hurt, eventually.'

Morales nodded sadly. 'The stock market crash of 'eighty-seven changed everything. It made me doubt for the first time that the project could be brought to the point where it was self-sustaining.'

For the following year and a half he had labored to salvage the project, convincing himself that for Jadwin's scams to succeed he had to keep up the appearance of progress until the economy recovered. But as time passed and the economy continued to stagnate, there were signs that Jadwin was going to cut his losses and bail out.

That had put Morales in a more desperate position. Without the Texans to serve as intermediaries with the foreign investors, he would be stranded. He had begun to search for alternatives. One of the bigger Wall Street investment banks had a fledgling Latin American department that was rumored to be aggressive and imaginative. Morales had met with the group's leader, but the banker had had serious doubts about the economic potential of the project, questioning Morales's basic assumptions. 'The bottom line, the way he saw it, was that we could build it but it would never get off the ground.'

Morales got up from the conference table and poured himself a cup of coffee. 'I hid from it. It didn't seem possible to me that the Europeans and Japanese who had already invested had been fooled so completely. That was stupid of me. What did they know about the real conditions in Brooklyn? It's easy to say that they had their own American advisors. That didn't keep them from overspending everywhere from Rockefeller Center to Hollywood.'

Morales stopped talking. He was silent, studying his coffee cup. Estrada could see in his face memories of hopes crushed, regret for self-delusion. Hard not to believe it was real.

'You knew all this, about the banker's opinion, before Jadwin told you about his plans to restructure?' Estrada asked.

'Months before. I kept beating my head against the wall anyway, looking for ways to salvage something. Even if that meant downscaling the project in a major way.'

'Were you making any progress?'

'You have to understand, my view of these things has changed since then. That was almost four years ago. My work then was making far-reaching deals involving large construction projects, large amounts of money to be spent over a long time. Today, I work for results that are much more immediate – a teenager saved from drugs, a poor mother and her babies fed and clothed for a week. I'm closer to the everyday life of the community. I remember something of what I thought in those days, and some of it I can reconstruct, but in many ways it's as if I were reporting a story told to me by a stranger.'

It was too clearly a speech, the first time Morales had let any contrivance show.

'To the best of your ability to remember it, then' – Estrada let some sarcasm leak into his voice – 'did you think at the time that you were making progress?'

'I did. I had an idea that involved a lot of sweat equity. Putting people in business for themselves.'

'Would it have worked?'

'No,' Morales said. 'I was fooling myself. In the economy as it was then and as it continued to be, it would have been a disaster. No, that's wrong, too. It would not have gotten far enough to be a disaster.' His smile was cold. 'At the time I didn't see that.'

'How much did Jadwin tell you about what he had in mind?'

'Not much. He said he was going to sell out a large chunk of the project to some Canadians and bail out. I thought it was a serious mistake.'

'Why?'

'For one thing, Jadwin's deal was going to disrupt the community.' Morales paused to look earnestly at Lisa Stein. 'I want you to understand that I'm not prejudiced in these matters. It's necessary to be realistic. There is tension in the community. People in a position to smooth the waters act instead as if they take pleasure in rocking the boat. Jadwin was selling out to religious Jews. They were not from the same sect as the Hasidim who have been a thorn in the side of Southside's Latinos. Jadwin thought that was significant. I didn't. The average person named José or Consuela doesn't make distinctions like that. Everyone in the Latino community would have been sure that once again they were getting the short end of the stick, and the Jews were walking away with everything good. It's not that simple, of course, but that is how people see it.'

Again, Estrada was disarmed by how much Morales was volunteering. It was a fascinating strategy, as if he were saying, 'Here are all my flaws. I'm putting myself at your mercy.' And yet, Estrada reminded himself, the man did not have much choice. Lying, if Estrada discovered it, would hurt Morales far worse than the truth.

'And is that what the Monday meeting was about?'

'Yes. Mostly that.'

'Where did Mariah stand?'

'That's the sad part. This one time, she was on my side and Jadwin's, both. She saw that I was right about how bad it would be for everyone if he went ahead. She wanted to save him from that fate.'

'Once he sold out, what difference did it make to him? Wouldn't he be long gone?'

'It's not like buying a car. There are several stages, and they extend over time. If there were obvious signs of trouble before the final steps were taken, Jadwin would have ended up with nothing.'

'He must have seen that.'

'I didn't think so, and Mariah didn't either. That was what we were going to talk to him about on Monday. That, and the possibility of an alternate purchaser.'

'Where did that come from?'

'Jadwin created it himself. The Canadians he was talking to were very respected. The logic was, if they're interested, maybe there's something good about this that everybody else has overlooked.'

'Did you actually have an offer?'

'All I had was more dreams. I had a conversation with that investment banker, the one who had been so clearheaded about the project before. He still wasn't interested for his own group, but he introduced me to some people at another investment bank who said they might be able to put together some of their clients to match whatever the Canadians were willing to do.'

'That's what you and Mariah were going to talk to Jadwin about on Monday morning.'

'Yes.'

Now Estrada had the opening he wanted. 'How did what you and Mariah were doing at the office Sunday night fit in? What were you working on that was relevant?'

Morales looked at him. 'What are you talking about?'

'You and Mariah were working on some papers that night. I assume it had to do with all this, and that's why the urgency.'

'I don't know what she was doing in the office.' Sliding neatly out of the trap. 'The papers that were found in her office had to do with finances. Some of them might have been helpful to what I had to say at the meeting Monday. Not all of them. In any case, I wasn't there, so I don't know what she had in mind.'

'But you did make a date to meet her there.'

'An appointment. We talked about getting together to prepare for Monday, and she said she had a new idea. I think that was what she was working on when she was killed. I don't know exactly what it was. From what I learned about the papers she had there, I couldn't figure it out.'

'Are you asking me to believe that you made a date with her, an appointment, and then stood her up for no reason, on the eve of this important meeting?'

'No, I'm not asking you to believe that. It didn't happen that way.'

Estrada stifled the impulse to ask another question. The man was on a roll – best to wait and see if he crapped out.

'I kept my appointment with Mariah that night. I was late, but I was there. I got there sometime around eight. She had arrived before me.' He closed his eyes and took a breath. 'She was dead.'

22

Estrada scarcely blinked an eye, keeping focused on Morales. Morales didn't have many choices, picking a story to tell. The revelation here was that this was the one he had chosen.

Stein reacted. Estrada could hear her sharply indrawn breath.

'That's right. I was there. I have not stopped grieving that I was too late to do Mariah any good. I don't know what went on there that night. I only know that if I had been earlier it might never have happened.'

A pretty speech, Estrada thought, with forced skepticism.

'How long did you stay there?'

Morales shook his head as if to clear away the memory. 'I don't know. I assume you've seen pictures. I saw the reality – someone I cared about deeply, brutalized and bloody. It made me crazy.'

'What did you do?'

'I stood there . . . a long time, I think. I kept looking at the body and looking away. I think I fell to my knees. I cried. Then it was as if I heard a voice in my ear. *Run*, the voice said: *No one will believe you if you stay*. So I ran.'

He put his head in his hands. When he looked up his cheeks were wet, but he was composed. 'I see now, I saw long ago, that it was crazy. I had no blood on me, and the office was a bloody mess. No one could have suspected me. But I ran. It was pure panic, pure horror at what I'd seen. I got out of there, and I went home.'

For a moment he seemed disoriented. He looked in his coffee cup and, finding it empty, handed it to Miller. Without a word she refilled it for him. He picked it up but did not drink. Put it down again.

'Once I had run away I was afraid to tell anyone. I didn't want to hurt my wife and children. My first thought was to deny being near there, to say I had been at home all night. But I was afraid that would involve my family even more than if I told the truth. Marti would walk through fire for me. She was savage about not answering anyone's questions, like a lioness. She would never say so, but I know how deeply it upset her, every minute of it.'

Now he was staring at the conference table, his voice a monotone. 'When I was accused . . . I didn't believe it at first. I was sure I would be cleared. I was also sure that anything I said in my own defense would hurt me, or my family. So I continued to say nothing except "I'm innocent." When I saw that once again I had made a mistake, it was too late.' He stopped. After a long moment he looked up at Estrada. 'Now I want to correct that mistake.'

'Why did you make it in the first place?'

'I had fled from the scene of the crime. I would have had to admit being there. Why did I run if I was innocent?'

'What did your lawyer say about all that?'

'I didn't tell—'

'Whoa!' came immediately from Miller, overlapping Morales's words. 'Hold on. Roberto doesn't want to talk about anything he said to his lawyer, or anything his lawyer said to him.'

Estrada nodded. She was right, once Morales breached the barrier of lawyer-client privilege there was no saying how far the prosecution would be able to go in that direction. Estrada might even be able to get Kubelik onto the witness stand.

Morales spoke up again. 'I thought that if I relied on my innocence everything would be all right. I was terribly wrong.'

'Tell me about the encounter you and Mariah had earlier, at the apartment.'

Morales looked at Miller, then fixed his eyes on the table again. 'It was . . . We got there around four and we spent almost two hours.' He closed his eyes. 'Excuse me, this is very difficult to talk about.'

Estrada made himself wait until Morales seemed more composed. 'Did she tell you she wanted to stop seeing you?'

'Yes.'

'How did you feel about that?'

'I wasn't surprised. It had been coming for a long time. But it hurt.'

'It made you angry.'

'Yes. Not so much the fact of it as the style.'

Estrada could not help thinking of Michelle. 'Did you fight?'

'As I told you, we were passionate with each other.'

'Did she call you names?'

'Yes, it was all part of it. As I told you.'

'And then you had sex? After the rejection and the fighting and the name-calling.'

'We made love. A way to say goodbye.'

'And that's when she got the semen on her body?' Wondering if Morales was going to mention condoms.

'Yes.' Eyes closed again. A sad shake of the head.

'Didn't she wash up?'

'I did. Marti knew about Mariah, but I thought it was grotesque to have another woman on me when I came home. I always took a shower.'

'Mariah didn't?'

Morales looked to his lawyer. 'Is this necessary?'

'It's why we're here.'

A deep breath. 'All right.' To Estrada: 'Mariah used to tease me about my showers. She was taunting me, in a way, when she didn't wash.'

Estrada sat in silence, waiting for more. Morales looked at him. 'That's all. That's how it was. She thought it was funny.'

Another pillar of the defense case revealed, a far stronger version of the story than Kubelik had used. He could not help feeling respect for Miller. She built well.

But what about Morales's condoms? Apparently he hadn't told his lawyer about his insistence on using them. Was he going to gloss over it in his testimony? Hope that no one else would raise it? Estrada rejected the idea of pressing him on it now. It was something to save.

He said, 'I want to go back for a moment to how you felt when you were there in the office with Mariah Dodge's dead body.'

Morales moistened his lips. Again, he did not look up from the table as he spoke. 'Let me tell you a story. Twice when I was young I saw people who had died of drug overdoses. One of them was in a vacant lot, I don't remember where, or why I went in there. Looking for a ball from a stickball game, maybe. I don't know how long the body had been there when I found it, but the rats had been chewing on it. The face was mostly gone. I can see it right now as clearly as I saw it then. It smelled . . . I can't describe it . . . I ran, just the way I ran from Mariah.' He stopped a moment. 'It was a horrifying experience for a young boy, to be face to face with the ugliest evidence of human mortality, the way we are all putrid and rotten in the end. That image never left me. After that I thought I was immune to the horror of death. I was wrong. There is nothing that prepares you for the sudden sight of someone you love who has had the life violently torn from them – and yes, I did love her. I stood there in that room with my feet at the edge of an ocean of blood, the same blood that had pumped through her heart that afternoon when it was so close to mine.'

His voice broke. He put his head in his hands again. After a time he looked up. In his dark eyes and in the downward curve of his full lips Estrada saw only sadness.

'No, Mr Estrada, I did not kill her.'

Estrada and Stein spent an intense hour going over her notes and filling in everything they remembered, getting as much down on paper as they could while the memory was still fresh and clear.

'What do you think now?' he asked her as they walked downtown past office skyscrapers like the one where Mariah Dodge had been killed. A front blowing down from Canada had scoured the air bright and had dropped the temperature back to a more springlike level.

'He's amazing. I don't know what to think. What about you?'

'He's got a good act going.' It was not what Estrada really thought; he could not tell her what he really thought. He said, 'If Kubelik hadn't been so intent on making the first trial into a circus about racist oppression, Morales might be a free man today.'

'You think so?'

'Suppose Kubelik had put him on the stand. Would you have voted to convict him if you were weighing our evidence on one side against the downstairs neighbor saying they'd made love in the afternoon plus what you saw just now?'

'It doesn't look very good, does it?'

They walked in silence for a while.

Estrada said, 'Let's assume he's telling the truth about what happened. Does it make any sense that he didn't take the stand the first time?'

'I can see why he'd be afraid to. If he didn't think his own story was believable, why admit he was there?'

'What's wrong with saying "I was there and she was dead and I got scared and ran"? How does it hurt him?'

'It makes him look cowardly . . . or as if he had something to be afraid of.' She said it tentatively.

'It puts him in front of the jury,' he countered. 'It keeps them from wondering why he's not speaking up in his own defense.'

'Don't they get an instruction about that? Not to make assumptions about it?'

'They get an instruction that no inference is to be drawn from the defendant's silence. But they want him to get up there and say he's innocent. And he didn't come across cowardly to me.'

'God, no. Me, either. I mean, it's hard not to believe him.' Struck by the implication of her words, she stopped walking. A man with a briefcase, coming up rapidly behind her, ran into her hard enough to knock her off balance. He barely apologized before hurrying on.

'You okay?' Estrada asked.

'Serves me right for being willing to believe the defendant. He couldn't really be telling the truth, could he?'

'Why not?' Estrada said it in the tone of a devil's advocate, but in his own mind the question was a real one.

'Why not! Because if he's telling the truth then we're trying to convict an innocent man. That's the worst. Would you do that?'

'Prosecute a person who's not guilty? It's not what we're there to do.'

There it was, unbidden and unwanted. And it was staring him in the face, a possibility he could not ignore.

To call for a dismissal of the indictment now was not a matter of exercising Joe Estrada's individual prosecutorial discretion. A lot was riding on restoring the public perception that the first trial had been fair, had been justified in the first place. He couldn't decline to proceed simply because the case was weak and Morales was potentially a convincing witness. He would need evidence clear enough to push the decision past Collins and Muir and the First Assistant and ultimately Bishop himself. Even then, from the little Estrada knew about Bishop, he could predict that although the D.A. might want to run from the case, he would insist on going ahead, preferring a courtroom defeat to an admission that he had allowed the prosecution of a man who might not be guilty. Knowing he could blame the result on any number of factors beyond his control. On Joseph Smithfield Estrada, if it came to that.

He became aware of Stein tugging his sleeve. 'Joe? You there?'

'Sorry. I went off the air for a minute.'

'Morales kind of got to you, didn't he? He sure got to me.

I guess that was Miller's idea. But it's not over yet. You'll find a way to nail him. Nathan is trying to get his boss to give him more time on this.'

'That's news.'

'He says he thinks there's something big. If there is, we'll find it for you.'

He looked around. They had walked all the way to Forty-second Street. To the east he could see the open sky above the United Nations plaza and the East River. The idea of going back to the office was suddenly intolerable.

'I tell you what,' he said. 'I'm giving you the rest of the day off. We've worked hard enough for one day.'

He did not want to go home any more than he had wanted to go back to work. On an impulse he took the subway to Brooklyn.

There was more litter on the grass at the Phoenix Project site, beer cans and discarded food wrappers. Aside from that nothing had changed. Across the water, sparkling in the afternoon sun, Manhattan still seemed poised to sail out to sea.

He wished his sense of the case were equally hopeful and unchanged. He did not like his impression that Morales was going to be a thoroughly credible witness in his own behalf. He liked even less the possibility that Morales had been telling the truth – shading it in his own favor, overdramatizing it, but basically telling the truth.

Estrada had gone into the meeting certain that he would come out knowing whether Morales had been lying, and when. He had trained himself to be good at making those judgments. Today he was sure of nothing.

Not sure did not mean he was without a sense of what he had seen and what it meant. It was getting harder to continue believing he was prosecuting the right man. A dangerous place to be.

More than ever, he needed to follow every hunch and lead he had, in the hope that something would cast enough light to clear the murk around the death of Mariah Dodge.

Walking toward the subway he saw a lone cab waiting at a light. He climbed in and had it take him to the old church that housed Adelante.

'Carlos is out leading the picketing at the municipal hospital,' a bright-eyed girl told him. Thanks, Estrada said and turned to go. The outside door opened and in walked Dolores Acampo, the head of Adelante's art and theater programs. He said hello and reintroduced himself.

It took her a moment to place him. 'Does Carlos expect you?'

'I came by on the spur of the moment.'

'Was there anything special you wanted?'

'I guess I've had enough of crime and punishment for today, and I need some hope and uplift.'

She laughed. 'You came to the right place. You're welcome to absorb as much of our hope and uplift as you want.'

She put him to work on stage scenery, wearing borrowed overalls. The teenagers painting large plywood panels thought it was a great joke to have a temporary assistant twice their age. He worked without urgency at the tasks they assigned him, enjoying the feeling of doing useful work with his hands and the unconcerned exuberance the five kids brought to their own tasks. They bantered in Spanish, their language so fluid and accented and colored with localisms that he understood almost nothing of what was being said.

After a couple of hours he put down his paintbrush and stood up to tell them he was leaving. Carlos Ramírez was standing in the doorway, grinning behind his beard.

'Doing some honest labor?'

Estrada stretched his shoulders and chest. 'I'll feel it tomorrow.'

'Dolores told me you were back here working. I thought she was kidding.'

'Next time she says it, she will be.'

He said goodbye to his five young bosses and went to change

back into his suit. Before he left, he stopped at the director's office.

Ramírez finished a phone call and waved him to a chair. 'We thank you for your volunteer labor.'

'It felt good. Those are terrific kids.'

'The best. Sometimes it takes them a while to let the goodness come out and take over from the darkness and suspicion they have when they come here. But inside they're all like that.'

'I see why a person might devote his life to this work.'

'If it was all pleasure and pride, everybody would do it. Mostly, it's frustration. No money, no cooperation from the city or the state, not enough facilities or physical space for all the things we want to do. And a constant battle with the temptations of drugs and drug money. It must be the same in your work – playing cops and robbers, putting away los malvados. A good idea, but not so simple in life as it is in theory.'

Estrada could not disagree.

At home he found three messages from Collins. The bureau chief's agitation increased from one message to the next. On the last one he left his home phone number, an honor Estrada would have preferred being spared.

'Where the hell were you?' The accusation was out of Collins's mouth before Estrada finished saying his name. 'Never mind that. What happened?'

Estrada gave him an abbreviated version.

'She was dead when he got there! What a crock.'

'He's very plausible.'

'You believe him?'

'He's going to make a good witness. A damn good witness.'

'You think he'll get up there?'

'Why else would Miller show him off to me?'

'Well, at least you know what to prepare for. It makes your I.D. witnesses important to pinpoint the times, especially the guy who saw him leaving late.'

Boynton, the janitor. 'He's strong. He'll be a good witness, but I'd be happier if he'd gotten a better look at Morales.'

'You think Morales is really going to testify about the semen? That she left it on her to annoy him?'

'If they think it will play.' Not a word to Collins about Morales and condoms, about Mariah Dodge's pleasure in the feel of sexual fluids, nothing about the diary Estrada still did not know how to handle.

The morning was over before Estrada and Stein were done reviewing and correcting the word-processed version of the Morales notes. A few minutes after Estrada had dispatched her to Collins's office with the finished report and a memo requesting more help from Masouros, the phone rang. Expecting Collins, he got Kassia Miller.

'I was in the office on other business. I thought I'd see if you had some time.'

'Come on up.'

Mariah Dodge's picture caught Miller's eye at once. She stood in front of it for some time. When she turned away sadness was clear on her small, precise features.

'I've never seen that picture. She looks so . . . vibrant. As if she were looking at you, seeing you from inside the picture. As if it were a window. It's hard to think of her as the woman in those horrible crime-scene pictures.'

'Not so hard that you have trouble representing her killer.' He regretted the cheap shot as soon as it came out. He wasn't going to gain anything by baiting her.

'You make me wonder if it was smart of me, not cutting off the idea of that meeting,' she said. In her soft white dress with its oversize black polka dots, a white headband in her dark hair, she could have been somebody's daughter visiting to see how her dad or mom spent the day at the office. Could have been, as long as you didn't notice the focused, mature intelligence in her intense brown eyes. 'Roberto had already told me he was willing to talk to you if I thought it would help, but I wasn't exactly encouraging him.'

'What changed your mind?'

'You did. You suggested a meeting. That wasn't something I was ready to do.'

You set me up for it, he was tempted to say. You fed me the straight line. 'Is there something particular I can do for you?' Everything he said to her today was coming out harsher than he intended.

'I came by to tell you that when you're ready to think seriously about finding better candidates for Mariah Dodge's murderer, I may be able to help.'

'Planning to finger someone for me?'

'Not exactly.'

'I'll bet "not exactly." If you had evidence somebody else did it, you'd be moving for a dismissal, not playing games with me.'

'I'm not playing games. I told you Roberto was innocent. Now you've seen him for yourself. Do you think anyone could believe he killed her?'

'I'll admit he's plausible. That doesn't mean he's not guilty, and you know it.'

'Tell me you don't have at least a reasonable doubt of his guilt.'

'That's a question for the jury, not the prosecutor.'

'I thought you were here to serve the interests of the community. Convicting the *guilty*.'

'That sounds right.'

'Not continuing a vendetta against a man who's been wrongly accused.'

'You really do believe that.'

She answered carefully. 'Yes, I really do.'

'If you're so intent on convincing me, why not give me what you have, now?'

'I have to be sure you won't try to use it against me.'

'How would I do that? And why?'

'You're a prosecutor. If I give you something that helps my

case and hurts yours I have to assume your first instinct will be to find a way to counter it, or to get it suppressed entirely.'

'Burying information that hurts my case isn't exactly my style.' Except recently.

'What about *Pandolce*? Billy Cakes . . . ?'

It caught him unprepared, though he had assumed she would do the usual research.

'. . . There's that fascinating place in the transcript where Kahn gets the snitch back on the stand, after he lied the first time, and has him testify about what he was really promised. His lawyer tells me you were the one who knew the real story and you didn't disclose it, not even to Kahn, until it was almost too late.'

She was too close to the truth for him to quibble about details. 'I learned a major lesson from that trial,' he said. 'From Larry Kahn, in fact. Give 'em what they want, he always said. You only get in trouble if you don't.' Count to ten without thinking of diaries. 'And I'm not in the business of convicting people who aren't guilty.'

'I'd like to believe you. But people tell me that's the ultimate test for prosecutors – you only really know you're good when you convict a defendant who's innocent.'

'I guess it takes a defense lawyer to take that one seriously.'

'I guess so.' She picked up her briefcase. 'I have to believe that you were impressed by Roberto. I know how hard it's going to be telling Collins and Muir and the rest of them that the indictment should be dismissed. If there's any way I can help . . .'

He did not try to suppress the smile that brought. 'Thanks.'

He walked her to the elevator. 'One of the things you learn over and over as a prosecutor is that the world is full of plausible liars.'

'I see a fair amount of that, too. On my bad days I think there's nobody in a courtroom who's telling the truth.'

'But Roberto Morales is different . . .'

She stopped by the elevator bank and turned to face him.

'Nobody's perfect. We all fudge a little here and there, on the nonessentials.' Her gaze was direct and intense. 'On all the parts that count, I believe him.'

Back at his desk, Estrada pulled out the police file. The DD–5's about Morales were as he remembered them: People had said a variety of negative things, mostly that Morales was full of himself, overbearing, insistent on having things his own way. Nobody had called him a liar. Then again, they had never seen him on trial for murder.

Estrada leaned back in his chair and consulted the portrait of Mariah Dodge. Miller was right, there was a vibrance about it, especially in the eyes, as if she were about to speak from within her two-dimensional prison.

'What really happened?' Estrada wanted to ask her, but she could not answer. Still, she had been more helpful than most murder victims, leaving behind pages of hints about the true nature of Roberto Morales.

That was the big question now: who was Roberto Morales, really? Most major-felony defendants came equipped with a long rap sheet that told you all you needed to know about who they were – career criminal, hard case, sociopath. There was an ugly logic to it. Billy Pandolce had been an FBI informant, perpetrator of dozens of well-worked-out robberies, a man who almost always got away with it. When he didn't, he would offer the phone number of his FBI-agent contact to the arresting officer and that usually did the trick for him – until he killed a prominent doctor from Boston at midday on a busy street.

First-timers were rare. Almost always they had been caught in the act or they had made a statement, or both. A case like *Morales*, at once highly visible and full of ambiguities and uncertainties, came to a prosecutor once in a career, if that. With these facts in a less prominent case Morales might never have been indicted. Maybe if Kubelik had tried harder to get Kahn not to indict, Kahn would have looked more closely at the diary before he gave it to the Dodges, and he would have discovered the value of talking to Johnny while he was still within reach. Who could say what the result would have been then?

Second-guessing was no help. He picked up the phone and dialed *Noticias Diarias*. Castillo was not at his desk. Estrada left a message, then called Clemente at the Task Force. 'How are we doing on Juan Alvaro?'

'Still nothing.'

'I need him, Tommy.'

'Yeah, you said. I'm spending so much time in gay bars the guys here are starting to look at me funny. I met a couple of people who say they knew him, but not from the bars. Introduced to him at parties, they don't remember where. At least the guy is real. Real, Cuban and rich, if it's the same guy, but nobody knows where he went, or if they do they're not saying.'

'Okay. Keep it up. Maybe one thing will lead to another.'

'The places I'm going, I hope not.'

Collins was skeptical about Nathan Masouros. 'You can have him for another week. He's been bugging his boss about it, too.' The bureau chief shook his head. 'What do you bet he's just looking for another shot at the juicy Ms Stein?'

Estrada did not say he'd had the same thought himself.

'Just remember, this is rape and murder, not fraud,' Collins warned.

Castillo returned his call. 'I thought you were mad at me.'

'It's not like I don't have reason.'

'I'm just doing my job. But all right, let's say I owe you one.'

'More than one.'

'Let's start with what you need today.'

'Suppose I wanted to learn more about Roberto Morales.'

'More than you learned from Carlos Ramírez?'

'More, and different.'

'Now? Then? When he was a kid?'

'All three.'

'What's happening?'

'Nothing worth talking about.'

Castillo was silent for a moment. 'Something's wrong. I can tell by your voice. You're worried about your case, aren't you?'

'You know I can't answer that,' Estrada snapped, then tried to redeem himself. 'The answer for publication is, I have every faith that Roberto Morales will be found guilty of the crimes he has committed.'

'Carefully not specifying what crimes those might be . . . if any.'

'You never stop fishing, do you? Make that of the crimes with which he is charged.'

'Fishing is my job. And my instinct. You want me to set up some meetings for you?'

'If you can.'

'If I *can*? You don't begin to know what I can do, my friend.'

23

Among the phone messages Estrada had not answered while he was preparing for the meeting with Morales were three from Tess Dodge. When he called at the end of the day she was not home, hardly unusual on a late June Friday in Manhattan. Less than eager to take his confusion home for the weekend, he took out a legal pad and made columns headed GUILTY and NOT GUILTY, began filling them with things he knew or suspected. It was uncomfortably difficult to keep NOT GUILTY from dominating.

The phone rang. Ginny, calling from downstairs. 'I was on my way out and I passed your friend Ms Dodge getting into the elevator to go up. I thought I should warn you.'

He thanked her and put the legal pad in a desk drawer under a pile of other papers.

Tess Dodge burst in. 'There you are. I thought you'd run off to join the foreign legion.'

'I've been busy.'

'I bet.' She had tied her hair back and escaped wisps of it curled around her damp, heat-flushed face, adding a dimension of wildness to her anger. 'I thought we were working together on this. I helped you with Mariah's diary and I tracked down Jadwin's little schemes for you . . .'

'It hasn't been that long since we talked, and I really have been busy.'

'Doing what?'

'Following up on Mr Jadwin's generosity, for one thing.'

'What does that have to do with convicting Morales?'
'I'm not sure yet.'
'Then why do it?'
'To see where it leads.'
'There's only one place any of this should lead – putting Roberto Morales behind bars for a couple of lifetimes.'
When he did not leap to agree, she looked at him closely. 'Am I missing something here? Is there some reason you look green around the gills besides that it's Friday?'
'Just tired. I ought to be getting out of here.'
'Something's up. You can't fool me, Estrada. Something's happening you don't trust me about.'
'Of course I trust you.' With the diary, she had more than repaid his trust. And with the rest of it, too. Most of what was bothering him he had learned through her. 'My only concern is getting the right result.'
'*The right result*? That's awfully damn cagey. Does that mean you don't think Morales killed my sister?'
'I didn't say that. I didn't say anything like it.'
'You're thinking it, though.' She stood up and advanced on the desk. 'You're supposed to be putting the man away.'
He had done this to himself, letting her get as involved as she had. He could not undo that now. 'If you'll sit down, maybe we can talk about this sensibly.'
'Tell me what's going on.'
There was no chance she would let him get away with temporizing. He had two choices: Try to shut her out of the process now, after having included her, even depended on her, or take her more completely into his confidence and risk her reacting badly to what he was doing.
Thinking about everything he had been through with her, he saw that the greater danger was in shutting her out. Like it or not, he had to keep her as an ally.
'There's one thing you have to understand. If I try Roberto Morales and it turns out he's not the killer, the real killer goes free. And I know that's not what you want.'

'Who's saying Morales isn't the killer?'

'Nobody is. But for the sake of argument, let me turn it around. Why do we think he *is* the killer?'

Anger flared in her eyes again. 'He was convicted of killing her.'

'Improperly, if you believe the Court of Appeals.' He waved away her protest. 'Make it a game. You're me and I'm Kassia Miller. Convince me he's guilty.'

'He was there. The security guards saw him.'

'In the lobby, not upstairs. But say he was there. It's his office, why shouldn't he be there?'

'*Her* office.'

'We don't know that he was in her office.'

'What about his semen and hairs on her body?' she challenged.

'From their lovemaking that afternoon.'

'Don't you dare call it that!'

'Sex, then.'

'His fingerprints were in her office and on the papers.'

'He worked there. He was the boss. Some of the papers were from his office.'

Her face darkened with frustration. 'Why are you doing this to me?'

'To show you we don't know as much as you think we do. All we have is a lot of circumstantial evidence, and almost all of it is ambiguous. When the judge instructs the jury about circumstantial evidence, she's going to say something like this – you can only draw an inference from circumstantial evidence if it excludes all other inferences to the point of moral certainty. We don't have anything like that.'

'Anybody can twist things around.'

'Not always. It's a lot easier to twist things when they aren't very strong.'

'Do you really think he's innocent?'

'If I did I'd be obligated to tell the court. I'm nowhere near ready for that. But I'm also past the point of taking it for granted that anyone can prove he's guilty.'

'There must be some reason you feel that way.'

'That's something I really can't talk about yet.'

'Oh yes, you really can. You're right, I want to see the real murderer convicted, Morales or whoever. You can't hold out on me now. I've done pretty good for you so far.'

'So you have.' She seemed to be taking this with surprising equanimity. It made no sense to antagonize her by holding back. 'There's a possibility Mariah may have been blackmailing Cuyler Jadwin.'

'What are you talking about?'

'I think that's why he arranged for her to get the apartment building. She knew about that scam you told me about, and she was in a position to send him to jail for it.'

'She could have sent him to jail for a lot of stuff over the years. She never did. Why should she change?'

'According to the diary, she and Johnny were up to something that had to do with Jadwin. The best sense I can make out of it is that they were putting pressure on Jadwin, right about the time he set it all up about the building.'

'So you put two and two together . . . and decided my sister was a criminal. Worse, a person with no more loyalty than a hungry snake on a hot day.'

Her voice was low; the words came out with icy clarity. He had been wrong to think she was taking any of this well.

'Do you really think Mariah owed Jadwin some kind of loyalty?' A new thought, surfacing from wherever it had incubated.

She started to shoot back an answer, stopped herself. 'That's a real interesting question. Real interesting . . . You're right, too. He was exploiting her from day one. She didn't owe him a thing.'

He said, 'There's still too much we don't know about this. For one, if Jadwin bought her off with the apartment building for that old land-price fraud in Texas, she would have needed something new to push him to murder. Johnny should be a big help on that when we find him.'

'If you can believe him.'

'That's a question with every witness. The important thing is to be sure we have the right defendant.' He stood up: interview over.

'There's something else that's important,' she said, not moving. 'I told you before I don't want you talking about my sister like she was crooked. She's not the villain here, she's the victim. You keep that right in the front of your mind.' She stood up. 'Didn't you say it was quitting time?'

'For normal people.'

'I'll wait and go downstairs with you.'

He took it as a truce offer. 'Okay.'

'Even if Jadwin had a motive,' she said as they walked uptown, 'why would he rape her?'

'Why would Morales?'

'Anger.'

'Anybody can be angry, if that's enough. And maybe there was no rape. The rape could have been faked to divert suspicion.' Even Morales might have faked the rape, on the assumption that no one would think he'd brutally rape his own lover.

'How do you fake a rape?' Tess asked.

'Doing what you'd do raping her for real, I suppose. Cutting her clothes off, to start.'

'She would have struggled.'

'I'd imagine that if a man was slashing your clothes with a razor-sharp utility knife you might be inclined to hold still. Particularly if the worst you were expecting was rape, not murder, and by a person who had been your lover.'

'Why? You think it's better to get raped by a former lover?'

'It's still rape, I'm not saying it isn't. But I'd think it might be slightly less loathsome, and there'd be less to fear from disease.'

The fear of disease was another reason to doubt that Morales was the killer. If he was as worried about AIDS as he seemed to be, how could he have committed such a bloody crime, cutting Mariah's throat not once but twice, standing his ground in a shower of blood?

'Rape is rape,' Tess said. 'That's the damn trouble – people talk as if it were some kind of sex, only less pleasant. It's like saying that if a guy jams a hot dog down your throat and holds your nose until you swallow, that's just another way of having lunch.'

They walked awhile in silence.

'Do you really think the rape was faked?' she asked.

'I think it could have been. Morales's semen was an extra touch of realism the killer couldn't have counted on. Or maybe he could. If he knew about the afternoon love match. Sorry. Sex.'

'How could he have known?'

'Maybe she told him.'

'Why would she do that?'

'Her telling makes more sense than hidden cameras. Or maybe Morales told the murderer about having sex with Mariah. Maybe that was part of the motive.'

'For Jadwin?'

'They'd been lovers. He'd be jealous of Morales.'

'He knew they were having an affair.'

'Suppose he thought they were going to stop and Mariah told him she'd changed her mind?'

'That's not right – she told her two friends she was going to break up with Morales that night.'

Except, Estrada thought, if Lynne Schelling had been telling the truth before she got worried about a perjury charge. 'People do change their minds.'

Tess stopped walking. Her eyes were fixed on his, a deeper green in the dusk shadows than he remembered them. He saw the challenge in them replaced by questions, by doubt. 'What do we do now?'

'Learn as much as we can as quickly as we can.'

When he arrived at the office on Monday, Ginny gave him

messages from Tommy Clemente and Pancho Castillo. 'Still no credit records,' Clemente's message said. 'Maybe bills sent to bank/accountant. Calling favors to see what I can get.' Castillo had left a name and a phone number for him.

Lisa Stein and Nathan Masouros were waiting to see him. Even first thing in the morning, the accountant reeked of cigars.

'We found something,' Stein announced excitedly. 'We worked over the weekend, and we came up with something important.'

Estrada settled in behind his desk. 'Okay. Let's hear it.'

'Jadwin was working a bigger scam than we thought,' Masouros began. 'I had assumed he was planning to skim money once the project got rolling – phony contracts, dummy purchase orders, that kind of thing. It's a natural in a big project like that. I never expected anything as wild as what we found. It looks as if at the beginning he was trying to finance the same costs over and over. Trying to raise multiples of what he needed, not letting one source of money know the others existed.'

'Wouldn't he have had to pay it all off, eventually?'

'Not if the project failed. That way no one expects to see any of their money back, ever. The amazing thing is, people do it and it works.'

'Did it work for Jadwin?'

'I don't know yet.'

'When is this from?'

'It began long before the murder, if that's what you mean.'

'After the stock market crash?'

'Yes, but we're not talking about American money.'

'It can't have worked, or why would Jadwin have been selling his piece of the company for loan guarantees and bridge financing?'

'Whether it worked or not, he had major larceny on his mind, and he went a good part of the way.'

'It's something to think about. Keep after it, see what you

find.' It sounded like Jadwin had an awful lot to protect. Motive for murder, and then some.

The man Castillo had arranged for Estrada to see about Roberto Morales was Father Gregory O'Neill, pastor of a church in the heart of Southside.

Walking south and toward the river from the subway station, Estrada passed quickly into an area where many houses had been demolished, leaving rubblestrewn lots. The buildings that remained had the forbidding look of abandonment. Even in the glaring summer sunlight there was something gray and chilling about these streets.

He had been told to go to the vestry building behind the church. Access was through a fenced-in, blacktopped yard webbed with cracks and fissures and pitted with holes. Once, it must have been a playground.

On the third floor, the stairway door opened into a large room that looked like an indoor version of the rubbled lots outside. Looking closer he saw that the litter might be of some use: a worn couch listing to one side where it was missing one of its stubby legs, an old doll house, a couple of battered plastic tricycles, a scattering of worn sports equipment.

A door opened at the other end of the room and a middle-aged woman stepped out; she was wearing a plain high-necked dress and a gray-and-white wimple. 'Hello. I'm Sister Martha. Can I help you?'

'I'm here to see Father O'Neill. My name is Joseph Estrada.'

'Come in, please.' She opened the door wider.

Father O'Neill was sitting behind a desk cluttered with books and papers. Bald, with only a fringe of gray hair, and comfortably into his sixties, he was wearing a plaid short-sleeve shirt and lightweight khaki trousers; nothing about him indicated his calling.

'Pancho Castillo tells me you want to know about the community.' The priest spoke slowly, in a voice so soft it was hard to hear. 'About how it is and how it was forty years ago and more. I don't go back that far, but we might find some of my parishioners who would talk to you. I have only one question – how does this help you prosecute Roberto Morales, and why should anyone here want to participate in that?'

Estrada decided to take a chance. 'I'm here as much for my own peace of mind as I am for Caesar.'

O'Neill smiled at the reference. 'Your peace of mind?'

'I hesitate to say my soul.'

O'Neill leaned forward, studying his guest, and for the first time Estrada truly saw the priest in the man. 'What's troubling you? Specifically.'

'Doubt. I want to do my duty, but I'm no longer sure in what direction my duty lies.'

'Your duty? To Caesar?'

'Would it be better if I said to right and justice?'

'Each of us has to choose his own master. Do you see any path to a resolution of your doubt?'

'Information.'

'Ah. I see.' The priest thought for a minute. 'You do want to know about Roberto Morales, then, after all.'

'Yes. About his origins, and the world he grew up in.'

'And you think knowing these things will help you resolve your doubts.'

'I hope so.'

'In which direction?'

Estrada spread his hands. 'That's why they're doubts.'

The priest nodded and leaned back in his chair. 'Roberto Morales came to Brooklyn before I did. I can tell you what I know from the stories I heard when I first came here, and the ones people have been telling since Roberto came back and made himself famous. Roberto's mother came here from Puerto Rico with two little boys and no man. She said she was expecting her husband to join her. While she waited she did her best to find work. She couldn't take care of the boys while she worked and looked for work, so she gave one of them to a distant cousin of her husband's and one to a woman she knew from home.'

'*Gave* them?'

'To raise them, as foster parents. She paid the women money for the boys' support. When the husband came north she was going to take them back.'

'If she could pay for their care, why not raise them herself?'

'It's common enough. A single mother can only afford to pay for her children's care by working jobs she couldn't hold if she had to care for the children. Two jobs, three jobs at a time, often.'

The priest's story matched Morales's, with added detail. 'What happened?'

'The husband didn't come, and the mother left the city in search of better opportunities, sending letters and money and then only money and after a time, nothing at all. The boys stayed where they were, growing up. Roberto's cousin was here, in the parish. I knew his foster parents well. Roberto I knew barely at all. He lived south of here, on the edge of the Heights. His people were not religious, and they were prosperous, relatively speaking. His foster father worked in construction, I believe, and the mother was a domestic. The couple had a daughter, a natural daughter, as well.'

'Really? He didn't . . . I didn't know that.'

O'Neill seemed not to notice the slip. 'I don't know much about her. I gather that she was an unhappy child. Her father was Italian, and she seems to have been torn between a need to affirm her Latino heritage and to be part of the so-called white world. She ran with the gangs here, sometimes.'

'Do you know where she is now?'

The priest shook his head. 'And her parents are no longer with us, I'm afraid.'

'So I understand.' That much was in the file. 'What about the others? The ones who raised the cousin?'

There was a knock at the door and Sister Martha looked into the office. 'I'm sorry to interrupt, Father, but Mr and Mrs Franco are here.'

'I'll be right there.' To Estrada, O'Neill said, 'I'm afraid

I have to tend to this. I hope I've been helpful with your doubts.'

'Very helpful. I wish we could continue.'

'We can. Next time perhaps I can introduce you to people who know more about this than I do.'

After the July Fourth weekend, Estrada went back to Father O'Neill's church. Late in the afternoon, he and O'Neill sat on folding chairs at a pair of flimsy card tables, drinking muddy coffee with Sister Martha and three of the priest's parishioners. All three had the condensed bodies and walnut-shell skin earned by living long lives filled with hardship. The two women wore unadorned black dresses and black lace shawls. The man was in a black suit worn shiny by the years and a graying white shirt. They spoke thickly accented Spanish that Sister Martha often had to interpret for Estrada.

O'Neill, whose smooth Spanish was a comfortable compromise between the harsh dialect of his three parishioners and modern newyoriqueño, led them into a general conversation about the old days on Southside when the Spanish-speaking population had swelled with people displaced from other neighborhoods by expressway construction and urban renewal, and with a wave of new immigration.

'Most of the newcomers were from Puerto Rico,' O'Neill explained. 'But there were quite a few in those days from Mexico, as well.'

That surprised Estrada. 'I didn't know there were Mexicans here. I thought it was all Puerto Ricans and Cubans and Dominicans.'

'We have a large Mexican community,' Sister Martha told him. Like O'Neill, she was speaking only in Spanish, out of courtesy for their other guests. 'The procession for the Virgin of Guadalupe is right here. They march on Broadway.'

One of the old women spoke up.

'Yes, Señora Rosales is right,' Sister Martha affirmed. 'In the time we are talking about it was much smaller. Only a few. It was harder for them.'

'It was hard for everyone,' said Señor de Passos. 'Too many people, too little money. Everyone came here to get rich, but they soon learned there was no gold in the street.' He stopped, as if tired out by the effort of speaking.

Señora Rosales and Señora Castro agreed with him vocally and at length. Estrada could not follow their anecdotes in detail, but the sense of hopes dashed and expectations unmet was inescapable. Now and then, Father O'Neill put in a word of agreement or encouragement. It took Estrada a while to realize that the priest was moving their reminiscences in the direction of the suffering of women with children and no husbands.

Even so, he began to drift, withdrawing from the effort of following a conversation spoken too quickly in a dialect he could barely make out. They had been talking for several minutes about a beautiful young girl named Elena and her children before something Estrada caught about her having to give the boys to friends and relatives made him realize he should be paying closer attention.

'Excuse me, but did you say she had two boys?'

'Beautiful boys,' Señora Castro said. 'It was a pity they had to be separated, and then their mother went away and never came back.'

'Such good boys,' Señora Rosales said. 'When they were young they were like peas in a pod. They were always together. Mis dos cuates buenos, poor Elena used to call them.'

'¿Cuates?' Estrada wanted to know. A word he had never heard.

'Sí. *Cuates*,' Señora Rosales affirmed. 'Compadres buenos. Gemellos.'

'¿Gemellos?'

'Sí.' She looked to the others for confirmation.

Señor de Passos seemed to be asleep, but Señora Castro nodded sagely. 'Es una palabra Mexicana,' she said. 'Los cuates son los gemellos.'

Gemellos, he understood. Gemellos meant twins.

* * *

'It was a surprise to me,' O'Neill admitted later. 'Both that the mother had spent time in Mexico and that the boys were twins. Odd that it's not more generally known.'

'Didn't Señora Rosales say that *cuates* could mean compadres buenos – good, close friends?'

'It's possible that they don't know it themselves,' the priest speculated. 'Their mother called them cousins. She couldn't have separated them so readily if it had been known they were twins.'

'What happened to the other one? You said you knew the family.'

'Yes. And he's still here in the community. You may have heard of him. He's called Carlos Ramírez.'

'Carlos Ramírez!'

'Yes, do you know him?'

'Only slightly.' Estrada was trying to assimilate the news. 'They sure don't look like twins. Not identical twins, at least.'

'Carlos hasn't had an easy life. Badly nourished as a child, where Roberto would not have suffered that way. And then Carlos is scarred by his years with the gangs and by the bombings and the jail time.'

'Jail?'

'Yes. He was a terrorist for a while, you know. Passionately political. After the Young Lords fragmented in the Seventies, he spent some time in Puerto Rico being trained by the FALN, the partria-ó-muerte people. There are stories that he was involved in bombings and a plan to kidnap the governor general. According to one story, one of his bombs went off prematurely – that's why he has those burn scars, and the limp. And he put in some jail time down there, as well. When you think about it, it's no wonder they don't look the same.'

24

Twins.

It was all Estrada could do to make a plausible exit and walk himself to the elevated subway station. He was wired from too much Cuban coffee and sticky with sweat from too long in the hot church; his hands were cold with anxiety.

If it was true, there was no way to convict Roberto Morales, not unless he could prove conclusively that Carlos Ramírez was nowhere near the offices of Phoenix Enterprises on the night of the murder. Because as far as Estrada knew, identical twins could not be told apart by analyzing body fluid or tissue samples.

He had nothing about a motive for Ramírez, but given their common involvement with the Southside Latino community it seemed likely that Carlos Ramírez and Mariah Dodge had not been strangers. And protecting Ramírez might have been a reason for Morales to have kept mum with his first lawyer. Who could say what the real relationship between the brothers was, what debts might be owed, what guilt Morales might feel?

Estrada made it back to the office in time to call Nancy Rosen and have her confirm that indeed, at the level of detail that the prosecution's experts reached with the samples available to them, they would not be able to distinguish between the DNA of identical twins.

He called Lynne Schelling. She did not recognize Ramírez's name, but she did remember Mariah talking about a Puerto

Rican she'd gone out with before Morales. 'I'd just met her then, and I think they'd had a nasty breakup. Then, when she got involved with Morales, she would refer to this other guy.'

'Do you know anything about any connection between the two men?'

'I think the first one worked for Morales for a while. Some kind of consultant. That's how Mariah met him.'

'What do you mean by a nasty breakup?'

'He may have hit her, I'm not sure. She didn't talk about it much, but I kind of had the feeling . . . And the other thing is, he wouldn't let her alone. He kept calling, sending flowers. Sometimes he was real sweet, and sometimes he'd yell at her.'

'Threaten?'

'What kind of threat did he need? Some guy won't leave you alone, that's bad enough.'

'How long did that last, not letting her alone?'

'Up to when she was murdered, you mean? I don't think so. She didn't . . . I don't think so.'

'Did you tell the police about him?' It was not in the DD–5s, as far as he remembered.

'No. It was something in the past. Besides, I was so sure who killed her, why would I confuse everybody? It's not as if the other guy ever did anything.'

He thanked her and got off the phone. So there it was. How did the old song go? *If the right one don't get you, then the left one will.* It was depressingly simple: consensual sex in the afternoon with Morales, as he had described it, murder by Jadwin or Ramírez in the evening. If it was Ramírez, add a rape and call it Ramírez's semen. For Jadwin, killing Mariah and making Morales look like the killer got them both out of his way. For Ramírez's motive, start with jealousy.

At home he took out Mariah Dodge's diary and went through the section covering the early days of Phoenix Enterprises. Sure enough, there it was: BIG DUSTUP WITH C. Reading it before, Estrada had taken C to be Carlyn Sims. Maybe not.

He called her. No, she did not remember any big fight with Mariah around that time. She did not remember any big fights with Mariah, period. They had bickered about all kinds of things, but nothing you could call fighting.

So the fight in the diary had been with Carlos. And given a pair of genetically identical twins with separate motives, the real world did not offer a way to prove either one of them guilty beyond a reasonable doubt. Not without an eyewitness or some other evidence more convincing than any Estrada had any reason to hope for.

Something was nagging at him. He went back to the cast file and Lisa Stein's index of the DD–5s. Under MORALES, IDENTIFICATION OF, he found four witnesses Kahn had not used. One of them, a woman named Rita Hazen, had told a detective doing a neighborhood canvass that she was regularly in her office on Sunday evenings. On her way home at about nine on the night of the crime she had seen a man leaving the building dressed in a long, dark coat over what appeared to be sweatpants and sneakers, carrying a gym bag – all of which had struck her as odd for a Sunday night. She had seen the man hail a cab and then, apparently agitated, decide not to get in. Instead, she said, he had walked off rapidly in the direction of the subway.

The basic description – a man in a dark coat – matched the other sightings of Morales, and the gym bag was an important addition. No bloody clothes had ever been found, and no murder weapon, and a gym bag was as good a way as any to carry them out of the building. But Rita Hazen's description of the man she saw had been vague at best. She had said she was not sure if he was white-skinned or light brown. Medium height, but he might have had a limp. A man as likely not to have been Morales as to have been him. It was no surprise that Kahn had not used her as a witness at the trial. Now, though, her uncertainties took on new meaning. Carlos Ramírez was medium height and had light brown skin and a limp.

Estrada had a momentary fantasy of bringing this Rita

Hazen in to show her a photo array with Ramírez in it. And Jadwin, for good measure. As if she would remember.

Larry Kahn was not yet in when Estrada called him in the morning. 'I have to see him first thing,' he told the secretary. 'I know he's busy, but he needs to hear what I have to say.'

In the Kahn Commission anteroom Estrada waited on the same uncomfortable plastic chair. This time a mountainous cop with a sweat-stained shirt and a 9mm automatic in a belt holster led him to Kahn's office at the rear corner of the big, bustling room, knocked on the door and ducked his head in. Re-emerging, he shook his head, not yet. Estrada could hear raised voices from beyond the partition.

Two lawyers came out, a man and a woman. They were so engrossed in conversation they almost ran into him. They went on across the busy office without apology.

Kahn waved Estrada into the office. 'Sorry to keep you waiting. What's the emergency?' He settled in behind his desk and waved Estrada to a chair.

Estrada went straight for it. 'There's a chance Roberto Morales is not guilty. I have to decide what to do about it.'

'It's a long time since April first.' Kahn was not smiling. 'What's really on your mind?'

'What I said. That Roberto Morales may not be guilty.'

'I really don't have time for games, Joe. I've got serious problems here, with serious consequences if I don't tend to them. Tell me exactly what you have.'

'For one thing, I have a convincing statement from Roberto Morales that Mariah was already dead when he got to the building that night.'

'And that's why you think—' He did not bother to finish.

'That's only the beginning. There are entries in Mariah Dodge's diary and other evidence to indicate she may have been conspiring against Cuyler Jadwin, that she probably blackmailed him successfully once and may have been about to try it again. Jadwin was in New York that night; his alibi is very thin.'

'You think he did it, then? Jadwin?'

'Possibly. There's another suspect.'

'Who?' Kahn's trademark fatherly manner was replaced by steely attention.

'Carlos Ramírez.'

Estrada watched for a reaction. There was none: Kahn was waiting for an explanation.

'He's a Southside community activist. He appears to have had an affair with Mariah Dodge. That's from Lynne Schelling, Mariah's health-club friend, who remembers Mariah telling her the affair ended badly, maybe with some violence. And I found apparent confirmation of that in the diary.'

'That's hardly enough to make him a serious suspect. How do you tie him to the crime?'

'There's a witness who saw someone who looked like him leaving the building at the right time. And he's Roberto Morales's brother. Possibly his *twin* brother.'

Kahn got the significance of that right away. 'Possibly?'

Estrada told him what he knew.

Kahn was shaking his head. 'This is nonsense. All nonsense. Roberto Morales killed Mariah Dodge, as sure as we're sitting here. But why are you bothering me with it? If this is what you believe, go to Lou Collins. Go to Natalie Muir. Hell, go to Bishop himself. I'm out of the loop, in case you didn't notice.'

'Not completely out.' Here it was: time to confront the man who had once been his ethical model with a challenge to the propriety of his actions. 'Part of the evidence against Jadwin and Ramírez comes out of Mariah Dodge's diary. I can't escape the conclusion that the diary is materially helpful to the defense. Is now, and would have been in the first trial.'

Kahn was shaking his head again.

Estrada said, 'There's more. I said Mariah Dodge may have been conspiring against Jadwin. The evidence for that conspiracy is all from the diary, and as of now, the co-conspirator is in the wind, and we're not finding him. But he was in New York for at least a few months after the murder, available to the defense if they had known he was worth talking to. Which means that if he's gone now and the defense has no access to him, they have a shot at getting the indictment dismissed for misconduct.'

'What have you been smoking?' Kahn's expression had changed to a weary tolerance. 'I read that diary. There was nothing in it about any conspiracy against Jadwin.'

'It takes a close reading to see some of this.' Estrada gave him examples.

Kahn listened impatiently. 'I don't know whether I should kick you out of here for disrupting my schedule or thank you for providing comic relief on a grim day. Do you think anybody but you, reading that kind of cryptic, ambiguous language, in a document of no known provenance or reliability, would see it as creating any possibility that the result in the first trial would have been different? Not on any planet in my universe.

'And this business of the alleged twin – you're basing that on the reminiscences of some aged Puerto Ricans about events more than forty years ago, hinging on the possible meaning of a single obscure word that may or may not ever have been spoken by a woman whose motives in the matter are suspect at best. That, plus the vague recollection of one friend that the deceased may have had a brief affair with this Ramírez, an affair that happened, if it happened, a year and more before the murder, and *may* have ended unpleasantly. Is that a fair statement of what you've been telling me?'

Estrada didn't think it was a fair statement of anything, but he could not think of a way to make Kahn see that.

'There's only one thing I want to know,' Kahn said. 'Why are you going so far out of your way on behalf of a vicious killer?'

'What makes you so sure that's what he is?'

'I prosecuted him the first time, remember? I investigated this pretty damn thoroughly.'

'I know how thorough you can be, but I've been going over

the evidence for months, and I don't see where we have a case against Morales. I've been reading and rereading that diary, prying it out of poor Mrs Dodge a page at a time, making excuses to myself for why I'm not turning it over to the defense. Telling myself you must have been right when you held it back in the first place. But now I'm coming to you to say I think you may have been wrong, honestly mistaken or too preoccupied to see what was there, and I want to see if we can figure out how to get this out in the open in a way that won't hurt anybody.'

'That's a great speech, Joe, but it's self-serving bullshit. I'm under fire from all sides on this Ellis indictment, and I have one coming up that's even more important and controversial. My people are taking so much grief that they're getting gun-shy precisely when I need them to be strongest.

'I have significant work to do here, trying to change the way a whole criminal justice system treats – mistreats, too damn much of the time – half the population it's supposed to serve. I don't have time to worry about some so-called diary that was junk when I read it and remains junk to this day.' Kahn's face was red but his voice was soft and controlled. 'If you don't get off this nonsense right now, you're putting all that in jeopardy, that and the hard work and commitment of the best lawyers and investigators I've ever been associated with. And you're putting both our heads in a noose – for no reason at all. Make no mistake, that diary is going to take you down too if you don't let it alone.'

'You're saying I should prosecute a man who may not be guilty.'

'I'm saying you should do your job. You don't know that Roberto Morales isn't guilty. If you're finding things that weaken your case against him you ought to be looking for ways to combat them. And if you don't have the stomach to make the best case you can, then you ought to step aside in favor of someone who does, while there's still time.'

Estrada was swept up by the strength and certainty in

Kahn's voice. Could he be right? Could all this be an elaborate version of cold feet?

'What about the diary?' Estrada still wanted to know. 'What about the man Mariah Dodge was plotting with? Am I supposed to pretend he didn't exist?'

'Unverifiable conjecture. Meaningless. What makes you think the diary's even reliable? How do you know she wasn't just trying things on for size? Embellishing and embroidering? Indulging in fantasy?'

'If it's so meaningless, why not let the defense know about it in the first place? Why give it to the family in secret?'

'I told you why.'

'You had to see it would be trouble.'

'We've been through this once, Joe. Either you get it or you don't. Believe me, revealing that diary now is pure death. Kill the family, kill my commission, kill yourself. And not do Roberto Morales any good, if doing him good is what you have in mind.'

'There's a way to avoid ever having to mention the diary,' Estrada said more calmly than he thought he could. 'If you said that the evidence in the first trial was circumstantial, marginal at best, and that if you had known then about Jadwin and about Carlos Ramírez you would have recommended the case against Morales be dropped. If we can get them not to proceed, then we can leave the diary out of it.'

'I can't do that. You know I can't. Even if I did, it wouldn't do any good.' His expression softened, slightly. 'Besides, if the case against him is as weak as you say, then he doesn't need any help.'

Estrada stood up to leave. 'You recommended me for this job. Why?'

'You're not supposed to know that.'

'Why not?'

'Confidential,' was all Kahn said.

'I'd like to know why.'

'Because I thought you were good. Because I thought it was your time, and you'd earned it.'

'Because you thought I'd hold back the diary. And you were right. Until now.'

Kahn shook his head sadly. He squared up some papers on his desk. 'If you'll excuse me, I have real work to do.'

'What's this about twins and DNA?' Nancy Rosen asked as she settled into the visitor's chair. 'Don't tell me Roberto Morales has a twin.'

'Hypothetical question.'

'Really.' Pure skepticism. She shifted, uncomfortable, tugging at her dress. Like much of what she wore at the office, it was loose and shapeless and covered with bright flowers; he supposed it kept her cool. Adjusted, she said, 'I'm going on vacation for a couple of weeks. I thought we should have a talk first, so we can get on with business when I come back.'

He wondered if Kahn had meant her when he suggested that Estrada let someone else try the case. 'What's on your mind?'

'We haven't exactly been a team so far. I've been blaming it on you but I realize it's as much my fault as it is yours. You probably think I hold it against you that I didn't get this trial as lead, that I'm second seat.'

'In all fairness, Nancy, you didn't make a secret of how you felt. It was all over the office.'

'It's true, I did think I deserved this one, and I did let off some steam about it. But I was mad at Bishop and his idiot advisors, not you. You're as much a pawn in this as I am.'

'All compliments gratefully accepted.'

'You know what I mean.'

'Look, you don't have to explain yourself. Bad enough they didn't give you the case, but then to put you under me . . .'

'No, no, that's all right. I mean, at least if I'm working on the case then what I know from the first trial can be of some use. Or it could be, if we were doing a better job of working together. I can't contribute if you keep avoiding me.'

'I haven't been avoiding you. I thought it made sense to have you running the forensics end of the case without any second guessing from me.'

'But I feel left out of what you're doing. That's where the real trial is, not the forensics, because Miller is going to give the jury an earful of love in the afternoon and then who cares about his semen? We'd better have more than that.'

And what if we don't, he thought. If the man is not guilty, what then? 'I'm going to ask you a question I should have asked long ago. What did you think of the evidence in the first trial?'

'It's a fair question. I thought we had a loser. Even though we didn't know about the afternooner until the trial, I wanted to expand the investigation, look for something besides the rejection motive, macho-man spurned, all that. Larry wouldn't hear of it.' She stopped talking, a look of mild surprise on her round face, as if she was unprepared to hear herself being so frank. 'Larry had his hooks into that one theory and that was all he wanted to know about. He was in a complete fog because of his wife, and there was nothing I could say. I was so frustrated, all the things I wanted to do and couldn't. So when the case got remanded, I thought I'd get a chance to do it right. It's true, when you got the case I was making everybody around me miserable. And then they told me I had to second-seat you. That was the worst. I was going to quit, but then I saw that was stupid. I could do better with you than I had with Larry. And then you turned out to have an agenda all your own, doing a lot of the things I wished we had done in the first place. And leaving me out. So that's my sad story. You think I resent you and the truth is you're doing it the way I would have, and all I want to do is help. I don't care about the glory. I just want to put the bastard away.'

He wanted to say something about the possibility that Morales was not guilty but there was no way he could do that now. He felt like a fraud, accepting her honest confession and repaying it with deception.

'Something bothers me,' he said. 'I understand Larry's being in a fog because of his wife. But why not let you investigate other motives?'

Her reaction was completely unexpected. She sat for a time staring out the grimy window, completely still.

'I think he wanted to nail Morales for being an adulterer, not a crook.' She said it softly, reflectively. Then she looked up. 'It was very important to him.'

'Why?'

She shook her head. 'I don't want to say more than that.'

The more Estrada pondered the situation, the surer he was that he had to take this to Collins and Muir. Even to offer Morales an attractive plea he would need Collins's agreement. That was the least painful way to deal with a defendant who might not be guilty: offer a plea and sentence too good to be refused. If the defendant took the plea, then the acceptance of guilt was on his own head, and the prosecutor was off the hook.

Collins was going to be furious. He was looking for a brave victory, not judicious disengagement. To keep this from torpedoing his chances to get Muir's job the bureau chief would have to be more creative than he had ever given any sign of being. The implications for Estrada's future were not pleasant.

The phone rang at three o'clock in the morning. He wanted to ignore it but it was too shrill, too insistent. He rolled himself out of bed and staggered down the hall, foggily assuming it would be Michelle.

'Hello?'

There was a woman crying on the other end – deep, racking sobs that obscured the words she was trying to say. Not Michelle. All he could make out was his own name and what sounded like the words *she* and *he*. He tried speaking soothingly into the phone: it's all right, catch your breath, it'll be all right.

Gradually the sobbing subsided. He heard the woman take great, gulping breaths; he knew then who it was.

'Tess. What's wrong?'

'Who . . . who . . . ?' She struggled to bring herself under

control. 'Who did you tell . . . about the diary?'
'Nobody. What do you mean?'
'Somebody . . . somebody told my father.' More sobbing.
'What? Told him what?'
'About . . . sex.'
'I don't understand.'
More gulping of air. Then, hurriedly. 'Can't talk. I'll call back.'
He sat with the dead phone in his hand, dazed, hung it up in case she meant soon. He hoped so, because he was not going to get back to sleep in a hurry if she didn't.
The phone rang.
'Tess?'
'This is her father. You've upset her enough over this. She has nothing more to say to you.' He hung up.
Estrada dialed the Houston number. It rang a long time, then was picked up and immediately hung up again. He did not bother trying again.

In the morning, having slept no better than he'd anticipated, he showered and dressed and drank two mugs of inky coffee, then called the Dodges.
Sylvia Dodge answered. 'Hello, Mr Estrada. Is there something I can do for you?'
'Is everything all right?'
'Why, yes. Shouldn't it be?'
He heard strain behind the sunny tones she was forcing into her voice. 'I had a call last night . . .' he began, abandoned that as going nowhere. 'Is Tess there?'
'I'm afraid she had to go out. She left a message for you. She said to tell you good luck in court.'
'I don't understand.'
'It's really been too much for her, worrying about the trial and all. She was *so* upset about her sister. The Doctor thought it might be best for her if she got away someplace nice with young people her own age where she could forget all this unpleasantness. So that's what she's done.'

'I thought she was there, with you.'

'Well, she's gone out, as I said.' Sylvia Dodge's voice was showing the strain more clearly. 'She's going to be awfully busy getting ready and packing. So much to do.'

'If you'd ask her to call me, please. I promise I won't take much of her time.'

'I'm sure she'd like to talk to you, and I know you'll understand if she isn't able to. It's really too upsetting. For me, too. In the future, if you need something please do feel free to call Dr Dodge at his office.' She recited the number. 'Goodbye now. We *all* wish you luck.'

Was it possible that Tess had actually had some kind of breakdown? Or was this the work of Dr Dodge? The result of Kahn's calling – it had to be Kahn – to tell Dodge . . . what . . . about the diary?

He shook off the thought. He had to do something right away to keep Samuel Dodge from destroying the diary.

The best protection against that was to get the Houston D.A.'s office to issue a search warrant and send cops in to seize it. Getting immediate action meant asking for a favor, and he knew no one in Houston. He did know someone in Dallas, his roommate at a training week run by the National College of District Attorneys. It had been two years since then, and Estrada had not kept up with him, but he was Estrada's best shot. He checked the clock, subtracted an hour. Perfect irony: too early to complete the call that might keep him from being too late.

It took him a morning's phone calls to get to the point of being on a senior Houston prosecutor's call-back list. Still seething with frustration he checked with Ginny to see what he had missed while he was on the phone.

'Lisa wants to know when you're going to be free. Nathan Masouros called, wants you to call back. Mr Collins said he'd be out all morning but he can see you after lunch. And Tess Dodge called.'

'What! When?'

'Just a couple of minutes ago.'

'Why didn't you let me know?' He was in danger of making a habit of yelling at secretaries this morning.

'You were on the phone. I didn't think . . .'

'It's okay. Don't mind me, I'm kind of on edge. Did she leave a message?'

'She said she wasn't going to be where you could reach her. She'll try again when she can. Something like that.'

25

'What's the emergency?' Collins wanted to know. 'You have something new?'

'Yes.' Like so much else, this was harder to do than to think about doing. 'It's not good news.'

'Sit down, sit down.' Collins came around and planted himself at his conference table. Estrada sat opposite him.

'This is something serious,' Collins said.

'Yes, very. Mariah Dodge was part of the Texas contingent at Phoenix Enterprises?'

'Right.'

'The man who brought her into it was Cuyler Jadwin. He was the financial guy, the banker.'

'And?'

'He was milking it. It was a scam for him, not a legitimate economic deal. Mariah Dodge knew, and she appears to have been blackmailing him about it. It looks as if he paid her off once, to protect an earlier swindle, and she was getting ready to hit him again, on Phoenix Enterprises this time.'

'Let me see if I have this straight. You think Mariah was blackmailing the banker, the one from Texas.'

'Right.'

'The defense know about this?'

'Not yet.'

'It's not going to help us. How sure are you?'

'Pretty sure.'

'Just pretty sure? Or do you have hard evidence?'

'There's the fact that Jadwin gave her an apartment building.'

'Larry Kahn must have known about that. It would have been part of her estate, right?'

'Hidden, undervalued. Nothing that would have rung any alarms at the time.'

'How did you find it?'

There were a lot of ways to answer that. Estrada chose 'Lucky, I guess.'

'Bad luck, if you ask me. Look, we all get jitters preparing a big case, it's nothing to be ashamed of. Just remember not to blow the negative stuff out of proportion. Murder victims are no cleaner than candidates for president, there's always something there if you look deep enough, somebody else they pissed off, somebody else they done wrong. It's meaningless, unless you give it meaning yourself. Go on, get back to work, and we'll forget we had this meeting.'

Collins got up. Estrada sat where he was. 'There's more.'

'Oh?' Collins sat back down.

'We're relying on Morales's semen. On DNA evidence.'

'Right.'

'He may have a twin brother.'

Collins blanched. 'What?'

'A twin brother with a motive.'

'You've verified this?'

'I have informal statements. I haven't been eager to nail it down any better, because it has to go straight to the defense and once it does there's no way in hell a jury is going to do anything but find reasonable doubt and send Mr Morales on his way.'

'Christ,' Collins muttered. 'I don't believe this. Does this twin brother have an alibi?'

'If he needs one, he can find one. This is a man who would have no trouble getting people to lie for him. None at all.'

'So then where's the problem? If he's got an alibi, he's no help to the defense.'

'But if he killed her, he's a problem for us.'

Collins's bulldog jaw tightened. 'I'm listening.'

Estrada gave him a quick sketch of the meeting at the church and what he had learned from Lynne Schelling about Mariah Dodge's affair with a possessive Latino.

'That's dumber than Morales's dumb story about finding the body, and lots dumber than the business about Dodge blackmailing her boss. At least that one makes some sense in the real world. The rest of this . . . twins that exist in some old lady's imagination. I think you're tired or something. Is everything okay in your life? That sexy girlfriend giving you a hard time?'

Estrada could not entirely wall out Collins's ridicule. It produced a surge of retaliatory anger, not the way he had wanted to approach this. He had been holding back about the diary, now he had to use it.

'There's more.'

'I don't want to hear it.'

'Mariah Dodge kept a diary. Larry Kahn knew about it, had it in his possession, and secretly gave it to the family, in the face of a discovery request for journals and diaries.'

'What are you saying? You accusing Larry Kahn of something?'

Estrada took a breath. This was the Rubicon for him: cross this and there was no going back.

'I've read the diary, and it corroborates the other things I've been telling you – the blackmail, the fight with the twin brother.' Giving it the importance Miller would if she knew about it. 'And there's a friend of Mariah's referred to repeatedly in the diary who was probably involved in the blackmail and whom she's likely to have told about Carlos Ramírez. This friend was available to the defense for several months after the murder, or would have been if they'd known about him, but he's gone now.'

'How do you know?' Collins was considerably subdued.

'I've had Clemente looking for him for more than a month. Nothing.'

'This isn't like the rest of the bullshit you've been feeding me today, is it? I mean, you've really got a diary that makes this missing friend clearly valuable to the defense.'

'Valuable enough.'

'And Larry Kahn knew about this diary.'

'Yes.'

'Have you talked to him about this?'

'Yes.'

'And he says?'

'He says the diary was junk when he saw it and it's junk now.'

'But you don't think so?'

'I think he had other things on his mind. The diary isn't easy to read, I had a lot of help from her sister. So I don't know if Larry intentionally buried the diary or if he was just careless. I don't expect the defense to make that kind of distinction.'

'You haven't told them?'

'I've been busy making up reasons why I didn't have to. I can't do that anymore. That's why I'm here. That and because I think that the way things stand there's so much doubt about Morales's guilt that people could think we're trying a completely innocent man.' Estrada stopped and took a breath. 'Frankly, at this point I'm not always so sure myself that he's guilty.'

Collins pushed his head forward. 'You don't do yourself a favor with that kind of talk. This diary is serious business if it's what you say it is. Let's stick to that.' He stood up. 'I want to bring Natalie Muir in on this. I don't know how much higher up we'll want to go, maybe all the way, but that decision isn't getting made right away. You did the right thing coming here.'

'We're going to want to have some verification on this diary,' Collins said as he headed for the door with Estrada. 'You have it, right?'

'I have a copy.'

'Here?'

'In the office?' Estrada's turn to be incredulous.

'Right. Smart. You'll need to bring it in now, so we can see what we're dealing with. Where's the original?'

'The family has it.' If it still exists.

'Does Nancy Rosen know about this?'

'So far, nobody knows about it except me and you and Larry Kahn. And the family.'

'Okay. Good. Let me see about setting up a meeting with Natalie. And don't say a word to anyone.'

He phoned the Houston prosecutor's office again, wondering as he dialed if trying to preserve the original diary was an exception to Collins's *don't say a word to anyone*.

Collins called Estrada back into his office at the end of the day. Natalie Muir, standing by the window, turned when Estrada came in.

'Lou told me about your problem. Nasty.'

Estrada nodded, wondering if she meant the diary or if Collins had told her more.

'There are a lot of considerations here.' She crossed her arms over her chest, making no move to sit down or offer Estrada a chair. 'My inclination is to suggest that you take a rest and let Nancy Rosen run the case from here on. She has the experience, she knows the evidence better than anyone.

'We've got Tommy Clemente on his way in to tell us about this missing witness of yours. I'm hoping we can do something about that, for starters. Meanwhile' – she glanced at Collins, sitting mute at his desk – 'Lou tells me that Nancy is going on vacation. That means you'll have to keep on with what you're doing, for now. Lou will be staying close to it with you. Giving you some backup.'

Muir made an attempt at a reassuring smile. 'This is no criticism of you, Joe.' Her tone was severe, the disclaimer unconvincing. 'You've done a great job finding all this, broadening the investigation, saving us from being caught by surprise if the other side came up with it first.'

She paused, her mouth pursed in distaste. 'Lou tells me you have some personal doubts about this. For now, just put that aside and assemble the evidence that supports the idea of Morales's guilt. That way, we'll be able to see our strongest case and weigh it against this other evidence you seem to have found. Starting with this diary. I want to focus on how seriously we need to take the *Brady* issue posed by the diary and your missing witness.'

'There's a new development there,' Estrada described his middle-of-the-night phone calls and his concern that Samuel Dodge might destroy the diary.

Muir and Collins traded glances, visibly calculating the possibilities this presented. Estrada, content to let them hang themselves on this one if they chose to, did not offer an opinion.

'What did you do about that?' Collins asked with a false ingenuousness that would not have fooled the densest witness.

'I called a friend in Texas to see about grabbing it before it was too late. The guy he put me onto in Houston won't move on it without something in writing, in advance.'

'Did you send anything?' the bureau chief asked tensely.

'No. I thought the two of you would have an opinion on how to handle it.'

'Didn't you think we'd have an opinion on talking to Texas in the first fucking place?' Collins was out of his chair, knuckles on the desk. 'Didn't I say don't talk to anybody?'

'I'd already made the first calls before we talked. It seemed to me I wasn't compromising anything by following up, and it could be a disaster if the diary was destroyed and the defense found out.'

'You should have cleared it first.'

Muir broke in. 'This isn't getting us anywhere. Joe, if you'll give Lou the details about whom you spoke to and what you said, we'll follow it up. We can come in at a higher level if it's helpful. You pay attention to getting the file together and going over it with Lou. Every single item.'

That was it. Natalie Muir had sketched the shape of the future, more by what she had left out than by what she had said. Joe Estrada would be quietly shifted into the background and there would be a circling of the wagons around the position that served the office best. Roberto Morales's fate would be a by-product of other, more important considerations. Larry Kahn, too, stood a chance of being saved. Probably better than Morales's, Estrada thought. He had the feeling everyone had already picked their villains, their decision perhaps made inevitable by the intolerable political consequences of having to admit being wrong from the beginning about Morales's guilt.

Muir might be leaving the office but she had the experience and instincts to be able to sense the prevailing winds, and she was not going to jeopardize her own smooth departure by bucking them. Her attitude was a clear sign that damage control was going to be the front office's first priority.

The question now was, what was Joe Estrada going to do?

In the heat of the moment the only answer he could see was to level the playing field a little. For months now he had been sitting on evidence that at least arguably he should have shared with the defendant. Sitting on it for good reason, or so he had been sure each time he made the decision to wait, but he did not expect the defense to see it that way. Now he was willing to err in the other direction, for balance, and disclose something earlier than he had to. Too soon he would be so far out of control of the case he would not be able to influence how things went at all.

He called Kassia Miller. 'I need to talk to you. In private and off the record. Can you meet me for a drink?'

'Tonight's not the best for me.'

'It's never the best. This won't take long.'

She suggested a place in their neighborhood where they could meet, an upstairs Caribbean restaurant he'd heard about but never tried. He climbed the stairs and found himself in a room that looked tropical and felt the next thing to arctic with air conditioning. The walls and windows were festooned with palm trees and oversize tropical fruits and parrots. Reggae played on the sound system. Kassia Miller was sitting in a booth reading when he arrived, a squat bottle of Jamaican beer in front of her. He ordered one for himself.

'Okay,' Miller said. 'I'm ready. It's your party.' She lifted her beer bottle in salute, but she did not drink.

He did. It felt uncommonly cool and refreshing.

'Do you know a man named Carlos Ramírez? He runs a youth center called Adelante.'

'I've met him.'

'I have reason to believe that Carlos Ramírez and Roberto Morales may be twins.'

She stared. Reached for her beer, knocked it over. They grabbed for the paper napkins propped between the bottles of hot sauce and used them in a hurried mop-up.

'Sorry,' she said as they mopped.

Their waiter arrived with a table rag and a concerned expression. She swept away the soggy napkins.

'It's okay,' Estrada told her. 'We'd like another beer, though. Two, in fact.' He was very thirsty.

'Fraternal twins.' Miller cast it as a statement.

'Not necessarily. Maybe identical.'

'They don't look like twins.'

The waiter put their beers on the table. 'On the house.'

They thanked her. Miller waved to the owner, a tall, handsome woman behind the bar.

'Try again?' Estrada raised his bottle. They toasted silently.

'According to what little I could learn, if they've lived different enough lives, identical twins don't necessarily look that much alike forty-odd years later. Malnutrition, accidents, scarring . . . Another thing you should know: I've heard that Mariah Dodge had a fling with Carlos before she got involved with Roberto.'

Miller's eyes widened. 'And I thought I'd had my quota of surprises for the evening.' She made circles of moisture on the table with the bottom of her beer bottle. 'You said maybe. Why are you telling me this before you even know if it's true?'

'Why not? If they're not identical twins, telling you is meaningless. If they are . . . I'd have to tell you eventually.'

'But not yet. So why now?'

He had decided what to say if she pressed him on this; it took him a moment to get it out. 'I'm anticipating trouble at my office. I may not be actively working on the case by the time of the trial.'

She did not hide her surprise. 'I'm sorry to hear it. I hope it's not going to be too bad for you.'

'However it comes out, this is information I dug up on my own. Right now it's a rumor, no more. There's no documentation of any of this, no formal statements, no proof at all. We both know I'm doing more than I have to, telling you about it now.' Because I don't trust my bosses to follow it up or to tell you about it themselves, he did not add. 'What I'm asking in return is that you develop it yourself and forget completely that anybody on my side ever had any knowledge of it.'

She thought about that. He could see the questions come to her mind, and he could see her hold them back.

'One more thing,' he said. 'If you get any confirmation on this, anything you could use in court, let me know. It will be more effective for your client if I can use it from my end, and it'll help me with my problems.'

'I can't promise you that.'

'Just keep it in mind. Try, if you can.'

'Nancy Rosen has been looking for you,' Ginny told him when he came in.

It was a call he did not want to make, but he knew he would be fooling no one but himself if he didn't. Collins and Muir had presumably already told her about their plans for a new regime on *Morales*.

She had the grace to volunteer to come up to his office.

'I had a meeting with Lou Collins and Natalie Muir,' she said in a low voice when she was settled in the visitor's chair. She was not looking at him. Her round face was blotched with red.

'They told me they were going to talk to you.' He did not want this to be any harder than it had to be, for either of them.

'They said they wanted me to take over the case.'

This part he could not help her with.

'I told them no,' she said.

He was not sure he had heard her. 'You told them . . . no?'

'You've been working hard on this, there's no reason to take you off it. I told them you deserve to be lead prosecutor. I want to work with you.'

'I don't understand.' An understatement.

'Isn't it enough that I feel that way, and I told them?'

'Last time we talked you were saying how upset you were I got the case and you didn't. Isn't this your chance?'

She started to cry, silently, her eyes squeezed shut.

Her tears confused him. What had he said? He tried to think of this as a witness interview: let her go through her emotions until the information he needed worked its way to the surface.

'You've looked all those places Larry never would,' she said. 'I don't know why they're upset about what you're finding. I was never a hundred percent convinced that Morales did it. But I couldn't say anything . . .'

'What are you talking about?'

She took a packet of tissues from her bag and blew her nose. Wiped her tears away. 'I suppose I can't keep this in forever. I hope you'll respect it, not go around telling . . .' The tears came again.

When she was dry-eyed she took out a small compact and looked at herself in its mirror. Dusted powder on her nose and cheeks, straightened herself in the chair. 'It was . . . I can't explain it in any way that makes sense. It was a hard time for me. I had just come back to the office from maternity leave for my second child, things weren't good at home, I was feeling fat and unlovable – fifteen pounds lighter than I am now! Larry was frustrated at work. The bench wasn't looking any closer for him, and he was full of envy about his classmates who were already in robes, particularly the ones he knew from law school who were on the federal bench presiding over huge cases. That's all changed now. He got onto the fast track going to work for the mayor and now with this Kahn Commission thing, but he didn't know that then.'

She shifted in the chair, tugged at her dress, wiped a sheen of sweat from her brow. 'I can't believe we were so stupid.' Bitterness in her voice. 'Working late, out for a nightcap. I suppose it happens all the time. Thousands of workplace adulteries every day in the big city. But ours was the only one we had. Not all that hot, even. We were . . . comforting each other, I suppose. I think I knew even while we were doing it – three whole times altogether! – that it was sad. Pathetic. But Larry didn't see it that way. Not that he saw it as some undying love, but it was *important* to him. And then he went home from our third time together and his wife told him she was sick.'

'Ouch,' Estrada could not keep himself from saying.

'New meaning to the word guilt. He became obsessed with two things – helping his wife through her ordeal and crucifying Roberto Morales. In fairness, Larry really thought Morales was guilty, and he may have been right. But it was crucial to him that Morales get it for fooling around. Except he had to be careful how he painted Mariah Dodge because he needed to have the jury feel sorry for her.'

'What about you? It must have been terrible for you.'

'It could have been worse, I suppose. Larry avoided me around the office – not as much as you did, if that's of any interest. The worst part was that there was nothing I could say about the case that he'd listen to. I was there to do my job on the forensics, period. And I felt too guilty, myself, to push it when I thought Larry was ignoring areas that needed attention. Ultimately he was doing a good job of making the case he saw, and he lucked out incredibly with Martinez's rulings on the hearsay, or so it seemed at the time.'

'That's a hell of a story.'

'Isn't it. So now you know why I haven't pushed harder for you to make me part of what you're doing, and why I don't think I should have the lead chair. It's because I don't deserve it.'

'It's not your fault . . .'

She tried a smile, almost made it work. 'I appreciate your saying that. But . . . look, I want to make up for what I did wrong the first time. I thought at the beginning I could do that best as lead prosecutor. But I've seen you work. I know a lot of what you're up to, even when you don't include me. I think you've earned the first chair.'

'Collins and Muir don't seem to think so.'

'They don't know what I do about how Larry handled the first trial.'

They sat in silence.

Estrada picked up a dart and threw it at the picture of Morales. It bounced off.

'We have so little, really,' she said. 'A couple of I.D. witnesses, hearsay about motive, and the DNA. But if they made love in the afternoon, the DNA doesn't necessarily tell us anything . . .'

'Suppose he admitted to being there but said she was dead when he got there?'

'Is that what he claims? A cynic would say it was fairly standard. But if he has a twin brother . . .'

'I'm trying to get verification from birth records, but nobody really knows where they were born.'

'There are better ways.'

'If we can figure out a way to get a tissue sample.'

'We could ask.'

'Just like that.'

'Why not?'

'Because he'd say no and he'd know we were after him and he'd be in the wind in a minute.'

'Not if we were clever.'

'I'm open to suggestion.'

'I'll think about it.' She gathered herself to go. 'They were real vague about why they wanted to make the change. Something about your not having enough faith in the case, or enough commitment. It's got to be more than that.'

Thinking of her as Larry Kahn's ally and, in a way, Joe Estrada's foe, he had never considered mentioning the diary to her. Now he thought he owed her that much, at least. 'I think Larry buried a piece of evidence that might be valuable to the defense. Muir and Collins don't like my attitude about it.'

Standing by the chair, she waited to hear the rest.

'There is a diary that looks to me like it might point to alternate suspects.' Softening it just a little. 'The entries are all kind of obscure, but not obscure enough to justify failing to make it available.'

'If it threatened Larry's theory of the case he would have been blind to it. He just flat out would not have seen what was there.'

'Unfortunately for all of us, understanding why he did it doesn't make it right.'

She sighed. 'Unfortunately.'

When she was gone he got up and retrieved the dart. The crisis was not past. Rosen might have turned down the first offer of his job, stood up for him, even, but it was only a temporary reprieve. He called Clemente.

'Big doings,' the detective said. 'You okay?'

'Surviving,' Estrada told him. 'We need to talk.'

'You name it.'

They met at an old Irish bar on Tenth Avenue with a

stamped-tin ceiling and a carved-wood back bar darkened with a century of tobacco smoke and wax.

'The bosses are awful interested in this guy Juan Alvaro all of a sudden.'

'We've got to find him, Tommy. He's the key to this case.'

'There's something you're not telling me.'

'What did you get from Collins and Muir?'

'All they did was ask. What did I know about this guy, what had I done to find him? If I had more resources for it could I do a better job? That was the part I liked best.'

'What'd you tell them?'

'Only what I had to. I said if I put a squad of guys on it I might do better but it still wouldn't be quick.'

'How'd they take it?'

'How do you think? They hated it. They want magic. They always want magic, these people. They're on your ass for something, right?'

'Did they make it that clear?'

'I'm a detective, remember?'

Estrada laughed. He was glad he remembered how.

'They wanted to know why you were looking for him. Something to do with motive, I told them.'

'And?'

'And nothing. Thank you, detective. They're not giving away a thing. Why *do* you want him?'

'Motive.'

'Dumb question. You want me to keep on looking, right?'

'Looking isn't enough. We need finding.'

'Maybe your bosses'll get back to me with a whole load of extra money and manpower, but I'm not exactly holding my breath.'

'There's got to be a way to find this guy. He can't just have disappeared completely. Why would he? Why would he want to?'

'You know, I've been wondering that myself.' Clemente finished his beer and waved to the bartender for another one.

'This guy has a good job, the company hasn't folded yet, and he's gone. Running from something. I figure it's because he can put Morales away and he's afraid Morales is going to do him like he did the woman.'

'Or he did it himself, and he's running from that. Or he knows who did it, and it's not Morales, and that's who he's afraid of.'

Clemente looked at Estrada appraisingly. 'No wonder they're putting some heat on you.'

'I'm not saying that's how it is.'

'But you think it's possible.'

'That's why I want Juan Alvaro so bad. Because I don't know what he knows, and I don't know what spooked him. I *do* know that there's a lot he can clear up.' Estrada waved for the bill. 'This one's on me.'

His beeper went off, unusual enough these days that it made him jump. 'It's the office. I'd better see what it's about.'

'I'll wait, in case you need a car.'

He got the cop on the desk. 'Mr Estrada, you had a call from a Detective Polk, uptown. There's some kind of trouble at your apartment.'

He raced out to the street. Clemente had a beat-up black sedan idling at the curb. 'Where to?'

'My house. Can we get the precinct on the radio?'

A break-in, the dispatcher told them. Polk was at the scene.

There were three radio cars and a plain black sedan double-parked outside his apartment house and a uniformed policeman in the lobby. Clemente flashed his badge and they went upstairs.

Polk was a heavy-set man in a wrinkled tan suit with the look of wishing he were somewhere else. He was standing in the living room.

'Estrada?'

He nodded. 'And Detective Clemente from the Task Force.'

'Kind of a mess, huh?'

'What happened?'

'Somebody broke in, looks like.' He gestured toward the splintered doorframe.

'Isn't this a big crew for an apartment burglary?' There were three more uniforms in the living room, no doubt having long since tread on any clues.

'Not just a burglary, maybe.'

'What do you mean?'

'They left you a message in the bedroom.'

Estrada started back that way.

'Be careful where you walk, and don't touch anything. Crime Scene is on the way.'

Estrada made himself walk slowly through the wrecked living room. In the bedroom, too, was chaos: drawers dumped, clothes everywhere on the floor. On the wall, spray painted in red it said MUERTE. A distinctive smell, out of place here, drew his eyes down to the bed, where he saw a pile of feces.

'They do that sometimes,' Polk said from the door.

Estrada pushed by him, back into the living room.

'Not very pretty,' Polk said. 'You're on that Morales trial, right? You got some threats, I hear.'

'Right.' They were still screening his mail at the office. He had not taken it seriously, had not even thought about it in weeks.

'You ought to get the bomb squad,' Clemente suggested.

'On the way,' Polk said.

Estrada went into the back bedroom. Papers had been swept from desktop to floor and the locked drawers of the file cabinet had been forced open, the files pulled out and scattered. Calling the bomb squad seemed excessive to him; he could not believe anybody wanted to kill him. He wondered if they had come only to scare him, or if they had been looking for something. He wanted to see if his copy of the diary was there, decided to wait until Polk and CSU and the bomb squad had done their jobs and left. He went back into the living room.

'Anything missing?' Polk asked.

'How can I tell, in this? It's going to take me a week to figure out what's here and what isn't. Any I.D. on the perps?'

Polk shook his head. 'Some old lady said she saw a couple of men, looked like they were in a hurry, carrying like a suitcase or a big leather bag. Couldn't tell how big or how old they were. White, she said, but they could have been Hispanic. Worthless.'

'Not much help. What about the doorman?'

'Nothing. The only thing he remembers unusual the whole day is a pretty blonde, broke the heel off her shoe walking by. Nice curly hair, he said. Nice set, too. He had to help her, you know, she kind of fell down. He probably copped a feel, made his day.' Polk shook his head. 'I don't blame him. It's not the best life.'

'A blonde?'

'He wasn't actually sure. Blonde or redhead. Kind of in between, he said. Why? That mean something?'

Estrada shook his head. 'Wishful thinking.'

Polk looked at him. 'Yeah, well, you come up with any names, nice-looking blondes, you let me know.'

26

He did not have Tess Dodge's phone number with him so he grabbed a cab across the park. Her doorman said he had not seen her in a week. Estrada started to reach for his D.A.'s office I.D., decided that was the wrong approach and palmed the man a twenty. 'I'm a friend. I'm worried about her.'

'What'd you say your name was?'

'Joe.'

'Joe,' he repeated, his brow creased in thought. 'Right. Joe. She's not here, Joe, but you want to come back around midnight, maybe the guy who's on then can help you.'

Estrada went back across town. The street outside his apartment house was clogged with double-parked cars and small vans crowned by microwave dishes. The press had arrived. A small crowd of impatient reporters, photographers and camera crews milled in front of the door. He paid the cabbie and walked the other way.

It was good to be walking, but he really wanted to be upstairs checking for Mariah Dodge's diary. Not that he thought he would find it, or his notes. He hoped CSU would have the courtesy and good sense to bag up the evidence on his bed sooner rather than later, but whatever they did he didn't see himself sleeping in that bed any time soon.

He called Mahoney. 'Had dinner yet?'

'I have a date.'

'The dancer again?'

'Yep.'

'Good for you.'

'Doctor's orders. He says if I don't start using it again, it's going to fall off.'

'Think you'll get lucky?'

'I give it one in three.'

'I bet it won't help your odds if I'm on your living-room couch.'

'It won't hurt either. If I strike it rich, it's her place or nowhere. Why? Who's sleeping in your bed?'

Estrada told him.

'Some world. I'll leave the key with the elevator guy.'

Estrada had a solitary dinner and went to a movie to take his mind off his troubles. When it was over he took a cab back across town to Tess Dodge's.

'Help you?' the night doorman asked.

'My name's Joe. The afternoon man told me to come back when you were here. Maybe he told you about me.' He came up with another twenty to refresh to doorman's memory. 'Tess Dodge?'

'Oh yeah.' He pocketed the bill. 'She's not here.'

The day's frustration surged to the surface; Estrada barely held in the anger. 'Don't play games.'

The doorman retreated a step. 'She said she'd call you. Said it was important.'

'She say when?'

'No, she was in a real hurry. Scooted in and got some stuff last night, then she was out of here.'

'Did you see the man she was with?'

'Look, mister, I don't want trouble.'

Estrada stared him down.

'Anyway, she was alone last night.'

'Before that.' Not letting up.

'Not to worry, okay? The guy was old enough to be her father.'

'Tall, white hair, impressive looking?'

'That's him.'

He palmed the doorman a ten. 'Keep your eyes open.'

The cop guarding his apartment door was just this side of sleep. Estrada showed him his D.A.'s office I.D. 'They finished in there?'

'They said you can go in and look around but not to move anything, they're coming back in the morning.'

The apartment felt alien to him, soiled beyond the indignity on his bed and the threat on his wall. It did not take him long to confirm that the diary was gone. He went downtown to Mahoney's and sacked out on the couch, woke up in an empty apartment. Mahoney's one-in-three shot had apparently paid off.

On his way to the office Estrada decided he wasn't going to tell Collins that the diary was missing, not until he knew more about what had happened, not until he had heard from Tess Dodge.

'That's really shitty about your apartment,' the bureau chief said. 'Sorry to hear about it.'

'Thanks.' Funny how what was in people's minds found its way to their tongues.

'Anything missing?'

'I've only had a chance to check superficially. It looks more like they were trashing things than stealing. They broke into my file cabinets. Maybe they were looking for more proof I'm not a Latino.'

Collins rubbed his chin, obviously uneasy. 'You know, Rosen says she doesn't want your job, she'd prefer to work under you. But after this maybe it would be best if you step down, anyway. Nobody would ask why.'

'And wouldn't that look great for the office, taking me off the case because some jerk wrote on my wall and took a dump on my bed? Since when did we start letting them frighten us off?'

'You're right about that.' For a moment, Collins seemed to tilt toward solidarity with Estrada. 'Look, Joe, we don't want to take you off this if we don't have to. If you stay on it, I'm going to be right there with you, help you make the hard choices. But if you don't think you can really put your heart into winning, let me know and we'll find someone who can step in for you, even if it isn't Nancy.'

I'm going to help you make the hard choices. That meant Joe Estrada would be on a very short leash indeed.

'I've never intended to give it anything but my best.'

'That's what I want to hear.' Turning to go, Collins was stopped by the photograph of Mariah Dodge. 'Do it for her. Do it for her family.'

If you only knew, Estrada thought.

He called Adelante. He had told Kassia Miller he would not follow up on Carlos Ramírez, but now he wanted to push things along any way he could.

'I'm totally buried,' Ramírez told him. 'We have a big show this evening. Music, dance, drama. I don't have a minute before then. Come out and see the show and we can go off in a corner and talk during the party after.'

On an impulse, he called Michelle. 'Surprise. I'm coming to see you this weekend. If I fly the redeye we can have almost two whole days.'

'That's terrific, Joey, only it's not a great weekend for me. Can we wait a week?'

'Who knows if we'll be alive in a week? I really want to see you. I really need to.'

'Well, if you put it that way . . .'

He had trouble containing his impatience as the day progressed. He answered questions for Polk on the phone, and at lunchtime he went home and verified that the diary was not there, packed up some clothes in a carry-on bag and left.

He did not know what to do about the missing diary. Collins was expecting it. If the copy was gone, Collins might decide he could back off on securing the original, figuring that if it was completely destroyed he could get by without letting the defense know it had ever existed.

Estrada walked down the hall to Collins's office and poked

his head in. 'I keep meaning to ask if you've heard anything from Texas.'

Collins frowned. 'They issued a warrant and when they went to execute it the house was locked and no one was home. The neighbors said the Dodges had all gone off a few days ago.'

'They ought to break in.'

'Why? If he took it with him, it's not there. If he left it there, he can't very well destroy it until he comes back. What about that copy of the diary you have? Weren't you going to bring it in?'

'I have to root around in the mess to find it and so far the cops haven't been letting me disturb things.'

Collins checked his watch. 'I've got a train to catch. Have that diary in here by Monday. No excuses.'

Estrada blessed the irresistible call of summer weekends and went back to his office to wait for Tess Dodge to phone. He checked his home answering machine repeatedly, with no success. If she did not call, he did not see how he could go to California.

The office was empty, deserted by the summering hordes. When the phone rang he plucked the receiver from its cradle.

'It's Tess.' Her voice was weak. He could hear street noises behind her.

'Are you all right?'

She hesitated. 'I need to see you.'

'Can you come here?'

'Someplace private.'

'It's empty here. They're all gone for the weekend.'

Another hesitation, longer. 'All right.'

She called back fifteen minutes later, sounding ragged. 'I'm sorry, I can't make it tonight. Tomorrow is better.'

'I'm going to be in California tomorrow.'

'I need to see you.'

'Come tonight.'

'I have to get off. I'll leave you a message where to meet me.'

'Tess, wait. Was that you at my apartment today?' He was talking to a dead line.

Reluctantly, he dialed Michelle to tell her he couldn't come. She did not take it well: once again she had disrupted her life for him, once again for nothing, and once again he didn't appreciate it.

He was not good at apologies; he did his best, but it had no noticeable effect. The hardest part for him was that he thought she was right to be angry. He called the travel agent and canceled his tickets, then booked himself into a small hotel the office sometimes used for expert witnesses.

The church building that housed Adelante was jammed with brightly dressed people. Tiers of temporary seats had been set up, boards on a pipe frame like the bleachers at a neighborhood park. The seats were full, and standees crowded the floor on either side.

It was a gray, muggy evening, threatening rain. The doors were open and three huge fans labored to move the air. From the back of the room, Estrada could barely hear the music over the enthusiastic buzz from the audience. He eased himself out of the crowd and went to wait on the front steps until the show was over. An hour later a few people straggled out; the rest were staying for the party. He went back inside. The air was thicker, and now there was the added fragrance of party food.

He caught sight of Ramírez, surrounded by admirers. Estrada did not like having to think of him as a murderer, liked even less the fact that the throng of celebratory humanity – the sweaty, backslapping, arm-squeezing camaraderie – seemed an opportunity to come away with something that might yield enough of Ramírez's DNA to be tested.

When finally Estrada was close enough to Ramírez to talk, it was in the midst of a crowd. Ramírez clasped him in an abrazo, breathed garlicky happiness in his face. 'What do you think, hey, Joseph? Something to be proud of, these kids of mine.'

'The best.'

'Did you see? Tanto talento, tanto pasión.'

'Sí. Maravilloso.'

'You wanted to talk?'

The crowd still pressed close.

'Maybe a different time.'

'Is it something serious?'

Estrada made a gesture of negation: nothing much. 'I was wondering about the time you spent as a consultant to the Phoenix Project. Whether you had a chance to get to know Mariah Dodge, see her with Roberto . . .'

Behind the beard, Ramírez's face clouded over. 'Serious enough. Of course I knew her, of course I saw them together. I have no stories to tell. You would waste your time to come back for that.' The sunny smile returned. He favored Estrada with another abrazo, more formal this time. 'Go, enjoy the party. I have to play gracious host.'

Estrada met Tess Dodge at the Staten Island Ferry terminal. She was late enough to make him worry he was in the wrong place, and when she arrived he almost did not recognize her, fooled by her mirror-lensed sunglasses and the wide-brimmed straw hat that covered her hair.

At the rail on the ferry's top deck a fresh wind tugged at her hat as they headed across the harbor.

'Okay. Now do you want to tell me what this is all about?'

She pulled her glasses away from her eyes with a sharp, nervous gesture, revealing a dark bruise and puffiness around one eye.

'My father made me tell him where your apartment was so he could get Mariah's diary.'

'It was the two of you?'

'He hired a private detective to do it.'

'Who?'

'His name's Mike, that's all I know. He's tall, taller than you, heavier, too. About forty or so, growing a gut, losing his hair. He looks kind of seedy, but tough and mean. I don't know how Daddy found him.'

'How did they work it?'

'Daddy knew I had your address, and he made me tell him things about you to help them plan getting into your apartment. Mike and his partner did all the actual breaking in. My father drove the car, and I distracted the doorman.'

'And you were the one who told them I kept the diary at home, not at the office.'

'No, damn it! I didn't tell him, and you have some nerve accusing me of anything.' She turned abruptly away from him and strode to the forward end of the deck. The breeze there was stronger, the spray heavier. 'My father already knew. I told Mom you kept it there when I was trying to get those pages. I had to, it was how I convinced her it was safe.'

'And she told your father.'

'He hit her, worse than he hit me. I never realized before how scary he is.' She tugged at the bow under her chin that held her hat, swept it off and shook her head and breathed deep as if more than her hair had been set free.

'Mariah was some kind of holy figure to him – his special darling. He made this huge fuss over her all the time. It was sort of creepy, but nobody thought like that, back then. People thought it was sweet when a father made a big fuss over his little girl. He was always buying her pretty things, feminine things. And he loved all that Homecoming Queen stuff. I think when she got killed it must have driven him over the edge.'

'Did he give you that?' The black eye.

'I tried to keep him from destroying your copy of the diary. He hit me.'

'Then he's destroyed it already.'

'Yes.' Leaning on the rail, she muttered something that was lost in the wind.

'Tess?'

She straightened up and faced him. 'I was saying it's a lousy damn way to talk about your own father. But I swear, when he heard that Mariah put her sex life in the diary, and that Mom never told him about it but she gave it to you to look at and maybe use in court, he just flat-out flipped. It was plenty scary enough just watching him and listening to him – he didn't have to hit her. But he did, he really walloped her good, and after that it didn't matter what he asked for, we'd either of us have given it to him.'

She began to sob, softly. Estrada pulled her head gently to his shoulder, not thinking about it, just following the impulse to be comforting. She leaned into him, crying harder. He stroked her hair.

After a time the crying subsided, and the tension of her body softened. He kept stroking her head. They stayed like that until it was time to disembark in Staten Island and pay their fare for the trip back. They rode most of the return trip in silence.

'I have some of it,' she said abruptly.

'What?'

'The diary. I have a copy of the part Mom sent to me. All the sex stuff and the "Johnny" notebook.'

'You really have it?' Not knowing whether to be relieved or upset. Part of him had been ready to hope the diary would disappear.

'Yes, really.' Her voice turned bitter. 'It's funny, of all the parts of her diary, that's the one he'd least want to miss. I copied it that first afternoon I had it, before you came to get it.'

'What did your father do about the original?'

'He burned the part my mother took out, the part I have the copy of. He made us watch.'

'What about the rest?' Joe Estrada's responsibility.

'I don't know. If he burned it, it wasn't when I was around. That's not saying he didn't, though.'

'Is there a chance you could persuade him not to destroy

the rest of it, once he's had a chance to calm down?'

'I might as well talk Chinese to a cow.'

'Maybe if you catch him feeling guilty.'

'I don't think guilty is on his list of emotions.'

He let it go. 'Do you have that piece of the diary with you?'

'Yes.' She patted her shoulder bag.

'We have to get copies made.'

'I already made a couple, yesterday. I put them different places, to be safe.'

'Good for you. We'll have to make some more. I'm going to need them.'

'This is all I have,' Estrada said to Collins, handing him a copy of the diary pages on Monday morning. 'The burglars got all of what was in my apartment.'

Collins pulled the pages from the envelope. 'How do you know this thing is a diary?'

'It's not a football. What else could it be?'

Collins flipped through the pages. 'Does it say it's a diary?'

'You mean, do all the entries begin *Dear Diary*?'

'Yeah. Anything like that.'

'Her friend in Texas says Mariah kept a diary, her parents talk about this as being her diary, her sister accepts it as a diary. What more do you want?'

'You sure about her parents?'

'I read the damn thing in their house. They knew I was there to see her diary.'

'So that's why you went out there.' Collins was not pleased. 'This is a great time to tell me.'

'It was *one* of the reasons I went out there.'

Collins handed him a letter. It was addressed to Hamilton Bishop on Samuel Dodge's office letterhead, and it was short and to the point:

> An employee of yours is falsely representing a part of my murdered daughter's unpublished writings to be a diary

of her life. This could not be further from the truth, and such misrepresentation must not be allowed to continue.

'You know why he wrote that, don't you?' Estrada said. 'He's worried about her reputation, and his own, if the diary comes out.'

'Has it occurred to you he wrote it because it's true?' The bureau chief took the letter back.

Is that why he broke into my apartment to steal my copy, and then destroyed it? Estrada was tempted to counter. 'What happens next?' he asked, knowing the answer.

'If this isn't a diary, if it's something she made up, then it's no kind of evidence and there's no reason for the defense to see it. Not now, and not three years ago at the first trial.'

'Suppose the defense hears that there's an *alleged* diary. Suppose they try to show that it's the real thing.'

'How are they going to do that? Who's going to tell them about it?'

'Try the people who wrote *muerte* on my bedroom wall – the folks who seem to have stolen my copy.' Estrada was happy that he had kept his mouth shut about Samuel Dodge's role in the break-in. 'Presumably they're on Morales's side, and exposing a diary the prosecution tried to hold back could be a way to get him off.'

'How are they going to know that?'

'They knew enough to take it when they came across it.'

'All right.' Collins was reluctant to yield the point. 'Let me take a look at the damn thing, this diary or whatever it is. Come back in an hour.'

'What am I supposed to make of this?' An hour later Collins looked as sour as Estrada could remember. 'It could be one of those subway ads – IF U CN RD THS U CN GT A GD JB.'

'The message I get is that there was a lot going on at Phoenix Enterprises, that Mariah Dodge had a good friend at work called Johnny with whom she may have been conspiring against Cuyler Jadwin, and that she and Jadwin had a falling out some time not long before she was killed.' He gave Collins a sanitized version of what WE'RE NOT IN TEXAS ANYMORE might mean, leaving out the possibility that Mariah Dodge might have been spying on Morales.

'You're trying to tell me this is all ammunition for the other side. If it's real.'

'I'm not ready to say what it is until we find Johnny and hear what he has to say. But you can see how easy it'll be for the defense to use it, as it is. And now maybe you can see why I get worried about whether Morales is guilty.'

'Not based on this, I can't. Maybe it's building blocks for some doubts if you push it real hard, but it's not proof of anything. Assuming it *is* a diary, which right now I am far from sure of.'

'Whatever you call it, it's an example of what Larry Kahn held back. If Johnny is gone, if the defense can't talk to him, they're sure to try to have the indictment thrown out.'

'I'll have to talk to Natalie Muir about it.'

Estrada returned to his office, gnawing on what Collins had said and his own responses. It seemed altogether likely that Collins was going to use Samuel Dodge's letter as a pretext for burying the diary, despite Estrada's bluff that the document might be revealed by the people who had defiled his apartment.

He checked with Ginny for his messages. Pancho Castillo had been calling since the break-in. He had called again. This time Estrada returned the call.

'Bad news,' Castillo said. 'You know who did it?'

'The list of people who claim they want to kill me is too long. I thought *you* might know.'

'Sorry. Nobody I speak to knows a thing. Don't the police have anything?'

'I'm talking completely off the record now – you don't print this in any form. Got that?'

'You're a hard man.'

'That's because I'm a man whose life has been threatened.' The Doctor's attempt to divert suspicion was turning out to have many uses.

'Okay, I never heard whatever it is you're not about to say.'

'I don't think the cops have a thing.'

'Is it true somebody shit on your bed?'

'Where do you hear such things?'

'I take it that's not a no.'

'It's not a yes, either. It's amazement at the imagination of your sources.'

'When are you ever going to make this easy?'

Estrada took a breath. 'There is one thing. I don't know what it's worth. Absolutely off the record. There's a rumor . . .' He stopped. There was time, he didn't have to do this yet. There were other ways.

'A rumor?' Castillo prodded.

'It's not even worth talking about. Forget I said anything.'

'Joseph, you have to honor your impulses. If you were going to tell me something, you must have had a reason.'

'It's nothing, believe me.'

Silence, then: 'You know where to find me when you're ready.'

As soon as he got off the phone with Castillo, Estrada called Larry Kahn.

'In a meeting,' his secretary said.

'Ask him to call me,' Estrada requested pleasantly and went straight over to the Kahn Commission offices.

The security guard barely looked up from the tabloid spread out on his desk when Estrada gave his name.

'Mr Kahn expecting you?'

'Not right now. But if you'll tell him it's urgent . . .'

'Urgent's all we got here, buddy.' He went back to his newspaper.

'Tell him Collins and Muir are interested in his diary.'

'Say what?'

Estrada repeated the message, and the skeptical guard

Estrada doubted the Houston cops would take the time to distinguish between a Sicilian-American and a Chicano, especially a Sicilian-American with a Spanish-sounding name working for an A.D.A. named Estrada. He took McMorris to Texas.

It turned out to be a good move. The rangy detective who met them at the airport introduced himself with a flash of his badge and a curt, 'Detective Sergeant Imes. Car's outside.' Estrada sat in back, letting McMorris ride shotgun. The two detectives were talking shop in obscene monosyllables before Imes had them off the airport exit road.

At the Dodge house they were met by a pair of uniformed cops and another detective.

'Nobody home,' the detective reported. 'And the doctor's not at his office.'

'Okay,' Imes said. 'The warrant says we go in anyway, but I don't have to like it. These people have their neighbors' respect, and they suffered plenty with their daughter getting killed. I want this quick and clean.'

Samuel Dodge came home while they were deciding what to do about the locked file cabinets in his study.

'What are you men doing in my house?' he asked Imes with near-perfect dignity. He glanced once at McMorris but behaved as if Estrada were invisible.

'Don't mean to startle you, sir. We have a warrant.' Imes handed it to him. 'We're looking for some notebooks we believe might be your daughter's diary.'

'I don't have any such thing. You're wasting your time.'

'Yes, sir, I appreciate your concern but I have to do my job here, and this warrant says to find these notebooks. I'd purely like to take your word for it that they're not here, but we're gonna have to look around before I can do that. It'd be a sight easier on everybody if you just told us where they are. You have all these books and files and papers, and all . . .'

Dr Dodge cleared his throat, but did not speak. He tried to stare the detective down. Imes stood his ground – nothing aggressive about it, almost apologetic in the way his thin shoulders stooped and his head tilted. He was no taller than Dodge but he seemed to be looking down on him.

'There's no need to tear everything apart,' Dodge said finally, his back even straighter than when he had been playing outraged lord of the castle. He dug into his vest pocket for a ring of keys attached to his gold watch chain and opened the file cabinets. Three notebooks were tucked into the back of each drawer, concealed by the files in front of them.

'This is all I have,' he said when they were piled on his desk. 'I destroyed the others. I should have destroyed them all.'

'What do you propose to do with these?' Collins asked. The notebooks were stacked in two neat piles in the middle of the bureau chief's small conference table. Muir was watching from near the window, arms crossed over her chest.

'Go to the judge for a protective order, so we can withhold them from the defense until we find Johnny. I know there's a risk we'll be turned down, but we need to make the application. If we don't, and the diary comes out somehow, we're all in trouble.'

'You've obviously been giving this a lot of thought,' Collins commented without a glance at Muir.

'It's our biggest problem.'

'All right,' Collins said abruptly. 'You've got it. But it means convincing Martinez that there's nothing in the diary, as it stands, to make it *Brady* material.'

'I understand that.'

'The question is, can you do it?' Collins prodded. 'I want to hear what you're going to say.'

Haltingly at first, Estrada ran through a rough argument in favor of keeping the diary a secret until Johnny was found.

'All right, it's an approach worth trying, but it means finding this Johnny, whatever resources it takes.' Collins stood up, ending the meeting.

They had it all worked out before I ever set foot in the

room, Estrada thought on his way back to his office: Muir had not said a word; Collins had never looked at her, never checked whether to go ahead. They've given me the rope, and now I have to keep from hanging myself.

Acting Supreme Court Justice Luz Martinez glowered at him from behind her desk. 'I don't like ex parte communications, Mr Estrada. The defense ought to be here, and if you don't convince me in a hurry that there's a good reason for this I'm going to pick up the phone and invite them to the party.' She waved a hand at the stenographer Estrada had asked to have present. 'You can start now, Rosemary.'

Estrada's dry tongue failed to moisten his lips. 'Your honor, I'm here to make a motion for a protective order under section 240.50 of the Criminal Procedure Law. My intention is to protect the court and the trial process from inflammatory material about the victim in this case, material that is almost certainly irrelevant but that once revealed could cause no end of mischief.'

'A laudable goal, Mr Estrada, but don't you think the defense would share it?'

'Nothing against Ms Miller, your honor, but I can't be confident of that, not where the potential exists to confuse the issues by creating an atmosphere antagonistic to the victim. Other defense counsel have in the past used personal diaries to stimulate vicious speculation in the press about the victim's sex life – on at least one occasion with no knowledge of the actual content of the alleged diary. I'll concede that in the future there may be a *Brady* issue here. Against that, there's the danger right now of impeding and distorting the progress of this trial if this material is disclosed prematurely. And it's sure to cause great anguish to the victim's family, whenever it's disclosed, a result that we all have an interest in avoiding if at all possible.'

The words rang in his ears, too much like soap-box oratory for this cramped room. But he was speaking as much for the record as for the judge. 'The language of the statute allows the court to limit discovery for any good cause, and it specifically mentions 'unjustified annoyance or embarrassment to any person' and 'an adverse effect on the legitimate needs of law enforcement.' That's 240.50 sub one. And taking unjustified annoyance and embarrassment first, I can assure you, judge, that does not begin to cover the effect this material would have on the victim's family. Even if it's never disclosed, consider the anguish of having the man they believe their daughter's murderer given access to her most private thoughts. That alone is reason to deny the defendant access unless it's absolutely required in the interest of justice, which is far from the case.'

Martinez raised her hand in a stop signal to the stenographer, took off her reading glasses and polished them with a facial tissue. 'You know, Mr Estrada, it's a wonder to me how nobody ever has an unimportant problem. How is it that everybody who comes in here has a direct line to such earth-shaking questions?' She stopped polishing her glasses and fixed him with a dyspeptic stare. 'I often wonder how many of us are fit for the responsibility of such weighty problems.' She put her glasses back on, nodded to the stenographer, and picked up a large black fountain pen. 'Go ahead, Mr Estrada, tell us your story.'

He kept it simple and to the point: There was a diary. Kahn had not thought it was worth bothering with. Estrada, on a close reading, felt that it might contain useful leads for the prosecution, but the language of the diary was incomplete and unclear. He believed, however, that a man named Juan Alvaro could clear up the questions raised by the diary.

In the meantime, he argued, it was vital to keep the diary's existence secret. Because if even its existence were known the diary would arouse a press already inclined to make the case into a media circus. If Alvaro's evidence indicated that the diary did not favor the defense, then the diary could remain private, as demanded by respect for the family and the memory of the deceased, and the best way to preserve the possibility of a fair trial. Even if Alvaro offered evidence that helped the defense, his testimony might well be complete enough in itself to make exposing the diary to the defendant, and possibly the world, unnecessary.

'Let me see if I understand you.' Martinez shifted her bulk behind the desk, the better to glare at him. 'You want to delay revealing this intensely personal but incendiary diary to the defense until you find this missing person who can tell you what it all means, and when you find him you'll know if the defense should see it.'

'Yes, your honor, that's how I'd like to handle it.'

'You're assuming you'll find him.'

'Yes, I am.'

'And when might that be?'

'As soon as possible.'

The judge leaned toward him, peering over the top of her glasses. 'Mr Estrada, if you'd try harder not to insult my intelligence it might help me appreciate your argument.' The stenographer's hands were still; she seemed to know this was another of Martinez's asides.

He felt his own hands go cold. This was the crux of it and he was starting badly. He resisted the impulse to apologize. 'I'm hoping to put Mr Alvaro on the stand to testify for the prosecution. If it turns out that he can help the defense, it's only fair that they know about it before they begin their case. That means that from both my point of view and the defense's I need to find him before I finish my case in chief. If I don't, then at that point it clearly becomes relevant that he's gone.'

'But you think it's fair to the defense, concealing all this until then.'

'Under the circumstances, yes.' He did not want to push her too far, but he could not back off, either. 'I do think it's fair. To everyone.'

'You can't truly believe that.' Her face was as sour as her voice. 'If Ms Miller were here, she would surely argue that she has a right to follow up much sooner than that on any leads she might find in this diary of yours. You're talking about the very last minute.'

'I'm not looking to sandbag anybody, your honor. That's why I'm here now. As to the witness, that's the second prong of my argument. I've only discovered this man myself because of the diary, your honor, but it's no secret to the defense that he was a friend and a co-worker of the deceased. If they had believed he would be valuable to them you would have seen him at the first trial.' A plausible argument as long as you didn't know that Johnny had made himself unavailable.

'Maybe they couldn't find him.'

'If they looked and didn't find him, then there's certainly no harm to them in what I'm asking. But I'm concerned that they may not want him found and if they knew I was looking they might interfere.'

'And you propose to withhold from the defense the existence of this diary.'

'For now, for the reasons I gave. And if Mr Alvaro's evidence doesn't support the conclusion that the diary is *not* helpful to the defense—'

'Yes?' she interrupted. 'What then?'

'As I've said, I don't expect that to happen. I expect to find him, as long as my efforts are not interfered with, and I expect his evidence to support the prosecution case.' In the face of her continued skepticism he felt increasingly uncomfortable maintaining the lie. 'If I'm wrong, the defense has to be told about the diary. I have an obligation under *Brady*, and I fully intend to comply with my obligation.'

'You should have given the diary to them the minute you knew it might have any value. As early as possible in advance of trial, isn't that how it goes? I don't see how you can justify any more delay.'

'In all fairness, your honor, I don't know yet if there's anything in it that's valuable to them, or even relevant to this trial. Mr Kahn very definitely believed there wasn't. He didn't turn it over to Mr Kubelik.'

She took a deep breath: her shoulders and chest rose and her head lifted as if she were inflating herself to a more imposing posture. 'Off the record, please,' she announced, no room for guessing this time. 'As you must know, Mr Estrada, Lawrence Kahn is not my favorite prosecutor. He has been known to argue quite forcefully for evidentiary rulings that later proved to be . . . ill advised, shall we say?'

There was the expected nettle: Kahn's luring her into error about Morales's hearsay statement. 'It's possible he made a wrong call on this diary,' Estrada conceded, 'but we have no evidence of that.'

'So Mr Kahn thought this diary was worthless. I suppose that means he didn't go looking for this man, either – the one you can't find now.'

'A detective interviewed Mr Alvaro at the time. Mr Kahn apparently didn't think he had anything relevant to add.'

'But you do?'

'I think it's possible.'

'So you don't always agree with Mr Kahn?'

'I've had to look at the diary much more closely than he would have. He thought he had a solid case, going in. For a variety of reasons, I haven't had that luxury.'

'You don't think you've got the goods, is that it?'

'Your honor, I didn't come here to bad-mouth my own case. I'm asking you for some time to develop it better.' Unable to admit his expectation that Alvaro's testimony would cast so much doubt on Morales's guilt that the case would dissolve without anyone referring to the diary. Or that Carlos Ramírez would prove to be Morales's twin and the killer, after all.

'You know, Mr Estrada,' the judge said sharply, 'if I were the defense, I'd say Larry Kahn told your Mr Alvaro to get out of town and then pretended he never knew about the diary. And I'd say he did it precisely because either the diary or Mr Alvaro or both of them could have destroyed his case.'

Estrada had no answer for that.

Martinez turned away from him and looked out her window.

From where he was, Estrada could not tell what she saw.

He had forgotten how slowly time could pass. When she turned back and regarded him, she was silent. Uneasy under her scrutiny, he focused on a corner of her desk.

'On the record,' she said: 'Why did you come to me with this, and why now?'

The words startled him.

'Why not just wait until your man Alvaro turns up? Or not.'

'I came because I don't want to be accused of sandbagging or of concealing the man's existence or of withholding the diary. I want it to be on the record that from an early date I have been actively and conscientiously trying to determine the status of this material and to locate this witness.' And for all the bobbing and weaving he was doing, that much was true and had always been true.

The judge shook her head, her broad, mocking smile glinting with gold bridgework. '*Early*, Mr Estrada? Take a good look at the calendar. It stopped being early a long, long time ago.'

He sat, silent. Again, there was no good response.

'And you expect me to take all this on faith?' she prompted.

'No, I don't, your honor. If you're at all inclined not to grant my motion, I'd urge you to examine the material yourself.' He pulled a thick manuscript envelope from his briefcase. 'I brought a photocopy of one of the diary notebooks with me, the most important one, anticipating you might want to begin right away.'

'One?'

'Yes, your honor, there are several. This one covers just under a year ending around five or six months before the murder. If any of them is relevant, this is the one.'

Martinez put the envelope on her desk without looking at it. 'Where are the rest?' Not pleased.

'We just retrieved the balance of them from Texas. There's too much to read at once, and as I said, this is really the most important.'

'I intend to make that judgment myself.'

'Yes, judge.' Agreeing – not apologizing. 'They're being photocopied now. I'm sure I can have them to you soon. And I'm confident you'll see that they support my position.'

She shook her head. 'All right, Mr Estrada. I'm taking your motion under advisement. As I'm sure you know, discovery of the matter in dispute is suspended during the time I'm considering the motion.'

'Thank you, your honor.' Better than he had feared, but only a temporary victory: this would not be over until she actually ruled on the motion.

He said, 'I'd like to request that the record of this hearing be sealed, pending determination of the motion and for as long thereafter as the protective order continues.'

'Granted.' She said it with closing finality. The stenographer folded the legs of her machine, picked it up and left.

As soon as they were alone, Martinez leaned commandingly toward Estrada. 'I want the rest of that diary in here inmediatamente. Ayer. ¿Está claro?'

'Absolutely. I'm not trying to withhold anything.' Anymore.

'All right.' She slid the envelope into a desk drawer as if she wanted it out of sight. 'For now, this is between us. For *now*, only. I want to read this thing, all of it, and decide for myself what its value is. And I want to monitor your progress finding your witness.'

Estrada stood up. 'Thank you, your honor.'

'Don't thank me. Get the rest of that thing in here today.'

'With your permission, your honor, I'll need more time than that. We're getting it photocopied, as I said, and there's a lot of it.'

She glowered at him. 'Mañana, Mr Estrada? Is that what you're telling me? Mañana?'

'I'm afraid so, your honor.'

'I get here at nine. Don't be late.'

Tess Dodge was waiting for him at the trial bureau, eyes

concealed behind her dark glasses. 'Where have you been?'

'In Texas.'

'Texas! You could have told me.'

'I didn't have time . . .'

She did not look mollified, but she waited for more.

'We got the diary from your father, the part he hadn't destroyed. I tried to convince Larry Kahn to intervene with him, and maybe that's what did it, I'll never know. What matters is that between the part your father had and the part you saved, we have the whole diary now.'

Something was nagging at him, a problem he had not yet faced. 'Except what your mother crossed out in the Johnny notebook.'

'Right,' she said gloomily.

'You know what's in it, don't you?'

'It's not about Mariah, it's about Johnny.'

'I don't care if it's about Santa Claus, we have to know what it says.'

She shook her head.

'This isn't a game. My bosses know about the diary. The *judge* knows about the diary. And she's going to find that section and she's going to ask what's in it.'

She stared at him. 'The judge?'

'I just came from her chambers.'

Tess looked down at her hands, folded in her lap. 'He likes boys,' she said in a voice he could barely hear.

'He likes . . . we know that.'

'No, I mean *boys*. Kids.' She looked at the picture of her sister, then down at her hands. 'It just seems so awful that Mariah could have a close friend who did that. She says he talked to her about how bad it made him feel to be like that, and you can't tell from the diary if it's what he did sometimes or all the time, but . . . how could she be his friend? Here she is helping sick little kids, and there he is . . . I mean, hell, I don't care what grown men do. I don't even care what kids do with each other. But grownups and little kids . . .'

Even behind the dark glasses she looked so desolate he wanted to console her, the way he had on the ferry. He changed the subject. 'I didn't see your mother at the house. Is she all right?'

'She went to stay with her sister in Ohio. She says she won't go back to Dad, but she will. It's a matter of time.'

'Has this kind of thing happened before?'

'Not that I ever saw. He used to get to where he'd yell real loud, and I've seen him go out the back and chop wood to work off a mad, but he wasn't a hitter that I knew about.' She sighed deeply. 'You live with somebody for years and you don't know a thing about them. Did you really give the diary to the judge?'

'The Johnny notebook. The rest tomorrow.'

'I thought you said you'd be in trouble on your case if anybody read it before you found Johnny.'

'Things change.'

In the morning he went straight to Judge Martinez's office. She was twenty minutes late.

'Were you here on time, Mr Estrada?'

'Nine o'clock sharp, your honor, as you said.'

'What do you have for me?'

He unpacked his bulging briefcase, a half-dozen thick envelopes.

'I see you weren't kidding when you said there was a lot of it.'

'No, ma'am.'

'I only had time to glance at what you gave me. It doesn't look exactly user friendly, as they say.'

'There are a lot of abbreviations, your honor. And there are a lot of references to things she knew about that aren't always clear.'

'Then how can you be so sure it's of no value to the defense?'

'Her sister explained some of it to me, some of it I had to investigate. That's how I came to my conclusion. But there's a lot that will be made even clearer if we have Juan Alvaro – the man she calls Johnny in the diary.'

'So you said. All right. If I need you to explain things, I know where to find you.'

It did not take her long to decide she needed him.

'Do you truly understand this gibberish, Mr Estrada?' They were in her chambers after she had adjourned her current trial for the day. Her favorite court reporter sat squeezed into a corner.

'A lot of it, yes, I think so.'

'Then you can give me some help with it.'

He sat with her for three hours, starting with an explanation of the short section Mrs Dodge had crossed out. She was not happy about it, not satisfied by Estrada's assurances that both Tess Dodge and her mother would testify to the original content.

Going over with Martinez the passages she had marked, Estrada walked a thin line, answering her questions as fully as he could and still keep the material from announcing itself as helpful to the defense. Where that was impossible – as with WE'RE NOT IN TEXAS ANYMORE – he pleaded uncertainty or ignorance.

It was the opposite of the tack he had taken with Collins. There, the diary's value was in creating doubt about Morales's guilt; here, he had to keep the judge from seeing it that way. He still hoped that his increasingly intricate dance of lies would ultimately result in justice's being done without further scarring the Dodge family and without raising the question of Larry Kahn's misconduct, or Joe Estrada's.

When they were finished, Martinez pushed herself back from her desk as if from a dining table where she had eaten too much. 'Exactly how do you think any of this is relevant to our murder trial?'

'As I've said, I'm not sure it is, your honor.' That was the best result: if the diary was not relevant to the trial, the issue of misconduct faded considerably – though it did not disappear. 'That's why I want to find Johnny. Juan Alvaro. Because I believe he can make that clear.'

'How are you doing?'

'I'm hopeful. I have a detective from the Task Force working on it. He's narrowing down the possibilities.'

'That means he's not making any progress.'

'It's not a fresh trail.'

'A word to the wise, Mr Estrada: Find this Johnny, and find him soon.'

28

He went back to his office and called the Task Force right away, left an urgent message for Detective Clemente to call A.D.A. Estrada. It was late and he was far from sure Clemente would call, but he waited around for an hour before giving up and going home.

Clemente returned the call first thing in the morning. 'Good news or bad?'

'Both. I need you full time again.'

'I don't know. I got stuff cooking here.'

'I can have Collins call Jack.' Boss to boss.

A pause. 'Nah. I'll handle it myself. What's up?'

'Juan Alvaro just made it to the top of the hit parade. You get all the help you need.'

Clemente whistled. 'And what's the bad news?'

'The bad news is he's not our dirty little secret any more. La Luz is monitoring our progress.'

'Shit.'

'Major shit if we don't find him. We need to set up a plan of attack on this.'

'I can be there after lunch.'

He called Michelle. She answered, sounding still asleep.

'Joe? What time is it?'

'Almost ten. Oops, sorry.' He had forgotten the time difference.

'It's okay. I had to get up at eight, anyway. You coming?'

'Looks that way.'

'I'll be there. Miss you.' She made tired kissing sounds into the phone before she hung up.

Collins called. 'Ready to start?'

'Five minutes.'

He checked for mouse turds in the file carton that held the trial transcript, added the police file and his own case file and carried it all to the bureau chief's office.

Going over the files with Collins, Estrada played it absolutely straight. He had decided against emphasizing the case's weaknesses to cast doubt on Morales as the killer: that would only push Collins to strip him of even the semblance of control over the case. He found it disconcertingly easy to slip into the accustomed role of eager prosecutor.

They worked through the I.D. witnesses: Boynton, the janitor, a plus; Petersen, the security guard, zero or less; and Santos, a potential major minus.

'This clown Santos still thinks he can change his story and get away with it?' Collins was incredulous. 'Did you give him a lesson in the penalties for perjury?'

'He claims he made an honest mistake.'

'And you let it go?'

'I have something on him.' Estrada told Collins about Santos's nose-candy business.

'Why haven't you used it to bring him around?'

'If I jam him up now, I have to put him on as a witness who's waiting trial on a drug indictment. And the defense tells the jury he's only testifying against Morales to get better treatment in his other case.'

'So?' It was a common liability. Prosecutors would be lost without witnesses who testified to buy themselves leniency.

'If I time it right, I might squeak in without actually having to offer him anything.'

'And in the meantime you're covering up evidence of a crime.'

Estrada tried another tack: 'You remember my push-in-robbery murder?' – the case that had made his reputation in the bureau – 'I got that guy to wear a wire on the housekeeper's best friend, Jamelle, her name was.'

'Right . . .' Collins had been deputy bureau chief at the time.

'I held onto that tape for *eight months* without ever confronting Jamelle with it. At the homicide meetings everybody told me I was crazy, I was going to lose her, every kind of disaster was going to happen. But I took my chances, because once I let her know I had it then every day after that was a day she could weasel out or the defense could cross me up on it. So I made sure I always knew where she was, and at the end of my case I made an ex parte application to the judge for an order of protection and a morning off, and I brought her into my office.

'I asked her what she knew. She gave me the usual song and dance – don' know nothin'. So I popped the tape on her, and five seconds into it she started crying. And that afternoon she sat there in the courtroom all composed and told the jury how she was in Louann's kitchen while Louann and her two friends planned the robbery, and how she watched them leave to go up to the old woman's apartment, and how she was still there in the kitchen when they came back with the four bucks they got for killing that poor, trusting old lady. Exactly the way she told it on the tape.'

Collins rubbed his jaw. 'I have to admit, it was good work.'

'My point is, if you've got a way to exert pressure on a witness, you hold it until the moment it can do you the most good.'

Collins did not seem inclined to argue. He checked his watch. 'I've got to go. On this Santos thing, play it however you want, for now.' He stood up. 'I'll be seeing Mr Bishop later. I'm going to say we've got some interesting evidence the judge is looking at, and a new witness we have to beat the bushes for. No reason for him to know all the gory details for now.'

* * *

Clemente came in to go over a plan for finding Juan Alvaro.

'What did we do to earn all this attention from the judge?' he wanted to know.

Estrada studied the detective. A Hawaiian shirt, baggy trousers, high-tops, the belt pack that held his notebook and cigarettes and wallet and gun. Still a fashion victim, still slightly out of date. And still hard-faced, pockmarked, with eyes as penetrating as lasers and a grimly knowing mouth. Tough guy. Estrada barely knew him, had no firm idea how far he could trust him. The prudent way to go now was to be stingy with specifics; he already needed a scorecard to keep track of who knew how much about the diary.

'We have some new documentary evidence,' he told Clemente. 'And our man Johnny may be the only living human who can read between the lines for us.'

'New evidence? Something we missed last time?'

'I keep saying, that's not what counts.'

'Then what is?'

'What we miss this time.' Closing the subject. 'Tell me about Johnny.'

Clemente pulled out his notebook and settled into the visitor's chair. 'Okay – until yesterday we had a guy with no known background, works as a finance expert, we can't trace him to a college, we can't find parents, we don't have friends.'

'Didn't Alexander Blair help you with college and the other credentials?'

'Oh, yeah, he was a great help.' Clemente flipped pages in the notebook. 'Said our man Juan went to some big football college in the south. Miami or Texas or Auburn or some other place like that. And he thinks maybe he was Cuban. Period, end of story.'

'Give me a break.'

'That's all the man told me, and we still haven't turned up the personnel records.'

'Why did he hire him?'

'An interview, and recommendations. He doesn't remember

who. Not the most cooperative guy in the world.'

'Until yesterday, you said?'

'I think maybe we got something. Juan Alvaro y Lobo, gold cards up the waz, address Banco Cubano in Miami. I've got a friend down there asking around about the family, make sure it's the right guy. From the credit cards, I gotta say it looks good. He was shopping in New York for five months after the murder, then down by Miami for a while, and then he went somewhere in Massachusetts for the summer' – he checked his notebook – 'Provincetown. Then he came back to New York and dropped off the face of the earth.'

'Before the first trial?'

Clemente did a quick mental calculation. 'Yeah.'

'Nothing since then?'

'Nada. Bupkis. No new purchases, no application for new cards someplace else. You have to figure something scared him off. If this is him, he left the job, then left town. Six months later he decided to disappear.'

'Could be it wasn't his decision.'

Clemente regarded him narrowly. 'You saying what I think you are?'

'Whatever made him leave could have kept him from coming back.'

'Dead men don't testify.'

'Something like that.'

'Morales?'

'Maybe. Frankly I hope this is a dumb theory and he's alive and well and being kept by somebody rich on Fifth Avenue.' Estrada doodled interlocking squares on a legal pad. 'We'll need to get a subpoena down there.' And if the bank didn't feel like cooperating, getting an answer could take forever.

'I didn't want to bother you with it till I had more.'

'Maybe we're finally making some progress.' He reached across the desk with the picture Tess Dodge had pulled from her shoulder bag after she gave him the diary – her trophy from Texas, a snapshot taken at a party. Mariah Dodge on a couch next to a strikingly handsome man with pale skin and light brown hair and eyes. They were both grinning at the camera, holding champagne glasses aloft. Confetti and streamers were festive litter on the couch and on their party clothes.

'This our guy?'

'I think so.' There was a New Year's party in the diary that she had gone to with Johnny.

'We better get some copies.'

'Whatever you need. What's next?'

'I'm going to keep pushing in Miami. And if I can get some manpower for a paper chase I figured to check for social contacts. Upscale gay organizations, AIDS charities, everything like that.'

'Good. AIDS might be a good place to look. He turned Mariah on to an AIDS volunteer group.'

'Did he? Where?' Clemente made notes as Estrada read off the location. 'Is there anything else you didn't tell me?'

Estrada remembered his conversation with Tess Dodge. 'There's one thing that might help. It could be he likes boys.'

'Yeah? So?' The detective considered it. 'You mean, *boys*? Like he's a chicken hawk?'

'Maybe.'

'You known this long?'

'Not very.'

Clemente gave him a sour look. 'Shoulda told me the first fucking minute.'

'My mistake. It got lost in other things.'

'Yeah, that happens.' The unspoken message was – if you *let* it happen.

'Finding Juan Alvaro is the key,' Estrada told Michelle the next afternoon as they lay entwined on the beach south of Marina del Rey. 'He's the only one who can unlock the mysteries in that diary and clear away all the ambiguity.'

It felt odd to him to be lying on this narrow, featureless beach with her, a beach they had reached by car in a choking ooze of traffic instead of bicycling past potato fields to the broad, duney Atlantic seashore where they had planned to be this summer.

'I still don't understand why you didn't leave the diary alone, the way we decided,' she said.

'Everything changed once I began thinking Morales might not be guilty. I need the diary to point the way to the real killer.'

Michelle disentangled herself and sat up to reach for a tube of sun block, holding the untied top of her suit with a forearm across her chest. 'Do my back?'

Her shoulders and back were a uniform toasty tan. 'You spend a lot of time out here?' he asked as he started to rub in the cream.

'No lectures,' she warned. 'I'm very careful. Not like you. Telling all those people about the diary seems awfully dangerous. The more people who know, the more people who are going to find out.'

'It *is* dangerous. For now, though, the paradox is that giving it to the judge protects it from disclosure.' Just as it virtually guaranteed disclosure if Johnny didn't show up. Estrada had a flash of worry about the process he had set in motion. *What if I'm wrong?*

'What're you thinking?' Michelle asked him.

'That I don't want to spend our whole weekend talking shop.' He put the cap on the sun block and reached around to kiss her. 'That's more like it.'

They had not even thought of driving to her apartment when he arrived in the predawn gloom. Instead they had pulled into the first hotel they came to, a stubby tower of sand-colored concrete immediately outside the airport. They had spent a tumultuous two hours getting reacquainted and then reacquainted again, after which Estrada had fallen immediately asleep, awakening to a lavish room-service brunch Michelle had ordered while he napped. Restored, they had proceeded to the beach.

When they'd had enough of the sand and surf they drove a

cursory tour eastward from Santa Monica and had dinner in a Brentwood Italian restaurant where they ate undercooked food swimming in expensive olive oil and Michelle interrupted their conversation to point out the movie stars. They closed the day with nightcap brandy on the terrace of her apartment, a one-bedroom in a building perched on the Valley side of the hills. He made her laugh with stories of living in a small hotel room and being chauffeured around by a bodyguard cop. It was funnier in the telling than in the living.

'Great view,' he observed in a quiet moment.

'It's temporary.'

'The view?'

'Living here. I want to be at the beach or as close to it as I can. I only took this because I knew we would be moving when you got out here.'

'Mmm.'

'I don't get the feeling that's number one on your mind,' she said.

'The case is so crazy. If I don't straighten it out, who knows what my prospects are going to be.'

'You aren't really worried about that, are you?'

'It's not like I can just walk out of the office into some great job. Not if *Morales* is a major public mess.' The truth was, a public mess was inevitable now. It only remained to be seen what kind and how bad.

'People would know it wasn't your fault if you lost. It's like anything else – being nominated means the most. Winning is nice, but it's icing on the cake.'

'This isn't Best Actor we're talking about, or Best New Recording Act, Country & Western.' Having kept her in the dark he did not feel he had much right to be annoyed, but he was, and he was tired enough not to be concealing it well. 'This is life and death. Getting a killer off the street. The *right* killer. Or else maybe convicting a man who isn't guilty, and putting him away for most of the rest of his life. Serious business.'

'Yes, and nothing else matters to you. I can't get your

attention more than a minute at a time, you don't care what I'm doing out here, what I'm going through – being alone, waiting to see what's going to happen with us when you're done with this big important case . . .'

He put his arm around her but she shrugged it off; 'It's not that easy. You know what I'm afraid of? I'm afraid you don't really want to quit that job. I'm afraid all the talk about becoming a real lawyer and making the kind of money you deserve for the great work you know how to do . . . I'm afraid it's all bullshit. What if the truth is that you like it fine right where you are?'

'The truth right now is that I'm exhausted,' he said with greater calm than he felt. 'The nap this morning helped but I only slept about two hours on that damn plane and I can't see straight, much less think straight. Let's talk about this in the morning.'

In the morning they made love again and ate breakfast and Michelle took him on another tour, this time of the best residential neighborhoods for the budding upper middle class. Neither of them mentioned the outburst of the night before.

Seeing him off in the evening, she said, 'I'm rooting for you to get what you want out of this case. Remember that, okay? All I want is the best for you, because I know that's the best for us in the long run.'

He put his arms around her. 'It's important for me to know you're on my side.' Oblivious to the noise and bustle around them, they clung together until the gate attendant called his flight.

McMorris came by to see him after lunch on Monday. 'Something interesting in the mail.'

Since the break-in all of Estrada's mail had been going first to McMorris and a Spanish-speaking detective from the uptown precinct named Taylor. Though he grumbled about it, Estrada was not completely unhappy with the attention being paid to his safety: Samuel Dodge might not be a threat, but there was no way of knowing who might be inspired by the widely reported MUERTE scrawled on the bedroom wall.

'I was real lucky on this,' McMorris said. 'I got it before Taylor ever saw it was there.' He took an envelope from his inside jacket pocket. The heat had wilted it considerably. 'It's about Morales.'

'Morales?' Tips came by telephone, not in the mail.

The letter was on a major energy company's letterhead, with a signature almost as regular and precise as the typewritten text. The writer's name was Andrew Flippo, and he gave himself the title Research Biologist.

He began with a paragraph of explanation: he had been late to see newspaper coverage of Roberto Morales's new trial because he had been out of touch while doing research. Flippo's writing style was as controlled as his signature. The second paragraph was similar to the first, an explanation of how traveling for work had also caused him to miss completely the results of Morales's appeals.

The next three paragraphs made Estrada sit down and reread the letter carefully.

> I am writing now to encourage you to apply all the resources at your command to the re-conviction of Roberto Morales. I believe that it is important for you to know that, assuming your defendant is the Roberto Morales I once knew, this is not the first time he has slashed a person's throat in an attempt to kill him or her.
>
> Many years ago, I was also his victim, although I was fortunate enough to escape with my life. I bear the scars of that experience to this day, both physically and emotionally. I did not make myself known during the earlier trial because I did not learn of it until quite late, perhaps too late to make a difference, and in addition I have always been reluctant to expose in public this episode in my past. Roberto Morales's conviction validated my opinion that my participation in his trial would have been superfluous.
>
> However, although I still cannot offer to participate

directly, I find that since Roberto Morales is now to be tried again I can no longer remain silent. Like the murder of which he is now accused, my own violent encounter with him also involved romantic rejection and ethnic defensiveness and anger. It was a miracle that I survived.

As Estrada read, he struggled to rein in his apprehension. There had to be a lot of Roberto Moraleses in New York, in the country, in the world: so what, if someone named Roberto Morales had slashed young Andy Flippo years ago? That didn't mean it was *this* Roberto Morales – even Flippo himself seemed to recognize that. Assuming the letter was anything more than pure fabrication.

'You've been reading these things,' he said to McMorris. 'What do you think of this one?'

'I don't know – guy like Morales does a thing like that, it figures he might've tried it before. On a guy, though. That's different, unless he goes both ways.'

'You think the letter's for real, then?'

McMorris shrugged, a gesture that involved most of his massive upper body. 'It takes all kinds. The letters from crazies, mostly you can tell, you know? This guy . . .'

'See if you can locate him. There's a lot in the letter about research trips. Let's hope he's somewhere we can reach him.'

Estrada called Lisa Stein and asked her to look for Flippo in the rosters of professional societies for research biologists. Anything that would verify his existence and give an idea of how legitimate this might be.

He sat staring at the picture of Mariah Dodge. He was breathing too fast, blood pounding in his ears. Take it easy, he told himself: you're exhausted from your trip, no sleep on the plane back, can't trust your reactions. He closed his eyes and concentrated on breathing steadily and smoothly, drifted into an unsteady half-sleep from which he was awakened by the telephone.

'Mr Collins is expecting you,' the bureau chief's secretary reminded him.

He stopped off in the men's room to splash cold water on his face, taking a good look to convince himself he had persuasive features, then went on to Collins's office to continue reviewing the case. He said nothing about Andrew Flippo.

Lisa Stein and Stash McMorris finished their research within an hour of each other. There really was an Andrew Flippo, and his credentials were impressive. At the moment he was on an oceangoing research ship in the Bering Sea. The only way to communicate with him was through his company's offices in San Diego, and they were not eager to disturb him.

They had a major division headquartered in New York, so it was easier than it might have been for Estrada to impress on them the value of cooperating with the Manhattan D.A.'s office. He had to press hard to get a direct phone conversation. Communicating with the ship was a luxury that had to be carefully rationed, the company maintained: all available channels were needed for the research that was the custom-built ship's only purpose for being.

Estrada spent most of the night before the call pacing the floor of the hotel room that was still his temporary home. Having had to confront the possibility that Morales was not guilty, he had put himself on the line to be sure nothing significant was kept from the defense, risking the slender prosecution case as well as the work of the Kahn Commission and his own future. Now he was faced with evidence that he had jumped too soon, that Morales was guilty after all. He needed to talk to Flippo, needed to know the details, but he dreaded the conversation.

The phone connection, by satellite relay from halfway around the world, was full of static and hampered by an annoying delay. Heard dimly, Flippo's voice was as dry as his prose. His story was simple: he had been going out with Roberto Morales's foster sister, Gina Coluccio. Flippo had learned she was lying to hide the Puerto Rican half of her background and decided that he wanted to break off the relationship.

Roberto had found out about it and had come with a friend to demand an apology. Flippo at the time had been a student of karate and in no mood to be bullied by a couple of street toughs. He had told Roberto where to go, and that he could take his lying slut of a sister with him.

Flippo confessed that his language had been laced with ethnic slurs. 'Pretty bad ones. This was a long time ago, attitudes were different, and I had a lot to learn about life and people.'

Roberto had responded instantly, without warning, whipping out a switchblade knife and slashing at Flippo's throat. Reflexes developed in endless hours of karate training had pulled Flippo back in time to take the knife across the collarbones instead of the throat. An off-balance kick had connected well enough to send the knife flying and maybe to break Roberto's wrist. Stumbling backward, Flippo had fallen; Roberto and his friend had fled, leaving Flippo to bleed to death. 'For all they knew, I did.'

It should have been the best of news. Not proof that Morales had killed Mariah Dodge, not by itself, and far from obviously admissible as evidence, but it opened a window on a pivotal aspect of Roberto Morales's character no one had suspected before. Unfortunately, ironically, the way things stood now it was not news Estrada would have wished for. 'I may need to have you testify about this.'

'Are you sure it's the same Roberto Morales? I assumed it might be from the fact that he slashed her throat, but . . .'

'A foster sister named Gina Coluccio doesn't strike me as a common characteristic of men named Roberto Morales.'

'I suppose not.' There was a brief silence. Estrada thought he might have heard a sigh over the crackle of static. 'I have a life to live, Mr Estrada, and a job to do. We've been planning this research cruise and doing preparatory work for a year. Conditions will only be right for a limited time. I'll try to help from here, but I'm not about to leave.'

Estrada did not press it, there would be time for that. 'I'll need to talk to you again.'

'Electronic mail is the best way to communicate. If you have more questions, please try to deal with them that way.'

Estrada reconstructed the conversation for his whole team. Nancy Rosen, back from her vacation, was as pale as the day she left, except for a thin strip of red along the top of her forehead that made her face look even rounder and more innocent than usual.

It was the first time they had all been together in his office since their kickoff meeting. This time the air conditioning was working but as he told his story Estrada had the feeling it would not have mattered if the ambient temperature had been in the nineties, everyone was so riveted by Flippo's story.

'We need the sister,' he told them. 'The sister, Roberto's friend, any records of the wound and treatment. The guy doesn't sound like a crazy, but I'm not taking any chances on this.'

'Twenty years ago,' McMorris groaned.

'More like thirty,' Clemente corrected.

'If it's too hard I can get somebody else,' Estrada said sourly.

'What about our man from Miami?' Clemente wanted to know.

'Keep after him. He's still the most important.' With everything suddenly turned upside-down, it was more crucial than ever to find Alvaro and defuse the diary, before it blew the case sky high. 'But this gets first priority for everybody else.'

McMorris's first report on Gina Coluccio was not encouraging. 'I talked to all the friends I could find. She moved away right after high school. She kept in touch with a few friends in Brooklyn for a while, when she was living in Manhattan, and that's it. The last anybody heard she was headed out west someplace. Oregon, maybe.'

'Anything there?'

'Zero.'

'Maybe she got married.'

'That's what I figured.'

'You talk to her friends about Flippo?'

'I found one that thinks she remembers him, on account of the weird name. Nothing about the slashing, though.'

'Keep pushing. We need it.'

'There *is* one thing. Another friend remembers her brother did something so bad she never talked to him after that. Said the reason Gina left New York was to go somewhere he couldn't find her.'

'That's more like it. Does she know what he did?'

'Not a clue.'

The final pre-trial motion from Kassia Miller arrived just as Judge Martinez was due to leave on vacation. Miller started by renewing all the previous demands the defense had made, including 'Disclosure of any prior acts of misconduct claimed on the part of the accused which the prosecution would desire (a) to examine the accused about if the accused chooses to testify, or (b) to use for any other purpose at trial.'

Estrada pulled the Criminal Procedure Law off the shelf. As he had remembered, the law did not require disclosure of prior bad acts until immediately before jury selection. He could keep Andy Flippo to himself for now.

On her last day at work, Luz Martinez called Estrada in to talk about the diary. He went, preparing himself to hear that she was denying his protective order. His concern was premature: she wanted to ask him more questions about what she had been reading.

'What's this about her going to the hospital? Was she sick?'

He told her about the pediatric AIDS ward. She was fascinated. 'Nothing like that ever came up in the first trial. I don't think it's ever been in the paper.'

'It hasn't. Strangely enough, as I understand it, that's one of the things that would cause her parents the most anguish.'

Carefully, bearing in mind he was speaking for the record,

he explained Samuel Dodge's aversion to AIDS victims, used it as a way into a longer review of the sexual content of the diary. He told the judge about Sylvia Dodge's attempt to keep her husband from seeing anything that had to do with his daughter's sex life, and about Samuel Dodge's destruction of the originals of those pages. He pressed hard on the idea that the Dodges' own actions were the best indication of how much grief it would cause them if the diary was exposed to the world.

Martinez was in an uncharacteristically reflective mood. 'Parents are so hard to predict,' she observed, waving for Rosemary to take a rest. 'You see some of them posing with their daughters for those centerfold magazines. I suppose they think they're being modern. And here you have people ashamed their daughter was helping sick babies because they have so much hate for how they think the poor babies' folks got the disease. You'd think, sitting where I do, seeing what I see, you'd get to understand people better. It doesn't happen.'

Estrada had no trouble agreeing.

'How's it going, finding this Johnny?' she asked, on the record again.

The question was so casual Estrada did not pump up his answer. 'Slowly. One step at a time. We're trying hard.'

'Well, keep at it. And let me know about your progress. I'll be gone, but they'll know how to reach me.'

He returned to his office feeling considerably relieved. It looked as if Martinez was not going to do anything about the diary at least until the pre-trial hearing.

He wondered if she might be trying to avoid the issue – and the possibility of a later reversal – by failing to rule at all for as long as she could reasonably keep the diary concealed.

29

McMorris came into Estrada's office, looking smug.

'I found our Gina.'

'Well done. Where? How?'

'Turns out she went back to school about ten years ago. The registrar at the high school found out they sent her transcript to a college. The college had her married name and her new address. Washington, not Oregon. She's still there. Gina Fiori.'

'You're sure it's her?'

'Sure as I can be without talking to her myself. She's been there about twenty years, has three kids – one grown, two still in school. Her husband works for a big aerospace company. The cops out there are real easy to talk to.'

'She work, or she stay at home?'

McMorris shook his head: don't know.

'Might as well give me the number.'

'Mrs Fiori, this is Joe Estrada,' he began, low key and friendly, when he got her on the phone. 'I'm a prosecutor with the District Attorney's office in New York.'

A moment's pause, then: 'How did you find me?'

'I didn't realize you were hiding.'

'If this is about Roberto, I can't help you. That was all in another lifetime, and I don't want to get involved.'

'I'm not asking you to get involved.' Not yet. 'I just want to talk to you about Andrew Flippo.'

There was a silence, then: 'The racist bastard. Is he still alive?'

'Yes, and not a racist anymore, to hear him talk.'

'Don't bet on it.'

Despite her apparent anger with Flippo, Estrada had heard curiosity in her question. He let it work on her.

'You talked to him?' she asked.

'Yes.'

'What did he say about me?' She was trying to sound nonchalant.

'That he treated you badly and it almost cost him his life.'

'Is that what he told you – it was me? That's a lie.'

'That's what I want to talk to you about. Your side of the story.'

'I'm not talking about any of this. I'm not letting Roberto ruin my life again.'

'If I have to serve a subpoena on you it will only be worse. This way it can be between us.'

'I told you, I've got nothing to say.'

'Roberto had a friend with him that night. Who was it?'

'I don't know. I wasn't there. Didn't Andrew tell you that?'

'If I can learn what I need to know from Roberto's friend, maybe I can leave you alone.'

That made an impression but he had to keep after her before she finally gave in, and then she had trouble coming up with the name.

'Alberto Quiñones,' Estrada told McMorris. 'Chances are he's got a yellow sheet as long as your arm.'

'You were right about the yellow sheet,' McMorris reported the next morning. 'Six burglary arrests, eight for possession of stolen property, all but three before he was thirty. Mostly he pleaded to burglar's tools and misdemeanor stolen property. He's had five indictments, one felony conviction and two acquittals. He's waiting trial as we speak.'

'When was the felony conviction?'

'Nine years ago. He's been clean since then, except for the one arrest.'

Fewer than ten years since a felony conviction meant Quiñones would be facing mandatory prison time on a new felony, no matter how clean he had been. It would make him extra eager for a deal that got him off with a misdemeanor.

'Who's got the new indictment?'

'It's in Brooklyn. A.D.A. name of Spadafora, defense lawyer's Gerard Lomax.'

It took Estrada a moment to place the name. 'You're kidding, right? Not Lomax.'

McMorris checked his notes. 'That's what it says here. Gerard Lomax. Why? You know him?'

'We don't have what you'd call a positive working relationship.'

He got on the phone with the A.D.A. in Brooklyn. Quiñones was up for being part of a plot to set a fire in a warehouse as cover for the theft of a truckload of whiskey. Caught behind the wheel a mile from the burning warehouse, he was claiming he had been hired only to drive the truck and that he'd had no idea what was in it or where it came from.

'I need to talk to him about another crime,' Estrada said. 'The statute of limitations ran on it long ago, but I'm still going to have to offer him something.'

'This piece of shit isn't worth a whole lot to me unless I can get him to roll over on his buddies. Seeing as he's a predicate felon, I have him jammed up pretty bad. I don't want to give away anything I don't have to. You're trying *Morales*, aren't you?'

'This is related. You and Lomax talking about a plea?'

'Is the pope Polish? That's all Lomax does is plead his clients out, and Alberto Quiñones is not your prime candidate for a happy stay at Attica.'

'Lomax and I have some history. If you can add this to your demands, don't mention me, just you need some details about a crime Quiñones witnessed twenty-five years ago.'

* * *

Spadafora called in the morning. 'Lomax says if you want something from him you have to ask for it yourself. Ask nicely, he said.'

'You told him it was me?'

'*He* told *me*. He knew exactly what I was talking about the minute I opened my mouth.'

'Then he knows he's got something to deal with.'

'Looks that way.'

Lomax took Estrada's call, then put him on hold for five minutes. Estrada decided to endure the punishment.

'Something I can do for you, Mr Estrada?'

'I had the impression you already knew.'

'In general terms. Why don't you be more specific?'

'Your client Alberto Quiñones witnessed an altercation involving Roberto Morales, not quite thirty years ago.'

'What are you offering?'

'It depends on what Alberto can tell me. In general terms, he's going to do better with Spadafora if he answers some questions for me, too.'

'Spadafora wants Alberto to give up his alleged partners in crime. He'll deal with us even if Alberto spits in your eye.'

'Don't be so sure. If it comes to a choice between nailing some mopes who stole a truckload of booze and Roberto Morales . . .' Speaking for Spadafora before he knew how cooperative the Brooklyn A.D.A. would be. 'Bear in mind, your guy is looking at mandatory prison time if he goes down for a felony, and the conversation with me costs him absolutely nothing.'

'That doesn't mean it isn't valuable to you, though, does it, Joe?' Twisting the knife.

'You have an obligation to your client to tell him about this.'

'Don't preach ethics to me.' There was venom in Lomax's tone. 'My obligation is to get my guy the best deal I can. I don't have to confuse him with every tricky bit of bullshit you happen to try out.'

'No bullshit. It could make a real difference for Alberto.'
'Try again,' Lomax said.

Pressing Gerry Lomax about Quiñones was a sure way to lose ground with the lawyer. Estrada went to Brooklyn and made his case to Spadafora, the A.D.A.

Lomax was not happy with the result. 'I'm going to nail your balls to the wall, Estrada. I had a solid plea agreement going until you walked all over it.'

'What are you talking about?'

'I'm talking about you interfering with a contractual agreement between me and Felix Spadafora.'

'You didn't have a deal, you had a conversation about a deal.'

'No difference.'

'You know better than that. Facts change, deals change. You want a deal to stick, try accepting it when it's offered, instead of holding out for better.'

'You fuck – you're not getting away with this shit.'

'Hey, I'm trying to do your guy a favor. Something for nothing.'

'Nobody gets something for nothing. Not Alberto Quiñones, and for sure not Joe Estrada.'

Pancho Castillo called. 'I understand you have the original of Mariah Dodge's diary locked up in the police evidence room.'

'What are you talking about?' Estrada tried to remember their last conversation. Hadn't he caught himself in time?

'Mariah Dodge's diary,' Castillo repeated. 'I hear you've got it in the evidence room.'

'I don't know what you're talking about.' Not sounding very convincing.

'On your desk, then. Isn't that the rumor you didn't tell me about?'

'This time you're really fishing.' The Dodges wouldn't have told him.

'You're not going to show it to me, then. Not even going to admit you have it.'

'You telling me you found some kind of diary?' Was there a leak in Collins's office, or Muir's? Or on the judge's staff?

'I'm going to do a piece about it.'

'You make it sound like a threat.' It *was* a threat, but Estrada could not let him know that.

'I'm going to report that prosecutor Joseph Smithfield Estrada flew to Texas last week, and with the help of the Houston police he confiscated about a dozen notebooks containing the personal reminiscences of Mariah Dodge, brutally slain in her office, allegedly by Roberto Morales.'

The Houston cops. 'I can't talk about that.'

'I think we have a mutual interest in keeping this story accurate, don't you?'

'We can't resolve this on the phone.' Estrada did not want this conversation overheard.

They met uptown, in Central Park.

'I can't tell you anything about this,' Estrada said as they walked along the chain-link fence around a pair of ballfields north of the reservoir. 'But if there was a diary I would need to keep it out of the public eye, at least until after the trial starts. Things like that can ruin people's lives.'

'Why? How?'

Estrada shook his head. 'That's all I can say.'

'If you cut me off like that, I'm going ahead with my story, and I can tell you I talked to Carlyn Sims. She's a lot of fun.'

The reporter broke off and leaned against the fence to watch a robust game of softball. Off to one side pungent smoke rose from a grill where a heavy-set woman was cooking sausages. Her bright yellow dress matched the jerseys of one of the teams.

Estrada and Castillo watched the game in silence.

'That's some pitcher,' Castillo observed after an inning and a half.

'The orange-team guy? He's sure got the batters guessing.'

'Like you and me. You never pitch me a straight one.'

'And how much have you told me about your book deal?' One of the details McMorris had finally come through with about the reporter.

Castillo gave him a sharp look. 'I forget, you have all those detectives. Okay – I have a deal for a book. So what?'

'So you might have an urge to stir things up, to make sure your story is really juicy.'

'Is that what you think?'

'I'm offering you the chance to prove I'm wrong – a choice between thoughtless sensationalism now and a better story later. I'm offering you a way to be a responsible journalist and at the same time show some compassion for people who have already suffered too much.'

'Very noble. But when some other reporter comes up with the story while I'm sitting on it, being noble, how do I explain that to my boss at *Noticias*, my book publisher and myself?'

'Nobody else is going to come up with it. You would never have found it, if I hadn't got you wondering what might be going on. How did you get onto it?'

'Long ago I made friends with someone who sees the travel vouchers. This is the first time it's done me any good. And now I have a story.'

'I'm not asking you to abandon the story, only to hold it awhile. Nobody's around to read it in August anyway.'

'No norteamericanos, maybe. Plenty of *my* readers.'

'Tell me you're not interested in being picked up by the mainstream press.'

'The Anglo press, you mean.'

There was a roar from the game they had stopped watching. A topheavy man in yellow with arms like watermelons was thudding around the bases to the triumphant shouts of his teammates and a score of fans, while the orange-team pitcher and his infield watched unhappily.

The next batter stepped to the plate. The pitcher wound up and threw. High and wide, almost out of the catcher's reach. The next one was in the dirt.

'Looks like the pitcher is losing his stuff,' Castillo observed. 'That's what happens. You get a little worried, you tense up, you make mistakes.'

Alberto Quiñones came into Estrada's office as if it were a strange bar frequented by people he owed money to. He paused just inside the door, his nervous eyes passing over Estrada and taking in the rest of the office before his head swiveled warily back to Estrada sitting at the desk. Gerry Lomax came in a step behind him.

McMorris and Felix Spadafora brought up the rear, herding Quiñones toward the visitor's chair and Lomax toward one of the other chairs Estrada had imported for the occasion. McMorris sat to one side, where he could see Lomax and Quiñones in profile but they could not see him without turning away from Estrada. Spadafora parked himself in the rear of the crowded room, present to prove that this meeting was important enough for him to let his negotiations with Quiñones rest on its outcome.

Estrada sat quietly, watching. Quiñones was a short, wiry man constantly in motion, even sitting down. His head and eyes continued to scan the room, and one foot, in a grimy high-top basketball shoe, rocked up and down as if it were working the treadle of an old-fashioned sewing machine. His dark brown skin bore a faint sheen of sweat.

Estrada introduced himself and questioned Quiñones to make sure he understood what was being offered: a sweetening of the sentence in any deal he made independently with Spadafora in Brooklyn. 'But you've got to deliver for both of us in a major way, or no deal.'

'Yeah, I got that.' Quiñones was trying for swagger and falling short. He looked at the picture of Mariah Dodge. 'That the one Robo killed?'

'That's the one.'

'¡Coño! Fuckin' waste.'

'I hear you saw him cut somebody else.'

Quiñones's head swiveled sharply back toward Estrada. 'Me? Yeah.' Quiñones had no more Spanish accent than his erstwhile buddy Roberto. Where Morales had adopted the careful speech of his upscale world, Quiñones's language was a gumbo of street talk and outdated slang, with Spanish words and phrases thrown in as if to insist that despite his chocolate skin and his aging-homeboy jive he was still a Latino.

'Tell me about it.'

Quiñones grinned. 'Which time?' He was missing three teeth in front; the rest were stained as brown as his skin.

'All of them.'

The bouncing of Quiñones's foot had become slower and more emphatic, more like tapping out a beat. 'Only one time he cut somebody real bad.'

'Okay. Let's start with that one.'

'It's a long time ago, man. My memory's not so good.' Like lawyer, like client.

'Tell me about you and your compadre Robo. How you got together, where you hung out. Warm up your memory.'

Quiñones squirmed. Estrada had the feeling that he wanted the deal but at heart he was no informant, however strong the motivation. He began slowly. 'Back in school everybody thought Roberto was, like, Señor Lambioso – kissin' everybody's ass. Good grades, all like that. Try'n'a be like he was white, you know. Then this one night I was over the other side of the bridge, this club in the city, Loisaida someplace. An' I seen him there. Un hombre muy diferente. He had on this black leather jacket an' motorcycle boots an' a bicycle chain. Like a fuckin' maricón, hey? But those days, it was muy macho. Soon as he sees me he grabs my arm, pushes me out the alley. He says, you say shit in there, you dead, same as if you tell about me in school. I was a kid, I di'n' know shit, I say sure, you got it, bro. After that, we hung out a lot. En la noche, party all the time. All the time goin' over the bridge – Loisaida, Spanish Harlem, all over. Lookin' for some blow, lookin' for pussy. An' he always had his cuchillo, mean motherfucker, pullin' it out all the time. He put that mark every place we went.'

'What mark?'

'Like Zorro, sign of the Z.' Quiñones whipped his hand through the air, slashing a wide, vicious X. 'Only Robo, his mark was X.'

'His trademark.'

'Yeah. Right.' Quiñones thought that was funny. 'His trademark.'

His trademark. So it was no coincidence. 'Did you see him do that a lot?'

'All the time. I told you. You shoulda seen, this one guy pissed him off, Robo cut all the seats of his car. Cut the paint, too. X, X, X . . . Sign of the X.'

'Did he say that? That the X was his . . . mark, his sign, anything like that?'

Quiñones looked out the window, then over at his lawyer, then at Mariah Dodge's picture. 'You want the story, or what?'

'I want the story and I want everything related to it.'

'Well, fuck that. I'm tellin' it the way I want.'

Estrada sat forward, elbows on his desk. 'No you're not, not if you want to get your deal out of it.'

Quiñones turned to his lawyer.

'You have to tell him what he wants, about this,' Lomax informed him sourly. 'That's the deal you couldn't live without.'

'That sucks.'

Lomax shifted in his chair as if he was about to get up. 'You change your mind, you want to walk out on the deal, I'm ready to go.'

Quiñones drummed his fingers on the arm of the chair. His foot was going faster than ever. 'Okay. Okay, I'm stayin'.' To Estrada, he said, 'I don' know. I don' know what he said about it. He did it, that's all.'

Estrada took him through the rest, going over his friendship with Morales and the incident at Flippo's. It was a halting performance, with the problem that Quiñones could not remember the name of the man Morales had attacked, could describe him only as 'tall, taller 'n Robo. He had a beard, a moustache, something like that.'

Estrada asked him what contact he'd had with Morales since that time.

'I went to him this one time, right out of jail. The fucker. *I don't hire convicts*. That's what he said to me. Like I'm a piece of dirt. He gives me money, says good luck. So a couple, three years ago, when he gets jammed up on killin' his tragona, I go see him.' He put a heavy weight of implication on the last four words.

'Alberto . . .' Lomax warned with a growling intensity.

His client looked at him blankly, then visibly realized what he was getting at. 'Yeah, right.'

'You were saying . . .' Estrada prodded.

Quiñones shook his head. 'I wasn't sayin' nothin'.'

'What's this about?' Estrada asked Lomax.

'We need immunity for anything further along this line.'

'I told you, Queen for a Day, that's it.'

'Not for this. We stop here.' Lomax turned in his chair. 'I'm not bluffing, Felix. You can tell him.'

'I'm just here to observe, Gerry,' Spadafora said mildly, 'make sure Alberto lives up to his end. It's Joe's office. Talk to him.'

'I don't buy pigs in a poke,' Estrada said. 'Before I give you anything, I need to know what we're talking about, what I'm buying, what kind of crimes are contemplated.'

'Nothing violent,' Lomax said. 'You don't have to worry about that. But I thought you'd want to know everything about Alberto there was to know. Everything Kassia Miller could use against him.' He leaned back in his chair and crossed his legs. 'Wouldn't you?'

'If we're talking about Alberto's extorting money from Morales in exchange for silence, you can have immunity on that.

Nothing else.' Estrada hoped he was guessing right. Bribing a potential witness was a compelling sign of guilt.

Lomax fished in his briefcase and pulled out a cassette recorder, leaned forward to put it on Estrada's desk. He poked the RECORD button and had Estrada repeat his offer of immunity. Lomax added the date and time and told his client to go ahead. 'About your conversation with Roberto Morales before his first trial, nothing else.'

Once more, Quiñones showed the gaps between his remaining teeth. 'I go to him. I ask him, you like how it feels, under arrest? How about the D.A. finds out you cut somebody before? He gets real mad, then he gives me money. A gift, he says, 'cause we're friends, he says, and friends don't fuck each other over. Coupla hundred dollars, big fuckin' deal, like I'm supposed to fall down happy. An' then he says don' ever come back for more. Next time you come back, I got other friends, you can talk to them – like I'm supposed to be scared. Fuck him.' He grinned again. 'Ese hijo de puta, ese pendejo, see how *he* likes it on the inside.'

The form was right, but Estrada was worried about the substance. *A gift 'cause we're friends* wasn't the best support for an allegation of witness bribing. He took advantage of Quiñones's anger to push him harder, looking for more explicit details, but got nothing.

After Quiñones and his entourage were gone, Estrada hunted in the case files for the crime-scene and autopsy photographs. He leafed quickly through until he came to a closeup of the left side of Mariah Dodge's face, the picture with the clear, staring green eye that had caught him on his very first pass through the crime-scene photos. It was not her eye that drew him this time; it was the two intersecting cuts on her cheek.

He pulled out the autopsy report. As he remembered, the medical examiner had described them as separate wounds probably made prior to the rape, to prevent a struggle or as a threat or both. But there had been no suggestion that the two cuts were related, and Estrada had seen them as described: a pair of cruel warnings. Now, with Quiñones's words fresh in his mind, Estrada saw something else. He saw an X. He picked up the phone to have Nancy Rosen talk to the medical examiner about it.

He gave his notes of the interviews with Alberto Quiñones and Andy Flippo to Lisa Stein to type up as the basis for affidavits giving the basic details of the slashing. Before he sent them off to be signed he gave copies to Collins.

'Still think Morales isn't guilty?' The bureau chief taunted.

Estrada held his peace.

'It's great gossip,' Collins said, 'but you know damn well it's no use to us. It's propensity evidence.'

'It goes to his identity.'

'Inadmissible. Even with the business about the trademark, you'll never get it in.'

'I'm damn well going to do my best. If I don't get it admitted as evidence, I can still use it cross-examining Morales if the defense opens the door on his peaceable nature. And I can use the payoff to Quiñones to keep quiet about it as evidence of Morales's consciousness of guilt, and that brings the Flippo slashing in with it.'

'What about Alvaro? He's still the key to the case.'

'Tommy's following up in Miami. It definitely looks like the right guy.'

'Let's hope. Meanwhile, you'd better find a theory for why it's really okay that we never found him. Just in case.'

Estrada noted that Collins had said 'we.' That was good news and bad.

'And you'd better start putting your case together for real. Next thing you know, it'll be time for the trial.'

30

Finding the right Juan Alvaro was not the same as finding Juan Alvaro. His family was not cooperating, and the Miami bank that had managed his money was even worse. Slow honoring Florida subpoenas, for a distant state they were almost inert.

Working through his list of what else was being done to find Johnny, Estrada saw nothing about the volunteer-placement agency that had arranged for Mariah to work at the hospital. According to the diary, Alvaro had put all that in motion, so he probably had friends at the agency.

'Nobody there ever heard of Juan Alvaro, and nobody remembers Mariah Dodge,' Clemente reported. 'Her name isn't anywhere on their lists. Nobody I talked to at the hospital remembers her either. I'm waiting to hear from the doctor in charge of the unit.'

Clemente called back in the late afternoon. 'I got the doctor. He'd rather talk to you.'

They met at a luncheonette across from the hospital. The physician turned out to be no older than Estrada, his brow divided by a premature furrow of worry. Estrada showed him the picture of Mariah Dodge. He stared at it for minutes, saying nothing.

'You know her,' Estrada said finally.

'Yes, I know her. At the hospital she wore her hair hidden under a baseball cap all the time and no makeup, and she used a false name. She didn't want anyone to know who she was. Not that anyone would have cared.' He sighed, rubbed his eyes wearily. 'She was very special, even by our standards. She seemed to really care about the kids, as individuals, not in some generic way. She wouldn't wear a surgical mask because she didn't want them to be frightened or to think she was avoiding them. She used to take the really tiny ones and put them inside her shirt, so they could be comforted by her body heat and the contact with her skin.'

He stirred sugar into his coffee. 'When I saw in the paper she'd been killed I couldn't believe it. If anybody's accustomed to death – to good people dying young – I am, but not like that. I remember once, a three-year-old girl was running across the ward and pulled free of her intravenous. Pulled the tap right out somehow. Blood all over. And the only person who would go near her was Theresa. That was what Mariah called herself here: Theresa deLancie. People used to kid her about how she didn't look like Mother Theresa. And there she was, holding this little girl's arm, applying pressure to stop the bleeding, hugging the kid to calm her down. Blood all over her.

'We test all our volunteers regularly. Theresa – Mariah – came up negative every time, even after that. They all do. Nobody's ever turned up positive from coming here to help the kids. You can't get people to believe it.'

He was silent again, staring at the picture.

Estrada said, 'I'm trying to find the man who first interested her in volunteering. Nobody at the agency seems to have known her. Maybe if I asked them about Theresa instead . . .'

'You'd only end up back here. She came to me first, and we don't like to take people directly. Some hospitals do, but we prefer to have an outside group handle the scheduling and all the rest of it, so I sent her there.'

'Wouldn't the person who recommended her have known to send her there first himself?'

'It wasn't that formal. I met her at a casual dinner party.

She said she was interested in helping out. We talked about what was involved, and I told her what to do.'

'Do you remember who introduced you?' Estrada showed him the picture of Mariah and Juan Alvaro.

'They were having fun, weren't they? So sad to see her so alive.' He passed the picture back. 'I think it was Juan who brought her to the party, yes.'

'You know him, then?'

'Yes. *Knew* him, I suppose. I haven't seen him in years.'

'Do you have any idea where he might be?'

'None.'

'Who his friends were? Anyone he might be in touch with?'

'What makes him so interesting?'

'They were very close friends. I think he may know some things about why she was killed.'

'I'm sorry I can't be more help.' The young doctor picked up his coffee cup, put it down without drinking. 'Tell you the truth, I don't see how any of this matters, now.' He stood up. 'I'd better get back.'

Estrada dropped a dollar on the table and took the check to the cashier.

'There's one person who might be in touch with Juan,' the doctor said as they left. 'Not somebody you'd know. A community activist in Brooklyn.'

'Try me.'

'His name is Carlos Ramírez.'

Halfway out the door, Estrada stopped. 'Carlos Ramírez knows Juan Alvaro?'

'Yes. I believe Juan spent a lot of time at Adelante. It was Carlos's party where I met Mariah. Why? Do you know him?'

'Not well,' Estrada said.

Not sure what to think, Estrada went back to the diary. It was as he remembered it: All the early references to the hospital were associated with Johnny. A few pages before the first entry about the hospital there was one about a party she had not wanted to attend. Johnny had persuaded her to go because there would be someone there he thought she would want to meet. There was nothing to indicate who the host had been. It was as if she had been blotting Ramírez out of her life entirely.

For Estrada it was now just the opposite. Dangerous as Ramírez could be to the case against Morales if the two men were twins, the community leader now represented Estrada's best hope for finding Juan Alvaro, who held the key to more than convicting a killer.

There was a message waiting for Estrada at the office: call Public Information. Intuition told him to go downstairs first for a copy of *Noticias Diarias*. Sure enough, there it was: ¿DIARIO DE SEXO? NUEVA REVELACIÓN EN EL PROCESO DE ROBERTO MORALES. New revelation, indeed.

Mouth dry and hands cold, Estrada skimmed through the piece in the elevator. Nothing of any real substance, mostly speculation. There was no byline.

Public Information wanted to know how to respond. No comment, Estrada told them.

An angry Kassia Miller was on the phone almost as soon as he hung up.

'What's this about a sex diary?'

'Sloppy guesswork and Latino hyperbole, I'd say.'

'In my dictionary, hyperbole means exaggeration, and that means there's something to exaggerate.' Her voice was sharp. 'I asked you more than once for journals and diaries and other writings.'

Too late now to keep her from knowing the diary existed. 'The only writings I know about I've already put in Judge Martinez's hands. She's considering a protective order.' Which he could hope might keep the diary's contents private long enough to find Johnny now that there was a solid lead.

There as a long silence. When Miller spoke again she was calm and distant. 'I consider this a betrayal. It's not the way I thought we were doing business with each other.'

'There's nothing in it for you. If there were, I'd have given it to you.'

'Then why are you looking for a protective order?'

'To spare the family the grief and anguish of having it pawed over by Roberto Morales and then possibly in court and in the press. They've suffered enough.' You sound like Larry Kahn, he chided himself: *I did it for the family*. Except this was genuine.

'It's already in the press, in case you didn't notice.'

'I don't want to confirm their guesswork.'

'Not good enough, Joe. We're serving another demand for it, and we're moving the judge to deny your protective order and make the material available to us immediately.'

Larry Kahn called next, furious. 'Every reporter in the city is calling me about your damn diary. I'm saying I can't comment because it's an ongoing criminal prosecution, but they're not making it easy for me. I won't bother asking you how you let it get out. Just bring this thing to a close.'

'It's out of my hands. The judge has the diary and a request for a protective order.'

'The judge!'

'That wasn't me, it was Collins and Muir.'

'And who told *them* about it?' Kahn was not mollified. 'Listen carefully: The Kahn Commission is an attempt to preserve racial peace in the city, and I'm about to put it to the test. This is very delicate, very risky, and the last thing I need is dumb press tricks about a mystery diary and what did I know and when did I know it.'

'I'm doing my best to make it go away. I may have a line on the friend who can explain the troublesome passages.' Stretching the truth. 'That should take you off the hook.'

'*May have* isn't good enough. If you're going to do it, *do* it. I'm trying to slow things down here, but I can only change my schedule so much. I'm taking a lot of heat, and I'm sitting on dynamite.'

* * *

Estrada took a ride out to Brooklyn. He found Dolores Acampo in Adelante's dance studio watching a lithe young man and four teenage girls rehearse a dance routine. She was not happy to see Estrada.

'The police are here looking for Carlos every day, and now private investigators. I don't understand why you brought us all this trouble. People think we've done something wrong. The kids stay away because they think they're going to get in trouble with the cops.'

'I apologize. I'll tell my detective not to come so often.'

'Why does he have to come at all?'

'It's very important to me to talk to Carlos. But that's not why I'm here today. I want to know if you remember a man named Juan Alvaro. I think he might have come here as a volunteer.' He showed her the picture of Alvaro and Mariah. 'This man. He would have been here three or four years ago.'

She glanced at the picture. 'Such handsome people. They seem happy together.'

'Yes. They were good friends. Do you recognize him?'

She hesitated before deciding to answer. 'A strange man. He looked so strong and sure, but he was . . . soft. He was good with the boys, but the girls liked him better.'

'What did he do here?'

'Everything. Painting scenery, like you did. Maintenance work. He supervised math in the tutoring program. He helped with the theater group. Then he left and never came back, not even to visit. Years ago.'

'Did he say where he was going?'

She shook her head. One of the dancers, standing at a respectful distance, took advantage of the brief silence to interrupt.

'I'm sorry,' Acampo told Estrada. 'I have to help my dancers.'

'Do you know when Carlos will be back?'

'By now, I thought. But now he says he doesn't know when. He's learning there, but I think more important is what he's teaching them.'

Without a goodbye she headed for the dancers sitting, stretching themselves, on the immaculately polished floor.

Estrada kept his mind off Larry Kahn's warning and the unavailable Juan Alvaro and Carlos Ramírez by preparing his case. He studied the transcript of the first trial, coordinated with Nancy Rosen about her witnesses, made and remade schedules, jotted notes for his opening and summation. At the end of every day he met with Lou Collins to give a report on his progress.

He was not cheered by a phone call from Kassia Miller.

'There's some news you ought to have.' From her tone of voice, it was news that was making her feel victorious. 'We turned up the birth certificates. Baby boys named Roberto and Carlos were born to Elena Maria Morales de Candelaria in Guania, Puerto Rico, on the morning of June fourteenth, forty-seven years ago. Flag Day. Morales was the mother's maiden name, as it turns out. The father's name was Pedro Candelaria, present whereabouts unknown.'

No more need to wonder whether Ramírez would be dangerous to the prosecution. With a birth certificate Miller might not even need the man himself to create a reasonable doubt. In a way, that made having Ramírez back in the country *less* of a problem, Estrada tried to convince himself. The damage was already done. Now there was only the hope that Ramírez could help find Johnny.

'What about Carlos? Have you found him?' Estrada asked her.

'Still in Cuba. They tell me he'll be back after Labor Day.' She paused. 'You know, Joe, if you really want to spare the family and keep that diary private, you ought to think some more about withdrawing the prosecution. There's really no point now going ahead, and your office will look a lot better acknowledging it now than making a public spectacle of trying to convict a man you have no case against.'

⋆ ⋆ ⋆

Off the phone, Estrada groped in his drawer for the magnetic darts and fired them violently one after the other at Roberto Morales. They bounced off the target and the wall, two of them with enough force to rebound all the way to his desk.

He collected the darts and put them on his desk. He was in no shape to keep working. He closed up the file he was working on and locked it away with the rest of his case materials, got his suit jacket from the back of the door. The phone rang: he ignored it.

Ginny stopped him on his way past her cubicle. 'Ms Dodge is on her way up. I tried to call you, but there was no answer. I knew you were here . . .' She saw the expression on his face. 'Sorry.'

He turned around and went back to his office. He sat behind the desk, closed his eyes and tried to blank the bad thoughts from his mind. When Ginny buzzed him he told her to send Ms Dodge back and went out into the blue corridor to meet her. Half the length of the corridor away, he could see she was not happy.

The newspaper in her hand told him why. His angry prediction to Castillo at the ballgame notwithstanding, the Anglo press had picked up ¿DIARIO DE SEXO? as its August sensation. Fires, earthquakes and floods – along with rest of the news-making world, it seemed – were all on vacation.

In his office, she placed the newspaper on his desk with studied calm. 'I see we made the news. Isn't that just dandy?'

'Why don't you sit down and tell me what's on your mind?'

She was visibly holding herself in check. 'On *my* mind? You want to know what's on *my* mind? Why don't we talk about what's on *your* mind?' She sat down abruptly in the visitor's chair, put her head in her hands and took a long breath, then raised her head to look at him. 'Isn't it bad enough my sister got murdered? What did she do to deserve having her private life in everybody's morning paper?'

'There's nothing there but speculation. Nobody has a clue what's actually in the diary.'

'That's bad enough. That's worse than bad enough.' She stood up and started to pace in the narrow office. 'Seems to me it's the defense that's supposed to slaughter the victim's reputation, not the prosecution.' She sat down again. 'How do you think my mom feels, being responsible for this?'

'She's not . . .' Estrada began.

'She sure thinks she is, and so does my wonderful father. And here's what's worse: I know who's fault it really is. *Mine*. I was pushing you so hard, and I was so full of tricks for getting that diary out of my parents – *for you* – instead of leaving everything alone to happen in its own time and its own way . . . And now my family's blown all to hell, my sister's being turned into the whore of Babylon . . .'

She stopped and looked at him blankly. 'Now what?'

'Now we do our best to salvage the situation.' Weak, but the best he could do in a hurry.

She did not acknowledge it. 'I've been thinking about this since I saw that newspaper, and I can't figure why you let that scummy reporter know about the diary . . .'

'I didn't . . .' He couldn't finish. It was too close to a lie.

'Here's what I came up with,' she ventured. 'You figure that if Johnny doesn't turn up, the defense can use the diary to get Morales off on a technicality. And since you don't think Morales did it anymore, the technicality is some kind of insurance for you so you don't have to try to convict him. Am I right?'

He was stabbed with the realization that he had not yet told her about Andy Flippo or Alberto Quiñones. About Roberto Morales's *trademark*. Her reasoning was exactly right, except the assumptions did not apply anymore.

She did not miss his reaction. 'You look like you just ate something meaner than you.'

'I'm as upset as you are about all this being in the papers. And as far as Morales, and whether he's guilty . . .' He took a breath and told her about Flippo and Gina Fiori, about Quiñones, all of it. He knew he should be careful but in the face of her emotion, knowing he was in large part responsible for the damage the diary had done to her family, he could not hold back.

She listened wide-eyed. 'You're saying Morales did it after all.'

'I'm saying he did something very much like it once before.'

'So then you ought to be able to convict him. If the jury knows he cut somebody . . .'

'We may not be allowed to tell them.'

'What are you talking about, *not allowed to tell them*? The man did the same thing before. He did it the same way – isn't that what you said?'

'Yes.'

'What could be a better sign that he did it this time than that he did it before?'

Estrada hated this. 'There's a rule that says you can't put a prior crime or any other bad act into evidence if all it does is show a person has a tendency to commit crimes. Not even if it's a certain specific kind of crime. It's called *propensity evidence*, and it's inadmissible.'

'That can't be right. You mean a person is guilty as sin, did the same crime before, and you can't let the jury know that? You have to let them think he's some kind of pure, innocent angel?'

'There are exceptions, but basically that's how it goes. I'm going to do all I can to convince the judge this fits the exceptions, but it's going to be an uphill battle.'

'I don't believe it. I just don't believe it. Is this what they call justice?'

'It's not over. We're not finished yet.' He put as much conviction into his voice as he could find, but he barely believed it himself.

When he left the office, Estrada detoured over to the pool. It was still early for the after-work crowd so he had a lane all to himself. He had not worked out in weeks, felt it in the heaviness in his thighs and forearms and in a tendency to wallow when he took a breath. He left feeling rubber-limbed, enjoying the freedom of no longer having a full-time cop watching over him. The post-rush-hour traffic was light, much of the city's workforce off somewhere on vacation. Estrada liked it that way.

He stopped by his apartment to check on the progress of the repainting. It still felt alien and hostile to him, furniture huddled in the center of the rooms under graying, paint-speckled tarps, the walls stripped of paint and paper and newly replastered.

At the hotel he nibbled yesterday's takeout Italian food from the half-refrigerator in the wet bar and returned a call from Michelle. He caught her at work, the first time they had connected in more than a week.

'I saw the diary in the paper,' she said.

'Not good news.' He started to talk about it, worried at first that she would say I told you so, then relieved that she had the grace or good sense to be all on his side. All at once he was telling her his concerns and misgivings, his guilt about what had happened in the Dodge family.

'It's not your fault, Joey, not your fault and not your responsibility. Every family has its own way to be unhappy, all on their own. They'd have found their way to this without you.'

He wanted to believe it, was not sure he could.

'Oh, baby, I hate to run,' she said, 'but I just saw the time. It's going to be okay – you're going to find Johnny, and your career isn't going to get ruined if you don't. You're too good for that. You'll see.'

What Michelle had said about families made sense to him. His own family certainly had a knack for finding its own misery without help from the outside. But that did not change how connected to the Dodges he felt, how responsible for bringing Roberto Morales to justice, *for them*. In that sense he could not accept Michelle's pragmatic view. He could not make this into simply a step in his own journey to success, or acceptance, or even to absolution by his dead father and the rest of his family.

He had started on this case with one foot in a hole. Trying to dig his way out, he had only made the hole deeper. Now he was so far down in it he could no longer see over the top. He remembered a line from one of the milder letters he had received at the office, a biblical warning: El que cava una hoya caera en ella – he who digs a hole will fall into it.

But there had to be a way to climb up out of it, and he was going to find it.

31

For the last week in August, the office was all but deserted. Natalie Muir was gone, after a farewell party reported to have been unusually sedate. Collins was on vacation, as were most of Estrada's bureaumates. Estrada continued to prepare for trial as well as he could without knowing about Juan Alvaro.

On the Tuesday before Labor Day, Nancy Rosen came into his office flushed with concern, carrying one of the morning tabloids. NO INDICTMENT FOR TIMMINS? asked the headline covering the front page. The story took up all of the lead news page; it was adorned with the familiar high-school yearbook photo of honor-student Timmins, an aerial view of his massively attended funeral, and head shots of the three cops and the A.D.A. most often mentioned in connection with his death. Veteran reporter Allen Crown quoted 'a source close to the commission' as saying that the Kahn Commission was unlikely to recommend any prosecution at all in connection with the crime that had prompted its creation.

This had to be what Kahn had been talking about when he said he was sitting on something major. The newspaper predicted that this could be the East Coast version of the disastrous acquittal of Los Angeles policemen on charges of beating a suspect – now the scary benchmark for any situation even vaguely similar. And at least those cops had been accused of a crime. If the Timmins case was closed with no one accused, without so much as an indictment, that would be very bad news indeed. With that possibility already being openly discussed, Kahn's concern about the diary did not seem exaggerated – an accusation of misconduct leveled at Kahn at this red-hot moment, especially misconduct involving apparent bias, could only inflame an already volatile situation. Rioting in the streets might not be far off the mark.

'They're out in the streets already,' Clemente said when he came into the office. 'I just walked by the building where Kahn's office is, and both sides of the sidewalk are jammed. They've got signs, JUSTICE FOR ABDULLAH, REMEMBER L.A., like that. Damned if I know how they get them made so fast.'

'You think Kahn's really not going to indict?'

'Where's he going to get evidence to indict anybody with? I mean, not unless somebody dropped a dime. Even if the M.E. says it was for sure a homicide, who do you blame it on?'

'All of them.' But without an eyewitness there was no case: it was the word of three live cops against one dead college student. 'You're right, it's a sure loser unless one of the cops turns.'

'And that's not happening in this lifetime.'

'What about Johnny? What's happening with him?' asked Estrada, thinking again how much worse the reaction to Kahn's handling of Timmins would be if people could accuse Kahn of bias.

'I was just talking to my guy down there. He's got one of the Alvaro sisters who might be willing to talk about her brother, but not to a local cop.'

'Then go down and see if she'll talk to you. And while you're down there you can check up on the bank, too. The state's attorney's office tells me they're doing everything they can, but I don't see the results.'

Clemente's visit left Estrada feeling better than it should have. He went back to work on a memorandum of law aimed at getting Morales's attack on Flippo admitted as evidence. Mahoney had provided the best case law he could find and his opinion that Estrada would be more likely to succeed mating a mouse to an elephant.

Lost in the 1901 case that had established the New York rules for evidence of past crimes and bad acts, Estrada was not immediately aware that there was someone in his doorway. He looked up to see a bearded man in a wrinkled summer raincoat leaning against the doorframe, his face mostly obscured by a slouch hat and the raised collar of his coat.

'Can I help you?' Estrada reached for the phone, wondering if anyone was on duty at the security desk down the hall.

At first the man said nothing, then he straightened up and took off his hat.

'I understand you want to see me,' Carlos Ramírez said.

Estrada was staring. 'Please sit down,' he said. Then, 'I thought you were in Cuba.'

'My absence from Adelante was causing too much trouble for me to stay. As I believe Dolores told you.'

'And as I told her, making trouble for Adelante was the last thing I had in mind.'

'What *did* you have in mind?'

'Making sure I can convict Mariah Dodge's killer.'

'And why am I so important for that?'

'A couple of reasons. Right now I have one, and your brother's lawyer has another.'

'My brother?'

'Roberto. Your twin brother.' Estrada was surprised to see a badly suppressed grin winking through Ramírez's beard.

'Where did you hear that?'

'Kassia Miller tells me there's a birth certificate.'

'That's true, there is a birth certificate.'

'I'm glad you think it's funny. It makes you a suspect.'

The grin wavered. 'Does it?'

'Not for me, not now. But it does for Kassia Miller. She's probably dying for a sample of your blood.'

'Is this what you had on your mind when you came to see me before I left?'

'Yes.'

Ramírez shook his head. 'I suppose I should set you straight. Roberto and I aren't twins, we're cousins. Second cousins. I'm told we looked alike as infants, even as small boys. I thought the rumor we were twins had died long ago.'

'The way I heard it, the story that you were cousins was something your mother made up so she could separate you.'

'That's a long story, for another time. For now, trust me, the truth is we are not twins, we are not brothers.'

'Would you give a blood sample so we could check it?'

Again, Ramírez shook his head. 'If that's the only way.'

'I'm afraid it is. I can have a detective drive you to any doctor you want and wait while they draw the blood.'

'Dolores tells me you want to know about Juan Alvaro,' Ramírez said.

'Yes. Whatever you can tell me.'

'Why?'

'He was a good friend of Mariah Dodge's. I have reason to believe that he knows . . . important things about what led to her death.'

'He wasn't at the first trial.'

'They didn't know about him then, didn't realize what he might know. And by the time of the trial he wasn't around.'

'That was my point. Do you think that was an accident?'

'No.'

'Then why would he participate in this trial?'

'To see justice done.'

A bitter smile. 'And where would he go for that?'

'Here, to start. Do you know where he is?'

'If I did, I wouldn't tell you.'

'Who do you protect that way?'

'I protect Juan, and I protect my own sense of honor.'

Estrada considered Ramírez carefully. 'I shouldn't tell you this, but I will, because I believe you *do* know where he is and because right now you're the best chance I have to get a message to him. I think he cared about Mariah, and I don't think he'd want to see her murderer go free. And there's a good chance that's what will happen if I can't talk to him.'

'And you think that fact would sway him?'

'I do.'

'But you don't know him, so how can you say that?'

'I know some things about him.' Taking another chance. 'I know he's gay, and I know he was . . . involved with underage boys, and that it troubled him.' Estrada realized for the first time that at Adelante Johnny would have been constantly working with young teenagers and pre-adolescents. He wondered how that fit with Ramírez's protectiveness. How would it affect Adelante if it got out that Ramírez had made a place for a man with Johnny's background?

Ramírez stood to take off his raincoat, sat down again. He was silent, his eyes on Estrada, for what seemed like a long time.

'Before we go further,' he said, 'you need to understand some things about Juan Alvaro. Before everything else, he's a man of intelligence and integrity.' Ramírez paused briefly, making a final decision to go ahead. 'Unfortunately, for most of his life he's had trouble accepting his own needs. He grew up confused about who he was, in a family, in a community where there was no room for any deviation from traditional masculine behavior. Growing up confused about your sexuality in a close-knit Cuban family in a prosperous Cuban neighborhood in Miami, under the eye of Mother Church, is not like growing up in Greenwich Village or San Francisco, and even in those places tolerance and understanding are nothing like universal.

'Juan was full of confusion and self-doubt, and he knew that if his family found out about him he would be disowned and worse. He saw everything he did as shameful, and every mistake he made as a sign of greater perversity and greater shame. He spent years hating himself, afraid of what he might be tempted to do next, especially because he had once been arrested for consorting with someone underage.'

'Arrested?' There was no record of it, nothing Clemente had turned up.

'A fourteen-year-old. Juan thought the boy was eighteen. A street hustler. I'm not blaming the kid, he had his own hard life, but I want you to understand that Juan was not seeing the reality when he decided that going with such a young boy meant he, Juan, must be horribly twisted. But that was what he thought and if you heard him talk about it you'd be sure his worries were based on real behavior. And he wasn't always careful who he confided in. There were people who found out about the arrest and his guilty plea who shouldn't have. In the end, the way he saw it, all he could do was run.

'It's sad,' Ramírez continued. 'Sad and unnecessary. And now he's afraid of what will happen to him if he comes back.'

Estrada jumped on that at once. 'If you mean legal consequences, criminal charges of some kind, I can probably help him with that. It's absolutely essential for him to be here. If he doesn't help us understand what he and Mariah Dodge were doing in the months before she was killed, the consequences are . . . I can't tell you how bad it would be.'

Ramírez nodded. He stood and shrouded himself again in raincoat and hat.

'I'll try to get word to him. I don't know what he'll say, I don't even know if I'll be able to find him, but I'll try.'

The preliminary results on Ramírez's blood came back in a day. His blood type and Roberto Morales's were not the same, the first unalloyed good news Estrada had had in far too long.

'No way they're identical twins,' the serologist said. 'You still want to bother with the DNA?'

'Absolutely.' Miller was bound to be skeptical of the simple ABO typing, and Estrada wanted to get her off Ramírez's back. It was one of the few favors Estrada could do for him.

Estrada called Tess Dodge. He thought she could use some good news. He was in the middle of leaving a message on her machine when she picked up.

'I'm here.' There was a quaver in her voice.

'You all right?'

'I just talked to my mother. My father hit her again. He went to Ohio to take her home and she didn't want to go, and he . . . he . . .' She broke into tears.

'Are your roommates at home?'

'No.' Sniffling. 'They're all off flying.'

'Will you be okay alone?'

'I'm fine . . . I . . .' She started to sob again. 'It's all so . . . so . . . lousy.'

'Look, I have some good news, I think.' Nothing to compare with the bad news. 'Maybe it'll do you good to get out. Why don't you come down here and I'll take you to dinner and tell you about it.' Knowing as he said it that his feelings of guilt about the Dodges were continuing to sabotage his judgment.

He arranged to meet her at the ballfield behind the courthouse where the D.A.'s-office softball league was playing its twice-weekly double header. The evening's first game pitted the Rackets Bureau against one of the support-staff teams. The lawyers were taking their usual beating.

Tess Dodge arrived during the fourth inning. She looked deceptively lighthearted in a sleeveless white blouse and a short, bouncy skirt, a sweater draped over her shoulder bag. Her curls were escaping from a white headband, and she had on a new pair of sunglasses with enormous lenses.

'It's okay if you want to stay and watch,' she said.

'I've had enough.' He could not help noticing the smooth muscles of her bare arms, lightly dusted with freckles. 'You look very nice.'

'Camouflage' – she touched the glasses. 'And distraction' – throwing her shoulders back with a self-mocking smile, straining the sheer fabric of her blouse.

Estrada tried not to succumb but his eyes betrayed him. 'That's certainly distracting.'

'Is that a blush I see?' Her smile was more like the real thing. She hooked her arm in his. 'Excuse me for being brazen and silly. I'm trying to fool myself into thinking the world's not such a rotten place.'

They walked in silence over toward the Seaport, Estrada uncomfortably aware of the soft warmth of her body against his elbow. As soon as he could do it unobtrusively, he took his arm back.

There was a jazz quartet playing on the pier to a crowd of Wall Streeters and tourists. He got beers at the outdoor café and they found a place to stand where they could talk without being overheard.

She touched her bottle to his. 'Better times.'

'Better times,' he echoed, with feeling.

'What's your news?'

'We found Johnny.'

'You . . . Really?' She was suddenly brighter.

'Don't get too excited. I talked to someone who's going to talk to him for us. I'm not in touch with him directly, myself. Not yet.'

'Can't you make this guy tell you where he is?'

'It's not a question of can't. It'd be bad strategy.'

'Strategy! Where did we get time for *strategy*?'

'That's how I have to play it for now.'

'How long is it going to take?'

'We have until the judge comes back. Then we can see about other approaches, if we have to.'

'That's not so long.'

Less than a week. 'I'm hoping it will be long enough.'

'Can we get out of here?' she asked suddenly. 'I want to walk.'

She headed downtown. 'Does that ferry we took run at this hour?'

It was after seven, the sun low in the sky. 'Sure.'

The evening was hot without being oppressive. Walking slowly, they arrived at the terminal just as an outgoing ferry was getting ready to cast off.

They stood at the top-deck rail again. Tess said nothing on

the trip out, just watched the water and the sky. He stood next to her, not looking at her but aware of her presence.

He thought of how much he had to do and how little time he had to do it. For the moment he was badly hampered by not knowing whether Johnny would emerge from hiding or what he would say if he did appear. And there was still the question of how Martinez would rule in the Flippo testimony. Estrada was doing his best to concentrate on what was available now, but there was really no way to draft an opening statement if you didn't know what was going to be in your case.

On the way back from Staten Island he and Tess crowded to the port side of the ferry with their fellow passengers to watch the sunset. After a few minutes, she pushed away from the congestion and wandered across to the starboard rail. He followed her.

With the sun going down, the breeze was cooler. Tess put her sweater on and wrapped her arms around herself, staring out across the harbor, her sunglasses pushed up on her hair. As he came to stand next to her, she shivered.

'Cold?'

For an answer she turned toward him and put her head on his chest. He let his arm go around her shoulders. They stood that way, awkwardly. Her shoulders shook slightly and he could feel dampness on his shirt: she was crying. He stroked her head with his free hand. Her body softened, molding closer to his, creating a confusion of responses.

If Lou Collins could see me now, he thought. Or Michelle.

She raised her damp face to him and kissed him softly. He knew he should pull away but he didn't want to be abrupt. The warmth of her breath seemed to envelop him. Her mouth moved on his, her lips soft and salty. Her kiss was hungry for emotional nourishment. After its first intensity passed her lips lingered on his.

She clung to him softly, her head nestled into the hollow of his shoulder and chest. His awareness of the contours and warmth of her body against his was vivid to the point of distress. He concentrated on breathing slowly and evenly, on keeping his hands and body still.

She shifted in his arms, her hands rising to curl her fingers in his hair and pull his mouth to hers. This time the kiss was deeper and stronger, her tongue exploring his.

His hands were moving on her back, helping her press their bodies together, while a voice in the back of his mind tried to shout warnings. He brought his hands up to caress her hair and her neck and her cheeks and in an act of will held her face steady so he could gently disengage from the kiss.

They stood that way – motionless, eyes locked, inhaling each other's breath. He was barely aware of the thump and bump as the boat docked on the Manhattan end of its run.

She turned her head in his hands to look. 'I guess we should get off.'

He relaxed, let go, stepped back. 'Right.'

She slipped her arm through his again as they disembarked. They walked out of the terminal into the gathering darkness in silence, the picture of a loving couple strolling toward Battery Park.

'We shouldn't, you know,' he said as mildly as he could.

She stopped walking. 'Didn't you like it?'

'That's not the point. It isn't ethical.'

'Why not? I'm not accused of anything. I'm not a witness. You're not forcing me to do anything, or taking advantage of me because of who you are.'

'You're a victim. A victim's family.' He had a mental flash of the picture of Mariah on his office wall, then one of a crime-scene photo.

Feeling his reaction she took her arm from his. 'Do I turn you off that much?'

'No.' He touched her cheek. 'Just the opposite. But I'd get fired in a minute if anything happened between us now. It's not just some abstract rule, it's office policy. Besides, I'm too emotionally involved in this case as it is.' He started to walk again. 'And I have a girlfriend.' Glad to have the excuse, the buffer, even one that was three thousand miles away.

'So I gathered.'

'Aren't you hungry?' she asked as they got to the park. 'I'm starving.'

He flagged a cab. 'We can get something to eat and then I'll take you home.'

They talked about the case over dinner, and her worries about her parents. At her door, she shook hands with him. 'Thanks for coming to the rescue. I needed it.'

'Happy to help,' he said.

In the morning there was a press conference, Lawrence Kahn and the mayor facing a roomful of clamoring reporters in City Hall while an estimated five thousand people marched outside demanding justice for Abdullah Timmins.

Kahn was wearing a dark blue suit and an air of righteous weariness, an honest man trying to do an honest job. 'A small vocal group is making irresponsible threats based on incomplete and incorrect information,' he said with more sadness than anger. 'This commission has compiled an impressive list of indictments, and we are investigating many other allegations. We expect significant results as the year progresses. Through all this, Abdullah Timmins remains one of our first priorities. No definitive action will be taken in his case until we have thoroughly investigated every aspect of it.'

The mayor repeated much of what Kahn had already said, closing with a testimonial. 'I have known Lawrence Kahn for years, and he's as good a prosecutor as this city has ever seen, as thorough and, most important, as honest as anyone I've ever known. He is an example to all of us who believe that we all have to work together if we're going to solve the problems that potentially harm us all.'

'I thought Kahn knew what you've got coming,' Mahoney said to Estrada at lunch.

'He does. He keeps telling me how much damage the diary's going to cause when it really gets out.'

Mahoney pulled a french fry out of the wicker basket that held his cheeseburger. 'You'd think he'd soft pedal some of this man-of-integrity bullshit. Put the emphasis somewhere else than on Lawrence Kahn, the last honest man.'

'You'd think so.' Estrada spread mustard on his hamburger. 'How's your friend the dancer?'

'Not great. I mean, she's okay, I'm just . . . I don't know. Kath wants to come back.' Mahoney looked bewildered, not an expression of his Estrada was accustomed to seeing.

'How do you feel about it?'

'I don't know why I don't just tell her to go to hell. Back to whoever it was . . .' Mahoney stopped and stared at his food. 'Ah, hell.' He made an effort to bounce back. 'How about you? How's it going with Michelle?'

A good question. Estrada wondered what the answer was. 'We're in some kind of holding pattern. She's all settled in, out there, looking for places we can live, scouting out the law firms for me. Doing great at work. But we don't talk even once a week, she's that busy.'

'How is it I don't hear great enthusiasm in your voice? Or impatience at not being out there with her?'

'I'm preoccupied. I can't think that far ahead.'

'It's the next step after you get out of this mess. That ought to be a great incentive to think about it.'

'Except I have my head wedged so tight into this damn trial. This *mess*.' But that wasn't all of it. Mahoney had picked up on something Estrada had not recognized.

He had been blaming himself for letting the tender moment with Tess Dodge get out of hand, when the important information in that event was that he would never have gone anywhere near that far if everything had been fine with him and Michelle. Something was off, and what bothered him now was that he was not letting himself see it.

Mahoney asked about progress on the Andy Flippo front.

Starting to detail his struggle getting the scientist to come and testify if Martinez held a hearing, Estrada had a sudden realization.

'I've been planning to spring this on Miller as late as possible, but I think that may be a mistake.'

'Oh?'

'The most important thing right now is keeping the diary from exploding in everybody's face.'

'Right.'

'And that's mostly up to La Luz, who we think doesn't want to rule on it because she sees what a keg of dynamite it could be.'

'Right . . .' Mahoney, out of french fries, snagged one of Estrada's.

'But she also has to be worried that she's helping me sandbag the defense. So the best thing I can do is convince her of my good faith. Get her to conceal the diary for me by proving that I don't really want to conceal *anything*.'

Mahoney saw where he was going. 'By giving her, and Miller, everything you have on Flippo, right now.'

'Well, I don't know about *everything*.'

Mahoney took another french fry. 'Now, Joseph . . .'

To go with the affidavits of the interviews with Quiñones and Flippo, Estrada finished his memorandum of law supporting the slashing story's admissibility. He carried the package over to Martinez's chambers himself, with a covering note asking that it be sent by express to her country house. With luck, it would get there before the Labor Day weekend. The copy to Kassia Miller went by regular mail.

He spent the next day with Nancy Rosen, starting with a rough overview of his part of the case: the cops, the building employees, Carlyn Sims and Lynne Schelling. Every time he reviewed it, it seemed thinner. He had Rosen challenge him everywhere she could, until finally he called a halt for a late lunch.

'If we keep this up we won't eat until Sunday.'

They talked jury-selection strategy over lunch. In the afternoon they went over the medical evidence. Rosen had drafted the section of his opening statement that would deal with the forensic evidence, and a proposed section of his closing argument covering what she expected from the defense.

'This is terrific stuff,' he commented as he read through it. 'I hope I can do nearly as well with my end of it.'

'You have the hard part. I don't envy you.'

He leaned back in his desk chair and looked at her. Her round face was flushed – not with heat, the air conditioning was doing fine – perhaps with the intensity of their day-long effort.

'That wasn't so bad,' she said with a smile. 'Was it?'

'Hell, no. In fact, I was just thinking we're going to make a pretty good team, in spite of everything.'

32

The press sniffed out the Flippo story almost immediately. Estrada had sent the papers informally to Martinez and Miller, waiting to file with the court because he was sure that Miller would want the papers sealed and because he himself was ambivalent about letting the story out too soon. The news that Roberto Morales had slashed someone's throat in his youth would give a big boost to the weakening public perception of Morales's guilt, but it would also open the door to formidable problems selecting a jury. Once the word was out, everyone who had read a newspaper or watched a TV news show would be challenged by the defense.

The first leak came from Gerry Lomax, whose unsubtle hints about playing a major role in the Morales case were ignored widely but not completely. Distorted details began to appear as filler items in the less careful news outlets. Estrada knew the news was really out when Ginny told him Pancho Castillo was on the phone. He did not take the call.

He spent the holiday weekend at the beach house where he and Michelle would have had a regular biweekly bedroom for the summer if she had not been on the opposite coast. The weather was bleak, hot and heavily overcast and rainy. Estrada played hermit, drafting two versions of a summation, one including Quiñones and Flippo, the other not. Unsurprisingly, the one that included the slashing attack on Flippo was much more convincing. What effect Juan Alvaro might have, Estrada did not speculate.

Promptly after Labor Day Martinez called him into her chambers. He went expecting questions about the diary or perhaps Juan Alvaro. When he saw Kassia Miller and a court reporter he knew more was up than that.

Martinez attacked immediately: 'Are you serious about this?' Brandishing his Flippo papers.

'Absolutely. The two slashing incidents are strikingly similar. I'm going to argue they amount to an identifying characteristic.'

'You *are* serious.' She studied him as if he were some odd creature that had wandered in. 'I assume you have something more convincing than these affidavits.'

'Your honor, those witnesses will give testimony at trial consistent with their affidavits. I think there's enough in the affidavits and supporting papers for you to rule on the legal issues, but if you want to hear argument . . .' Hoping that she would not want a full-scale hearing – to keep Miller from getting a shot at Quiñones on the witness stand and because he doubted he could get Andrew Flippo to New York. With any luck, Miller would be happy to forego a hearing, too, to avoid the beating her client would take in the media.

Miller handed him and the judge a copy of her response. 'We're moving to seal these papers.'

'Consider them sealed,' Martinez said. 'I suppose it was foolish of me to expect a simple, straightforward trial. As you may remember, I saw my quota of interesting new theories the first time.'

She asked Miller to excuse her and Estrada so they could discuss the prosecution's ex parte application. 'Where's Juan Alvaro?' she asked him.

'I'm happy to say it looks like we may have him.' It was an answer he had spent some time on; hearing it come out, he thought he should have done better.

'Translate that for me, Mr Estrada. It sounds like it means you *don't* have him.'

'He's not available at the moment, but we're working on it.'

'*Working on it* is what you were doing last time we talked about this.'

'We've made progress. I've spoken to someone who's in contact with him. He's in hiding, but this intermediary is opening a communications channel for us. We're trying to move things along as fast as we can.'

'You're saying this person knows where Alvaro is.'

'He appears to.'

'Then slap him with a subpoena and if he doesn't come through I'll be happy to hold him in contempt.'

'I considered that, your honor, but I don't believe it's the best way to get cooperation from this individual.'

'They say the immediate prospect of incarceration is great for concentrating the mind.'

'Yes, judge. But I'm trying to do this on trust. I remember you said once I'd do better with honey than vinegar.'

'Did I? And are you going to tell me who this gent might be?'

'His name is Carlos Ramírez. He runs a youth center in Brooklyn, and he seems to be Roberto Morales's cousin, though their birth certificate says they're twins. And based on his history – Young Lords and FALN – I don't think going to jail for contempt is likely to scare him much.'

'¡Madre . . . !' The truncated curse was pure exasperation. 'All right, Mr Estrada, I'll give you some more rope. Just be sure you don't try my patience past the breaking point.'

'Some setup down here,' Clemente said from Miami. 'Four, five houses inside a wall, gardens, swimming pools. Rich people, these Alvaros. Not too friendly, either. The sister talked to me, but we had to meet in some bar on the beach. Not what you'd expect, not an old folks home in sight.'

'Did you get anything?'

'Yes and no. This sister is the only one in the family who talks to him, even admits he's alive. Nice woman, feels bad for her brother, hasn't heard from him in a year.'

'Where was he then?'

'Paris. Before that, South America, working with poor people and sick kids. That's what she said.'

'Does she think he's still in Paris?'

'She says last time she was there, in the spring, she looked for him at his old address. Not there.'

'What about friends? She know any?'

'The only one she knew died of AIDS a couple of years ago. She doesn't know anything about his family and she isn't even so sure about his name.'

'So that's it. Dead end.'

'Looks that way.'

'What about the bank?'

'They claim they'll have the records next week. And this time I think the state's attorney is going to keep after them. I . . . helped him see how important it was.'

Estrada called Adelante and learned that Carlos Ramírez was on the picket lines at City Hall. A lot more convenient than Brooklyn. Estrada went over.

Ramírez was standing to one side conferring with the leaders of the Timmins demonstration. He excused himself to join Estrada.

'Have you talked to Juan?' Estrada asked.

'I sent a message.' Ramírez limped across the small park, away from the demonstration.

'Time's getting short, Carlos.' Estrada had no better way to press him. Given his presence on the picket line, Ramírez didn't seem likely to care about the danger Johnny's absence posed to Larry Kahn and his commission.

'This has to take its own time,' Ramírez said.

'Too much of that and it'll be too late.'

'Don't push,' Ramírez said, and went back to the demonstration.

At day's end Cuyler Jadwin finally returned one of Estrada's daily phone calls.

'We're starting the trial soon,' Estrada told him. 'I may need you to testify.'

'Nobody needed me the last time.'

'That was Mr Kahn's mistake. We're buying the ticket, and I won't need much of your time. Think of it as a free trip to New York.'

'Kind of you to offer, only I don't have much call to be in New York these days.'

'Then think of it as something you can do for Mariah, a tribute to her memory. I'll do my best to work around your schedule.' He gave Jadwin the rough dates of the trial and said he would call back to make arrangements.

'You'll be wasting your boss's dime,' Jadwin said.

'I'll take the chance.'

Reviewing the files to be sure he had not missed anything that might be of use, Estrada saw a long shot he thought might be worth taking. He put in a call to Rita Hazen, the woman who had seen a man carrying a gym bag on the night of the murder, the unused witness whose DD–5 had caught his eye when he was still thinking that Carlos Ramírez might be a suspect.

'Is this about that murder? Mariah Dodge?'

'Yes. There's going to be a new trial.'

'I know. I think about it a lot. I'm glad you called.'

'Really?'

'I think I was wrong about not being able to say who it was. I thought . . . maybe if I could come in and look at some pictures . . .'

'Whenever you want.' Before she could respond, he added, 'The sooner the better.'

She hesitated. 'I'm in the middle of a crazy deadline at work . . . I don't know . . .'

'How about right now?'

She sighed. 'All right. I suppose.'

Estrada put in a call to McMorris and then dug through the file for the photo arrays used in the first trial.

An hour later, the downstairs security guard called to find out if he was expecting anybody named Rita. He met her at the elevator. She was a slender woman of about fifty in a loose, floral-print summer dress and thong sandals. Her gray hair was long and straight, and she wore round-lensed eyeglasses with plain metal frames.

As he led her back to his office he thanked her for coming and asked what had caused her change of mind.

'I've been thinking about it a long time. Once I'd said what I said . . . I was afraid people would be upset with me if I said anything different.'

'All that matters is that you tell the truth as you remember it, as fully as you remember it.'

'Won't I get in trouble for changing my mind?'

'Not for an honest mistake.'

Two steps into his office, she stopped. 'That's him.'

'What? Who?' Not McMorris, sitting in an extra chair, waiting.

'Him.' She pointed at the dartboard Estrada had forgotten to take off his wall.

He stepped between her and the dartboard. 'Let's not jump into this, let's do it right.'

It was too late to do it right. The identification was already tainted – the suspect's picture presented alone, so literally depicting him as the target of suspicion it could almost be a parody. He introduced her to McMorris and showed her the photo array anyway. She picked out Morales immediately.

Estrada went to sit at his desk. 'Tell me what you remember from that night.'

Her story was virtually the same as it had been when

Clemente first interviewed her: She had seen a man coming out of the office building wearing a dark coat and sweatpants and sneakers, carrying a gym bag, looking agitated; he had hailed a cab and when it stopped for him he had waved it on and walked off toward the subway. The only difference was that now she was sure she had seen Roberto Morales.

He asked her why she had not been able to identify the man at the time but thought she could now. She was vague and evasive about it, and he was sure she was lying.

'Are you willing to say in court that it was Morales?'

She bit at her lower lip. 'Yes.'

'Before you do, you'll have to be a lot more complete about why you changed your story.'

She nodded, nibbling more intently, her attention absorbed by the tile floor.

He stood up. 'Why don't you give it some thought and get back to me when you've made up your mind?'

Judge Martinez was late for the final pre-trial conference in her chambers. Estrada, unwilling to sit virtually knee to knee with Morales in the cramped office waiting for her, prowled the hall. Nancy Rosen stayed inside, taking refuge behind one of the paperback novels she always had in her briefcase.

There was a minor press case underway in a courtroom on the same floor – a composer accused of pushing his musician wife out the window. A single small TV crew lounged around their tripod and lightstands and silver equipment boxes, probably from some specialty court-news show on cable. The case wasn't important enough for broadcast news to cover it except as a sound bite on the courthouse steps. *Morales* would be different.

He saw the judge sailing down the corridor toward him from the elevators, a battleship in a gray suit. He turned to go back to her chambers.

'Mr Estrada,' she called. He waited for her.

'Just arriving?'

'No, your honor. It was a bit crowded for the four of us to sit around inside.'

'Anything new on your Mr Alvaro?'

'Not yet,' he had to admit. 'I've been preparing a list of written questions so I can give you an offer of proof as to what his testimony will be, while I continue to work on actually getting him here for the trial.' True as far as it went, but writing questions was not the same as getting them asked, much less answered.

The exaggeration failed to impress her. Holding the door for her, he wondered how much harder he could push Ramírez in the face of his warning not to.

As the first order of business, Martinez told them that she was still considering the papers they had filed about the admissibility of the prior bad act. 'I expected this to be more straightforward. You've both done your homework. I'm going to schedule oral argument and I'll give you notice if I want to hear the witnesses.'

It was not a request for comments. She moved on immediately to other questions. 'I've decided that to preserve the presumption of innocence it would be best if the jury did not know that Mr Morales has already been tried and found guilty.' Everyone, she said, lawyers and witnesses, was to call the first trial only a 'prior proceeding,' and she would give the jury an instruction not to speculate about the nature of that prior proceeding or its outcome.

Morales, dressed again in a blue blazer and gray trousers, listened alertly and with apparent understanding, now and then taking notes with a heavy black fountain pen like the one Judge Martinez favored.

Estrada was surprised when the judge ruled against Miller's request to select jurors by questioning them individually. 'Practically speaking, if there's a question or series of questions that either side feels it's *essential* to ask at the bench, I'll rule on the request at the time. But I don't think the benefits of questioning every juror separately are worth the cost in time and effort. I want to cover as many of the sensitive areas as possible with a written questionnaire so we'll have our answers without any worry that one juror's response will affect the others.

'Of course,' the judge added, 'if as we proceed it begins to look necessary to do it Ms Miller's way I may change my mind.'

Estrada hoped not: he did not want potential jurors, one by one, sitting in a small room with the judge, the lawyers, and Roberto Morales. Estrada did not trust the jurors to be immune to the defendant's charm at that close range.

The crime scene photos were next. The judge excluded more of them than Estrada had expected her to. He wanted to challenge the decision but he decided to wait until after she had ruled on the diary.

Before they got to that, Martinez suggested they come to final agreement on what evidence they would stipulate to the jury to avoid having to call all the first trial's witnesses again.

'We've only had preliminary discussions so far, your honor,' Miller volunteered. 'I've told Mr Estrada that the defense is willing to stipulate all the testimony that establishes the existence of the crime, from the 911 operator up through the medical examiner. I think it could save us a great deal of time.'

Nice try, Estrada thought. 'It seems to me that the jury is entitled to get a firsthand account. It's important that they have a good picture of the crime scene, and I'd like a chance to question the witnesses in my own way. I may not choose to bring out the same points that Mr Kahn did the first time around.'

'With respect, your honor, a parade of policemen describing the bloody corpse – evidence that's merely cumulative, at best – adds nothing to the jury's understanding. It only inflames them. I'm willing to concede it's a heinous crime, but that has nothing to do with the guilt or innocence of my client.'

Her client had been sitting virtually motionless. At the

words 'bloody corpse' his eyes closed, as they did again at 'heinous crime.' Otherwise his expression was neutral. Estrada was impressed again by the man's self-control.

'I'm sure we can find a compromise here,' the judge said.

Ultimately, they did. Estrada agreed to stipulate all the cops except Clemente, and Miller accepted the authenticity of the crime-scene diagrams and model, and the identification of the fingerprints found at the crime scene.

'While we're at it we ought to stipulate the blood and semen, too,' Nancy Rosen suggested as if it were the most natural thing in the world. Estrada did not expect Miller to consider it.

'Can I have a brief talk with my client, your honor?' she requested.

They were gone less than five minutes. 'As to Mariah Dodge's blood,' Miller said, 'we'll agree to having the jury told that both parties agree that Mariah Dodge's blood was found on the rug and in the shower drain. But we'll agree to that only if the jury is not told how the match was made.'

The judge glanced at Estrada. Before he could okay it, Rosen jumped in. 'Your honor, we'd like to go outside, too.'

'She's clever, I'll say that,' Rosen observed when they got out into the corridor. 'I thought it was worth trying to get her to stipulate the semen, but you have to watch her every minute.'

'What am I missing?'

'Well, look at it from the jury's point of view. There's a woman all bloody, and there's blood on the carpet and in the shower drain. Whose blood can it be? Mariah Dodge's. Hers, or the murderer's, maybe.'

'Right.'

'Okay. So if we get up there and show a DNA-print match to Mariah, that fits the jury's expectations perfectly. The result is, their confidence in the method goes way up, because it gives the answer they expected. And the best part is, if Miller tries to attack the quality of the lab work, she helps us, because she shows that DNA-printing gives the right result even when the lab work is sloppy.'

'Very neat,' Estrada said. 'If she gets us to agree that it's Mariah's blood without mentioning how we know that, it's easier for her to challenge the DNA-print of the semen.'

'Which we now can guess is part of her strategy.'

Martinez was not prepared to have Estrada refuse the stipulation. 'You sure, Mr Estrada? It seems harmless.'

'Both blood and semen or neither,' he said.

'Neither,' Miller said in a flat voice.

Miller next offered to stipulate the medical examiner's testimony about the bruises on Mariah Dodge's body. 'I have no trouble with the idea that she died a violent death.'

Estrada weighed it. Her strategy was most likely to be selling the jury the idea of another killer. If so, the bruises cost her nothing: her alternate killer could be a rapist as well as a murderer. But she could not afford to have the jury's attention directed too closely or for too long at the evidence that supported the rape charge, on the off chance that the jury might decide Morales was the killer, after all. The result Miller had to avoid at all costs was convictions for both rape and manslaughter, which the jury could then combine to make felony murder, with a possible life sentence. In a way it was similar to the question of Mariah Dodge's blood: having the bruises admitted as unobtrusively as possible was best for Miller.

For his part, stipulating the bruises would be worth it to him if he could use the stipulation to get something else he wanted.

'The way things stand I can't even consider it,' he said. 'Not unless I can use additional pictures to establish all the bruises and their relationship to each other.' He made a case for reinstating some of the gorier pictures Martinez had excluded.

Miller fought him on all of them. Martinez, out of patience, cut it short by picking three additional pictures as the price of the stipulation.

She breezed through the rest of the necessary business, covering her initial instructions to the jury and procedures for drafting the jury questionnaire.

'Is there anything we missed?' she asked, peering down through her reading glasses at a list on her desk as if unaware that everyone was waiting to hear what she had to say about the diary.

'Oh yes. The diary.' She raised her head and looked over the tops of her half-glasses, first at Miller and Morales, then at Estrada and Rosen. 'I'm withholding my decision on that pending an offer of proof which Mr Estrada has promised me by the end of the week.' She looked straight at him. 'Right, Mr Estrada?'

'Yes, your honor, that's right.' He was as stuck with the promise as if he had actually made it.

'Good. All right, that's it for now.'

For Estrada, every minute now was lived with the knowledge that it was too short. Being aware of the importance of each one did not keep them from blending into a featureless morass of work and anxiety in which he felt himself being engulfed.

No day passed when Collins did not come by for updates at least three times. Bishop was proving to be in no hurry to fill Natalie Muir's vacant job, and Collins was sweating out the promotion more visibly with every passing day.

Nancy Rosen, her forensic evidence assembled and organized, worked with Lisa Stein on making sure all their witnesses, out of town and local, would be prepared and in court at the right time. Together the prosecution team assembled and prepared the exhibits: photos, diagrams, models and all the physical evidence from the crime scene.

Stein was fascinated by the stand-in murder weapon. 'It looks so harmless.'

She took the utility cutter from its transparent evidence bag: a flat rectangle of orange plastic an inch wide and five inches long, with a rounded black plastic cap at one end. She turned it over to loosen the black locking wheel and slid the blade up half way, exposing almost three inches of steel razor. 'People use these every day. And one just like it killed someone.'

'Why not?' Estrada said. 'People get killed with kitchen knives, baseball bats, all kinds of everyday things. That's what keeps us busy.'

His daily calls to the assistant state's attorney in Miami finally got results. Not quite a year after Mariah Dodge's murder, just before Roberto Morales's first trial, Juan Alvaro had transferred the principal of his trust fund to banks in Switzerland. All his business correspondence was now handled by a firm of solicitors in London.

Predictably, a transatlantic phone call brought a polite refusal to provide any information. The clerk took a message for Alvaro without saying whether he was a client.

'Another dead end,' Estrada told Clemente. 'If Alvaro were a fugitive, we might have a chance to get some information out of Switzerland, but a witness . . . I don't think so.'

'Then it's all up to friend Carlos.'

'Who isn't exactly setting any cooperation records.'

'Want me to talk to him?' Clemente looked eager.

'Not yet. He can clam up on us in a minute if we push him the wrong way.'

'How about some electronic eavesdropping, then, see who he talks to?'

'What do we use for grounds?' But there were possibilities. Hindering prosecution, bribing a witness. Stretches in both cases, but maybe worth it. 'Not yet.'

Two days' unreturned phone calls later, Estrada began to reconsider.

In the meantime he heard from a lawyer who said he represented Cuyler Jadwin. 'I want you to know that if you subpoena Mr Jadwin, he won't resist the subpoena and he won't flee, but if he testifies he expects to rely on his privilege against self-incrimination. And we *will* resist a material witness order. I'm assuring you that he'll appear if called, so if you have it in mind to soften him up by putting him in custody, you can expect a lawsuit.'

Having seen the writing on the wall, Jadwin was playing

this to get himself immunity for crimes he was no doubt eager to get away with. Estrada could put him on the stand and get nothing but refusals to answer. If Estrada then compelled him to testify, Jadwin would end up immune from prosecution on any subject they covered.

'It would help if I knew what he was going to say.'

'I can't talk about that,' the lawyer said.

'I'll let you know if I need him.' Not something he would rush to do.

When Martinez announced she wanted a hearing on the Flippo slashing, Estrada knew he was facing a hard fight. And when Lomax brought in Quiñones to prepare for the hearing Estrada saw more clearly than ever that even with testimony from the medical examiner he would need more. He sent electronic mail messages to Andy Flippo on his research ship in the Bering Sea, urging him to come to New York and testify. The only response was notification that the messages were being held in the ship's communications center until such time as Mr Flippo would be in a position to read them. Estrada wished for someone he could grab by the lapels and shake some sense into.

With that in mind he sent McMorris to Brooklyn to sit on Adelante until Carlos Ramírez showed up. Clemente, Estrada thought, would have been overkill.

While he waited for results, he worked on his list of questions for Lynne Schelling and Carlyn Sims, looking for ways to sharpen the picture of Mariah Dodge's intention to 'give it to Morales with both barrels.'

After his months of effort he was stuck with the case he'd had at the beginning. He knew much more than Larry Kahn had about the lives of Mariah Dodge and Roberto Morales and the people close to them, but he had not been able to assemble the pieces into a convincing picture of the crime he could use with the jury. Not unless he could use the Flippo story; not unless 'Johnny' Alvaro came through with something important. Assuming he came through at all. If he remained among the missing there was still the possibility that there would be no trial to win or lose, a result that Estrada had been doing his best to keep out of his mind but that increasingly seemed a danger.

'The end of the week,' Martinez had said, inventing Estrada's promise of answers from Johnny. Now it was Friday and Estrada had nothing for her. McMorris had come back from Brooklyn empty-handed. Carlos Ramírez was hiding, or away, and no one was being helpful about it.

Estrada drew up a subpoena for Ramírez, though he had no idea where to find him. One more time, he picked up the phone to call Adelante.

'Carlos isn't here,' Dolores Acampo told him.

'What a surprise.'

'He left you a message,' she said.

That *was* a surprise. 'I'm listening.'

'He said he spoke to Juan. He said Juan has no information that can help Roberto Morales.'

Estrada said nothing. That he was relieved to hear it made no sense. It was meaningless, would carry weight with no one. Still, he had harbored for so long the concern, at times the conviction, even briefly the hope that Alvaro would be full of information helpful to the defense, that even something this insubstantial seemed like good news.

'It would help if I could have it in writing.' Only in the most illusory way. A pretend bone to bring to the judge.

'Carlos mailed you a letter.'

'Do you have a copy you can fax to me?'

'I think, yes.'

'Please.'

He went down the hall to wait for the fax to arrive. The letter was short and simple: 'Mr Juan Alvaro tells me that he does not believe he possesses any information that would be in any way useful to the defense of Roberto Morales.'

He made a quick photocopy and brought it straight to Martinez's chambers.

The judge read it. 'What is this supposed to be?'

'It's Juan Alvaro, or it will be. Johnny. The missing witness. I'd hoped to have more for you today, but this indicates that we *will* have more, and soon. And it ought to take some of the pressure off, since it doesn't appear the defense has been deprived of anything.'

She glanced down at the letter again, took off her reading glasses and polished them. 'Are you saying you expect me to take this seriously? A secondhand conclusory statement by people who don't know the first thing about it?'

'Your honor, I'm trying to convict a brutal killer, and I have very meager tools. I'm asking you to hold your decision on the diary until we have more information.' He saw her about to protest – something about the lateness of the hour, he was sure. He hurried on: 'I know we're close to trial, but there's a limit to how much quicker I can make things move. Given Mr Ramírez's evident cooperation, serving a subpoena now would be more likely to slow things down or halt them entirely than it would be to help.'

She scribbled something on a small yellow sticky pad and stuck the note to the letter. 'All right, Mr Estrada,' she said sourly. 'Just be aware that I'm being very generous with you on this. I'm not one of those judges who weighs her rulings on a balance scale – so much for the prosecution, so much for the defense. But you have to admit that by now I owe the defense a large amount of leeway.'

33

The day before the hearing on Andy Flippo, Estrada told Ginny to hold his calls so he could concentrate fully on the law he would be arguing. He spent the morning with the cases, but the beauty of the day – the cloudless, deep blue sky and the first touch of coolness that signaled the end of summer – drew him out of the office for lunch. He picked up his message slips from Ginny on his way out and leafed through them waiting for the elevator. One, marked URGENT, made him turn back.

'I don't know who it is,' Ginny confessed. 'The connection was the worst. I think he said he was calling from an airplane. He said he'd call back in an hour. That's fifteen minutes from now.'

'Mr Andrews?' he read on the message slip.

'I think so. It was just the worst connection.'

He went back to his office and waited, filling the time with work. The call came forty-five minutes later.

'This is Andrew Flippo,' he thought he heard the caller say through a rush of noise.

Over the static, they managed a short conversation. Flippo had read Estrada's messages urging him to come east to testify, had found them convincing and had rearranged his work schedule so he could do it. His time was limited but he wanted to be as much help as he could. Even if he made all his connections he would not arrive in New York until late at night, but he hoped to be available first thing in the morning.

He said he was sorry to be cutting it so close.

'The important thing is that you're coming.' Estrada told him. 'Call me as soon as you can so we can make the most of the time we have.' However much it was, it would not be enough.

Martinez had called the hearing for nine-thirty in the morning. Estrada got to the office at seven. At five after nine McMorris brought in Alberto Quiñones and Gerry Lomax and a cardboard tray of donuts and coffee from outside. There had been no word from Flippo.

Estrada, already on his fourth cup of vending-machine coffee, felt a twinge in his stomach. His heart was already beating too noticeably and his palms were cold and sweaty. He assembled his notes and his court opinions in file folders and tucked them into his briefcase, left Lisa Stein to hold the fort and went for a walk in the corridor to calm himself down.

At nine-twenty, Nancy Rosen came in with the medical examiner, who had flown in the night before from California. Flippo still had not called.

'Stay here and wait for him,' Estrada told Stein. 'Knowing La Luz, we won't start till ten the earliest. The important thing is to get Flippo into that courtroom.'

Coming down the corridor from the elevators, Estrada saw a small throng of reporters lounging behind a barricade erected by the court officers. One of the reporters saw him coming and they all snapped into action. He braced himself for the insistent brightness of TV lights that glared into his eyes as soon as he came within range. He tried to look confident and businesslike.

Miller and Morales were already at the defense table in the packed courtroom, talking in low voices. Barry Burns sat with them. There was no clerk and only a single court officer, a brawny man whose shoulders and paunch strained against his white shirt, leaning against the rail that separated the well of the court from the spectators' gallery.

Estrada nodded hello to Miller and sat down, taking his papers out and arranging them on the scarred oak counsel table. Rosen came in and sat next to him. 'Lomax and client are comfortably settled in the witness room, along with the good doctor,' she reported.

Judge Martinez was, as predicted, a half hour late. She entered without comment, preceded by a clerk and a court stenographer, and got to work immediately.

'Mr Estrada, you ready?'

'We are, your honor.'

'Ms Miller?'

'Ready, your honor.'

'All right, Mr Estrada, let's get on with it.'

A court officer brought Quiñones in. Lomax had dressed him up in a gray suit with a white shirt and a blue tie, and his hair had been cut and combed, but the real Alberto Quiñones showed through the camouflage. He vibrated while he took the oath and as soon as he sat down his body began to move in response to his bobbing knee.

Estrada took Quiñones quickly through his pedigree, listing all his crimes including the one on which he was currently awaiting trial. He asked the questions you had to ask an informant – was he expecting any benefit as a result of his testimony, what was it, and would he lie in order to get it? That bullet bitten, Estrada asked a few questions about Quiñones's apparently law-abiding life over the past nine years. Presenting his case to a judge on the issue of admissibility, it was the content of the testimony that mattered: credibility was for the jury to decide. Still, he did not want Quiñones to look like a total skell.

When it came to the story of Morales's attack on his sister's ex-boyfriend, Estrada came as close as he could to letting the witness tell it himself. He did not want to feed him his lines, or even prompt him with cues. If he got the emphasis wrong, that could be fixed with follow-up questions.

Quiñones did a better job than Estrada had expected. He was clearly nervous, his body bobbing at an increasing rate, and his language was again that odd mix of Spanglish, pseudo-homeboy and slang from his youth. The story was compelling enough as he told it to take Estrada's mind partly off the missing Andy Flippo.

Listening to Quiñones, Estrada watched the judge, trying not to be too obvious about it. She was keeping an admirable poker face, he thought, leaning back in her tall leather chair, the reading glasses pushed up on her helmet of hair, fingertips poised under her chin.

For all her apparent judicial distance, she was intently focused on Quiñones. It looked as if his story was making an impression on her.

When Quiñones was done with his narrative, Estrada asked a few questions about what Morales had said as they left to go after Gina's boyfriend. He had Quiñones tell the judge about the X as Morales's trademark, like the mark of Zorro, and about Morales's attempts to bribe and threaten Quiñones into silence. Then it was Kassia Miller's turn.

She was wearing a red-and-white silk dress loosely tied at the waist with a matching sash. She looked bright and summery. Watching her approach the lectern, Estrada could not remember when he had last seen a lawyer in a criminal case wearing a dress appropriate for a garden-society luncheon. Not the kind of thought he would have had about a male defense lawyer, and yet it seemed relevant to him. Kassia Miller's style was likely to have an impact on the trial, and on its outcome.

Her questioning was easygoing to begin with. She followed up on Quiñones's testimony about his criminal past and about the deal he was expecting on his pending case, including the immunity he had been offered in return for his testimony about soliciting cash from Morales for his silence. She quickly succeeded in making Quiñones look a lot more desperate. She did it so deftly that Quiñones did not seem to realize he was hurting himself.

'You testified that Roberto Morales had a trademark,' she said next. 'Is that right?'

'Yeah.'

'Did you ever tell anybody that before?'

Quiñones seemed perplexed. 'The D.A.?' he ventured.

'Do you mean Mr Estrada?' She smiled in the direction of the prosecution table.

'Yeah.'

'You told him that when you saw him recently?'

Again the answer was slow in coming.

'Yeah . . .'

'Did you ever tell anybody else that before?'

'What?'

'That the X was Roberto Morales's trademark.'

Quiñones shrugged.

'You have to answer out loud, for the court reporter. Did you ever tell anybody else?'

Quiñones shook his head. 'Nah.' He seemed captivated by her.

'You never said it before because it was a new idea.'

'I guess.'

'Did you see Roberto make that mark a lot?'

'I said.'

'Where?'

Quiñones looked blank.

'Where did you see him do it?'

'I don't know. Places. This one dude, Robo messed up his ride.'

'Anywhere else? At school?'

'No.'

'At parties?'

'No. We didn't—'

'That's all right, Mr Quiñones, no is enough.' She was smiling at him, indulgent and unthreatening. She pushed that line a few questions more, stopping just as Quiñones's bobbing began to accelerate.

'Did you see Roberto Morales slash a lot of people?'

'No.'
'Just one time?'
'Yeah.'
'You testified that he made that mark.'
'Yeah.'
'On one person.'
'Yeah.'
'Once.'
'Yeah.'

Asked and answered, Estrada was ready to say, but she moved on.

'Before you went to see this person, did Roberto say anything about intending to cut him?'

'I don't remember.'

'But you testified that he said, "I'm going to show him he can't get away with that," isn't that right?'

'Yeah, if you say so.'

'Don't you remember your testimony?'

'Yeah, that's what he said.'

'Were those his exact words?'

Quiñones was confused. 'I don' know.'

'Isn't it true that you don't remember what he said at all, you're just telling us what he *might* have said.'

No answer.

'Mr Quiñones?'

'I don't know.'

'When the fight happened, did you actually see the cutting?'

'What do you mean?'

'Let's try it another way. Tell me where you were in the room.'

Giving Quiñones all the help he needed, breaking it down into small pieces, she took him through the layout of the room and the locations of the participants. He remembered only sketchily. The picture she coaxed from him, full of probablys and must've beens, had him standing near the apartment's entrance hall, with Morales between him and Flippo, about ten or twelve feet away.

'You said before that Mr Morales *went for* this person.'

'Yeah.' Quiñones was bobbing faster than ever. He seemed eager to be agreeable, if only to get the ordeal over with. Earlier he had glanced frequently at his lawyer in the spectators' gallery; now he looked only at Miller.

'When Mr Morales went for him what did you see?'

'He cut him.'

'But Mr Morales was between you and him.'

'Yeah.'

'So how could you see if he cut him?'

No answer.

'Wasn't your view blocked by Mr Morales's body?'

No answer.

'Mr Quiñones?'

'Yeah, I guess.'

'So you didn't see Mr Morales actually cut him.'

Quiñones shrugged, sullen now. 'Maybe not.'

'What did you actually see?'

No answer.

'You saw blood, is that right?'

'Yeah.'

'Blood. Anything else?'

'Yeah. The guy kicked Roberto. He was fallin' down but he kicked him.'

'And then you ran, didn't you?'

'Yeah, sure did. That was a lot of blood.'

'But that's all you saw.'

Quiñones was studying the floor at his feet now. No part of his body was moving. He looked up at his lawyer.

'Mr Quiñones,' Miller said pleasantly. 'The answers aren't out there. Was the blood all you saw before you ran?'

'Yeah.'

'You didn't see the knife, or the cutting, or anything like that?'

'No.'

'Thank you, Mr Quiñones, that's all.'

Disaster, Estrada was thinking. He stood up. 'Mr Quiñones,

when you said Roberto Morales messed up somebody's ride, how did he do it?'

'Con su cuchillo. With his knife.'

'Did he do anything in particular with his knife?'

'He cut the seats and the paint.'

Nerves, Estrada thought. He can't be this stupid. 'How?'

'Oh. Yeah. Like an X, you know. Like Zorro, only an X.'

'Thank you.' Too little, too late. Miller had leached the story of its convincing similarity to Mariah Dodge's murder by the simple expedient of confusing a witness about an event that had happened in the dim past. Hardly brilliant, he reassured himself, but effective nonetheless and bound to be more convincing than Estrada's attempt to rehabilitate him.

Pushing his concern out of mind, he called the medical examiner who had done the autopsy on Mariah Dodge and turned the floor over to Nancy Rosen.

They started with a reprise of the testimony Kahn had used in his attempt to show that the slashing of Mariah Dodge had been intentional within the meaning of the law on intentional murder. The jury had not been convinced on that score, but now the testimony was meant to prove a different point.

Dr Gail Martin – formerly of the Chief Medical Examiner's Office of New York City, now coroner of a mid-size city in California – was a Maine Yankee, thorough and precise. In crisp tones she testified that the first cut had produced a pulsing fountain of blood, and that if the attack had been prompted by sudden anger she thought that the torrent of arterial blood would have discouraged a second cut, except if the attacker was in a frenzy of the sort that resulted in multiple wounds. In that case she would expect ten or more wounds, and on occasion she had seen as many as thirty or forty. For there to be two cuts only, in a clear X-pattern, she had said, indicated to her what she called 'at the very least, a certain savage determination, and very possibly an intention to make a symbolic wound.'

'And what about motion on the part of the victim between the first cut and the second?' Rosen asked. 'In your opinion with a reasonable degree of medical certainty?'

'The two short cuts at her jawline on the left side may be indications that she was trying to move her head and that the assailant tried more than once to make that second cut.'

'Would she have been able to move her head much?'

'With these large muscles on the right side cut through, she would not have had a full range of motion. But from the bloody smudge on her forehead and the way her hair was twisted, it's possible to deduce, and it's my medical opinion that at some time after the first cut the assailant grabbed her hair, here at the hairline in the middle of her forehead, to expose her throat for the second cut.'

'Is it possible to tell if the second throat wound was made before death?'

'Not strictly speaking, not from what I saw in the autopsy. I can say with confidence that the second cut was made some time after the first.'

'Why is that?'

'Primarily, the shape of the cut. I'd do better if I could draw a picture.'

'Your honor?'

'Go ahead, Ms Rosen. But let's not extend this unnecessarily.'

A court officer helped Rosen set up a large drawing pad on an easel. Dr Martin came down from the witness stand and sketched the wound, a long, asymmetrical X with the crossing at the bottom of the legs.

'You see how the stroke that comes from right to left as you look at it – that's equivalent to the victim's left side – is broken slightly where it crosses the other stroke. We get this slight zig-zag effect when we reassemble the skin. A discontinuity like this is a clear sign that the broken cut came second. It happens because the skin is not taut and not supported in that area after the first cut is made.'

She handed the marker to the court officer and resumed the witness stand.

Rosen moved on to ask about the cuts on Mariah Dodge's

cheek, questions Estrada had suggested Rosen pursue with the pathologist after his first meeting with Alberto Quiñones.

'Dr Martin, I'd like to ask about the wounds on Mariah Dodge's left cheek. In particular, how deep were they?'

'Not very deep at all. I believe the autopsy report calls them superficial – two relatively superficial, linear incised wounds of uniform depth, crossing each other at their forward ends in the approximate form of a rough letter X.'

'Can you tell her honor how such a wound might be made? Between slashing wildly at someone and making the cuts deliberately, which is more likely in your opinion, with a reasonable degree of medical certainty?'

'That's an interesting question,' the pathologist said. 'When I testified at the first trial I was of the opinion that those two cuts were essentially unrelated. I'm no longer of that opinion.'

'What is your current medical opinion?'

'I believe that it's an intentional X, just as the neck wound is.'

'Why is that?'

'The cheek wound is far too regular and the depth is too uniform to be the result of random slashing.'

'Can you explain that?'

'In a slashing wound, you commonly see some parts of the wound that are deeper than others. In wounds like the ones on her cheek, that deeper part might be in the middle, or at the beginning.'

'Would it be easier if you illustrated that for us?'

'If I might.' She used the large sketch pad again to make diagrams showing the curved sweep of an arm and how a blade might enter and leave a convex skin surface. 'The longer such an incision is, the more likely it is that the wound would *not* be of uniform depth.'

'Can you compare that with a cut that was deliberately made?' Rosen asked when the witness had resumed the stand.

'Certainly. If you're making the wound deliberately, by which I mean with full intentional control of its placement and so on, you can clearly make it as uniform as the steadiness of your hand will allow, depending also on how still your subject – or perhaps I should say victim – is.'

'And did you observe anything in that regard?'

'Yes. I looked at the autopsy photographs with a magnifier when I was reviewing the materials prior to testifying here, and I saw something I had missed before, and that's a tiny notch-shaped cut at the upper rear corner of the X – that is, the point nearest her ear.'

'And do you have an opinion what caused that, with a reasonable degree of medical certainty?'

'Yes, I believe it was caused when the assailant first began to make the incision, and Mariah Dodge flinched as the blade first cut into her skin.'

'And you can form any opinion from that as to the relative motion of the two people?'

'Yes, it confirms for me that she was not moving at the time the blade was applied to her face, and that the cut was being made slowly and deliberately.'

'Thank you.'

On cross-examination, Miller went straight for the marks on Mariah Dodge's cheek. 'When you say they were uniform, does that mean you measured their depth at every point?'

'Well, no, that was an observation based on a visual examination.'

'And by that you mean you took a look at it and recorded the observation?'

'I suppose you could put it that way.'

'So when you say those cuts were uniform, that's a relative judgment. It means there was nothing *obviously* irregular about them.'

'I think it's more precise than that.'

'Let me put it another way. Roughly how deep would you say those scratches were?'

'I don't think you can call them scratches.'

'How deep?'
'I don't know.'
'Roughly.'
'Not more than a millimeter.'
'That's what, in inches?'
'About a twenty-fifth of an inch.'
'But it could have been half a millimeter?'
'Possibly.'
'Or one and a half millimeters?'
'I doubt it was that deep, but I suppose it's possible.'
'And if it varied by that much over its length, would you have noticed it?'
'Probably.'
'Would possibly be more accurate?'
'Yes.'
'You'd possibly have noticed it?'
'Yes.'
'And that means you quite possibly would *not* have noticed it.'
'Yes.'
'So the depth of the wound could have varied by as much as a hundred percent, or more, in just the way you illustrated.'
'It could have, yes. But I don't—'
'It could have.' Cutting her off. 'The last time you testified about this was roughly three years ago, is that right?'
'Roughly.'
'Much closer in time to the autopsy itself?'
'Yes.'
'And at this time you have no independent memory of this cut, just what's in the autopsy report you wrote back then?'
'Yes.'
'Then we don't have to dwell on this further.' Miller was dismissive, almost contemptuous. 'Suppose we go back to the major wounds to the neck of Mariah Dodge. At the first trial you testified as to the order in which they were made based on the distinctive shape of the cuts.'
'Yes.'
'When you say it's distinctive do you mean you and other

pathologists have seen many times before two cuts in which one crosses another in the rough shape of an X?'

'It's often two cuts out of several which happen to cross. There may be dozens altogether and some cross in pairs.'

'Then you're saying people tend to make cuts in pairs?'

'Not necessarily.'

'Sometimes.'

'Yes.'

'And sometimes it's just two cuts, and they cross.'

'Sometimes.'

'In the cases where it's just two do you think that those people were all trying to make the letter X?'

'Objection,' Rosen said.

'Sustained.'

'Can I ask you to stand up and demonstrate for the court the kind of motion a person might make, slashing with a knife or a straight razor?'

Dr Martin turned to the judge. Given a positive nod, the pathologist shrugged and stood up.

'Can you start with a backhand slash?' Miller requested. 'I believe that's the kind you said caused the first cut?'

Starting with her right hand by her left ear, the witness slashed it rapidly across her body.

'Don't sit down,' Miller said. 'Now give us a cut in the other direction.'

Martin raised her hand to shoulder height and slashed it across.

'Thank you.' Miller waited for her to sit down. 'Now, I saw your hand go from high on your left to low on your right, and then you lifted your hand and cut downward again, this time from high on your right to lower on your left.' Miller repeated the motions, faster. 'Is that correct?'

'Yes.'

'And doesn't that look like an X to you?'

The pathologist clearly felt trapped. 'Well, yes, but I was giving—'

'Doesn't that look like an X?'

Let it go, Estrada thought: give it to her and let her move on. As usual, the witness did not respond to his telepathy.

'Yes,' she said grudgingly after hesitating too long.

Miller kept on. 'Isn't it true that if you make two rapid cutting motions, one in each direction, that they're *likely* to make an X, or something close to an X, whether that's your intention or not?'

'I don't think you can say that.'

'Can you say that it's *un*likely?'

'Well, no, not *un*likely . . .'

'Then would it be accurate to say that if you make two rapid cutting motions, one in each direction, that they're not unlikely to make an X, or something close to an X, whether that's your intention or not?'

'Well . . .'

'Doctor?'

'Yes, you could say that.'

'I'm asking if *you* would say it.'

'Yes, I suppose.'

'Thank you, doctor.'

As Miller was finishing with the witness, Estrada heard the courtroom door open and close. It was a strain to keep from swiveling to see who it was. Hearing heavy footsteps approach, he turned. It was a court officer. He let himself through the gate in the rail and handed Estrada a slip of paper, a note from Lisa Stein.

'Your honor,' Estrada said, 'I've just been informed that Andrew Flippo has arrived at my office. With the court's permission, I'd like the afternoon to confer with him before I put him on the stand.'

'Mr Estrada, we have a trial to get underway here in just a few days, and I have a full schedule until then. You've had ample opportunity to get this witness here on time. You can have half an hour.'

They used the jury room. The scientist was tall and thin,

bald but with a heavy brown beard, as if he had put his hair on upside down. He wore a wrinkled tan suit with a blue shirt and a red tie, and he seemed relatively fresh and alert, considering the amount of time he had been traveling.

Estrada explained quickly what was about to happen and fielded Flippo's questions, then had a few of his own – things that needed clarification, and also a way to warm Flippo up a little. Estrada's biggest concern was that Flippo would come off too stiff and scientific, when what was needed was drama.

'Just talk naturally,' he advised. 'Not like you write. Like sitting around in a bar.'

Flippo nodded, his eyes narrowed as if he were working out an equation in his head.

'I'll try,' he promised. 'I'll do my best.'

Lisa Stein came in to say, 'Time.'

Estrada put Flippo on the stand and asked him briefly about his education and his job experience, to put him in context for the judge. Flippo started out stiff and uncertain, his eyes still narrowed in concentration. He was not helped by Martinez's impatience with the pedigree questions. 'There's no jury to impress, Mr Estrada. Let's get to the heart of it.'

'Yes, your honor.' He smiled encouragingly at his witness, the best he could do with Martinez watching from the bench.

'In the course of your life . . .' he started, then said, 'Withdrawn.' If he wanted Flippo to give a natural and relaxed answer, then stiff, formal questions were not going to help. 'Did you ever know a girl named Gina Coluccio?'

'Yes.'

'Tell us about it.'

'Well . . .' Flippo again got his look of concentration, working out how to begin. Then his face relaxed slightly. 'I dated Gina when I was in graduate school. She was living with some other girls in an apartment on the West Side, and we met at a bar on Broadway where they had jazz and cheap beer. I thought she was Italian. I knew she had a brother named

Roberto who was at Harvard and that her father lived in Brooklyn. That was really all I knew until I got a visit from three very tough-looking Puerto Ricans who said they were members of a gang called the Shadow Phantoms. They told me to stop fooling around with Puerto Rican girls. I told them I didn't know what they were talking about. They said I should wise up – that's how they put it – or I would be dead.'

He stopped and looked up at the judge. 'Can I get a glass of water?'

Martinez motioned to the court officer. He poured water into a paper cup and brought it to Flippo, who drank it down and asked for another one. Estrada decided Flippo was doing well enough on his own not to need any prompting, for now.

'I didn't know what they were talking about,' the scientist resumed. 'So I asked Gina about it. She got upset and started to curse about crazy people who wouldn't leave her alone. There was someone in Brooklyn who had a crush on her, she said. She thought she had discouraged him. She cried and told me it was true that her mother had some Puerto Rican blood, but her father was all Italian and she had always thought of herself as just being Italian. I did what I could to comfort her even though I didn't understand. She promised me she'd talk to this guy and get him and his friends to back off. As you might imagine I was very nervous about continuing to go out with her, not least because I believed the Shadow Phantoms were quite serious. But I didn't want to do anything until she spoke to this person, whoever he was. Nothing happened for about a week. Then, one night when I was walking home, five or six of these Shadow Phantoms cornered me in an abandoned lot. They were going to kill me, for dishonoring their sister, they said. Something like that. I would have thought it was a bad joke, except for the fact that they had chains and lead pipes and knives. I was a brown belt in karate but there were too many of them to fight, so I feinted one way and ducked the other and ran. I never ran like that in my life.'

He stopped to drink more water. Estrada smiled at him: You're doing great. Keep it up.

'That was all, for me,' Flippo went on. 'Gina was nice enough but she wasn't worth having my face rearranged, or worse. I called her and said I could never see her again. The next night, I was coming home from my karate workout and when I opened the door to my apartment someone pushed by me and stormed in. I followed, shouting for him to get out.'

Estrada interrupted with a question. 'How many people were there?'

'I only really saw one, but I'm fairly sure there was a second. My memory of the peripheral activity is pretty vague.'

'Could there have been more than two?'

'No. Two, maybe. Not more.'

'Would you recognize either of those people today?'

Flippo nodded, his lips pressed into a thin line. 'One of them is sitting right over there.' He pointed. 'Roberto Morales.'

Instinctively, Estrada paused, allowing for a reaction from the nonexistent jury. The roomful of spectators obliged, and Martinez exercised her gavel to quiet them.

'Did you know who he was?'

'Yes.'

'How?'

'I'd seen him once or twice when I picked up Gina and he was home on vacation, visiting her. And he told me.'

'And what happened when he was in your apartment?'

'He started to yell at me about how nobody could treat his sister the way I had, and how he wasn't going to let me get away with it. I hadn't recovered from my scare of the previous night, and the adrenaline came pouring back. I called him some colorful names, the way you do in the heat of anger. And then I said, "You may go to Harvard but you're no better than those punks in the Shadow Phantoms, and your lying slut of a sister is no better than you are." And a lot more like that. I'd call it racist, now. I'd probably have called it racist then, too, if I hadn't been so pumped up with fear and anger.'

'What happened then?'

'He got really mad. It happened all of a sudden, like throwing a switch. He jumped me, shouting curses in Spanish. He came for me with a switchblade knife, so fast I couldn't get set. And he cut me. Put me in the hospital.'

'Where did he cut you?'

'He tried to slash my throat, but I was backpedaling to get away from him and he slashed my collarbones instead.'

'What happened next?'

'I kicked him. I was aiming for his wrist, and I think I got him. The knife went flying and he ran.'

'And the others?'

'They ran, too. I collapsed and I was lying there, thinking I was going to die. That didn't seem like a good idea, so somehow I got myself out of there and over to an emergency room. They patched me up and gave me blood, I'd lost a lot of blood by the time I got there. And that was it.'

Estrada stood there, sure there was something he had left out in his rushed questioning. Nothing came to him. Then, as he sat down, he saw what it was.

'When Roberto Morales cut you, what – if any – scars did it leave?'

'Across the collarbones,' said Flippo. 'At the bottom of my neck. An inch higher and I would have been dead.'

'Can you show us?'

For a biologist, Andy Flippo was turning out to have a fine sense of the dramatic. He stood in the witness box and turned away from the judge while he unbuttoned his shirt. Then he turned with his upper chest revealed. The scar, old and faded though it was, stood out pale against Flippo's ruddy skin – thick white lines connecting his collarbones, a scar in the shape of a long, lopsided X, like the cuts on Mariah Dodge's neck.

Estrada thanked him and turned him over to Miller. He wondered if she would risk playing memory games with Flippo the way she had with Quiñones.

She did, but carefully.

'This person you claim was Roberto Morales, how long was he in your apartment?'

Flippo took a moment to think about it. 'About five minutes.'

'That long?'

'I think so.'

'It could have been less.'

'Not much less.'

'You said you'd seen him before once or twice.'

'Yes.' Flippo was regarding Miller with great interest, eyes narrowed in concentration.

'For a few minutes, at most.'

'I suppose . . . yes.'

'You were a brown belt in karate?' Changing the subject before Flippo could work out where she was headed.

'Yes.'

'You used some of your karate that day, didn't you?'

'Yes.' Flippo looked across at Morales. 'A very little.'

Miller turned to the judge. 'Your honor, could I ask you to instruct the witness.'

Martinez looked down at him. 'Mr Flippo, please just answer the question that's been asked. Don't embroider it.'

Flippo thought about it for a moment. 'I see, your honor. I apologize.'

'Now, Mr Flippo,' Miller resumed. 'You used your karate on this person. Did you hurt him?'

'I don't know.'

'Is it possible that you broke his arm?'

'I was trying to. I don't know if I succeeded.'

'The question was, is it possible?'

'Possible? Yes.'

Flippo looked at Estrada, perplexed.

'Mr Estrada doesn't have any answers for you,' Miller said at once.

'That isn't why I was—'

Miller cut him off with, 'Nobody asked a question.'

Flippo clearly wanted to say more but he nodded instead.

'Did you see this person again any time in the next, oh . . . twenty-five years?'

'No.'

'And did you report this incident to the police?'

Flippo did not answer.

'Mr Flippo? Did you report this to the police?'

'Not all of it.'

'What part didn't you report?'

'Who it was.'

'Somebody cut you with a knife so badly it put you in hospital and you didn't tell the police who it was?'

'That's correct.'

'What did you tell them?'

'They came to the hospital, asking questions. I said somebody attacked me and I didn't see who it was.'

'And did they believe you?'

'Objection,' Estrada said. 'He can't know what was in their minds.'

'Rephrase that, Ms Miller.'

'Did they challenge you when you told them that?'

'I don't remember.'

'You've read about this case?'

'Not at first.'

'But you *have* read about it.'

'Yes.'

'And you know it's about a knifing?'

'Yes.'

'Thank you, Mr Flippo, that's all.'

Estrada stood up for redirect.

'Why did you tell them that, at the hospital?'

'The Shadow Phantoms would have killed me if I told anybody what happened. He was one of them.'

'And was that why you didn't tell the police who it was?'

'Yes, it was.'

'Could it have been because you didn't know who it was?'

'No. I was sure who it was. It was Gina's brother, Roberto.'

'How did you know that?'

'He said so. He called her *my sister*. And then when I started to mouth off about Puerto Ricans, he said his name was Morales, and that I should remember it. And then he attacked me.'

Estrada thanked him again and sat down.

'One more question, your honor,' Miller said, standing. 'Mr Flippo, you just said Mr Morales was one of them. Do you mean he was in the gang?'

'I don't know if he was a member, if that's what you mean, but he was one of them. I was sure they would kill me.'

One of them. That was not going to endear Flippo to Luz Martinez.

'I see that it's time for lunch,' Martinez announced. 'I'll hear your arguments at two.'

34

Estrada and Nancy Rosen spent an hour and a half reviewing the testimony and modifying Estrada's arguments based on their best guess about the approach Miller seemed to be taking. They were back in the courtroom before two. Again, Morales and his lawyers were there first, and again the gallery was packed.

Martinez came in at two fifteen. 'Mr Estrada?' she said before she was even seated.

Estrada stood up slowly and stacked his notes in front of him, giving her time to get settled.

'Your honor, there are two items of evidence the People are asking to have you admit today. The first is the testimony by Alberto Quiñones that Roberto Morales paid him money in return for his silence.

'The payment of hush money to potential witnesses has always been considered evidence of a consciousness of guilt – like fleeing to avoid prosecution, or trying to conceal that a crime was committed – and evidence of a consciousness of guilt has always been held to be relevant and material to the jury's deliberations. I'm not suggesting that this evidence alone would be enough to convict, but it's something that the jury has a right to hear. The law here is clear, and the evidence is squarely within it. If the defendant thought he had something to hide and wanted to hide it so badly that he tried to prevent a witness from giving evidence about it, the jury ought to know about that.

'In addition, the People seek admission of evidence that shows the defendant's identity as the person who committed the crimes charged in the indictment.'

Martinez was watching him as he spoke, but he doubted he was getting through. He felt stiff and his voice was flat. He thought of a line spoken by a character he'd once played in a college production. 'My words fly up, my thoughts remain below. Words without thoughts never to heaven go.'

'The People acknowledge that a similar *modus operandi* in an earlier crime does not by itself identify a given person. The fact that a robbery defendant had previously held up the same kind of convenience store with the same kind of gun, even a gun similarly concealed in the same kind of brown paper bag, probably would not make the grade. The example used by the Court of Appeals to show something that *would* meet the test of an identifying or "signature" crime was' – he picked up a heavy book of reported opinions and read – ' "the type of crime committed by Jack the Ripper".

'The crimes we're considering today come uncomfortably close to the crimes of Jack the Ripper. Roberto Morales used a sharp-edged instrument to inflict a distinctive wound on a specific anatomical part of a specific kind of victim. It's important not to be distracted by the fact that Andrew Flippo is a man and Mariah Dodge was a woman. What counts is that they were both hurling ethnic insults at Roberto Morales at the time he was provoked to carve his X-shaped trademark into their necks as a way to silence them. And in both cases the object of Roberto Morales's rage had romantically rejected him or someone close to him.

'The medical examiner's testimony makes it clear that this kind of X-shaped throat slashing is not something just anyone could do. That provides a second reason the earlier slashing should be admitted as evidence in this trial: It's evidence of an unusual skill. Past behavior, including vicious and criminal acts, should be admitted into evidence if it shows that the defendant has a *skill* that's material to the commission of the crime at hand. Unpleasant as it is to think of throat-slashing as a skill, in this case, as the medical examiner made clear, that's not too much to say. To do what Roberto Morales did requires a very special kind of determination. It requires the ability to make the first cut and to stand your ground in the face of blood and gore and the struggles of your victim so that you can make the second cut in exactly the place you want it. And this was a carefully placed cut made at close range, not the product of some generalized arm-waving. An intentionally made X.

'That X is no small part of how Roberto Morales identifies himself. With Andrew Flippo, even in the heat of attack – not with his victim pinned and helpless on a couch, but pursuing him across the room, pursuing a man who proved well able to defend himself – Roberto Morales made an X-shaped cut. Not the quick slash-and-withdraw of the knife fighter. Not, as I said, some generalized arm-waving. No, he kept up his pursuit so he could make the second cut, just as he held his ground in a torrent of blood to cut Mariah Dodge's neck the second time.

'We're not here to talk about credibility. The question is what value does this testimony have for the jury, assuming they believe it. Does this evidence go to identify Roberto Morales as the person who killed Mariah Dodge? Ms Miller attempted in her cross-examination of Dr Martin to cast doubt on the idea that the X shape of the wound on Mariah Dodge's neck was deliberate. But the demonstration that Ms Miller arranged – a medical examiner standing in the witness box – has nothing to do with a man kneeling astride the woman he is about to rape and making a deliberate X, first in her cheek and then, when he's done, slashing another X into her neck.

'Small variations in the depth of the wound on Mariah Dodge's cheek do not make it into the kind of wound that Dr Martin described as resulting from an unrestrained slash. And nothing can erase the two cuts on Mariah Dodge's chin made when Roberto Morales kept trying to make that second cut that would complete the X in her neck. Certainly he didn't keep trying because he thought she might survive if he didn't. Not with all that blood on her and on him. And he kept trying until finally he held her head steady and finished his trademark.

'The evidence shows strongly that Roberto Morales deliberately and intentionally cut his trademark X into Mariah Dodge's cheek and neck. As for what Alberto Quiñones saw or didn't see of what Roberto Morales did to Andrew Flippo, we need only ask Mr Flippo to show us the X-shaped scar just below his throat to disperse Ms Miller's smoke screen. This is strong and unambiguous evidence, and highly probative.

'Look at the wound on Mariah Dodge's neck. And then look at the wound on Andrew Flippo's neck. Consider that Roberto Morales had made that mark often before, even if not in human flesh. The mark of Zorro, Alberto Quiñones said. And if a Z can be an identifying mark, so can an X.

'If you were to ask who is Roberto Morales, it would not be unreasonable to answer that Roberto Morales is the man who, when he is provoked to the point of losing control, slashes an X into the throat of the person provoking him. An X that is literally his signature.

'If this evidence is ruled inadmissible, the jury will reach its verdict in ignorance of that essential fact.'

He paused, to put a period on it. Shuffled through his notes and resumed. 'Apart from the fact that the slashing of Andrew Flippo *identifies* Roberto Morales by its form and its circumstances and so should be admitted in evidence as part of the prosecution's case in chief, this incident should also be available for use in cross-examining the defendant.

'The Court of Appeals has said that an act of calculated violence could significantly reveal a disposition of the defendant to put his own individual self-interest ahead of principle or the interests of society.

'Now, Alberto Quiñones testified that Roberto Morales told

him, "We're going to show the fucker he can't get away with that shit." Having made that threat, Morales then traveled from Brooklyn to the Upper West Side of Manhattan, armed and angry, to see the man who had shown disrespect to his sister. He forced his way into the man's home, over his protests and objections, and then provoked him with fighting language. "I'm gonna make him sorry he was born," is what the defendant said on his way to see Andrew Flippo. How much more calculated could that violence have been?

'Does that calculated violence show that the defendant was willing to place the advancement of his individual self-interest ahead of principle or the interests of society? Absolutely. Whose interest was the attack against Andrew Flippo meant to aid? Not the sister whose honor Roberto claimed to be defending. We heard from Alberto Quiñones that she urged him to stay away from Flippo. Defending his sister was simply a pretext. The interests of Gina Coluccio, or Andrew Flippo, or even Alberto Quiñones, did not matter to Roberto Morales. Certainly the interests of society did not matter. Principle did not matter, not in any sense in which we understand principle.

'The Court of Appeals said it best: "A demonstrated determination deliberately to further self-interest at the expense of society or in derogation of the interests of others *goes to the heart of honesty and integrity*." And make no mistake – the slashing of Andrew Flippo by the defendant was a deliberate and calculated act, and a totally selfish one.'

Estrada stood silent for a moment before he closed his argument.

'For the reasons just given, the court must allow the admission of this evidence to show an identifying characteristic of the murderer of Mariah Dodge. Even more clearly, and whatever the court's decision as to the admissibility of this incident as evidence in chief, reference to this prior act is appropriate in cross-examining the defendant should he choose to testify.

'Apart from that, the court must allow the testimony of Alberto Quiñones about the bribe he received from Roberto

Morales, a bribe specifically intended to keep Alberto Quiñ-ones silent about the very evidence the court is ruling on here – as clear an indication as there could be of the strength of this evidence and of the defendant's consciousness of his own guilt.'

As soon as Estrada sat down, the judge turned to his opponent. 'Ms Miller?'

She stood at the defense table, looking as fresh as she had first thing in the morning, the deep burgundy of her dress made richer by the afternoon sun slanting through the court-room's high windows. She began speaking without looking at the ring binder open on the table in front of her.

'Long ago, this state's highest court said that in our system of justice "in a very real sense a defendant starts his life afresh when he stands before a jury." Not long after that, it said, "One may not be convicted of one crime on proof that he probably is guilty because he committed another crime." Nothing in what Mr Estrada has said today, or in the evidence he's presented, is enough to contradict that principle.

'All the cases on this subject, from the very beginning of the century until now, agree that in deciding questions like this the court has to ask two questions: how useful is evidence of this prior act in proving something against the defendant now? And how much unwarranted prejudice against him will be created in the minds of the jurors if they hear about it? To decide if the evidence should be admitted, the court weighs one against the other – prejudice against probative value.

'What are the standards?' she asked, and answered herself: 'Lapse of time since the prior act is an important measure of how much value the prior act has as proof. If you look at the statutes and cases on this question around the country, you find that ten years is a kind of benchmark. After ten years, evidence of past criminal behavior is generally thought to be too remote to be admissible.

'Just as an example, in the Federal Rules of Evidence ten

years is the limit in the case of *convictions* for prior crimes. Crimes *proved* in court, not *alleged* bad acts for which the proof is scant or problematic.

'The question naturally arises, if a person shouldn't be burdened with questions about a *proved crime* after ten years, how can we seriously consider raising against him a mere allegation of a bad act supposedly committed almost thirty years ago, twenty-five years before the crime that is the subject of this proceeding?

'There is no theory to support using an event so far in the distant past for *any* of the reasons recognized in New York as sufficient to overcome the inadmissibility of prior bad acts as evidence against the defendant.

'I was interested to hear Mr Estrada quoting *People v. Sandoval* in support of using this alleged prior act in cross-examination. If he had looked at that case more carefully he'd have seen that the court made a point of saying that acts of violence seldom have any logical bearing on the defendant's credibility, *particularly if they're remote in time*.'

She moved a few steps across the well of the court, placing herself next to the empty jury box. 'What about the so-called *evidence* Mr Estrada is relying on to establish this prior bad act? We have the medical examiner who admits, even demonstrates, that if you make two cuts, forward and back, one after the other, you're going to get an X, like as not, and who tells us that we cannot draw reliable conclusions about intention from the mere fact that two cuts cross each other.

'We have Alberto Quiñones, who does not know what he saw – he said as much – and who does not know whom he saw it happen to. We have Mr Flippo, who has a scar but who cannot substantiate how he got it, or from whom. He cannot even say, despite Mr Estrada's attempt to pull it out of him, that Alberto Quiñones was there at all. He had seen Roberto Morales only once or twice before the incident he described, and only briefly. He never reported that the person who tried to kill him was someone he claims he could identify at the time. Why? Because, he says, he *imagined* that someone would wreak retribution. Nobody ever threatened it. Even if we believe him, all we know is that someone who *claimed* to be Roberto Morales visited him that night.

'Besides all that, Mr Quiñones has a clear motive to fabricate his testimony, to make his story fit Mr Flippo's, or the suggestions of some law enforcement officer. He wants to stay out of prison. And Mr Quiñones's own prior crimes are acts of dishonesty – stealing, dealing in stolen goods. It's true that the court is not primarily concerned with credibility in this hearing, but that doesn't mean it has to give weight to apparent fabrications.

'The truth is that nothing in what these two men have said is at all persuasive that they are describing the same incident. Nothing helps us decide what's true in their stories and what isn't.

'Because the event, if it *is* one event, is so remote to begin with, and because the testimony is too weak to be believed, we have to conclude that the probative value of this alleged bad act is already as low as it could be. But we have to ask, too, what relationship it bears to the crime charged here. The answer is: very little. The alleged prior act and the crime charged now are noticeably different, in a significant way. The story we heard today – assuming we accept the Quiñones and Flippo versions as the same story – is about a male reacting to being personally insulted in front of a male friend, and at the same time having his sister insulted in front of his friend. In the murder of Mariah Dodge, the previous prosecution case was based in the absence of an audience: no one saw the crime, no one heard the alleged insult. This is a major and significant difference, where the prosecution is alleging an act of violence supposedly involving macho self-image and sexual jealousy.'

She stepped back to the defense table again and turned a page in her notebook. For effect, Estrada thought: a reason to move. She did not take time to read anything before she resumed her argument.

'What about the amount of prejudice that would be created by admitting this evidence, or even alluding to this alleged bad act in cross-examination?

'In truth, what Mr Estrada is urging on the court today is the most blatant and unacceptable form of propensity evidence. It says, clearly: convict this man because of what we claim he did in the past. That is precisely the evil against which this principle of law is aimed. And what the prosecution has represented here as evidence is weak and hard to believe. It isn't even decent propensity evidence.

'As for referring to any of this in cross-examination, the Court of Appeals warned particularly against cross-examination based on past conduct similar to what the defendant is presently charged with, "in view of the risk that the evidence will be taken as some proof of the commission of the crime rather than be reserved solely to the issue of credibility." The prejudicial effect is not diminished by the court's instruction that the particular act should only be considered in assessing the defendant's credibility. As another court put it, "A drop of ink cannot be removed from a glass of milk."

'The court should have no trouble discarding Mr Estrada's arguments and declaring that any reference to an attack by Roberto Morales on Andrew Flippo is inadmissible for any purpose, either as evidence in the prosecution's case in chief or as material for questions in cross-examination.'

Miller paused long enough for Estrada to think she was finished, but she did not sit down. She resumed in a milder, less clipped tone.

'Mr Estrada also talked about an alleged attempt by Mr Morales to bribe Alberto Quiñones to prevent him from being a witness against Mr Morales. I admire Mr Estrada's imagination, but I don't think a court of law is the place where he should be exercising it.

'The story told us by Mr Quiñones, vibrating in fear of a prison sentence as he spoke, was the story of a desperate man gouging a handout from a former acquaintance who'd had the fortitude, skill and courage to make something of his life. To Mr Morales's credit he did not send Mr Quiñones away empty-handed. Nor did he encourage him to come back. There is nothing, even in Mr Quiñones's account, to make this transaction into a payment of hush money, especially since – as I have pointed out – Mr Quiñones's story about an alleged slashing in the distant past is not and could not be evidence in this trial. This sordid tale of manipulative panhandling has no place here.'

She sat down.

'Thank you, Ms Miller,' the judge said. 'Mr Estrada? Any rebuttal?'

'Yes, your honor.' He stood in his place at the prosecution table. 'In her zeal to protect her client, Ms Miller has misstated the law and mischaracterized the evidence. There is nothing stale or over-age about Roberto Morales's clear attempt to buy silence from Alberto Quiñones. It happened more recently than the crime we are here to try. And what matters about that bribery attempt is not whether the Flippo slashing is admissible or inadmissible evidence. What matters is whether Roberto Morales *thought* at the time he offered the bribe that it might be evidence against him. Similarly, for Roberto Morales's threat against Mr Quiñones to be relevant, we do not need to show, or even to believe, that Mr Morales had a staff of kneecappers ready to do his bidding. All we need to believe is that Mr Quiñones found the threat to be credible, which he certainly did. This incident clearly shows a consciousness of guilt on the part of the defendant, and it should be admitted as evidence against him.

'As for the slashing itself, the lapse of time in no way diminishes its value as proof that the defendant had the skill and ability to make such a precise double cut, persisting in the face of a fountain of blood resulting from the first cut. Nor does the lapse of time diminish the probative value of the slashing as a signature crime, and the other instances Mr Quiñones described of the defendant's *trademark* X cut, as identifying characteristics. The defendant himself made clear how fresh and important that past act is and how immediate and relevant it seemed to him. Why else pay Alberto Quiñones to remain silent about it?

'The People concede that Alberto Quiñones expects to benefit from his testimony. That goes to the weight of his testimony, not its admissibility, though Ms Miller appears to be arguing, incorrectly, that it should be considered in assessing the probative value of this event.

'Most important, the rules of law are not meant to provide the defendant with a shield, they're meant to insure a fair trial. And the exclusion of this evidence as inadmissible and, even more, any decision that precludes me from cross-examining on this incident will inevitably deprive the People of any chance to receive a fair trial before any jury.' He held Martinez's gaze a long moment before he sat down. He read no encouragement in her eyes, but nothing negative, either. Maybe, he thought. *Maybe*. Trying not to think about the impressive job Miller had done on the witnesses.

Miller did not immediately rise to reply. When she did, she said, 'I stand by my argument. There is no reason to allow blatantly unfair and prejudicial allegations to pollute this trial. No alleged youthful escapade of thirty years ago has any place in this court, nor does any empty allegation of witness bribery or intimidation, which in reality has been trumped up merely to put a gloss of freshness on doubtful charges otherwise too antiquated to be heard. And it is the defendant to whom the law guarantees a fair trial. The law says nothing about the prosecution.'

There was a silence in the courtroom when Miller sat down. Martinez looked at the two prosecutors and the two defense lawyers. She gathered the papers in front of her into a neat stack.

Estrada put his own papers into his briefcase, getting ready to be dismissed.

'I thank you both for your learned arguments,' Martinez

said without apparent sarcasm. 'It's always good to hear smart lawyers debate an interesting point of law. The prosecution's motions are denied.'

Estrada started to offer pro forma thanks for the compliment, and then the judge's words registered. 'Your honor?'

'I think that's clear, Mr Estrada. I'm denying your motions. You will not enter into evidence any of this business about slashing his foster sister's ex-lover, nor will you use it in cross-examination. You will not put Mr Quiñones on the stand to talk about bribery or intimidation.'

She leaned forward across the bench to talk to the court reporter. 'Hearing adjourned. We're off the record now.' She sat back. 'I'd like to see Mr Estrada and Ms Miller in chambers briefly.'

She started talking as soon as they were all in the room. 'One thing I want to get absolutely straight. I decided this in favor of the defense because I believe the defense argument is the correct one. This story, true or not, is inadmissible. Inadmissible in any court in the state, I'd guess. Inadmissible in my court for sure.' She paused to take off her black judicial robe and draped it over the back of her desk chair. 'I have the impression that people are worried I'm going to roll over for the defense in this case because of the way I got slapped down on the appeal after the first trial. Some people think I'm too much of a defendant's judge, anyway. As a result of those two theories these same people think I ought to throw a couple of decisions the prosecution's way just to show I'm being fair.

'Well, the hell with what people think. I call them the way I see them. Always have and always will. If people don't like that, and they think they've got a better judge to sit in my chair, I say let them use her.'

She sat down heavily at her desk. 'I'm perfectly aware that the entire dog-and-pony-show Mr Estrada just put on for us was intended to get me thinking the defendant is guilty. I want you to know that it's not going to affect my ruling on the diary, or on anything else in this case.

'Speaking of the diary, I have begun to prepare an edited version for the defense. I do agree with Mr Estrada that there are aspects of the diary that are so private they should not be revealed to the writer's accused killer. But there are also parts where I can't tell whether they might be useful to the defense or not. And I'm tired of waiting for the phantom Mr Alvaro to appear out of the blue and clear up the questions.'

'Excuse me, your honor, but I don't understand,' Miller interjected. 'Who's Mr Alvaro?'

'A question we'd all like to have answered for us. Soon, Mr Estrada?'

'Yes, judge, very soon.'

'So you keep saying.'

'I had hoped to have a little more time before discussing this in this way.'

Martinez turned stern. 'I'm going to give you until the end of jury selection to come up with this missing person, or a reasonable facsimile. If not, the defense gets the diary, edited as I see fit.'

And without Alvaro the defense also gets to accuse Lawrence Kahn of misconduct, Estrada thought. And maybe me, too. Carlos Ramírez's letter would not begin to forestall that.

'With respect, your honor,' Miller protested, 'if there's anything in this diary I need to follow up on, seeing it for the first time on the immediate eve of trial doesn't begin to give me adequate time.'

'I think you'll find, Ms Miller, that you'll have time enough to do what you need to. As you know, I have no desire to protract this trial unnecessarily, but this is a sensitive matter, and I want to give Mr Estrada all the rope I reasonably can.' To Estrada, she said, 'I don't care if a dozen saintly people say they're going to talk to him. I want to hear what the man himself has to say. ¿Está claro?'

'Yes, your honor, it's clear.'

Miller pressed him for more as they headed down the hallway to the elevator.

'I asked for a protective order precisely so I could avoid telling you any of this,' he pointed out.

'The fact that the judge needs testimony from a missing witness to make a decision about the diary is no subject for a protective order.'

'There's nobody missing. And the judge said you'd get what you needed in time to use it.'

'*In time* is a matter of opinion. If there's so much as a *word* of that diary that's ambiguous, that even *hints* it's valuable to me, I should have seen it long ago.' The elevator bell rang. 'And I intend to file a motion to that effect first thing in the morning.'

So that was that. Roberto Morales would enter the courtroom as a man with no violent history, and he would stay that way unless Kassia Miller was unheeding enough to make his peaceableness an issue in the trial, or unless Morales himself was careless enough to say he had never done anything like what he was accused of doing to Mariah Dodge. Neither mistake seemed likely.

The judge had been right to say that Estrada had been hoping to sway her – and Miller – toward believing that Morales was guilty. He wished he could banish his own lingering doubts. But the idea of Morales's signature X was persuasive, if not absolute proof, and the fact that Martinez had ruled the slashing inadmissible did not mean it had never happened.

The evening news anchors kept their correspondents standing in the rainy dusk in front of the courthouse to explain why the law did not wish a jury to conclude that this prior act of violence made Roberto Morales's guilt more likely. For balance they showed all of Miller's statement on the courthouse steps. 'These charges are false and malicious and have no grounding in the truth,' she had said. 'They are the result of a grudge held by a lifetime cheat, thief and liar against an honest man who has overcome the disadvantages and obstacles that life put in his way. As for Mr Flippo, I don't know what his motives are, but I do know he's mistaken. I also know that even if the law allowed these charges to be heard, no jury would believe them.'

Estrada's own statement got less play, but he was not unhappy with the appearance of sincerity he gave saying he regretted the judge's decision and felt that it meant the jury would be deprived of important evidence.

The morning papers gave him even less space, mostly playing the story as an implausible allegation properly kept out of court. They seemed more willing to show their bias in favor of Morales now that the trial was about to begin. Only one treated Flippo's story as seriously as Estrada thought it deserved.

The front page headline in *Noticias Diarias* said simply, PRUEBAS PROHIBIDAS. Inadmissible Evidence.

TRIAL

1

The first morning of the second trial of Roberto Morales greeted Joseph Estrada with unseasonable heat and a steaming downpour. By the time he got to the subway, his pants were soaked to the knee.

At the courthouse, Kassia Miller did not look at all wet, nor did her client, or her associate. That was one of the differences between the prosecution and the defense in a case like this one: the defense did not take the subway.

But the jurors did, and they were bound to be resentful that the System had dragged them out to get rained on and sweaty and then made them sit, damp from head to toe, in an uncomfortable room in a dim and soulless building. As representative of the government, part of the System, Estrada knew he would be a target for their resentment. So he had not taken a cab or brought a change of clothes, hoping that by looking as soaked and miserable as the jurors felt he could help them think of him as one of them, instead of one of Them.

Surprisingly, Acting Justice Martinez came in only a few minutes after the appointed hour of nine-thirty. The rain had partly collapsed her helmet of hair, and her attempts to repair it had left her looking dented on one side. The experience had also left her surlier than usual. Gruffly, she took care of some housekeeping details and gave Estrada and Miller copies of the pre-trial jury instructions she intended to use. One of the court officers had a large cardboard box full of juror questionnaires ready to be distributed; the final version was sixteen pages long, full of questions about racial attitudes, attitudes about family life and exposure to press accounts of the crime and the prior proceedings.

'All right,' Martinez said. 'Let's get them up here.' She patted her hair, trying to do it so no one would notice.

A court officer led the jurors in. Even in this long and broad courtroom, with ceilings high enough for a double-decker of lesser courtrooms, a hundred and fifty potential jurors in clothes still damp from the rain quickly filled the air with the odor of wet cloth. They crowded into the benches like errant congregants at Christmas and Easter. To make room for the oversize jury panel Martinez had temporarily restricted spectators to a single row of press seats. A throng of press and spectators waited in the corridor for seats to become available.

Martinez began with the standard pep talk for jurors, a paean to the importance of jury duty and the need to serve with honesty and full attention. She talked briefly about the burden of the prosecution to come forward with proof, and told them that the proof had to be beyond a reasonable doubt as to each necessary element of the crimes charged. She told them, too, that until all the proof was in, the defendant had to be considered an innocent man. Listening, Estrada could not avoid the memory that not so long ago he himself had been ready to believe that Morales was not guilty.

Despite the bad mood Martinez had inflicted on the lawyers, she was showing the jurors a pleasantly engaging side that Estrada had never seen. With his chair turned sideways he had a view of the jurors listening attentively to her, nodding in the right places, smiling in the right places.

After the basic indoctrination Martinez gave the jurors a quick rundown on the questionnaire they would be filling out. Court officers passed the questionnaires around. Martinez told the jurors that there were no right or wrong answers, and swore them to answer honestly. By the time the questionnaires were completed and the court officers had collected them it was time for the lunch recess. Martinez sent the jurors home until the next morning.

The lawyers came back early from lunch to begin reading through the questionnaires. When Martinez arrived they culled out the jurors they agreed had valid reasons not to serve on this jury. They lost twenty-three that way, with another forty-one writing in excuses that required a conversation with the judge.

Those forty-one and the remaining eighty-six were checked for obvious bias. A few of the answers were outrageous enough to crack the attorneys' professional reserve, and even the judge's. Morales remained aloof, not joining in the laughter.

The light moments aside, it was a grueling afternoon. Miller was eager to strike any juror whose answers veered slightly toward the bigoted, especially when the prejudice involved stereotypes of Hispanic behavior. Estrada saw himself being deprived of every juror who might be willing to entertain a guilty verdict. Finally he let himself blow up about it.

'This is too much. Here's a woman who thinks African-Americans are athletic, oppressed and poor; Jews are intelligent, greedy and clannish; Catholics are religious, bigoted and powerful; and Hispanics are sexy, creative and impulsive. And you want to strike her as biased against *Hispanics*?'

'She also says that having sex with a woman not your wife is a sin,' Miller said.

'A lot of people think adultery is a sin. That doesn't make her an unfit juror.'

'She thinks Hispanics are impulsive.'

'Impulsive isn't dishonest. Impulsive isn't a liar.' Though it might be a murderer. 'Look, if you want to ask her questions to get deeper into this, fine. You want to use a peremptory challenge on her, fine. But this is not bias enough to excuse her for cause. They only have the words we gave them – we can't strike everyone who picks *anything* negative, not unless you want a bunch of sycophants and liars. At least this one's an equal-opportunity bigot.'

'I have to agree with Mr Estrada,' the judge said. 'We can't expect these people to have sanitized opinions.'

That improved things, but not much. They still lost thirty-nine jurors because of their answers, and the vast majority of them were likely to have been pro-prosecution. The next big cut was for exposure to press accounts of the crime. Only a few claimed never to have heard of it. Most were aware of the recent testimony of Flippo and Quiñones. Miller wanted almost all of those excused. Estrada fought to keep the ones he thought would be assets, with almost no success.

After eliminating jurors by agreement based on a first look through the questionnaires, they were left with a panel of eighty-eight possible jurors, of whom twenty-one were claiming hardship excuses that required further explanation.

The prosecution team spent the next few hours photocopying the eighty-eight questionnaires for the defense and the judge and themselves. They took their own copies to Estrada's office and pored over them until midnight, sorting and characterizing, getting a feel for the panel and the individual jurors. Estrada was enjoying working with Nancy Rosen. She was a good lawyer, organized in a way that he would never be.

He left a message for Michelle before he went to sleep, disappointed she wasn't there and at the same time relieved. If they had talked he might have told her he wished she were here, not there, that he needed comfort and support and a partner who lived on the same edge of the continent as he did. And that would have surely led to an argument, the last thing he needed now.

The alarm blasted him awake at seven. He stood himself under a cold shower then and spent ten minutes shaving, studying himself in the mirror and telling himself that the face he saw was clear-eyed and strong-jawed. He smiled a few times and failed to find himself captivating.

In the hall outside the courtroom would-be spectators clustered behind a police barricade separate from the one that restrained a pool television crew there to record the comings and goings of the main players. Estrada walked past briskly, trying out his smile – more to keep his face from feeling frozen when he began with the jurors than out of any desire to court the TV audience.

He had discouraged Tess Dodge from attending the jury selection, but today she was in the courtroom, sitting on the aisle in the front row of the gallery, the row reserved for the D.A.'s office. He stopped to say hello and saw that she looked tired and drawn.

Martinez had done a better job of avoiding this morning's lighter rain: her hair was only slightly askew. She dismissed the jurors who had already been excused and gave the rest a short, sharp reprise of her lecture about civic duty and not avoiding jury service.

She adjourned to the jury room with defense and prosecution to see the jurors with hardship claims one at a time. The first three called had been sufficiently cowed by the judge's warning that they withdrew their excuses.

Roselle Alden, a fiftyish woman from 120th Street, was the first potential juror to press her excuse: she had a physical disability that made it hard for her to travel to and from the courthouse.

'We're not expecting a long trial, Mrs Alden,' Martinez assured her.

'What if we have to stay over in some hotel?' She glanced nervously at Morales, then back at the judge. 'You said that – stay over in a hotel. I don't sleep except with my hospital bed that I got on my disability.'

'Jury duty inconveniences everyone to some degree,' the judge said mildly. 'You can go back into the courtroom. Please ask the clerk to send someone else. And try to remember to bring your cane if you need it.'

The next juror was a sixty-four-year-old woman named Yetta Fink, from lower Riverside Drive. She was worried about the publicity.

'I'm afraid. I see what happens. If people don't like the answer – guilty, nor guilty, whatever it is – you could have God knows what on your head. Killing, rioting. No thank you.' There was an edge of panic in her voice.

Martinez tried to put it in perspective but Mrs Fink only got more agitated and the judge saw there was no point continuing. She excused Mrs Fink with an admonition not to discuss her excuse with any other juror.

Martinez handled the rest with similar dispatch. By the time she had rejected twelve excuses while approving only four, others began withdrawing their requests. In the end she accepted only seven of the twenty-one excuses.

'That was quick,' Nancy Rosen commented over lunch.

'She cut them no slack.' Estrada munched without interest on a turkey sandwich. 'I think it's a good sign.'

'You were right about having them in the room with Morales,' Lisa Stein said. 'They can't keep their eyes off him, even the ones that look like they want to.'

The question came up again when they got back to the courtroom.

'Your honor, I'd like to renew my request for individual questioning of jurors,' Miller said as soon as Martinez came in. 'It went well this morning, and I feel more strongly than ever that the questions I need to ask won't get straight answers in a more public setting.'

'Mr Estrada?'

'I'm still opposed, your honor. This morning was a simple yes-or-no decision by the court on a single issue, and it still took us half a day to get through fewer than twenty people.'

'That's only another day or two at the most, then.' Miller said it as if it were self-evident.

'Only if you can do it in a couple of minutes a juror.'

'I haven't changed my mind,' Martinez said. 'Let's start with the group. We can go to individual if we have to.'

Miller was not happy. 'Your honor, I have to follow up on

some of these questions about family values. If I do that in front of the panel, there's a risk of prejudicing them all and almost no chance of getting a reliable answer. And no one will answer a question about race prejudice in front of a roomful of strangers.'

'That's why we put all those questions into the written questionnaire, and it's why we excused thirty-nine people, if I have the number right. I don't see any need to ask a lot more questions on those subjects.'

Estrada was pleased by the decision, though he would have been interested to see how Miller planned to dig out the anti-Latino prejudice of a juror sitting in a small room face to face with a judge named Martinez.

The jury panel filed into the courtroom and took seats.

'I know you've answered a lot of questions already, but now we're going to ask you some more,' Martinez informed them. 'You're still subject to the oath you all swore before the questionnaires.'

The clerk drew sixteen names to fill the jury box. Estrada watched them file up from their seats in the gallery. At the other end of the prosecution table Stein was pulling their questionnaires and flipping through them to find any responses the prosecution team had highlighted as needing a follow-up.

Martinez smiled at them. 'I want to ask you some questions about the law, to be sure you're comfortable with how we're going to do things. I mentioned before that we presume that a person is innocent until he is proved otherwise. Does everybody understand that? And does everybody understand that that means the defense doesn't have to prove anything? If you have any questions about that, please ask them.'

Nobody did.

'Good. Now, another thing that means is that the entire burden in this trial is on the prosecution. That's Mr Estrada, sitting over there, and his colleague Ms Rosen. It's up to them to prove to you that the defendant is guilty, and they have to prove it beyond a reasonable doubt. If they don't, you have to vote not guilty. Is that clear to everybody?'

She asked more questions about reasonable doubt, and asked if anybody would have any trouble being a juror subject to those rules. None of the sixteen said they would.

'I know from your questionnaires that none of you is acquainted with any of the prosecutors or defense lawyers, or the defendant or the prosecution witnesses. I just want to double-check on that. No? Okay, then I'm going to turn you over to Mr Estrada. But before I do that I'm going to make a request. I'm going to ask you to promise that you'll keep an open mind, that you'll wait to discuss the case until after I give you my final charge as to the law and how to deliberate, and that you'll pay attention during the trial and not fall asleep.'

That brought some laughs. 'Promise?'

They all nodded; some said yes.

'Good. And the other thing I want you to promise is that when it does come time to deliberate you'll all participate.' She gave them a chance to nod assent to that promise, too. 'Good. Then we can begin.'

Estrada led off with a quick round of personal questions to warm the jurors up, then got to the day's serious business by asking about their experiences with people overreacting, especially in anger. 'Has any of you ever known a person who reacted to things more strongly than you did? Emotionally, I mean. Somebody who really blew up at what seemed like a small provocation? Ms Casirer?' The fashion designer in seat twelve had responded to the general question with a nod and an imperfectly suppressed smile.

'Yes, I have.' The answer was restrained, accompanied again by the partly suppressed smile.

'You've seen someone overreact seriously?'

'Yes.'

'Just once? Or have you seen people blow things out of proportion more than once?'

'Many times.'
'Would you say you're comfortable with the idea that other people might react more strongly to certain events than you would?'
'Yes.'
'Mr Yussuf?' A twenty-one-year-old African-American college senior. Estrada did not want college students of any race on this jury, especially liberal-arts students. An accounting major might be all right, one working days and going to school at night.
Yussuf's response was a snort and a shake of the head. 'People blowin' up all the time. Make a mess for somethin's no way worth it.'
Estrada nodded. 'I know a lot of people in Manhattan don't have much chance to drive a car, but I want to ask if you've ever been in a situation where you were in a car and somebody cut you off, raced into your parking space, anything like that?'
'Oh yeah. Once or twice.'
'And did it make you angry?'
'Yeah, it did.'
'And did you imagine doing something violent to the person who cut you off?'
Yussuf took a moment to relish the thought. 'I sure did.'
'Would you actually do what you imagined?'
'Never.'
Good. Mr Yussuf might not make it onto the jury but he had already done his duty as a citizen, educating his fellow jurors. 'Have you ever heard of that happening? People shooting each other over a parking space, or over some argument in traffic?'
'Sure. I remember, in L.A. a couple of years ago they were poppin' each other once a day like that.'
'So even though you wouldn't do it yourself you could believe someone else would.'
'No problem.'
Estrada moved on to asking how the jurors would react to

the lack of an eyewitness to the crime. His lead-in was the usual exorcism of TV trials. 'The real world isn't always as neat and tidy as television. For example, I can tell you now not to expect anybody to come into this courtroom and say "I saw it happen. I saw *that man* do it." So my next question to you is, can you bring yourself to vote for conviction in a case where there's no eyewitness to the crime itself? Ms Domsky?'

'Um . . . you know, if you can prove it some other way . . .'

'That's an excellent point, Ms Domsky, and I thank you for it.' She was a thirty-two-year-old beautician with dyed black hair and bright red lipstick that matched the polish on her lethal-looking fingernails. 'If the People prove the charges to you beyond a reasonable doubt – as the judge said, she'll be telling you more about what that means – even though there is no eyewitness, could you vote to convict?'

'Is there some reason I shouldn't?'

'No. The judge will tell you the law, but I can predict that she'll say there's no reason not to convict once you're satisfied of the defendant's guilt, even if there's no eyewitness.'

'Okay. I could do that.'

'And could you stick to that vote, and not be bothered by some annoying feeling that you'd be even *more* certain if somebody testified who actually *saw* it happen.'

'If that's what I'm supposed to do.'

He asked each juror in turn about eyewitnesses, getting all of them to think in terms of conviction, building a consensus that the absence of an eyewitness was not enough reason to doubt anyone's guilt. He watched them closely as they answered, trying to see past the easy and obvious affirmatives to the misgivings they might be concealing.

He asked, too, if anyone found the severity of the crime a problem, if any of them would be hindered in reaching a guilty verdict by the likelihood that such a violent and final crime would carry a heavy penalty. They all said the right thing, not all of them convincingly.

'Mr Nissensen.' A forty-year-old car salesman. 'Have you

ever seen anybody do something and not understand why?'

'I'm not sure I understand what you're asking.'

'Let me put it differently. If I have it right, when you're making a sale, you try to figure out what the customer is looking for and help him or her to see how the car you're selling meets those needs.'

'That's how it's supposed to work.'

'Okay. So the idea is that people act more or less rationally, in their own interest?'

'Yes. That's the idea.'

'And in your experience is that how most people act?'

'No. Not at all.'

'Can you explain that?'

'I wish I could.' Grinning. 'I'd have sold a lot more cars.' He laughed at his own joke, and several of the others chuckled.

'But you're saying it's your observation that people aren't necessarily acting in their own interest even when they think they are?'

'That's right.'

'So would you have any trouble believing that a person might do something extreme out of anger even though it might have a bad effect on his life later on? That he might not stop to think of all the consequences right at the moment he acted?' His most important theme, one he wanted to get at often.

'I have no trouble believing that, none at all.'

'That a person might do something that, if he stopped to think about it, he might not do.'

'Right.'

Estrada tried variations of that question on the other jurors, again building a consensus as he made the transition into the area of motive, establishing that the prosecution did not have to prove motive, testing their level of comfort with that idea.

'Ms Casirer?' The fashion designer. 'Have you ever known a situation where a woman wanted to break up a love affair, and the man didn't?'

'Once or twice.' Smiling, as she had before.

'And where the man might have wanted to continue the sexual part, in spite of the rejection?'

'Yes.' She stopped smiling.

'Do you think the woman has a right to refuse, even though she's been intimate with the man before?'

'Of course!'

'Mr Bellino?' A stockbroker, twenty-eight. 'What about you? Does the woman have a right to refuse?'

'Are they married?'

'No. Lovers.'

'Well, I don't know how it is if they're married, but if they're lovers, I guess she does.'

'You guess?'

'No, I'm sure.'

'Ms Kim? Do you think a man should be punished for forcing his ex-girlfriend to have sex with him?'

Ms Kim, a forty-three-year-old Korean woman, an electrical engineer for the MTA, took a long time to answer. 'Yes, I do, I think he should be punished.' Her words were clear and accentless.

Estrada ran the date rape question around the jury box. The last juror for a rape question was number six, an earnest woman with a thick Spanish accent.

'Ms Olivera, if the judge told you that rape means having sexual relations without consent, using force or the threat of serious bodily harm, would you be able to apply that rule even if the man and woman used to be lovers?'

She was looking at him, puzzled. 'I'm sorry. Say to me another time, please.'

'Let me ask you something else, for now. I see by your questionnaire that you were born in Ponce and you've been in New York for fifteen years. Did you live on Puerto Rico until you came here?'

'Yes.'

'Do you think you have a good understanding of Latino men?'

She looked puzzled again. 'I'm sorry?'

'Do you think you know how Latino men act?'

'Ah. Yes. Sometimes.'

'Is it different from . . . Anglos?'

'Yes.'

'How is it different?'

'More . . . passion.'

He gave that a moment of its own, then resumed. 'Let's go back to the other question.' He took it slowly. 'The judge may tell you later that rape means having sex with someone who doesn't want to. Forcing a woman to have sex. Do you think you could decide if the defendant is guilty based on an instruction like that? Even if the woman was his lover in the past?'

'They had sex together?'

'Yes, they did, before. But now she says no.'

'She can do that?'

'Is that a question? Do you want to know if she can refuse once she has said yes?'

She looked at the judge, troubled, then back at Estrada. 'I'm sorry. I think, yes. She can say no.'

'And if he continues? If he says I'll hurt you, or I'll kill you.'

'No, that is not good.'

'Rape?'

'If rape is how you say it.'

He decided to sit down while he was ahead. 'Thank you, ladies and gentlemen, for your patience.'

Kassia Miller smiled at the jurors as she stood up. Today's dress was a deep yellow, in the kind of soft fabric she favored. She stepped up to the lectern without notes or questionnaires and introduced herself.

'I'm going to talk to you about unconventional marriages. That might not be what you expect to hear about today, but this isn't an everyday trial.' Her manner was easy and conversational. 'I want to start by asking each of you if you're aware of the growing concern for what some people call traditional family values?'

She went quickly around the jury box, and Estrada realized with a jolt that she had memorized all the jurors' names. It was a dazzling trick, nicely underplayed, one that was sure to make the jurors feel important. They all said they knew that people were concerned about family values.

'Good.' She seemed genuinely pleased by her pupils' quick answers. 'Now, I wonder if you would agree that the traditional family the politicians talk about is two married parents bringing their kids up at home?' The jurors all seemed to agree. 'And I wonder if you would also agree that even if that's the way of life you prefer, there might be other ways of life that make other people happy? Ms Schwartz?'

'I'm sure there are.'

'That's not what it says in the Good Book,' volunteered Mrs Walker, an African-American woman who listed her age as sixty-two but who looked older. 'Holy matrimony is the only way for good Christians.'

Miller turned to the judge. 'Your honor?'

Martínez looked over at the jury. 'Ladies and gentlemen – and this includes all of you, the ones who aren't up here in the jury box yet, too – I want you to remember only to answer the questions that are posed to you. And I want you to put out of your mind and out of your memory what Mrs Walker said just now.'

Miller kept on with her family-values questions, offering the jury a hypothetical family with two kids and a special sexual arrangement. 'A happy family, the kind you see on some of the TV shows you watch. Only there's one problem. The mom, for some reason, can't enjoy having sexual relations with her husband. True, she had the kids . . .'

Estrada stood up. 'Your honor.' He said it without heat. 'Can we approach?' He started for the bench. 'I'm willing to be forbearing with hypotheticals, your honor, but the defense is getting far too close to the facts of this case.'

'Your honor, my client and I have to decide if he should take the witness stand. If he were a drug addict, I could ask the panel if they could believe a person who takes drugs. My client's situation is more complicated than that, so I have to use a hypothetical.'

'Judge, if Ms Miller wants to ask them if they'll believe an adulterer, I won't object. That's pretty much the same as her drug-addict analogy.'

Miller's cheeks colored, but she kept her voice down. 'I resent the characterization. This isn't about adultery, or cheating, because that's not what Roberto Morales was doing, and I want to see how these people react to the real situation.'

'Unbelievable.' The word jumped from Estrada's mouth. 'Why don't you just argue your whole case now and be done with it?'

'Enough! I don't want this turning into a cat fight before we even get a jury.' The judge let them stand there for a minute, then turned to Miller. 'Mr Estrada has a point. There's a limit to how much indoctrinating you can do and pretend you're just trying to learn about the jury panel. I've already told you that we've covered a lot of this in the questionnaires, and I can't let you use a hypothetical so specific that it amounts to arguing facts that may be the object of proof in your case.'

'We could avoid a lot of this, your honor, if we examined these people one at a time.' Her main objective, Estrada was sure.

'I'm not ready for that, Ms Miller. Get on to your question and do keep it quick and general.'

'Sorry for the delay,' the defense attorney said to the jurors. 'Mr Helman, I want to ask if you think a mom and dad in a happy family might agree that dad could have a limited sexual relationship outside the marriage? And I want to ask if you can accept the idea that – even if you would never do it yourself – it might still come closest to making everyone in that family happy?'

'I suppose.' Helman, a grizzled, middle-aged taxi driver, did not seem sure.

'Ms Casirer?'

'I don't know if something like that would actually make people happy, but I believe they might do it.'

'And if the husband testified here, would you be less inclined to believe him because of that arrangement he had made with his wife?'

The fashion designer looked at Morales, then back at his lawyer. 'Not necessarily, no.'

'Mr Bailey?' The juror who had been giving the strongest signs he did not want to serve. 'Do you think a man who has permission from his wife to have a sexual relationship with another woman is any less worthy of belief than anyone else?'

'It's a lot of nonsense, you ask me.' Mr Bailey had clearly seen a way to get out of this case. 'People carryin' on like that. You ask me—'

'Mr Bailey!' The judge's voice stopped him.

Martinez shook her head. 'Ladies and gentlemen, please disregard what Mr Bailey just said.'

Miller half turned toward the judge, about to say something, but instead turned back to the jury. 'Ms Domsky? Would you be less likely to believe a man who had that kind of arrangement?'

The beautician popped her chewing gum. 'I don't know. You got to hand it to the guy, getting himself a deal like that, but I wouldn't want to be the other woman.'

'Would you hold it against the man, or think he might not be truthful, as a result?'

'No.'

'You wouldn't blame him in some way?'

'I'd blame the women. Both of them.'

From what Estrada could see of Miller's face from his seat next to the jury box, she was not as pleased as he thought she should be. Blaming the women was exactly what the defense needed to have the jury do.

Miller turned to the parochial-school math teacher in the last chair. 'I don't see how you can expect anyone to think that's all right,' he said in righteous tones. 'It's not all right, and I don't think any man who behaves that way is worthy of belief by me.'

'Thank you,' Miller said quickly and turned to the judge. 'Your honor?' *I told you so* in her voice.

Martinez called them to the bench. 'I'm convinced, Ms Miller. You've got someone blaming the women, so I think you came out all right with this group, on balance, but starting with the next bunch I'm going to allow individual questioning on this topic.'

Questioning potential jurors individually – putting them in close quarters with Morales while asking about their attitudes toward his special marital arrangements – turned out to be an even bigger problem than Estrada had envisioned. Most of the sixteen people they interviewed in the afternoon could not keep their eyes off the defendant. Three of them contorted themselves to avoid having to look at him; Miller challenged all three. One woman, one of the jurors who seemed to be reacting acceptably, stopped in the middle of an answer and said directly to Morales, 'You're better looking than I thought from your picture.' Estrada found it small consolation that Martinez immediately excused her for cause. He used the incident as an argument for returning to questioning the panel only in the jury box. Miller dug in her heels, and Martinez did not change her ruling.

By the end of the afternoon, they had selected a total of five jurors; prosecution and defense had used six peremptory challenges each. With twenty-eight peremptory challenges left between them, and seven jurors to pick, plus four alternates and an additional sixteen challenges, Estrada calculated that there was almost no chance they would get a jury from the forty-nine people left in this panel. In two days, or three, they would have to spend at least a half day on a new questionnaire, new preliminary instructions and new hardship excuses. That might allow stretching jury selection out past Friday, giving him the extra weekend days to get Carlos Ramírez to produce Juan Alvaro and avert the possibility of a serious defense motion to dismiss the indictment, with all its unhappy implications.

And if there was any chance Alvaro might be a witness for the prosecution, Estrada wanted to know as soon as possible. The kind of people he was looking for on the jury now – socially conservative people, religious people, people concerned about law and order – were not likely to be impressed by the testimony of a man who had been convicted of having sex with an underage boy.

Tess Dodge was waiting in the corridor outside Estrada's office. He had her come in.

'How did you think it went?' she wanted to know.

'It's always dangerous to make predictions about juries at this stage. Nothing major went wrong.'

'I didn't think it was going to be this hard for me, the second time. All that about the nice Morales family and their sad *arrangement*. I wanted to scream.'

'It's going to get worse before it gets better.'

She put a hand on his arm. 'I wanted to say thank you. I know I've been difficult. It was a pleasure to watch you today.'

She left as Nancy Rosen was coming in.

'How sweet,' Rosen said.

He dropped himself into his desk chair, suddenly exhausted. 'I forget how tired this can make you.'

'A lot of concentration. That was gutsy, keeping the designer on the jury.'

'Or reckless. Sometimes I get fed up with the conventional wisdom. And the truth is, we're going to be asking the jury to make a fairly large leap, connecting the dots. Smart people may not be the worst idea in the world.'

He started to pack papers into his briefcase. 'I'm going home to work. I need to get out of these clothes. Your assignment for tonight is to think of ways to keep us selecting the jury past Friday.'

There was a message from Michelle on his machine. 'On my way to New York. See you tomorrow.' He felt a warm thrill of anticipation followed by the chill of reality. Eager as he was to see her, he would have no time for romance, especially complicated romance.

He worked on his opening and wrote new questions to ask tomorrow's jurors. He remembered the late news barely in time to catch the lead stories. One of the local network affiliates was opening with the trial. He missed the first minute, but from what he saw the emphasis was on Miller's questions about the nontraditional family. He watched it through and then flipped channels. He caught one more *Morales* story, this one followed by a pre-commercial chat between the anchors and yet another correspondent on the dark street in front of the granite columns at the courthouse entrance, debating how closely Miller's questions approximated the real Morales household.

Estrada saw that he had been too close to the event to realize its significance. This was the first glimpse of Roberto Morales's side of the story the public had been given in the nearly four years since the crime. There were going to be screaming headlines tomorrow. What had seemed like a questionable tactic in court turned out to be a major media coup. It would get – what had Tess called it? – *the nice Morales family and their arrangement* into the public mind faster and more thoroughly than any press conference.

He had been so buried in worries about Juan Alvaro, Mariah Dodge's diary and the possibility that the indictment might be dismissed, that he had lost sight of a more immediate danger: he was facing a formidable opponent – one who had beaten him in their first courtroom encounter and who seemed still to believe completely in the rightness of her cause.

In the morning, Centre Street in front of the courthouse was clogged with TV-remote vans and a dense, slowly circulating loop of pro-Morales demonstrators. He gave them a wide berth and circled around between the civil courthouse and the federal court to approach the D.A.'s office entrance from behind.

Upstairs, the corridor outside the courtroom was only slightly more controlled. The corridor TV crew had grown, as had the crowd of would-be spectators behind the blue sawhorses. Court officers were keeping everything quiet and in order, but the atmosphere was charged with expectation in a way it had not been the day before.

With the jury panel trimmed to forty-nine, there was room for a full complement of press – three rows on the right side of the aisle, behind the prosecutors' table, and some rows of spectators at the back of the room. Judge Martinez began with a short speech to the newcomers about keeping quiet and not interfering with the wheels of justice.

The sixteen names picked by the clerk for the morning were an older group than either of the previous two. Getting them qualified was an uphill battle. Miller was deft at helping them trip themselves up on one kind of prejudice or another. She picked only five for the trip to the jury room for individual questioning. She did not have to bother impressing the others with her client: there was no chance they would be serving on the jury.

The morning was good and bad for Estrada. He did not like feeling that Miller was controlling the rhythm of things, but if that meant slowing down to one new juror out of sixteen he would not complain.

As he gathered himself to go down to his office for lunch someone called his name from the rail. Castillo.

'I have nothing to say to you,' Estrada told him.

'I have something you're going to want to know about. Something important.'

'I don't want to hear it.' Not from you.

'Suit yourself,' Castillo said, and walked away.

* * *

The reporter was at the rail again when the judge dismissed the jury panel for the afternoon. The jury had gained two more members, giving them eight so far, the two women and a man chosen today fresh from close and personal exposure to the defendant.

'Look, I know you think I'm a rat's ass because of the diary. But this is different, and I promise you'll see how important it is to you.'

'We have some business with the judge,' Estrada said. 'Try my office in an hour.' Curious, in spite of himself.

Turning to leave, Castillo almost collided with a woman standing behind him in the aisle. Estrada went back to his table.

'Joey.'

He bolted up. 'I didn't see you.' Taking Michelle in his arms right there, across the rail, was hardly the proper thing to do in the still-crowded courtroom, but at that moment he could not make proper matter. He hugged her so hard he could feel the rail between them biting into his legs.

'What brings you?' For the moment, the bustle of the courtroom faded into background noise.

'Big meeting. Meetings. Can you get away? Even a little?'

'Not till late.'

She made a face. 'I have to see some people later. I won't be done till . . . ten, maybe later.'

'Where are you staying?'

The question surprised her. 'With you, I thought.'

'How about a fancy hotel room? My place stinks of paint. And it still gives me the creeps.'

'I'll see what I can do.'

'Let me know. I've got to go see the judge.'

The meeting in Martinez's chambers was short, not sweet. 'We're taking too long with this,' the judge said sharply, 'and it's not necessary. I'm calling for a new panel first thing in the morning, and I've arranged to have the questionnaire administered to them while we're working. So they'll be ready for us by tomorrow afternoon if we need them, and you can have their questionnaires at lunchtime.'

So much for having the weekend before the deadline on Alvaro. Estrada hurried back to his office to call Carlos Ramírez. Again he got Dolores Acampo.

'I have to see Carlos.'

'He's not here.'

For a change. 'Do you know when he'll be back?'

'Over the weekend, I think. He went to see Juan Alvaro.'

Security called: Mr Castillo wanted to see him. Waiting with the reporter at the security desk was a tall, slender man with sparse white hair and weathered skin a shade darker than Castillo's. Something about him was naggingly familiar.

'This is Joe Estrada,' Castillo said.

The man held out his hand.

'Este es el Señor José Estrada,' Castillo repeated in Spanish.

'Encantado de conocerle,' Estrada said, very formal, as they shook hands. The older man said nothing. His hand was dry and firm, the grip strong.

Estrada, waiting for the man's name, was surprised when Castillo said, 'Can we go back to your office?'

Estrada led the way. He offered the older man the visitor's chair and let Castillo stand.

'What's this about?'

'José wanted to meet you. He's sort of a fan.'

'Gracias. That's very flattering. Did I miss something?'

'Like what?' Castillo was all innocence.

'Your friend José's last name?'

'It's what I said.'

Estrada did not like the feeling he was getting. 'Maybe you should say it again.'

'Sure.' Smiling. 'Este es el Señor José Estrada.'

The older man was studying him, dark eyes surprisingly bright in the deeply eroded face.

'José seems to think he's your grandfather.'

2

Estrada's first impulse was to throw them out. 'My grandfather's dead.'

'How do you know?'

A fair question. 'My father told me.'

'You never saw him?' Castillo had switched to Spanish.

'Never.'

'Then if your father was lying, lying about that and everything else, you have no way of knowing.'

'Everything else?'

Tess Dodge knocked on the door frame and came in. 'I'm sorry, am I interrupting?'

'It's not the best time,' Estrada told her. 'We can talk tomorrow.'

'I . . .' she started to protest. 'Never mind. Tomorrow.'

'We should go somewhere else,' Estrada said when she was gone. 'And I have some work to do first.'

He made a reservation at a restaurant he frequented in his neighborhood. Watching them leave he wondered what Castillo had meant by *if your father was lying*. José Estrada – if that was really his name – had said not a word, but the intensity of his gaze had been unsettling.

Estrada made notes about the day's jury selection, solidifying his impressions of the jurors they had picked: a woman recently laid off from her job as a marketing executive for a computer software company, a schoolteacher, and a bus driver. Ages from thirty-three to fifty-seven, and Estrada thought they would get along relatively well with the people already on the jury. The group was still too young and too female for his taste, though he told himself that none of the women seemed likely candidates for developing a crush on Morales.

He wrote some new questions, modifications of what he was already doing, and then went out into the world. The reporters had dispersed, and the demonstrators were gone. He walked over to the subway and got a train uptown.

As Estrada had suggested, Pancho Castillo and José Estrada were in a booth at the back of the restaurant, where no one would have any reason to pass by except their waiter. José's story emerged gradually over a bottle of dense red wine. As he told it, he had been born José Maria Peña Escobar, in Cuernavaca, Mexico. His family had been neither rich nor poor, merchants in a place where rich people from Mexico City and, in those days, an occasional American, came in the summer, but José had shown an early talent for getting into trouble and had left home at sixteen.

Working on a huge ranch in the north, he had fallen in love with the owner's daughter. She had become pregnant but had kept secret the father's name. Her family had sent her away, and a year later she had returned to the ranch married to a distant cousin, the mother of a baby boy.

José had been driven mad by the knowledge that he could not see his son, though he was sometimes only yards away. He had found a way to sneak into the house at night and go to the baby's room to look at him. It had worked well for a month and then one night the crib had been empty.

Looking for the child, José had been caught by the night watchman and taken out and beaten, then kicked off the ranch. The baby's mother had not betrayed him, and the foreman had accepted his story that he was there to steal.

He had stayed away, growing ever more angry that he could be beaten bloody for wanting to look at his own child. For more than a year he had planned what he would do. One morning, when the family was asleep and the guards were dozing, he had taken the baby in its blankets and some clothes he had found in a chest, and – on impulse – some family heirlooms that had been hung in the baby's room.

With the clothes and the heirlooms in a knapsack and the baby in his arms, he had fled the house. Once, the baby had cried and José had been sure he would be caught, but he had quietly sung in the baby's ear and it had become calm.

Being on the run with a baby was almost impossible, he said. In preparation he had stashed food and clothes and some money in a roominghouse about fifty miles from the ranch. He had reached there on the third day. By that time, though he had been giving the baby water, and dry bread that he chewed himself before feeding it to him, the child was feverish and crying constantly. Arriving at his rented room he had washed the baby and himself and fed the baby real baby food. Almost at once, the baby had thrown up violently.

Afraid to go to a local doctor with the child, he had stolen a car in town and driven to Juarez. There he had ditched the car and taken the baby, by then as hot and dry as a little furnace and too exhausted to cry, to a doctor. The doctor had treated the baby at once and told José he had arrived barely in time.

It was a month before the doctor said the baby was well again. José had paid the bills by laboring for the doctor, had slept in the basement of the office and eaten scraps from the doctor's table. His life had been consumed with worry about the child and fury at a country where a man could be made a criminal and a fugitive for claiming his firstborn.

Sneaking across the border and making his way north with a small child had been difficult, but José had learned a lot in his month working for the baby doctor, so there had been no real trouble. Once they had found a place to live in San Antonio things had begun to get better. Clever with his hands and a fast learner, José had found a job as a mechanic.

In the early days in Texas, José had thought about how to

give the child a place in his new country. He had seen that it would not do simply to make the boy an American – he would still be the son of a wetback. They both needed a new history. To create one he had taken his inspiration from the heirlooms he had impulsively stolen. With his first savings he had paid for forged birth certificates for himself and the boy, in the name of Estrada to match the name engraved on the coat of arms, the name of the boy's mother's maternal grandfather. He had kept his own first name and called the boy James, for Santiago, the patron saint of Spain. As soon as José was sure he had scoured all the Mexico from his speech and replaced it with some of the twang of the Southwest, they had moved farther north.

Everything had gone well until James was about twelve. Incessantly curious, especially about his father's illustrious family, he had figured out that José could not be a third-generation American, as he had claimed. Looking for a safe lie, José had told his son that they had both come to the United States from Mexico after his mother died.

As time passed the boy's desire to make some connection with his aristocratic Estrada past had turned into an obsession. Certain that the boy's mother and her family had long ago erased the episode of the baby from the official story of her life, fearful of what would happen if the boy found her, José had had no choice but to tell James most of the truth. In only one matter had he continued to lie: telling the boy that his mother had died in childbirth and that her family had sworn eternal hatred for both José and the niño who had killed their darling daughter.

The boy had stopped talking to his father after that. A year later, on his fifteenth birthday, he had run away, taking with him the Estrada family heirlooms and two thousand dollars José had kept stashed in an old motor-oil can. José had continued to live in the same house, gradually losing hope that his son would ever return. Finally, José had gone back to Mexico, where for many years he had refused to have anything to do with norteamericanos. Before long, he had lost almost all of his English. He had married late in life and had no children. His wife had died after ten years of marriage.

And then, weeks ago, a friend to whom he had long ago told the story of his years in the United States as if it had all happened to another man had shown him a newspaper clipping from New York. It was about a young man named Estrada, and the newspaper story of his family's history brought back to José's mind all the lies he had told his own son.

'It's strange,' he said now. 'As I become older, the days of my youth spring into my mind more and more, with the freshness of yesterday.'

Castillo picked up the story from there. The friend's cousin had helped José get in touch with *Noticias Diarias*. At Castillo's urging the paper's publisher had decided it would be a newsworthy event to have A.D.A. Joseph Estrada meet this man who might be an important piece of his past. 'I'm sorry about that part of it,' Castillo said, his conscience strengthened by the wine. 'It was the only way I could get them to pay the expenses.'

'Then you won't mind when I say that all this is off the record. Not to be quoted or referred to. Not background. Nothing.' Estrada waited for an acknowledgment.

'You're right. This is private. It ought to be private.'

'Do you expect me to be grateful to you for dumping this on me just as I'm about to go to trial?'

'We're going to publish a major front page update and retraction of our *Latino falso* piece. It has to be before the trial and we could hardly do the piece without making you part of it. Besides, I assumed you'd want to know.'

'You're also assuming there's some truth to this. I don't see why.' That was a lie, it was not hard for him to believe José's story. He could think of no better explanation for Big Jim Estrada's pathological aversion to all things Latino, and his constant fear that he would be mistaken for a Puerto Rican or a Mexican. Would a real fourth-generation American worry seriously about such phantoms? Estrada did not know why he had never before seen the oddness of his father's concern.

He himself had been the subject of that mistake regularly, and it had never been more than a petty annoyance or a source of bitter amusement, a window on prejudice he would otherwise never have had. An excuse to flaunt his noble ancestry the way he had when Big Jim had made him take the ducal crest to school once a year for show and tell. Even that, he saw now, that passion of his father's to spread the family story, should have been a sign.

He remembered his Mexican cousins' first reaction when he told them who he thought he was: We don't have any relatives in the States. He had assumed that they had lost touch with the emigrant part of the family. He had insisted on his version of the family history and they had decided to accept it. Or had they simply decided it was impolite to call him a liar to his face?

Castillo said, 'It's easy to find out if José's story is true, you know. All we have to do is look at that family crest of your father's and see if it's the one José says he took.'

'And suppose it is – what do we accomplish?' Estrada snapped. And then, remorseful, he turned to the man who was almost certainly his grandfather. 'I apologize for being impolite. This is difficult for me.'

'It is nothing. Less than nothing. It is I who apologize. That is why I came here. To apologize.'

When he got to Michelle's hotel room he sat in the single armchair and told her about José Peña and his story of a stolen child.

'I kept thinking he looked familiar, and I couldn't figure out why.'

'The way you say it, it sounds like you did.'

'It's probably my mind playing tricks on me, or the wine.'

'Tell me anyway.'

'He's thin, you know? Gaunt, almost.' Even as he started

to describe him, Estrada was sure he was imagining things. 'There's something about the way he looks, the skin stretched over the bones, the lines by the corners of his mouth. Even the way he smiles, with his lips closed and not much of a curve, reminds me of my father when he was sick. Except for the vitality in José's eyes. The only glow in my father's eyes was fever.'

'Poor Joey.' Michelle uncurled herself and got off the bed, came over to kiss him. 'It really blew you away, didn't it?'

'It sure looks that way.'

She led him to the bed and put her arms around him. It was what he needed.

He awoke at dawn next to her in the queen-size bed, naked. He pushed himself onto an elbow so he could admire her, chestnut hair splayed out over the pillow, her face tranquil in sleep, the curve of one breast just visible at the top of the blanket. He moved close to her so her head was nestled against his chest.

The phone woke them both. An automated wakeup call, six forty-five.

'You think of everything,' he said.

She got up and padded, naked, to the bathroom. She came out with a towel wrapped around her and went to the door, returned at once wheeling a room-service cart. 'Juice and coffee. And bagels.'

'You really do think of everything.' He sat up in bed.

She dived onto him. 'You bet I do.' Grabbing him and pulling him down with her, rolling him over on top.

By the time they got to their juice and coffee, they had no time left to drink it. Solid sleep and morning sex had left him with a clear head, despite the red wine. Missing dinner had left him ravenous. He took a bagel with him as he left for work.

He deflated on the subway going downtown. His problems had hardly been solved by a night with Michelle, however delightful it had been. He was glad he had been able to avoid going home. He would have spent most of the night awake, still a stranger in his own apartment, brooding over the Estrada coat of arms.

He told himself that it didn't matter who his grandfather *really* was – what counted was that he had spent all his life thinking of himself as a certain person with a certain heritage, true or not. That was what had formed him, and that was who he was. Besides, the truth – if José's story was the truth – was not that different from what he had thought. He *was* descended from a noble Spanish family, even though they would never acknowledge him.

Even as he tried to convince himself, he knew he was rationalizing. If he was not who he thought he was, if he was struggling to fulfill a legacy based on a lie, he would ultimately have to face the real questions it raised.

Somehow he got through the rest of jury selection. By the middle of Friday afternoon they were still two alternate jurors short of finishing. Martinez was furious, but there was nothing to be done but to finish on Monday.

'Put Tuesday down for opening arguments,' she mandated. 'No way is this going past one more day.'

After court Estrada met with Pancho Castillo and José Peña to show them his family coat of arms and the other mementos of the sixteenth-century Spanish Estradas he had inherited from his father. The process made him uneasy; he still had no idea how to assimilate this new history.

Castillo said at once that the real objects bore a striking resemblance to the verbal descriptions José had already given and the sketches he had worked on with a heraldic artist hired by the newspaper. More convincing was José's reaction to the objects – the warmth and sadness in his eyes as he looked at them, the longing with which his thick, gnarled fingers touched them.

Watching the older man, Estrada saw small gestures that

reinforced his impression of a resemblance between José Peña and Big Jim Estrada – the angle of his head as he studied the coat of arms, the way he stroked the side of his nose with a forefinger when he was thinking about something. That one had made it all the way to the current generation, Estrada realized, sensing his own finger beside his nose.

If he had not been convinced before, he was now. His impulse was to embrace the older man, say some words to bridge the odd gap between them. The words were not there, and as he searched for them he had the feeling that this rush of emotion was premature: they were still strangers even if they were connected by blood. He shook José's hand warmly and asked him to have patience, 'until I finish this work.'

The work immediately at hand occupied all of the weekend. Most of Saturday went to rewriting his opening and practicing delivering it. Mahoney brought his dancer friend over on Saturday night, and Estrada gave them and Michelle a dress-rehearsal version. The three of them poked it full of holes that Estrada spent Sunday patching. As he worked he kept getting up and pacing around, telling himself to keep at it, it was worth the effort, even though the fact that Juan Alvaro was still missing made it possible that Miller could get the trial stopped and the indictment dismissed. The only thing that kept him sane, he thought, was how well things were going with him and Michelle. She seemed more relaxed, more at ease when they were together. For the weekend they had moved into his apartment. She was mostly out at her seemingly endless series of meetings, and when she was there and he was busy she kept occupied with her own work. Yet it seemed there was no time when he wanted her that she was not there. Their lovemaking, as abundant and varied as they could make it in the time available, left him energized.

Sunday night he could not stay asleep. His restlessness made no sense: the only business left for Monday was the selection of the final alternate jurors. It took him too many sleepless hours pacing the dark living room or staring out the window across the pale white spires of the church across the street to realize that it was not jury selection he was worried about, it was Carlos Ramírez, off somewhere with Juan Alvaro.

He called Adelante as soon as he got to the office Monday morning, having no-commented his way past the press waiting for him at the D.A.'s office entrance.

'I haven't heard from him,' Dolores Acampo said.

'Do you know where he went? Is there any way to reach him?'

'I'm sorry.'

For the first time, Martinez was in the courtroom when Estrada arrived. The defense team came in only a few minutes later.

Martinez had the thirteen people remaining in the second jury panel brought in immediately. From the beginning, she stepped in to take charge of the questioning. She covered most of the topics both lawyers had harped on during the first five days of jury selection. She had to give them a chance to ask questions as well, but she made it clear that she did not want them going back over the ground she had already covered.

Even with Martinez's pushing, it took them most of the morning to get one alternate. Miller was insisting on individual questioning for every candidate, and Estrada was as interested in going slowly as he was in the jurors' qualifications: the third and fourth alternates were unlikely to be part of the jury's deliberations.

At lunch he filled in a subpoena for Dolores Acampo. She had to know where Ramírez was, and Juan Alvaro with him. And maybe putting pressure on her would get something out of Ramírez. He wasn't sure what their relationship was but he suspected they were lovers.

When McMorris arrived to pick up the subpoena, Estrada told him it was a false alarm and tore it up. His panic about

Alvaro was beginning to hamper his judgment. The last thing that would work was trying to strong-arm Carlos Ramírez, man of conscience and former terrorist.

The last juror was selected just before three o'clock. Estrada was as satisfied with the jury as he supposed he could be. Only one choice worried him, a fifty-year-old woman magazine writer whose questionnaire had rated the importance of religion in her life as four out of a maximum of five, but who had said on being questioned that her most important and abiding belief was in the innate goodness of every human being. Estrada, with one challenge left to Miller's three, had been reluctant to leave himself with none just before a fresh batch of sixteen was seated. Confident that Miller would strike the writer because of her strong commitment to religion, he had pronounced her acceptable. He had guessed wrong. Apparently Miller had decided that belief in innate goodness would be more persuasive than concern about adhering to the ten commandments.

'You were going to have something to give me today, weren't you, Mr Estrada?' Martinez reminded him when the jurors had been sent home for the day.

'Yes, your honor. I expect to have it later.' Stretching things out to no real purpose – Alvaro might as well be on the moon, as likely as he was to show up today.

'Later won't do.' The judge peered through her reading glasses at some papers on the bench. 'Ms Miller, I've prepared an edited version of a document that purports to be the diary of Mariah Dodge. The document is written in a sort of private code. Mr Estrada has been helpful deciphering it, but some of the interpretations are unclear even so. We had been expecting further help, which does not seem to be forthcoming. In the absence of a strong showing by the People to the contrary at this time, I feel that I have to make this available to you so you can examine it to see if it contains information that may be of material value to the defense. I am releasing it to you for that purpose only, and subject to strict confidentiality. I've prepared an order covering all this.' She held out copies of the order to the court clerk, who brought one to each side.

'The edited diary is in my chambers. It will be here in a moment.'

They spent the next minutes in silence, waiting for the clerk to fetch the diary. Estrada stared at the edge of the table beyond his folded hands. Images floated in his mind: Miller brandishing diary pages and declaiming in an outraged voice, Larry Kahn denying any wrongdoing to a tribunal of unsympathetic judges, Morales walking out of the courthouse with his hands clasped overhead like a champion prizefighter, demonstrations in the streets turning into a riot. The Dodge family permanently sundered, Sylvia Dodge hospitalized in a depression born of unshakable guilt at not having destroyed the diary long before. *For want of a nail . . .*

The binder of photocopied pages the clerk handed him was thinner than Estrada had feared it might be. He looked across at Miller. She was packing her binder into a briefcase, not looking toward the prosecution table.

'We begin in the morning,' Martinez said. 'Is there any last-minute business?'

Estrada said, 'I want to go on record that I plan to file a motion that the so-called diary be declared inadmissible as evidence and I'd like the motion papers to be under seal. If I can't prevent Ms Miller and her client from having access to these personal writings of the deceased and from using the information they find there, I do want to keep it out of the courtroom and out of the public eye.'

'Duly noted. Much as I believe in open proceedings, I'm sympathetic to keeping this under seal, though I think you'll find I've been as careful of the family's sensibilities as possible. Ms Miller, anything else?'

'Yes, your honor. I've noticed some spectators wearing buttons that say JUSTICE FOR MARIAH. I think we have to exclude those from the courtroom, along with any other similar indications of support. Frankly I'd like to see them excluded from the neighborhood of the courthouse altogether, but I don't suppose we can do that.'

'No, but I can certainly keep them out of my courtroom.'

'That goes both ways, your honor,' Estrada said. 'We've already had trouble with one serious disruption by partisans of the defendant. If we have any more of those, we're likely to end up with a mistrial. And I also think we should consider what can be done to shield the jurors from the demonstrations in the street as they enter and leave the courthouse.'

'I can tell you now that I'm not happy with anything that makes the jurors feel this is something out of the ordinary,' Martinez said. 'My first suggestion is that both of you use your influence with these demonstrators to keep them out of the area before nine-thirty and after four-thirty.'

'I don't have that kind of influence, your honor,' Miller demurred. 'These are spontaneous demonstrations of support and have nothing to do with us.'

'That goes double for me, your honor,' Estrada added.

'Someone has to control them. If you can't, find out who can. I'm putting you both on notice: I won't tolerate any outbursts or demonstrations in this courtroom. And I will hold you both responsible.'

She pushed herself to her feet and stomped from the room.

Estrada went through the diary pages in a fever of apprehension. Martinez had included all the passages about Morales, plus the Church of the Heavenly Blessing and anything recognizably to do with Phoenix Enterprises. Nothing about being a landlord. Neither IT FEELS LIKE TEXAS AGAIN nor WE'RE NOT IN TEXAS ANYMORE. Almost nothing about sex except references to Mariah's unhappiness about having to use condoms. The only other problem area he saw was the entries about Johnny – everything about his and Mariah's seeming conspiracy against Jadwin was there. More than enough, Estrada thought, to let Miller claim that without Johnny there could be no fair trial.

He had been amazed in the first place that Martinez had

put as much effort into reading it and culling out pages as she had. Most judges he had dealt with wouldn't have. She had not seemed happy about turning it over, and he suspected her hand had been forced by the press speculation. He would never know how much his barely held back hint to Castillo had contributed to bringing that about.

He and Nancy Rosen went over their projections of the defense strategy one last time, and they reviewed his opening statement a paragraph at a time, making final adjustments. Then he went home and rehearsed some more, until at nine-thirty Michelle interrupted him.

'Okay, soldier, at ease. I'm buying you dinner, and I'm taking you to bed. Slaving away right up to the last minute never helped anybody.'

He kissed her. 'I appreciate it, but I don't have a choice on this one. There's too much at stake. And I don't think I'm going to be much fun in bed.'

'Nobody asked you to *be* fun. I want you to *have* fun. You're wound up so tight you're going to snap if you don't relax.' She led him by the hand into the dark bedroom and pushed him down on the bed. Slowly she untied his shoes and took them off, then unbuttoned his shirt and helped him off with it. She did the same with his trousers and his socks.

He started to sit up. She pushed him back, then stood up and undressed, folding her blouse and skirt and placing them over the arm of a chair, moving in and out of the moonglow. Not a striptease, but the chiaroscuro of the room turned her smooth, precise movements mysterious and erotic. When she was naked she lay down next to him and eased her body against his, her skin soothingly cool.

'Let's get these off while we can,' she said, and tugged at his shorts. He lifted his hips to help, but she still had to pull them over an obstruction. Laughing, she said, 'Just in time. And you said you wouldn't be much fun.'

He reached for her.

'No, no. You just lie there. This one's on me.'

She turned him over and began by massaging his neck and back and legs. He was acutely aware of her hands and the soft, rounded parts of her that drifted or pressed against him as she kneaded his muscles. Then she kissed him, top to bottom – lightly, her lips barely touching his skin, her warm breath tantalizing him.

She turned him back over and repeated the process. After a while he lost contact with everything in the world that was not his skin and hers, her hands and mouth.

'Well,' she said when they were done and lying in each other's arms. 'That wasn't so bad, was it?'

He hugged her tight. 'It was perfect. You're perfect.'

'Well . . .' she said in different tone, 'I don't know about perfect.'

'Okay – how about damn good?'

'How about some food?'

'Oh no. No getting up and going out.'

'I'll order in.'

They ate the food out of its tinfoil and cardboard containers. When they got back into bed he was surprised to find that he was ready again.

3

'Ladies and gentlemen,' began Assistant District Attorney Joseph Estrada after Acting Justice Luz Martinez had instructed the jury, 'we are here to do justice in the murder of Mariah Dodge.'

He was standing at the lectern, conscious of every sensation: the weight of his opening-statement suit on his shoulders, dust motes in the light streaming through the high windows, the cloying tang of perfume wafting off juror number eight. A police siren wailed somewhere to the east.

'Nothing can bring Mariah Dodge back, nothing we can do will return the life that was torn from her so early. We are here, instead, to assign the blame for that horrible and premature death.'

He turned to look an accusation at Roberto Morales, sitting impassive at the defense table. He did not point, as many prosecutors would have.

'This is not a pleasant story,' he told the jurors, his voice harsher, stronger. 'The evidence you hear and see in this trial will show you that this is the story of a man in a rage. This is the story of a man scorned. A man who in his anger and humiliation struck out against an innocent woman who only wanted the freedom to go her own way. In his anger – not a heated anger, but a cold and vicious fury – in his fury he violated her as horribly as he knew how. First he violated her sexually and then he violated her life. He slashed her throat, not once but twice.

'The evidence will show that the murderer stood his ground when Mariah Dodge's blood erupted from his first merciless cut. A medical examiner, expert in these matters, will tell you that the murderer had to be so intent on carving this double cut, this X of death in Mariah Dodge's tender throat, that he slashed her a second time even as her heart, in its final frantic moments, pumped her lifeblood at him as if it were using that gruesome fountain to ward him off.'

He moistened his lips with a small sip from the cup of water on the lectern. He could not tell what the jurors were thinking, but so far they were definitely paying attention.

Somewhere out in the gallery were Tess Dodge and Michelle. He could not imagine what listening to this would be like for them. Perhaps only for José Peña the rhythms and colors of his voice would be intriguing, unblemished by the brutality of the words.

He resumed in a softer tone. 'Over the next days you will come to know Mariah Dodge, a woman in her thirties just entering the prime of her life, a talented and beautiful woman who came to New York from Texas to work for a company that hoped to build housing and stores and small factories on the Brooklyn riverfront – a place where the local people could find new direction and new opportunity in their lives. Mariah Dodge had a responsible position with Phoenix Enterprises, as you will hear. Her title was Assistant Director of Finance, and she worked with the company's top management.

'On the night of October sixteenth, a Sunday night not quite four years ago, Mariah Dodge went to her office to prepare for an important meeting that was to take place the following morning. You will hear that she went there expecting to meet her boss, Roberto Morales, the defendant, who was then the president of Phoenix Enterprises.

'You will hear that people working in the building where Phoenix Enterprises had its offices saw the defendant that night, saw him entering the building and saw him leaving. And you will hear that at some time that night Mariah Dodge was brutally assaulted in her office. Her clothes were cut from her body while she lay helpless on the couch in her office, sliced off her by the same razor-sharp blade that later killed her. Her body was badly bruised.

'And then she was murdered. The medical examiner will tell you that her throat was slashed savagely, two deep cuts in the shape of an X that sliced open the vital arteries and veins of her neck' – with a forefinger he drew an X across his own neck – 'causing the lifeblood to pump out of her body until she died.'

He paused, looking not at the jurors but down at the lectern, a moment of respectful silence.

'You will learn that the cuts slashed deeply into Mariah Dodge's throat are consistent with the cut that would be made in a human throat by a simple, common tool found in many offices, a utility knife – a long razor blade that slides out of a plastic handle and locks into place – that Mariah Dodge was using that night to cut and paste documents in preparation for the important meeting she didn't live to attend. A kind of knife that was used regularly at Phoenix Enterprises. And you will learn that one of those utility knives was found to be missing by the defendant's secretary the following morning.

'You will learn, too, that semen was found on Mariah Dodge's body. Biological scientists, experts in their field, will tell you that sophisticated tests have matched the most fundamental patterns from the semen cells found on Mariah Dodge's body to the building-block patterns in the blood cells of Roberto Morales. The tests these scientists will describe to you are the best that modern technology can offer, capable of matching patterns in different cells from a human body to an accuracy of one in many, many millions.'

Despite the variety Estrada was trying to put into his opening – passionate and rational, persuasive and commanding – his face felt stiff, and his voice was rough. Sweat stung his chin and upper lip where he had nicked himself shaving. He tried to chase away the idea that the nicks on his face were bleeding again, and to ignore the trickle of sweat down his sides and the center of his back.

'The police found semen, ladies and gentlemen, because the defendant's crime of brutalization was a sex crime as well as a crime of violence. The defendant raped her in anger and he killed her in anger.'

'Objection.' Miller's voice was sharp and precise. 'Argument.'

'Restrain yourself, Mr Estrada,' the judge told him. 'You're way over the limits.'

Estrada turned and nodded at the judge. There were lawyers who thought it was smart to say thank you when the judge rebuked you. Estrada was not one of them: he could not let himself believe jurors were stupid enough to be fooled by a stunt that transparent.

Being more careful to assign his promises and predictions directly to the evidence, he talked to the jurors about the elements that made up the crime of rape, and promised them that the evidence would show both sexual contact and the threat of force. 'We will prove to you that the defendant had a weapon capable of inflicting serious bodily harm or death, and we will prove that the defendant demonstrated the fearsome sharpness of this blade to Mariah Dodge by using it to cut her clothes off as she lay petrified beneath him.'

'Your honor?' Miller prompted.

'Mr Estrada,' the judge obliged. 'I warned you once.'

Estrada turned slightly and nodded to acknowledge it but he did not break stride. 'The evidence will show more than that. It will show that the murderer left a trail of bloody footsteps on the carpet of the office. These bloody footprints led from the body of Mariah Dodge, lying on her couch with the blood still draining from her slashed neck, straight to the office of the defendant.

'Without a detour, without hesitation, as you will see, the trail of bloody footprints went from the bleeding body to the defendant's office and then into his office and straight to the private bathroom and dressing room that, as president of Phoenix Enterprises, was his and his alone, a room with an outside lock to keep anyone but him from using it. And in that private bathroom there was a stall shower.

'And, you will be told, there was blood in the drain of the defendant's private shower. Experts will tell you that they can judge with a certainty of one in many million that both the blood that made the footprints and the blood in the drain of the defendant's private shower was the blood of Mariah Dodge.'

He paused, letting the jurors complete their mental picture of the murderer hurrying to his own private shower to wash off his victim's blood. Making the jury stretch a little kept them alert and engaged. The only danger was in confusing them, possibly losing them entirely.

As far as he could tell, none of these jurors was lost, and they were all still paying attention. Beyond that he did not try to gauge how the jury was responding. He was happy to get through his opening without having driven anyone to counting the tiles on the floor.

'It's always tempting to try to figure out why people do things,' he said in a more conversational tone. 'We talk all the time about the motives people have for the things they do. But we can't really look inside people's heads. Too many times we can't look inside our own heads. How often do you ask yourself, why did I do that? But even so, we have this impulse to know *why*.

'The judge will tell you that the crimes we're considering in this trial are principally crimes of action, not intention. Rape is forcible sex – no more, no less. It doesn't matter what the defendant had in mind when he did it, which of the many things we hear about as motives for rape – sexual gratification, random violence, the desire to control the victim or punish her, the pleasure that some people feel when they inflict fear and pain. It doesn't matter *why*. Only the defendant's actions matter.

'Murder in the second degree, as it is presented in this indictment, is also a crime of action. The judge will tell you that if the defendant committed a rape, and if he caused Mariah Dodge's death as part of that crime or part of his flight from that crime, then he is guilty of murder in the second degree. It does not matter what was in his mind when he caused her death. It does not matter what he intended. Or why.

'Manslaughter is primarily a crime of action, too, as the judge will also tell you. That the defendant caused the death of Mariah Dodge is the central question. When it comes to the manslaughter count, you will also have to find that the defendant acted with the intention to cause serious physical injury. But even this is a question of *what* the defendant intended, not *why* he intended it. The judge will tell you that you can find this intention simply by examining the defendant's actions. When the time comes, you can ask yourselves if cutting a woman's throat twice with a razor-sharp knife constitutes intending to do serious physical injury to her.'

Estrada stopped to take another drink of water and share with the jurors the absurdity of thinking there could be any question whether the killer had intended to cause Mariah Dodge serious personal injury.

'I know that the kind of intention that satisfies a legal definition doesn't necessarily satisfy our human curiosity. We want to know *why* on a more basic level than that. We want to know why a person would want to inflict any injury at all. The judge will tell you that satisfying this curiosity is not what any of us is here to do. Your verdict must be based on the law and the evidence, and on those alone.

'The law does not require that the People prove anything at all about the defendant's motives. But despite the fact that I don't need to, I will try to help you satisfy that curiosity.

'You're going to hear from Mariah Dodge's friends that she had told them she was having an affair with Roberto Morales.

Why would a man rape a woman he was having an affair with, you're bound to ask. The witnesses will tell you that Mariah Dodge said she intended to break off the affair. That she had talked about wanting to break off the affair for some time. That she told her friends on the day she was killed that she was going to break off her affair with the defendant that very night.

'And if Mariah Dodge was through with the defendant, she was *through* with him. As soon as she said no, the moment she said no more sex, that ended it, no matter what had gone before, no matter if somebody tells you they had already been in bed together that very same day.' Alluding to it, dismissing it in advance, so the idea would not gain strength from surprise.

'And Mariah Dodge's friends will tell you not just that she said she wanted to break up with the defendant, but that she said she wanted to do it so he would be certain she meant it. And to do that, she planned to say things to him that were hurtful, things that are fighting words to some people, bound to inflame him to anger.

'What she could not know was the horrible and painful and final way he would act out that anger.'

He stopped, eyes down, actually feeling the sadness and loss he wanted the jury to see. *Don't overdo it*, he warned himself, but this emotion was not voluntary. He looked up at the jurors, all sixteen of them waiting for what came next.

'You've already heard that the prosecution has a burden of proof in this trial. The prosecution has the burden of proving beyond a reasonable doubt that the defendant is guilty of the crimes charged against him.

'On behalf of the People of the State of New York, I accept that burden. I intend to prove, no, I *promise* to prove to you that Roberto Morales, the defendant, the man sitting there' – and now he turned and pointed – 'I promise to prove to each and every one of you *beyond any reasonable doubt* that Roberto

Morales committed rape, and that he committed murder in the second degree, and that he committed manslaughter. I promise to prove to you that the defendant had sexual intercourse with Mariah Dodge by threatening her with a deadly weapon, a razor knife, and that then, in the course of the crime of rape and as part of that crime, as a terrible finale, he slashed her throat with that same knife, causing her death.

'The prosecution has a burden in this case, and because we represent the People, we have an obligation. Our obligation is to prove that the defendant is guilty of rape and guilty of murder in the second degree and guilty of manslaughter, and to prove it beyond a reasonable doubt.

'You have an obligation, as well,' he told them. 'Your obligation is to follow the law as the judge gives it to you, and the evidence as you see and hear it presented in this courtroom. And if you fulfill that obligation, faithful to the evidence that will be presented here, then you will – you *must* – find the defendant guilty as charged.'

One last time he looked at them all, then he turned and walked slowly back to his seat at the prosecution table. His shirt was soaked through and his knees barely held him up long enough to get into his chair, but he felt good. He had always liked that ending, ever since he had first heard Larry Kahn use it in the Pandolce case. It was gutsier than the usual: stressing the prosecution's burden, emphasizing the obligation. But the defense was going to hold you to that standard anyway. You might as well show the jury you were not afraid of it.

He was vaguely aware of Nancy Rosen pushing a legal pad toward him. She had written a note on it: *Nice work*.

Maybe. He pushed his chair back from the table and closer to the jury rail so he could have a better view of Kassia Miller. She was wearing a light beige dress that looked like linen. It had a notched collar like a suit jacket or a formal shirt-dress. There was a red silk handkerchief in her breast pocket, and her shoes were red. She wore only a touch of red lipstick.

'Good morning,' she said. As Estrada had, she looked at each juror in turn. 'The prosecutor just told you that he has an obligation in this case, an obligation he bears as a representative of the People of the State of New York. Well, I have an obligation to the People as well. I have an obligation to make sure that an innocent man is not sent to prison for a crime he did not commit. I have an obligation to make sure that an innocent man is not convicted due to the thoughtless carelessness of the police and prosecutor, acting in the People's name, who have seized on a suspect because that was what seemed easy and obvious to them at the time, not because it was right. I have an obligation to the People not to let such a miscarriage of justice occur, because I know it is not what the People want.'

Estrada was impressed. Miller had picked up on his personalization of the trial, which she could not have anticipated, and immediately turned it against him. He voiced no objection to her characterizing the cops and the D.A.'s office: he preferred to have her get off this and go on.

'The judge has already told you that before you can vote to convict Roberto Morales you must find that the prosecutor has proved each element of each charge against him *beyond a reasonable doubt*. And the judge has told you that if you can *not* find him guilty of *each* element of *each* crime charged beyond a reasonable doubt, then you *must* vote to acquit him. Because according to the law Roberto Morales is presumed to be innocent.

'The judge has also told you that because the defendant is presumed to be innocent the defense does not have to prove anything. But I'm not going to rest on the fact that I don't have to prove anything.

'Instead, I'm going to prove to you that the police did a sloppy job investigating this crime. I'm going to prove to you that the police failed to follow important leads, and they failed to find important suspects. I'm going to prove to you that, as a result, no one can say with any confidence *who* killed Mariah Dodge.

'That's way beyond what the law requires me to do. It's far more than what you need in order to find Roberto Morales not guilty. But when this trial is over you will see that all you have been shown by the prosecution is a series of unconnected allegations that, taken together, prove nothing.'

She allowed a pause to let that register.

'Guessing who actually committed the crime is not my job, and it's not yours, either. It was the job of the police to find out who could have done it, and they failed. But I'm going to demonstrate to you that if you have to guess, there are much better guesses you could make than the one the police and the prosecutor settled for because it was easy and they thought they could get away with it.'

'Objection, your honor,' Estrada said. 'That's improper, and Ms Miller knows it.'

'Yes, Ms Miller,' the judge said. 'Try to be careful. And Mr Estrada, please leave the editorials to me.'

Miller smiled at that, but she did not comment.

'The prosecutor said a lot about the things he wishes he could prove against Roberto Morales. Well, I'm going to make a prediction. I predict that the prosecutor is not going to prove those things to you. He's not going to prove them beyond a reasonable doubt, as he said he would. Far from it. In fact, he's not going to prove them at all.

'I'm going to predict something else. I'm going to predict that while the prosecutor cannot prove what he said he could, the evidence *will* contain some of the facts the prosecutor talked about. But as you listen to the witnesses you will see that those facts – *as the witnesses testify to them* and *not* as the prosecutor will try to twist them around – do not even begin to indicate that Roberto Morales is guilty of any of the crimes charged against him. Not anything like it. Instead, the facts introduced by the prosecution will point in many directions,

directions in which the prosecution and the police have unfortunately failed to look.

'How can that be? Well, we're all human, and we all make mistakes. For some of us, those mistakes have greater consequences than for others. For the police and the prosecutor, those mistakes can mean an innocent man is brought to trial while the guilty one goes free. It's sad to admit that such things happen, but they do. That's what happened in this case, as the evidence will show.

'I'm going to prove to you that the investigation that led to the arrest of Roberto Morales was seriously flawed. As I've said, I will prove that the police failed to find important evidence and failed to follow up leads that pointed to important suspects. And because of that failure, the story you will hear from the prosecution witnesses is not the whole story. The most important parts are missing.

'I promise that by the time this trial is over you will see that the murder of Mariah Dodge could have occurred in any number of ways not included in the prosecutor's artificial and farfetched scenario.

'But I also said that I'm *not* going to reveal the real murderer. Mr Estrada himself told you during jury selection that tying things up in a neat package before the ending is for television, not real life. I *am* going to promise you that by the time all the evidence is in you will have some good, solid ideas about who the real murderer might be and that you will not think that it was Roberto Morales. Not only that, but you will wonder why the prosecutor ever thought so.

'I'm going to prove to you that Roberto Morales should not be here in this courtroom at all, that Roberto Morales is sitting here only because, as I'm going to prove, the police and the prosecutor failed to do what they should have done to find out who really should be sitting here.

'When we're through presenting our evidence I'm going to ask you to send Roberto Morales home to his wife and children where he belongs. And maybe the police will have to follow up some of the things we found, things they should have found for themselves and followed up on years ago. And maybe then a different jury will hear the trial of the person who *really* killed poor Mariah Dodge.'

4

'Important suspects?' Estrada asked his prosecution team, gathered for a lunchtime meeting. Mahoney's Bayard Street hideout had been the first place Estrada could think of where they would not have to worry about Lou Collins descending on them. 'Tommy, do you have any idea what she was talking about?'

'None. It's pure smoke.'

'Nobody blows smoke as the centerpiece of their opening statement. That woman has something.'

'Don't ask me.' The detective pulled out his cigarette case, shook one free and poked it into the corner of his mouth, unlit. 'If it's something we missed, it's something we *missed*.'

'All that about a sloppy investigation could be bluffing,' Nancy Rosen suggested. 'Defense lawyers love to blame the cops. All she needs is one lead we don't have police testimony on.'

'Like what?' But Estrada knew of at least one person who might do: Cuyler Jadwin. All the more reason Estrada needed to know what Johnny had to say about himself and Mariah Dodge and Jadwin.

And then Estrada remembered Miller saying that she would point him in the right direction when he was ready. Had she meant Jadwin then, or were the revelations she had promised in her opening about someone else? Either way, Clemente was right: they would only learn about it when Miller revealed it in court.

Estrada called Charlie the waiter over and asked for an

extra-large takeout container of dumplings.

'Tommy and I have to prepare,' he told the others. 'Nancy, you all set with Dr Martin? Did she get in okay?' He had spent the evening so wrapped up in fine-tuning his opening and getting it straight in his mind – and then so wrapped up in Michelle – that he did not know if their autopsy witness had returned from California.

'She's here. I spent some time with her last night, but we need another hour with the diagrams and photos.' She checked her watch. '*This* hour, if we're going to get done in time for the afternoon.' She stood up.

'I can't promise we'll get to her today. Depending on what Miller has up her sleeve for Tommy.'

'She understands that.'

He dropped some money on the table. 'Sorry to eat and run,' he said to Stein and McMorris.

Collins was waiting for him in his office. 'Where have you been?'

'War council.' Estrada had been making a science of avoiding the bureau chief.

'What was that business in Miller's opening about other suspects? Is it the one we know about? The Texan?'

'We don't have a clue.' Estrada did not have to wonder where Miller would have come up with the inside information about Mariah Dodge's ten-year relationship with Jadwin, Jadwin's scams, all the rest of it. Morales would have given her the broad strokes, and she would have followed up with the best investigation Morales's money could buy. And whatever she had learned could have been given new life by the diary. No time to worry about it now. 'I need to talk to Tommy about his testimony.'

Collins was not happy to be put off. 'I'll be here after court. You be here, too.'

Clemente shook his head as Collins left. 'He doesn't add a lot, does he?'

'I think they call it management style.' Sometimes Collins was enough to make California look attractive. 'Let's talk about how you're not going to get mad on the stand when Miller tries to make you look lazy and careless.'

Clemente was a good witness as cops went. He was more willing than most to drop the stiff, multi-syllabic jargon that cops spoke in court, and he was hard to rattle. The downside was that he had an attitude problem with defense lawyers.

In response to Estrada's questions he told the jury what he had found when he arrived at the offices of Phoenix Enterprises that Sunday night. As in his opening, Estrada did not hold back on the gore. There were two emotional themes he wanted to develop for the jury – that Mariah Dodge was a decent woman with a promising future who knew she had made a mistake becoming involved with Roberto Morales and was eager to correct it, and that her rape and murder had been an unspeakably horrible experience. Pity for the victim and revenge for what had been done to her were theoretically taboo in a criminal trial, but they could be great friends of a prosecutor who knew how to use them.

By agreement, the testimony of the other cops was read into the record while Clemente was on the stand. To help the jury visualize the crime, Estrada used the old model of the Phoenix Enterprises offices that the Engineering Department's model-builder had crafted for the first trial, hand-detailed down to the tiles on the bathroom walls and floor. A large chart showing the layout of the offices and the location of the body and the trail of bloody footprints was set up on an easel next to the model.

Taking Clemente from the discovery of the crime through the investigation by the police Crime Scene Unit, Estrada regretted having agreed to stipulate so much police testimony. If he'd had any idea that Miller was going to build her case so clearly around police negligence, he would have preserved every police department witness he could, buried Miller in a blizzard of blue. As it was, all he could do along those lines was to have Clemente talk about the thirty-nine detectives who had been involved in some phase of the investigation, and how thorough they had been, interviewing 267 people.

Miller's first question for Clemente was, 'In the course of your investigation, did you run a check on the backgrounds of the building employees?'

'What building is that?' Clemente asked her, deadpan.

'The office building where the crime was committed.'

'I believe so.'

'Does it appear in your notes?'

'I don't recall.' Clemente had his arms crossed over his chest and was leaning back in the witness chair, his face a tough-cop mask. Estrada was not happy to see it.

'Can you look in your notes and see?'

'Well, you know, it was a long investigation, a lot of personnel involved.' Clemente favored her with an imitation of a smile. 'I can't just flip through a notebook.'

'Would it surprise you if I said nothing appears in your notes about checking on the building employees?'

Clemente appeared to consider it. 'No, not really.'

'It wouldn't surprise you?'

'That's what I said.'

'It wouldn't surprise you that you had no record of checking out the building employees.'

'Right.'

'Wouldn't that be a standard thing to do, trying to find out who might be a suspect?'

'We went to the building office. The personnel office. They had all the records.'

'You didn't double-check them?'

'That would be in my notes, the ones you seem to have read already.'

'Then you didn't double-check the personnel records?'

'If you say so.'

Estrada concentrated on keeping his face neutrally

interested in the testimony, concealing his dismay at Clemente's attitude.

'It's not what I say, detective, it's what *happened* that I'm interested in.'

Clemente's expression did not change. 'The way I recall it, the company had good records.'

'When you went to the building office did you check about temporary staffing in the security department?'

Clemente, caught off guard, gave the question a moment of apparent thought. 'Not that I remember specifically.'

'Detective, you testified you've been on the force eighteen years and a detective for twelve. In that time, have you investigated other crimes that involve the violent death of a woman?'

'Yes, sure.'

'A lot of them?'

'You could say that.'

'Would you say that the woman's lover or husband was often a suspect?'

'Sure. Mostly, they *did* it.' Getting in a dig, not threatened, not thinking about it.

'Would your investigation have shown that members of the security staff sometimes hired friends to substitute for them?'

'It might have. I don't remember.'

'Do you have any record of any employee at that building with a history of spending time in jail?'

Clemente made a show of thinking about it. Is this her secret weapon? Estrada wondered, or just a way to distract the jury?

'There was one that I remember,' Clemente testified. 'A guy who had been in for assault. Beat up his wife and kid, I think. That'd be in the notes, too. I don't remember a hundred percent, but I'd say he was in maintenance, not security.'

'But you were interested in finding out about people like that.'

'Yes.'

'Because they're natural suspects, too.'

'Sometimes.'

'And you only found that one? No others?'

'Not that I remember off the top of my head. If I can have some time with the file to refresh my memory, maybe I can tell you then.'

Miller looked surprised. 'Didn't you spend time with Mr Estrada preparing your testimony?'

'We talked. Not about this.'

'About what?'

'About the murder.'

Miller turned to the judge. 'Your honor, can we strike that?'

Martinez was already looking at the jury. 'Ladies and gentlemen, when we talk about murder in a courtroom, we're talking about a crime with a very specific meaning. Murder is for the prosecutor to prove. All we have here is a killing, unless and until you, the jury, name it murder by your verdict.' She looked down at Clemente. 'You ought to know better, detective.'

Miller thanked the judge and asked Clemente, again, 'What did you and the prosecutor talk about?'

'The case.'

'And did you talk about the investigation?'

'Yes.'

'Interviewing witnesses?'

'Yes.'

'Finding suspects?'

'Yes.'

'And what suspects did you find?'

Clemente pointed. 'The defendant.'

'No others?'

'None.'

'How long did that take?'

'What?'

'Deciding the defendant was a suspect.'

'A serious suspect? The third day, I think. Maybe the fourth, early.'

'And did you immediately stop looking for others?'

'The next day, day after that.'

'Isn't that very fast?'

'No.'

'You usually solve crimes that quickly.'

'Yes. Often.'

'You're accustomed to it.' There was a note of respect in her voice, Estrada thought, just enough for Clemente to catch. Sure enough, the detective straightened noticeably in the witness chair.

'We do our best,' he said.

'And you often get your man within a day or two, or three?'

'Mostly.'

'Isn't there even some kind of rule about that, about catching somebody in the first seventy-two hours?'

'It's not a rule, no.'

'I don't mean something in a book of regulations. More like a rule of thumb, a principle.'

'I suppose you could say that. That the longer it takes to find the killer, the less likely it gets that you'll ever find him. And mostly, it's within the first day or two. Or three.'

'Or four?'

'Four might be pushing it.'

'That means that when you decided to make Roberto Morales your prime suspect, it was only barely within the time that you're comfortable with?'

'I guess you could say that.' Clemente shifted in his chair, as if becoming aware for the first time that Miller was going somewhere with this.

'But at more than three days it would be late to start looking for a new suspect, wouldn't it?'

'No, not really.'

Easy to see, now, where she was headed. Next she would remind him that he had said four days was pushing it.

But she didn't; she left it where it was. Estrada was impressed. She could make the point herself later on, in her closing argument, and for now she had left the jury with a conclusion they could reach on their own. Involved them in creating her case, just the way Estrada thought it should be done. Which did not mean he was going to let her get away with it.

On redirect he asked: 'Detective Clemente, were you rushing to find a suspect because you thought time was running out?'

'No.'

'Would you do that?'

'Never.'

'Thank you, detective.' But Estrada knew the seeds of doubt had been sown.

Collins was not pleased with the way the afternoon had gone. 'Tommy's a good cop, but he needs mouth training. What are you doing about Miller's mystery suspect?'

'I've got a call in to Jadwin and a subpoena ready to serve if I need to. I'll use him for rebuttal if she targets him.' He was trying to convince himself that the Texan was too vulnerable to be anything but cooperative. 'If she's after somebody else we may be in trouble.'

'Who else could there be?'

'Nobody I know about.'

'What about friend Johnny from the diary, whatever his name is?'

'Juan Alvaro. I don't see him helping them.' Except with a motion to dismiss the indictment because he's unavailable.

'I thought you were going to have a statement from him.'

'I will, any minute.' When in doubt, bluff it out.

They went over the planned witnesses for Wednesday: Dr Martin, the pathologist who had done the autopsy, an expert on bloodstain patterns, and then Carlyn Sims, Mariah Dodge's friend from Texas, to give the jury a glimpse of the living Mariah Dodge and a first look at Morales's motive.

The next two hours went to preparing Sims for her testimony. Estrada had expected a cross between the Tess Dodge he knew and the Mariah Dodge he imagined. In reality she was short and round-cheeked and matronly, years older than Mariah.

She caught the perplexity in his eyes. 'I bet you expected Miss Texas. Well, heck, honey, I *was* Miss Brazoria County one time, but I gave all that up long ago.'

She proved to be as willing and eager to help in person as she had been on the phone, without apparent bitterness, enthusiastic in her desire to avenge her friend.

After Sims, he and Nancy Rosen went over their main questions for the next day. They quit at eleven to watch the late news. The two reports they caught featured a clip of Miller on the courtroom steps, looking feisty and surprisingly fresh after a day in court. 'I think it's nothing short of shameful that the police settle for the first suspect that comes along. This is what happens when the pursuit of arrest statistics is more important than doing justice.'

The two news shows split on who had won the openings, one giving it to Estrada on points, the other by a wider margin to Miller. But both courtroom reporters agreed that the day had gone to Miller, on the combination of her opening and the intriguing questions she had raised cross-examining Clemente.

'Just be glad they're not the jury,' Rosen commented. But that was the point: you couldn't be sure the reporters' judgments were much different from the jurors'.

Estrada took a cab uptown. Michelle was in the living room reading the early edition of a morning tabloid.

They kissed hello. 'Anything interesting?'

She showed him the front page.

KAHN ON TIMMINS – NOT ENOUGH, the headline blared. Allen Crown's article, attributed to 'exclusive sources close to the investigation,' said that Lawrence Kahn would definitely announce no later than Monday of the next week that his investigation had not found sufficient usable evidence to indict anyone in Abdullah Timmins's death. It was not much different from Crown's first rumor-ridden piece two weeks before – more detailed and more definite, but the same basic message. The last paragraphs talked about the demonstrations earlier in the month and the possibility of upheaval if the rumors proved true.

'Bad?' Michelle asked.

'The worst.' He did not doubt that Kahn's decision not to prosecute was a conscientious one. It was the timing that was deadly.

5

Wednesday morning as Estrada was about to leave the office for the courtroom, he got a call from Dolores Acampo.

'Carlos wanted me to tell you he's back. He has a million things to catch up on but he wants to see you. He has a videotape to show you.'

'Tell him thank you. I'm very grateful and I'm eager to see it as soon as possible. Did he say what was in it?'

'No, I'm sorry.'

'Do you know if he'll be there at lunchtime?'

'I don't think so, but you can try.'

On his way into the courtroom Estrada passed the press people lined up to get in and the far longer line of ordinary citizens waiting behind the police barricade, some squatting, some sitting on the floor, backs against the wall, reading, knitting, a few chatting with each other. He marveled at the power of morbid curiosity to bring people out of their homes and away from their jobs to an event like this. It seemed to him hardly different from the skin-crawly compulsion to see the three-headed baby or watch a man eat a live mouse. Not a thought to dwell on, or he might be tempted to apply it to himself.

Distracted by the idea of a videotape of Juan Alvaro, Estrada was glad Rosen was scheduled to question the medical examiner. A videotape would be useless as proof, inadmissible for any purpose, but it might take some of the pressure off, and there was a lot it might clear up. Where Cuyler Jadwin would ultimately fit in the trial, for one thing.

The pathologist was making even more use of her Maine Yankee heritage with the jury than she had testifying just for Martinez. Simply and precisely she listed Mariah Dodge's wounds, using blowups of some of the crime-scene photographs and closeups made just prior to the autopsy, showing the cuts in greater detail.

'Before the first cut, the skin on her neck was intact,' Dr Martin said, 'and the blade sliced through in a clean line. The wound is deepest on the right side of the neck, just past where the blade first made contact, and it becomes somewhat shallower moving to the left.

'This was a very sharp blade. It made a clean cut going in, and it cut through several layers of muscle as well as major blood vessels. It even cut through part of the thyroid cartilage at the center of the throat, that's the bump we call the Adam's apple. It may have bound slightly, or stuck, going through the cartilage, possibly twisting the handle in the assailant's hand. If you look closely there's an indication that the wound, which is slightly curved, changes direction at about that place. But the stroke was forceful enough, and the blade was sharp enough, to cut through the skin and muscle to the veins and arteries on the right side of the neck before it hit the cartilage, and to do some damage as well to the more superficial blood vessels on the left, toward the end of the cut.

'The second cut, from the other side, did considerably less damage. It's a shorter stroke and more vertical than the first cut, and also much shallower. It crosses the first, in this X shape that echoes the cut on her face.'

'Can you tell us, with a reasonable degree of medical certainty, how these cuts were made?' Rosen asked.

'I can tell you that they are consistent with a right-handed man kneeling over the victim, straddling her on the couch, making the cuts with a sharp-edged weapon like this' – the utility knife – 'with a powerful backhand stroke followed by a shorter, less forceful forehand stroke.'

'And can you tell us how you came to that opinion?'

'Primarily from the angle and direction of the cuts and the position of the body when it was found.' The pathologist sat forward, slipping her right arm out of the sleeve of her suit jacket as she talked to the jury. There was something about her – not just her appearance but the restrained, almost stiff way she moved – that reminded Estrada of his mother. He wondered if Abigail Smithfield Estrada was following the trial at all.

'You can see why there could be a lot of power in that first backhand stroke,' the pathologist said. 'You've got the muscles behind the upper arm, and the muscles in the shoulder' – wearing a sleeveless blouse, she used her own slender arm as a model, bending it and straightening it, pointing at the muscles – 'and in the position of being over the victim, you can also twist your torso slightly and that adds more power. It could be a very forceful cut, and very fast.'

'Why do you mention speed?' Rosen asked her.

'Speed is important because the penetrating power of a blade goes up with the blade's speed relative to the skin it punctures. But it's not just one to one. The force goes up according to the square of the speed. That means twice as fast gives you four times the force.

'When the point of a blade hits the skin, the skin is pressed in – the kind of dimple you'd get if you pressed a fingertip against the head of a drum. Once the blade breaks through that initial resistance, no additional force is necessary to continue cutting through the tissue underneath – except for bone and calcified cartilage, which provides more resistance. Also, if the wound runs at an angle to the skin's natural lines of elasticity, as these wounds do, the wound tends to gape open on its own. The edges of the wound are pulled back by the skin's elastic fibers.'

'Is that consistent with what you observed at the autopsy?'

'Yes, it is. And it's important to note that in making the

second cut, the assailant's hand-and-arm motion was limited by the back of the couch. That's one reason that the second wound has the form it does.'

'Objection,' Miller said. 'Is that a fact or an opinion?'

'Ms Rosen?' the judge asked.

'Sorry, your honor. Dr Martin, is that your opinion as a pathologist?'

'Yes. I didn't mean to imply anything else.'

Rosen next took her through some of the testimony she had given Martinez about the wound on Mariah Dodge's cheek at the hearing, carefully avoiding any emphasis on the inadmissible X formed by the two intersecting cuts. To prevent a repetition of Miller's earlier cross-examination the pathologist explained that the wounds were so shallow compared to their length that even a variation of a hundred percent or more in their depth would not affect her opinion that the cuts were made slowly and deliberately.

'No one is precise enough to make a wound that long that's uniform to within a millimeter. But that kind of variation is different from what you'd see in an uncontrolled slash.'

'I see,' Rosen said as if she had just learned something important. She shuffled papers on the lectern to let the jury consider the revelation.

'I'm going to move on now to some of your testimony from a prior proceeding. We're going to put it in the record by stipulation, if you'd help us do that.'

Dr Martin read excerpts from her testimony at the first trial about the bruising of Mariah Dodge's right wrist and the bruises on her thighs. Then the pathologist described finding fragments of paper and cloth in the wounds and read the stipulated testimony of the technicians who had matched the fragments to Mariah Dodge's slashed clothes and to the papers on her desk and the table near the couch.

'What can you conclude from that, with a reasonable degree of medical certainty?' Rosen asked her.

'I conclude that the same knife was used to cut the paper,

the clothing, and the throat of Mariah Dodge.'

'Did you ever have the knife itself to test?' Miller asked when it was her turn.

'No. As I testified, I was given a knife that I used to make comparison tests to see if that kind of knife could have made the wounds.'

'Then you can't say for sure that it was any specific knife or razor, or anything else specific.'

'As I testified, the wounds were completely consistent with the sort of knife I tested.' She pointed at the utility knife on the evidence table. 'The one that's been entered in evidence.'

'Could the wounds also have been made by a straight razor?' Miller asked.

'I suppose.'

'You suppose it could have been a straight razor.'

'Yes.'

Miller stepped over to her table for a shallow box of knives of different sizes – utility knives with plastic or metal handles, kitchen knives with thin, flat blades, a long-bladed folding knife. 'Your honor, I'd like to mark these for identification.'

When the knives were marked, Miller asked, 'What about these?'

Dr Martin looked them over. 'I suppose, yes.'

'You suppose any of these could have made the wounds?'

'Yes.'

'In fact, is it possible to determine with any confidence which specific smooth-edged knife or razor made incised wounds like these?'

'No.'

'You testified that the wound on Mariah Dodge's right, the one you call the first cut, was made very rapidly. Is that correct?'

'Most probably.'

'Why do you say that?'

'Based on its depth and length and how straight it is.'

'Is it possible that a rapid stroke might have come as a surprise?'

The pathologist hesitated.

'Is it possible?' Miller prodded.

'Yes.'

'Is it also possible that a rapid stroke, if it was well aimed, might have cut through her neck in a straight line even if her head was moving?'

'Yes, that's possible.'

'So you can't really say whether her head was moving or not at the time of that blow.'

'I believe what I said was—'

'The *question* was, can you say if her head was moving immediately before or during the time that cut was made?'

'No.'

'Thank you.' Miller started for the defense table. 'Oh. One other thing. In your medical opinion, is it possible for a man to rape a woman and not leave any traces behind?'

'Do you mean a sexually experienced adult woman?'

'Yes, I do,' Miller said.

'Yes, it is possible.'

'That's all.'

'It's early for lunch,' Judge Martinez observed. 'But it's a beautiful day out there, and this has been a hard morning's testimony, so I think the jury ought to get some extra time. See you at two.'

Estrada was glad to have the time, on the off-chance that he could catch Ramírez and see the tape.

Standing to leave he saw Michelle waiting for him. Tess Dodge stood off at a little distance, as if she was unsure whether to approach. A court officer was herding the spectators out; Tess turned and left before he got to her. Castillo and José were already gone.

Estrada went through the gate and joined Michelle, kissed her lightly on the cheek. 'I have an emergency to attend to over lunch. I don't know how tonight's going to be, either.'

'Don't worry about me,' she said. 'You just do what you have to.'

He kissed her again and double-timed down the stairs to his office. Ginny stopped him on his way in and handed him a phone slip that said, 'Come at seven. Carlos.'

Rosen started off the afternoon with an expert in analyzing the patterns made by bloodstains. Using blowups of the crime-scene photographs and her own diagrams, she described the crime as she read it in the blood splashed on and around the body.

The X cut into Mariah Dodge's cheek had been the first wound, she said, because the blood smeared over it was not disturbed the way it would have been if a knife had been drawn through the blood. And she had concluded that the assailant had been holding Mariah's right wrist at the time he made the first cut in her throat, because there was a blank space on the wrist where the assailant's hand had protected it from the major spraying of arterial blood, which was evident from the characteristic zig-zag pattern on the carpet.

The bloodstain-pattern expert's opinion reinforced Dr Martin's about the timing of the second throat wound. Using the diagrams and photographs, she showed that the wound on the left side of Mariah's neck had not bled much, relatively speaking.

'Mariah Dodge was almost certainly, if not dead, then very close to it, at the time that cut was made.'

'Can you tell us, with a reasonable degree of professional certainty, your opinion of what happened that night?' Rosen asked.

'Yes, I can.' The witness, a rotund African-American woman with a harsh, high voice, settled herself more comfortably in the witness chair before she elaborated.

'I believe that the assailant, at some time after he cut Mariah Dodge's clothes and assaulted her sexually, knelt on top of her while she was in a position much like the one in which she was found, with her left arm immobilized between her body and the back of the couch. By that time he had already cut her cheek. Then he grabbed her right wrist in his left hand, holding it down and away from her body, and at approximately the same time he delivered a cutting stroke to the right side of her neck with the knife in his right hand, making the wound that we see there.

'He then tried to make a cut from the other side, but he was hampered by the back of the couch and whatever struggling she was doing. So he continued to hold her wrist, protecting it from the further outpouring of blood and causing the bruises, until her struggles grew weaker or stopped. Then he grabbed her by the hair at the center of her forehead and pulled her head back so he could make the second cut.

'He then got up and stood next to the couch for a period of time during which blood dripped off his clothes and hands onto the carpet. It was at about this time that he used a piece of cloth to wipe and smear the blood on the back of the couch, leaving behind some black threads. The smears on the end table are more consistent with wiping with a balled-up piece of paper than wiping with a cloth. Standing there by the couch, he also took off his shoes. And in his stocking feet, carrying his shoes, he walked on his heels to his office—'

'Objection!' Miller called out almost before the phrase was finished. 'The witness has no idea who this person was.'

'Sustained. Strike the last sentence. Ladies and gentlemen, pay no attention to anything the witness just said about whose office the assailant went to.'

'Is it your expert opinion that the assailant walked through the offices of Phoenix Enterprises in his stocking feet?' Rosen asked, getting back on track.

'Yes, because of the absence of a distinguishable heel or sole print in the bloodstains. And he walked on his heels, because there are no forefoot or toe prints whatever. He then went into the office identified on the diagram as M, into the bathroom there, and into the shower itself, opening the doors with a piece of cloth, leaving those small smudges of blood but no handprints. And then he showered, and after that there are no more bloodstains. He also appears to have been careful about stepping clear of the bloodstains once he was out of the shower.'

Rosen said thank you and sat down.

Miller approached the lectern with a wary eye on the witness, as if she was not sure what to make of her unusual expertise. It was, Estrada knew, a tactic, since the unraveling of Miller's biggest previous case had depended on the analysis of bloodstain patterns.

'About that cut on Mariah Dodge's cheek,' the defense lawyer began. 'In your professional opinion is there any way to tell when that cut was made except that it was before the cuts in her throat?'

The answer came slowly. 'No. I'd say it could have been . . . any time before. I mean within . . . a few hours, say. A pathologist could—'

'That's fine, just answer the question I asked you. Can you tell when her cheek was cut?'

'No. Only that it was before the rest of it.'

'And is it consistent with the bloodstains you analyzed for the assailant to have had sexual contact with Mariah Dodge while the wounds were being made or afterward?'

'No. The absence of any smearing of the blood or any transfer of blood to parts of her body that were protected from bloodstains because of the assailant's position indicates that no one disturbed the body after the cutting.'

'Are you aware of the fact that semen was found on the body?'

'Yes.'

'Can you say whether one person or two was responsible for the evidence of sexual contact and the killing?'

Another pause. 'No. No, there's no way to tell whether it was one attack or two.'

Miller sighed audibly. 'Your honor?'

'Strike the last part of the answer. Ladies and gentlemen,

it has not been established that the sexual contact was the result of an attack. That's for you to determine.'

'Thank you, your honor. Could I have the question read back, please?'

The court reporter read. 'Can you say whether one person or two was responsible for the evidence of sexual contact and the killing?'

'No,' the witness said flatly.

Miller sat down and Estrada waited for the court officers to clear away the easels holding diagrams and crime-scene photos before he called Carlyn Sims. Letting the jury absorb what they had heard before he returned them to the land of the living.

In a dress with a muted flowery print, Carlyn Sims looked like somebody's mother, much better for Estrada than the hot Texas number he had originally anticipated. Her southern accent and the light girlishness, almost innocence, of her voice were assets, too.

He took her quickly through her personal history, then led her up to her friendship with Mariah Dodge.

'We were like sisters, together all the time. I was an only child, and she was just like the little sister I always wanted.'

He was happy to expand on that theme until Miller stood up and protested and the judge told him to get on with it.

'When Mariah went to New York to work, what happened to your relationship with each other?'

'Well, you know, it was funny, we stayed in touch and it was like – maybe because we couldn't see each other and all? – it was like we got closer to each other, I'd say. Talking about important things. I mean we didn't do that when we were younger. Boys – giggling about boys? – we always did that. But this was different. This was more serious.'

'Toward the time she was killed, did you talk about anyone in particular?'

'Yes, we did. We talked about Roberto Morales.' She pointed at him.

'Okay, now, without saying exactly what she said, could

you say anything about Mariah's tone of voice when she spoke about him, or anything else about how she sounded?'

'Well, I mean to tell you, she was rippin' mad at that man sometimes, especially at the end. But when they started up together, she was . . . real positive.'

Estrada led her through the growth of Mariah's negative state of mind toward Morales, going from there to the specific intentions she had expressed the night before she was murdered.

'She was mad, and she said she was going to tell him off. Tell him how no good he was. Tell him she didn't want ever to see him again.'

'She said those words?'

'Near as I can remember.'

'Anything else specific, that she said she intended to say to him?'

Sims looked down at her hands in her lap. Her neck reddened. 'It's not the kind of talk polite people say in public. It's not the way Mariah talked, mostly, either.' She did not look up.

Martinez saved him from having to figure out how to handle it. 'This is a special circumstance,' the judge told her. 'We can report things in court we might not otherwise.'

Sims looked up at her. 'Can I say she said dirty spic?'

'Objection,' Miller said over a hostile murmur from the spectators.

'Sustained. Disregard that, ladies and gentlemen.'

'You see,' Sims said.

'It's not the word,' Martinez explained. 'It's how you told us about it. You can tell us what she said she *intended* to do or say, but not any accusations she made or anything else she said that might be taken as a statement of fact. Mr Estrada should have explained all that to you.'

'Oh, he did explain it, judge,' Sims said at once, to Estrada's relief. 'I'm just a little bit slow understandin' these technical things. That's all I mean to say, was she said, "If I call him a dirty spic or anything like that it'll drive him right up the wall." '

Martinez told the jurors to disregard the part about Morales's reaction. 'You can say what she said she intended to do, not what she said about anyone else's thoughts. Mr Estrada, you can lead a little if it will help.'

In that way, a step at a time, Estrada got Sims to tell the jury the harsh words Mariah Dodge had said she was going to use with Roberto Morales when she next saw him.

'Did she say when it would be that she was going to say these things to him?'

'Tomorrow. She said tomorrow.'

'And was that on Saturday that she said that?'

'Yes, it was.'

'The day before she was killed?'

Sims looked down into her lap again and said in a tiny voice, 'Yes, sir.'

'Thank you,' Estrada said softly, and sat down.

Miller took her time standing up and started with some benign follow-up questions about Sims's friendship with Mariah Dodge, letting the emotional moment pass and trying to dissipate the initial hostility of a prosecution witness for the defendant's lawyer.

When Sims had begun to relax, Miller asked her, 'Have you ever promised to do anything you didn't do later?'

Sims looked at Miller sharply, then looked at the judge, who smiled down at her and nodded.

'Yes.' Reluctantly.

'A lot?'

'Sometimes. Not much.'

'If you haven't kept promises, what about times when you didn't actually promise anything, you just . . . bragged you were going to do it?'

'I don't brag.'

'Sorry. Things you just . . . *said* you were going to do, then. Do you always do those, where it's not a full promise?'

'No, I don't suppose I do, not always. I try to.'

Miller let her get away with the addendum. The defense lawyer did not seem to be trying to demolish Sims. In fact, Estrada thought, Miller had so far been disturbingly benign, as if to tell the jury that the prosecution witnesses were not saying anything that mattered very much.

'Do you think you're unusual in that way?'

'In what way?'

'Missing out on a promise here and there, and not following through on things you say you're going to do?'

'Object, your honor,' Estrada said. 'That calls for an opinion.'

'The veracity of other people is well within the exceptions to that rule,' Miller argued. 'And the opinion I'm asking for is the witness's opinion of herself.'

'In that case, it's irrelevant,' Estrada came back.

'That's enough!' Martinez was not hiding her anger from the jury. 'We don't need to confuse the jury with this jabbering. From now on, if you have an argument, make it at the bench. I'm going to allow this, but don't dwell on it, Ms Miller.'

Miller had the question read back.

'No. I don't think I'm any different that way,' was Sims's reply. 'I think everybody does it.'

'Mariah, too? Did she miss out on keeping promises and fail to do things she said she was going to?'

'I suppose.' Sims said it so softly that Miller had to have her repeat it.

Estrada stood partway up, as if to object.

'I'm done on that subject,' Miller told him and turned back to the witness. 'Ms Sims, you said a moment ago you try to keep your promises. Do you try to tell the truth, too?'

'Yes, I do.' Chin up, with a note of pride.

'And were you recently the subject, in your current place of business, of a consumer protection action against you for . . .' Miller let it hang there while she went to the defense table to pick up a sheet of paper and read, 'false advertising, bait and switch, and selling goods that did not meet specifications?'

Silence. Sims was looking at her hands again.

'Ms Sims? Were you fined for false advertising and selling goods that weren't what you said they were?'

'Yes, I was. But—'

'Just yes or no.'

This was not what Estrada wanted to hear. He had asked Sims more than once if there was anything the defense could use against her, and she had said no.

It wasn't really her fault. The problem was his: he had believed her. He wondered if he dared try to rehabilitate her. There had been that 'but,' except he had no idea where it led. He decided to leave bad enough alone, and ask the one question he thought might be safe.

'Ms Sims, did any of those accusations deal with statements you made when you were under oath, as you are today?'

She glowed with relief. 'No, sir, they most surely did not.'

Before Estrada could go out to Adelante he had to get past Collins's daily postmortem. The bureau chief praised Rosen, had not much criticism of Estrada. 'Did you know about that fraud thing?'

'She said she was clean.'

Collins made a sour face.

'We ran a criminal check,' Estrada told him, 'and a docket check for civil suits. This was administrative.'

'No excuse. But you pulled it out, sort of. Damn it, be careful. What about your other motive witness?'

'Schelling? She'll be fine.' If she doesn't change her story again.

'She'd better be, for everybody's sake.'

Collins put them through a rundown of the coming day's agenda, then asked Rosen to give him a minute alone with Estrada.

'I had a call from Mr Bishop. He wants to know what's

happening with the diary and the missing witness.'

'We'll know soon.'

'Any minute, you said yesterday. I don't see anything happening.'

'Tonight. We should know a lot more after tonight.'

Collins grabbed his arm. 'Don't play games. We're hanging by a thread here.'

'Alvaro made a taped statement.' Estrada hated to talk about it before he saw it. 'I'm going to get a look at it later.'

'I want to be there.'

'It's not like that.'

Collins did not like it, but Estrada did not flinch.

'Call me at home tonight,' Collins ordered. 'Any time.'

6

Juan Alvaro, Mariah Dodge's 'Johnny,' looked neither short nor tall on the TV screen. Recognizably the strikingly handsome man in the New Year's Eve snapshot, he had straight brown hair combed to one side prep-school style and wore sunglasses with tortoise-shell frames. Wherever he was, it was warmer than New York in late September: he was wearing white duck trousers, boat shoes, and a mint-green short-sleeved shirt. He was lean and craggy and yet somehow looked as if he had never had an athletic thought in his life. In the tape's first shot, he was standing by a swimming pool. The camera followed him to a white metal table and chairs, where he sat down. In the upper right corner of the frame, dangling palm fronds added a tropical note.

Alvaro cleared his throat and said to the camera 'My name is Juan Alvaro. I was friendly with Mariah Dodge. She called me Johnny.' He stopped and looked away from the camera.

'Excuse me,' he said when he looked back. 'I've never talked about this before.' He cleared his throat again. 'I understand there are some questions raised by her personal diary that people want me to help answer. I don't know very much, really, but I'll do my best.' His voice was a rich baritone that went with his cigarette-cowboy good looks. His accent sounded more East Coast prep school than Latino. He glanced down at a sheet of paper in his lap.

'Several of these questions have to do with whether Mariah Dodge and I were blackmailing Cuyler Jadwin.' He was talking to a place somewhere on the ground in front of the camera. 'The answer is no, we weren't. The person who was being blackmailed was me, and certainly not by Mariah.' He glanced again at the paper in his lap. 'A related question is about the building in Texas that Cuyler gave to Mariah. I didn't know a lot about it but as far as I know it was a kind of bonus for years of good work and loyalty. I have no reason to think there was anything more to it than that. It might have been intended as a way to keep her on his side, except I don't believe that he had any particular reason to doubt her loyalty.' Alvaro's delivery was stiff, consciously stripped of emotion. He looked again at the sheet of questions.

'If Mariah wrote that there was something I wanted to tell Cuyler that she thought would make him angry, I can't be sure what that is. Again, it had nothing to do with blackmail or extortion. She and I were not plotting anything like that. There was a time, not long before Mariah was killed' – he paused, lips pressed together, his eyes a blank behind the sunglasses – 'a time when I was worried about certain financial improprieties I had been coerced into, and at that time I talked to Mariah about telling Cuyler my concerns. She was against my doing it, and that may be what she was referring to. At one point I also thought of telling him about my own past indiscretions – the personal things I was being threatened with – as a way out of what I was being forced to do. She was against that, too, because she was afraid Cuyler wouldn't understand.' He stopped again, looked away. 'She was a wonderful woman, and the best kind of friend. She was very protective of me.'

He read another question. 'I'm asked if I have any idea about anyone who might have had a reason to kill Mariah. My answer to that is absolutely not. No one at all. Except that on that horrible night Roberto Morales *thought* he had reason. We all underestimated him, I'm afraid. He was a more evil and more dangerous person than we ever guessed. He was ready to see the Phoenix Project destroyed, even though he made everyone believe it was his life's goal to make it succeed.'

Estrada paid closer attention. That Alvaro had been blackmailed into some kind of financial manipulations was interesting, but this was something more. Did Alvaro know something about what had happened that night?

'Mariah was wonderful, and she was also capable of great anger. She had been growing increasingly angry with Roberto during her last few weeks – not that anybody knew it would be her last few weeks.' He squeezed his temples between the thumb and long fingers of a graceful hand. 'She thought he was not responding the way he should to Cuyler's ideas about restructuring the company. Even though she was finished with Roberto as a lover and weary of the fact that he persisted despite her hints, she felt she had to make common cause with him on this issue of the restructuring, for the sake of saving the project.'

He looked briefly into the camera, then resumed talking to the ground. 'I was with her the day she was killed. I went with her to the office that night to prepare for the meeting with Roberto that would be a strategy session for Monday's meeting with Cuyler. While we were working, using some papers from Roberto's files, Mariah found something that should not have been there. A misfiled page of notes and calculations. What she read in it made her furious. Because of my work in the financial end of the company I knew where we could look to follow up her suspicions.' He paused. Beads of sweat were appearing on his forehead; he seemed oblivious of them. Estrada, leaning forward in his chair, felt the clamminess of his own hands as he awaited Johnny's next revelation.

'As soon as Roberto arrived, she confronted him. He evaded her questions but she was too tenacious to be put off and finally he admitted that she was right. He was trying to sabotage Cuyler's restructuring not because it was a way for Cuyler to milk the project dry and abandon it, which it was, but because before it could proceed the outside financiers would have to do heavy research into the company – due diligence, it's called – and that was bound to expose the way *Roberto* was preparing to milk it dry. He was planning to come out of it not only with money but with the public image of a hero, the man who had tried heroically to save a doomed project. The bottom line was that the project was too big to get approval for sewage disposal. Not just our specific plan – anything big enough to have a decent economic return would have had that problem. The Phoenix Project had been doomed from the beginning, and apparently Roberto had known it from day one.' Alvaro stopped talking and looked off-camera, pointed at something. A hand entered the picture to give him a tall insulated glass. Estrada restrained himself from fast-forwarding the tape.

'It's a strange thing about Mariah,' Alvaro resumed, 'considering where she came from and what her background was, but she was very committed to the Phoenix Project as a way to accomplish something worthwhile. Volunteering at the hospital opened her eyes to a lot of things. The project had started for her as a job she was doing because Cuyler Jadwin had asked her to, but after she began to understand the problems some of these people have she became passionate about it. She couldn't abide the idea that Roberto was using it as a way to get something for himself at the expense of the hopes and efforts of all the community people who believed in what he was doing and who were turning their lives inside out to make it happen, in some cases jeopardizing other projects, other approaches to community improvement they had devoted their lives to up to then. The Phoenix Project was very controversial in the community, and to say you were for it was to make enemies where you used to have only friends.

'So when Mariah learned what Roberto was up to, it made her even angrier than finding out that someone was embezzling from the company she worked for. And she really laid into him. She said he was a traitor to his people and not fit to be on the same streets as they were, and there was a depth of contempt and disdain in her voice that I have rarely heard in my life. It was really as if she were talking to some slimy, disgusting *thing*.' He paused to take his glass from the table and drink again.

'Roberto got very angry. Very cold and very angry, as if he was matching her heat with his iciness. It was chilling just to look at him. He told me to get out, this was none of my business, but I wasn't about to leave them alone together, not until the rage died down. The tension was incredible, and I knew that either somebody was going to explode or else they were simply both going to fizzle, because you can't maintain that level of emotion forever.

'Roberto really wanted me out of there. He threatened me, and I think that was some kind of last straw for Mariah. Whatever restraint she was exercising she abandoned at that moment. She began to say the most awful things about his ancestry and about his ability – inability, I should say – as a lover. As angry as he was, he got angrier. He ordered me again to leave and the threat was worse this time, because he knew things about me he shouldn't have. I wasn't going to go without Mariah. I kept saying Mariah, let's get out of here. As long as she wasn't leaving, I wasn't either. At that moment I didn't care if he ruined my life. But she turned to me and said, as calmly as if nothing was happening—' His voice cracked. He shielded his face with his hands and when he looked up again his cheeks were damp and his voice was shaky. 'She said it's okay, I'm fine here, go on home and I'll see you in the morning.

'*I'm fine here. I'll see you in the morning.*' His anguished voice stopped short, and he lowered his head again. 'I left,' he said in a voice so strained it was hard to make out the words. 'I left. She was so sure . . .' He stopped again, this time to take off his sunglasses and bury his face in a handkerchief. His shoulders shook. He blew his nose, balled the handkerchief up in one hand. 'I apologize. I have to get over this . . . this feeling that I killed her, that I'm responsible for her death, that if only I'd stayed there he wouldn't have . . . wouldn't have been able to do what he did.'

He wiped sweat from his forehead with the wadded cloth, put the sunglasses back on and then looked at the camera. 'That's all. That's what I know. I hope that it clears up any questions you have.'

Estrada sat in the dark until Carlos Ramírez came back and turned the lights on.

'Does that answer your questions, Mr Estrada?'

Estrada took a moment to come back to the present. 'Yes, it does. And it raises new ones.' He was lightheaded, operating on automatic. 'And it comes just in time.'

'There's a signed and sworn transcript that goes with it, and an affidavit by the cameraman to say this tape is original and unedited.'

'You've really gone out of your way for him.'

Ramírez sat on the arm of an easy chair. 'When he came to me, he had spent his life confused and tormented. He wanted to feel better and the only way he could see to do that was to help other people, particularly boys and young men in trouble. It was as if he had a personal demon and he had to confront it directly . . . I was sympathetic. I told him that if he got out of line he would have to answer to me, but I never thought he would, and he never did.'

Ramírez took the tape from the machine. 'I think he made this . . . confession . . . as a kind of expiation. But he still wants it to be kept as private as possible. He's very concerned about that.'

'Of course. But realistically there's only so much I can do.' He had to get Ramírez used to the idea that Johnny could not hope to have both his expiation and his privacy, too, because the next step was convincing him to come and testify.

'I have to consider my obligation to Juan,' Ramírez said. 'If this gets out in the wrong way he'll feel that he can never come back.'

The tape was not the real issue, the testimony was. But for now the tape was the only way Estrada saw to buy the time he needed to get Alvaro to New York.

'That tape is relevant material in a murder trial. You can entrust it to me now or I can subpoena it. In fact, I brought a subpoena with me, all ready to go, and I'll be happy to serve it so that you're clear that I'm acting under the court's authority.'

'I never doubted that you were,' Ramírez said with a wry smile. 'I told Juan I thought you were a man of conscience and you would not betray his trust.'

'If I can help it, I won't. But I have a more important trust to protect.'

Estrada took the subway back to the office. He called Collins to give him a brief summary of the tape and fended off for the moment the bureau chief's insistent questions about getting Alvaro to testify. Before Estrada could worry about that he had to prepare for his next day in court.

The day's big witness for Estrada was Ramon Santos, the reluctant security guard whose testimony would either be central to the verdict or so eclipsed by Alvaro and Morales as to be insignificant. But until Alvaro was in New York – if he ever was – Estrada had no choice but to treat Santos as pivotally important.

He put the transcripts and notes away at midnight. On the way home his initial elation about Alvaro returned. The tape might not be evidence, but if it was true – *if* it was true – there could be no more doubt in Estrada's mind: Roberto Morales had to be guilty. That fact brought with it a bleak realization. In his eagerness to follow every lead and explore every motive he had come frighteningly close to letting Roberto Morales get away with murder.

Michelle was waiting up for him.

'What happened after court? You look more relaxed than I've seen you in a long time.'

'That's strange, because all I have is new problems.'

'Tell.'

'Right now I just want to forget about it.'

'Not fair. I can't be in court tomorrow. Work again.'

'You wouldn't see it tomorrow, anyway.'

She put her arms around him and tickled his neck and ear with her tongue. 'Pretty please?'

He laughed. 'I should know better than to hold out on you.' He told her about the tape.

'Joey! That's incredible! I mean, it is, isn't it? It proves he did it. It means you don't have to worry about that any more.'

'*If* Alvaro's telling the truth. *If* I can get him in front of the jury. If, if, if.'

'You're being silly. *You* know, and that has to matter. And it means the defense wasn't hurt any because he wasn't available . . . We have to celebrate.'

Estrada got to the office at seven-thirty in the morning, groggy from too much energetic celebrating in bed and too little sleep. He spent a half hour getting organized for the day in court. At eight Collins arrived, looking eager, and ten minutes later McMorris was there to drive them to one of the apartments the office kept as a safehouse for witnesses, where he had already dropped Carlos Ramírez.

Estrada watched with as much fascination the second time as he had the first. Collins started out sitting back in his chair; by the time Alvaro was well launched on his story, the bureau chief was leaning forward eagerly.

'That's great,' Collins said when it was over. 'Perfect. When can we get him up here?'

There was an awkward silence.

Collins glared at Estrada. 'Didn't you talk about this? We need to have him up here, right away.' Collins aimed it at Estrada, but Ramírez was the real audience.

'I don't think he'll come,' Ramírez said mildly.

'Where is he now?' Collins demanded.

'I can't tell you that.'

'You don't seem to understand how this works,' Collins said. 'If you get a subpoena, you come and you answer the questions. Or you go to jail.'

Ramírez just shook his head.

'I've got to get back to court,' Estrada said quickly. 'Carlos and I will talk about this later.'

'That stuff is dynamite,' Collins said in the car on the way back to the office. 'I say find out where the guy on the tape is and get him here. Hell, if he won't come voluntarily, kidnap him.'

The first two witnesses of the morning were Rosen's, repeating testimony they had given at the first trial, mostly an explanation of how DNA-printing worked. Rosen broke the technical difficulties into pieces small enough not to confuse the jury. Estrada was confident enough in how she was doing to let himself worry about how he was going to structure the rest of his case. He had the two building employees and Roberto Morales's former secretary scheduled for the afternoon and it was likely they would be done testifying before the day was over. Even if he drew it out so they ran over, he only had Lynne Schelling left for Friday. Unless he could get an adjournment from Martinez to find a way to get Alvaro to New York, there was only one way he could stretch things to the weekend.

He had two witnesses on call: Rita Hazen, the woman who might have seen Morales hailing a cab that night wearing sweatpants and carrying a gym bag, and Bernd Petersen, the sluggish and oblivious security man who had been on duty in the office building during Santos's shift at the desk. Ordinarily he would not have considered putting either of them on. Weak witnesses were worse than no witnesses at all. They were likely to make the jury think that weak witnesses were the best you could do and from that the jury was likely to conclude that you couldn't have much of a case.

But at the moment, he had to disregard those considerations. The first order of business was drawing the trial out long enough to get Juan Alvaro to New York to testify. Once again, a weekend was tantalizingly close, two crucial days, and using weak witnesses might be the only way to make it that far.

The cross-examination of the DNA witnesses was being done by Miller's associate, Barry Burns. Not much more than two years younger than Estrada, his courtroom manner was still awkward but his questions were effective.

'Do you remember a study done by the California Association of Crime Laboratory Directors approximately a year before these DNA comparisons were made, in which your laboratory used the same technology?'

'Yes, I do, but I don't know if I remember the details.'

Burns had the report marked for identification and handed to the witness to refresh his memory.

'Do you remember now if there was a sample in the study that included mixed semen from two donors?'

'Yes, I believe so.'

'And was that sample correctly identified as matching the donors?'

'As to one donor, yes.'

'As to the other?' Burns asked.

'No.'

'Was pure semen from the second donor tested as well?'

'Yes.'

'And was *anything* matched to it?'

'No, it doesn't appear so.'

'So this blind test of DNA-matching on a mixed sample yielded a match for a single donor.'

'Yes.'

'With no indication that it was a mixture.'

'Apparently.'

When Burns was done, Rosen asked to look at the report.

'What's the sample size in this test of mixed semen?' she asked her expert.

'One,' he said.

'Is that a reliable statistical test, in your scientific opinion?'

'No.'

Burns got up for redirect. 'Of the one sample tested, how many yielded incorrect results?'

'One.'

'And what percentage is that?'

'A hundred,' the expert said grudgingly. 'But—'

'A hundred percent wrong. Thank you.'

Burns struck again with Rosen's second DNA expert. 'Mr Manoogian, didn't you say that those statistics you used are only reliable if all of the characteristics you tested for are randomly distributed in the human population?'

'Yes.'

With a perplexed expression, Burns leafed through some papers on the lectern. 'I'm trying to find where it says that you tested representatives of all racial and ethnic groups to be sure that the characteristics you test for really are random.'

It was potentially good theater, though clumsily executed. Rosen broke it up. 'Objection. Mr Burns knows he has to ask a question.'

'Sustained. I know this is cross-examination, but try to phrase your questions as questions, Mr Burns.'

Burns continued shuffling through his papers. 'Mr Manoogian, let me ask you this. Did you ever test representatives of all racial and ethnic groups to be sure that this randomness exists?'

'I don't do that sort of thing,' Manoogian said it as if the idea were distasteful.

'Has anyone done studies like that?'

'Not that I know of.'

'So you're guessing.'

'Making an assumption,' the scientist corrected.

'Doesn't that mean you're guessing?' Burns persisted.

'Yes, but—'

'Yes or no will be fine.'

'Yes.' Grudgingly.

'Isn't it true that there are some scientists in your field who say that certain racial and ethnic groups – African-Americans, certain national groupings of Latinos, various other groups – show a greater frequency of some of these patterns within the group than across the general population?'

'Yes.'

'So it's not random.'

'It may not be.'

'And that means your statistics are not reliable.'

'Well . . .'

'By your own definition.'

'Yes, but—'

'Your statistics are not reliable. Yes or no.'

'Well, the way you put it, I suppose I have to say no.'

'No, your statistics are not reliable, is that right?'

'Yes.'

'Thank you, Mr Manoogian, that's all.'

On redirect, Rosen asked him, 'Is there anything unusual about the assumptions you've made in calculating these probabilities?'

'No, they're the assumptions that are regularly made in this field.'

'And what about the regular use of the statistics?'

'Yes, the statistics are the ones customarily used in this field.'

For lunch, Estrada grabbed a quick hot dog from a sidewalk vendor and then presented himself at Judge Martinez's chambers. She had arranged for them to have the use of a television and a VCR. Her law clerk was setting it up when Estrada got there. Martinez was at her desk having lunch out of a plastic container from a salad bar. Rosemary was wedged into her usual corner, ready for whatever the judge wanted on the record.

'This better be good,' Martinez warned. 'I don't like to miss my lunch when I have a long afternoon ahead of me.'

The videotape played to another unblinkingly fascinated audience. When the law clerk turned the lights back up, Martinez had her chin resting in her hand.

'Well,' she said. 'That's very interesting. I have several things to say about it. The first is, this man should be here to testify. The jury is not going to have a complete picture of this crime without him.'

'That's my feeling exactly,' Estrada agreed.

'And are you talking steps to get him here?'

'Well, your honor, that's really up to Mr Ramírez right now. He's the one who's in contact with Mr Alvaro, and he's the only person we're aware of who knows Mr Alvaro's current whereabouts.'

'And where is Mr Ramírez?'

'I can produce him if you'd like, your honor.'

'Why isn't he here now?'

'If your honor please, Mr Ramírez has been very cooperative. As we said before, this is more a question of honey than vinegar.'

'We're well past that, Mr Estrada. Do what has to be done. I'm not going to look kindly on delay. We've got a jury that was not easy to select and I'm not going to send them home to cool their heels and forget the testimony they've heard while you play nice with Mr Ramírez. ¿Está claro?'

'Yes, your honor.'

'All right. Now I want you out of here doing something productive. Court starts in twenty minutes. I intend to show this tape to the defense this afternoon, after we adjourn, and I want to see Mr Ramírez here. If it will help you with him, you can say I'm issuing a protective order for now, so no one can discuss this outside the ambit of these proceedings, and especially not with the press. And now, if you don't mind, I'd like to finish my lunch in peace.'

Estrada went back downstairs to his office and called Larry Kahn to tell him about the tape.

'We're about to get this cleared up. If you can hold your

announcement, we'll know soon what the outcome is going to be.'

Kahn did not seem to be listening. 'Didn't I tell you there was nothing in that diary for the defense?'

What about what's in it for the prosecution? Estrada kept himself from saying. 'I'm trying to get Alvaro here to testify. With luck I can drag my case out over the weekend and have him here on Monday. If I do, the whole threat of misconduct evaporates.'

'*If* isn't good enough. I have to get my problems here out of the way before this mess you've made explodes. That means you're the one who has to stall, not me.'

7

Lisa Stein had assembled the afternoon's potential witnesses while Estrada was in Martinez's chambers. The only one missing was Ramon Santos. McMorris brought him in as Estrada was leaving his office for the courtroom. The security man was in his work clothes. Except for the brightly embroidered shoulder patch of the security company that employed him, he looked like a gas station attendant. A sullen, uncooperative gas station attendant.

Estrada risked being late to ask Santos some last minute questions. 'Ramon, did anybody ever ask you if you saw Mariah Dodge come in that night?'

Santos glared at him.

'Stash, do you want to have a talk with Ramon before he testifies?'

'You mean about his little side business?'

Santos looked at the detective warily. 'What business?'

McMorris pinched his nose and sniffed. 'I don't know, Ramon, what business do you think?'

'I don' know what you're sayin'. I don' do nothin'.'

'Well, that's good, Ramon, 'cause I'd sure hate to have to bust your ass and run you out to Rikers. What would Mrs Santos and the kids do? And poor Rosita?'

Santos looked from one to the other. 'I don' remember.'

'You don't remember who asked you?' Estrada pressed.

'Maybe somebody asked. I don' remember. Maybe nobody.'

It was possible no one had – for different reasons, neither

Miller nor Kubelik would have had any reason to establish when Mariah had arrived that night. As for Kahn, any opportunity for Santos to say he had missed seeing her when she came in was a problem. If he didn't see Mariah Dodge, the defense would ask, who else didn't he see?

'I'll ask you now,' Estrada said. 'Did you see Mariah Dodge come in that night?'

'Yeah, sure.' It was too offhand.

'Was she alone, or was someone with her?'

Santos saw his mistake. 'I don' remember.'

'Stay with him,' Estrada told McMorris. 'I'll need him in court in maybe ten minutes.' And as a parting shot to Santos, in Spanish: 'All you have to do is tell the truth, Ramon. There is no shame if a man tells the truth about a coward who cuts the throat of a woman.'

Judge Martinez was late, as usual, and preoccupied. She skipped her usual attendance-taking and called for the jury.

Santos looked no less sullen and no more cooperative when he took the oath. Estrada led him through his pedigree information and established his routine on the job. Every step was an effort. It did not get easier when Estrada started asking about the night Mariah Dodge was killed. Through a series of questions Santos pretended not to understand, Estrada's frustration increased until he decided he had to underline for the jury what was going on. 'Your honor,' he said, 'could you please admonish the witness about cooperating?'

Martinez peered over her reading glasses. 'Señor witness, please try harder to answer the questions. If you have trouble understanding we can have an interpreter for you. You don't have to be ashamed,' she added in Spanish.

'I understand okay.'

'Good.' Martinez sounded pleased. 'Then let me ask you, did you have your dinner delivered to your desk most nights?'

'Yeah, I did.'

'And on the night Mariah Dodge was killed?'

'Yeah.'

'Gracias,' the judge said. 'That was easier, wasn't it?'

'Yeah, well, you asked me straight.' Santos almost smiled.

'Verdad. Mr Prosecutor, you can go ahead now. And feel free to ask him straight.'

'Thank you, your honor.'

But Santos continued to resist. When he failed to remember if anyone had come into the building while he was paying for his dinner, Estrada stepped away from the lectern to pick up a transcript from the prosecution table and asked him, 'Ramon, did you testify at any prior proceedings about this crime?'

Santos looked at the judge.

'Were you in court to talk about this before?'

Santos nodded and turned to Estrada and pointed. 'You have it in that paper, right?'

'Are you saying you did testify in the past?'

'Yeah, that's what I'm saying.'

'How many times did you testify on this subject before today?'

Santos shrugged in ignorance, but he said, 'Two times.'

'And were you under oath?'

'Yeah.'

'And do you remember now if anyone went through the lobby at the time your dinner was delivered?'

'I remember. Somebody came in.'

'Who?'

'I don't know.'

'Man or woman?'

'Man, I think.'

'Can you describe him?'

'I don't remember.'

'Ramon, when you testified before, under oath, did you tell the truth?'

'Yeah.'

'Was there a stenographer there, writing down what you said?'

No answer.

'Like this man is taking down what you're saying?'

'Yeah.'

Estrada handed him the transcript. 'Would you take a look at this document on page 237? Read the third paragraph, where it says your name.' He waited for Santos to find it and read it. 'Does that help you remember who came in that night while your dinner was being delivered?'

Santos shook his head, no. 'I still don' remember.'

'When you testified last time, did you lie?'

'No. I don' lie.'

'Did you testify truthfully?'

'Objection. Asked and answered.'

'Sustained.'

'Ramon, could you just read through that paragraph again, and the next two, and see if that refreshes your memory?'

'I see what it says, but I don' remember.'

Estrada wanted to wring Santos's meaty neck. He turned away to walk over and put the transcript back on the prosecution table, slowly, so the anger and frustration would have time to drain away, aware of how close the jury was and how carefully they were probably watching him now.

The stolen moment helped Estrada find his balance. Whoever had coached the security man had made a mistake. Santos should have appeared cooperative, answering the unimportant questions willingly, undercutting only the important ones by not remembering or by remembering something slightly but significantly different from what he'd said at the first trial. Instead, he was merely being as big a pain as he could, and the jury would see it.

Ready to let him go, Estrada decided there was profit in giving the jury a further demonstration. He asked Santos the same questions about Morales he had been asked in the grand-jury testimony and then the questions about his familiarity with Morales. Santos obliged by being unwilling to repeat that testimony, too, even when his memory was refreshed by the transcripts.

'Thank you, Ramon,' Estrada said when he thought he'd drawn it out as far as he could. 'That's all.'

'No questions,' Miller said.

Estrada's next witness was Willard Boynton, the night-shift janitor. He was wearing a jacket and tie, as he had the other times Estrada saw him. He looked at home dressed that way, as if it was how he always dressed when he was off work.

'Hello, Mr Boynton.' Estrada felt better just seeing his bright eyes and eager expression.

'Mr Estrada.'

'Have we met before?'

Boynton cocked his head, a smile teasing his lips. 'Don't you remember?'

'I wondered if you did.'

'Yes, I do.'

'How many times?'

'Just the once.'

'And when we met that time, did I tell you what to say here in court?'

'No, you sure didn't. Just talked to me some about how you did things in here, what to expect. Asked me if I remembered some things.'

'And do you?'

'That I do.' He looked at the jury and smiled again, confident in his memory.

Estrada had him tell the jury about his Alabama background and his family's move north to Harlem, his steady employment and his raising a family of four successful children.

'And you're still a janitor, is that right?'

'Man has to do some kind of work. That's what I know. That and having a family and reading books when I have the time. People don't pay you for having a family or reading books.'

Perfect. Time to get to the meat. 'Does the name Phoenix Enterprises mean anything to you?'

'I remember there used to be a company by that name in the building, a few years ago.'

'At the time, did you recognize any of the people who worked there?'

'Anybody works real late, I get to see them. I'm a night-shift man. There are some night owls most places in that building. A lot of hard workers.'

'Does any incident stand out in your mind, thinking about Phoenix Enterprises?'

'There was the time that nice, pretty woman got herself killed.'

Got herself killed. Estrada told himself it was just a way of speaking – it would probably go right by. 'Was she one of the people you recognized?'

'She was real nice. Said hello and all, every time she saw me, like I was a real person.'

'Do you have any memories of that night, the night she was killed?'

Boynton had the presence of mind to take a moment before he answered. 'Yes, I do.'

'Can you tell us about them?'

'Well, I saw the fellow who was boss in her company walking out of the building. Had on a dark overcoat, dark gray, I think it was. Didn't say hello or anything, just looked straight ahead and out into the night.'

'Do you know who that was? His name?'

'It was Mr Roberto Morales.'

'Is he in the courtroom today?'

'Right over there.' Boynton pointed. 'Sittin' there next to the little lady in the red dress.'

'Indicating the defendant,' Estrada said, deadpan, for the record. 'Can you say about what time it was that you saw him?'

'About. It was way after eight, that's the time I take my break, eat a sandwich, have some coffee. Past nine, I'm pretty sure. Could have been ten, not later.'

'Did you notice if he was carrying anything?'

Boynton shook his head sadly. 'I can't say I did. He might have been, but—'

'Objection,' Miller interrupted.

'Sustained. Don't speculate, mister witness.'

'Sorry, judge.'

'Jurors, you should disregard that.'

'Was there any doubt in your mind who it was that you saw?' Estrada asked, to close on a better note.

'Nope. Not a bit.'

Happy with how Boynton's testimony had gone, Estrada turned him over to Miller.

She walked to the lectern but stood next to it, so there was no barrier but distance between her and Boynton. She started with a few easy, friendly questions about his work and the books he liked to read and the effects of age on his ability to do his work. Boynton was having a good time, flirting with her as he answered.

Estrada remembered an exchange they'd had during their initial meeting. He had warned Boynton not to be complacent about facing a woman defense lawyer. 'I don't know how you are,' he had said, 'but I get fooled easier by women than by men.'

Boynton had laughed. 'I been gettin' fooled by women sixty years now. I can't say I'd mind gettin' fooled by 'em another sixty.'

Estrada had let it go. He wondered now if he should have been stronger about it.

Miller said, 'I want to ask you about what time it was when you say you saw Mr Morales. You said it was around nine but not after ten.'

'I did.'

'But it could have been earlier.'

'No.'

'You were saying before that as the years pass some of the things you read in books blend together in your memory.'

'Yes, ma'am. You get some interesting stories that way, ones the writers never intended. Better, a lot of 'em.'

Miller smiled. One of the jurors laughed out loud.

'And other memories blend that way, too?' Miller asked.

'Some.'

'You say you knew Mr Morales by sight.'

'I did. I do.'

'And that wasn't because you went drinking together, or talked about books.'

'It surely was not.'

'It was because you saw him coming and going, to and from work.'

'Right.'

'Many times?'

'Many times.'

'How many, would you say?'

Boynton did not have to think about it. 'I couldn't say a number. It was a couple of years. He worked late a fair amount.'

'Could it have been fifty times that you saw him?'

'Easy.'

'Seventy-five.'

'Maybe. Maybe more.'

'Was it always at the same time of the evening?'

'All different times. Evening, night.'

'So in remembering that particular evening you could be confusing it with any one of those seventy-five or more times you saw him over the years.'

Miller did not wait for an answer. It was the kind of more-or-less rhetorical question that tied up a seemingly diffuse cross-examination. At a similar point questioning Clemente she had left the final question unasked.

'I remember all right,' Boynton said in a clear, strong voice, catching her headed back to her chair at the defense table. 'You *think* about stuff like that, knowing you saw a murderer walk right past you, the blood still on his hands.'

Miller was on her feet again. 'Move to strike.'

'Granted. Ladies and gentlemen of the jury, you never heard that.'

When Boynton was off the witness stand, Martinez took

time to give the jurors further education on the subject of putting out of their minds the improper questions and inadmissible answers and outbursts that were stricken from the record.

'I know it sounds artificial, and we don't really expect you to forget these things, not literally. All we expect is that, if or when you remember anything you're not supposed to, that you say to yourself, I'm not allowed to take that into consideration. And of course you can't make it part of your deliberations.'

All well and good, Estrada thought, but they had heard this one, and it was not an image they were likely to forget.

Morales's former secretary showed up to testify in a long white shift printed with large pink flowers, a straw hat tied with a broad pink ribbon, and white high-button shoes. This eccentric flamboyance was a surprise to Estrada, and not a welcome one. She testified offhandedly about Morales's private filing system, from which had come some of the papers found in Mariah Dodge's office the fatal night, and about who had access to Morales's office.

'Mr Morales was real careful about that. He didn't want people in and out of his office. *He* had keys, of course.' She grinned at the jury to share the joke. 'And so did I. Plus, Mariah Dodge had a set, too. Not because of her job. Mr Morales wanted her to be able to come and go in his office as she pleased. And as he pleased.'

That Mariah had had the run of Morales's office was information that had to come out. Kahn had put it in front of the jury himself, and Estrada agreed that it was a good idea to introduce the inevitable weaknesses in your own case. You wanted to keep the jury thinking you were playing straight with them.

'Who else had keys to the office?'

'Nobody,' she said airily. It was not the right answer.

'Are you sure about that? Nobody at all?'

She looked at him oddly, as if she knew he was getting at something but could not guess what it could be.

'Security? Maintenance? Anybody like that?'

Miller did not bother to object.

'Oh, I see what you mean. Security didn't need keys. All they had to do was come by every hour or so and check to see that the door was locked.'

'What about maintenance?'

'Yes, they had a key.'

Estrada wished they had gotten past this quickly, the way he had intended. Miller's questions to Clemente about checking on the building employees had made the prosecutor wonder if this might be a bigger problem than he had anticipated. Still, there was no help for it.

'Anybody else?'

'No, not that I know about. And when I said nobody before, I meant nobody in the company.'

Estrada finished by having her tell the jury about the workout clothes and gym bag Morales kept in the dressing area next to his shower, and how they were gone the morning after Mariah Dodge was killed.

Miller had no questions for her. Martinez checked the clock and Estrada wondered if he was going to have to start using his reserve witnesses already.

'I think it's too late to start a new witness,' the judge decided. 'Thank you, ladies and gentlemen. We'll see you tomorrow at nine-thirty. Counsel, in my chambers, please.' For the next viewing of Johnny Alvaro's talk show.

8

Kassia Miller's reaction to the tape was immediate and angry.

'This is ridiculous, your honor. To spring this . . . this contrivance on us at this late date and expect us to accept it. Even granting that this man is who he says he is, he has worked up this obvious *performance* – with no one knows how many false starts and discarded takes – under controlled circumstances, with no adverse party present, with no one to cross-examine him, giving us no chance to investigate any of these allegations, all of which may perfectly well be the product of some grudge he bears against Mr Morales, or an attempt to cast suspicion on someone else so he can avoid it himself. He says it himself, at one point – *I killed her*. Are we certain that he didn't? Do we know these stories aren't the fevered imaginings of a guilty mind? A gross lie built on a framework of truth and half truth? This is not something the court can take seriously.'

The judge was clearly impressed. Without directly acknowledging what Miller said she turned to Carlos Ramírez, standing against the closed door of the inadequate room.

'Mr Ramírez, I'm afraid the only way we can resolve this is to have your friend here to testify. As you can see, there's some question about his veracity.'

To Miller, Ramírez said, 'No one who knows Juan Alvaro at all could make such charges.'

Miller returned his intense gaze coolly. Her fingers drummed lightly on the arm of her chair, the only sign of her impatience as she waited for the judge to answer for her.

Martinez obliged. 'That's exactly Ms Miller's point. She doesn't know him. None of us knows him. And we don't know what he would say if Ms Miller had a chance to ask him some questions.'

'Your honor, I'm sorry but I have to rely on Mr Alvaro to communicate with me. I don't even know where he is.'

'Let me tell you something, Mr Ramírez,' the judge said. 'Whatever your reason is for obstructing this court, it isn't good enough for you to interfere with a murder trial. I want Juan Alvaro in my courtroom tomorrow. And Mr Estrada, this is your responsibility, too. Anything less than full compliance will earn you a contempt citation.'

She squeezed a stenographer into the room and repeated the salient parts of her ultimatum for the record.

'Ms Miller, if you have any motions on this subject, or any renewals of motions you've already made, I'd like to have them before we start tomorrow. Say, eight-thirty, if you can.'

'No problem, your honor.'

'I assume you still want a chance for your client to see this.'

'Right away.'

'That's all, gentlemen,' the judge said to Ramírez and Estrada. 'The gag order stands. Goodnight.'

Estrada walked to the elevator with Ramírez, waiting for him to react.

The elevator bell rang and the doors slid open on the usual packed car. Neither man made a move to get on. The doors closed.

Ramírez perched a hip on the windowsill at the end of the elevator lobby. 'She's formidable.'

'Kassia Miller? Very.'

'I can't tell Juan to come up here knowing he'll have to face her in court.'

'He says on the tape that he feels responsible for Mariah's death,' Estrada reminded him. 'And that he believes Morales killed her.'

'Yes . . .'

'Does he know that if he stays away Morales may well get away with it? Have you talked to him about that? Have you given him a chance to make that choice himself?'

'He made that choice. He left. He could have stayed and testified at the first trial.'

'When he left, he had no reason to think Morales would get off,' Estrada pointed out. 'In fact, Morales was convicted. That's different now.'

Ramírez stared out the window. 'Juan is still worried about being treated like a criminal,' he said to the view. 'For whatever he did at Phoenix Enterprises and whatever Morales was threatening him with.'

He turned to look at Estrada. 'I owe it to Juan to tell him what you've said. But I won't tell him to come. It's up to him. If that means I have to deal with the charming judge . . .' He shrugged. 'I've been in jail before. Tougher ones than here.'

'Don't forget to tell Juan I'm offering immunity.'

'For what?'

'Anything he did before he testifies.' Nothing was important next to nailing Morales and preventing the mess a dismissal for misconduct would cause. 'Anything except violent crimes.' For a prosecutor there was no nightmare worse than giving someone immunity to get answers, and then finding out he'd committed the very crime you were investigating, and because you'd given him immunity you could never prosecute him for it.

'Immunity might help,' Ramírez allowed.

'Just get him up here.'

'I can't promise. I'll need it in writing, about the immunity.'

'When I know what flight he's on.'

'No promises. And not by tomorrow.' Ramírez looked at his watch. 'I can't even reach him until tomorrow.'

'Why the hell didn't you tell the judge that? Call her first thing in the morning. Let her know what you're doing. Don't ask for more time in so many words. She'll only turn you down, and then if I try to drag my case out, she'll know what I'm up to.'

'Juan will either say yes or no. If he comes, he can be here Monday. We're only asking for the weekend.'

'And most judges would grant it without a thought. But I don't think this judge will, not at this point in this trial.'

'I'll let you know how it goes.' Ramírez limped over to the elevator and punched the DOWN button. They waited in silence, neither man trying to make small talk.

Tess Dodge was in one of the blue chairs at the entrance to the bureau's almost-deserted offices.

'I'm going nuts, not being able to talk to you about it,' she said when they got to his office. 'It's almost over, isn't it? Our part of it.'

'Almost.'

'There's still her friend, the one she talked to right before she went to the office.'

Estrada had to readjust to recognize that she meant Lynne Schelling, not Juan Alvaro. 'In the morning.'

'Will she help?'

'I think she'll be a big help.'

Tess nodded, accepting it for the moment. 'Was that your girlfriend sitting in my row? She seems nice. We ride down together when the guards hold an elevator for us after court.'

'Haven't you talked to each other?'

'I'm not very good company right now. I thought I'd be all right after all this time, but it's awful sitting there listening to the witnesses testify over and over about how Mariah died.' She fumbled in her shoulderbag for a tissue and blew her nose. 'Excuse me. I'm such a mess over this.'

'You've been through a lot.'

She stood up. 'I should let you work.'

He walked her to the elevator.

'Do we stand a chance?' she asked on the way. 'I mean, I can't tell for sure, but if I was on the jury I don't know if I'd vote to convict him.'

That was not the best thing to hear from the victim's sister, but he was not surprised. 'Lynne Schelling was Kahn's star witness. I think she'll be ours, too.'

'I hope so.' She pressed the elevator button. 'Thanks for putting up with me.'

'I don't think of it that way.'

She put a finger on his lips. 'Shhh. You don't have to humor me. I think you're doing a great job. You and Nancy, but especially you. I only wish you had more to work with. Most of all I wish I could help some way. In the summer, when I thought I was *doing* something . . . I don't know, I just felt better.'

Back in his office, Estrada pulled out the transcript of the first trial and went back over Lynne Schelling's testimony, preparing for the morning.

The phone rang. He was surprised to hear his mother's voice. 'Joseph, do you know a man named Castillo?'

With all the turmoil about Alvaro, Estrada had lost sight of Grandpa José. 'He's a reporter. He's writing a book about this case, and he likes to pretend he has a personal interest in the Estrada family. He's the one who wrote about Spain and all the rest of it.'

'How unpleasant. He wants to come and see me. I can't imagine why.'

Estrada took a breath. 'Mother, how much do you know about Father's background?'

'What do you mean? I know the same things you do.'

'Was there ever anything besides the stories and a couple of heirlooms?'

'Joseph, what's this about?'

'Mr Castillo has found a man who claims to be Father's father.'

'I don't understand. Your grandfather died before I married your father.'

'I know this is going to sound strange, but I think you should meet this man. You and John and Jeff and Betty. All of you should go and listen to his story. Ask him questions. Just remember that Castillo is a reporter. He can be charming, but he's going to write about what you say. So ask questions, but don't answer them.'

'Are you sure about this, Joseph?'

'No. But I think it's worth the risk.'

'Well . . . We'll see.'

Not ready to get back to work, he called Lynne Schelling for an attitude check. He had been walking a fine line with her, calling occasionally to keep her on the team while trying not to badger her too much. This time he could not tell if her equanimity was real or a way to get him off the phone. He tried to resign himself to the fact that this was one more thing over which, ultimately, he had no control. She would be fine on the witness stand, or she would fall apart, and – short of being careful how he questioned her – there was nothing he could do about it.

He quit when the words began to blur in front of him, and realized he was starving. Michelle, in meetings until not much before he got home, had not eaten either. They went out in the neighborhood, just catching the kitchen at the wood-paneled restaurant where Estrada had heard José Peña's story. This time he picked a small table at the back corner of the front room, where the music was louder and the congenial crowd at the bar was close but not too close.

Michelle, in a giddy mood, told him she had news. 'But first tell me about you. How did your day go?'

'The judge put the heat on Ramírez to get Johnny for us.'

'Do you think he'll deliver?'

'Could be.' This was not a time to be realistic.

'That's great.'

'I hope he's in time. Tell me about you.'

'I think I'm getting a promotion.'

'No kidding? What kind of promotion?'

'A *big* promotion.'

'That's terrific. I didn't know there was any room for that. Aren't you running the store out there already?'

The owner came over to say hello and chat about the trial. Estrada told him Michelle was getting a big promotion.

'It only counts if they bring you back here,' he said. He gave her a congratulatory kiss and sent over a bottle of champagne.

'He's so sweet,' Michelle said.

'He has the right idea, too.'

Surprisingly, she did not rush to proclaim her allegiance to California. She smiled at him and sipped her champagne.

'You still haven't told me about your new job.'

'It's not definite, and it's not right away. But things are going so well in L.A. that they're giving me more money and a bigger staff. And they're letting me hire someone who can be my deputy and spend some time learning my methods while I keep building the business and get it all on a more solid footing.'

'Then what?'

'That's what's so exciting. It's why I've been here so long, working out the details. They're making me vice-president in charge of sales and marketing.'

'Not bad.'

'I'd have to travel a lot, back and forth.'

'Nothing new about that.'

'No, I mean really travel. But I'd be based in New York.'

'That *is* news.' He lifted his glass in salute, leaned over to kiss her. She was as happy as he had seen her since before he got *Morales*. He was happy, too, but not as happy as he thought he should be.

'There's only one problem,' she said as they strolled back to his apartment. 'I have to fly back tomorrow, and I'll be there for at least four months solid, maybe longer, before I can come back to New York again. There's a lot happening, a lot to get ready for, expanding the whole West Coast division. And then when I hire my eventual replacement, I'll have to stay to help him take hold. Actually, I'm not going to hire him, I'm going to promote him. He already works for us.'

'You're saying we're going to be apart even more.'

She stopped to kiss him. 'Let's not fight about it. It's good news and we have time to work out the details. Everything has been so good for us this trip, let's just enjoy it.'

'You're right.' They kissed again. Suddenly it seemed important to get home quickly.

They undressed in a tangled hurry and grabbed for each other, toppling onto the bed to make rollicking, exuberant love. The bed creaked and thumped under them and for a moment he wondered about the downstairs neighbors, and the neighbors beyond the bedroom wall.

Spent, they lay in each other's arms, letting the night breeze cool the sweat they had worked up.

'There's something else,' Michelle said in a small voice.

He drew back enough to see her in the glow compounded of moonbeams and muted lamplight. She was on her back, staring at the ceiling. He waited, sensing that this was not the preamble to good news.

She looked at him, then back at the ceiling. 'I don't mean to drag this out. It's just hard.'

He sat up and crossed his legs like a kid sitting by a campfire waiting for a ghost story.

Finally she turned toward him, looked up at his face, then cradled her head in her arm. With her free hand she touched his leg tentatively, then withdrew it. Speaking to the mattress, she said, 'I've been seeing somebody at work.'

'Seeing?'

She picked at the bedsheet.

'Who?'

'Nobody you'd know. Somebody out there.'

'Once?'

Silence.

'More than once?'

She went on staring at the bedsheet. He thought of

Mahoney. What had he done? How had he handled this when it happened to him?

'How long?' He felt compelled to pursue it, though he didn't really want to know. 'A week? A month?'

She sighed, as if to say *do we have to?* 'A month.'

'Why?'

'I had this huge decision to make, whether to stay out there or not. My whole life depended on it, really. And you were too busy. You had this big case. All you had to do was say you loved me and ask me to stay with you, but you were too busy.'

'It's your life. Your career. What right did I have . . .'

'That's not the point. You could have said you'd come with me, too, but all you could do was talk about how much you'd be leaving behind and how different the law was out there. How different can it be?' Her voice was full of sadness. 'I needed somebody who cared. You weren't there.'

'Why are you telling me this?' His own voice sounded oddly normal to him, as if he were asking out of ordinary curiosity. 'And why now?'

'I know it's not a good time.' Her voice broke.

She's crying, he thought. She's telling me this, and *she's* crying.

'It's been so good between us,' she said, calmer. 'It's never been this good before. It's as if . . . the moment I started to . . . After that, all the pressure was off between you and me, and I could be with you and it was all right. Better than all right. Great.'

'Are you still . . .'

'No. I couldn't. How could I? I feel so close to you. I couldn't be with anybody else.'

'You were sleeping with him?' He did not know why he was still asking questions, but he knew he had to stay calm. He didn't want this to turn into a shouting match and he didn't want to put her on the defensive. Once that happened he would no longer be able to trust what he was hearing.

Trust. As if the word had real meaning.

'I wasn't going to tell you.' Her voice was small again. 'But everything is going so well for both of us, in our work, and what's between us is so good. I couldn't live a lie.' She picked at the sheet. 'I had to tell you in person, and I'm going away for months . . .'

'Who is he?'

She touched his leg again. For some reason, he did not shudder. 'What difference does it make?'

He didn't know the answer to that, but he did know the answer to his own question. 'It's the guy you're going to promote, isn't it? The one you'll be grooming to take over for you out there.'

'It doesn't matter.' Barely audible. 'Really. It's not as if I'm ever going to go near him again, that way.'

There was something he was supposed to feel now. Some kind of rage or fury. Didn't people kill over this kind of thing?

'It's late,' he said. 'I've got another hard day tomorrow.'

He got under the covers, surprisingly ready for sleep. He did not bother to brush his teeth.

9

Dressing for work, he watched Michelle sleep. He knew they couldn't leave things the way they were, but for the moment he had nothing constructive to add. He woke her to say good-bye. She clung to him, warm with sleep. He endured it.

'Are you okay?' she asked.

'I need some time.' Not really answering the question.

'Remember that I love you.'

He checked his watch. 'I've got to run. Have a good trip back.'

'I'll be thinking of you. I'll call.'

He paused at the bedroom door. 'Do me a favor – not until the trial's over. I don't think I could handle it.'

The morning was crisp and clear, nearly perfect, as if nature were mocking him. Less than eager to be immersed in the hustle and anxiety of the courthouse, he took a longer detour than usual around the marchers demanding Justice for Morales.

Clemente brought Lynne Schelling in at nine. Estrada's idea had been for them to sit around with coffee and donuts, getting comfortable. Now that it was time, that was the last thing he was in the mood for. Schelling was not eager for small talk, either. In a suit of deep, muted red with a dark, pinkish-gray blouse, she was six feet plus of badly contained anxiety. She sat in the visitor's chair shredding a facial tissue in her hands, looking out the window at the grime-obscured view of water tanks and tarred rooftops, oblivious of the white lint falling in her lap. Clemente was leaning against the door jamb, enjoying the view in the office.

The phone rang. 'Carlos Ramírez?' Ginny offered.

'Put him on.'

'I spoke to Juan. I don't think he's going to come.'

'I don't want to hear that,' Estrada raged into the phone, all his anger coalescing. 'That's not acceptable.' In answer to Clemente's inquiring look, he tilted his head toward the door. Clemente sprang to Schelling's side and invited her to wait out in the corridor.

'Did you tell him we'd give him immunity?'

'He doesn't seem to be interested.'

'Then he doesn't understand. Or you don't. This way he's going to be a fugitive forever. If he makes the deal he can come back and start over with a clean slate.'

'And a dirty reputation.'

'Let me tell you a sad truth. Nobody out there is going to remember your friend's name after the first month. We don't deal in lasting celebrity over here.'

Ramírez said nothing.

'Let me talk to him myself,' Estrada urged. 'Get him to call me now, before I go to court.'

'He won't do that.'

'Listen to me – some time this afternoon Justice Martinez is going to want an answer. We won't be able to temporize: she's going to want an *answer*. For everyone's sake, the answer had better be yes. For your friend Juan's sake, most of all. People all over the world bribe and lie and leave their families and barter their children so they can get to live in this country. All your friend's got to do is testify in court one afternoon.'

'All right, you've made your point. I'll talk to him again and see what I can do.'

Off the phone, Estrada put his head on his desk, searching for a moment's peace.

Lisa Stein startled him back to the real world. 'I came for

the evidence cart. It's time to go.'

'So it is. Did you see Tommy out there?'

'With Ms Tall America?'

'Right.'

'They're headed upstairs. Tommy looked like he was in love.'

'That's all we need, to have him make a pass at our star witness.'

While Estrada was getting settled at the prosecution table, Clemente came in to say that Schelling was in the witness room, looking pale. 'Maybe you should send Stein to hold her hand. I wasn't doing much good.'

'Good idea.'

As she left, Estrada twisted in his chair to look at the people filing into the spectators' gallery. The crowd was predominantly Latino, as Clemente and Stein had reported on previous days. There was a woman who looked like a prominent TV personality, a movie star he recognized and several representatives of the young street patrollers who had made themselves local heroes over the years, berets decorously in their laps, out of sight of the jury. And Señor Condado, Estrada noted with a brief stab of alarm. Tess Dodge's seat was empty.

He took a last-minute look through his notes. He had trouble concentrating, the previous night's bedtime conversation blocking his thoughts with every reference to lovers or breaking up or being cruel. *I couldn't live a lie.*

Too soon, Martinez came in, and Schelling was walking toward the witness stand. Rosen, sitting next to him, slipped him a note. 'From Lisa.' It said: *Last-minute trip to the loo – be careful.* He was sure it meant something; in his state of mind he had no idea what.

'Good morning, Ms Schelling,' he said, and stood a moment straightening his notes before he asked her where she was from and what she did for a living, and what jobs she had had before that. The pedigree questions were intended to help her relax and to help the jury see what a solid, reliable person she was. They were also to help him gauge her emotional state.

She seemed considerably more controlled than she had been earlier, in his office. Her hands were out of sight in her lap, but he knew from the motion of her forearms that she was fidgeting with something – another tissue, or the clasp of her handbag. Her eyes were bright and her answers were quick. She was animated in a forced way he did not remember from their previous meetings, a way that he was afraid explained Lisa's note. This would not be the first time he questioned a stoned witness, but it would be the time that mattered the most.

It puzzled him that this woman, ordinarily so self-possessed – headhunter for high-ranking executives; formerly an executive herself in a movie company and before that, briefly, an actress – could be so undone by the idea of testifying in court that it took a noseful of cocaine to get her into the room.

Remembering how compelling he had found her in their first meetings, he had been planning to take her through a narration of how she had become acquainted with Mariah Dodge at their health club, and how their friendship had grown. It was the kind of gossipy story that juries liked, but the danger was too great that she would go on a talking jag, so he asked short questions that encouraged short answers. They also encouraged Miller to object repeatedly on the grounds that he was leading the witness.

The barrage of objections had an effect on Schelling, who began to glance toward Miller before answering any question. Estrada tried to give Miller less reason to object. He did not think that Schelling's nervous mannerism was helping her with the jury.

The questioning itself went reasonably well, establishing that Mariah had, for a while, talked constantly about Morales, but then had seemed to lose interest in him as a topic of conversation.

'On the day Mariah was killed, what if any contact with her did you have?'

'We talked on the phone.'

'How many times?'

'Twice.'

'What subjects did you talk about the first time?'

'About getting together to go to the gym, and about her love life.'

'What about her love life?'

'She said she was fed up with Morales, and she wasn't going to let him treat her badly anymore. She was done with him.'

Miller objected, and Martinez called them up to the bench.

'It's hearsay,' Miller charged.

'It goes to her state of mind, your honor, and it also goes to the intention she had at the time to do certain things in the future, which we'll be exploring next.' It was also the very testimony that the Court of Appeals had allowed when it was dividing the admissible from the inadmissible evidence, an argument Estrada did not want to make unless he had to.

'I'm going to allow it,' the judge ruled. 'But be careful, Mr Estrada. This is an area that's been marked out for us by our betters, and I'm not going to let you go beyond those boundaries.'

So much for not bringing up the appeals. Luz Martinez had just announced, in a voice full of resentment, that she was not going to risk being reversed on the same grounds a second time, which meant that Joe Estrada would get away with nothing.

Back at the lectern, he smiled at Schelling, hoping it looked like a real smile, hoping it would dissipate the panic he had seen in her eyes when he and Miller went up for the sidebar. He had the last question and answer read back to get her restarted, and because it did not hurt the jury to hear it again.

'If Mariah said anything else about her intention not to let Roberto Morales treat her badly anymore, anything on that general subject, can you tell us about it?'

'Yes. She said she didn't know why she had kept going out with him so long. She said she thought it had been a big mistake and she wasn't going to go on with it for another minute because being with him made her feel dirty.'

'And what, if anything, did she say about her specific intentions?'

'That she was going to break up with him, absolutely no doubt about it. She said she was going to do it that night.'

'When she said she was going to break up with him that night, was that in the first of your phone calls with her the day she was killed, or was it the second?'

'It was the second call, the one where she called to say she couldn't go to the gym with me because she had to go to the office to—'

'Ms Schelling,' he interrupted. 'Forgive me. I just wanted to know which call it was.' Trying to keep from scolding her. 'If we need to hear the substance, I'll do my best to ask a specific question about it, which I'm about to do.'

'Oh.' She sat up straighter, her eyes wide. 'Did I do something wrong?'

'It's all right. We'll just go ahead from here, all right?'

She nodded. 'Okay.'

'Good. Now, at the time, during your second phone call with Mariah on the day she was killed, when Mariah said she was going to break up with the defendant that night, can you tell the jury, if you remember, how she put it?'

'Yes, I do. She said she was going to the office that night and she was going to do it then.'

'What, if anything, did she say about why she was going to the office?'

'Objection,' Miller said and started toward the bench. Martinez waved Estrada up to join her. This time, the judge also motioned to a court officer, who led Schelling off the witness stand to a corner of the room near the jury box, where she would not be able to hear the sidebar conference.

'I'm going to anticipate Ms Miller's objection,' Martinez said. 'We're working under strict guidelines on this issue. There is to be no testimony about any report by Mariah Dodge of the defendant's intentions with respect to meeting her, or with respect to anything else that night. You can lead her a little, but don't overdo it. And remember, if your witness even slips you're looking at a mistrial. Now go out there and be careful.'

Estrada waited for Schelling to be escorted back to the witness box. She towered over the court officer. Estrada hoped her pre-testimony toot had worn off.

'The question was what, if anything, did Mariah Dodge say about why she was going to the office that night? Just *her own* reasons, now, not what anyone else was planning to do.' Thinking, be careful.

'He says we've got to have that presentation ready for Monday is what I think she said. Something like that.'

Estrada let out a breath he had not known he was holding. It was the one question and answer he had gone over with her specifically. 'He? Who did she mean?'

Miller stood. 'Your honor, I object.'

Again, Martinez had Schelling removed from the witness stand. As she stood, Schelling leaned towards the judge and whispered a request. Martinez's expression was skeptical. Schelling renewed her request, and an unhappy judge motioned the court officer over. 'Take this witness down the hall, please.' To Schelling she said, 'Make it quick.'

Estrada could not believe this was happening, knew he could not say anything.

'I just warned you about staying away from this subject,' the judge said to him. 'Is there a good reason why I shouldn't hold you in contempt the next time you do it, and declare a mistrial?'

'Your honor, all the witness said was that Mariah Dodge told her that Morales said *we've got to have that presentation ready for Monday*. That's offered as Mariah's reason for going to the office that night. It's an instruction from him to her; it has nothing at all to do with the defendant's intentions for that night. He could've been telling her to prepare it herself. He could have intended to work on it at home while she was at the office. I understand your desire to stay well within the guidelines you mentioned, but even by those standards, this does not cross the line.'

'All right, Mr Estrada. But if I were you I wouldn't push this topic any further.'

Estrada returned to the lectern and a few minutes later watched Lynne Schelling walk back to the witness stand, her every move followed by the jury. She tripped on the step going up, grabbed for the rail in time to catch herself. She smiled at the judge and at Estrada.

Estrada gave her time to get settled before he repeated the earlier question.

'She meant Roberto Morales,' Schelling said.

'Is there anything else you remember specifically from that conversation?'

'Like what?'

'For instance, about the manner in which Mariah Dodge intended to break up with the defendant, or anything else?'

'Objection. Leading.'

'Sustained.' Martinez glared at him. 'Your leading license expired with the last topic, Mr Estrada.'

'Anything about the manner in which she was going to carry out any intention that she told you about?'

Schelling looked completely blank.

'I don't . . .'

This is the punchline, Estrada thought: you can't blow it, you said it in the other trial.

'Oh. Yes. I remember now. Mariah said, I'm going to give it to him with both barrels.'

Estrada let it hang there as long as he thought he could get away with it. 'What if anything did she say that might explain what she meant by *give it to him with both barrels*?'

'She said she was going to tell him how slimy she thought he was and that he was lousy in bed.' Morales had heard it before, but Estrada was still curious about his reaction. He steeled himself against turning to look – Rosen would have a report at lunch. 'How he was stupid to act like this great macho guy, when he didn't do it for her at all.'

'Objection,' Miller said. 'Move to strike.'

'If your honor please,' Estrada countered, 'the witness is testifying to what Mariah Dodge said she *intended* to say. That's well within our . . . guidelines.'

'If that's what she's testifying to, then let her say so. It doesn't sound like that to me. I'm sustaining the objection as to the form of the answer. Ladies and gentlemen, please disregard what you've just heard.' Martinez turned to the witness. 'If you're going to talk about what Mariah Dodge intended, please try to speak in those terms.'

'But I did.' Schelling was indignant, and for the first time since she took the stand the combined power of her size and the force of her personality was evident. 'I said . . .'

'We heard what you said,' the judge snapped at her. 'Just try harder next time.'

'My exact words were, she said *she was going to tell* him—'

'Enough! Mr Estrada, do you have any further questions of this witness?'

'Yes, I do. Ms Schelling . . .' He took his time, speaking in a soothing tone. 'Can you tell us about what Mariah Dodge said she was going to say to Roberto Morales? And can you tell us in that form?'

'Yes. She said she was going to say' – Schelling was speaking with exaggerated distinctness – '*she was going to say* that Morales was a lousy lay and a hypocrite and a liar and the lowest form of life on the planet.' Talking straight to Morales now. 'Dirty and smelly and hateful . . . How's that, Robo, you like that?'

The judge was instantly furious. 'Control yourself, missy. You do that again and you go to jail for contempt of court, and you run the risk of causing a mistrial.' She turned to the jury. 'You can disregard the last part of that.'

Estrada decided to quit before things got worse. 'After she said she was going to tell the defendant that he was bad in bed and a hypocrite and a liar, what if anything further did she say on the subject?'

'That she was going to tell him so that night, no matter what.'

He said thank you and sat down.

10

Miller took her time about getting up and walking to the lectern.

'Good morning, Ms Schelling,' she said warmly. 'I'm Kassia Miller. I represent Roberto Morales.'

'Good morning.' Schelling seemed fascinated by this advocate in a soft blue dress, no taller standing up than Lynne Schelling was sitting down.

'Ms Schelling, forgive me if I repeat some of Mr Estrada's questions, but how long did you know Mariah Dodge?'

'A year, a year and a half.'

'And where did you meet?'

'At the health club.'

'And how well would you say you knew her?'

'Very well. We were good friends.'

'Did she have other friends?'

Schelling hesitated. 'I suppose.'

'Did you meet any of them?'

Another hesitation. 'No. It was just the two of us.'

Miller smiled at her. 'If you can answer yes or no, I'd prefer it. Okay?'

'Okay.' Despite Miller's congeniality, Schelling was wary, Estrada was pleased to see. As long as she wasn't wary to the point of seeming to be hiding something.

'How often did you go to the gym together?'

'Twice or three times a week, depending on our schedules.'

'And did you go out afterwards, sometimes?'

'Yes.'

'And make dates to go to the movies, or a play?'

'Yes.'

'When you had those dates, did they always work out?'

'What do you mean?'

'I'm sorry if I wasn't clear.' Miller was still the soul of agreeability. 'I meant, did it ever happen that something came up and you had to cancel, or postpone?'

'Yes.'

'Mariah, too?'

'Sure.'

'Now and then?'

'Now and then. We were both busy.'

'You just said you didn't know her other friends. Did you know their names?'

'There was an old friend in Texas. And a man at work she mentioned a few times. And her sister.'

Sister, Estrada thought, and saw a way Tess could be helpful again, the way she wanted to be. He jotted a note to Rosen: *For Tommy – Is Tess here?* Rosen reached it back to Clemente, sitting behind them.

On the witness stand, Schelling had a question. 'You're talking about friends, not lovers, right?'

Estrada wanted to go up and muzzle her. Lovers was not a subject that could do the prosecution any good. But Miller passed over it.

'Friends. People she talked to about her life.'

'Those are the only ones I know about.'

'Did you ever know her to change her mind?' A quick change of subject.

'Well . . .'

Estrada waited, remembering his first meeting with Lynne Schelling, and their lunch together, wondering if her second toot was wearing off, and how that would affect her.

'. . . Doesn't everybody?'

Brava! Estrada thought.

'That's not the question,' Miller said. 'The question is, did Mariah Dodge ever change her mind?'

'Sometimes.'

Miller paused, seeming to consider her next question.

'You're in the executive placement business?'

'Yes.'

'And before that you were in the movie business?'

'Yes.'

'What did you do there?'

Schelling brightened. 'I did a lot of things. At the end I was in charge of creative affairs for a production company. That's finding stories and screenplays, and finding writers and directors. It's very exciting.'

'It sounds it. How long did you do that?'

'Seven years.'

'And why did you leave?'

'They call it creative differences.'

'Before that you were an actress, is that right?'

'Yes.'

'Did you have a lot of roles?'

'Not many. That's why I stopped.'

'But you went to a lot of acting classes.'

'Yes. I did better in class than I did in auditions. I have stage fright. Isn't that great? An actor with stage fright.'

Estrada did not know where Miller was going with this line of questioning: all he knew was that it was someplace that would not make him happy. He stood up to object.

'Your honor, I really don't see the point. The jury's already heard about Ms Schelling's career.'

'Can we approach the bench, your honor? Out of the hearing of the witness?'

Martinez had a court officer lead Schelling off the witness stand and over to the corner. Estrada was happy to see the male jurors enjoying her journey and relieved she hadn't asked for another chance to powder her nose.

'Why are we here, Ms Miller?' the judge wanted to know.

'Your honor, this goes to the witness's credibility, and that's obviously not something I want her to know.'

'Her success or failure in acting class does not strike me as bearing on her truthfulness,' Estrada protested.

'Stick with me, I'll show you how.'

'All right, Ms Miller,' the judge conceded. 'But don't draw it out too long.'

Estrada scanned the audience as he walked back to his chair. He did not see Tess Dodge. There was a note waiting for him that said, *Not here.*

'Please correct me if I'm wrong,' Miller said to Schelling when she was back in the witness chair. 'But isn't part of an actor's training to learn to be very involved in the character she's trying to create?'

'Yes, that's right.'

'I've been told that being involved in the character that way can sometimes mean discovering underlying motivations for your characters that aren't written in the lines you speak, or anywhere in the play. Is that right?'

'Yes.'

'Is that necessary a lot of the time?'

'Always.' Her answers were clear, if a bit slow in coming.

'Then is it fair to say that you learned to supply this motivation from your own artistic imagination?' Miller was full of respect.

'Yes.'

Estrada stood up. 'Your honor, I fail to see where this is getting us.' It was not true. He could see now where Miller had to be going, and he wanted to derail her.

'If your honor will allow me another handful of questions.'

'All right, Ms Miller, but interesting as this is, please try and tie it in.'

Miller nodded, then turned back to the witness. 'We were saying that you learned to exercise your artistic imagination supplying motivation for your characters to add truth to your performances.'

'Yes.'

'And would you say that was a skill you acquired in the course of your training?'

'Well . . . that was what I worked at.'

'Does that mean your answer is yes? That you learned to use your imagination to supply truth and drama to your characters?'

'Yes. I guess so. Yes.'

'And sometimes you were given material that was rather flat as you read it on the page?'

Estrada stood up again. 'Your honor . . .'

Martinez waved him down.

'You were given material that was flat, on the page?' Miller repeated.

'Yes.'

'And in that same way did you learn to extract drama from even flat or unexciting material?'

'Yes.'

'And that's what you've been doing here.'

'Yes,' Schelling said without thinking. 'No, wait.'

'Thank you, Ms Schelling,' Miller said, obscuring the attempt to have second thoughts. 'Thank you very much.'

Estrada was on his feet. 'One question on redirect. Ms Schelling, were you making anything up here today?'

'No.'

'Thank you. That's all.'

Martinez sent the jury out for lunch and called the lawyers into her chambers.

'Well, Mr Estrada?'

'Your honor, I have witnesses to call for this afternoon, and I'm in touch with Mr Alvara. I'm hoping to have him here on Monday.'

'I distinctly remember saying he should be here by today.'

'He's not in the country, and frankly he's not eager to come. But I think we all know that he's a crucial part of this trial.'

'That may be, but you've had half a year to find him and get him here.'

Miller had been listening in silence. Now she spoke up.

'Your honor, the State has had *four years* to find this man and bring him forward. From the very beginning of this case they've withheld the diary in which he's named. Wrongfully. In bad faith. If they had revealed it in the discovery period of the first trial, as they were obligated to under the *Brady* cases, we wouldn't be here today.'

'I don't see *Brady* in this,' Estrada countered. 'The evidence this man is going to give is going to put your client away for the rest of his life.'

'I doubt it.'

'Enough,' Martinez ordered. She leaned back in her chair and looked from one to the other. 'I suppose it's admirable to find two lawyers who are such committed advocates, but quite honestly it makes me tired. Life would be easier for all of us if you'd both lighten up a little sometimes.'

'Your honor, my client's whole future is at stake,' Miller protested.

'I know, I know. I'm not suggesting that you do less than your best on his behalf. I mean . . . never mind.' She pushed herself forward again, elbows on her desk. 'Ms Miller, I suppose you have a motion to dismiss this indictment that you want to give me.'

'I do, your honor. Based on prosecutorial misconduct. Mr Estrada's, and especially Mr Kahn's before him.'

The door opened and Martinez's law clerk burst in. He saw the crowd and stopped short. 'Sorry.'

'What's that?' Martinez asked him.

He held out a newspaper. Martinez took it and put on her reading glasses. She peered through them a moment and then turned the paper so Estrada and Miller could see the front page. The headline said: TIMMINS – NO INDICTMENT.

'We're in for a grand weekend,' the judge observed. 'With Mr Kahn right at the center of things.' She took off her reading glasses and looked again from Estrada to Miller and back. 'Tell me about these witnesses of yours, Mr Estrada.'

'To tell the truth I'd rather not put them on unless I have

to. If I've got Alvaro, they're redundant.'

'I appreciate your honesty. They're here to stretch things out till Monday, am I right?'

Estrada did not contradict her.

'All right. Spare them the trouble. I'm tired. I'm going to adjourn for the weekend. My original deadline stands. I've said it before – it wasn't easy getting a jury for this trial and the publicity since then is likely to make it impossible to do it again. And I'm not going to open up a hope in the middle of the trial because this jury deserves better and we'd lose half of them anyway. Ms Miller is right – four years is long enough. I want Señor Alvaro in this court first thing Monday or you rest your case. Ms Miller, you can give me your motion Monday if Mr Estrada doesn't produce his witness. Have a good weekend.'

'You lead a charmed life, Estrada,' Miller said when they were out in the corridor. It was not a friendly remark.

If you only knew, he thought.

He hurried to his office and called Adelante. Ramírez was not in. 'It's an emergency,' Estrada told the teenager who answered. 'I have to talk to him right away. Is there *anybody* who knows where he is?'

She put down the phone and went to check. Five minutes later Dolores Acampo picked it up. 'Who's this?'

'It's Joe Estrada, and I need to talk to Carlos right away.'

'About Juan Alvaro? I don't think there's any more to say. Carlos tells me he won't come back.'

'Tell Carlos I want to talk to him, wherever he is. I only have the weekend. I have to do it before Monday.'

Ramírez called an hour later.

'Suppose I bring Mariah Dodge's sister to talk to him?' Estrada proposed immediately.

Ramírez was silent long enough for Estrada to wonder if he'd hung up. 'Carlos?'

'I'm still here.'

'They were soulmates, Juan and Mariah, or whatever you

call that kind of closeness. She was wonderful, he said. Cared about him, protected him. Suppose her sister spoke to him and made an appeal for him to do this for Mariah. And I'd be there to promise him the world. Immunity for everything.'

'And deliver it.'

'And deliver it,' Estrada agreed. 'In writing. But we need to set this up right now.'

'I'll call you back as soon as I can.'

'I need to get airplane tickets. Where am I going?'

'This isn't a trick?'

'No. That would be stupid of me . . .' Collins came in and sat in the visitor's chair. Estrada remembered the bureau chief saying if he won't come, kidnap him. 'I need his cooperation. I need him to testify willingly.'

'Go to Miami,' Ramírez said. 'I'll arrange the rest. If Juan agrees.'

'Tomorrow.'

'I'll try. I can't promise. Make alternative return reservations if you can.'

'What was all that about?' Collins wanted to know when Estrada got off the phone.

Estrada told him about it. 'I want to go down with Tess Dodge, if I can find her. And that's all there is. It's in the laps of the gods, as they say.'

'I'll get you the tickets,' the bureau chief said, standing to leave. 'I still think you should kidnap him. Take Clemente instead of the sister.'

'Take me where?' Clemente came in with Nancy Rosen and Lisa Stein, toting bags from the sandwich shop and extra chairs.

'To Miami for the weekend. Nice and romantic.'

'Gee, too bad I'm busy.'

'Where's Tess Dodge?'

'Don't know. Not in court today.'

Estrada dialed her number. No answer.

'That's your assignment. Find Tess Dodge.'

'Can I eat my sandwich first?'

'If you eat fast.'

They reviewed the day in court as they ate. The consensus was that the jury had stayed interested, with only a couple of them tuning out. Rosen and Stein did not think Schelling had done too badly on the stand. Clemente disagreed. 'I hate to say it, but she looked stoned to me.'

'Everybody who isn't dead looks stoned to you,' Rosen pointed out.

Clemente shrugged. 'I mean, hey, I think she's just fine, you know – I can think of worse ways to spend an evening. But I don't know what the jury thought about her testimony.'

'How about when she laid into Morales?' Relieved that Schelling had not caused a mistrial, Estrada was trying to think of her outburst as funny.

'I'll tell you,' Rosen said, 'that's one cool customer. He didn't bat an eye.'

'And when she was saying he couldn't make it in bed?'

'The same. As if she were giving a weather report.'

'You think that's going to help him with the jury?' Estrada asked. 'It sounds kind of bloodless to me.' He balled up his sandwich wrappings and lofted them toward the wastebasket, overshooting by a foot.

'Stick to darts,' Clemente advised.

'Okay, gang,' Estrada said. 'Here's the weekend. With any luck, I'm off on a witness hunt. Tommy, after you find Tess Dodge, you belong to Nancy. She's going to be making sure we're ready for the opposition. Stein, the first thing I need is some copies of the Alvaro transcript. Then you may have to do some work with Dan Mahoney, he'll call if he needs you. Otherwise, work with Nancy. Questions?' There were none. 'Okay. Dismissed.'

He went down to see Mahoney, letting Ginny know where he would be in case Clemente came up with Tess Dodge.

'Aren't you due back in court?' Mahoney wanted to know.

'Afternoon off.'

'So you came to interrupt the work of the less fortunate.'

'Exactly.'

Mahoney laced his hands behind his head and put his feet up on the desk. 'Hey, nothing I like better.'

'Actually, I do have some work for you.' Estrada got up to hand him a page of notes.

Mahoney accepted it without disturbing himself, glanced over it and said, 'Monday, I assume?'

'If you can.'

'No problem. How's it going with you? You look a mite . . . peaked. Face all tense or something. Martinez giving you a hard time? Michelle *not* giving you a hard time? You can tell Uncle Danny.'

'I'm okay.'

Mahoney cocked his head. 'Maybe you want to try another reading on that, for realism?'

Estrada, still on his feet, closed the door then sat down again.

'Ah – mystery and intrigue,' Mahoney observed. 'I love it. You don't close the door for legal research questions.' He swung his feet off the desk.

Estrada told him about Michelle. In the telling he heard some of the hurt and anger that had been suppressed when it happened.

Mahoney listened with his full attention, his lips pressed into a grim line. At the end he was silent for a moment before saying, 'I sure do sympathize. It's probably good you can talk about it, 'cause I sure held mine in way too long. Only, I've got to disappoint you if you were hoping for my sage advice. I've got zero to say about what to do or how to feel.'

'I don't suppose I expected magic. You still seeing the dancer?'

'Right now I'm seeing Kath, as a matter of fact. Don't ask me why.'

'You said she wanted to come back.'

'Heck, Joseph, I can remember when little Danny Mahoney wanted to be an astronaut.'

The phone rang. Mahoney answered it. 'Who?' he said with a sour face. 'Who's that?' He listened. 'Oh, *that* Estrada.' He listened some more. 'Let me see if I can find him.'

'Not funny.' Estrada grabbed the phone but Mahoney had already hung up. 'Frisky today, aren't you?' Estrada was not amused.

'That was somebody named Tommy who said he's got somebody named Tess waiting for you in your office. He says she was too nervous to come to court today, but now she's waiting to talk to you.' Mahoney cocked his head. 'Has it ever occurred to you that having detectives bring in dates for you might not be the best way to go about it?'

'You've got a point there. And I've got to get back to work.' He headed for the door.

'Joe,' Mahoney said. 'I do have one piece of advice. Don't forget that you hurt. Don't forget that *she* did it. Let yourself get mad, dude. You're entitled. Take it from me, this modern *understanding* bullshit is strictly for the birds. It only makes you feel worse.'

11

They arrived in Miami on Saturday afternoon. Ramírez's message at the information desk gave them only the name of an island-hopping airline. The attendant at its single small gate could not find any record of their names.

'It must be there,' Estrada said, not in the mood to be stranded.

She looked again. 'Oh yes. I don't know why they stuck them there. Two tickets. Plane leaves in an hour.' She handed him the envelope, a note paper-clipped to it gave the name of a hotel. 'Luggage?'

'Just carry-ons.'

'We check those, too. Plane's too small for carry-on.'

Three hours later they were on the verandah of a small hotel used mostly by deep-sea fishers, watching the sun slip into the ocean.

'I should have brought a bathing suit,' Tess said.

'I'm sure they'll sell you one.'

'Gift shop's closed.'

'Wait till it gets darker and go skinny dipping.'

She squinted at him over the umbrella in her drink. 'Why wait?'

'Good point. Bad enough we have to wait for friend Johnny.' He looked at his watch. 'Speaking of waiting, I'm supposed to let Nancy know where we are.'

He went to find a phone and left a message at the office saying where they were and that it looked like they were staying until Sunday. Tess was still on the verandah, still fully clothed, when he came back.

'Do you think he'll come tonight?' she asked.

'The sooner the better. I don't want to be lying awake wondering if he'll show up.'

They finished their drinks and went into the dining room. Hungry, they started immediately with conch chowder, a rich broth with generous chunks of conch and the bite of pepper. Estrada gave the wine list to Tess.

'Last time you complained about the wine. This time you pick it.'

She laughed. 'Do I have a limit?'

'Whatever you think the State of New York can afford.'

The waiter came over to tell him he had a phone call.

'Johnny?' Tess guessed.

'Let's hope.'

It was Nancy Rosen. 'Was this in the plan?' she asked. 'I don't remember anything about tropical islands.'

'I'm following Carlos's script, gritting my teeth and enduring the hardship.'

'I'll bet. You picked a great time to leave. There was a huge demonstration in front of City Hall demanding justice for Abdullah Timmins. Mostly peaceful, but some kids got out of hand afterward and there were a couple of dozen arrests. Three kids hospitalized, two cops. And they hanged Larry Kahn in effigy.'

'Just what we all needed.'

'Monday should be interesting,' Rosen speculated. 'The Justice for Timmins demonstrators and the Justice for Morales demonstrators right down the block from each other.'

'Maybe they'll draw some of our crowd.'

'Or maybe they'll come over and join them. Stash went to see his Polish lady. She's still not eager to testify about Censabella's drinking, or his taking money from Morales. I've got our Morales notes organized. That's about it here. Señor Castillo called to ask if you read what he sent you.'

'I forgot all about it.'

'Too busy planning your trip to the sun, no doubt. And Michelle called. Three times. I told her you were away, but she didn't believe me the first two times. She said to tell you she left a message on your machine.'

He knew it was a mistake but he could not keep himself from calling home. Michelle's voice stung badly. 'I don't know where you're hiding, but I don't blame you. I can't stand the way we left things. I don't want to interrupt the trial, I know it's important, but I have to talk to you. I'm getting tickets for New York for next weekend, just for a night and a day. If your trial isn't over I won't come. You don't have to return this. Only, please don't shut me out. Let me talk to you.'

He hung up and went back to the table. The waiter was just pouring a straw-colored wine for Tess to sample. She tasted it and pronounced it excellent. The waiter poured for both of them. 'Fish be out soon.'

Estrada lifted his glass in a toast. 'To Johnny. May he wait until tomorrow.' He drank off half his glass of wine.

'What's the matter?'

'Nothing.'

'You look awful.'

He shook his head. 'It's nothing.' He didn't sound so good, either.

'You can tell me.' She picked at the tablecloth. 'After all we've been through.' Smiling at him.

He squeezed his eyes shut to close out the image of Michelle picking at the bedsheet. He felt Tess's hand on his and opened his eyes.

'It's really bad, isn't it?'

He did not answer.

'The girlfriend?'

He nodded, started to take his hand back, stopped. She withdrew hers.

She looked at him for a long time. 'She cheated on you.'

He stared.

'How did I do it? Right?' The green of her eyes deepened with the flickering of the candles. 'I don't know, really. Something about what I saw in her, or something about the way you look, now. Like somebody smashed all your Christmas presents. Hurt, confused, bereft. Angry, too, but you don't have that fierce look that comes with arguing over something dumb. So it was either she left you or you found out she cheated on you. And I don't think she'd leave. I was watching her watch you in court. She's . . . I don't know if I'd say she's in love with you, but she sure wants to have you.' Her hand made a grasping motion. 'Really *have* you.'

'You're very perceptive.' The words came out sounding strangled.

'Only for other people.' She picked at the tablecloth again.

'This is going to sound weird,' Estrada said, 'but I'd appreciate it if you wouldn't play with the tablecloth.'

She looked up. 'Sorry.'

They sat in awkward silence until the waiter brought their fish. Tess thought it was delicious. To Estrada, it tasted like styrofoam.

'This is paradise,' Tess said, most of the way through their silent dinner. 'I'm sorry you can't enjoy it more.'

The waiter poured out the last of the wine. 'Another one?' he asked.

'You bet,' Estrada said. 'Live it up.'

'Are you sure?' Tess asked. 'What if Johnny shows up?'

'He'll meet a drunk prosecutor.'

She smiled at the waiter and told him they would decide later. 'You're feeling sorry for yourself,' she said to Estrada. 'It's understandable, but it's a mistake, and I'll bet you know it.'

'Right again, Dodge. You keep surprising me.'

'We do our best.'

He looked closely at her in the candlelight. 'Are you blushing?'

'Probably.'

The waiter came back. 'Phone call.'

Estrada started to get up, Tess beat him to it. 'I'll get it.'

He finished his wine while she was gone. She was right; he was feeling sorry for himself and he shouldn't. And Mahoney was right, too, he ought to get mad and he hadn't. Not yet. But maybe he would, now. She couldn't even restrain herself a whole week. *Please don't call until the trial's over*, he'd said. Not a lot to ask. He drank the rest of Tess's wine.

She came back. This time he could see for sure that her cheeks were flushed. 'It was Johnny.' She was out of breath. 'He sounds . . . scared. He says he wants to talk to me first. Just me. But he *is* coming – ten in the morning.'

It pulled Estrada momentarily out of his mood. 'Good for him. Good for us.' He waved his arm. 'Waiter, champagne.'

'Are you sure?'

'Why not? I drank your wine, anyway. You'd be dry the rest of the meal. And Johnny isn't coming until tomorrow.'

After dessert and espresso, Estrada picked up the champagne bottle and the glasses and they went for a barefoot walk in the sand and the surf. The water was warm and caressing and a light breeze blew in off the water to ruffle Tess's hair and play with her skirt. The sky was cloudless; a nearly full moon lit their way. They stopped and sat on the bottom of an overturned rowboat and drank champagne.

'How are you feeling?' she asked.

'Better. Kind of lit' – he hefted the champagne bottle, still half full – 'but better.'

'I'm excited about Johnny.'

'You said he sounded scared.'

'Yes, but I think he'll be all right as long as we don't frighten him off. I don't think he'd have called if he wasn't most of the way to coming back with us, do you?'

'I think you're right. And I promise I'll try not to scare him.'

She leaned over to kiss him on the cheek. 'Good.'

'We should get back.'

They walked slowly, Tess taking occasional detours out into the mild surf, standing there looking out to sea. He stood on the cool sand and watched her.

They said goodnight at her door. 'We share a bathroom, right?' she asked.

'I think so,' he said. 'Between the rooms.'

'You go first. I'll probably take longer.'

They stood on the balcony that connected the rooms on the upper floor, neither of them moving toward a door. She lifted her head and offered him a goodnight kiss. It was warm and soft. He wished her sound sleep and went into his room.

He took off his trousers and hung them up so the sea water would dry, washed up and got into bed. He lay on top of the sheets, enjoying the easy wind off the ocean and the gentle downdraft of the wood-bladed ceiling fan on his body. Moonlight filtering through the slats of the wooden window blinds made stripes on the floor and walls and ceiling.

There was a tapping at the bathroom door. He pulled the sheet up over his waist. 'Yeah?'

The door opened and Tess slipped into the room, elusively beautiful as she came to his bed in the silver light.

She lay facing him, silent and unmoving. For long minutes he watched patterns of moonlight on the ceiling, absorbing the sensation of her presence in the bed next to him. He could feel her exhalations, feathery on his shoulder.

He took a slow breath, let it out gradually as he rolled to face her. She was watching him seriously, almost somberly, her green eyes pale in the faint light, her body a composition of rounded shadow.

Her hair spread on the pillow gave him a momentary flash of other hair, redder and less curly, fanned out around a pale face. He shuddered, closed his eyes against the image.

'What?' she asked.

'Your hair . . . I got this horrible flash of . . .' He could not say it.

She sighed. 'Mariah?'

'I knew it was going to haunt me.' He shook his head. 'But I never . . .'

'But you never expected this.' She kissed her forefinger and pressed it to the corner of his mouth.

He lay still, watching her watch him, letting the image of the dead sister recede, growing more and more aware of the living one, until she was all he was aware of. All, except Michelle, who lurked in the back of his mind, equal parts goad and reproach.

'This isn't about anyone else,' Tess said softly. 'Just you and me, here and now.'

He closed his eyes and reached for her. Her skin was impossibly smooth and soft, and she smelled fresh and lush, like a tropical forest of exotic flowers and rich soil. He buried his face in her neck in her skin in her boisterous hair, tasting sweetness and the faint salt tang of sweat. He felt her arms and legs wrap around him and the warmth of her body all along his. He breathed her scent and stroked the skin of her shoulders and back as she rocked him and pressed tighter against him.

He felt his own urgency and the ache of knowing he was not prepared.

She drew back. 'Something's wrong.'

'No.' He kissed her, long and intense, immersing himself in the sensations of her mouth on his, the strength of her body. He nuzzled her neck and her cheek and told her what had bothered him.

She kissed his ear, drew back again, keeping her legs twined around him. 'I brought something.' She buried her face in his neck, suddenly shy. 'In case I got lucky.'

He had to laugh. She scrambled to her knees, bent to kiss him lightly on the belly, then bounded off the bed. He watched her go, marveling at how she was at once firm and bountiful and sleek, and soon she was back.

'We shouldn't,' he said, prepared to hate himself one way or the other. He might as well not have spoken. She tore open the foil and dressed him and joined herself to him, with a soft *oh!*

Only then, when they were fitted together, did she encourage him to wait, to be slow and patient, to draw out their pleasure, and their need. Her legs locked around him again and they lay entwined, on their sides, rocking slightly and making small adjustments that heightened the sensation until finally it was too much for him and he galloped to a finish.

They did not separate but lay there together, breathing each other's breath. After some unknown time he asked if there was anything he could do for her.

She chuckled: a low, affectionate sound. 'Another time. This was just fine for now. Just fine.' She tightened around him. 'Think we can sleep this way?'

'We can try.'

She nestled closer to him, her head on his shoulder. He pulled the pillow further up under his head. 'Comfortable?' he asked her.

'Mmmm.'

He kissed her eyelids and drifted into sleep.

The glare of morning woke him. Tess had rolled away from him and was sleeping curled up at the edge of the bed. He got up and checked his watch: six-fifteen. He pulled on his boxer shorts and went out for a swim.

Tess was awake when he came back, still in bed. 'I thought you'd run off without me.'

He felt oddly uneasy, unsure how to behave. She smiled up at him. 'Are you going to take those off and get back into bed, or what?'

Still uneasy, he followed the program. The uneasiness dissolved when he was in bed with her.

'That's more like it,' she said.

'Your turn,' he told her after a time. She did not protest.

* * *

They went to breakfast at eight-thirty. The hotel's other guests were already finished, a few still lingering over coffee. They were greeted by their waiter of the night before.

'Mornin' folks. Slep' late?' His smile wider than ever.

'Must be the clean ocean air,' Estrada said.

Breakfast was sweet fresh fruits, savory sausage and eggs, and dark coffee. This time Estrada could taste it all.

As Juan Alvaro's ten o'clock arrival time approached, Estrada began to get tense. 'We ought to get our stuff and check out.'

After they packed and paid, Tess proposed a last walk on the beach. 'We've got' – she checked – 'twelve minutes.'

'If he's not early,' Estrada said, and then, 'Sure.'

They left their bags with the bellman and walked out to the ocean.

'It's so beautiful,' she said.

He put an arm tight around her shoulders. 'Thank you,' he said into her hair.

She pulled away. 'Thank you?'

'Is something wrong with that?'

'It's not as if I was doing you some favor.'

Weren't you? he didn't say: Comforting the wounded? 'Okay. Don't get mad.'

'I'm not mad!' She heard herself and laughed. 'Well . . . a little.' She looked at him. 'What now?'

'When we get back,' he began awkwardly, 'we can't . . . Back there we have to pretend this never happened.' He saw her face tighten and reached for her, hating that he had to stop this now. 'I told you, my office has rules.'

'Okay . . . okay.' She was calming herself down as much as she was agreeing with him. 'I can deal with that. And I'm the one who said it was only here and now. But I'm not pretending it never happened.'

They heard the bellman calling from the hotel verandah. 'Miss Dodge. Miss Dodge. Visitor.'

Estrada took her shoulders and gave her a last kiss, held

her at arm's length to appreciate her. Reluctantly, he let her go.

'Okay,' he said. 'Heeeere's Johnny!'

12

Juan Alvaro had to spend almost three hours getting to know Tess Dodge before he was ready to meet Estrada, who spent the time watching the ocean and making notes to keep his mind on the questions he wanted to ask, sentence fragments drifting off into doodles of sailboats and skyscrapers.

They all had lunch together, Estrada warned by Tess in a single whispered sentence to go slow in pressing him about testifying. Juan Alvaro in person was not unlike his image on videotape, stiff and uneasy, not looking at Estrada when he talked though he was noticeably more relaxed when he spoke to Tess. It was something to work on in the few hours they would have before he testified, if he testified.

The lunch conversation was mostly a history of the arrest and trials of Roberto Morales, as narrated by Estrada in response to Alvaro's low-key questions. Estrada tried to emphasize the tenuousness of his case against Morales without making it an obvious sales pitch. And he explained how Miller might get the indictment dismissed if the diary's 'Johnny' was no longer available to the defense as a witness.

'It's a long shot,' Estrada admitted, 'but it'll cause big trouble if they try. And pain for Tess and her parents because it will all revolve around Mariah's diary. And they might win.'

'I don't understand how. There's no way in the world that I would have said anything helpful to them. I'm sure Roberto killed her. I said that in my videotape.'

'But your videotape can't be used as evidence, and the judge has already said she won't rely on it in making rulings. One way or the other, if you don't come back to testify, Morales walks.'

'They convicted him the first time.'

'A fluke. And my case is even weaker than Kahn's was.'

Alvaro fell into a troubled silence. He asked for the immunity agreement, read and reread it and asked questions about what he would have to do, until it was time to leave the island. After three hours with Tess and four more with Estrada he agreed to fly as far as Miami with them to continue talking about it.

On the plane he balked at the idea of having to cooperate with federal prosecutors. 'More ways to humiliate myself. And how does talking about phony invoices at Phoenix Enterprises help Mariah?'

'It's all a part of making sure Morales doesn't get away with what he did,' Tess told him.

'That was a struggle,' Estrada commented to Tess when Alvaro was off in the men's room. 'I don't think he'd have listened to word one if you hadn't softened him up.'

'I like him,' she said. 'I know you can't tell from what you've seen, but I really think he cares about people. And he's smart and funny when he relaxes. I can see why Mariah liked him so much. It's sad the way life screwed him up . . . Can you imagine being in a place in your head where having sex with hustlers in public places was the only thing that felt safe? He was afraid of taking home someone dangerous from the bars, and anywhere else he was afraid he'd say the wrong thing to the wrong person. And then, the way he describes it, he was so desperate and so confused he let himself be fooled by kids pretending to be older. And he hated himself for it.'

'It doesn't sound like fun.'

'He said Mariah and Carlos Ramírez were the first people who helped him see it was possible to lead a normal life – stable relationships, people meeting each other through friends and getting close because they liked each other. When he was talking about it, I realized I'd never thought about any of that before, what that part of it would be like. It must have been awful for him.'

Estrada remembered something Clemente had said, talking about his frustration hanging out in bars and not finding Johnny: 'Maybe he's not that kind of guy. For all we know, trying to find him in the bars could be like looking for a first baseman at the Super Bowl.'

The flight back to New York told Estrada more than he expected to learn. He had reason again to curse Larry Kahn for assuming that the trial of Roberto Morales could proceed effectively without Mariah Dodge's cryptic diary. Alvaro claimed that in the aftermath of Mariah's death Morales had arranged for him to be trapped yet again, and had threatened him with exposure if he did not leave the country. Intimidating a witness was a crime. It was also evidence that Roberto Morales thought Alvaro had information that could hurt. Just like Alberto Quiñones, only a lot clearer. Evidence of a consciousness of guilt.

'Why didn't you threaten him right back?' Estrada wanted to know. 'You had information about the rigged finances.'

'What was I supposed to do – trade him revelation for revelation? I couldn't *prove* anything against him. At most I could make his life uncomfortable. He could ruin mine forever.' The futility in Alvaro's eyes was magnified by his glasses. 'I'm always forgetting how hard it is for the straight world to understand – even for some big-city gays. I spent the first two-thirds of my life confused and ashamed. And scared. For the longest time I couldn't let myself believe what I was feeling and then, when I couldn't hide from it anymore, I knew that if anyone found out they would treat me like the spawn of the devil, or worse. Laugh at me, shut me out, maybe hurt me. And *nobody* is sympathetic to kiddie diddlers.' He said the phrase with disgust. 'With help from Carlos I've come to understand that's not really what I am, but that's how Morales was going to paint me to the world. And the worst of it was, he knew where my family was. They've treated me badly, but still, I've always hoped . . .'

Me, too, Estrada thought, and realized how minor his own estrangement from his family was by contrast.

Alvaro's face filled with resolution. 'I'm glad you pushed me so hard. As long as I don't have to worry about prison, I can face the rest. *I* know who I am, now, and that's a solid enough place to stand.' A smile flickered briefly in his eyes. 'At least, on my good days I feel that way.'

Estrada spent the rest of their time aloft going over the information they could use to give Alvaro's testimony the depth of detail that would make it ring true. Where he did not have a fact, he checked it with Alvaro.

'When did the two of you meet that day?' he asked as the pilot announced that they were making their final approach. 'I know you went to the office some time before seven, but when did you actually get together?'

'She called me right after she got off the phone with Roberto. They'd decided to meet that night to prepare for the meeting that was coming up on Monday, and she wanted to talk to me about it before she saw him. So we got together and had a late brunch.'

'What time was it?'

'I don't know exactly. One-thirty? Two? After we ate we went for a walk. And then eventually we ended up at the office.'

'How long were you together?'

'However long it was. About five hours.'

'The whole afternoon?'

'Yes.'

'Didn't she spend any time with Morales?'

'Not before we went to the office.'

Estrada turned to a new page in his notebook. 'Let me be sure I understand. You met Mariah between one-thirty and two in the afternoon and you were with her until you left her alone with Morales in the office at some time around eight. She never left you to be with Morales?'

'That's right.'

The remains of Sunday passed in a blur of preparation, going over Alvaro's story with him, anticipating how the defense would treat him on cross-examination. By ten, after twelve solid hours with Tess and Estrada, Alvaro was exhausted. Estrada sent him off to his hotel room to get some rest. Tess went along, worried that being escorted by a detective would make him feel like a prisoner. Collins, who had come down mostly to see Johnny in the flesh, was pressed into service by Estrada before Alvaro left. The bureau chief stayed long enough to grill him briefly about the financial manipulations, preparing for a conversation with a friend in the U.S. Attorney's office in the morning.

Estrada had dragooned Mahoney to come down to the office and sit in with him and Rosen and Stein and the two detectives. They worked on strategy for Alvaro's testimony and how to track down the people involved in Morales's blackmail intimidation of Alvaro.

At ten to twelve, Estrada got through to Lynne Schelling after having left three messages on her answering machine.

'Haven't I done enough?' she challenged. 'I thought this was over.'

'I just have one question. When you talked to Mariah the second time that Sunday, what did she say about having been with Morales in the afternoon?'

'That's why you have to talk to me at midnight on Sunday?'

'It's important.'

'Nothing. She didn't say anything.'

'Nothing?' He had to keep any hint of censure out of his voice now. 'Did you talk to Larry Kahn about it at all?'

'He called me, just like this, days after I'd testified. He told me somebody else testified Mariah was with Morales that afternoon. I told him I didn't know a thing about it, but if somebody saw them together, I'd believe it. I told you, consistency wasn't her middle name.'

'But she never actually told you about it?' He remembered her describing it in detail at their first meeting.

'I told you at the lunch we had that when I remembered her telling me about that I was confusing it with a different time. All she said to me that day was that Morales wanted to meet her at the office and that was why she couldn't go to the gym with me. And that's *all* she said.'

Estrada reported the conversation to the others. 'My question is, can I call her on rebuttal?'

'The dog that didn't bark in the night?' Mahoney asked. 'It might be worth trying.'

'If you can scrape her off the ceiling,' Clemente said.

At one in the morning Rosen pointed out that Alvaro wasn't the only one who needed to be well rested in court. As they were leaving the building, she dug into her briefcase and gave Estrada a folded Sunday-supplement magazine. 'I forgot all about this.'

He stopped to open it. It was from *Noticias Diarias* and one of the cover lines was LATINO VERO. Estrada turned to the inside pages and saw a telephoto picture of himself hurrying out of the D. A.'s office. *Publicity-shy prosecutor*, the caption said. There were also pictures of his mother, sister and brothers, and a shot of Grandpa José posed by one of the granite slabs that dominated the courthouse entrance.

'I suppose that's what Castillo's message was about,' Rosen speculated.

'I suppose.' Estrada wondered how well his family had understood that they were cooperating with the reporter on this. 'Maybe it'll help our image,' Estrada said, but he doubted it.

His skepticism was confirmed immediately. There were two police radio cars double-parked in front of his apartment building and a TV station's remote van across the street.

Lights illuminated a dozen or so picketers circulating in front of the building. The message of their signs and subdued chanting was that Joseph Estrada was a traitor to his people, and that he was deficient in Latino pride.

'Pull up next to the police cars,' he ordered his reluctant cabby, holding his D.A.'s office I.D. past the seatback so the man could not miss it.

One of the cops came over to investigate as soon as the cab stopped. Estrada held out the I.D. like a talisman. 'I need to get in there in one piece and get some sleep.'

'We can get you in, sir. The sleep is up to you.'

He did not do as well at it as he would have liked.

In the morning he broke a personal rule and took a cab from the Chambers Street subway station to the office. He told the driver to go around the back way; he had too much on his mind to risk being waylaid by an aggressive reporter or a demonstrator who had gotten past the regulated picketing area.

Everything was normal for eight o'clock on a Monday morning in the office. The prosecutors and support staff who had reason to arrive early went about their tasks with typical Monday bleariness, unaware that Estrada had returned from the wilds with a prize witness, unconcerned about the public change in his ethnic status. The normalcy of it all took some of the bounce from Estrada's step. *Morales* might be the highest-profile case in the office right now, but no matter how it came out the system would keep grinding along. People's lives would be changed irrevocably, Joe Estrada's among them, but the massive wheels of what passed for criminal justice would keep on turning.

He tried not to worry when Tess and Alvaro were late. He called her apartment and the hotel to make sure they were on their way. He went to the men's room to make sure he was presentable. When he got back to his office he called Justice Martinez's chambers and got no answer. It seemed he was the only one who was treating today's court session as anything out of the ordinary.

Lisa Stein was the first one to let him know that outside the courthouse things were not at all normal. 'There are about five times as many people picketing today. A huge crowd. And I heard that people started lining up to get seats at five in the morning.'

That could only mean that Morales's supporters were going to pack the courtroom, with what in mind he did not care to imagine.

'A lot of the signs downstairs are about you,' Stein informed him.

He told her about *Latino Vero*.

'Wow. Is that true? Are you really a Latino?'

'I don't have a clue. Right now all I'm worried about is convicting Roberto Morales.'

'Why are they so upset, though? Isn't this better than if you're a phony Latino?'

'If I understand it right, the idea is that as a phony Latino I was the dumb, possibly racist pawn of the racist District Attorney.'

'Right. I get that.'

'But if I'm the genuine article, then I'm a self-hating traitor turning his back on a blood obligation so I can be the dumb, racist pawn of the racist District Attorney.'

'Oh. Okay, that makes sense.'

'Thanks,' he said.

She turned an immediate bright red. 'No, I didn't mean . . .'

He laughed. 'It's okay. I know what you mean.'

He did not laugh when his mother called. 'I had a call from that nice Alva Garcia down at the library. She told me about the newspaper . . . We met that man, Joseph, the way you told me we should, though I must say I don't know how you could possibly have thought it was a good idea. I suppose he must be some kind of crank, though how a grown man could have any pleasure slandering people he doesn't know . . .'

'I'm sorry, Mother, I didn't think it would upset you.'

'I don't see how you could think anything else.' Her tone was the sharpest he could remember hearing it. 'I don't understand it, and though I've never said this before it's only the latest of many things I don't understand about you. We've all tried to be as good as we can about your poor father's dying wishes, though sometimes I've had trouble making your brothers and sister see that you're not taking advantage of us all, the way you're ignoring the whole point of what your father intended. But this . . . this raving old man . . . is really too much. The way the boys and Betty feel they've been held up to ridicule . . . And it's your fault, I can't say it's not. I'd be surprised if they would be at all happy to hear from you.' She stopped for breath. 'Well . . .'

Well, indeed. It was a long speech for her, and he could not doubt that it had been sincere. 'I'm sorry you all feel this way,' was all he could think of to say. 'I never intended to take advantage of any of you.'

'That's all well and good, Joseph, but the world doesn't run on intentions, it runs on deeds. I'm your mother, but I understand why the others think we've already seen too much of how you conduct yourself. And I don't like to lay blame, but it's my belief you owed us all better . . . especially your father who did so much for you. Frankly I think you'd do well to give us all a wide berth until you get a better sense of where your obligations lie.'

It intrigued Estrada that this did not surprise him or upset him more than it did. It made him sad, but he was less willing than he used to be to feel he was at fault. He was discovering that some old ties had to be cut, old assumptions challenged.

He had respected Larry Kahn, had not forgiven himself for almost bringing his sometime mentor to grief, and yet Larry Kahn had persisted in denying a mistake in the face of mounting danger to himself and others. It was only by separating himself from whatever had bound him to Kahn and acting independently that Estrada had been able to try to salvage the situation . . .

There was a call from the downstairs guard. 'I have a man and a woman here for you,' he said warily. 'Tess and Juan?' Something else was different today: Security was being careful.

'If it's a beautiful strawberry blonde and a brown-haired guy in his thirties, give them an all-day pass.'

'*A beautiful strawberry blonde*,' Stein mocked. 'Did I miss something interesting? Last I looked I thought she was kind of a pain.'

'Remember, she brought us our key witness. That makes up for a lot.'

He put in another call to the judge's chambers and this time got her clerk. 'Please tell Justice Martinez that Mr Alvaro is here, and that I'll need a day's adjournment to get him federal immunity before he can testify.' He did not want her wondering about Alvaro any longer than necessary.

'Come on, Stein,' he said. 'Let's go greet our guests.'

13

Martinez gave him only the morning to do his business at the U.S. Attorney's office – and that much with reluctance. Collins had been working on his contact in the Major Crimes Unit, laying the groundwork. A pair of Assistant U.S. Attorneys took Alvaro through a gruelingly detailed Q&A and extracted promises of full disclosure, absolute truthfulness and whatever testimony might be requested; only then did they give the nod to a short, general immunity letter. Collins had put himself on the line to keep the Q&A informal. No notes were taken and no record kept. That part would come when the Morales trial was over.

'After this, how bad can cross-examination be?' Alvaro joked wanly.

Worse than you think, Estrada did not say. He put Alvaro and Tess Dodge in the care of Lisa Stein for lunch, with his wishes that they relax and enjoy themselves – and with separate instructions to Stein to make sure, tactfully, that they ate moderately and avoided alcohol. He grabbed a sandwich on the way back to the office and munched it while he went back over his plans for Alvaro's testimony.

Waiting for the afternoon session to begin he glanced around the courtroom at a multi-hued audience that tended heavily toward brown. The TV personality and the movie actor were there, and the vigilantes. And Señor Condado. And scores of people he did not recognize who were sitting in a stillness unnatural for this informal part of the judicial day. In the back row he saw Carlos Ramírez with Dolores Acampo and two others from Adelante.

The judge was only ten minutes late. As soon as she was on the bench she waved the lawyers up. 'Mr Estrada? Did you settle everything with your witness?'

'Yes, judge.'

'Ms Miller, I assume we can do without your motion to dismiss.'

'For the moment, your honor.'

'All right, let's get to work.'

As the lawyers took their seats, Martinez rapped sharply with her gavel, though the room was quiet. In English and then Spanish she said she knew that many of them had been waiting since early in the morning and explained that a fair trial sometimes required delays. She pointed out the extra court officers she had arranged for and threatened the assembled spectators with contempt citations and thirty-day jail terms 'if you speak out of turn or do anything else but watch and listen.' Then she called for the jury.

The first questions Estrada asked Juan Alvaro were about his upper-class Cuban-American upbringing and his parochial-school education. Estrada used as many of the standard tricks of repetition and emphasis as he could, looping back to remind the jury of the homey facts he wanted them to remember. He expected to draw objections from Miller, and he did. He thought she was tenser than she had been before, her responses quicker and more edgy. It was the first time he'd had any sense that he was getting to her.

At a sidebar conference with the judge, Miller said, 'Haven't we had enough of the witness's insular, sheltered youth? This case is not about Juan Alvaro's catechism classes.'

'Your honor, it's important that the jury have an accurate picture of this man, because they're going to be asked to make a difficult and crucial decision about his credibility, and it ought to be an informed one.'

'There's a limit,' Miller maintained.

'Indeed there is,' the judge agreed. 'It's time to move on, Mr Estrada.'

Back at the lectern, Estrada had Alvaro testify to his immunity deal, then returned to his earlier line of questioning. 'Let's jump ahead some years. When your academic training was over, where did you go?'

'I went to Chicago for a few years and then I came to New York.'

'How long ago?'

'Almost ten years.'

'And what did you do?'

'I worked as an accountant and a financial officer for several different corporations.'

'Where were you working between four and five years ago?'

'At Phoenix Enterprises.'

'What sort of company was that?'

'Real-estate development. It had a plan for mixed affordable and luxury housing and commercial and light-manufacturing space on the Brooklyn riverfront. It was a much more interesting company than the others I worked for.'

'What did you do at Phoenix Enterprises?'

'I was associate financial director.'

'I'm going to ask you more about that in a minute, but first I want to know about another aspect of your work. Were you ever acquainted with a woman named Mariah Dodge?'

'Yes, we worked together at Phoenix Enterprises.'

'And was that the extent of your acquaintance with Mariah Dodge, that you worked together at Phoenix Enterprises?'

'No, we were friends as well.'

'What sort of friends? Casual friends, good friends . . .'

'We were very close.'

'How long did you know her?'

'Not quite two years.'

'And for how much of that two-year period would you say you were very close friends?'

'Almost all of it.'

Alvaro was doing well. More often than not, he was looking at Estrada when he answered, as instructed. He had been stiff at the beginning, but almost all civilian witnesses started stiff. Estrada decided to take a chance on an open-ended question. 'Can you explain to us how it was that you became close friends so quickly?'

Alvaro sat in silence long enough for Estrada to worry that the question had been a mistake.

'Well,' Alvaro said. 'It makes me sad to think about it too much, but there was something about us that drew us together. It's hard to explain that sort of thing. People talk about chemistry, sometimes. That's usually physical. This was a sort of mental, temperamental chemistry. We both knew right away—'

Miller objected.

'Mr Alvaro,' the judge said. 'It would be better for our purposes if you told us what you saw and heard, and what you did. The mental processes of other people are not usually a good subject for testimony.'

Estrada took him through how he and Mariah Dodge had had lunch together, had gone out together after work, and had quickly began to share confidences.

'What sort of things did you talk about?'

'All sorts of things. Movies and plays. Books. Work, of course.'

'Anything else, of a non-work nature?'

'Yes, we talked about our love lives.'

'And did you have a lot to talk about, about your love lives?'

'You can always make it into a lot, talking about that, but yes, we generally did.'

'And were you lovers?'

'No. We weren't lovers.'

'But you were very close friends.'

'Yes.'

'Objection, your honor. Asked and answered.'

'Yes, Mr Estrada, once is enough.'

Estrada nodded to the judge, then asked Alvaro, 'How did it happen that you were such close friends but you weren't lovers?'

'We weren't lovers because . . . I'm gay.' Alvaro's reserve did not keep the revelation from prompting laughter in the gallery. Martinez gaveled the room quiet.

'Have you been gay for long?'

Alvaro had flushed at the laughter. It took him a moment to regain his composure. 'I've been gay all my life. I didn't recognize it until rather late, though, because in my family, in my culture, it wasn't an accepted way to be.'

Estrada was expecting an objection, on the grounds of relevance if nothing else, but one did not come. Miller was giving him the rope, hoping he would loop it around his own neck. Which he was about to do, if he wasn't careful.

'Mr Alvaro, have you ever been convicted of a crime, or did you ever plead guilty?'

A pause. 'Yes.'

'Can you tell us about it?'

'It's a very painful part of my life.'

'Move to strike,' Miller said.

'Ladies and gentlemen, you can disregard that. Mr Alvaro, please just answer the question.'

'I pleaded guilty to minor crimes three times between when I was twenty and twenty-eight. And I was convicted of a felony once since then.'

'What did you plead guilty to?'

'Disorderly conduct twice, and once to public lewdness, I think it was called.' Minor offenses either not listed in the national crime registries or likely to slip by, which was why Clemente had not found them.

'And what were you initially charged with?'

'Sodomy.'

'All three times?'

'Yes, and indecent exposure.'

'And were these charges based on consensual acts?'

'Yes.'
'Voluntary homosexual acts?'
'Yes.'
'And can you describe your partners, in general?'
'They were prostitutes.'
'How old were they?'
'Young men. Around eighteen, as far as I know.'
'You paid them to have sex with you?'
'Yes.' The color in Alvaro's movie-star face had subsided. The only sign of strain was the exaggerated rise and fall of his chest as he breathed.
'And the conviction, was that in New York?'
'No, it wasn't.'
'Did you make it part of your résumé?'
'No.'
'How did you answer questions about your criminal record?'
'I said that I had none.'
'On job applications? Licensing applications?'
'I always said no to those questions.'
'Would you say that most, some or none of those questions had a warning about answering truthfully under the penalties of perjury?'
'I don't recall precisely but I'm sure some of them must have.'
'And in those cases, did you lie about your criminal record or did you state it accurately?'
'I did not state it accurately.'
'Do you mean you lied?'
'Yes.'
'Why was that?'
'I was too frightened of the consequences to ever admit the truth.'
'Weren't you afraid your employers would find out?'
'The felony conviction wasn't under my name.' Which was why, without Alvaro's fingerprints, Clemente had missed that one, too.
'How did that happen?'

'I was carrying false I.D. at the time.'

'What was that conviction for?'

'I was convicted of inducing an underage person to have sex with me.'

'And how did you induce him?'

Alvaro allowed himself a pale smile. 'I didn't induce him. *He* induced *me*.'

'What do you mean?'

'He was a hooker, like the others. A professional.'

'How old was he?'

'Fourteen is I think what the indictment said. He told me he was eighteen, and he looked it.'

Miller stood. 'Can we approach, please?' At the bench she said, 'Your honor, either this is irrelevant or Mr Estrada is impeaching his own witness.'

'Your honor, I'm only trying to present the entire picture, to put it all in its proper context.'

'I'm sure Ms Miller concedes your right to do that, Mr Estrada, but within limits. Fast-approaching limits.'

'Yes, your honor. Thank you.' He went back to the lectern, not feeling particularly triumphant. 'How did you feel about being with a person that young?' he asked Alvaro.

'Object, your honor. Irrelevant.'

'Sustained.'

'Do you still frequent prostitutes?'

'Not for years. It was crazy then, it's suicidal now.'

'What's the nature of your current intimate relations with other men?'

'Objection.'

'Your honor,' Estrada said louder than he intended.

Martinez motioned them up.

'It's irrelevant,' Miller argued, 'and, as your honor said, there are limits.'

'The jury needs this information, judge.' Miller had timed her objections perfectly. 'Without this, they have an incorrect and distorted impression of the witness.'

Martinez considered it. 'All right, I'll let him answer this one question, no more. After that, move on.'

'Thank you, your honor. Mr Alvaro, what's the nature of your current intimate relations?'

'They're limited to one adult with whom I have an emotional connection. There's no one like that right now.'

'Were your co-workers at Phoenix Enterprises aware of your earlier preference for relatively youthful male prostitutes?'

'Only two who knew directly from me. Mariah Dodge and Alexander Blair.'

'Who is Alexander Blair?'

'He was my immediate superior at Phoenix Enterprises, and he hired me.'

'What was the nature of your relationship with Alexander Blair prior to his employing you?'

'We were . . . I guess you'd say acquaintances, or a little more. We had friends in common and we sometimes were at the same parties.'

'How did he know about your preferences?'

'He was present on one occasion when I indulged myself.'

'Did he have similar preferences?'

'Objection.'

'Your honor, Alexander Blair's habits are relevant to the circumstances of Mr Alvaro's employment at Phoenix Enterprises.'

'You've established enough in that line, Mr Estrada. We get the point. Objection sustained.'

'Why did Alexander Blair hire you?' Estrada asked.

'Objection,' Miller said again. 'Speculation. Mental process.'

'Sustained.'

'Did Alexander Blair tell you why he hired you?'

'Objection. Hearsay.'

'Sustained.'

Estrada was feeling battle-weary. He could only hope that

Miller's repeated objections might be losing her points with the jury.

'To your knowledge, were there other applicants for the job, or were you the only one?'

'There were others.'

'How do you know?'

'Mr Blair showed me the file of applications.'

'How many were there?'

'I didn't count. At least twenty.'

'When Alexander Blair hired you did he say anything that indicated to you that the job had special requirements, or that you were particularly suited to it?'

'He said he could trust me.'

'What's special about that?'

'Objection.'

'Your honor, I'm laying a foundation here. I can make an offer of proof if you'd like.'

Martinez shook her head impatiently and waved him on. 'Go ahead.'

'What did you take that to mean, that he could trust you?'

'I thought he was threatening me.'

'With what?'

'Public exposure.'

Laughter. The judge quieted them down.

'Was your conclusion that he was threatening you confirmed, or not?'

'It was confirmed.'

'How?'

'As part of my job, working with Mr Blair, I was required to set up a system of internal accounting controls that would not pick up various kinds of false billing. He offered me a bonus out of the money that was being skimmed. I refused the money, but he told me it would be a dangerously self-destructive mistake to say no to doing the work. He mentioned something about the good parties we'd been to together, he and I. He didn't have to spell it out.'

'Did you go ahead with it?'

'Yes.'

'What kind of scheme was it?'

'Basically it was an accounting trick. Certain money was shown as spent to pay bills, but they were phony bills and the money was transferred to another account. I was told it was to cover extortion payments to organized crime people in the construction business.'

'How much, if any, construction did Phoenix Enterprises ever do?'

'None.'

'Then why pay extortion to the construction business?'

'We were sending out requests for preliminary bids, to put together budgets for our investors.' On safer ground now, Alvaro was answering crisply in a strong, clear voice.

'To your knowledge, what happened to the money?'

'I don't know.'

'To your knowledge was it ever used to further the company's purposes, illegally or otherwise?'

'Not that I know of.'

'What did you tell Mariah Dodge about any of this?'

'Nothing at first. Eventually I told her what I knew.'

'What was her response?'

'It upset her. She said she wanted to do something about it, but she didn't know what.'

Estrada took a breath. On the witness stand, Alvaro asked for a glass of water.

Estrada waited for Alvaro to finish drinking his water, then asked, 'Did there come a time when there was a change proposed in the company's financial structure?'

'Yes.'

'Can you tell us about that?'

'Cuyler Jadwin, the chairman of the board of directors, had arranged for some outside investors to come in and take over part of the project. In mid-October he came to New York from Texas to hold a meeting at which the new arrangements would be discussed, to be sure there was no unforeseen obstacle.'

'And what, if any, preparations did you make for this meeting?'

'There were reports to prepare and statistics about the financial operation of the company to be assembled. That occupied most of the week leading up to the meeting. Then, on the evening before the meeting was scheduled, I went to the office with Mariah Dodge to discuss a new idea she had for a compromise solution to the company's problems.'

'What was this a compromise between?'

'There was the plan proposed by Cuyler Jadwin, and there was opposition from Roberto Morales. Mariah told me she thought she could reconcile the two, and keep them from draining away money the project needed.'

'When did you go to the office?'

'About six or six-thirty. It was a Sunday night.'

'Was the office open?'

'No.'

'Who had the keys?'

'We both had keys to the main part of the office. I also had the key to my office and the clerical and filing area and the room where we kept the copier and the fax. Mariah had those keys, and the keys to her office and to Morales's.'

'Was anyone else there when you arrived?'

'No.'

'What did you do?'

'We went to Mariah's office and set up to check some files and to do some cutting and pasting of documents and so on, so Mariah could make her ideas clear to Morales at the meeting on Monday.'

'Why didn't you use a computer?'

'It wasn't practical at that point for what we were doing. It was easier to make a bunch of photocopies and throw something together in a hurry, and Mariah was more comfortable working that way. Computers intimidated her.'

Estrada showed him the utility knife. 'Do you recognize this?'

Alvaro looked at it briefly, looked away. 'It's the same kind as the one we were using that night.'

'Did all of the documents you used come from the main part of the office, or did they come from other places as well?'

'Some came from my office, some came from Roberto Morales's.'

'How did you get into the defendant's office?'

'We used Mariah's keys.'

'How did you leave the door after you got the documents you needed?'

'We made more than one trip. Each time, we locked the door behind us.'

'How can you be sure?'

'We were careful about it because we didn't want anybody to be able to get in, and it was a nuisance to have to open it again every time.'

'Were you able to do what you had come for?'

'Not entirely.'

'Why was that?'

'Mariah found something that upset her.'

'Objection.'

'Sustained.'

'What happened?'

'Mariah found something that made her stop.'

'Did you see what it was?'

'Yes. It was a letter with some handwritten notes on it.'

'Was the handwriting strange to you, or was it familiar?'

'It was familiar.'

'Whose was it?'

'Roberto Morales's.'

'Where and when had you seen his handwriting before?'

'Many times and many places. In particular, he made a practice of responding to memos at work by making notes in the margins. We both had seen that kind of thing many times before.'

Estrada had him examine the file of documents found at the crime scene, already in evidence. 'Is the letter in that file?'

'No.'

'Can you give the jury your best recollection of what the letter said?'

'The letter was addressed to Morales at home, from someone whose name neither I nor Mariah recognized and I can't remember now. It was about some investors – something about the investors being in place, ready to go, and that their documentation would withstand scrutiny. And it asked something like how long did he need them for? That was odd. It might not have been that explicit, but that was the feeling we got.'

'Objection to the feeling.'

'Sustained.'

'What else was in the letter?'

'It said thank you for the check, and if Morales wanted the reports they'd discussed then more money would be required. It was quite cryptic, as if they both knew—'

'Objection,' Miller interrupted. 'Move to strike.'

'Sustained. No opinions about other people's knowledge, please.'

'What is your best recollection of what the defendant's handwritten notes said?'

'There were several handwritten words, and each one was connected to typewritten words in the letter by a line or an arrow. I remember there were some cash amounts, and abbreviations for air pollution and sewage disposal, and something about a letter of credit.'

Estrada had a court officer set up the four-foot-high pad of paper that Rosen had used with the medical examiner and then had Alvaro come down off the witness stand and write on it in large letters so that the jury would have a visual image to go with the testimony.

'To the extent that you remember the handwritten notes and what words in the letter they were connected to, could you put them down for us?'

The words Alvaro wrote gave the clear impression that Morales was paying for phony reports on the air pollution that would be caused by the Phoenix Project and the amount of sewage it would generate. Under the abbreviation POLLU/SEWER he drew a rough skull and crossbones. 'That was there, too, I remember that clearly.'

'Do you remember anything else?'

'Yes.' Alvaro wrote *L.C. – offshore – SECRET* in the place he was using for representing Morales's marginal notes and connected it to DOCUMENTATION in the letter. He drew a double box around *SECRET*. 'L.C. is Letter of Credit,' he explained.

'This is what you remember from the letter that Mariah Dodge found that made her stop what you were doing?'

'Yes.'

'These specific words and abbreviations?'

'These or something close to them.'

'What did she do after she read the letter and the notes?'

'She asked me about the financial manipulations I was involved in.'

'Were these the same manipulations that you testified about earlier, or different ones?'

'The same. She asked me to tell her in greater detail.'

'And what was her reaction?'

'She became very angry. She wanted to follow up on the conclusion she had come to as a result of reading this other document. I helped her with that.'

'Was everything you looked at a financial document?'

'No, we looked at planning proposals and correspondence with the community planning board. A lot of different things.'

'As the two of you continued your research, did she become less angry, or more?'

'More angry. She was as angry as I had ever seen her.'

'How did the anger manifest itself?'

'She became very intense and focused, and at the same time very agitated.'

'Did there come a time when someone else arrived?'

'Yes.'

'Who?'

'Roberto Morales.'

'And what happened then?'

'She confronted him immediately with her suspicions. She said he was lying to everybody about the Phoenix Project, using it for his own selfish purposes even though he knew it would never get built.'

'Objection, your honor.' Miller was heading for the bench. Martinez waved her off.

'Overruled. Mister witness, did the defendant deny the accusations?'

'Yes, he did.'

'Ladies and gentlemen, please bear in mind that these accusations are not being offered to you as evidence that they're true. This is just to establish the words the witness says he heard.'

'What was her demeanor?'

'She was speaking in a loud, agitated voice. She was angry.'

'And where was her anger directed?'

'At Roberto Morales.'

'Beyond what you've already told us, how was her anger at Roberto Morales expressed, speaking generally?'

'Generally? She called him names.'

'Can you give us your best recollection of what was said, being specific as to the words if you remember them?'

'She said he was a traitor to his people, a liar and a thief. She said he disgusted her and she couldn't believe she had ever let him touch her. She said he was not a good lover. Pathetic, I believe was the word she used.'

'What was his reaction?'

'He got very angry with her. He said she didn't know what she was talking about. Yelling at her. He called her a stupid bitch and said she should stick to things her tiny mind could handle.'

'Was he yelling only at her, or did he say something to you?'

'He demanded that I leave.'

'What did you do?'

'I stayed.'

'Why?'

'I was afraid to leave them alone, they were that angry. He was, especially.'

'Did you leave, eventually?'

'Yes.'

'Why did you leave?'

'Two reasons. The first was that Morales began to attack me directly. He said he would tell the world how much I enjoyed young boys.'

'Did you leave the office as soon as the defendant threatened you?'

'Objection,' Miller said quickly. At the bench she said, 'The prosecutor is drawing improper conclusions, and he's testifying for the witness.'

'Your honor, Mr Alvaro has testified that the defendant said he would tell the world . . . would make accusations against Mr Alvaro involving practices that are widely thought to be depraved and indefensible. That's a threat, in my book.'

'I'll allow it.'

Estrada had the earlier question read back.

'No, I didn't leave the office right away,' Alvaro testified.

'What did you do?'

'I urged Mariah to leave with me.'

'How did she respond?'

'Not at all, at first.'

'What was she doing?'

'She was yelling at Morales.'

'Do you remember the substance of what she said?'

'Some of it.'

'It's important for the jury to hear whatever you remember.'

'She was cursing him, mixing Spanish and English. She said

that he was the son of a whore and that he was impotent and that he was . . . malparido – misbegotten, or misborn . . . not born whole.'

Miller stood. 'Objection . . .' She sat down without finishing it. 'Withdrawn.'

Alvaro looked confused.

'You can continue, if there's more you remember,' Martinez instructed.

'There's one part of it I remember especially well. Mariah said to him, you think you're better than all the people out there you think of as filthy spics, the ones you're so afraid will taint you by association. Then she said, I know people who are heroin addicts and needle-sharers – the kind of people you think are the lowest scum of the earth, of the Puerto Rican earth – and you're not fit to shine their shoes. They may be sad and troubled, she said, but there's not one as filthy, dirty evil as you are. And cowardly – she said cowardly, too – there's not one of them as big a coward as you are. She said it made her skin crawl to think of him touching her, that she was never going to make that mistake again.'

The courtroom had the special quality of silence that comes with complete attention. Wrapped up as he was in questioning Alvaro, Estrada sensed it.

'And how did the defendant respond to her saying that he was ashamed of his heritage . . .' Estrada took a breath to let Miller object, hoping for a chance to have Alvaro repeat it all, but Miller held her peace. '. . . and to her saying that he was evil and a coward and that she would never let him touch her again?'

'He was shouting at her to shut up.'

'Was that all, or was there more?'

'Mariah kept demeaning his manhood. At one point she told him I was a hundred times the man he was. That was the worst . . . angry as he was already, he got even angrier. And it made him focus on me. He threatened me again, this time much worse, because the threat was to tell people about my arrest and conviction in another state under another name. Until then I'd had no idea he knew about it. His saying that terrified me, because I've always been sure it would ruin me if it ever got out.'

'What happened then?'

'Mariah repeated her threat that she would tell the world what an exploiter Morales was. That he was willing to keep people believing in the Phoenix Project when he knew it was a lie. No, not just that he *knew* it was a lie, that he was *creating* the lie, letting people ruin their lives for a dream that would never happen, just so he could come out looking like a hero. And he said I *am* a hero. I'm the biggest hero you ever saw, and nothing else matters. And she said, People matter, all these people. And he said, I never did anything to the people – investors aren't people.'

'What did you take him to mean when he said, I never did anything to the people – investors aren't people?'

'Objection.'

'Sustained.'

Estrada tried again. 'What was the subject of the conversation at the time the defendant said "I never did anything to the people – investors aren't people"? Leaving aside the name-calling.'

'They were talking about the letter Mariah and I had found, and Mariah was accusing him of falsifying everything about his proposal for the meeting on Monday, and she was saying he had been falsifying important information about the project from day one.'

'And did he say anything else at that time?'

'He started calling her names, and me, too. Worse than before. All this was in English.'

'Do you remember any of the words he used?'

'He was saying he wasn't going to listen to a fag baby-fucker and a white-trash cunt tell him what to do. And she said, you're nothing, less than nothing, a pile of excrement pretending to be a man. And more about how it made her sick to think she ever let him touch her. And *he* said if she ever talked about him like that to anybody she would see what it was to be sorry. When he said that she went off the scale. Her language became very . . . Texas colorful.'

'Objection.'

'Sustained. Disregard the characterization.'

'What specifically did she say? If you remember?'

Alvaro looked doubtful, but he went on. 'She called him a scum-sucking, worm-fucking, maggot-ridden, asshole – or something very close to that – and then she turned to me and said I should leave. She said it in her normal calm, steady voice. And I saw that I might be making things worse by staying, because it would bother him more that she was saying these things to him in front of a maricón.' Using the slur for homosexual. 'So I left.'

'And how would you describe the defendant's tone of voice at the time you left, from what you could observe?'

'He sounded furious.'

'And his demeanor in general? His facial expression?'

'I never saw anyone so mad. He was . . . foaming at the mouth.'

'Objection.'

'Sustained. Keep it literal, please.'

'He was furiously angry.'

'And when, after that, did you next see Mariah Dodge?'

'After that?' Alvaro seemed perplexed by the question. 'I never saw her after that.'

'Why is that?'

'That was the night she was killed. Right in that office.'

Estrada gave that a moment of silence before he turned to the judge to request a sidebar conference. At the bench he said, 'Mr Alvaro just returned to the country late last night, so he hasn't had a chance to look at the documents my office has assembled from Phoenix Enterprises. We'd like to request an early adjournment this afternoon to give him a chance to examine them.'

'I already gave you the morning off. And Friday afternoon.'

'Your honor, I can't conclude my examination of this witness until he tells me how much of that information he can help me present to the jury.'

Miller protested that the prosecution had had more than ample time to prepare a case and shouldn't be given free rein to conduct fishing expeditions in the middle of the trial.

'This is the first time we have a cooperating financial officer of Phoenix Enterprises to look at these documents,' Estrada argued. 'Clearly, from Mr Alvaro's testimony this afternoon we have to expect that we'll find information relevant to the motive in this case.'

'Limits, Mr Estrada, limits,' the judge scolded, shaking her head unhappily. She put on her reading glasses to make notes on the pad in front of her, then turned to the jury and reminded them not to discuss the case with each other or anyone else and to avoid news reports of the trial. The court officer took them out and Martinez rapped her gavel. 'Adjourned until tomorrow at nine-thirty sharp.'

Carlos Ramírez waited for the defense team to leave by the inner door before he bucked the departing crowd to come to the rail.

Estrada gripped his hand. 'I haven't had a chance to say thank you.'

'It's an ugly business, isn't it? I thought it would be hard for him, but not this hard.'

'He did a terrific job up there. It's going to make a big difference.'

'I'm worried about how this is going to affect him. He's a complicated man. This isn't over for him yet.'

'It's something I never get used to – the way the grief and the pain don't stop with the crime.'

Ramírez shook his head, as if to clear it of the unpleasantness. 'I see by the newspapers that you're one of us after all,' he said, smiling behind his beard.

'I want to talk to you about that. Does that story in *Noticias Diarias* make any sense?'

'Why not? It's not so different from how Roberto and I got to be twins. I'll tell you about it someday.'

Clemente was waiting in the corridor. 'No luck on Alexander Blair. Out of the country, nobody's saying where, or when he'll be back. His phone's on temporary disconnect.'

'When did he leave?'

'About a week after the last time I talked to him.' Clemente popped a mint into his mouth. 'One too many questions about Juan Alvaro,' he said, disgusted.

14

Back downstairs at the office Estrada introduced Juan Alvaro and Tess Dodge to Nathan Masouros, the accountant pulled off his other job yet again to work on *Morales*. They kept at it until midnight without coming up with anything conclusive. The documents they had were adequate to show both double billing and phony invoicing, but they were worthless when it came to pointing the finger at Morales.

Some of the double billing that Masouros had found was new to Alvaro. 'The systems I set up allowed this to happen, but I wasn't aware anyone was using them this way. You have to imagine a situation where there's no good way to cross-check the money that's going out against the goods and services and so on that are coming in. You can do a lot with that if you're creative. But it's hard to know who's benefiting from it unless you have some way to see who's taking the money out at the other end of the pipeline.'

'Mr Alvaro's been very helpful separating the real suppliers and contractors from the phony ones,' Masouros said. 'And he's shown me some places where I was adding one and one and getting eleven, but the bottom line is we don't have a smoking gun. We have some guns, but they're cold and we can't read the fingerprints on them.'

'Could Blair unravel it?' Estrada wanted to know.

'Some of it,' Alvaro guessed. 'But it's possible that he doesn't know much more about the executive side of it than I do. All I knew was that Blair told me to set up a system that made cheating easy. I assumed he was one of the cheaters. Blair and Morales. But I could be wrong. Blair doesn't have to have known much more than I did.'

'He knows who told him to do it. The next person up the line.'

'Suppose it was Jadwin,' Masouros proposed. 'He was the one behind the manipulations on the site buyout.'

Alvaro was skeptical. 'It *could* have been Jadwin . . .'

'Let's remember this is a murder trial,' Estrada pointed out. With Alvaro found, Cuyler Jadwin was the last person he wanted in the courtroom. 'I know you financial sleuths want to unravel the mystery, but that's not what we're here for. We have only one goal – to help the jury understand and believe that Roberto Morales had something valuable to protect that Mariah Dodge was threatening. But that only helps me if I can do it without confusing them or diverting them from the question of murder. There's a real danger they'll turn any doubt or confusion they have about the financial manipulations into doubt that Morales is guilty of murder.

'Our assignment for tonight is getting our evidence ready. Evidence against Roberto Morales. And we need to do it without depriving Juan of a good night's sleep.' Because nothing was more important than his getting through cross-examination in one piece. The way things looked now, this trial was coming down to Juan Alvaro's word against Roberto Morales's.

In the morning, Estrada and Alvaro reviewed a small pile of tax returns and investment prospectuses, a slightly larger pile of invoices and bank statements, and three four-by-six-foot charts showing the flow of money and the way the accounting system allowed expenses to be billed more than once and bills to be paid for work not done. Masouros and Stein had spent until three in the morning culling out the papers and creating and refining the charts, based on information Alvaro had given them.

'It tells the story,' Estrada judged. 'It's a brilliant job. But it still doesn't point a finger. We can't show who got the money, and we don't have marching orders from whoever was the general. So if we put it on, Miller says: okay, Juan Alvaro participated in a scheme to defraud, but who's to say it wasn't Juan Alvaro's *own* scheme to defraud? What connects any of this to Roberto Morales except Juan Alvaro's accusation? So who's to say Alvaro didn't kill her to keep her from blowing the whistle on *him*?'

'What about Morales's personal records?' Alvaro asked. 'Can't we find out what kind of money he had coming in, how much he spent? Show that there's unattributed income?'

'If there is, he buried it somewhere in his real-estate holdings. Nathan's looked at what we have and there's nothing obvious. And if there's anything we don't already have from those days, it's long gone.' Estrada had no confidence that Larry Kahn had done a thorough job: he had not been looking for a financial motive.

'Sorry, folks,' Estrada said, wishing it were otherwise. 'I know you worked hard, and you did a great job, but we can't afford to take a chance on this.'

Miller started asking Juan Alvaro her first question on cross-examination before she reached the lectern. 'Mr Alvaro, did the police ask you the significance of the papers that were found in Mariah Dodge's office?'

'Yes.'

'What did you tell them?'

'I don't remember.'

Estrada felt the presence of the jury, close enough to read his response to Alvaro's blunder. Miller jumped on it immediately.

'Just yesterday weren't you reporting conversations to us word for word from longer ago than that?'

'From around the same time.'

Alvaro had done relatively well on direct. Now he was returning to his bad habits, looking everywhere but at Miller and resisting her questions when yielding would have worked better, clearly afraid she was out to hurt him. She was, but this wasn't the way to avert it.

'If you don't remember, I've got a police report you can use to refresh your memory.'

Estrada turned to a new page in his yellow pad and reached for a file at the end of the table. His arm hit his paper cup of water and knocked it over. Quickly he snatched his papers from the path of the water. Rosen pulled tissues from her purse and blotted.

'Sorry, your honor,' he said, sure that Miller and probably the judge, too, knew what he was up to. At no time did he look at Alvaro. He had to hope the diversion would remind the witness of his friend the prosecutor, refocus him on the instructions he'd been given.

'Mr Alvaro, would you like to refresh your memory?' Miller asked.

'No, that won't be necessary,' Alvaro said. 'I can remember generally.' He was looking at Miller now, the way he was supposed to. 'I told them the papers were financial documents. I believe they asked me why Mariah might have been looking at them on Sunday, and I told them about the meeting that had been scheduled for Monday morning. But I don't remember the exact words.'

'You didn't tell them you had been there?'

'No.' Turning away from her accusing stare.

'Or that you had been stealing from the company?'

'I wasn't stealing from the company.'

'Didn't you testify yesterday that you were participating in bookkeeping schemes designed to provide phony invoices for expenses the company never incurred?'

'Most of the schemes—'

'Yes or no,' Miller interrupted sharply.

'Yes.'

'You knew Roberto Morales at Phoenix Enterprises?'

'Yes.'

'Would you say you were allies there?'

'No.' For the first time, the corners of Alvaro's mouth turned up slightly.

'You were aware of his relationship with Mariah Dodge, your close friend?'

'Yes.'

'Did you approve?'

'No.'

'Did Roberto Morales ever speak to you about Mariah Dodge?'

'Yes.'

'What did he say?'

'I don't remember his exact words.'

'The general tone.'

'It was negative.'

'He didn't approve that you and she were friends?'

'No.'

'So it's not that you and Roberto Morales weren't allies. You were enemies.'

'Well . . . I don't . . .'

'Yes or no? You were enemies.'

'All right. Yes.'

'You were arrested three times for sodomy.'

It took Alvaro a moment to adjust. 'Yes.'

'With teenagers.'

'Yes.'

'Teenage boys.'

'Young men.'

'Do you consider fourteen to be the age of a young man?'

'They weren't—'

'Mr Alvaro.' Miller cut him off right away. 'I asked, yes or no, if you consider a male person of fourteen to be a young man?'

'No.' There was no good answer to that one.

'And the time you had sex with the fourteen-year-old boy, the time you were convicted of a felony for that sex act with a minor, you had false I.D. on you?'

'Yes.'

'And you lied to the police about who you were?'

'Yes.'

'And they had arrested you for having sex with this boy?'

Alvaro started to protest, but answered yes. He was staring fixedly at the rail of the witness box.

'You had sex with him.' Accusing now, not asking at all.

'Yes.'

'A fourteen-year-old boy.'

'Objection. Asked and answered.'

'Sustained.'

'And could the court please direct Ms Miller to ask questions,' Estrada requested, 'and admonish her not to testify for the witness or browbeat him?'

'I'm conducting cross-examination,' Miller said. 'This is how it's done.'

'Yes, it is,' the judge agreed. 'Overruled, Mr Estrada.'

'Thank you, your honor,' Miller said crisply. Estrada noticed a new note of mastery in her voice. Tiny, charming Kassia Miller, in her well-tailored feminine dress, was beginning to assert control over the courtroom.

'You knew what a bad a thing that was to do, didn't you, Mr Alvaro? Having sex with a fourteen-year-old boy?'

'Well . . .' Alvaro seemed confused.

'Bad for the *boy*.'

'Yes.' A straightforward acknowledgment, as Estrada had advised. Good.

'But you did it anyway, didn't you?'

'Yes.'

'And you'd done it before, hadn't you?'

'Yes.'

'More than once.'

'Yes.' Alvaro's responses were taking on a mechanical tone as if he were trying to numb himself to what he was saying. His gaze stayed locked on the rail.

'And you knew it was illegal, didn't you?'

'Yes.'

'But you did it anyway, didn't you?'

'Yes.'

'Knowing it was harmful to *all* those boys.'

'They were *prostitutes*,' Alvaro protested in anguish.

Miller stared at him for what seemed like a long time, letting his cry reverberate in the minds of the jurors. She looked at them for a moment before turning back to Alvaro.

'Do you suppose, Mr Alvaro, that these young boys were prostitutes *voluntarily*? That they *wanted* to be . . . ?'

'Objection,' Estrada said, not soon enough. 'Mr Alvaro doesn't know what was in their minds, and neither does Ms Miller.'

'Sustained.'

'Mr Alvaro,' Miller began again, 'do you suppose being a prostitute is *not* harmful to a fourteen-year-old boy?'

'Objection.'

'Overruled. You can answer.'

'No.'

'No, what? Is it harmful?'

'Yes, it's harmful.'

'You knew it was harmful, and you did it anyway.'

'Yes.'

'Because you wanted to.'

'Yes, but–'

'Knowing it was harmful and illegal.'

'Objection. Asked and answered.'

'Sustained.'

'You kept doing it even though you knew it was harmful and illegal, because it was in your personal interest.'

'No.'

'No? It *wasn't* in your interest, *as you saw it then*?'

'Well . . . no. Yes.'

'It *was* in your interest?'

'Yes . . . but–'

'And that's why you did it.'
'Yes.' Resigned.
'And continued doing it.'
'Yes.'
'And now you've made a sweetheart deal with the prosecutor, haven't you?'
'I don't know if it's a sweetheart deal,' Alvaro struck back, desperate to make any kind of points he could. Right into her trap, Estrada thought, and watched her close it.
'Let's explore that. You're testifying here in return for immunity, isn't that right?'
'Yes.'
'Immunity from any crimes you may have committed.'
'Yes.'
'Financial crimes.'
'Yes.'
'Fraud?'
'Objection, your honor. May we approach?'
At the bench, Estrada said, 'Ms Miller has no basis for putting the witness through a litany of possible crimes. Taking immunity does not impute unproved crimes to him.'
Miller was not even slightly ruffled. 'Your honor, I'm asking only about crimes I have been given a basis for in the witness's own testimony-in-chief.' Still asserting her control.
'She's right, Mr Estrada,' the judge said. 'I'm going to let her continue.'
And continue she did, getting Alvaro to admit – one crime at a time – that he was being given immunity by the D.A.'s office for embezzlement, state tax fraud, conspiracy, grand larceny and perjury. Estrada objected again at the length and repetitiveness of the list, and the judge finally cut Miller short, making her lump together in a single question her list of sex offenses and offenses against minors.
'You're immune from prosecution for all these crimes?'
'Yes.'
'And for all the federal crimes you may have committed, as well.'

'Yes.' Tentatively.

'Because you have immunity from federal prosecutors as well.'

'As far as I know.' Alvaro slumped in the chair.

'And what do you have to do in return for that immunity?'

'Testify.'

'In return for your immunity from all those crimes all you have to do is testify. And you don't know if that's a sweetheart deal? Do you want to reconsider that answer?'

'I suppose it is.'

The judge leaned across the bench toward him. 'You have to speak up, Mr Alvaro.'

'I suppose it is,' Alvaro repeated, too loud.

'You've made a sweetheart deal by which the prosecutor is allowing you to go free for whatever you've done in the past.'

'Yes.'

'You're going to walk out this door a free man.'

'Yes.'

Miller was giving him cause to object but Estrada did not want the jury to think he was hiding anything about this, and he wanted Miller to get on with it.

'You weren't happy about being in danger of arrest and conviction for your crimes, were you?' Miller resumed.

'I didn't think I was in danger. Not until—'

'You *didn't*?' she interrupted. 'You didn't think you were in danger.' She paused there, with a significant look at the jury. Then she said in a neutral voice, 'You're not living in this country anymore?'

'That's right.' Warily.

'When you left the country, how long was that after Mariah Dodge was killed?'

'About ten months.'

'And during those ten months were you aware of any official actions or proceedings with respect to her death? Just yes or no, not what they were.'

'Yes.'

'You said you spoke to the police at that time.'

'I did.'

'But you didn't tell them your story, the one you told here?'

'No, I didn't.'

'Did you give formal testimony at any prior proceeding in this case?'

'No.'

'Were you in the country at the time of any prior proceeding?'

'One, that I know of.'

'And are you aware of a second?'

'Yes.'

'Where were you then?'

'I was living out of the country.'

'And after that?'

'I've continued to live outside the country.'

'You left the country without telling anybody this story of yours.'

Alvaro hesitated.

'You didn't tell anyone what you now *say* happened that night.'

'No, I didn't.'

'You didn't tell your story until you got your sweetheart immunity deal.'

'Yes, but—'

Miller spoke over him. 'You went to live in foreign countries so no one would know about your past, didn't you?'

'Well . . . yes, in part.'

'So you could avoid the shame of what you'd done.'

A silence. Estrada wished he would answer and get it over with. They had covered this, preparing.

'Mr Alvaro?' Miller persisted. 'So you could avoid the shame of what you'd done?'

'Partly, yes.'

'Just as you lied so people wouldn't know.'

'Well . . .'

'You lied on job applications.'

'Yes.'
'You lied to your co-workers.'
'I didn't talk about it.'
'But that's lying, too, isn't it?'
Again, Alvaro hesitated.
'It was lying to let people make assumptions you knew were wrong.'
Still no answer.
'Wasn't it?'
'I suppose . . .'
'Did you ever escort a woman to a business function?'
'Yes.'
'And that was a lie, wasn't it?'
No answer.
'Wasn't it?'
'Yes.'
'And did you ever tell anybody you went on a date?'
'Yes.'
'And that was a lie.'
'Yes.'
'And you understood that all these were lies, the lies you told by implication and omission as well as the direct outright lies.'
'Yes.'
'And you perpetuated all those lies because you thought it was in your self-interest.'
'Yes.'
'And that's the story of your life, isn't it?'
'Objection,' Estrada said.
'Sustained.'
'You victimize people and you lie about it, isn't that right?'
'Objection.'
Martinez considered it. 'No, I'll allow that.'
'You victimize people and lie about it. Don't you?'
Estrada stood again. 'Your honor, there's really no need for defense counsel to browbeat the witness.' Risking another

repetition of the question in the hope he was making it seem unreasonable.

'I think she's within the limits, Mr Estrada.'

'Thank you, your honor . . . Mr Alvaro, you victimize people and lie about it?'

'Yes.' Looking at the floor.

'And now you're going to take your free passes from the District Attorney and the U.S. Attorney and you're going to go out of here a free man, aren't you . . . ?'

Estrada was standing to object again, but her timing left him momentarily silent. Maybe she was done.

'*And you're going to do it again.*'

'Objection!' Too late.

'Withdrawn,' Miller said before the judge could rule.

Still standing, Estrada said, 'I have some redirect, your honor,' and immediately started questioning Alvaro. 'Did you come to the D.A.'s office looking for immunity?'

'No.'

'Who first suggested it?'

'You did.'

'How did you learn that I was offering immunity?'

'A friend told me.'

'Before the idea of immunity was proposed to you, what were your thoughts about coming forward?'

'I was considering it.'

'How did you feel about the fact that you had not come forward sooner?'

'I regretted it. I thought it was a mistake.'

'Did being offered immunity make a difference in your decision, or not?'

'Yes, it did.'

'Was it the only reason you came forward?'

'No.'

'Did you solicit immunity at any time, and if so, when?'

'I never did.'

Estrada asked to approach the bench. 'Judge, I'd like to

make an offer of proof outside the hearing of the jury. I'm getting into an area where I'm sure your honor will want to rule on whether the jury should hear it.'

'I appreciate your consideration, Mr Estrada, but what I *do not* want is to protract these proceedings. Your case has already been a festival of surprises and last-minute evidence.'

'Your honor, believe me, that's not how I want it.'

'No doubt.' Martinez did not sound happy. She turned to the jury. 'We're going to have a little conference here, ladies and gentlemen, some technical matters that don't concern you. I'm going to excuse you now, for a few minutes, and then we'll invite you back.'

The jury filed out, casting inquiring looks at the judge and the lawyers. Estrada took a moment to confer with Clemente, then returned to the lectern.

'Mr Alvaro, why did you leave the country?'

'I left because I was threatened.'

'Your honor!' Miller protested.

'Mr Estrada,' Martinez fumed. 'I don't like to be sandbagged any more than Ms Miller does. Is this the subject you're planning to inquire on?'

'Yes, judge.'

'Mr Alvaro, you're under oath,' she admonished. 'Take care you remember that.'

Estrada asked, 'How were you threatened?'

'I was threatened with criminal prosecution as a . . . corrupter of minors. I don't know what you call it, exactly.'

'What specifically were you threatened with?'

'I had . . . been with a young man, not long after . . . after Mariah was killed. I thought he was eighteen or nineteen. I was told later that he was fifteen. I was told he was going to accuse me of raping him. That he had already told a clergyman about it, and someone in his family. I was told that they were being bought off, but that if I didn't leave the country they would go to the police.'

'And did you believe this?'

'Yes. That they would go the police if I stayed, yes.'

'Your honor, this is completely irrelevant,' Miller said.

'A few more questions, your honor, and I think it will be clear. Mr Alvaro, who introduced you to this young man?'

'Alexander Blair.'

'Your superior at Phoenix Enterprises?'

'Yes.'

'And afterward, who delivered the threat?'

'Stanley Gilbert.'

'And who is Stanley Gilbert?'

'He was head of security for Phoenix Enterprises.'

'What did Stanley Gilbert tell you about how he learned of this allegation?'

'He said that the boy and someone from his family came to Mr Morales, and Mr Morales arranged this deal. He said I should be grateful to Mr Morales.'

'And were you grateful?'

'I was angry and frightened. I realized, far too late, that they had set me up.'

'Who set you up?'

'Roberto Morales, with help from Alexander Blair. I knew too much, and they wanted me gone.'

'Your honor,' Miller interjected, 'this is a waste of the court's time. It's no more than conjecture and hearsay, and it has no relevance whatever, in spite of these contortions Mr Estrada is going through.'

'Intimidating a witness is hardly irrelevant, your honor.'

'Spare us!' Miller's tone was pure ridicule. 'All I've heard so far is an allegation by the witness that he heard some stories about things the defendant allegedly said, hearsay, all of it, things that even if they're true indicate only that Mr Morales *did him a favor*.' Miller gave him a look of disdain. 'What's next, a list of Mr Morales's other charities?'

Estrada stifled the desire to strike back. Now was the time to call Alexander Blair and get him to confirm the setup and the threat, to keep this from being altogether too much like the secondhand hearsay that had gotten Martinez into trouble before. But Alexander Blair was not available.

'Off the record,' Martinez said to them at the bench. 'Mr Estrada, I assume you're a better lawyer than to argue that you've in any way connected this alleged threat to the defendant. Or that this is more than hearsay.'

'Your honor, Alexander Blair is out of the country indefinitely but we're still looking for the boy and for Stanley Gilbert. I think we can find Gilbert soon, and he should be able to help us find the boy. I'm sure they can give us a better picture of the conspiracy.'

'Spare us, Mr Estrada – as Ms Miller might say. As it stands, these allegations are every bit as inadmissible as your sideshow about the mark of Zorro.'

Estrada asked to go back on the record. 'Your honor, Ms Miller has tried to impeach Mr Alvaro's credibility before the jury by exploring his state of mind when he left the country. She opened the door. The jury has a right to hear the real reason he left. The real reason *in his mind*, without regard to its objective truth.'

Martinez did not like it. 'All right, but I don't want *any* of the hearsay. We can get his state of mind without the specifics.'

Like so much else in this trial, the specifics of Morales's threat, having been declared inadmissible evidence, would be in all the papers and on every television news show, but the jury would not hear about them. The statue of Justice was a blindfolded woman holding a balance scale, but any prosecutor or defense lawyer who had been at it awhile knew that the important blindfold was the one on the jury.

'Ladies and gentlemen,' Martinez said to them when they came back, 'the evidence you're about to hear is about the witness's state of mind. To the extent that there are any details about reasons for that state of mind, please remember that this testimony is not offered to prove the truth of those reasons, but only to show whether the witness believed them at the time.'

'Mr Alvaro, why did you leave the country when you did?' Estrada asked.

'Because I was threatened.'

'What were you threatened with?'

'Criminal prosecution for having sex with a minor.'

'What if anything did you understand the connection to be between the threat and your testifying or failing to testify about what you observed the day Mariah Dodge was killed?'

'Objection.'

'Sustained.'

Estrada looked at the judge, but he kept his mouth shut.

'Did you believe the threat when it was made?' he asked Alvaro.

'Yes.'

'And why did you stay out of the country all this time?'

'Because of that threat.'

'Thank you, Mr Alvaro, that's all.'

'Call your next witness, Mr Estrada.' Martinez said.

'That's the People's case, your honor.'

15

Martinez sent the jurors out while Miller made a motion to dismiss the charges against Morales for lack of a legally sufficient prosecution case.

'Denied,' Martinez said dispassionately. 'If the jury believes what they've heard, I think there's enough here.' She looked at the clock. 'We have a lot to do if we're going to get this to the jury by tomorrow or Thursday. I don't think anybody wants the jury to start being locked up on Friday night.'

Nobody disagreed.

She called them to the bench. 'On admitting the diary, I've decided that Mr Estrada is right, by and large, to say it's inadmissible. The diary is hearsay as to anything that involves what Mariah Dodge heard from others. If you want to use it to refresh a witness's memory, Ms Miller, I'll want to know about it first, and I want you to be very careful about not publishing the content when you use it for that purpose. If you have anything from it that's just about Mariah Dodge that you want to use in evidence, I'll want a specific application and time to consider it, but I'll warn you that the document itself doesn't give you much to support its use. No indication of how regularly the entries were made, and nothing to show they were made close in time to the events or thoughts they describe.'

'Your honor—' Miller began, but the judge cut her off.

'This was a *Brady* problem, not an evidentiary one. You've had it for producing leads. It produced Mr Alvaro, as you know, and I'd think that alone would make you think twice about using it further.' She checked the clock. 'Ms Miller, have you got a witness you can put on in the time we have left before lunch?'

'Yes, your honor, I do.'

The jury came back looking like they'd had a half-time break and were ready for some more action.

Kassia Miller stood up at the defense table and turned so she could see the bench and the jury. It was one of Estrada's rare chances to see her full on from the front with no distractions. She was wearing a navy-blue dress, almost severe by her standards; her cheeks were slightly flushed and her eyes were bright. The excitement of battle.

'Your honor, the defense calls David Dexter.'

Who? Estrada looked at Rosen. She didn't know, either.

David Dexter proved to be a lanky, dark-haired man of about thirty dressed in green workshirt and workpants. In answer to Miller's questions he said that he was a building superintendant, but that four years before he had been on the security staff at the building where Mariah Dodge was killed.

'Was there anything unusual about the hours you worked?'

'The only thing was sometimes I didn't work my shift.'

'Does that mean you swapped shifts with someone else, or do you mean something else?'

'It means I had my brother-in-law sometimes go in and do my job for me and then I'd pay him for taking my shift.'

'Who at work knew you did this?'

'My supervisor and my co-workers, that I told about it myself. It was a thing we all worked out. Nobody minded as long as the work got done.'

'Where is your brother-in-law now?'

'I don't know.'

'How long is it since you've seen him?'

'Almost four years.'

Estrada stood up. 'Your honor, I fail to see the point.'

'Your honor, if I can have a little leeway . . .'

'A few more questions.'

'Mr Dexter, do you remember anything important that happened around the last time you saw your brother-in-law?'

'Yeah, a woman got killed on the thirtieth floor. It was real messy.'

'Was that before or after the last time you saw him?'

'Before. Not long before, though. He left New York a week or two later. We heard from him for a few months, then nothing.'

'Can you tell us his name, please?'

'Kenneth Charles.'

'At the time the woman got killed on the thirtieth floor, did Kenneth Charles work for you at that building?'

'Yes.'

'What shift were you working then?'

'Days, Wednesday to Sunday.'

'Do you remember if you worked on the day the woman was killed, or had someone substitute for you?'

'Yeah, I sure do remember. I didn't work. I remember it was good she wasn't killed on my shift because I'd have been in deep shi . . . real trouble, not being there and all.'

'Who worked for you that afternoon?'

'Kenny.'

'Did Kenneth Charles have access to the keys of various offices at that time?'

'He could have.'

'How?'

'There was a key rack with different master keys that the maintenance department had.'

'Was that key rack kept locked?'

'Sometimes, sometimes not.'

'Was there any reason why it was or wasn't?'

'Not that I ever could tell.'

'Do you know if your brother-in-law has a criminal record?'

'Yes.'

'How do you know that?'

'One time he was arrested in my house. I was always having to bail him out. I been to court when he was on trial, and I visited him in jail.' Dexter looked as exasperated as he sounded. 'I do it for my wife.'

'Have you ever been present when he committed a crime for which he was later convicted?'

Estrada had been letting this go as long as he thought he could afford to, getting a sense of where Miller was headed. Sensing danger now, he asked to approach the bench.

'This is ridiculous.' He pushed the righteous indignation as hard as seemed safe. 'A man who was in the building once or twice, or even ten times, has a criminal record. Where do we draw the line?'

'Mr Estrada has a point,' Martinez allowed. 'There's a limit to how far afield we can go.'

'This is a murder case,' Miller said, more than ever with an air of control. 'If Roberto Morales is convicted of the top count of the indictment, the minimum sentence you can impose is fifteen years to life. That's the *minimum*, and Mr Estrada is sure to ask for more. The least I should get is a chance to show that someone else may have committed the crime.'

'How does this witness accomplish that?'

'If I can show your honor a document I'm about to use . . .'

'Please.'

Miller left and returned with a certified arrest record from North Carolina, with front and side mug shots. The record covered arrests for sexual assault and for aggravated assault with a straight razor.

'This is the man we're talking about.'

'Your honor' – Estrada was not going to let this one get by him easily – 'this is clearly going to be propensity evidence. Ms Miller wants to tell the jury that this man, a man she can't produce or we wouldn't be listening to his brother-in-law, is likely to have committed this crime because in the past he committed some sex crimes and a slashing somewhere else.' He turned to Miller. 'Right?'

'Yes . . .'

'Judge, you just ruled that I can't put Andrew Flippo and Alberto Quiñones on the stand to show that the defendant committed *exactly* the kind of crime charged here. If that's inadmissible evidence, then so is this. Take away the criminal record and this man is no different from anybody else who was in that building.'

'Your honor, my client's life is at stake. How can you limit me? I'm showing, in the first place, that the security in the building was lax, anybody could have come and gone that day, and, if your honor permits, that there was a specific person with access to that specific office plus a history of opportunistic sexual assault and violence that amounts to a motive.'

'Mr Estrada has a point about propensity,' Martinez said. 'If you were defending this brother-in-law you would certainly argue against the admissibility of his criminal past.'

'It's not the same. I'm trying to raise a reasonable doubt here, and I believe this man is a credible alternative suspect not found by the police. Mr Estrada's own police witness testified that people with prison records are natural suspects. If nothing else, I should be able to introduce this to show how sloppy the police investigation was.'

Martinez nodded. 'For that purpose, I'll let it in.'

With permission from the judge, Miller had Dexter identify the picture on the criminal record as being a likeness of Kenneth Charles. Then she asked her witness about the crime he had seen his brother-in-law commit.

'It was a bar fight. Kenny cut a guy pretty bad.'

'How did he cut him?'

'He cut him across the face with a straight razor.'

'Thank you, Mr Dexter.'

Estrada stood. 'Mr Dexter, did your rounds as a security guard require you to go into the offices of the companies in the building as a regular part of your routine?' Taking a small chance based on what he had seen when he visited the building and what Morales's secretary had said on the stand.

'Not as a regular part, no.'

'How often did you use the key rack downstairs?'

'Any time there was something wrong.'

'Not often.'

'Not very.'

'When your brother-in-law was working, were you there?'

'No. That's why he was working.'

'So you don't know what he did when he was there.'

'Well, he did the job.'

'He made the rounds of the security stations in the hallways outside the offices.'

'I guess.'

'Aside from that you don't know anything about what he did when he was there.'

'No.'

'You don't know if he ever used the key rack.'

'No.'

'Or if he even knew that Phoenix Enterprises existed.'

'No.'

'Or even if he was there on any given day.'

'He was, the days he worked for me.'

'Really? Were you there those days?'

'No.'

'Then you couldn't have seen him there, could you?'

'He punched the clock.'

'You don't know that. Anybody could have done it for him.'

Confused, Dexter chewed on that.

'Kenny could have hired someone to work for him just the way you hired him to work for you.'

'Yeah, I guess . . .' More fascinated now than confused.

'So you don't know if he was ever there.'

'Wait a minute.' Something dawning. 'He knew the other guys.'

'Your honor?' Estrada said.

'Strike that.' Martinez told the jury to disregard the outburst and warned the witness.

'The truth is,' Estrada resumed, 'you don't know when he was there.'

'No, I guess not.'

'Thank you, Mr Dexter.' Maximum disdain in his voice. 'Your honor, I have no more questions for this *important* witness.' Sitting down with a *what next?* smile and a shake of his head for the jury.

'All right. A short lunch,' Martinez informed everybody before she left the bench. 'Back at one-thirty.'

Clemente hurried over to the prosecution table, talking fast. 'Some guy's wife's brother. How're we supposed to—'

'It's okay, Tommy. Nobody's blaming you.' Knowing about Santos, Estrada thought, I should have anticipated something like this. 'I want you to get on it and find the guy. I want everything we can get on him, and I want you to talk to the wife and the rest of that family, too. If you need bodies to help, I'll have Collins call Jack.'

'Okay. We'll find him, don't worry.'

Back at the office Estrada discovered that Alvaro had not stayed for lunch.

'He went somewhere with Tess and Carlos Ramírez,' Stein reported. 'He was kind of a mess from testifying.'

'He knows he has to come back,' Estrada said.

'I reminded them all.'

'I don't see why Miller's relying on the brother-in-law to tell about him,' Stein said over lunch. 'Why not get the guy himself on the stand?'

'She's trying to create doubt – maybe Kenneth Charles did it. If Kenneth Charles himself is here, where's the doubt? Accuse him and he denies it. That's why I'm so hot to have Tommy find the guy.'

They were wrapping up their sandwich scraps when Stash McMorris called 'I have some news. Bad news or good news, I don't know. Bad, most likely.'

'Try it and see.'

'Old man Censabella's dead.'

'What!'

'Yesterday. Fell down the stairs and broke his neck.'

'How convenient.' Estrada did not like how he felt about this. 'Where?'

'In the house where he lived. He was upstairs on the floor where Morales's apartment used to be, and he tripped or got dizzy and by the time he hit the bottom his neck was broken, plus a lot of other old bones.'

'What was he doing upstairs?'

'Don't ask me.'

'I *am* asking you, and I want you to find out.'

'Hey, hey – I'm only the messenger.'

'See if the autopsy's been done. If not, alert the M.E. that the neck may have been broken before he was thrown down the stairs.'

'You think?'

'I don't know what to think. I want to be certain, if I can.' Not likely: certainty was not a plentiful commodity in this case. 'Maybe Mrs Iannacone knows something.'

'I'll see what I can do.'

'Fast. We're running out of time here.'

Miller's next witness was Craig Lawrence, her investigator. He was over six feet and brawny, a fullback to Estrada's halfback. Unlike Joe Estrada, Craig Lawrence had been a college star before *his* football injury sidelined him: second-team all-America one year. Then he had gone to law school and from there to the FBI.

'What is your current occupation?' Miller asked him.

'I run an investigation agency.' He sat easily in the witness chair, tall and straight without being stiff. His answers were matter of fact, almost completely free of the old-style FBI habit of looking at the jury with each answer. Instead, he carried on a dialogue with Miller, glancing at the jury only occasionally. He did an impressive job of describing the effort his agency had put into finding David Dexter and otherwise covering the bases that the cops had missed, closing with their efforts, unsuccessful so far, to locate Kenneth Charles.

On cross-examination, Estrada took him through his paces all over again, this time emphasizing how much it all had cost.

'Mr Lawrence,' he said mildly, 'when you were in the FBI you were paid by the taxpayer, weren't you?'

'Yes.'

'The taxpayer paid you to find out the truth.'

'Yes.'

'And who pays you in this case?'

'I bill the law firm of Pane, Parish, Eisen and Legler.'

'That's the defense, isn't it? The defense pays you.'

'Yes.'

'To find out things useful to the defendant.'

'If I learned anything unfavorable to the defendant, I'd tell them that, too.'

'You'd tell *them*. But the jury would never hear it.'

'Objection,' Miller said.

'Sustained.'

The investigator was reluctant to say how much the total bill had been. Estrada pressed him.

'I guess it was about a hundred fifty thousand dollars altogether.'

'*A hundred and fifty thousand dollars*. And more than a year's work. And all you came up with of any interest is Kenneth Charles?' Estrada turned to the jury to share his amazement. 'Is that right?'

'We found what was there.'

'A man you can't even demonstrate was there the night of the murder.'

'Well . . .'

'Isn't it a fact, Mr Lawrence,' Estrada said, 'that you spent a hundred fifty thousand dollars of the defendant's money and all you showed was how thorough the police were?'

'Objection.'

'Sustained.'

'Did you make any attempt to connect David Dexter or Kenneth Charles with Mariah Dodge?'

Lawrence hesitated. 'Yes.'

'What did you do?'

'Mostly it was a process of canvassing the building, interviewing people who knew them . . .'

'You tried hard, didn't you?'

'We did our job.'

'You were looking for that connection, weren't you?'

'Yes.'

'How much money did you spend looking for that connection between Kenneth Charles and Mariah Dodge?'

'I couldn't separate that out.'

'A fair percentage of the time you billed?'

'Some, yes.'

'You never found any connection?'

'Nothing specific.'

'No connection with her anywhere near as close as the defendant's.'

'Objection.'

'Sustained.'

'No connection at all, even though you spent all that time and all that money.'

Lawrence hesitated again and Miller stepped in with an objection.

'Sustained. Move on, Mr Estrada.'

'How much time and money did you spend looking for Juan Alvaro?'

'I couldn't say.'

'None, isn't that right?'

'I don't remember the name at all.'

'Your client knew how close Juan Alvaro and Mariah Dodge were, didn't he?'

'Objection.'

'Sustained.'

'Didn't you think Juan Alvaro would be helpful?'

'I don't think it came up.'

'You didn't think he would be helpful because that's what your client told you, isn't that right?'

'Objection.'

'Sustained.'

'You took your cues from the defendant.'

Miller asked to approach the bench. 'Your honor, all these questions are improper, and Mr Estrada knows it. He's throwing in everything from the mental processes of third parties to tampering with the attorney-client privilege.'

'She's right, mister prosecutor. Find something new or sit down.'

'I have nothing else for him, your honor.'

With Craig Lawrence off the stand, Miller asked for a sidebar conference to talk about her deceased witness.

'I'm sorry to hear it,' Martinez said. 'I assume you'll want to use his testimony from the first trial.'

'It's essential.'

'I see no problem with it. Mr Estrada?'

'I have a problem. The man was a surprise witness in the first trial. Mr Kahn didn't have any real opportunity to prepare for cross-examining him, a fact made clear by my investigation. It's unfair to bind the prosecution today to Mr Kahn's inadequate cross.'

'Do you have any reason to believe you could do better?'

'I do, judge, because I have information that Mr Censabella was paid regularly by the defendant, to the tune of hundreds of dollars a week. At the very least I'd like to have a stipulation to that effect to go with this testimony.'

'Would I be wrong in guessing that this information is hearsay, Mr Estrada? The deceased told somebody about it who told you?'

'Let me say this, your honor, I have reason to be confident that if the defendant were to take the stand and if he were asked did you pay Remigio Censabella, that he would not deny it.' The closest he could come, for now, to using what Morales had said about it in their meeting. 'So I would say that we should either have a stipulation to that effect, or you should exclude the testimony.'

'Mr Estrada, the rule is that there has to have been an opportunity for cross-examination. If it was poorly done or badly prepared for, you can blame bad lawyering on Mr Kahn's part or bad investigation by the police, but the People had their chance at this witness and that's all that counts.'

After some quibbling about who should read the testimony to the jury, Martinez impatiently decreed that the court reporter would do it.

In that way the jury heard that Remigio Censabella had lived forty-six years in his apartment in Little Italy, and that for slightly more than one of those years he'd had an upstairs neighbor who was rarely there and, then, only with a woman, a beautiful woman with long, thick red hair. Censabella had talked about the various noises he could hear through his ceiling: music sometimes, some walking around, and – if he went into the back room – rhythmic noises that sounded like a rocking chair or people exercising.

The talk of rocking chair noises and exercise amused the gallery, again packed with Morales's supporters. They and the jury heard that on a Sunday afternoon in mid-October Censabella had been sitting in the window watching the neighbors go about their business, and he saw his upstairs neighbor – whom he had picked out in the courtroom as the defendant, Roberto Morales – come into the house with his woman friend. They stayed for between one and two hours, Censabella had said, and then left. He had identified the woman as Mariah Dodge, from a picture. During the time they had been there, Censabella had had reason to go into the back room several times, and each time he heard the noise like a rocking chair or exercise.

'Did you ever hear, through your walls or ceiling, the sound of people arguing?' Walter Kubelik had asked him on behalf of Morales.

'Yes,' Censabella had answered.

'Which people did you hear arguing?'

'Next door, all the time. Downstairs. Upstairs.'

Censabella had gone on to testify that he sometimes heard Morales and his friend arguing, that he had heard loud voices on the Sunday in question, but that it had not been a long argument and it had ended before the rocking noises began.

Kahn had cross-examined on the obvious issues: the number of Sunday afternoons and their similarity, the number of pedestrians on the street, the state of Censabella's eyesight and hearing and memory and general awareness of the outside world. Kahn had pushed hard and tripped him up, though to Estrada's mind the victories had been hollow ones. His main concern was that the court reporter, in reading Kahn's questions aloud, might give the impression Kahn had been persecuting a poor old man. Now a poor, dead old man.

'You heard the rocking chair noise,' the court reporter read.

'Yes.'

'Could you hear that sitting by the window?'

'I don't know.'

'Where could you hear it?'

'I don't know.'

'Didn't you testify that if you went into the back room you could hear the noise like a rocking chair?'

'Yes.'

'So if you were in the back room, you weren't looking out the front window?'

'I don't know.'

'How hard is that, Mr Censabella?' The court reporter read flatly. Estrada was glad the jury was spared what must have been Kahn's disdainful tone. 'If you were in the back, you weren't in the front.'

'Yes.'

'And if you weren't in the front, you weren't looking out the window.'

And so it went, this particular attempt to befuddle the witness leading to the admission that Censabella might have missed somebody coming in or going out. It was the natural thing to try under the circumstances, Estrada supposed, but it did not have much relevance. Judging by their inattention, the jury shared his opinion.

Estrada did not want them to miss Censabella's flaws, because he was the only person besides Alvaro and perhaps Morales whose testimony covered the specific events of the murder day. The absent Mr Censabella confirmed Morales's version of events in a way that no one confirmed Alvaro's. It was impossible to know how that would affect the jury.

Reading the testimony went more quickly than live testimony with its often interminable delays for finding papers or setting up displays or conferring about arcane legal points at the bench. When the court reporter was finished, Miller stood up and went to the lectern.

'Your honor,' she said, 'the defense calls Roberto Morales.'

16

There was a moment of silence. The jury members were all suddenly wide awake. Abruptly, the gallery rocked with whistling, cheering and applause.

Martinez rose in her chair, pounding with her gavel, motioning to the nearest court officer to take the jury out. Before he took a step the demonstration stopped, tumult yielding swiftly to quiet, the courtroom silent except for the banging of the gavel and the shouts of court officers.

'All right,' Martinez said. 'I warned you. If you think there's safety in numbers, you're wrong. Anything like that again and you *all* go to jail. *Todos*. En la carcel. Inmediamente. You can straighten it out in your cells who participated and who sat on their hands. And if you don't like those terms you can leave now.'

Estrada saw two elderly men he recognized as trial buffs get up and squeeze their way out to the aisle. There was a scattering of laughter and applause as they left.

'Enough!' Martinez said. 'Behave or I'm clearing this courtroom – straight over the bridge into the jail next door.'

She turned to the jury. 'Ladies and gentlemen, I know you're all smart enough to disregard this childish outburst by people who have nothing better to do with their time than get themselves seats in a courtroom hoping to cause a disruption. I trust that you will not let it make an impression on you, either favorable to the defendant or unfavorable to him. Ms Miller, you may proceed.'

Estrada watched Morales take the oath. He had been anticipating this from the beginning, certainly since Miller had brought Morales in to talk. He had previsioned it and prepared for it, but he felt unready. Cross-examining defendants was a rarity. Cross-examining a defendant in a case like this was something some prosecutors never got to do.

Miller started at the beginning, asking Morales where he had been born and when he had come to New York, about his foster parents and his education.

Morales answered clearly and precisely. He seemed serious and attentive, a touch nervous. He was wearing a single-breasted blazer with a blue oxford button-down shirt and a conservatively patterned tie, and soft gray trousers. His hair was styled as conservatively as his clothes, medium-length and carefully combed; whatever held it in place did not make it look stiff or styled.

Miller was cooler than usual, with no sign of the playfulness she occasionally allowed to show through. 'Mr Morales, before I ask you more about your past, I want you to turn your attention to the present. I want to ask if you heard the testimony of the prosecution's final witness, Juan Alvaro?'

'Yes, I did.'

'Did you hear the part about the night Mariah Dodge was killed?'

'Yes, I did.'

'How much of what he testified to – as to that night and your participation in those activities – how much of that was true?'

'None of it.'

'None at all?'

'The part involving me? No. None of it was true. I can't tell you about the rest.'

'We'll come back to that, but first I'd like to ask you some more about your background.'

In response to Miller's questions Morales outlined the same history he had described to Estrada in their conference.

Estrada felt as if he were holding his breath the whole time, following Morales's every word, hoping he would open the door for questions about Andy Flippo. Or contradict his earlier words. Everyone on the prosecution team had the same assignment.

As Morales progressed from Brooklyn to the Ivy League and then to housing rehabilitation and Phoenix Enterprises, Estrada began to see that Miller was being very economical in her questions, getting the maximum punch for the minimum effort. They had obviously rehearsed well. Morales was keeping his answers short and to the point, and his demeanor was proper and respectful of the process without being rigid. They dwelled predictably on his wife and children, to the point where Estrada reconsidered his decision not to object on that subject and asked for a sidebar.

'I've been giving you plenty of room on this,' the judge told Miller, 'but I think Mr Estrada is right, it's time to move on.'

'How did you meet Mariah Dodge?' Miller asked, back at the lectern.

'She was with Cuyler Jadwin at one of our early meetings. He told me she was going to be his eyes and ears in New York, and he said she was going to do a good job for us at Phoenix Enterprises.'

'When did you begin to work together?'

'She came to New York to stay the following month. At first our work lives didn't intersect much, but gradually I saw more and more of her.'

'What information did you give her or did you know she had about your marital status?'

'She knew I was married, right from the beginning. Everybody knew. Marti was with me at all the public occasions we had, and there were many of them, for the community, for potential major tenants and for our investors.'

'What information did you give your wife about Mariah Dodge?'

'I told her everything. She knew Mariah and I were going

to have an affair before Mariah did, in a way.'

'What do you mean?'

'I told Marti I could sense that Mariah and I were attracted to each other, physically, before I did anything about it.'

'Was that common, or unusual, for you to tell her that?'

'It was both. She knew I had affairs. That was the basis of our marriage. Can I explain?'

'Please do.'

'Marti had a terrible childhood. She had been through a lot. She wanted children of her own, but aside from that she wanted me to satisfy my sexual needs somewhere else. All she cared about was that I be steady and discreet.'

'Does that mean it was usual for you to tell her whom you were sleeping with?'

'We talked about it the way you talk about anything that's part of your life. I wasn't hiding anything from her. But I didn't usually tell her much about who my partner was. It was different with Mariah, because they knew each other.'

'How did she know Mariah Dodge?'

'From parties and receptions and so on. They would both come, Marti because she was my wife, Mariah as a corporate officer.'

'How would you describe your relationship with Mariah Dodge, from your point of view?'

'It was stormy, because we were both driven, active people. But Mariah was a terrific woman and being with her was the best thing in my life, next to my family. And my work. In a way it was part of my work. That's one reason it was so good for me, while it lasted.'

'When did you meet Juan Alvaro?' Miller asked. Estrada was surprised to hear the question.

'When he came for a final interview for his job.'

'Did you work together?'

'Not really. But we were at meetings together and I was aware of his job performance.'

'How would you characterize that?'

'Poor.'

'Did he know you felt that way?'

'Yes.'

'How?'

'I told him so. I had more than one meeting with him to say that if it was up to me I would fire him.'

'Who was it up to?'

'I would have had to convince Alexander Blair and Cuyler Jadwin.'

'Did you and Juan Alvaro have any particular personal problems with each other?'

'To speak frankly, I didn't like him, and I didn't like the fact that he attached himself to Mariah.'

'Did you have any reason to believe he knew you felt that way?'

'Mariah and I had a couple of conversations about it. After that he came to me and asked why I was trying to come between them. He said I had no right to run her life.'

'Were you trying to run her life?'

'No.'

'Did you have any other difficulties with Juan Alvaro, or were the problems about his job performance and about Mariah Dodge the only ones?'

'No, there were other complaints.'

'Were they made directly to you?'

'I was told about them by others at first, but then they were made directly to me.'

'Who made the complaints?'

'Some of the boys in the mailroom.'

'How old were they?'

'Some of them were still in high school.'

'And what was the nature of those complaints?'

'Objection.' Enough was enough. 'Hearsay.'

'I'm not asking for the substance, your honor.'

'I think you've made your point, Ms Miller. Sustained.'

'What happened then?'

'I tried to have a serious talk with him about it. He wouldn't listen. He denied it and accused me of trying to destroy his life. I told him if he didn't stop he'd be out of a job.'

'What came of that?'

'Nothing. I didn't hear any more about it after that. It was only a few weeks later that Mariah was killed and I was too upset and too busy to deal with anything like Juan Alvaro's perverted sex life.'

'What was the state of your relationship with Mariah Dodge at the time of her death?'

'Actually, it had just changed. She'd broken up with me that afternoon.' Morales allowed himself the ghost of a self-deprecating smile.

'Where were you and Mariah Dodge when she broke up with you?'

'We were in the apartment I'd rented for us.'

'Was there anyone else at that address you knew or spoke to?'

'Remigio Censabella.'

'How would you describe your relationship with him?'

'We were neighbors, we traded small talk when we saw each other. And I paid him to look after my apartment when I wasn't there.'

So Miller was going to pull the sting on the payments even though Censabella was dead. She had Morales describe the chores Censabella had done for him.

'You say you paid him. How much?'

'It varied. A hundred dollars a week, most weeks. Sometimes more, if there was an extra-important job for him to do. Never more than two hundred.'

'Did you pay him for anything else?'

'No.'

'Did you ever pay him, directly or indirectly, in relation to his testimony at any proceeding in this matter?'

'No.'

'You testified that you were at the apartment when Mariah

Dodge broke up with you. How did she go about breaking up with you?'

'Mostly she called me names.'

'What kind of names did she call you? Can you give me some examples?'

'Pompous, self-satisfied greaseball. That I was a spic and I hated myself for it. Things like that.'

'Anything else?'

'She said I thought the whole world worshiped my . . . my penis. Like all men, she said.'

'Like all men? Is that all?'

He hesitated. 'Well . . . no. She said I was worse that way than other men. She said I was the worst she ever saw. She said I was . . . Do I have to do this?'

'Yes,' Miller said.

Was the reluctance scripted, Estrada wondered, or was Morales finding his lines harder to say in performance than in rehearsal?

'She said I was . . . puny . . . and that I made her sick.'

'How did this make you feel?'

'It made me feel angry . . . very, very angry.' Something was awakening behind Morales's eyes. 'I am a man. I have my pride.' He sat fractionally straighter, as if the words were animating him. 'A man can't allow a woman to call him names and laugh at his manhood.'

Estrada held his breath. This might be a place where he had a chance.

'I was very angry.' Testifying about it now, Morales sounded angry. 'But not so angry that . . .'

Estrada waited.

There was no more. Miller, seeing the potential for trouble, jumped in with a new question. 'How did you express your anger?' The question this had all been aimed at.

'I expressed my anger with my voice. I yelled at her. I told her she couldn't talk to me that way. I called her names in return.'

'What names?'

'Ugly names. Slut. Bitch. Worse names than that. I called her some names in Spanish.'

'How did she react?'

'She yelled back. We went back and forth like that, yelling, calling names.'

'Was that the first time something like that happened between you, or had it happened before?'

'It happened before. We both had tempers. We both had nasty mouths when we wanted to.'

'What happened next?'

'We made love.' He said it as a punch line, and he got a laugh. Martinez rapped once with her gavel.

Miller asked, 'Was this lovemaking forced, or was it voluntary?'

'We made *love*. That can't be by force. What we did was how we always fought and made up.'

'How did you leave it, about her breaking up with you?'

'If Mariah wanted us to end it, I wasn't going to make her stay. I respected her. I wanted to keep her friendship if I could, and if not her friendship then her trust.'

Miller paced out from behind the lectern, then back. She stopped with her hand on its angled wooden top, standing out in the open. 'Mr Morales, I don't want to embarrass you, or invade your privacy, but these next questions are necessary. What, if any, protection did you use when you and Mariah Dodge made love that Sunday afternoon?'

Morales looked at the jury as if appealing for their understanding. To Miller he said, 'None.'

'Why was that?'

'Usually we were very careful. But this was our last time and she said she didn't want that rubbery condom feeling. She always hated it. This time she said she had to have my skin next to her. We were both very careful about . . . diseases, but I was tested regularly and she was too, and we told each other the results.'

'And what happened when you had this unprotected intercourse?'

'I got worried at the end and I . . . I pulled out. To protect her.'

'Did you ejaculate, or not?'

Morales's neck and cheeks colored. Harder to rehearse than the specifics of testimony, Estrada thought. Morales put his hands on the witness-stand rail and studied his fingers as he spoke.

'I did, yes. I did.'

'Where?'

'On her . . . body.'

'And what happened then?'

'She . . . rubbed it around. She . . . did that, sometimes.' He stopped, seemingly at a loss for how to proceed.

'Where?'

'On her stomach, mostly. Her thighs.' He looked up. 'As a way to tease me. She did that sometimes. Played that way.' The jury was spellbound. 'It made me uncomfortable, and she knew it. She was smiling at me, and she said, "All over, all gone." Because it was the last time for us.'

'And how long did you stay there that afternoon?'

'Not much longer. She said she had things she wanted to do, and so did I. We got up and left.'

'Did either or both of you shower before you left?'

'I did. She didn't.'

'What if anything did she say about that?'

'She said it was the last time so she'd wear me awhile. I remember that was how she put it. And she said she was going to the gym and she would shower there.' His composure slipped. 'But she never got there.'

Estrada rose. 'Your honor?'

'Strike that remark,' Martinez ruled. 'Ladies and gentlemen, you'll ignore that please.'

Miller moved on. 'Was the whole time you were at the apartment devoted to talking about breaking up and making love, or did you discuss other things?'

'We talked about work.'

'What, about work?'

'About the meeting the next morning.' His answers had a slightly dazed quality now.

Miller took her time about asking the next question, giving him a chance to get back his equilibrium. 'What did you discuss about the meeting?'

'I told her about some conversations I'd been having with Cuyler Jadwin about restructuring the company. She was more interested than I thought she was going to be. So we talked about getting together that night at the office to work out some things to say to Jadwin in the morning.'

'And how did you leave it with her?'

'That we'd meet at the office around eight.'

'And did you keep that appointment.'

'Yes,' he said. 'In a way.'

'Can you tell the jury what you mean?'

'Yes. I mean I went there, but she wasn't . . . she was . . .' He stopped and cupped his forehead in one hand, elbow propped on the rail. After a moment he sat straight again and looked at the jury. 'I apologize. This is difficult.'

Estrada half-stood. 'Your honor,' he said mildly.

'Indeed. Ladies and gentlemen, disregard that, please,' Martinez turned to the witness. 'Mr Morales, don't address the jury on your own. Wait to be asked a question. Ms Miller, try to keep your witness under control.'

Miller nodded to the judge. 'Mr Morales, when you went to the Phoenix Enterprises offices, what did you find?'

'When I first got there I headed for my own office, because that was what I always did when I arrived. But I saw that the light was on in Mariah's office so I changed my route and went there. I expected her to be working, and I expected her to be expecting me. I knocked on the doorjamb before I went in, and called her name, so she wouldn't be startled.' He blew out a long breath and shook his head.

'Mr Morales?' Miller said to get him back to the present. 'What did you find when you entered her office?'

'I found her lying there on the couch.' His face and voice were bleak. 'You saw the pictures. You all saw the pictures . . .' He stopped for a moment, gathering himself, but he was not finished. '*I* saw the reality – someone I cared about so deeply, lying there brutalized and bloody.'

Miller gave him a moment before she asked, 'Could she have still been alive?'

'No. No, she couldn't have been alive. Her eyes were open. And all that blood, from that horrible ugly gash in her throat.' He closed his own eyes, shook his head again as if by denying it strongly enough he could erase the reality.

'What did you do?'

'I stood there. A long time, I think. I think I may have fallen to my knees. I must have cried. Then it was as if I heard a voice in my ear. *Run*, the voice said, *No one will believe you if you stay*. So I ran.'

'Why did you run?'

'I see now, I saw long ago, that it was crazy. I had no blood on me, and the office was a bloody mess. No one could have suspected me. But I ran. It was pure panic, panic and pure horror at what I'd seen. I got out of there, and I went home.'

Estrada had the sense that he was hearing an echo. Not only was Morales sticking to the story he had told in their conference, but these specific words and phrases were strikingly familiar.

'Did you go straight home?' Miller asked.

'No, I don't think I did. I don't have a very clear mental image of what happened when I left. I know I left, I left the building in a hurry, and I know I ended up at home. In between I may have gone to a bar or two. I don't know how much I drank or what I drank. I don't know what bars. I think I wandered the streets for a while. I think that was the first thing I did.'

'And what did you do when you got home?'

'I took a very long shower. Maybe I thought I could wash away the memory. I told Marti I needed to sleep in her bedroom with her, that I couldn't be alone. We have separate bedrooms, but sometimes to comfort each other we sleep in the same bed.'

'Did you tell her what was wrong?'

'No. She guessed it had to do with Mariah, so I told her that Mariah had broken up with me, but not the rest of it.'

'Did you tell anyone at that time what you had seen and done that night?'

'No. I was too confused and frightened. And I didn't think I knew anything that was helpful. I assumed the police would catch the killer, and that would be that.'

'Mr Morales, did you rape Mariah Dodge?'

'No, I did not rape Mariah Dodge.'

'Did you kill Mariah Dodge?'

'No. No, I did not. I did not kill Mariah Dodge.'

Miller took her time turning to Estrada. 'Your witness.'

Martinez looked at the clock. 'I think that's plenty for one day.'

17

Estrada hurried out of the courtroom with Rosen and Stein. As soon as they were in the D.A.'s office wing of the courthouse, Stein said, 'It sounds to me a lot like he's repeating the same things he said that time with us.'

'My thought exactly,' Estrada said.

'Isn't that good for us?' Stein asked eagerly. 'I mean, isn't there a way to get the jury to see it, and then they'll know it's made up?'

'That's when you've got two people conforming their testimony to each other, and you can get one of them to repeat word for word what the other one said.'

'Oh.' The paralegal pulled a long face. 'It's just that I have this fantasy that you're going to get up there and blow him away.'

Estrada smiled at her: a brief, warm smile, not a happy one. 'Wouldn't that be nice.'

Rosen said, 'We've all got that fantasy tucked away somewhere, and we'd all better forget it. It's not going to happen.'

'I appreciate the vote of confidence.'

'You'll do better if you start out realistic. I'm trying to let you off the hook.'

The one who needed to do that was Joe Estrada. 'I keep having these flashes of good prosecutors humiliated by plausible defendants.' He felt sour juices at the back of his throat. 'Morales looks pretty solid up there.'

'The worst thing is to try too hard to demolish the defendant and be seen to fail,' Rosen commented.

'And the second worst is not to try hard enough.' Estrada pushed it away. 'Stein, what happened to our friend Johnny?'

'Tess took him for a walk. They'll be back soon.'

McMorris dropped in to say that the autopsy on Censabella was inconclusive. He had been found at the bottom of the flight of steps, but no one knew why he had been at the top or why he had fallen to the bottom. Suspicious, but not enough to call it a homicide.

'The M.E.'s got it down as a CUPPI.' Circumstances unknown pending police investigation.

'Did you talk to Mrs I?'

'Not yet. She wasn't around.'

'Get back over there and wait for her. And do a canvass. See what you can turn up.'

McMorris had barely left when Clemente called to report no progress on Kenneth Charles. 'No further arrest record, at least nothing that's in the FBI's computer.'

'Keep looking,' Estrada said, not expecting much.

When Alvaro came back, Estrada cleared the office temporarily to ask him about the mailroom boys and the fights with Morales.

'None of that ever happened. It's a complete fabrication.'

'Did he tell you he thought you weren't doing your job, anything like that?'

'Not explicitly. But he was always hateful to me. I must have threatened him in some way, something to do with Mariah, I think, though it couldn't have been sexual jealousy, Lord knows.'

'Would anybody from the company be able to testify that you *didn't* make passes at the mailroom boys, that Morales didn't try to fire you, anything like that?'

'You have to be kidding.'

'At this point, I'll try for anything. I'm definitely going to need you to testify again. I'm going to need you later tonight, too, for preparation. Not for very long, but I need to do some other work first.'

Estrada and Rosen spent the next hours going over Morales's testimony, reconstructing it as best they could. They reviewed the notes from Estrada's meeting with Morales and the cross-examination questions he had sketched out based on what Morales had said then. Estrada wasn't sure he was helping himself for the cross-examination, but this was the way he knew how to do it. As they worked he was listening with one ear for a call from McMorris.

When Alvaro came back for his preparation, Tess put her head in the door long enough to say hello. Estrada had been trying not to think of her, had been avoiding her in the days since they had returned. He felt a shock of pleasure seeing her scrubbed face and wild hair and her bright green eyes, was sorry to see her hurry away.

After a quick supper with Rosen and Stein, Estrada returned to the office and went over the freshly delivered rush transcript of Morales's testimony with them and Mahoney, who arrived looking rumpled and smelling like a brewery.

'Cheer up, Joseph,' he advised. 'Someday you'll be able to relax and party, too.'

'Just so it hasn't dulled your brain.'

'Sharpened it, my boy, sharpened it.'

In the morning, Estrada got up earlier than he wanted to and could not get back to sleep. He spent a half hour on the ski machine for the first time in memory and took a long, cool shower. He came out surprisingly refreshed.

Shaving, he scrutinized himself carefully. He was going to cross-examine Roberto Morales this morning: he wanted to be sure he had his face under control. It was not quite the same as he remembered it. The intense brown eyes were more bloodshot, and there was an unfamiliar furrow atop the straight nose, no doubt the gift of all the stress he was under. He pushed his jaw forward Collins-style, did not like the effect. He smiled, liked that better. Frowned. Lowered his brow. He tried saying 'Mr Morales' in different tones, accompanied by different facial expressions. It was all he could do to keep from laughing at himself, and in the end it wasn't going to matter. In the heat of the fray, he would have no idea what his face was doing and less control of his voice than he thought.

He approached the courthouse from the front, on the theory that he should have some firsthand sense of Morales's support. More people than he had ever seen marching there carried signs in Spanish and English varying from somber black and white to the bright colors of the Caribbean, under an ugly sky the same dirty gray as the towering slab of courthouse. Their messages were a mix of support for Morales and antagonism for the criminal justice system. Rosen had been right: the pro-Timmins people had come over to join the Morales supporters.

A news crew recognized him as he was making his way between the blue sawhorses that restrained the demonstrators and the tangle of cables and jumble of equipment that clogged the sidewalk at the curb. He no-commented the reporter and broke free into the road, preferring to dodge traffic than journalists. He was followed by jeers and curses from the crowd, alerted now to who he was.

The heavy clouds beyond the tall windows enclosed the courtroom in gloom. Estrada stacked up the bound sections of transcript and the notes from his meeting with Morales, each newly indexed by Lisa Stein, each labeled so he or Nancy Rosen could quickly find what was needed.

Morales came in with his wife and his lawyers. The defendant was looking fresh and rested, in a double-breasted blazer and darker gray trousers than the day before. In a creamy yellow tie with tiny red-and-blue medallions and a pale yellow shirt, he was a spot of visual optimism in the otherwise grim surroundings.

Martinez was uncharacteristically prompt, and she wasted no time getting the jury seated. The gallery was full, again packed with Morales's supporters. The front row behind Estrada, reserved for the court and the D.A.'s office, was full, too – for the first time. Too many of Estrada's colleagues, Lou Collins among them, wanted to watch the show.

Morales resumed the stand with a warning from the judge that he was still under oath. Estrada pushed himself to his feet and walked stiff-legged the short distance to the lectern, shuffled papers for a moment to let his heart slow down.

'Mr Morales, you testified that after you found Mariah Dodge's body you left the building in a hurry and that at this point you don't have a clear idea of where you went. Is that right?'

'Yes.' Morales let the word out reluctantly, not knowing where it was headed.

'Were you carrying anything when you arrived at the office that night?'

'Not that I remember.'

'No briefcase? You were going to work.'

'No. The papers I needed were at the office.'

'Were you carrying anything when you left?' Setting up for rebuttal on that subject if he needed it.

'No.'

'Mr Morales, you testified that you and your wife went to parties for Phoenix Enterprises, isn't that right?'

'Yes.' Not expecting such an apparently benign question.

'And you testified that your wife is a fashion model, is that right?'

'Yes.'

'Is it fair to say that she's glamorous and beautiful?'

'Yes, that's fair.' Morales looked into the gallery to where his wife sat in her usual seat on the aisle; his incipient smile of pride dissolved immediately when he remembered that helping him show off was not what the prosecutor had in mind.

Estrada watched the transition, then asked, 'Did the two of you do other things for Phoenix Enterprises besides go to parties?'

'Like what?'

'Did you give joint interviews, did she accompany you when you made speeches, things like that?'

'Yes.'

'And in general the two of you posed as the perfect couple.'

'Objection.'

'Overruled.'

'I'm not sure we were perfect.'

'Does that mean yes, you *did* pose as the perfect couple? Yes or no?'

'I suppose . . . yes.'

'That was a lie, though, wasn't it?'

'No.'

'No? Mr Morales, did you testify here yesterday that you and your wife had separate bedrooms?'

'People do that.'

'Did you also testify that you had affairs that your wife knew about?'

'Yes.'

'And that in the case of Mariah Dodge, the three of you socialized together, and both women knew about the arrangements among you?'

'Yes.'

'And you testified that you had a full-time mistress?'

'Yes.' Reluctantly.

'And did you tell anyone about that?'

'No.'

'So the public image you cultivated of your happy marriage was a lie, wasn't it?'

'No, it wasn't. We were very happy.'

'And your supposedly *normal* marriage was a lie.'

'Objection. Speculative.'

'Sustained.'

This was not going well. 'You were having an affair with Mariah Dodge, right?'

'Yes.'

'And she was your subordinate at work, wasn't she?'

'Yes.'

'In other words, she reported to you.'

'Not directly, no.'

'But you were her boss.'

'Yes.'

'At work every day, you conducted yourself with Mariah Dodge as if you were no more than colleagues, isn't that right?'

Waiting for the yes, Estrada remembered Miller doing almost the identical cross-examination of Alvaro the day before.

'Isn't that right?'

'Yes.'

'And that was a lie, wasn't it?' Miller's rhythm had been better than this.

'Yes,' Morales conceded.

'You rented an apartment in Little Italy.'

'Yes.'

'And you pretended to be Italian, didn't you?'

'Yes.'

'You gave your name on the lease as Messina.'

'Yes.'

That felt better. 'And that was a lie, too.'

'Yes.'

'A lie you told to get an apartment.'

'Yes.'

'Because that lie served you at the time.'

'Yes.'

'Your lie served you because you needed that apartment to conceal your illicit relationship with Mariah Dodge.'

Morales seemed about to contradict Estrada, but he said only 'Yes.'

'A relationship that was itself a lie.'

'No, we were honest with each other.'

'As you presented it to the public and your colleagues, it was a lie.'

No answer.

'Didn't you? You lied about your relationship with Mariah Dodge.'

'Yes.'

'Because it suited your purpose at the time.'

Morales hesitated again.

'Because it suited your purpose to fool people about it, didn't it?'

'Yes.'

'Speak up, Mr Morales.'

'Yes.' A lot louder, and then quickly, 'Because we had to work together, too.'

'And people would have objected.'

'Yes.'

'People would have claimed favoritism.'

'Yes.'

'You didn't want that.'

'No . . .'

'You lied to keep that from happening.'

'Yes.' Morales's perfect control was slipping.

'You lied to get what you wanted.'

'Objection,' Miller said, gaining her client a momentary pause. 'Asked and answered.'

'I'll allow it. Answer the question.'

'Yes.'

Estrada followed up quickly to minimize the break in his rhythm caused by the objection. 'In your direct testimony, didn't you say you were very angry?'

Morales looked blank.

'Talking about your final conversation with Mariah Dodge, did you say you were angry?'

'Oh. Yes, I believe I did.'

'Very angry with Mariah Dodge?'

'Yes.'

Taking a chance now: 'Did you say *I was very angry but not angry enough* . . .'

'Those words, I don't know.'

'I can have them read back for you . . .'

'No, it's all right, if you say I said them.'

'When you said you were not angry enough, you meant not angry enough for what?'

Risking the open-ended question because if Morales said *not angry enough to kill her*, or *not angry enough to hurt her*, then from there Estrada could go to: Have you *ever* been angry enough to kill anyone? To hurt anyone? And from there, perhaps, to Andy Flippo's X-slashed collarbones, with Miller certain to object but at least he would have a chance to get Morales's past violence in front of the jury without a mistrial. But Morales was saying nothing.

'Not angry enough for *what*?' Estrada prodded.

'Not angry enough . . .' Morales repeated slowly and distinctly, his face without expression as he tried to conceal his hunt for an answer. And then his stare relaxed and he said confidently: 'Not angry enough that I didn't understand her. She was not getting what she wanted and she was unhappy in her life, and she took it out on me. I could understand that. People do that.'

Estrada was sweating, hands cold, knowing that he was way behind the witness now, knowing that if it didn't get better soon it would get a lot worse.

'When you said not angry enough, are you sure you weren't going to say not angry enough to kill her?' Asking the question so the jury would at least understand where he had been headed, though it meant giving Morales a free denial.

'Yes, I'm sure I wasn't going to say that.'

'You testified that you were successful in real estate.'

'Yes, I was.' There was a note of belligerence in the answer, Morales's annoyance at the earlier questions surfacing now that it was safe.

'You rehabilitated housing.'

'Yes.'

'You made a lot of money doing that.'

'Yes.' Morales was getting himself back under control.

'Getting started, you profited from programs for minorities.'

'Yes.'

'At the same time, you were able to succeed because you pretended to be an Anglo, a norteamericano.'

No answer.

'You pretended *not to be what you are*, yes or no.' Estrada squeezed as much venom into it as he safely could.

'No.' The answer popped out.

There it was. Small – but there it was.

'You didn't?' Estrada was trying to sound innocently surprised. 'You didn't pretend to be an Anglo?'

'I am who I am.'

To keep from showing his relief Estrada looked down at the lectern. 'Mr Morales, did you and your attorney meet with me prior to this trial?' He asked it mildly, setting the record straight.

'Yes.'

'And at that time, even though you were not under oath, did you represent to me that everything you were going to tell me was the truth?' Still mild.

'Yes.'

'You talked about your real-estate success.'

'Yes.'

Estrada turned from the lectern and reached out a hand toward the prosecution table. Rosen handed him the notes from the meeting with Morales.

'And you said . . .' Estrada turned to the indexed page in the notes that held what he was looking for. 'You said that you chose to work in cities where the racial problem was with African-Americans.'

Morales took a moment with it. 'Yes . . .' Tentatively. 'I may have said that.'

'Either you did or you didn't.'

'I don't remember everything I said in the exact words.'

'If I told you you said it, would you deny it?'

'No.'

'I took care to dress well and talk respectfully. Did you say that?'

'I suppose.'

'You *took care*?'

'I might have said that.'

'I hired local contractors.'

'Yes, I did that.'

'And you *said* it, having represented to me that you were telling the truth.'

'Yes, I suppose.'

'I look white. Did you say, I look white?'

'Yes.' Morales accompanied the word with a mildly exasperated sigh, a signal to the jury that this was all so unimportant.

'The neighbors didn't have to worry about me. Did you say that, too?'

'If you say I did.'

'And you said that you did all that so the neighbors wouldn't worry when you bought houses near them. Isn't that right?'

Morales nodded.

'You have to answer out loud.'

'Yes.'

'And did you mean that the neighbors weren't going to be worried because you weren't black?'

'Yes.'

'Did you mean that the neighbors weren't going to worry because even if somebody figured out you were Puerto Rican, you looked and acted white?'

'Not in so many words.'

'That's what all that means, isn't it? I look white so the neighbors don't have to worry.'

'If you take it that way.'

'Yes or no.'

'Yes.'

'That's what you told me about the secret of your success, that it was built on lies.'

'Objection,' Miller said, breaking in to give her client a rest. 'Conclusory and argumentative.'

'Overruled. Answer the question.'

'Yes.' Noticeably calmer.

'Did you tell your neighbors about your true background?'

'They didn't—'

'Yes or no.'

'No.'

'And that was a lie of omission.'

'Yes.' Grudgingly.

'And when you said, "I look white and I took care to dress well and talk respectfully," that was a lie of behavior you were describing.'

'Well . . .' He saw Estrada ready to strike again. 'Yes.'

'Did you use your name on your company?'

'No.'

'And you said, I hid behind local contractors.'

'Yes, I might have said that.'

'And those were lies of commission.'

'Yes.'

'So the secret of your success was an elaborate structure of lies. Lies to conceal your ethnic identity. Lies to conceal the very ethnic identity you were using—'

'Objection!' Miller interrupted. 'Mr Estrada knows not to argue his case now.'

'Sustained.'

'Mr Morales,' Estrada began again, 'didn't you say that your success depended on lies of commission, lies of omission, verbal lies and lies of behavior? All lies.'

'No.'

'They weren't lies?'

'That wasn't why I succeeded.'

'Are you telling this jury that you would have succeeded without the lies?'

'Yes.' And then, quickly. 'I didn't think of them as lies.'

'*You didn't think of them as lies.*' Estrada abandoned for now the structure he had planned. 'Did you think they were the truth?'

'Well . . . no, I don't think . . .'

'You knew they weren't the truth.'

'It wasn't a question of lies or truth.' There was an edge in Morales's voice.

'Because it makes you more comfortable not to think of them as lies.'

'No, that's not it.'

'Just what do you consider a lie?'

'I shouldn't have said that.'

'Why shouldn't you have said it? Isn't it the truth?'

'Not exactly, no.'

'So when you said you didn't think of them as lies, you were lying.'

'No—'

'You're under oath here. Was that the truth or not?'

'Objection, your honor. He's badgering the witness.'

'Overruled.'

'You said it so we wouldn't think you were a liar? So the jury wouldn't think you were a liar?'

'I meant to say, I didn't think of them as significant lies.'

'Not *significant* lies?'

'Right.' Morales seemed to be regaining his poise.

'That made it okay?'

'Not entirely.'

'By that you mean it's okay sometimes and sometimes it's not.'

'Yes.' Relieved to see a way out.

'Then you're saying it's okay to tell lies you don't think are significant?'

'Under some circumstances. Not often.'

'How do you know that other people wouldn't think your lies were significant?'

Morales, brow creased, looked for an answer. Estrada did not give him time to find one. 'Maybe your *investors* would think they were significant.'

'I don't lie to my investors.'

Estrada turned briefly to the jury to underline that, then shifted back to a conversational tone. 'In our prior conversation did you also tell me about Cuyler Jadwin's plans to steal money from Phoenix Enterprises?'

'Not from Phoenix Enterprises.'

'But you said he had plans to steal money.'

'Not so much steal as manipulate things for his own benefit.'

'Whose money was he *manipulating* that way?'

'Some foreign investors'.'

'Cuyler Jadwin was your boss.'

'In a sense.'

'Yes or no.'

'Yes.'

'And didn't you tell me Cuyler Jadwin was a crook?'

'I don't remember.'

Estrada handed him the notes from their meeting. 'Does this refresh your memory?' Trying to keep Morales off balance and out of touch with his prepared responses.

He did not look. 'I suppose I might have said that.'

'You knew that Cuyler Jadwin was planning to steal money? Manipulate, as you put it.'

'Yes.'

'You were willing to see it happen, didn't you say that?'

'I was unwilling to see Phoenix Enterprises be destroyed in order to prevent it.' Firmly, on track again.

'You were willing to see Cuyler Jadwin steal substantial amounts of money?'

'Yes. For the right—'

'Yes is enough,' Estrada interrupted. 'Did he steal money, yes or no?'

Morales turned to the judge. 'It's more complicated than that.'

'It's not complicated,' Estrada insisted. 'Did he or didn't he steal money?'

'No, he didn't *steal*.'

'Did he inflate the price of the option on land he owned

and sell it to Phoenix Enterprises at an inflated price?'

'Objection. Hearsay. Not in evidence.'

'Sustained.'

Estrada took him through the steps by which he acquired his knowledge, twisting through a barbed jungle of objections from Miller before he reached his objective.

'You're saying that you knew Cuyler Jadwin had stolen two million dollars.'

'It was more like overcharging than stealing.'

'So you knew that Cuyler Jadwin had set things up to *overcharge* your investors by a couple of million dollars, and you said nothing.'

'To save the Phoenix Project.'

'You condoned fraud because it was in your interest.'

'I said, to save the project.'

'Did you have occasion to speak with those investors or their representatives?'

'Yes.'

'And every time you did, you lied, because you weren't telling them what you knew.'

'Well . . .'

'Yes or no. You didn't tell them what you knew.'

'Yes.'

'Is that what you meant when you testified just now that you don't lie to investors?'

'No. I mean—'

'Is that what you meant when you told Mariah Dodge that investors aren't people?'

'No! That's not—' Morales shot back and stopped himself and pulled it out with: 'I never said that.'

'Didn't you?' So close . . .

'I wasn't even there.' Under control again.

'You did lie to your investors, though.' The near miss filled Estrada's voice with scorn. 'Lied right in their faces. Every time you didn't tell them they had been defrauded of two million dollars.'

'Objection,' Miller said.

'Sustained.'

'Mr Morales, you testified earlier about an argument you said you had with Mariah Dodge on the last day of her life, that you said occurred in private in your apartment in Little Italy, is that right?'

'Yes.'

'And you described it to me in our earlier meeting.'

'Yes.'

'And in both instances you were telling the truth?'

'Yes.'

'You said that Mariah Dodge demeaned your background.'

'Yes.'

'She said she found you disgusting.'

'Yes.'

'She said bad things about what kind of lover you were.'

'Yes.'

'And she ridiculed your sexual equipment.'

'Yes.'

'She said you're self-satisfied and think you're better than others.'

'Yes.'

'And you're ashamed of your heritage.'

'Yes.'

'And did you hear the testimony in this courtroom of Juan Alvaro?'

'Yes.' Clearly wondering where this was headed.

'And he said he heard Mariah Dodge say you were ashamed of your heritage.'

'I suppose, yes.'

'And that you're self-satisfied.'

'Yes.'

'And that she said bad things about what kind of lover you are.'

'Yes.'

'But you said that Mr Alvaro wasn't there during this argument.'

'Yes.'

'Then how is it possible that he knows *exactly what was said*?'

'Objection,' Miller said immediately.

'Sustained.'

'Mr Morales, are you aware of the charges against you?'

'Yes.'

'You're aware that this is a serious crime.'

'Yes.'

'You don't want to go to prison, do you?'

'No, I don't.' Morales said strongly, prepared for this one. 'Especially not for something I didn't do.'

'Really? And what about something you *did* do? Would you happily go to prison for that?'

Morales stared at him.

'Mr Morales, would you happily go to prison for a crime you did commit?'

'No.'

'If you could pay to get out of going to prison, you would.'

'Objection,' Miller said. 'Can we approach?'

The judge nodded reluctantly. 'What's your problem, Ms Miller?' she said when they were at the bench.

'He's already asked if Mr Morales wants to go to prison. Besides, where's his good-faith basis for the question, your honor?'

'Try Alberto Quiñones,' Estrada said. 'He may not be admissible, but he's real.'

'Inadmissible and not to be the subject of cross-examination,' Miller shot back.

'I'm not making any specific reference to him.'

'Overruled, Ms Miller,' Martinez said.

'Thank you, judge,' Estrada said. 'And before we go, can I ask that you instruct Ms Miller to make her objections clear so we can skip the sidebars? This is obviously just to interrupt my rhythm.'

'He's got a point, Ms Miller.'

She did not respond.

'Mr Morales,' Estrada said, back at the lectern, 'would you pay to stay out of prison?'

'Yes, I suppose.'

'And telling lies to avoid embarrassment is something you've done, right?'

'Well . . .'

'Yes or no.'

'Yes.'

'Telling lies to get an apartment is something you've done.'

'Yes.'

'Covering up a serious crime – covering up a two-million-dollar fraud – you've done that, too, because if it came out it would interfere with your business plans. Isn't that right?'

Morales sat in silence.

'Isn't that right?'

'Not the way you put it.'

'Your honor, can I have some questions and answers read back, please?'

'Never mind,' Morales said. 'Whatever knowledge I had, I kept to myself, that's true.'

'And compared to the things you bought with those lies that you were so good at telling – freedom from embarrassment, a secret apartment, an illicit love affair, the continuation of your business plans, even your desire to be thought of as a hero – all those things are insignificant compared to staying out of prison, wouldn't you say?'

'Yes.' He was not avoiding it any longer.

'No one wants to go to prison, right?'

'Yes.'

'Staying out of prison is worth a fair amount of effort.'

'Yes.'

'Worth telling a few lies today, isn't it?'

'I don't have to lie. I'm telling the truth.'

'Then the answer is *yes*, isn't it? You would lie to stay out of prison.'

'Objection.'

Estrada started toward the prosecution table as if he might be finished, not caring what the ruling was. Then he turned and went back to the podium. 'One more thing, Mr Morales.' His tone of voice, too, made this seem like an afterthought. 'I'm interested in your *story* about what happened that night . . . You say you were there, at the office. Is that right?'

'Yes.'

'You say Mariah Dodge was lying on the couch when you arrived.'

'Yes.'

'You say you could see that her throat was cut and there was a lot of blood.'

'Yes.'

'Was that dry blood?'

'I don't know. I suppose not.'

'You *suppose*.'

'Objection.'

'Sustained. Disregard the prosecutor's remark, please.'

'So she was lying there and the blood was not dry. And what did you do to help her?'

'I . . . she was dead.'

'Did you go near her?'

'No.'

'Did you touch the body?'

'No.' Morales was showing some discomfort, as if the memory pained him.

'Are you a doctor?'

'No.'

'You know that medical science is making great strides in saving people, in healing them?'

'I don't *know*, not really.'

'But you know there are Emergency Medical Service crews who are trained to deal with traumatic wounds.'

'Yes.'

'And you know that people have severed limbs sewed back on?'

'Yes, I suppose.'

'And you know that people have hearts transplanted, and have other organs transplanted, and live.'

'Yes.'

'People are resuscitated from having drowned?'

'Yes.'

'And would you know from a quick look at a drowned person if they could be revived?'

'No.'

'Or if a heart attack victim could be saved?'

'No.'

'Or how much blood a person can lose and be saved?'

'No.' Forcing himself to say the word.

'In fact you have no medical training that would allow you to know if a person was beyond help.'

'No.'

'But you didn't give Mariah Dodge the benefit of the doubt.'

'I . . . no, that's wrong.'

'You say you loved her?'

'Yes.'

'You say you respected her?'

'Yes.'

'But you wouldn't go near enough to make sure she was beyond help. You just assumed it from what you saw.'

'Yes, but—'

'Despite your lack of medical knowledge.'

'I *knew* she was dead.' Anguished.

'Let's look at what you *said* about what you did next. Your *story* is that this was a woman you loved, and yet you didn't lift a finger to help her, right?'

No answer.

'Your *story* is that instead of helping this dying woman you loved, you ran. You fled.'

No answer.

'Didn't you?'

'Yes.'

'You said you had no blood on you.'

'Yes.'

'You saw the blood.' Estrada had a court officer hand Morales the crime-scene photos. He waved them away.

'I saw the blood. I said I saw it.'

'Then if you had no blood on you, how close could you have gotten to this woman in this bloody place? To this woman who was dying?'

'Not very close.'

'How close?'

'I don't know.'

'Fifteen feet? Twenty?'

'I don't know.' An edge of annoyance now.

'Not close enough to this woman you had been having an affair with for more than a year even to get a drop of her dying blood on the tips of your shoes.'

'It wasn't like that.'

'Yes or no. Not close enough to get a drop of her dying blood on the tips of your shoes.'

'Yes.' Looking away, trying for control.

'And that's how much effort you *say* you put into finding out if she was alive.'

No answer.

'That's how moved and concerned you *say* you were by her injuries.'

'I *was* concerned. I just didn't get close.'

'But that isn't the truth is it? You *did* get close. You got close to her in a murderous rage and you raped her and you slashed her throat.'

'No. No! I didn't.'

Miller's shout of *Objection!* failed to drown any of it out. 'Move to strike.'

'Sustained.'

'Did you see the trail of blood leading to your office?'

'I don't remember.'

'You noticed the blood on the floor.'

'Yes.'

'You kept clear of it.'

'Yes.'

'How could you miss the trail of blood that led from the room?'

'I don't know.'

'You had to see it just to avoid stepping in it.'

'I can't remember any of that. I definitely don't remember seeing any trail of blood.'

'A trail of bloody footprints that led straight to your office. Straight to your shower.'

'I didn't see it.'

'You saw the blood flowing and you knew that even if she was dead, it was only recently.'

No answer.

'Didn't you?'

'I suppose.'

'But you didn't notify anybody about it because you knew nobody else was in danger.'

No answer.

'You knew nobody was in danger because *you were the murderer*. The only person in danger, once you'd killed Mariah Dodge, was *you*, and that's why you fled.'

'No, that's not right.'

'And what did you do after you left her dying and fled, according to your story? When did you inform building security that a murderer might be loose in the building?'

'I didn't.' Talking to the floor.

'When did you call 911?'

'I didn't.'

'When did you contact the police?'

'Never. I didn't do any of that.' Head up now, almost defiant.

'If it had been your wife or one of your children would you have called 911 or the police?'

'Objection. Calls for speculation.'

'Sustained.'

'You passed the building security station on your way in?'
'Yes.'
'You passed it again on your way out.'
'Yes.'
'You passed Walter Boynton, the janitor, whom you heard testify that he saw you.'
'I didn't see anyone.'
'You saw no one?'
'People might have been there and I didn't see them. My mind wasn't working right.'
'And then you went for a drink.'
'I wandered around in a fog.'
'You went for a drink.'
'Yes. I needed something . . .'
'More than one drink, more than one place.'
'Yes.'
'There are telephone booths in the street.'
'I don't know.'
'Telephone booths in the bars.'
'I don't know.'
'Did you call 911 from any of those telephones?'
'No.'
'And after that you went home?'
'Yes.'
'You took a shower?'
'Yes.'
'Did you tell your wife what had happened?'
'No.'
'No you didn't tell your wife. You acted as if nothing had happened.'
'No. I told her I needed to have her stay with me.'
'Did you tell her why?'
'No.'
'And after the night you *say* you saw Mariah Dodge's body and wandered around in a daze, did you help the police in their investigation?'

'No.'

'Did you come forward to say what you'd seen and what you'd done?'

'No.'

'You professed to care deeply about Mariah Dodge, but you couldn't be bothered to help find her murderer?'

'I didn't see what I could do.'

'The real reason is that you were deeply concerned about Roberto Morales, isn't it?'

'No.'

'No? But didn't you tell me – I was afraid that they would think I did it?'

'Did I?'

Estrada offered him the meeting notes. Again, he refused them.

'I suppose I might have said that.'

'So then you *were* deeply concerned about Roberto Morales.'

'Yes . . . I suppose, in a way.'

'Because you knew that *you* were the murderer.'

'Objection.'

'Sustained.'

Estrada sat down.

Miller stood to say, 'I have a few questions on redirect, your honor. Mr Morales, the prosecutor asked you about some business practices of Cuyler Jadwin. Did you participate in any way in any fraudulent activity?'

'No.'

'Mr Estrada asked if you knew about Cuyler Jadwin's plans to add to the price of the land option and if you told the investors about that. And you said you didn't tell. Why not?'

'In the real-estate market as it stood I thought that inflating the price of the land would get lost in the quantities of money that would be generated once the project was under way. What Cuyler was doing was more like sharp dealing than like any kind of fraud. And my goal was to preserve the Phoenix Project.'

'Do you believe you made the right decision not to tell the investors?'

'No. I should have told them. I regret that I didn't.'

'And have you been lying here today?'

'No.'

'Did you kill Mariah Dodge?'

'*No.*'

'Thank you. That's all.' She sat down.

Estrada stood for re-cross. 'You say you didn't participate in the fraud committed by Cuyler Jadwin?'

'That's right.'

'But you suspected it.'

'Yes.'

'And you never lifted a finger to find out more, even though you were the president of the company.'

'Well . . .'

'You ignored your obligations to your investors and the people of the community because it wasn't in your interest to know more.'

No answer.

'Isn't that right? It was another example of how you always look out for the interests of Roberto Morales, wasn't it?'

'No.'

'You ignored the fraud.'

'Yes.'

'And by ignoring it you lied about it, didn't you?'

'Yes.'

'Just as you lied about the fact that the project would never get built, because it would interfere with your being a hero.'

'No.'

'But you weren't a hero at all, were you? You were a thief and a liar, weren't you? And ultimately a murderer.'

'Objection.'

'Sustained.'

Estrada sat down again.

'Ms Miller, do you have any more?' Martinez asked.

'No, judge. That's all of my witnesses.'

'Mr Estrada? Are you going to have any rebuttal?'

'Yes, judge. Just one or two witnesses, and they won't take long.'

'Ms Miller?'

'I'll have to hear Mr Estrada's evidence.'

'But we can finish today?'

Both lawyers agreed with that.

'Good,' Martinez said with evident satisfaction. 'Then let's take an early lunch, and we'll start again at two-thirty. That should give you time to prepare anything you need to give me – jury instructions, motions, what have you. We'll sum up in the morning. Please try to be brief. I'd like to charge the jury after lunch tomorrow, at the latest.'

18

Everyone congratulated Estrada on the cross-examination. Even Collins seemed to be pleased. Estrada did his best to enjoy the backslapping. Depending on the next few days, it might be the last round of congratulations he would get for a long time.

He cleared his office so he could concentrate on the business at hand, going over his final requests for additions and modifications to Martinez's instructions to the jury. He had no motions of his own to prepare, but he had consulted with Mahoney to be prepared for one that Miller was sure to make. He called the squad room and got someone to go out and collect Rita Hazen, the woman who had seen Morales carrying a gym bag the night of the murder. She had said she was coming in but he was not in the mood to take chances. A sandwich sat uneaten on his desk while he went over his questions for Juan Alvaro's rebuttal testimony.

The detective came back with Rita Hazen just in time for the afternoon session. He spent fifteen minutes with her going over what she had seen and why she had been so reluctant to tell anyone at the time. 'When I got to work the next morning and learned what had happened all I could think was mind your own business,' she said, still uneasy about it. 'The longer I didn't say anything, the easier it got not to. You tell yourself, they'll get him anyway. And what if you're wrong and you help convict somebody who's not guilty? But I guess you don't have to worry about thoughts like that.'

* * *

Before he left for the courtroom, Estrada made sure he had a copy of Rita Hazen's DD–5 to give Miller. The impulse to call Hazen after all had struck him while he was questioning Morales. Now, waiting for the elevator, he put himself through a Q&A about it, to be sure he was doing the right thing.

What evidence would she provide? The gym bag. How valuable was it? Her story of the nervous man with the gym bag hailing a cab and then not taking it was vivid and credible. In a close argument in the jury room, that kind of corroboration for Alvaro could make the difference. How believable a witness was she? Estrada believed her, but that didn't mean a jury would, especially if she spent her time on the stand nibbling her lip and worrying that they would blame her for not coming forward. Downside? That the jury *would* blame her for not coming forward, or doubt her word because she had lied to the police about how well she had seen Morales. Miller's strategy? That initial lie, plus the dart board.

That was the problem, Estrada saw as he waited for the judge to arrive in the courtroom. If he put Rita Hazen on the stand Miller was going to make it all about the dart board. Not just to impeach Rita Hazen, but to make Joe Estrada into a man with an unreasoning vendetta against Roberto Morales. And he had no one to blame for that but himself.

When Martinez called the session to order, Estrada stood at the prosecution table and said, 'The People call Juan Alvaro.'

Estrada started by asking him if he had ever made any sexual advances toward anyone in the Phoenix Enterprises mailroom.

'No, I never did anything like that. For any number of reasons. I wouldn't have dreamed of it.'

'Tell the jury, if you will, about your relationship with the defendant at work.'

'We stayed out of each other's way.'

'Did you get along?'

'No.'

'Did he tell you you weren't doing your job, or that he wanted to fire you?'

'No.'

'How much did you argue?'

'Not really at all. As I said, we avoided each other.'

'Would you characterize him as a friend or enemy?'

'Neither. I do believe he might have liked to fire me, but that was his problem, not mine.'

Estrada expected an objection; Miller let the answer go by.

'Let's turn our attention to the day Mariah Dodge was killed,' Estrada said. He asked Alvaro at what time he had met Mariah Dodge on the fatal Sunday, and where they had gone and what they had done. Alvaro took the jury on a trip through Manhattan's upscale East Side and midtown: brunch on Madison Avenue, a walk in Central Park, Fifth Avenue window-shopping, afternoon tea at an expensive midtown hotel. And from there, some time after six, to the offices of Phoenix Enterprises.

'Were you and Mariah Dodge apart at any time that afternoon?' Estrada asked him.

'No, we weren't.'

'Was there any other person she went to see, for any length of time?'

'No.'

'Is it fair to say, then, that from around two o'clock in the afternoon until you got to Phoenix Enterprises the two of you were together without a break?'

'Except when she went to the ladies room,' Alvaro answered. 'And she made a couple of phone calls.'

'Could she have had time to visit Roberto Morales in Little Italy and make love with him?'

'No.'

On cross-examination Miller asked Alvaro if the activities he and Mariah had enjoyed that Sunday were the sort that they had shared regularly as part of their friendship. Alvaro said they were. Miller had no other questions.

The judge gave the jury a quick rundown of how the next day was going to go, and what to pack for their deliberations; she reminded them more severely than usual not to discuss the case with each other or anyone else, then she sent them home.

With the jury gone, Martinez called for final motions. Miller renewed her motion to dismiss the indictment.

'Given what we've heard I don't think I can do that,' Martinez said. 'Any juror who believed Mr Alvaro and disbelieved Mr Morales could certainly vote guilty on at least one count.'

'There's absolutely no case for rape, your honor,' Miller argued, as Estrada had expected she would. 'No rational person can find beyond a reasonable doubt based on any evidence before this jury that Roberto Morales raped Mariah Dodge. Even if, as you said, a juror were to believe Mr Alvaro and disbelieve Mr Morales – which I don't think is likely or even possible – there is no reason, no evidence at all to believe that any sex act between Mariah Dodge and Roberto Morales was anything other than voluntary.'

Estrada argued that the slashed clothes and the X on Mariah Dodge's cheek were ample evidence of forced sex. 'Women don't have voluntary sex with men who cut their clothes off their bodies with razor sharp knives, or who cut a trademark into their face.'

'There's no evidence here of a trademark,' Miller interjected.

'That's right, Mr Estrada. And I warn you to remember that fact during your closing argument.'

'I will, your honor. But to return to Ms Miller's motion, the only question we have to be concerned with is the bare legal sufficiency of the evidence. And where there's any doubt at all it has to be resolved not in my favor or Ms Miller's but in favor of the jury. And any juror who believes Juan Alvaro, the medical examiner and the crime-scene reports has enough evidence to convict on rape.

'It's always problematic to take a decision on the facts away from the jury. That's the jury's function, and once they're out of the picture there's no way to tell if a decision on the facts was correct.' Mahoney had set it all out, and the reasoning felt persuasive to Estrada as he delivered it. 'The prosecution can't ask for appellate review. We have no recourse. We have no way to find out what a jury would have thought. But if the jury considers the evidence and *convicts* despite what the defense claims is insufficient evidence, the defense *still* has the benefit of an appeal. They can claim that the jury was wrong, that the verdict is unsupported by the evidence and the motion to dismiss the charge was incorrectly denied.

'So where there's *any* question, *any* possibility at all that the evidence *might* support the charge, the jury must have a chance to reach its own decision. That's settled law, and I have some cases here that support that theory.' He gave a copy of Mahoney's research to Miller and handed one up to the judge.

Martinez skimmed over the pages impatiently. 'All right, Mr Estrada. I don't think you have much of a case for rape, but you've got a good case for letting the jury decide. Denied, Ms Miller. That all for today?'

It was. The two sides handed up their final suggestions for jury instructions, and Martinez adjourned until nine-thirty the following morning. 'Nine-thirty sharp,' she said. 'We have a busy day. I'm even going to be here on time myself.'

McMorris was waiting for Estrada in his office.

'News,' the detective said.

'I'm ready,' Estrada was suddenly exhausted. 'After I sit down.'

'I finally got Nada to talk to me,' McMorris told him. 'She said Censabella was supposed to see Morales some time on the day he fell down the stairs.' He picked a dart off the corner of Estrada's desk and flipped it at the board. It stuck, then dropped off. 'Time to retire that thing.'

Estrada sat forward. 'If there's more, I need to hear it now.'

'Not much more. All he said to her was he was going to talk to Morales.'

'Not why, or who set it up?'

'Not a thing. Not that she's telling us, anyway. She's very upset. She blames us for what happened.'

'She blames *us*?'

'She says that Censabella was all upset about having to testify again. He was worried that his memory wasn't as good as it was three years ago. He didn't like being yelled at by Larry Kahn in the first place and wasn't hot to do it again with *you* yelling at him. She says all this happened, his falling down and all, because all that other stuff was on his mind.' The detective flipped another dart. This one stuck and stayed.

'What else?' Estrada was too tired to be polite.

'Yeah, sorry. I'm kind of bummed about this myself, actually. I was getting kind of fond of the old guy, and I hate to see Nada so broken up. She's a nice old lady.'

'Does she know why he was at the top of the stairs?'

'No.'

'Did you canvass the neighborhood?'

'Yeah. Nobody saw nothing.'

'Nobody saw Morales anywhere nearby?'

'A couple of weak maybes. Not worth a thing in court. You want my opinion, Morales was afraid the old man wouldn't stand up for him, so he heaved him down the steps.'

'That's my opinion, too. Ten more of us and we can convict.'

'Yeah, and that's as close as we're coming, too.'

'What about under his fingernails?'

'Censabella? Nothing. No sign of a struggle. Except the broken neck.'

'Okay, Stash, thanks. I know you're beat, but can you get back out there tomorrow and do some more canvassing? Maybe get some help from the precinct?'

McMorris hauled himself to his feet. 'Right.'

A few minutes later the phone rang. 'Lisa's on her way with

Ms Dodge and Mr Alvaro,' Ginny informed him. 'If that's okay.'

'It's fine.'

'I can't believe it's over,' Tess said when they came in.

'It's not over yet,' Estrada reminded her.

'I mean the testimony part of it. I thought you were great.'

'I hope the jury agrees with you.'

'It's all up to me, isn't it?' Alvaro sounded forlorn. 'I saw some of the newspapers, and the TV news. They treat it like an Old West shootout – Alvaro versus Morales at the O.K. Corral.'

'The truth is, right now it's between Kassia Miller and me,' Estrada said. 'We each get to talk once to the jury and they go off and decide. And I've got to do some preparing, so I'll say thank you and goodnight.'

He read through the two draft summations he and Rosen had been working on, and picked the more analytical one. He worked on it for a couple of hours, bringing it up to date and boiling it down to a set of outline points on note cards. At ten, exactly on time, Mahoney showed up. Estrada let him get settled in the desk chair and stood by the window to deliver his argument. He stumbled here and there, but basically it went smoothly.

When he was done, Mahoney looked at him and said, 'Very good. Very precise. Very well argued. Perfect structure. A textbook summation.'

Estrada was beginning to feel a little better. Maybe this was going to be all right.

'One problem,' Mahoney said. 'It needs more heart. I know I'm not the one to talk, being a legal mechanic and all – an arguer of dry technicalities before a bench full of old farts – but listen to me anyway. Pull out some stops here and there. Be an emotional advocate. If you're going to try to win this one on logic, you might as well stay home tomorrow.'

19

Estrada had assigned Lisa Stein to what she laughingly called hospitality-suite duty so he could be alone in his office with his summation notes and the picture of Mariah Dodge. He was intrigued to find that where Tess had once reminded him of Mariah, now Mariah's picture reminded him of Tess. Fitting enough, because for all the sympathy he felt for Mariah, it was for the living that he was going into court today.

With ten minutes to go, as Estrada was checking to make sure he had not left out any important points, Stein called from Ginny's desk. 'We've got a crowd.'

'Crowd? How?' Tess Dodge was the only one he expected.

'Come out and see.'

Just what he needed: games. He took a last run through his notes and went out to join them. Nancy Rosen was there with her husband, adding to the congestion in the narrow corridor. He saw Tess, and a short woman he did not immediately recognize as her mother, and Juan Alvaro and Carlos Ramírez. And a man in his late twenties Estrada did not recognize at all, tall and fit, in a banker's suit.

'This is Seth,' Stein said, blushing. 'I told him there might not be enough seats.'

'If he won't fit with the family he can sit in the front row, but only if nobody from the office wants the seat.'

'Thanks.'

'Mrs Dodge, it's good to see you,' Estrada said. 'I wasn't sure you'd want to be here.' He thought he detected the traces of bruising under her makeup, decided he was imagining it: that was too long ago.

'Tess tells me you're doing a fine job. She said I shouldn't miss it.'

'She's been very helpful. If we succeed, we'll owe a lot to her.'

'You're kind to say so, Mr Estrada. I'm glad to hear that at least one member of the Dodge family has been helpful.'

Alvaro and Ramírez were waiting patiently on the fringes of the activity.

'I just came to say good luck,' Alvaro said. 'I know I can't be in the courtroom.'

'I wish you could be, but I don't think it's worth the risk that the jury might see you and decide you had too big a stake in the outcome.'

'It's all right. Carlos promised to tell me all about it. He can have my place.'

'If there are too many . . .' Ramírez said.

'No, you belong here. We'll find room.'

The corridor outside the courtroom was a model of controlled chaos, would-be spectators lining one wall behind a police barricade while the other wall was headquarters for the press people who had not made the first cut. A television crew was encamped beyond the courtroom door, spread out so it could assault all comers.

The courtroom was full, except for the half-row reserved for the family and special friends of the victim.

'Your friend will have to squeeze in if he can,' Estrada told Stein. 'The office row is almost full.' Even from the back he had immediately spotted Lou Collins, Nancy Rosen's bureau chief, the First Assistant D.A., Dan Mahoney and – another surprise – Lawrence Kahn. Clemente and McMorris were there, as expected. The remaining seats held some of the more senior members of Estrada's trial bureau.

For only the second time in the trial, Kassia Miller was

wearing an outfit that included a jacket: loose and collarless, it draped gracefully over a matching pearl gray dress; her gray shoes were simple and unadorned. She looked effortlessly composed, Estrada thought, a person who could be trusted to know right from wrong, innocent from guilty.

Almost true to her word, Luz Martinez was only five minutes late. She got the jury in and with no delay gave them a quick outline of what to expect from the day and turned the floor over to Kassia Miller.

'Good morning,' Miller said to the jury when she reached the lectern set at the center of the jury box rail. 'You've all been very patient and attentive these past days. I thank you for that. It's a pleasure to work with a group of people who take their obligations seriously.

'We've been here together all these days to observe the evidence offered as a result of an indictment charging Roberto Morales with rape and manslaughter and murder. As the prosecutor himself has told you, he comes to court with a heavy burden, the burden of proving guilt on each of those charges beyond a reasonable doubt. At the beginning of the trial, I predicted that he wouldn't prove the things he promised you he would prove. I predicted he would not carry his burden successfully. And I was right: he hasn't.

'*Beyond a reasonable doubt*. Judge Martinez is going to tell you what that means. Basically, she's going to tell you that you need only a small degree of doubt to throw these charges right into the garbage where they belong. That instruction may seem superfluous by the time you hear it, because I think you all know already that your doubt about who committed this horrible crime is not small, your doubt is substantial, and nothing you've heard in this courtroom has made it less.

'This is an unusual case, in a way. On a lot of points, both sides agree. It's only on the most important ones that we disagree.

'I'm going to start by telling you a story. It's a story that is supported by all the believable evidence you've heard in this trial. It starts with Mariah Dodge telling her friends that she's going to break up with Roberto Morales, and that she's going to call him some harsh names when she does, because she wants him to know she means it.

'So, on an October Sunday almost four years ago, she and Roberto Morales get together, in the apartment he maintains for them to use as a place to be alone together. She tells him she doesn't want to be his lover anymore. She calls him names. She yells at him, he yells back at her. They say the cruel things that only lovers know how to say to each other and when they've exhausted themselves that way they make love. It's a kind of farewell salute to what they've had together in the past, the way people sometimes do. The downstairs neighbor overhears them arguing and he overhears them making love.

'Intending to go to the gym with a friend and to shower there, Mariah dresses, but before she leaves she and Roberto talk about work. There's a big meeting coming up and he has an idea she hasn't heard before. She's excited about it. They agree to get together at the office later on that night to work on it. Mariah calls her friend to cancel the gym date, but having already dressed she doesn't bother to get undressed again to shower. So she leaves with the dry residue of their lovemaking still on her body.

'Some time later she goes to the office. She uses her keys to get into her office and into Roberto's office as well and begins to work on a presentation for the meeting the next morning. She's invited her friend and co-worker Juan Alvaro to help her. They assemble the papers she needs and begin to cut and paste the sections that will be helpful.

'At some point, she is interrupted. Later, we'll talk about who might have interrupted her, but I'll say now that it was almost certainly a man and that it was *not* Roberto Morales. The man takes the knife she's been using – or one of his own – and threatens her with it. He makes a cut on her cheek to show he's serious. Terrified, she waits for what's coming next. He cuts her clothes. Perhaps he rapes her, perhaps not. Perhaps he tries and fails. What he does, without question, is to cut her throat.

'When she is dead her killer goes to the nearby office where he knows he'll find a shower. It happens to be Roberto Morales's office. A coincidence. There is no evidence to show he had any reason to go there except convenience. He washes himself off and he puts his bloody clothes in a gym bag he finds in the dressing room. He steals some clothes from the closet: the workout clothes Roberto Morales keeps there. And this killer who is *not* Roberto Morales wraps up the bloody clothes he was wearing and puts them into Roberto Morales's gym bag. Dressed in Roberto Morales's clothes, the killer leaves the office. We don't know if he leaves the building immediately.

'Not long after the killer leaves the office, Roberto Morales arrives to work with Mariah. He sees her lying there, dead, and he is stunned, grief-stricken. In shock. In that state, barely able to move, he stays in the office for some unknown period of time, until his paralysis changes to unreasoning but understandable panic and he flees. He wanders around in a daze, has a drink or two and finally goes home, where he is comforted by his wife, though he is afraid to tell her what he has seen.'

Miller stood in silence, her eyes slowly scanning the jury. 'That is the story the witnesses have told you. With one exception even the prosecution witnesses agree with it. There has been only *one* witness who contradicts that story directly, and we'll talk about him in a minute.

'First I want to talk about the prosecutor's case. What does the prosecutor rely on?

'In the first place, the prosecutor is relying on a police investigation that I would call laughably inadequate, except that there is nothing laughable about the way it has nearly ruined an innocent man's life, and there is nothing laughable about the tragic injustice it could lead to.

'How do we know that the police investigation was inadequate? We heard it from the mouth of the only policeman whose voice we actually heard in this courtroom. Detective Thomas Clemente told us that when it comes to murder cases the police feel pressure to have a suspect – an *arrest* – within days of the crime. Four days was *pushing it*, he said. So the police, by the admission of their own spokesman, were in a hurry, and because they were in a hurry they took the first suspect they could find close at hand. And Detective Clemente admitted that the police automatically consider the victim's lover a suspect in cases like this, whether there is any specific reason to suspect him or not.

'How else do we know that the police investigation was inadequate? We know it was inadequate because the police failed to uncover important facts that a private investigation was able to find years later. The police missed the very important fact that there were people working as security guards in that office building who were on no official payroll. You heard Craig Lawrence, who was here to testify – a man with years of experience in the FBI, a top investigator. He told you how he and his staff of private investigators found out about those unofficial employees and tracked some of them down. Craig Lawrence found these people long after the crime. Not three days after it, three *years*. But the police were in a hurry after three days.

'You also heard one of the men who was turned up by Craig Lawrence and his private investigators. David Dexter talked about the practice of letting friends and relatives substitute for the security staff. David Dexter worked in that building at the time of the police investigation. At that time, his brother-in-law, Kenneth Charles, was substituting for him now and then as a security guard in that building. David Dexter told us that Kenneth Charles worked in his place the very afternoon of the crime. Kenneth Charles, whose trials for sexual assault David Dexter says he attended. Kenneth Charles, a man David Dexter saw commit assault with a straight razor. A man the police didn't bother to find.

'Now, as we sit here, Kenneth Charles is almost four years gone. But he wasn't gone then. For two weeks after Mariah Dodge was killed he was in New York. He was still around long after Detective Clemente's three or four days. And for four months after that he was in touch with his sister and his brother-in-law, and he would not have been hard to find.

'Did the police ever find him? They didn't even look. By the third day they'd already found somebody they thought they could hang this crime on, so they stopped looking. Imagine that: a man who because of his past should have been a suspect in this crime, as Detective Clemente himself told you, a man who worked in the office building where she was killed, a man who knew the building's layout and its security routine and who had access to the maintenance department's keys – David Dexter told us all that about Kenneth Charles. And that man was within reach for weeks and months, and clearly should have been a suspect in this crime. But the police couldn't be bothered to find him when he was right there in front of their eyes. And if the police didn't bother to find Kenneth Charles, who else might they have missed?

'The prosecutor ridiculed Craig Lawrence because Kenneth Charles was the only suspect he found. But that's exactly the point. Even *three or four years* later it's possible, by being diligent, to find someone who is a plausible suspect. Who might the police have found if they had been willing to exert themselves a little bit more only three or four *days* after the murder?

'And where is Kenneth Charles now? Not here. He's not here, where he should be. Nor are any of the other suspects the police may have missed. Roberto Morales is here instead. Roberto Morales who has *no* criminal record' – Estrada waited for her to say *Roberto Morales who is not a slasher* and braced himself to object, to say, 'We don't know that, your honor.' But she moved on 'Roberto Morales is here. Because the police couldn't be troubled to do their job.

'That's the kind of police work that brought us here today.

Police work that failed even to learn of the existence of a man who may well have committed this crime. And yet the prosecutor is going to get up here in a few minutes and insist that you take these charges seriously.'

Miller left a moment of silence to put a point on that topic and then, with considerable disdain, she dismissed the DNA expert who had not done population studies on Latinos. 'Ridiculous,' she said. 'You've heard of voodoo economics,' she said. 'Those people practice voodoo statistics.'

Estrada, still smarting from Miller's attack on Clemente and the cops and her strong advocacy of Kenneth Charles as an alternate killer, did not care about DNA. He was not going to rely on it, anyway. That was from the days before he had Juan Alvaro.

'What else is the prosecutor going to ask you to believe?' Miller continued. 'He's going to ask you to believe that there is some significance in the way bloody heelprints lead from the body of Mariah Dodge straight to Roberto Morales's bathroom. But Kenneth Charles worked as a security guard in the building, so he must have known the way. Juan Alvaro *certainly* knew the way. So did many of Phoenix Enterprises' employees, maintenance employees . . . any number of people the police did not bother to consider as suspects. Knowing the way to that shower was not a classified secret. Lots of people knew it was there.

'But those are the small things. The prosecutor had something else up his sleeve, something he hoped would convince you to ignore the weakness of the rest of his case. The prosecutor had a *star witness*.' Her scorn increased: 'Juan Alvaro, the man who was supposed to explain it all for us. Juan Alvaro, the most interesting person we saw in the course of this trial, and I do not mean that as a compliment.

'What can we say about Juan Alvaro? A remarkable man is Juan Alvaro, able to repeat lengthy conversations between other people after four long years. The prosecutor is going to go on and on about Juan Alvaro, about all the things that

Juan Alvaro had to say, and about their implications for this trial. There's only one problem: everything Juan Alvaro said concerning Roberto Morales's activities on the day and night Mariah Dodge was killed is a *lie*.' She paused and let her eyes scan the jury.

'Now, in a way, getting into the specifics of Juan Alvaro's lies is like debating the life history of Mickey Mouse before Walt Disney, unreal speculations about unreality. But it's something we have to do.

'The prosecutor will try to sell you the idea that Juan Alvaro's story has the ring of truth. He'll tell you that no one could make up such an elaborate and detailed story. Even though Juan Alvaro did just that.

'So we have to think about where such elaborate lies might have come from. Well, everybody who has experience with lying and liars knows that the most convincing lies are usually based on truth in some way. Why? Because it's easiest to fill a lie with details – and to remember what those details are, in case it's necessary to retell the lie later – if the lie is also a description of something real, with just a few crucial details changed. You tell as much of the truth as possible, and make changes only when you have to.

'I submit to you that that is exactly what Juan Alvaro has done. My Italian friends have taught me an expression for stories like the one Juan Alvaro has told here. They say *non é vero, ma é ben trovato* – it isn't true, but it's cleverly put together. Just so with Juan Alvaro's story.

'Let's look at how Juan Alvaro put his lies together. Juan Alvaro testified that he had spent many Sunday afternoons with Mariah Dodge. He testified that he talked to her about her love life. When he tells us things like that, which have nothing to do with the killing, we can give him the benefit of the doubt.

'So we accept that he has details from all those Sunday afternoons he really did spend with Mariah Dodge to put together when he tells us about what he claims happened on one particular, fatal Sunday – a Sunday on which he *did not* see her, at least not in the afternoon.

'Juan Alvaro told us that he and Mariah Dodge talked about her love life. The evidence also shows us that Mariah Dodge told at least two of her friends about her intention to break up with Roberto Morales and about the words she was going to use to do it. Lynne Schelling told us about that – the tall woman in red, an actress with a dramatized story. A woman who by her own admission was not a very good friend of Mariah Dodge's. She had never met any of Mariah Dodge's other friends and didn't know the name of Mariah's sister or her close male friend Juan Alvaro. Basically, the two women climbed stair machines together, and did aerobics in a gym. But Mariah Dodge told her a lot about what she wanted to say to Roberto Morales.

'Now, if Mariah Dodge told that much to Lynne Schelling, we have to conclude that she told even more to Juan Alvaro. We can suppose that when she saw him later that day, she told him about how she broke up with Roberto Morales. It's human nature to tell your juiciest, *newest* story to the person who's your confidant. So when Juan Alvaro put together his made-up story about the breakup between Roberto Morales and Mariah Dodge in the office – which never happened – he had plenty of material to work with. All he had to do, telling us about it, was to repeat what Mariah Dodge told him. The only change he needed to make was to transfer the location from the apartment to the office and place himself there as a witness.

'But what about the other argument he described between Mariah Dodge and Roberto Morales? The one that had to do with Phoenix Enterprises. That has a basis in reality, too. All of that happened. The only change Juan Alvaro made there, and an important change it was, was to substitute Roberto Morales for himself.

'Think about it that way and everything you heard in this courtroom, from both sides, fits seamlessly into a single story.

There *was* a fight in the office that night. Mariah Dodge *did* find out that someone was manipulating the Phoenix Project, threatening it with destruction, for his own greedy reasons. But that person was *Juan Alvaro*, not Roberto Morales.

'It was Juan Alvaro who had betrayed Mariah Dodge and disappointed her. It was Juan Alvaro who was enraged by her reaction to what she had learned. It was Juan Alvaro whose angry threats did not make Mariah Dodge back off from her intention to expose what she had learned.

'*It was not Roberto Morales.*'

Miller paused to let her last sentence resonate. When she resumed, it was in a cooler tone. 'Does that mean that Juan Alvaro killed Mariah Dodge? It may very well mean that. But we have to remember that arguing is not killing, though the prosecutor will try to tell you that it is. He'll try to convince you that whoever argued with Mariah Dodge must have killed her, too. But arguing isn't killing. Arguing is arguing. So I can't tell you the evidence says beyond a reasonable doubt that Juan Alvaro, who argued with Mariah Dodge, killed her, too.

'Juan Alvaro may have killed Mariah Dodge, or Kenneth Charles may have killed Mariah Dodge. And when I say Kenneth Charles I don't just mean Kenneth Charles, the man David Dexter saw slash another man's face, the man whose rape trials David Dexter attended—'

'Objection,' Estrada said finally, risking calling attention to it in the hope he would get a corrective instruction.

'Sustained. Ladies and gentlemen, the specific crimes committed by this person are not of any interest. They are not relevant to your deliberations, Ms Miller, be careful.'

'Yes, your honor. I apologize if there's any misunderstanding. I'm only trying to make it clear the *kind* of man the police didn't find. When I say Kenneth Charles I also want you to think of all the *other* people who had access to the building, access to the key rack, all the men the police never bothered to find or question or suspect.'

She had slid out of it neatly, and Estrada was not sure his objection had bought him anything.

'Kenneth Charles or someone like him may have been lurking around the building looking for trouble. He may have seen Mariah Dodge on her way in and been tempted to follow her to see if he could catch her alone and vulnerable. Or he may have been drawn by the brightly lit office in the mostly dark building, or by the noise of an argument. He may have waited for the fuss to die down and then, when Juan Alvaro left – if he did – Kenneth Charles may have entered the office and attacked Mariah Dodge and killed her after raping her or trying to rape her. Because he could have raped Mariah Dodge without leaving any noticeable traces on her body. The medical examiner told us that, and the prosecutor's DNA expert admitted that even if Kenneth Charles or someone else did leave semen behind, and if that semen mixed with the semen left that afternoon by Roberto Morales, the oh-so-sophisticated DNA test might not have detected it at all.

'And let's not forget Juan Alvaro himself – enraged at Mariah, feeling betrayed by her, sure that she was going to expose his crimes. Juan Alvaro himself could have intimidated her, cut her cheek, slashed her clothes. Why? To create the impression of rape. To divert suspicion from himself. After all, he knew Roberto Morales was on his way, he knew that Mariah and Roberto had quarreled, and he knew that Roberto Morales would immediately be suspected by the police. So he faked a rape and he cut her throat. Not knowing that the deception would be enhanced by the residues of lovemaking Mariah did not have a chance to wash off.

'The evidence doesn't tell us enough to know which of those two plausible scenarios to believe: someone like Kenneth Charles as the killer or Juan Alvaro as the killer. There's a huge gap in what we know. No one, not even Juan Alvaro in his fantasy scenario, tells us anything about who was present when Mariah Dodge was killed. If the police had not been so eager to lock up the first person they thought of for this crime, we might know more. But they took the easy way out. And the result is that we do not know what happened in those final minutes of Mariah Dodge's life. Was it Juan Alvaro who killed her? Was it Kenneth Charles? The prosecutor wants you to think it was Roberto Morales. But we don't know. We can't know. As it stands, the only thing we *know* from the evidence – the lack of evidence, really – is that there is no proof that Roberto Morales had any part in the horrible things that happened to Mariah Dodge.

'Now, in telling you this story – the story of how after Mariah and Roberto had their afternoon together, Mariah went to the office with Juan Alvaro and discovered things about Juan's dishonesty that led them into a vicious argument – I am attributing important lies to Juan Alvaro. I feel perfectly comfortable doing that. The evidence, including the admissions of Juan Alvaro himself, amply supports the idea that Juan Alvaro is a self-serving liar.

'The prosecutor is going to tell you that Juan Alvaro had no choice but to be dishonest in his life, and in his employment at Phoenix Enterprises. But that's Juan Alvaro's story, and it's as twisted, as deviously put together, as everything else he's said. Based on truth, perhaps. True? No.

'Let's consider Juan Alvaro's dishonesty at Phoenix Enterprises. He himself says he was creating accounting systems that allowed false invoicing and double invoicing, systems that had no proper accounting control to catch those and other abuses. Cooking the books, some people call that.

'But Juan Alvaro wasn't cooking the books for the reasons he says. Not to pay off the construction unions. The Phoenix Project was still no more than an idea. No ground had been broken, no construction begun. It is simply not credible that anything substantial in the way of bribes would have been necessary to secure a bid. No, Juan Alvaro was cooking the books for himself. Himself and whatever accomplices in theft he may have had. Juan Alvaro was a man experienced in lying. Experienced in lying to himself, experienced in lying to others.

'The prosecutor is going to bend himself into a pretzel to justify Juan Alvaro's lifetime of lies. He has to. Think of what the prosecutor's case would look like without Juan Alvaro. A couple of security guards who aren't sure of what they saw or when they saw it, and two friends of Mariah Dodge's, a woman not her close friend who's trained in dramatizing her stories, and a friend from the past who only talked to her on the phone and whose tendency to lie in important matters had come to the attention of the consumer protection authorities where she lives. Both of these women, like the police, were eager for a quick solution to this tragedy. They are not too careful about their facts or about picking a person to blame.

'Not much of a case. Not enough to convince anyone of anything beyond a reasonable doubt. So the prosecutor relies on Juan Alvaro. What choice does he have?

'But Juan Alvaro admitted to concealing and lying about his criminal record. Juan Alvaro admitted to participating in dishonest accounting practices. Juan Alvaro admitted to harming and corrupting children to gratify his sexual desires. Juan Alvaro admitted to continuing these vile practices even though he knew the harm he was doing as he went on satisfying himself. There are no words to describe how awful, how reprehensible, how unforgivable was what Juan Alvaro did.

'Now he comes here and presents himself to you and asks for your understanding and for your belief. And he asks you to accept the notion that he is here to see that the truth is served.

'But the only truth that Juan Alvaro serves is the truth of his own interests. He is here seeking to be legally absolved for all the crimes of his past. Sexual crimes and financial crimes. He was tired of hiding and he saw this as a way to come back with everything forgiven.

'And while he's at it he gets to strike what he hopes will be a deadly blow at a man he has reason to hate. Roberto Morales saw through Juan Alvaro's incompetence and told him so. Roberto Morales wanted him out of Phoenix Enterprises and out of the life of Mariah Dodge. Roberto Morales knew about his need to have sex with children and about the cruel and exploitive behavior this led him to. And Roberto Morales told him to straighten himself out or be fired. Can we doubt that Juan Alvaro is eager to do whatever damage he can to Roberto Morales?

'And all Juan Alvaro has to do to get himself a clean record, to wipe away the stain of the unspeakable things he's done, indeed to make himself the darling of law enforcement *and* to get back at his enemy Roberto Morales is to put together a story out of parts of other days spent with Mariah Dodge and pieces of things she told him about her breakup with Roberto Morales. And then add to it his own last, violent fight with Mariah Dodge, which he describes for us with his own part played by Roberto Morales and himself as spectator.

'And he peddles that story for his thirty pieces of silver and walks away free.'

She stopped, her voice full of loathing, and resumed in a more conversational tone.

'Roberto Morales was up on the witness stand in front of you, too. You heard what he had to say, and you watched him as he said it. You've been watching him during the whole trial. You don't need me to tell you about Roberto Morales.

'The prosecutor is going to tell you that Roberto Morales is a liar. He's going to push hard on how high the stakes are for Roberto Morales, testifying here before you. Yes, Roberto Morales said he wants to stay out of prison. Who wouldn't? But the fact that a man wants to stay out of prison doesn't mean that he's lying on the witness stand. If the truth is what will keep him out of prison, then he has no reason to lie.

'You have to make your decision about Roberto Morales's truthfulness based on other factors: on how consistent what he says is with the rest of the *believable* evidence, and on his demeanor when he speaks to you.

'Roberto Morales admitted that he had lied in the past. But there is no lie that Roberto Morales talked about here that is not minor and excusable. He shaded the truth and kept private things private out of concern for his wife and his small children. Private matters *that harmed no one*. Is that a fault in a man? If it is, then it's a fault that Roberto Morales has. Because Roberto Morales is a family man. His affair with Mariah Dodge was no threat to that family. I don't ask you, ladies and gentlemen, to adopt his way for yourself, or even to approve of it. All I ask is that you understand that Roberto and Marti Morales have love and respect for each other which is not diminished by their special arrangement. You watched Roberto Morales and listened to him as he talked about his children. You know how much his family means to him.

'The prosecutor made a fuss about the way Roberto Morales dealt with his ethnic identity in conducting his business. Pure nonsense. Look at the evidence. For years Roberto Morales was one of the most visible Latino businessmen in the East. It was a status and a reputation he built with hard work. If he seems to have had his mind on racial questions when he was starting, they were not questions of his own making.

'Real estate is a racially sensitive business. This is a sad fact, and not something anyone can be proud of. But it isn't something that is going to be changed in a day, or by the efforts of a single person. A young man making his way in the world is not necessarily in a position to cure all the world's ills. Later, perhaps, when he is better established, he can address these problems.

'Roberto Morales addressed the legacy of racism prominently and powerfully with the Phoenix Project. He is doing that now, with his drug rehabilitation program and his community housing efforts. But in his early days, struggling to establish himself, he quite understandably selected areas to work in where he would not be the subject of prejudice. I ask you to consider if a young man trying to get his first foothold would do himself or anyone else a favor by seeking out a place to do business where prejudice against him would be a significant barrier.

'Roberto Morales worked long and hard to get to a place where he could be an example and an inspiration to his people, and where he could provide a secure future for his family. Where he could know that his actions would matter in the world. The prosecutor wants you to believe that a man who worked so hard and achieved so much would throw it all away because of an insult, because a woman rejected him.'

She paused again, her head momentarily bowed as if in mourning for the world's folly.

'It's a sad and sordid tale we've played out for you here. Saddest by far for Mariah Dodge but sad, too, for everyone involved.

'One thing is undeniable about it: there is an overwhelming amount of uncertainty here as to the identity of Mariah Dodge's killer. There is no credible evidence here to justify finding that Roberto Morales is guilty of any of these crimes. No evidence whatever that Roberto Morales ever had sex with Mariah Dodge except by mutual consent. No evidence whatever that he committed any violent act toward her, much less that he raped her or that he killed her.

'The prosecutor has now had the opportunity to hear what I have to say, and when it's his turn he's going to tell you to disregard it. I ask you this favor: listen to the prosecutor's argument with skepticism, on my behalf. I don't get to talk after he does, so I'm going to trust that when he makes a point you'll ask yourself, what would Kassia Miller have said to that?

'You all saw horrible pictures here in this courtroom. You all heard a horrible and heartrending story: the details, one after the other, of the pain and terror Mariah Dodge must have gone through. It is impossible not to feel sadness and pity for Mariah Dodge, and profound anger at anyone who would treat a fellow human being that way. It is understandable if you feel those emotions – sadness, pity, anger – and feel them strongly.

'Sometimes when people feel that way the very anger they

feel makes them strike out at the most available target. We want to make *somebody* pay for this. We don't want it to go unpunished. Everyone connected with this trial knows how that feels. Everyone connected with this trial has had to live for many months with these pictures, with the autopsy report, with all the horror of what happened. How could any of us not want to see Mariah Dodge's killer punished? But we must be sure it's the *real* killer, not an innocent stand-in.

'So I ask you, I implore you, do not let those justified and righteous emotions of pity and anger lead you to convict an innocent man. Do not make the same mistake the police made and the prosecutor made. Do not take out your anger on Roberto Morales simply because the prosecutor has been wrongly led to offer you Roberto Morales as a sacrifice, compounding the mistake of the police. Do not add a tragic injustice to the terrible loss of Mariah Dodge.

'When we started this trial, I said to you that like the prosecutor I have an obligation to the People of the State of New York. My obligation to the People is to prevent a miscarriage of justice, to see to it that you, the jury, have enough information to avoid convicting an innocent man.

'I'm confident that if you consider carefully what I've had to say – and I know you *will* consider it carefully – you will agree that there is nothing the prosecutor can tell you, consistent with the evidence as you have seen it unfold, that will hinder you in returning the only just and proper verdict in this case: *not guilty* of rape, *not guilty* of manslaughter and *not guilty* of murder in the second degree.'

20

Estrada stood up and went to the lectern. He found himself thinking, unwillingly, of the bureau chief who had told him he had the right kind of eyes for working with a jury. 'Intelligent but not cold. People forget how sincere brown eyes can look. There's nothing more compelling to a jury than a strong prosecutor with compassion.' That memory brought back, as it always did, the trial-practice professor who had told him to cultivate his smile. As a result, no facial expression seemed natural, and he was sure that his stiffness and discomfort were unavoidably obvious.

He stood for a moment, looking at the jury, hoping his expression was neutral, willing his jaw to unlock and release his formula opening, taught to him and a bureauful of others by Larry Kahn, who himself had learned it from a former star A.D.A. now on the federal bench.

'Ladies and gentlemen,' he made himself say, 'at this point in the trial it's my duty and my privilege to sum up the evidence on behalf of the People of the State of New York. I'd like to add my thanks to those you've already heard for the patience and the courteous attention you've shown all of us during the course of this trial.' He was warming up gradually, carried along by the familiar words. 'A trial is nothing more or less than a search for the truth under the rules of evidence, truth which I have the legal requirement to prove beyond a reasonable doubt.'

He skipped the part about what the summation was going

to contain, eager to get to the point.

'The issue in this case is, did this defendant, Roberto Morales' – he turned and pointed at Morales and was surprised by the surge of emotion he felt. The drive to win had always run strong in him, and the desire to get the bad guys, but this was deeper and more powerful – 'did Roberto Morales brutally rape Mariah Dodge and murder her by slashing her throat?'

For a moment that was all he could say. He wondered if the jury would see the frozen pause as rhetorical mastery.

There was more in the formula, more he should say now about the crimes; it was the logical next step in the closing argument he had been using successfully for years. But he remembered Mahoney's advice and thought, Maybe he's right, maybe this isn't the time for logic. There was only one thing going on here and he wanted to call it by its name.

'You've got a straightforward choice to make when you sit down to deliberate, ladies and gentlemen. You have to decide which of two men to believe. That's really all there is to this trial. The rest is window dressing.' He paused, and this time it was because he wanted to.

'Life would be easier if murderers wore a sign on their foreheads, or a certain color hat. In old movies there was a whole catalog of ways to tell the bad guys from the good guys. We don't have that luxury. If we did, a lot of people would be spared pain and anguish.

'If there were some radar that let you tell a person who might become murderous from a person who wouldn't, Mariah Dodge would be alive today. And you, ladies and gentlemen, would not be here being asked to examine the evidence and to conclude that this man who seems to be a pillar of the community is in fact a brutal rapist and murderer.

'It may be to some degree that Mariah Dodge walked in harm's way. If she had been less moved by righteous anger, if she had been less eager to stand up for what she thought was right, she might not have been so outspoken. She might have kept a rein on her anger and found some other way to express it. But she had no way to know that the defendant would turn into her killer if she challenged him. She couldn't see into the future.' Or into the past, he wanted to say, where she would have seen Roberto Morales slashing Andy Flippo. But he couldn't say that, because that was inadmissible.

'She couldn't see that if she challenged Roberto Morales he would turn violent, she couldn't see that he would force her to have sex with him, and she couldn't see that when he was finished and she thought the ordeal was over that he would slash her throat. Slash it with the same knife she had been using to cut out sections of the documents she hoped would save their company. A knife like this one.' He held up the utility knife, its flat, razorlike blade extended four inches, ordinary tool turned chilling weapon. 'The same knife he had used to cut his X-mark into her cheek.'

He expected an objection from Miller. Instead, he got a reprimand from the judge. 'Be careful, Mr Estrada. I made a ruling about that.'

'Yes, your honor.' Not the kind of emphasis of the trademark X that would do him any good.

'I was saying that Mariah Dodge could not see the future. She could not tell that this man with whom she had been having an affair would take the knife she had been using for constructive purposes and use it to put a warning cut in her face and then slash her clothes, as a way to force her to have unwanted sex with him – at a time when she had vowed never to let him touch her again. And she could not know that when it was all over, when she *thought* it was all over, he would snatch up that knife and swiftly and viciously slash it across her throat. Before she could react, before she was even aware of what was happening.

'And then she was aware. Too aware. In pain. Dr Martin, the assistant medical examiner, told us she was in pain. Struggling as best she could while the life pumped out of her. And it's horrifying to think about what those moments were like, feeling that pain, seeing your own blood shooting out of your neck – and you saw, ladies and gentlemen, you saw that pattern on the rug, the zigzag track as the blood spurted from her body, you saw it in the pictures and you heard the medical examiner and the expert in bloodstain patterns describe how it happened. That's a strong pump we have in our bodies, and Mariah Dodge's heart was pumping desperately. And at the same time she was trying to get her free hand up to ward off any more pain, in a desperate attempt, already too late, to save her own life. But the murderer held on to her wrist as he tried to make another cut in her neck. And when he saw that she was weakened by the loss of blood and the shock of what had happened to her, he took her by the hair and he made the second cut on her throat, completing . . . what he wanted to do. The expert witnesses described all that.

'Now, Roberto Morales sits here before you accused of manslaughter and rape and murder. But before I say more about the specific crimes that are charged against him, I want to talk about the two stories you've heard over the past days, and the two men who told you those stories.

'The defendant and his lawyer want you to believe that the defendant had an amicable parting with Mariah Dodge after she broke up with him. They want you to believe that she made love with this man, the same man she told her friends made her feel dirty. They want you to take the defendant's word for it when he says that when he arrived at the office that night Mariah Dodge was already dead. And they want you to believe him when he says he doesn't know where he went or what he did after that. It's a story full of vagueness and holes and illogic.

'But that isn't all the defendant and his lawyer want you to believe. Ms Miller has had to make up a complex story about Juan Alvaro as well, to explain away his testimony, which so completely contradicts the defendant. She has had to concoct a whole complicated lie-producing system to attack the plain truth spoken here by Juan Alvaro.

'Ms Miller would have you believe that lying is a complex

art, but it isn't. Lying is simple and brutal. Roberto Morales's lie is inevitable – it's the only story he has. Except, of course, the truth. In the Bible it says: *the truth shall make you free*. In a spiritual sense I suppose this applies to Roberto Morales as much as to anyone. But not in the legal sense. Not for this defendant.' Pointing at him again. 'For Roberto Morales, the truth shall put him in prison. And so he sits here before you and lies.

'Let's look at how he came up with the lie he told here:

'He was at the office that night, so he can't prove he was somewhere else.

'Ramon Santos saw him arrive at some time around eight, so he can't say he was never there.

'Walter Boynton saw him leave between nine and ten so he can't say he came and left right away.

'So he says the only thing he can say – I came and I stayed awhile.

'Now it gets even tighter for him. He's in an area where he has a choice. He could tell the same story that you heard from Juan Alvaro, up to the point where there are no more witnesses, and begin his lie there. He could say that he left the office right after Juan Alvaro did, when Mariah was still alive, and that he knows nothing about what happened after that.

'If he tells that story, he has to hope you will believe that relatively soon after he was gone an unknown person came and raped and murdered Mariah Dodge. But even though his lawyer has come up with a candidate – a sort of symbolic candidate, a stand-in for unknown and unknowable hordes of suspects' – voice full of ridicule – 'that's a theory not much different from blaming invaders from Mars. And the idea that Juan Alvaro faked a rape and killed his closest friend is even more farfetched.

'So that story won't fly, and the defendant has to do what he did: claim that Mariah Dodge was dead when he got there and that he spent the time he was there not arguing with her, slashing her clothes, raping her and cutting her throat, but grieving over her death. The big problem with *that* story is Juan Alvaro, who can testify that it's not true. But when the defendant was deciding which lie to tell, he knew that Juan Alvaro was fleeing his own demons and hadn't been heard from for years. So the defendant gambled that Juan Alvaro wouldn't come back from wherever he was hiding, and that if he did come back he could be discredited.

'That left the defendant with only one problem: explaining the semen left on Mariah Dodge's body when he raped her. They had been lovers, so that part of the lie might have been easy, except for the fact that she told her friends she was going to break up with him, as her friends testified.

'So the defendant added an afternoon spent with Mariah at his secret apartment, with a noisy breakup followed by a farewell interlude of lovemaking. He created this with the help of the late Mr Censabella, a man the defendant admits he paid hundreds of dollars every week for watering his plants.' A smile at what a ridiculous notion that was.

'Luckily for the defendant, we didn't get to see poor Mr Censabella, who had the misfortune to die only a few days before he was scheduled to testify. And when you don't get to see a witness testify it's hard to judge how believable he is.' Estrada took a defensive breath, anticipating an objection to his implication that the death and the testimony might be connected. None came. 'We have only Mr Censabella's words to go by, read aloud by a court reporter far younger and clearer-minded than he was.' Still no objection. Miller was letting it pass, possibly in deference to the custom of not objecting during summation but more likely to avoid calling attention to it.

'But even Mr Censabella's naked words tell us that he was generally befuddled about the things he saw and heard,' Estrada went on. 'And confused about when he saw and heard them. Still, the late Mr Censabella, who was on the defendant's payroll, is the only peg the defendant has to hang that crucial part of his story on.

'So there it is, crudely put together from the materials at hand: one story for a defendant. The story that goes: We argued and we made love in the afternoon. She didn't want to wash, or she didn't have time – he seems to want to have it both ways on that one – and when I got to her office later that night she was dead and I went into a funk and stayed awhile, and then wandered around and didn't tell anyone what I'd seen because I was afraid no one would believe me. And if I didn't try to help her and I didn't do anything to help catch the killer . . . well, he doesn't really have an explanation for *that* part of his story, does he?

'Can you imagine that, ladies and gentlemen? This man who expresses tender sentiments for the deceased wants you to believe that he made no attempt to get close to his beloved, though he admits that for all he knew she could still have been saved. Even so, he did not get close enough to see if she was alive or dead. According to *his story* he did not get close enough to soil his shoes with her blood.

'And then he fled and he told no one. Warned no one. Called no ambulance. Called no police. Why? Because, he wants you to believe, he was in a fog.

'There's nothing cleverly put together about any of that. It's a crude and obvious lie. Unfortunately for the defendant, it's the only lie available to him. It's the lie he *has* to tell.

'And bear in mind that Roberto Morales is a man who lies even when he doesn't have to. Right here, on the witness stand in his own murder trial, he lied about something completely unrelated to his guilt or innocence. A lie in which he was caught, as I'll remind you in a moment.

'I said earlier that you're being asked to choose which of these two men is telling the truth and which isn't. How do you make such a judgment?

'We all judge liars and truth-tellers every day of our lives; you don't need any lessons from me. We watch people to see how they act. We listen to what they say to see if it makes sense, and if it agrees with other things that we know. And we weigh any other evidence we have about their truthfulness or their lack of truthfulness, especially in similar situations.

'You saw the two men testifying here. You saw how they behaved. Juan Alvaro was emotional. The things he said had meaning to him.

'Roberto Morales sat here cool and easy. Not only when he was on the witness stand – he sat here cool and easy for the whole trial. Nothing made Roberto Morales angry, nothing filled him with grief. Oh, sure, he pulled a long face or two, but that man was in control of himself the whole time. Even when he was caught lying on the witness stand. And make no mistake about it, he was caught lying when he was up there.

'I'm not talking about the big lie, the lie that's at the heart of his defense, the lie that he's been telling for four years. The lie that he *has* to tell because his freedom depends on it. That lie – the lie that he did not kill Mariah Dodge, the lie that he has rehearsed for so long, and so often, that it's second nature to him now – that lie is one that he was prepared to be challenged on.

'No, when I talk about his getting caught lying here on the witness stand, I'm talking about the small lie, the *unnecessary* lie. The defendant wanted you to believe that he was proud of himself and his heritage. He wanted you to believe that his reaction to ethnic slurs was just the kind of reaction any person proud of his heritage would have. *I am who I am*. That's what he said. But the fact is that when he said that he was trying to sneak a lie past us all. And he got caught.

'What was the lie? The lie that Roberto Morales never tried to pass as what he wasn't. The lie that he didn't try to cover up who he was. That he wasn't ashamed of his heritage.

'Being ashamed of your heritage,' Estrada was surprised to hear himself say, 'being ashamed of your heritage is a powerful thing, ladies and gentlemen, more powerful than we sometimes imagine.' He heard the emotion in his voice, knew he was in danger of getting carried away by his own history. A father who made a lie of his own life and the lives of his children. A mother who . . . He focused on the jury, waiting to hear him continue. 'Being ashamed of who he was was one of the things that drove Roberto Morales to murder, and he himself told us about it.

'*I am a hero*. That's what he said to Mariah Dodge when she challenged him about the ways he was betraying his people. Juan Alvaro reported that to us, and even in Ms Miller's complicated theories about stories cleverly put together out of pieces of other, truer stories, she has to admit that Juan Alvaro is an accurate reporter.

'And what did Roberto Morales do when he got caught in that unnecessary lie? He let us know how he deals with the truth. He's got whole families and hierarchies of lies, does Roberto Morales. Significant lies and insignificant lies. Lies he thinks of as lies and lies he doesn't think of as lies. One thing is clear – lying is a familiar part of his life.

'*I am a hero*. That's what mattered to Roberto Morales. To be a hero, to be a symbol. But only if it served his purposes. If it served his purposes to be a coward, that was okay, too. But he didn't want you to know that. And he forgot that he'd already admitted it to me.

'You can check this. Have the testimony read back. Roberto Morales was on the witness stand, under oath. I asked him a simple question about his early days in real estate. I said: "You were able to succeed because you pretended to be an Anglo, a norteamericano." And he didn't answer. So I prodded him. I asked the same question in a slightly different form. I said: "You pretended not to be what you are." This time, he answered. He said "No."

'Frankly, I was surprised to hear him say no, because I had good reason to expect him to say yes. So I gave him another chance. *You didn't?* I said. *You didn't pretend to be an Anglo?* And that's when he said, *I am who I am.*'

This felt good, this was something to relish. Nailing the bastard.

'*I am who I am*. The problem with that answer is not only

that it's a lie, but that he and I had talked about the very same subject in an earlier conversation, when he had promised to tell the truth. There was no jury then, but Roberto Morales had promised to tell the truth all the same, and he told a different story then from the one he swore to here. As you may remember, I had to remind him of that. It took me several questions, and you can have them read back any time you want.

'This man who said that he picked places where there was prejudice against another race, who hid behind local contractors, who tried to look white and took care to be respectful, all so the neighbors wouldn't worry, this is the same man who sat here and said, full of self-righteousness, *I am who I am*. He said that so you would admire him. He said that so you would see how upright and honest he was. But he was lying when he said it. Lying and caught at it.

'You can't say anything like that about Juan Alvaro. Nothing he said here was a lie. Nothing he said here was contradicted by anyone but the defendant himself, except for poor Mr Censabella's opinion that he had seen Mariah Dodge at the apartment that afternoon.

'The defendant's lawyer tells you that Juan Alvaro made up a story. Why would he do that? She wants you to believe he did it to get back at Roberto Morales for . . . something. And that he did it to fool the D.A.'s office into giving him immunity.

'But consider the immunity that Juan Alvaro is getting. There are many kinds of immunity. We hear that word and we take it at its everyday meaning. Juan Alvaro is immune, he's free and clear, nothing can touch him. Not so. Some immunity works like that, but not all. Juan Alvaro has his immunity – both from the District Attorney and the U.S. Attorney – as part of contracts he made with those two offices. He only gets his immunity if he tells the truth. If he were to lie, the deal would be off. If he were to lie he would get indicted for perjury. Not only that but, according to the deal he made, lying means that everything he's said that's incriminating can be used against him. If Juan Alvaro had it in mind to lie he would have been better off, far better off, to have stayed where he was and let the wheels of justice do their grinding without him.

'Besides if he's lying to hurt Roberto Morales or for whatever other reason the defendant's lawyer wants you to believe, he could have put together a much better lie. He could have said that the defendant admitted the financial misdeeds Mariah Dodge was accusing him of. He could have said he actually witnessed Roberto Morales doing the killing and that he kept silent until now because he was afraid for his own life. Unlike Roberto Morales, who has only one lie he can tell, Juan Alvaro has multiple choice.

'But Juan Alvaro isn't telling *any* of those lies. He's telling the truth.

'The defendant's lawyer wants you to believe that Juan Alvaro could have killed Mariah Dodge. But to suggest, as Ms Miller does, that Juan Alvaro came here to tell this story because *he* is the murderer is the most ridiculous of all. Juan Alvaro doesn't have immunity for murder, or any violent crime, and he can't get it. If he were the killer he would be putting his own neck in the noose. For what? Juan Alvaro was long gone. He was history as far as the NYPD was concerned. *In the wind*, the police call it. If he were the killer would he come here? It's not worthy of belief.

'The defendant's lawyer heaped scorn and vituperation on Juan Alvaro. By her tone of voice as well as her choice of words she made it clear she wants you to think of him as lower than God's lowest creature.

'This treatment cannot have come as a surprise to Juan Alvaro. He had to know that it would happen. Juan Alvaro has struggled for years to put behind him the mistakes he made. And they were mistakes, no question about that. And those mistakes were no less grievous because Juan Alvaro's young partners were paid, and they were not innocent boys.

What they were doing can only have been out of desperation, and for him to have patronized them was only to exploit that desperation.

'But that has nothing to do with testifying at a murder trial. Nothing except this – the last thing Juan Alvaro needed or wanted was to have all of the shameful mistakes in his past paraded before the world.

'Immunity? Sweetheart deal? Getting back at his enemy? I said it before: He could have stayed where he was and lived peacefully and unchallenged. For more than three years he was content to stay where he was. Only one thing changed: during that time he saw that if he did not come forward, Roberto Morales might get away with murder. So he made the hard decision, and he chose to endure public humiliation, and to suffer a lifelong stigma. Why would he make that choice? Because his conscience would not have rested otherwise.

'Yes, he is being given a sort of immunity. And yes, in the past he has been guilty of a particular kind of cowardly and exploitive act. But that's the past. Consider what he is doing now. What he has done here in this courtroom, exposing himself to shame and ridicule for the sake of the truth, is genuinely an act of courage.

'Both Juan Alvaro and Roberto Morales lied to the world about behavior related to sex. The behavior that made Roberto Morales lie is not so unpleasant, not so shameful in the eyes of the world as Juan Alvaro's. In some places arrangements like the one between Roberto and Marti Morales are commonplace. But Roberto Morales lied about that just as he lied about so many other things. Including the very essence of who he was. By his own admission, as we have seen, Roberto Morales is a man who cynically used his ethnic identity when it could do him good and hid it when he thought it might cause him problems. By his own admission, Roberto Morales lied about almost everything. His whole life was a lie.

'Not Juan Alvaro. Juan Alvaro only lied about and because

of one thing. Any dishonest behavior of his had its source in shame about the way he had at times acted out his sexuality. That's why he lied about it and concealed it from friends and employers. It's even why he let himself be forced into helping with the financial misdeeds at Phoenix Enterprises, even though he refused to take the money offered to him for the minor and mechanical part he played in those dishonest goings-on.

'By coming here to testify, Juan Alvaro has exposed to the world everything about that part of him that makes him feel ashamed.

'So here you are, with one man with a sadly flawed past whose demeanor says he's telling the truth, who has told you a story that is believable and consistent and is far from the most damaging story he could make up about Roberto Morales if he wanted to lie. A man who has no motive to lie to you and every reason to stay away from this courtroom. Every reason to stay away, except for his desire to see his closest friend's murderer brought to justice.

'And in contrast you have another man who has an apparently exemplary past – a past that turns out to be built on lies – whose demeanor is artificially controlled, who you know has lied to you about something with no direct bearing on his guilt, something he could freely have told the truth about. And this man has told a story that flies in the face of common sense and of the evidence you've heard. A story that is the only one he could tell under the circumstances – except the truth. A man who has the strongest possible motive to lie to you – the truth would put him in prison.

'All you need to do to reach a verdict is pick one of these men to believe.

'But don't let me mislead you, it's not that this is some kind of debating contest. You've heard other evidence, some of it supporting one side or the other. The defendant's testimony is corroborated in small part by the late Mr Censabella, a man the defendant was paying significant amounts of money to help him in his lies.'

'Objection.'

'Sustained. Ladies and gentlemen, no one testified that the defendant paid anyone to lie. Be careful, Mr Estrada.'

'I will, your honor.' He took a break and turned back to the jury.

'Juan Alvaro's story is supported by evidence from people with no reason to help him. His story is consistent with the testimony of Ramon Santos. Ramon didn't want to testify here, but the truth is the truth, however reluctantly conveyed. And Juan Alvaro's story is consistent with the testimony of Walter Boynton, who has no reason to do anything here but tell the truth.

'The defendant's lawyer would have you believe that either story is consistent with the testimony of Lynne Schelling and Carlyn Sims. If you think about it you will see that it's not true. Ms Schelling and Ms Sims spoke of more than the Punch-and-Judy breakup the defendant described here. They spoke of a woman who found her former lover intolerable.

'From the totality of the evidence, and from common sense, if you have to pick one of these men as a truth-teller and one as a liar – and the differences in their stories leave you no choice – I submit that Juan Alvaro is the only possible candidate for truth-teller.

'All right, you might say, suppose he *is* telling the truth. His story stops short of the murder itself. Doesn't that leave room for a different murderer, someone other than Roberto Morales? I won't deny there's a gap in the story. But how much doubt does that gap create? Not much, is the answer. Not enough to be a reasonable doubt.

'It's true that no one came back from the offices of Phoenix Enterprises and reported that he or she actually saw this crime. But don't make the mistake of thinking that you can't convict the defendant just because we have no eyewitness to the crime itself. The judge will tell you that isn't so. If it were, we'd be in trouble convicting a big percentage of murderers. It's something we talked about at the beginning, and you agreed you could convict without an eyewitness.

'I once heard a defense lawyer say: murder is just assault with one fewer witness. The witness who's missing in a murder, the *victim*, is the most important witness of all, especially when the murder is committed in private. Then, if the killer doesn't confess, we have to deduce what happened from whatever evidence – whatever legally admissible evidence – we can muster. Because the victim's tongue is stilled forever.

'But though Mariah Dodge cannot speak to us directly, her wounds cry out. They cry out but they cannot tell us who her killer is unless we listen with special ears. We have to listen carefully to her wounds and to the other indignities she suffered.

'We have to listen to the semen on Mariah Dodge's body as, with help from the technique of DNA-printing, it tells us the name of Roberto Morales. And we have to listen to the semen on her body as it tells us, with help from the testimony of Carlyn Sims and Lynne Schelling, that Mariah Dodge would not have had sex willingly with Roberto Morales that day, and she would certainly not have walked around with his semen on her body.

'The judge is going to tell you to consider whether the testimony you hear is reasonable. This part of the defendant's story isn't even close to reasonable. Mariah Dodge told not one but at least two of her friends that she had reached the point where being with Roberto Morales made her feel dirty. She told them that she was sorry she ever let him touch her. *Being with him* made her feel dirty. Made her skin crawl. Do you suppose she would let him have sex with her, much less play with the results and walk around with the residue on her body?

'We need to listen as well to the position that Mariah Dodge's body was found in and to the condition of the room around it. Here, too, we have the help of experts and trained observers. We have the testimony of the Crime Scene Unit experts – which you heard by stipulation, because the defendant accepts that testimony. The Crime Scene Unit says there was no sign of a struggle in Mariah Dodge's office. And the medical examiner says that the only signs of physical resistance came after or at the same time as the first cut in her neck. The fatal cut. The cut that took Mariah Dodge completely by surprise.

'But that was after she was raped. The medical experts told us that. Just as they told us that she was not struggling when the cut on her cheek was made. Whoever made that cut was able to get close enough to her to make that cut without any struggle. The defendant's lawyer told you about a man who worked once a month or so as a night security guard. There is no way in the world this man could have gotten near Mariah Dodge under circumstances that would have allowed him to make that first cut. It's completely unreasonable. It's beyond any belief.

'And what about the end table? Ms Miller is silent about it, because she can't explain it. Why did her imaginary killers wipe off the end table with a crumpled piece of paper? Even invaders from Mars wouldn't do that. But Roberto Morales would. He would because that end table is where the letter was. The letter that Juan Alvaro told us about. The incriminating letter. So on his way out he picks it up and he crumples it and he wipes the table to remove any sign that the letter was ever there and that he ever touched the table. Thinking to cut the only tie that bound him to that murder scene, just as he cut Mariah Dodge's throat. But he didn't do as complete a job with that as he did on Mariah Dodge, because we know, if we think about it, that he is the only person with a reason to do that.'

Estrada looked at the jurors. He had been thinking of them for so long as a group, as a force for good or evil, that he had forgotten that they were people. Now, for some reason, he saw them clearly: not so much as a beautician, a car salesman, an engineer, a teacher, and all the rest, but as people sitting in a place where they had not chosen to be, performing a chore they did not relish, and doing it with good will despite all that.

'I said in my remarks at the start of the trial that motive is not a part of these crimes. The judge is going to tell you that, too. The People don't have to prove the defendant's motive. We don't have to look inside his head to see why he did what he did. But the defendant's lawyer has raised a question that I want to help you answer. She asked why a person who has everything Roberto Morales has would risk it all by raping and murdering his former girlfriend in response to some insults and a threat to uncover financial manipulations which he denies he had anything to do with.

'Her question implies that there ought to be something rational in all this. That if the People can't offer you a rational explanation for the defendant's outrageous actions, that somehow that makes the People's case weaker. I submit to you that there is no truth to that. It's an attempt by the defendant's lawyer to confuse you.

'Let me be clear about this: the People are not contending that Roberto Morales was acting rationally when he killed Mariah Dodge, or when he raped her. Rational people don't rape and kill.

'And we have evidence that Roberto Morales, for all his achievements, for all that he has earned respect in some quarters, is not always a rational person. Here on the witness stand, as I've shown you, he could not restrain himself from lying about small and unimportant matters. Why does a person do that? It's hardly rational. Here, where everything depends on his convincing you that he is telling the truth, where his future hangs on getting away with the big lie despite its complete implausibility, he risks telling a small lie? Why? Could he think that telling a big lie makes him immune to discovery when he tells a small one?'

He thought again of Big Jim Estrada and José Peña, and drew from his own pain a stronger link to the truth of his argument. 'There's a key here to this man's mind. What does Roberto Morales tell us about himself by telling this lie? He tells us that his whole life depends on appearances. And that when his idea of what he should *appear* to be is threatened, he behaves irrationally and self-destructively. Because if that little lie he told here was anything, it was self-destructive. Self-destructive and irrational.

'Roberto Morales is a contradiction – a man ashamed of what he is and ashamed of that shame. A man who wants to be a hero. A man who insists on it, who *says* I am a hero. I *am* a hero. A man to whom appearances are so instinctively important that he will risk everything on a point of no significance.

'And look what he faced on the night he killed Mariah Dodge. She was threatening everything that mattered to him. She was going to expose him as a fraud. She was going to show that he was an exploiter of the very people for whom he claimed he was a hero. Never mind the criminal charges that might come out of it: he can hire expensive lawyers to deal with that—'

'Objection,' Miller said, breaking his rhythm.

'Sustained. Ladies and gentlemen, the defendant has a right to counsel, and what he pays or doesn't pay is none of anybody's business.'

Estrada took a moment and started again. 'What mattered to Roberto Morales when he was confronted by Mariah Dodge was that she would destroy his status as a *hero*. Now that he had decided that being the savior of his people was what he wanted, she threatened that. Not only did she threaten it, she demeaned it. She laughed at it.

'And to make matters even worse from his point of view, she demeaned his manhood, too. She demeaned his manhood in front of a man whose own manhood Roberto Morales holds in contempt and worse than contempt.

'Did Roberto Morales have a motive? Sexual and romantic rejection are classic motives for murder. Surely we have that here, but that is only the beginning. Mariah Dodge threatened everything that mattered to Roberto Morales. Mariah Dodge was going to make him a laughingstock, a public object of ridicule and scorn. She was going to do all this to a man who cares so much about the smallest aspect of his public image that to defend it he risks being convicted of murder, destroying the very thing he's presumably trying so hard to protect.

'Being held up to public ridicule is also a classic motive for murder. For Roberto Morales it is a motive multiplied many times.

'Is it rational? No. No, it's not rational. It's kind of scary, in fact. It raises the question of whether it could happen again if Roberto Morales were allowed—'

'Objection!' Miller said. 'That's completely inappropriate, as the prosecutor knows perfectly well.'

'That's true,' Martinez affirmed. 'Ladies and gentlemen, please disregard those last remarks. And Mr Estrada, put a leash on it.'

'Yes, your honor,' Estrada said, and to the jury: 'Not rational. An act of outrage and anger. And fear. It's visceral, it comes from someplace deep inside. It's an immediate response to a threat and an affront. You've seen it here in a much smaller, more controlled version. It has nothing to do with rational, but it's what killed Mariah Dodge.'

Estrada stopped and turned pages in his notes, squared them up on the lectern. It was time to return to the formula.

'When you go into the jury room to deliberate, you're going to have three crimes to consider: rape in the first degree, manslaughter in the first degree, and murder in the second degree. Justice Martinez will explain these in detail to you after lunch, and tell you how to proceed. But it's part of my job to help you see how the evidence proves each and every one of these crimes. To do that, I'm going to ask you to look one more time at the photographs of this crime.' He waited while Rosen and a court officer set up an easel holding the blown-up photos.

Estrada started with first-degree rape – sexual intercourse by forcible compulsion – showing the jury a closeup of the X cut into Mariah Dodge's cheek and one of her slashed clothing. For manslaughter he showed them enlarged closeups of her neck. Two of the jurors looked away. He took the photo off the easel and put it on the floor resting against the easel legs: no longer prominently displayed, but not out of sight, either. When it came to the second degree murder charge, he made a chart:

RAPE or ATTEMPTED RAPE	+	CAUSED DEATH	=	MURDER

'Once you have decided that Roberto Morales raped or even tried to rape Mariah Dodge, and once you have decided that he also caused her death, the rest is essentially automatic. A specific intention to kill is not required for this crime. If the killing took place at all close in time to the primary crime of rape or attempted rape in the first degree, that's all that is required.

'If he killed her to silence her cries, real or anticipated, if he killed her to keep her from telling the police or anyone else that he raped her, if he killed her because she was resisting, if he killed her in fury because she did not respond, if he killed her as part of the same angry act that prompted the rape, if he killed her so she could not delay his escape . . . As long as he killed her close in time to the rape for virtually any reason related however remotely to the rape or its precursors or his concern about its consequences – even if he killed her without intending to – he is guilty of murder in the second degree. He is guilty of murder in the second degree, as her honor will tell you, even if you do not or would not find him guilty of manslaughter.

'The evidence is clear that Roberto Morales is guilty of murder in the second degree.

'I told you, and the judge will tell you, that the People are obligated by law to prove these charges beyond a reasonable doubt. The defendant's lawyer told you that you should doubt the defendant's guilt because the defendant's story offers a denial of that guilt, and – though she didn't put it this way – because you can distort almost all the other evidence so the defendant's story is not completely inconsistent with it. But that causes a doubt only if you believe Roberto Morales. And, as we have seen, he is most definitely not to be believed.

'The fact that he made up a story does not create a doubt. When a guilty defendant takes the witness stand, all he can do is make up a story. The very point of doing that is to create a doubt. That's what he's there for, and he couldn't have a stronger motive to lie. He's up there to save himself. He told the truth about that. But that doesn't mean he told the truth about anything else.

'Because Juan Alvaro did not see Roberto Morales kill Mariah Dodge, the defendant's lawyer also wants you to create doubt out of the idea of someone like Kenneth Charles lurking out in the hallway, having coincidentally come upon Mariah Dodge . . . But that is a doubt so remote, so contrived, that it is not worth considering.

'The judge will tell you what we mean by reasonable doubt. She'll tell you it's a doubt that would affect your decision in a matter of importance in your own life. I ask you, would fear of a Kenneth Charles out there in the world somewhere affect anything you did in your life? Kenneth Charles and the other phantoms like him are the very definition of a doubt that is *not* reasonable. A phantom killer. A man who is conveniently not even in this courtroom. Kenneth Charles or a player to be named later. I said it before, you might as well blame this on invaders from Mars. By no means a *reasonable* doubt.

'Ladies and gentlemen, this is not a case that needs to be decided by fine shadings of doubt. If you believe Roberto Morales, you have to acquit him. If you believe Juan Alvaro, as the evidence indicates you must, then there can be no doubt that Roberto Morales is guilty. There can be no doubt at all.

'We know Roberto Morales is guilty beyond a reasonable doubt by virtue of the evidence offered by the prosecution witnesses. But we know he is guilty beyond *any* doubt because he felt the need to get up here and lie to you.

'If he were not guilty, he would have no need to lie.

'The evidence shows that Roberto Morales is guilty of rape in the first degree. The evidence shows that Roberto Morales is guilty of manslaughter in the first degree. The evidence shows that Roberto Morales is guilty of murder in the second degree.

'At the beginning of this trial I asked each of you to promise that if we proved our case beyond a reasonable doubt you would not hesitate to return a verdict of guilty. At this time I hold you to those promises in the name of the People of the State of New York, and in the interest of justice.'

21

Estrada was drained when he sat down. He checked his watch and saw that there was enough time left in the morning for Martinez to charge the jury if she was willing to give them and herself a late lunch. 'I'm going to call a lunch recess now,' she said. 'Ladies and gentlemen, I want you to come back promptly at two, and at that time I'll tell you the law and give the instructions you need for your deliberations, and you can begin. I caution you now very strongly not to discuss the case with each other or with anyone else. I know you're impatient, but you do need to be properly charged before you can start.'

The cluster of reporters demanding comment was denser than usual and far more insistent. There were more questions than he would have liked about his dismissal of Kenneth Charles as a possible murderer. Didn't that fit all the evidence? Molly O'Hara demanded, looking uncomfortably like one of the Dodge sisters. Wasn't it possible that if Morales lied it was simply out of fear that the truth would *not* set him free even though he was innocent?

'I don't see it that way,' Estrada told her. 'But my opinion doesn't count anymore. From now on it's up to the jury.'

The office seemed aswarm with excited people, euphoric simply because the active part of the trial was over. Estrada endured their congratulations and invented last-minute preparations in order to avoid joining everyone for a lunch he could not possibly have eaten.

His mail had been delivered while he was in court, the usual interoffice nonsense and ads for law books and conferences and prosecutors' associations. And a letter already opened and read by his guardians, written in Spanish with a broad-nib fountain pen in an elegant, old-fashioned hand.

My esteemed grandson,
This old man is sorry to have made trouble in your life. I regret that your dear mother has so much unhappiness because of my story. I am very proud to have such a grandson, and I am very sad that your grandmother – God grant her happiness – cannot see you as I can.
Go with God,
José Peña Escobar (Estrada)

There was a knock on his door. 'Go away, I'm busy,' Estrada said without looking up.

'Just take a second,' Lawrence Kahn said. 'That was a good job you did in there. A little on the emotional side, but I think it worked. Good thing the diary didn't come up more than it did. I told you it was a waste of time. But I have to say, I was proud to be there.'

'Thanks.' Estrada reached for the phone so he would not have to say anything else.

Judge Martinez spent the first minutes of the afternoon in an informal talk to the jury, explaining the deliberation process and the verdict form they would be using to record their votes. Then she gave them their formal charge, explaining each count of the indictment and the relevant law. She talked to them at length about the standards they could use to decide whether a witness was telling the truth or not – including the charge that the defendant had an interest in the outcome of the trial and the jury might consider that interest in determining the credibility and weight they gave to his testimony. It was the mildest version of that charge she could have given, a response to constant pressure from Miller, who had argued that the general interested-witness charge was enough by itself, and that there was no need to single out the defendant for special mention.

Martinez told the jury that where two witnesses' testimony disagreed, they did not necessarily have to accept everything said by one of the witnesses and reject everything said by the other, but could pick and choose as long as they did not accept two specifically contradictory pieces of testimony.

She repeated that Morales was to be presumed innocent unless and until they decided that the prosecution had proved otherwise beyond a reasonable doubt. Her explanation of the standard of proof was no worse for Estrada than it had to be, but it was one that he always dreaded. The judge's charge on circumstantial evidence made him wince, too.

'There are two kinds of evidence,' she said. 'Direct and circumstantial. Direct evidence is the report of the witness's perceptions through her own senses, or his own senses. If I describe what I can see from this bench – sixteen people sitting in an enclosure on my left, two small groups of people at tables in front of me, a roomful of other people in pews beyond a rail, and armed men in blue trousers and white shirts watching over it all – that's all direct evidence. It's what I can see. That there is a trial going on in this room is an inference you might draw from being given that direct evidence. That inference is what we mean by circumstantial evidence. Scientific evidence, photographic evidence, all that is direct evidence. If you believe it, you can draw inferences from it. In a case of an armed robbery with a gun, if a fingerprint expert tells the jury that a fingerprint on the gun matched a fingerprint of the defendant in twelve significant points, and that there's only a one-in-so-many-million chance of such a match, then if you believe that the matching was done properly, you have direct evidence that the fingerprints matched. It is *not* direct evidence that the defendant ever held the gun. That requires an inference, and where an inference is required that is what we call circumstantial evidence. So the fingerprints are circumstantial evidence that the defendant held that gun. As it happens, we take that particular circumstantial evidence to be so strong, to exclude so thoroughly all other inferences, that it's hard to remember it is circumstantial evidence. Does everyone understand?'

She waited for them to nod that they did. To Estrada's eyes, several of them looked blankly confused, but there was nothing to be done about it. Their fellow jurors would explain, or try to, if it ever became a point of contention among them. That depended on what came next.

'Where proof of guilt is based on circumstantial evidence,' Martinez continued, 'as it is in this trial, where no one testified to having seen the crime committed, the law requires that each and every one of the circumstantial facts from which the inference of the defendant's guilt is drawn must be inconsistent with his innocence. We say that all the circumstantial facts must not only point in the direction of guilt, they must exclude *to a moral certainty* every reasonable hypothesis *but* guilt.

'I'm going to repeat that so I'm sure you have it down, and don't hesitate to ask to have it read back if necessary.'

And repeat it she did, slowly and with emphasis on every word. She did not leave it at that, but broke it down further, pointing out, among too many other things for Estrada's comfort, that no inference could properly be drawn from circumstantial evidence unless each and every fact necessary to support that inference had been proven beyond a reasonable doubt. Listening to her, Estrada wondered why she did not simply direct a verdict for the defendant.

He knew that in reality the circumstantial-evidence charge did nothing worse than repeat the need for proof beyond a reasonable doubt, but the meaning of a charge to the jury was as much a matter of emphasis and tone as of literal reality. This time, Estrada was hearing it with especially sensitive ears, and it sounded to him as if no jury listening to those instructions could possibly find *any* defendant guilty.

After the jury left to begin deliberating, Estrada went back to his office. He sat at his desk looking around at piles of papers, files, yellow legal pads covered with notes: all of it meaningless to him now. Direct evidence of a clutter of files and papers, nothing more.

He reached for the phone to call Michelle but his hand drew back. The pain of their last time together – temporarily walled off – broke through to him again.

He thought about his failure to yell and throw things, or whatever was right to do. Get mad, Mahoney had told him. But he wasn't raging with anger. He felt . . . unreal. This was happening to him but it had an otherworldly quality. As a college actor he had once played a man confronting his wife about a suspected infidelity: *Not caring is a lot like not loving*, the character had said. Joe Estrada cared. And maybe he was more angry than he knew.

He fired darts at Morales's face and watched as they bounced off the board.

'Hey,' Lou Collins said, coming in the door. 'People get hurt that way.' He looked at Estrada. 'Or is that the idea?'

The bureau chief dumped a stack of file folders on Estrada's desk. 'Something to do while you're waiting for the verdict. Micki Becker went rock climbing last weekend and got herself in traction and we have a speedy-trial problem with some of her cases, so I'm kind of passing them around.'

Estrada let the files sit. He had his September monthly report to do, and the *Morales* files and papers needed sorting before they got put away. And he was nowhere near ready for anything new.

There was no word from the jury before dinner. Estrada went out with Mahoney.

'You did good,' his friend told him.

'Emotional enough for you?'

'I liked it.'

'That's what counts.' They toasted each other. 'Better days,' Estrada said.

'Fuck the days,' Mahoney came back. 'Let's see some better nights.'

Estrada thought about Michelle, due in the next evening for her one-day visit, decided not to bring it up. There was nothing new to say. He and Mahoney talked about the baseball playoffs. Having missed most of the season, Estrada had no clear idea who was doing what to whom, but it was easy enough to pick up the essentials from what Mahoney was saying and soothing to talk about an artificial world where there was little real change from one year to the next.

They walked around to the front of the courthouse on the way back, keeping a discreet distance. There was a loop of demonstrators circulating behind the blue sawhorses, each marcher carrying a lighted candle against the gathering gloom of late dusk – a vigil for Roberto Morales. One man carried a pole from which dangled a male doll, hanging by its neck, a sign bouncing against its chest. Estrada could not read the sign from where they were standing. He did not have to, he knew what it said.

'They're hanging me in effigy. Progress, I guess.'

'Fame is a fleeting thing,' Mahoney declaimed. 'Enjoy it while you can.'

Mahoney left for home and Estrada went back to his office. He did mechanical chores, sorting through the case files and beginning to put them into storage boxes. After an hour he got restless and went upstairs to the courtroom.

There was no line of waiting spectators, but the television crew was still encamped at the end of the hall. Reporters stood in small groups, chatting. They noticed Estrada, but with one exception they did not react. The frenzy was past and no one was looking for a verdict tonight. Estrada waved off the one reporter who seemed inclined to approach him.

The same air of lethargy prevailed inside the courtroom as in the corridor. The spectators' pews were mostly empty. Morales was sitting well back from the defense table, slouched in his chair as he had never been when court was in session, his jacket draped over its back and his sleeves rolled up. Miller, next to him, seemed engrossed in paperwork.

Estrada nodded hello to Tess and her mother and went to join Nancy Rosen at the prosecution table.

'What brings you?' he asked.

'I got so I felt like I was in jail sitting in my office, so I came up here for a change of scenery.'

'Anything interesting while I was gone?'

'Morales took off his jacket. Officer Moore farted and pretended he didn't. A regular madhouse of activity.'

Leaving for the night, Estrada saw Carlos Ramírez in the last row of the gallery. They went to a luncheonette and sat at the counter over coffee.

'I promised you a story,' Ramírez said. 'Are you still interested?'

'To learn how you are the cousin of the man whose birth certificate says you're twins? Very.'

Ramírez smiled. 'It's not so complicated. As I said, not so different from your own history. It begins like this – once long ago in Puerto Rico there was an almost-rich girl who was pregnant. She was pregnant without marriage at a time and in a place where that was not a possible state for a young woman. So she went away and her family thanked God that they found a relative close in blood who was the same age as the poor not-quite-rich girl and only slightly less pregnant: Roberto's mother. They arranged to have her go away to join her cousin, and then some time later Roberto's mother returned home with two sons. Twins, everyone said, with great thanks to a variety of saints. My own mother's family had enough money to pay support for the extra child – at first. But no one imagined that Roberto's mother would run away to New York with both sons.'

'Quite a story.'

'Shame, shame everywhere. In your case and mine, the shame of fornication and illegitimacy. Quaint, here and now, but there, then . . .'

'How long have you known this?'

'Years. Since I first went back to Puerto Rico after college. For all that time I have known that Roberto's mother stole me from my family. I was lucky I met my mother before she died. Not long before, but enough so we had a few precious months together. After her death I became a zealot for Puerto Rican freedom, and then what some would call a terrorist.'

'Why didn't your mother come after you?'

'Where would she have looked? And by then she was engaged to a man who didn't know . . . But she was glad to see me again before she died. That was a precious time for both of us. She was too young to die. But you see that a lot, don't you?' Ramírez finished his coffee and dismounted from his counter stool. 'I thought you would want to know one of the reasons why my concern for Juan Alvaro was stronger for me than the tie of blood I have to my dear cousin Roberto.'

Court the next morning looked a lot like it had after dinner the night before. From the small number of spectators and the lethargy of the press corps, expectations of an early verdict had not increased. Within limits, that was all right with Estrada: he did not think a guilty verdict could come quickly. As long as the jury did not go past two or three days, he would not be worried. Assuming there was nothing distressing in the testimony they asked for, or in the judge's instructions they wanted repeated.

He looked in on the courtroom to see who was there. Tess had Alvaro with her this morning instead of Sylvia. 'Mom decided to stay home. Too much strain sitting here with nothing to distract her, jumping every time the door opened.'

Estrada went back to his office. Not long after he got there, Clemente dropped by. With the cooler weather, he was back in his slightly-out-of-date suits. The cigarettes had disappeared some time during the trial.

'I got a line on Stanley Gilbert,' the detective offered. 'The guy Alvaro says carried the threat from Morales.'

Estrada waited.

'Died two years ago.'

Estrada sat up straight. 'How?'

Clemente popped a mint into his mouth. 'Boating accident.'

'Right. Sure.' Estrada was full of skepticism. 'And that means that unless we can find out what happened to the kid, we're out of luck on the whole issue of witness tampering.'

'Too late to use it on Morales, anyway.' Clemente said. 'Trial's over, if you didn't notice.'

'The murder trial, maybe. But witness tampering has some value. As a way to nail him for conspiracy on the financial stuff, say. In case this one doesn't come out right.'

'You really want to get this guy, don't you?'

'Are you surprised?'

'Well, yeah, a little. Time was, you were going pretty soft on him.'

'Time was, maybe . . . but not anymore.'

'What happened?'

'I got a dose of reality.'

22

The jury sent out a note before lunch asking to hear the entire testimony of Remigio Censabella – his testimony-in-chief and the cross-examination.

'What does it mean?' Tess asked Estrada as they waited for the jury.

'Hard to say. It's better than if they just wanted the defendant's half of it, but if they're focusing on this then we have to presume they're looking for help deciding who to believe.'

'That's not good, right?'

'It's inevitable.' But it wasn't, and he decided not to coddle her. 'Inevitable is too strong. They could have found something convincing when they first heard the testimony, or something in the closing arguments. This probably means that at least some of them are really confused about it, looking for a crutch.'

The judge came back and Estrada went to sit at the prosecution table with Rosen, spared having to decide whether to say what he really feared: that this was not a matter of confusion but persuasion – convinced jurors using this as a way to persuade those less sure of what to believe. That would account for the evenhandedness of asking for all of Censabella's testimony.

'What do you think?' he asked Rosen when the reading was over.

'I gave up trying to analyze jury requests a long time ago,' she told him. 'I never got it right once.'

* * *

He took a walk at lunchtime, over to the Friday greenmarket at City Hall park. Not hungry, he made himself buy a muffin and some fresh-pressed apple juice. It was likely to be a long day.

When he got back to the office he left an outgoing message on his home answering machine so Michelle would know to look for him in court. He did more mindless clerical work, still avoiding the case folders Collins had left him. If he wasn't going to stay in the office, there was not much sense starting new cases. The thought startled him. He had not consciously considered his next step in a long time.

The jury sent out another note. They wanted to hear Morales's testimony about his afternoon lovemaking with Mariah Dodge. Estrada requested some of the cross-examination or a section of Alvaro's testimony for balance, but Martinez turned him down. The jury would hear no more than what they asked for.

'This really isn't good, is it?' Tess asked after the jury had gone back to deliberating.

'Maybe they wanted some comic relief,' Estrada said.

He took another walk. The whole courthouse seemed oppressive to him. On his way back to the office he found Juan Alvaro sitting in one of the blue chairs, waiting for him.

'Can you spare a few minutes?'

Estrada motioned him down the hall. 'We can sit in my office.'

'I wanted to say thank you, and to apologize,' Alvaro began.

'I'm the one who should be saying thank you.' As he had, several times now. 'You did a brave thing.'

'Sure, an act of courage.' Bitter. 'I understand that you said that for the jury's benefit, not mine, but the truth is I was a coward. If I'd've come forward years ago, this whole trial wouldn't have been necessary.'

'The important thing is you came forward now, and you didn't hold anything back. You did a good job – for Mariah, for the People, and for yourself. It'd be crazy to go around now hating yourself for what you did or didn't do years ago.'

'Crazy? I don't know. It fits the pattern.' Improbably, Alvaro smiled. 'That's what this is all about. Hating yourself for what you are. That's why I did what Alex Blair told me to, and that's why I ran. And that's what drove Roberto. It's easy enough to blame society, but ultimately we do it to ourselves, and that's the real shame.'

Estrada thought again of his own father, making up stories about his past, hating himself for what he was.

'Roberto Morales was as bad that way as anybody I ever knew,' Alvaro said. 'You didn't go nearly far enough with it. He wasn't just ashamed, he loathed himself for being a spic. Even Mariah, bless her, cursing him out the way she did, only touched the surface.

'The odd thing was that he could make himself a hero Latino and somehow that didn't keep him from thinking of himself as an Anglo. Better than an Anglo.

'That's really why he killed Mariah – the fury that she would show him to himself the way he really was. In front of me – mariposa, picaflor, maricón. And to threaten to expose him to the rest of the world. He couldn't have lived with it. He would have killed me, too, I think, if it had gone on much longer and I hadn't left.' Alvaro stopped for a moment, looking at the floor. 'It's easy to see all that now. But then, at that moment, I was blinded by my own self-hate.' He looked at the picture of Mariah Dodge. 'God forgive me, I *wanted* to leave that office, to be away from the anger, from the hate and contempt in Roberto's eyes like the hate and contempt in my father's eyes when he found out what I was. And I wanted to be away from Mariah's anger, too.' His eyes met Estrada's. 'She gave me an excuse to leave and I took it. I wake up with that every day.' Alvaro was dry-eyed, but there was a hollowness in his voice.

A call from Collins caught Estrada on his way to dinner at

the jury's usual early hour. 'Stop by the office for a minute?'

Estrada stood at the door, expecting a grilling about his progress on the new cases. Collins was rearranging file folders. 'Bureau meeting on Tuesday,' he said without looking up. 'It's time you rejoined the family. I wanted to be sure you'd be there. Assuming your jury's come in, of course.'

Estrada did not say anything.

'Any progress on those files I gave you?'

Estrada took a breath. 'Lou, in all fairness to everybody, I don't know how long I'm going to be around. I've been thinking of leaving for a long time.' He sounded more tentative than he had thought he would.

Collins put down the file he had in his hand. 'That would be too bad, if you left. I was just talking to Talley about you. He thinks you'd be good in his job when he moves up to bureau chief.'

'You got the promotion?'

'Didn't I tell you?'

Estrada shook his head, knowing that Collins knew he hadn't.

'It's official next week.' Collins picked up the file folder. 'Think it over. Take a few days off after the verdict. You earned it, whatever the jury thinks.'

After dinner Estrada went back to the courtroom. Tess was there, alone. He slid into the empty pew next to her.

'Anything new?'

'Not much. After the last testimony, Miller's husband brought their little boy to court and she played mommy for a while. I couldn't believe it, the lady of steel being maternal.'

'The lady of steel? Is that how you think of her?'

'I'm sure she must be a nice person out of court and not just a collection of contrivances to fool the jury. I don't happen to like her choice of clients, is all.'

'I think she really believed he was innocent, at least at the beginning. I thought he might be, too, if you remember.'

She made a sour face. 'Unfortunately, I do. I never said you were smart, just because I think you're sexy . . .'

'I'd better go sit at my table,' he said, sliding out of the pew.

Tess grinned. 'Why? Do I make you that nervous?'

He was alone at the table, which was fine: some thinking time would be welcome. At the defense table Kassia Miller was knitting, while Morales played cards with Barry Burns and Pancho Castillo. Just like a reporter, Estrada thought.

'Joe?' a familiar voice called quietly. He turned, half-rose, to see Michelle at the rail, leaning toward him. Her carry-on was on the floor next to her. The courtroom was almost deserted. As he went to the rail he glimpsed Tess watching with interest.

'Hi.' He took Michelle's shoulders, intending a public kiss. She embraced him mightily before he could disengage.

'I've been thinking about you so much,' she said.

'I've been thinking about you, too.' Not completely a lie. 'It's going to be another couple of hours here.'

'That's okay. I'll sit in the back and read. Who knows, maybe something exciting will happen.'

'Probably not. The jury isn't giving any sign they're done.' Which would begin to be worrisome if it went on much longer.

Michelle gave him a quick kiss. 'I'll go sit down now. I'm looking forward to later.'

He watched her walk up the aisle, provocative as ever. Turning to go back to his chair he noticed that Tess had left the courtroom.

Nancy Rosen plopped herself into the chair next to him. 'Good evening,' she said, laying a stack of newspapers on the prosecution table. 'Seen these?'

'I've been avoiding newsstands.'

'We're picking up some friends.'

He looked through the stack. There were two morning tabloids: one headline said HERO? over a nearly full-page picture of Morales, and OR NOT! below it. The other headline was: FRAUD RISES FROM THE ASHES.

He pondered them. 'Not bad.' The third paper was *Noticias Diarias*. Its headline said: YO SOY HÉROE.

'You seem to have struck a chord.'

'With the press. That's not my intended audience.' He paged through the articles. 'And they're not saying they think he's guilty. It's more like they're having fun with the idea of another phony Latino.' He folded the papers so the headlines didn't show, in case the jury came back.

The jury stayed out. At ten-thirty the judge's clerk came in to say that they had retired for the night and that they would not resume until ten-thirty in the morning.

There was a cop in plainclothes waiting outside the courtroom for him. 'Mr Estrada? Gil Thomas. I'm your driver tonight.'

'What's this about?'

'Your office got some more threats. I guess they're playing it safe.'

It had been weeks since he'd had to put up with a constant police escort. He wasn't eager to start again. 'Thanks, Gil, but I don't think . . .'

'I go where they send me. Tonight, you're it. I don't have to be in your apartment, but I've got to be outside, and I've got to drive you around. My relief will take you back in the morning.'

'The trial's over,' Estrada grumbled. 'Too late to shut me up now.'

'There's always revenge.'

They compromised, Estrada and Michelle enjoying the cool night air, the cop crawling along behind them in the issue sedan.

They walked in silence. He could feel her next to him, all of her, could *see* her without turning to look. They crossed Canal Street and walked into Little Italy, past the house where Remigio Censabella had lived and died, then turned west through Soho, passing the blank-faced and forbidding loft buildings that held who-knew-what marvel of art studio or opulent residence.

'Hungry?' Michelle asked. 'Or did you go out when the jury did?'

'I didn't eat much. I never can during deliberations.' She knew that. Or, he had told her that. He no longer had any idea what she knew about him. Maybe he never had.

'We ought to stop,' she suggested. 'There are some great places to eat right near here. That place on Prince Street, with the tile walls? Something with a Z? And I'm starving.'

'You're right,' he said. 'We ought to stop.'

'Okay. Where?'

'No,' he said. 'I mean stop. Really stop, I can't do this. I thought I could, but I was wrong.'

'What are you saying?'

'I'm saying goodbye.'

'What are you talking about? Right here in the street? With your bodyguard in the car three feet away? Goodbye? That's crazy.'

He did not answer. He'd said what mattered.

'Joey! Don't just stand there!' She hit his chest. 'Joey!'

He couldn't move. She grabbed his lapels and shook him. 'Joey, you can't just do that. Not now. We have plans.'

We have plans. But they didn't, not really. *She* had plans, and that was the way it had always been. He existed for her only as a character in her pre-planned domestic drama. Joey the bed partner. Joseph the soon-to-be rich litigator, full of amusing courtroom stories. Her affair in California was only a symptom: he had been slow picking up his cues so she had found a stand-in.

She shook him harder. Her knuckles dug in below his collarbones.

He put his hands on hers, firmly. Squeezed them and pressed them to him to keep her from shaking him anymore. They stood there, immobile, her hands in his between their chests like lovers pledging their troth.

'You're hurting me,' she said in a small voice.

You hurt me, too, he thought. Seeing now why they'd had to play so much phone tag and what she must have meant the time he'd planned to fly out there and she told him it wasn't a great weekend for her. She'd said it herself: I don't tell you everything, either. A symptom. Of the way she lived her life, of the way they had never truly connected with each other. There was nothing to be gained trying to put it into words.

Estrada dropped her hands and walked away.

'Joey,' she called after him. 'Joey, I'm sorry.'

He made himself keep walking. Many dark blocks later he stopped for the car to pull up next to him and he got in.

23

On Saturday morning, Morales's supporters were again holding their vigil outside the courthouse. A much smaller group of counterdemonstrators marched silently in the park across the street carrying signs with legends like NOT MY HERO and JUSTICE FOR MARIAH.

Tess was in the corridor outside the courtroom when he got there. He saw her begin to turn away to avoid him, then change her mind and stand her ground.

'How's the girlfriend?'

'I sent her home.' Trying for casual.

'How sweet. To your house?'

'To her house. In California.'

She looked at him a moment, her expression softening. 'It hurts, doesn't it?'

'Some.'

'Natural enough.'

'That's me, Mr Natural.'

'Don't be hard on yourself. You do all right.' She looked at her shoes. 'If you want some company tonight, it's available . . . no assumptions, no strings.'

He tried to smile. 'I appreciate it, but I don't think so.'

'Right. Alone is probably better. You'll heal, though. Remember that.'

That morning the jury asked for the cross-examination of Juan Alvaro. It did not make Estrada happy.

After that, there was nothing more from the jury until they came back from dinner, when they sent in a note saying that several of them wanted to go to church in the morning. Notes went back and forth about an appropriate church near the Queens motel where they were being sequestered and security arrangements to be sure the sanctity of their deliberations was not breached.

Estrada slept fitfully, went for an unsatisfying swim in a pool crowded with morning regulars. He arrived at court at noon, the time the jury was set to begin the day's work, and found the courtroom almost full, the reporters and news crews tense with anticipation. Nancy Rosen was at the prosecution table, looking worried.

'What's happening?'

'There's a rumor Miller is going to ask for a mistrial.'

'Why?'

'Something about the sermon.'

'I don't believe it. It's not happening.'

Miller marched in with her associate and her client. She was carrying her briefcase instead of her knitting bag, and her face was grimly purposeful. Martinez arrived not long after.

'What is this I hear, Ms Miller?' The judge shifted her shoulders to settle her hastily donned robes, her expression at least as grim as Miller's.

'Your honor, I know we've all been through a lot and it's no time to see it all go down the drain, but I'm afraid I have no choice but to move for a mistrial.'

'Get on with it, please. I don't like the suspense.'

'Your honor, I took the precaution of having a colleague attend the church service that five members of the jury were taken to this morning. He recorded the sermon and played it back for me. I'm sorry to inform the court that its content is such that we can't ignore its influence on the jurors.'

Martinez shook her head, exasperated. 'We warn the clergymen, we always warn the clergymen. All right, let's hear what it's about.'

'Apparently, your honor, the sermon was based on verses from the first chapter of the New Testament book called the General Epistle of James. I have them here. With your permission, I'll read them.'

Martinez, increasingly sour, waved her on.

'Blessed is the man who endureth temptation,' Miller read from a typed transcript. 'For when he is tried' – *when he is tried*, she repeated – 'he shall receive the crown of life, which the Lord hath promised to them that love him. Let no man say when he is tempted, I am tempted of God: for God cannot be tempted with evil, neither tempteth he any man: But every man is tempted, when he is drawn away of his own lust, and enticed. Then when lust hath conceived, it bringeth forth sin: and sin, when it is finished, bringeth forth death.' She read the last verse again. 'Then when lust hath conceived, it bringeth forth sin: and sin, when it is finished, bringeth forth death.'

She paused, and in the wake of her reading the courtroom was silent.

'Your honor, this language speaks directly to the charges made here by the prosecution. We have to assume that any juror of a religious turn of mind hearing those verses and the sermon based on them would have been influenced against Mr Morales.'

'Mr Estrada, can you think of some reason why I shouldn't give serious consideration to this motion?' An appeal, not a challenge: anything to save her from a mistrial.

He stood. 'Your honor,' he began slowly, trying to give himself time to think. 'I didn't hear about this until this minute, and I think that gives my adversary an unfair advantage, but . . . I do think, if I could just have the verses to look at for a moment . . .' He held out his hand to Miller for the transcript. He read it over quickly once and then slowly reread it. And saw what he thought might be an answer.

'Your honor, these verses are about resisting temptation. Specifically, they're about resisting sexual temptation. It's Ms

Miller's contention that her client was nowhere near sexual temptation on the night of the murder. According to her he wasn't there, so he could not have felt lust, which could not beget sin, which could not beget death.'

He glanced over the verses again. 'Also, Ms Miller has made the temptations of Juan Alvaro as pivotal a part of this trial as the lust of Roberto Morales. So I think, in fairness, that if these verses say anything to us they say "a plague on both your houses." No juror would be swayed in either direction by them, but rather, if anything, confirmed in the opinion he or she already held.'

'Thank you, Mr Estrada. That was very helpful.' Martinez looked considerably relieved. 'Here's what I am going to suggest. I am going to have a quiet chat with each of the jurors who went to that service, and then we'll see what we do.'

It took the judge fifteen minutes to decide that the jury had not been contaminated by the words of the Bible. 'I think they were much comforted by the opportunity they were given to pray about the hard choices they had to make, and quite frankly I'm of the opinion that they neither heard nor absorbed most of the sermon. They certainly did not seem to think it had much to do with the case at hand.'

A half hour later, the jury sent out a note. They wanted to hear again the judge's instruction about being able both to believe and disbelieve testimony given by the same witness.

'That's no surprise,' Rosen said as they were waiting for the jury to be brought in. 'We knew this was about who they believed and how much they believed him.'

'Right,' Estrada acknowledged. 'But I don't think we can win if they only believe part of what Alvaro said up there. Look at what else they've asked to hear. Censabella. Morales's testimony about the afternoon lovemaking.'

'And Alvaro's cross-examination,' Rosen added.

'Right. All that about his ugly past . . . I don't like it.'

He watched the jury carefully as they came in, but they all kept their eyes down, looking at none of the participants.

Otherwise, he thought they looked alert and full of energy in the early-afternoon sun streaming through the high windows. Some of them were still in their Sunday clothes.

In a flat voice, Martinez read them the instruction they had asked for. 'Should you in the course of your deliberations conclude that any witness has intentionally testified falsely to a material fact during this trial, you are at liberty to disregard all of his testimony on the principle that one who testifies falsely as to one material fact may also testify falsely to other facts. You are not required, however, in all circumstances to consider such a witness unworthy of belief. You may accept so much of his testimony as you believe to be true and reject only such part as you conclude is false.'

She asked if they had any questions. They conferred silently among themselves and the foreman said that they wanted to hear the last part again.

She read it all. 'I don't want to distort it by reading only part.' Being careful, Estrada thought, not to repeat the kind of mistake that had brought her to grief in the first trial.

The jury left, followed by the judge. Almost everyone else stayed. Estrada thought they were making a mistake. If the jury did not yet know whom to believe, they could not be close to a verdict.

Around four the gallery started to empty out, an exodus prompted by the press as the gradual ebbing of expectation led them all out into the corridor for phone calls, cigarettes and conversation.

Tess called to Estrada from the rail and he got up to join her.

'That was good, about the Bible,' she said. 'Fast on your feet.'

'If I'm not careful, I'm going to drown in compliments.' But he was pleased. 'How's your mom?'

'She wants to be here but she's afraid of what she might do if the verdict goes the wrong way. What do you think it means, that they wanted to hear that instruction again?'

'I think it means they're confused.'

At five, the jury sent out a note: they were at a crucial point in their negotiations – could they have dinner brought to the jury room? Arrangements were made.

Estrada knew he would not be able to eat but he was too edgy to sit in the courtroom. He went out for a walk only to discover that the early-fall evening had suddenly clouded over and rain had begun to fall.

He retreated to the main lobby of the courthouse and was waylaid by a small crowd of reporters looking for comment on the church service. 'I said all I had to say upstairs,' he told them. All he had to say, but not all he thought. In truth, he thought the sermon was like a message aimed straight at the jury. As he had argued in court, it might not change minds, but it would still affect the deliberations by stiffening people in their opinions. The jury's 'crucial point' might be the realization that they were deadlocked.

Back in the courtroom he found Nancy Rosen and Tess Dodge trying to figure out what the jury might be having trouble with, and what the result might be. 'If they believe Morales about the afternoon, and Censabella to back him up,' Rosen was saying, 'that means no rape. And no rape means no murder.'

'But Juan testified that he was with Mariah all afternoon,' Tess countered. 'If they don't believe him about the first part, how can they believe him about the second? And if they don't believe him that means no guilty verdict at all.'

Rosen had no answer for that, and Estrada didn't, either.

'How can you break up his testimony?' Tess asked. 'Or Morales's? It doesn't make sense.'

Martinez's law clerk came into the courtroom and checked to see that the prosecution and defense were all there. He walked to a spot between the two counsel tables and said, quietly, 'They're coming in.'

He reported it to the court clerk, who called the press room downstairs. Ten minutes later the courtroom was full. Nothing happened for another fifteen minutes, and then Martinez arrived and announced to the impatient throng that she had called for additional court officers to deal with any demonstration. 'I anticipate that some of you will be tempted to express yourselves whether you like the verdict or not. Be warned that I will not be lenient.'

Estrada watched the four extra officers file in, depriving him of one of his early-warning signs on the verdict. Extra officers were often called in for a guilty verdict, and they tended to be alert. For an acquittal, the usual contingent lounged around unconcerned. That wasn't going to be how it went today.

The jury came in looking considerably less fresh than they had six hours earlier. Again, they looked straight ahead, sparing no attention for the parties.

'Case continued on trial,' the clerk said. 'People versus Roberto Morales. Present are the defendant, defense attorney, prosecutor, her honor Acting Justice Luz Martinez. All sworn jurors are in the box. Mr Foreman, will you please rise?'

Nissensen stood up, poker-faced. Estrada strained to get a look at the verdict form. Sometimes you could see the check marks through the paper.

'Has the jury reached a verdict?' the clerk asked.

'Yes.'

'How say you as to count one of the indictment, charging rape in the first degree?'

'Not guilty.'

The air left Estrada's lungs. His mouth felt dry. In the split-second before the courtroom burst into cheers he could feel the relief coming from the defense table. Martinez banged her gavel furiously, and the noise settled. 'If that happens again, I'm clearing this courtroom.'

'How say you as to the lesser included offence of attempted rape in the first degree?'

'Guilty.'

Estrada took a moment to assimilate it. Attempted rape? Could this be some sort of consolation prize, a compromise to placate a faction that wanted Morales convicted of *something*?

'As to the count in the indictment charging manslaughter in the first degree . . .'

Estrada's heart was pounding as furiously as Martinez's gavel. He thought: whatever the jury says I get to go home tonight, and even so I can hardly breathe. How must this feel to Morales?

'. . . how say you?'

'Guilty.'

Yes! Sitting at the prosecution table, Estrada could see Morales's profile over the top of Kassia Miller's brown hair. He was looking straight ahead, not at the jury or the judge, with no expression Estrada could read. Miller was watching Nissensen, calmer than Estrada would have been in her place.

'As to the count in the indictment charging murder in the second degree . . .'

This was the big one. If the jury had stopped at manslaughter, Morales's sentence could be as low as two to six years, eight and a third to twenty-five at most. For murder, he got a life sentence – no better than fifteen to life, with twenty-five to life not unlikely. Manslaughter combined with attempted rape was enough for murder if the jury was willing. Estrada tried not to expect it. Attempted rape was not a good sign . . . they had been holding back. He had a sudden antic image of being at an Oscar-night party, watching to see which movie got the early awards to guess if a trend was developing.

'. . . how say you?'

Nissensen clearly knew this was his moment. He drew himself up tall and played to the gallery. 'As to the count charging murder in the second degree, we the jury find the defendant guilty.'

There was a brief silence, broken by a crescendo of boos and shouts in Spanish, the sound of crying, the banging of Martinez's gavel. Morales did not move. Miller was looking at him now, so Estrada could not see her. He turned away from them to share an awkward hug with Rosen and Stein.

The booing and cursing dwindled to uneasy silence. Martinez warned the spectators again and told them they would not be allowed to leave until the jury was clear of the building.

She polled the jury. One by one they affirmed that they agreed with the verdict as read. They were all somber and contained, some of them more forceful than others, none seeming either triumphant or regretful. Estrada used the time to get a rein on his galloping relief. This was not over yet.

Martinez thanked the jury for a good job done under difficult circumstances. 'This is a citizen's most important duty. We could not have a system of laws without people who give up their time to perform the unpleasant task of sitting in judgment on their neighbors. In a better world, this would not be necessary, but until we get there, we rely on you.'

The jury left quickly. Miller stood to make a motion to have the verdict set aside as against the evidence. Martinez denied it. Miller handed up a notice of intention to appeal.

'At this time, your honor,' Miller said, 'in the interest of Mr Morales's two small children I respectfully request that he be given the night with his family. He is not a danger to the community and steps can be taken to insure there is no risk of flight.'

For the first time Estrada detected a lack of fire in Miller's delivery. He remembered a thought he'd had about his own argument in the Flippo hearing: *Words without thoughts never to heaven go.*

'He can visit with his family for an hour here in the jury room,' Martinez said curtly. 'And we'll keep him overnight in a cell next door so they can see him tomorrow before he leaves.' She banged her gavel. 'Defendant is remanded to the custody of the Department of Corrections. This court stands adjourned.'

24

There was a loud, happy party at the Italian restaurant where all the A.D.A.'s hung out and where Estrada could remember a harrowing lunch with Lynne Schelling, five months or a lifetime ago. The long table in the center of the room was full of people who had been in the courtroom and people who had convened when they heard about the verdict. The few other patrons on a Sunday night regarded the rowdies with the tolerance reserved for the blessed mad.

It was not until past ten, almost four hours after they had started, that the revelers began to disperse. Estrada, not yet ready to let go of the warmth of celebration, offered Tess Dodge and her mother a ride home in his police car.

At Tess's apartment building Sylvia Dodge said goodnight and thanked him again before she got out of the car. Tess stayed where she was, watching her mother walk to the door.

'Want some company watching the news?' she asked Estrada.

He did. This was his big victory. He could not imagine trying to enjoy it alone in his empty apartment with all the ghosts that new paint and plaster could not exorcise.

The news faded in as the television warmed up. Molly O'Hara was reporting on the verdict. Estrada flipped quickly through the network affiliates. All three were leading with the *Morales* story, all as interested in the jury's failure to convict for completed rape as in the fact that Morales had been found guilty of murder. Morales and his family were not commenting. The word *exclusive* caught his ear and he stopped flipping channels to hear Molly O'Hara say '. . . two members of the jury when we come back.' He endured the commercials, unwilling to miss any of what came next.

The first juror came on, shrouded in shadow. It was a woman, and Estrada knew immediately it was the beautician.

'We were in trouble right from the start on account of nobody was ready to believe anybody,' she said. 'It was this guy the prosecutor put on who liked little boys. And Morales, well, he had to stay out of jail . . . So nobody could really believe either one of them.'

'Was there anything in particular that gave you trouble?' O'Hara asked.

'It was the whole business about the afternoon. We could believe Morales was with her then, except some of the things he said about what they did – I can't say it on television – they didn't make sense to a lot of us. But one person said she knew some people who did those same kinds of things, and that helped.'

'I bet that's herself she's talking about,' Tess said.

'So once we had that part of it sort of figured out, how it might have happened, there was still this one woman who didn't know what to do. And she said she had to go to church on Sunday, and then she'd know. So she went, and some of the others went with her, and then when she came back, she was, it was like she was all different. I mean, she was all, like, tense before she went to church and then when she came back she was all, Okay, let's vote, I'm ready.'

'Did she say what had changed her mind?'

'She said she went to church and prayed and the Lord showed her the way, and now she knew that anybody who was so full of pride and self-hate at the same time could do any bad thing.'

'Some people have expressed surprise that you found him guilty of murder and attempted rape but not rape.' O'Hara said. 'How did you come to that decision? Why *attempted* rape?'

'Well, you know, that was the hardest. There were people who thought that the . . . that Alvaro wanted to get back at Morales, and that's why he said he was with Mariah all afternoon. To get Morales in *worse* trouble. And those people weren't going to change their minds. But then, other people were sure Morales killed her. So we couldn't get anywhere. Then, after the judge told us we could, like, pick what we wanted from the different witnesses if we thought they were only lying part of the time, we all agreed that probably they *had* been together in the afternoon – Morales and Mariah Dodge. So then we had to figure out what happened and most of us didn't think he'd be able to, you know, *rape* her only three, four hours later. I mean, he's what? Forty-seven or something. Some people thought he could've raped her anyway, but more didn't. We all agreed that he *attacked* her, and that he *wanted* to rape her because he was so angry. And then when he *couldn't*, it made him even angrier and he killed her.' The juror took a moment to catch her breath. 'It's really sad, you know. Such a pretty woman, so smart. She had so much to look forward to.'

The second disguised juror was the computer software marketer, and she confirmed the beautician's story. 'It was a compromise only to the extent that some of us thought he raped her there in the office and some didn't. There were three opinions, really. That he had sex with her in the afternoon and raped her in the office, that they had sex in the afternoon and later he tried to rape her but couldn't, and that it all happened in the office and there was no afternoon rendezvous. It got easier for us once we understood that, as far as our verdict was concerned, it really didn't matter which of those three it was. Any way you sliced it the man was guilty of murder, and we all thought so.'

The station went to commercial and Estrada hit the OFF button. 'I'll come down and help you get a cab.'

‘Don’t be an ass, Estrada,’ she said, and took him to bed.

Monday morning dawned indecently bright. He opened his eyes and regretted it immediately. Next to him on the bed was a pillow full of curly red-blonde hair that made him happy for the moment he was awake. The next time he woke, the sun was in full possession of the sky and Tess was in the kitchen making coffee.

A brisk shower failed to revive him. ‘Nobody’s supposed to look so wide-awake after a night like that,’ he announced.

‘I can’t help it if pleasure makes me bouncy. Have some coffee.’

It was delicious. After the first jolt, he sipped it slowly.

‘Don’t you have to go to work?’ she asked.

‘My boss gave me some time off.’

‘What are you going to do?’

‘I’ll decide when I return to the human race.’

She did not seem inclined to leave, and he was not eager to see her go. They went out and found a newsstand on Broadway that still had the Travel section from Sunday’s paper. He bought all the morning papers, too. The headlines were big and bold and mostly said GUILTY. Pancho Castillo’s article in *Noticias Diarias* had a subhead that said NUEVO HÉROE over a picture of Joe Estrada.

‘You ought to keep these,’ Tess said. ‘Put them in your scrapbook.’

He had never kept one but he thought she was right, now seemed not a bad time to start. And while he was at it he ought to arrange for a compilation tape to be made of the newscasts the office routinely recorded.

They looked through the ads for hurricane-season specials in the islands, until Estrada realized that was not where he wanted to go. He spent an hour tracking down Pancho Castillo before making a hotel reservation and buying himself an airline ticket.

In the afternoon he called Collins to make sure it was all

right for him to take the rest of the week off and generally made sure his life at the office would not fall apart while he was gone. Because there was no doubt in his mind that he was going back. There was, he had discovered, a simple reason why he had taken so long to leave the D.A.'s office for a more lucrative job: The D.A.'s office was where he wanted to be.

He was not sure what the key had been to his finally seeing the truth that others – Michelle among them – had seen before he had, but now that he saw it, it could not have been more obvious. He liked his job. He thrived on it. If he had ever belonged anywhere in his life, the D.A.'s office was it.

At this point he no longer knew if he owed Big Jim Estrada much of anything except anger for the lies he had inflicted on the family, but whatever moral debt he had to the rest of his family seemed well paid by the work he was doing. He would be glad to get away for a few days, but he knew that when it was time to go back to work he would be ready.

He and Tess watched the late news again. Roberto Morales was no longer the lead story, but two of the three major stations carried his dry-eyed farewell to his family as he left on the first leg of his journey to prison. A prominent criminal defense lawyer made pro-forma remarks: Morales had not been given a fair trial and the new appeal would, once again, vindicate him. The lawyer took care to point out that the fault was entirely with the judge and the prosecutor, and not with his admired colleague at the bar, Kassia Miller, who would not be participating in the appeal. Miller herself said only that the jury had spoken and she would have no comment.

'Did she jump or was she pushed?' Tess asked.

'A little of both, I'd say.' But he thought that Miller had probably left Morales's defense on her own. Those last minutes in the courtroom he'd been sure she'd had enough of her 'innocent' client.

In the morning he and Tess had eggs and toast and coffee

together, in a silence that got progressively louder until he knew he had to break it.

Before he could speak, she said, 'This is over, isn't it?'

It wasn't exactly what he had been about to say but it was right. 'Not because I don't think you're terrific.'

She took his face between her hands and kissed him softly. 'All you know about me is I'm a warm body on a cold night.'

'Nothing wrong with that,' he said. 'That's terrific all by itself. But I know a lot more about you than that. I know how smart you are and how passionate. I know you're a force of nature when you get it into your head.'

'No, those are just words. You've been around me, but you've been too busy to see who I really am. And that's not criticism. You were doing what you had to, and I'm grateful for it. All us Dodges, even my crazy father, are grateful for what you did. But you missed getting to know me while you were at it.'

'Maybe I'll figure it out,' he didn't stop himself from saying.

She kissed his nose and stood up. 'Or maybe not.' She picked up her shoulder bag and headed for the door. 'And maybe I'll hate you for a while, too, for being so dense.' She began to cry. 'Shit. I swore to myself I'd never cry in front of you again. Shit.' And then she was gone, leaving behind a bigger emptiness than he had expected.

He made his plane with no time to spare and slept the whole trip. In the Pacific Coast fishing village where José Peña had chosen to live out his life, grandfather and grandson took long walks on the beach, sometimes talking, often silent. They made excursions to the interior to visit ruins left by people who were as much part of Estrada's heritage as any duques de Estrada.

His last full day in Mexico, Estrada went up the coast alone to think. On the way back he stopped at a deserted beach to watch the sun go down.

This might have been Michelle's vacation too, he reflected.

Anger at her continued to elude him: sadness was all he could muster. He thought about the Kahns, weathering her illness and his affair with Nancy Rosen, and about Mahoney and Kath, struggling toward a reconciliation. But they were couples with a kind of history he and Michelle had never had.

Redness spread over the water as he watched, tinting the foam tops of the waves. Red had been the color of the Morales trial: red hair, red blood, the red of Lynne Schelling's suits and sometimes of Kassia Miller's dresses.

Even without Kassia Miller on Morales's team an appeal was nearly certain. Estrada was sure Mahoney would do the best anyone could to make sure it did not succeed. This time would be different: there would be no reversal prompted by the weakness of the prosecution case. And even if Morales won both appeals, he would have to stand trial again.

However all that came out, for now Estrada could enjoy the solid sense that he had put a bad man behind bars where he belonged, and the knowledge that, no matter what, Roberto Morales would never again be a hero to anyone.

Estrada could only marvel at Tess Dodge, streaking through his life all brightness and intensity. A younger Joe Estrada might have tried to hang on, but he knew that making their magic permanent was an illusion. The sweetness they had shared had begun as a kind of mutual comforting and reassurance, then become a reward they were giving themselves and each other, physical pleasure and satisfaction as a metaphor for other kinds of pleasure and satisfaction. Right and good as it all had been for them, it was not, without more, the basis for a life.

He watched the last sliver of sun dissolve into the darkening water and thought how odd it was for him to be here, celebrating victory by looking for a past he had never known was there, in the company of a gentle, solitary man who was still barely more than an interesting stranger. Spending his last night alone on a deserted beach.

This kind of sunset demanded both a hero and a heroine, he thought, two loving and triumphant people walking off together hand in hand.

But maybe that wasn't the only happy ending. Maybe it was just as important to enjoy some sunsets alone . . . if you could do it knowing who you were – where you'd come from and where you were going. Master of your own soul at least until the next time you had to wrestle with it.

If you had that – really and truly had it – he saw with unexpected clarity, the rest would surely come in time, and when it did how much sweeter it would be.